Also by Paul Boyce:

Black Harlequin   (currently under re-editing)

FAR
FROM
HOME

FAR
FROM
HOME

PAUL BOYCE

authorHOUSE®

AuthorHouse™ UK
1663 Liberty Drive
Bloomington, IN 47403 USA
www.authorhouse.co.uk
Phone: 0800.197.4150

Published by AuthorHouse 09/03/2015

ISBN: 978-1-5049-8855-1 (sc)
ISBN: 978-1-5049-8856-8 (e)

My sincere thanks and appreciation...

... goes to my lovely wife Jane who has had to tolerate my periods of silence, no doubt glad of it at times, and many late nights while I tap away on my keyboard. Without her encouragement and support I might never have inflicted this publication on an unsuspecting public.

... goes to Alex, my delightful new daughter-in-law for her design of the map of the continent of Baylea on the world of Amaehome, and the design of the website, with assistance from my son Andy, all for her technologically-naïve father-in-law.

... goes to Valerie, Merly and the team at AuthorHouse UK for their patience, inspiration, advice and preofessionalism, and a little nagging at times.

PART 1
THE GATHERING

PROLOGUE

"SO, MY FRIEND, ye ask me who is this young elf of whom tales are being told in this peaceful place? If ye buy me a cool mug o' mead for I have a king's thirst upon me on this hot day, we shall sit here awhile and I shall take delight in telling you a little of this most colourful of elves. If the luck of the Lady Neilea, the Lady of Serendipity, is with us then he will be in here shortly. Well, where to begin? For a start, he is young. Barely eighty years of age. Thou hast the face of bewilderment! Does this fact surprise thee? Nay? Nor should it by the great gods! As aforesaid, he is a princeling elf of a high and noble race, from the ancient but troubled realm of Faerhome, the race of High Elves who live long indeed. And him being uncommon tall for all that, having been also blessed by Tambarhal, the Deity of all things considered normal in nature and, by the natural intervention of his parents of course, endowed with a wiry but muscular and athletic physique. There! Look yonder, he enters – aha! And with an entourage of young elves and human lads and of course, the flock of maidens! Look at him! Being broad-shouldered - which is also unusual for an elf – dost thou not agree? Aye, but then many years of swinging blades and shooting arrows will do that to a warrior. Oh, has this been mentioned by me yet? Nay? Aye indeed; there walks a proud warrior of growing ability and some notoriety already in one so

young. A leader of a successful warband at that! And with many an orc ear to his credit! But how might thou recognise him, dear traveller? There - take a look at him again — over there, yonder, by the pillar, surrounded by those panting maidens as usual — hah! Observe his features if thou hast a care to! His typically long elven face is tanned and extraordinarily handsome, thou must surely agree. Aye, that is so! His hair is golden and very long but with those side braids such as a dwarf may be partial to; unlike other elves he doesn't tie his hair back except for when he is hunting goblins and those other despicable creatures of the wooded hills, caverns and valleys. His agility is legendary amongst his peers and many young elves and men aspire to be like him; they emulate him and swagger hither and yon but they do not have his flair and self-assuredness. It is said that his father does not consider him to be the best role-model for the youth, however. Silmar is wont to be flirtatious with the girls and a terrible show-off and it sets his father in a terrible lather at times. There, observe thou? He does juggling tricks with the pretty little dark-haired maiden's bauble! The back of his hand lightly presses her plump breast as he shows his dexterity, and she laughs! Aye, indeed, how they all laugh but she will be bedded before the day wanes. Mark thee my words well. Oh, were I but a score of years younger and my hair not quite so grey…"

Crystelle Brightblade, Travelling Bard
Writer of the "Freemen of Carrick Cliffs"
Town of Refuge in the Home Territories
Year of the Brown Bear

CHAPTER 1

YAZAMA JIUTARÔ (RONIN)

I, YAZAMA JIUTARÔ, Samurai warrior in the service of the *daimyo* Lord Asano Takumi no Kami tell this story in the hope that it offers inspiration to you, my students. It tells of hierarchical injustice that resulted in the enforced death of my honourable master. But also of the very patient and calculated revenge by his forty-seven Samurai retainers, of which I am proud to be one, I shall tell later. Be patient for much adventure occurred between these two tales, which I insist are true, and these shall shortly be recounted in the tale to be told by others and no doubt in song. But where?

Know only that the core of this tale is that these forty-seven *ronin* (ah! You ask the meaning of this term? Masterless Samurai - literally meaning *wave men!* That is what we were to become) fully knew that their plan of revenge would certainly result in the deaths of every one of us and at *our* own hands. However, know also that the code of the Samurai revolves around the sense of honour, duty and sacrifice in order to achieve a higher end.

April, the month of late-winter at the Asano *Han* in the town of Ako in the Harima province of Japan was usually cold and windy with knee-deep snow. This year, 1701, was different. Instead of the wintry conditions, there had been two weeks of torrential rain which had washed away the deep blanket of snow that had covered the forests and rice-fields in the area. At this time however, I was too overwhelmed with my duties to be bothered by the weather.

Traditionally at this time the Han's *Ryū*, or training school, took on a batch of students who aspired to be, or rather their fathers aspired them to be, future Samurai warriors. Each year, training was offered to eight boys aged eight years but they would, if found to have the necessary determination to succeed, take eight to ten years to become competent to bear the coveted *Katana*. In reality, only one student, two on a rare occasion, would achieve this remarkable feat. Our captain and principal counsellor, Oishi Kuranosuké, would oversee the progress of the training; it would be two years before the students even placed their hands on the *bokken*, the bamboo practice sword. By this time, the number of students would have diminished to four.

At thirty-four years of age, our esteemed master, Asano of the once influential Naganori family, was young to inherit a *daimyo*, or estate, such as this. The value of a *Han* is measured in *koku*, that is the amount of rice necessary to sustain one man for a year. A *Han* of a very wealthy warlord, such as the revered Tokugawa Shogun, could be as great as half a million *koku*, that of the Asano *Han* was a mere fifty-five thousand. To protect his Han, Asano-san had a retinue including forty-seven Samurai warriors. I, Yazama Jiutarô, am proud to be one of these men. Many of us, though sadly not I, have experience in battle. I am yet to use my sword in the defence of my master. When my time comes I hope to die with honour. I would dearly wish for my master and fellow warriors to speak in the future with pride of my own courage in the face of the enemies of my master.

It was before dawn one Sunday morning that I was summoned to speak with Oishi-san. Further to being our leader, he was the adviser and counsellor to our revered master. I stepped onto his porch and removed my swords from my obi, the large blue sash around my waist, and placed them to the side of the doorway. I removed my dusty sandals then adopted the customary *Za-rei* kneeling position, rapped on the door, announced myself formally and waited. A minute later the door slid to the side and Oishi-San was similarly kneeling on the other side.

We bowed to each other; Oishi-San had a beaming smile this day, one that the students never saw. He had been given a nick-name by students some years earlier - *the man who never smiles*. I think he rather liked that and, to preserve the dignified stern image, he always took care not to show a smile in front of the students.

To look at, he was tall, though a little shorter than I, and broad-shouldered. He carried scars on his face, one from the centre of his left eyebrow to the bottom of his left ear, which gave his face an almost lopsided appearance. I have seen students blanch as his gaze passed across them, just as mine did some years ago when I was a young student. His prowess with the katana was legendary. Unusually for these times, he encouraged the use of the *yumi* asymmetrical bow and its arrows with us Samurai. This has proven to be an advantage with me – it may sound like I am boasting but I have, I like to think, a competency with this weapon that has impressed my captain. In no way though, can I begin to match the bow-skill of Oishi-san – I have seen him on horseback, at full gallop, put three arrows into a straw figure at one hundred paces in as much time as it takes to count to ten. I can only achieve this at the canter. I will better myself in time. It is only recently that I discovered the trick of success in this art – to release my bow-string as the horse's hooves are all off the ground; that is when there is a pause in the jolting.

"Yazama-san," he began. "Come in, leave your swords inside my door and make yourself comfortable here. Partake of tea."

An honour indeed and for only the second time. I settled down onto a cushion on the *tatami* mat while Oishi-San sat down on the *futon*. Like me, he was wearing a thick kimono with a dark-blue *obi* about his waist. He carried no weapons when in his own house but I could see they were within arm's reach. No Samurai would have his weapons more than a couple of paces away from him. I had made every effort since achieving my manhood to emulate this man, taking every opportunity to hone my fitness and stamina just as I know he did every single day.

Oishi-San ordered tea from his housemaid. I knew that he would make this a formal occasion.

"You have a rather important day today, young warrior. Have you prepared your presentation?"

"I have, Oishi-San."

"We are pleased that you have volunteered to give the opening demonstration and speech to the new students, I look forward to your katana display in the dojo. Make sure you keep it short enough to whet their appetites."

The '*we*' signified that he had spoken with our master. I sat up straight and squared my shoulders.

"I shall, Oishi-San."

"I have some news that I shall speak to all Samurai about during the morning. As you will be occupied with the introductory presentation, I shall briefly tell you of it now. Our honoured master has been given a special task for the court of the *Mikado*, Tokugawa Tsunayoshi."

I immediately focussed; Tokugawa was the supreme military dictator, a member of the ruling class and a man of high nobility. This could contribute greatly to raising the status at court of our master.

The tea arrived and Oishi-san carried out the formal serving of it.

He continued with his dialogue. "I am sure that you know of Kira Kotsuké no Suké – a warlord of greater seniority than Asano and a man greedy of money and prominence. It is no secret however, that he has a coarse manner at times, but he has the ear of the Dog Shogun at Yedo himself."

I confirmed my knowledge of this man and am sure that my face would have betrayed my dislike of his reputation. For the purpose of etiquette though, I said nothing of it.

"Well, Kira Kotsuké no Suké has been commissioned to entertain envoys of the emperor at the Kyoto court. Our esteemed master has been summoned to assist in order to get instruction from him and thus avoid any errors of etiquette."

"Oishi-San," I said, "with respect, what effect on our duties will this have?"

"I, together with thirty of our Samurai, will accompany our master to Kira-San's mansion and then onto the court of Tokugawa Tsunayoshi. I would like you to come with us. We leave tomorrow. Make your preparations and pack what you need to sustain you for the journey there and back, probably about fifteen to twenty days in all."

I was so happy at this time. If I knew of the events which were to unfold perhaps I would have been better prepared than I was, perhaps we all would have been.

"Yazama-San, I shall detain you no longer, this is an important day for you, I shall be in attendance but please, do not let it affect your presentation."

With that, we gave the formal bow, standing this time. I collected my weapons, bowed again at Oishi-San's door and returned to the *dojo*, the practice hall. I had a nervous feeling in my stomach; this would be the first time that I would stand in front of students and give them formal presentation. I must be firm and assertive – how would Oishi-San do this?

I arrived at the *dojo*. This hall was large, probably measuring forty paces by thirty although I had never measured it. The practice area covered much of the floor of the dojo although there was seating area down one side. In the centre of this seating area was a raised dais with a low seat mounted on top of it – this would be for our captain, the senior teacher. On the practice area, on the opposite side away from the high seat, I had placed a man-sized straw dummy supported on a wooden frame. The students had already arrived and were kneeling in line at one end of the practice area. They were fidgeting, laughing and poking each other.

I dimly remembered my first day as a student.

"Silence!" I roared sharply, just as my teacher had done then. The effect was wonderful, I had total control.

I modulated my voice so they would have to remain quiet in order to hear my words.

"You are not here to play. If you wish to play then return to your homes now, otherwise you will give full attention to your studies. This way, one or two of you may become a Samurai."

I paused to let this information sink in as I took up a formal kneeling position in front of and facing the students.

I called the formal command to bow.

The dojo was now quiet except for a low rustle noise from the end of the hall behind me.

I remembered that I had omitted to introduce myself. "I am Yazama Jiutarô. From this moment you shall address me as *Sensei* but only when invited to speak."

I turned to face the straw dummy. Bringing my right foot forward I leaned forward with my weight onto it and brought my right hand in an exaggerated swing to the grip of my katana. I then swept myself up onto my feet and withdrew my blade. Swinging the sword in the double-slash butterfly stroke, I removed all four limbs from the straw dummy. I then executed the upward left-to-right diagonal with one hand, the swordsman's second most difficult stroke, which sliced the dummy into two pieces from right rib cage to left shoulder. Re-sheathing the sword with a flourish, I returned to the kneeling position. The whole demonstration had taken no more than three heartbeats.

The faces on the students were worth a purse full of gold.

"If you wish to be a Samurai, an elite warrior, you must abandon play and childish behaviour; you must embrace discipline – self discipline. Is that clear?"

The students gave anxious looks to each other. I raised my voice once more.

"Is that clear?"

"Hai!" came their anxious response.

"In future, you will answer *Hai, Sensei* to all teachers. Is that clear?"

"Hai, Sensei!" they responded.

"Better," I said, softly again. "You will at all times show respect and courtesy to teachers and all Samurai here at this *han*. Is that clear?"

"Hai, Sensei!"

"At no time shall you make eye contact with the Master of this han, His Excellency Asano Takumi no Kami. You shall bow deeply until he has passed by. Is that clear?"

"Hai, Sensei!"

"It is expected that at all times you will show respect to each other. It takes anyone courage to learn the arts that you will achieve. Petty squabbles and bullying between yourselves and with other students will not be tolerated. Is that clear?"

"Hai, Sensei!"

"You will obey your teachers in every task given to you; it is for your advantage and betterment. Is that clear?"

"Hai, Sensei!"

"Good," I replied. I felt that now they knew where they stood, it was time to ease off slightly.

"Your training will take some years, I am sure you are aware of this. You will be expected to fetch and carry, wash and clean, exercise daily and learn from everything you do. These duties are designed to develop your abilities and attitudes. Do not become disheartened. I was where you are now not so many years ago. Every Samurai here today has been where you are now. Some of these Samurai are heroes who have already proven themselves in war and battle."

I paused for a moment and observed as they gave each other looks then returned their gaze back to me. I could hear a soft noise from the gallery at the end of the dojo but chose to ignore it.

"Do not expect to be wielding swords and other weapons in the near future, you will not be swinging katanas for a long time to come. This will be the last time you step on this practice area for a long time, unless you are wielding a cleaning cloth, so make the most of it. You will be assigned a senior student who will act as counsellor for you. If you have problems of any kind, fears, difficulties, illness or anything else, do not hesitate to speak with him. You will find him a source of inspiration as well as advice. This person will make himself known to you later this morning."

I paused once again as their young faces looked towards me with bewilderment. "I shall speak to you of the *bushido* code," I continued. "Can anyone tell me of the meaning of *bushido*?"

One student nervously raised his hand. I pointed at him to answer.

"S-Sensei, it m-means the w-way of the warrior," he stammered.

"Hai, well answered," I replied. "The way of the warrior commands a man's entire being without concession, it demands *total* loyalty, courage and etiquette, inspires inner dedication and outer composure without equal. You will learn that it is more sentiment than a belief. I can tell you that writings about *bushido* over the last few centuries are found more in poems by countless Samurai than in books of learning. Read these poems, they will all have the same theme: the purpose of a Samurai's life is death – to die properly at the proper time."

The mouths of the students were hanging open, I continued with my speech.

"Having spent his boyhood training to die in the right way, a Samurai will spend his manhood waiting to die at the right moment. Take heed, this is the Samurai spirit – knowing when and how to die. Not only does the Samurai have no fear of death, he considers it his sacred moment of honour. If cheated of the honour of dying for his lord in combat, the he will receive the honour of performing his own death. For him, life and death are not two things but one. And this contradiction is the strength and character of the Samurai."

I could sense that the young students had some difficulty in fully understanding the terminology of what I was explaining but I knew that in time they would come to comprehend and accept the bushido code, provided that they managed to continue with their training. I slowly and reverently withdrew my katana, in its sheath, from my obi. Holding it horizontally in two hands in front of me, I continued with my dialogue.

"I have one or two final things to discuss with you. Understand that the soul of Nippon, our sacred land, is the Samurai and the soul of the Samurai is the katana. To the Samurai, failure only occurs when the swordsman fails the sword, because the sword shall never fail the swordsman. A man's will and a man's act must be one, thus sword and swordsman must be one."

I allowed my rather clever observations, as I thought them to be, to sink into the minds of the students.

"Does anybody have any questions for me?"

A couple of hands were raised. I gestured to one student. "Speak!"

"Sensei, why is the ritual act of suicide carried out on the belly?" This one spoke with self-assuredness.

"This is to release the soul, which followers of Buddhism say resides in the belly. It is said that it is why Buddha has such a large belly!" This brought one or two low chuckles from the students.

"This now concludes my talk with you. *Ja-mata*, I shall see you soon."

I concluded with a formal kneeling bow and left the training area. Yoshida Chiuzayémon, a good friend of mine with a couple of years more experience than I, was ready to take over the teaching from me.

"Good sword-play, my friend," he commented with a grin. "Pity about your ugly face though!"

"This face will make the maidens swoon with delight one day," I replied.

"With pity, more likely." We both laughed.

I stepped out of the dojo into the cold, damp air. Oishi Kuranosuké was there waiting for me. I bowed deeply to him and he returned the compliment.

"I witnessed all of the presentation, including the speech. Don't be so hard on them, they are only young. Well done though Yazama-San, I shall make a teacher of you yet!"

"I am grateful for the opportunity, Oishi-San," I replied.

"Showing off a bit with you sword demonstration, weren't you?" he commented. "Your second stroke was nicely done but I do not approve of showing a single-handed technique to students as young as these. They may be inclined to think that this is the norm."

"My apologies, Oishi-San, but it seemed the most expedient way of finishing off the enemy."

A broad grin appeared on Oishi Yoshio's face. "It was good to see that you continue with your sword practice to such good effect," he answered. "You and I will practice together perhaps this afternoon."

"I shall be honoured, Oishi-San." An honour indeed!

At that, he bowed and strode away, I bowed too.

Early next morning, with our master Asano Takuni no Kami in his carriage and Oishi Kuranosuké riding on his horse beside him, together with the thirty other mounted Samurai closely behind, we rode out through the gates of Ako on the long road to Kyoto. This would be a nine-day ride at least and that was assuming the roads had not been damaged by the inclement weather and that adequate accommodation was available in the wayside inns and taverns on the way. We could see that our master was engrossed in reading scrolls and parchments. Our captain reckoned that he was reading up on etiquette. Although this would be a learning experience for him, he would not want to show his ignorance of these matters to an oaf such as Kira Kotsuké no Suké.

We need not have worried unduly. Our group was large enough to deter any wandering bands of *ronin*, those masterless Samurai who, as criminals, were known to wander the highways and rob travellers of weapons and belongings, sometimes even food and clothing. They kept well out of our way. From time to time, some of us would be sent out into the countryside to track down and put an end to these itinerant bands, I was somewhat disappointed that I had yet to be asked to go.

The weather, although cold, stayed quite dry which was a bonus to us Samurai because the *yoroi* armour we were wearing tended to become uncomfortable in the wet. We eventually arrived at Kyoto and, at the suggestion of Kira Kotsuké no Suké, the Samurai were accommodated in the local militia barracks but, fortunately, our master, together with our captain of Samurai, were allowed to stay in the mansion of Kira-San.

That evening, Kira-San held a reception to welcome his visitor, our esteemed master. A deep embarrassment spread across the face of our master when he realised that he had brought no gifts for his host. This was a grave failure of etiquette on the part of our master who should have shown appreciation for the fact that he was to be given instruction by his host in matters of protocol. Kira was deeply offended and proceeded to pour insults on our master.

We later heard that Kamei Sama, another young Lord receiving instruction from Kira, had also neglected to provide a present. He remarked to his own counsellors at a secret conference "Kotsuké no Suké has insulted Takumi no Kami and myself during our service in attendance on the Imperial envoy. This surely is against all decency and I was tempted to kill him on the spot; but I bethought me that if I did such a deed within the precincts of the castle, not only would my own life be forfeit but my family and vassals would be ruined. So I stayed my hand. Still, the life of such a wretch is a sorrow to the people and tomorrow when I go to Court I shall slay him – my mind is made up and I will listen to no remonstrance."

One of Kamei Sama's counsellors was a man of much perception and when he witnessed his lord's enraged manner that it would be useless to dissuade him, he said "Your lordship's words are law – your servant will make all preparations accordingly. And tomorrow, when your lordship goes to Court, if this Kotsuké no Suké should again be insolent, let him be the one to die the death."

However, the counsellor was deeply disturbed at his master's words and as he reflected on them, it occurred to him that since Kotsuké no Suké had a miserly reputation, he would almost certainly be open to a bribe. It would be better to pay any sum of money, no matter how great, rather than his lord and his house and family be ruined.

He collected all the money that he was able and, with his servants carrying it all, he rode off to Kotsuké no Suké's castle and said to the man's retainers "My master, who is now in attendance upon the Imperial envoy, owes much thanks to my Lord Kotsuké no Suké, who has been at so great pains to teach him the proper ceremonies to be observed during the reception of the Imperial envoy. This is but a shabby present which has been sent by him, but he hopes that his lordship will condescend to accept it, and commends himself to his lordship's favour."

With these words, he produced a thousand ounces of silver for Kotsuké no Suké and a hundred ounces to be distributed among his retainers. Thus was Kamei Sama's position strengthened in the eyes of Kotsuké no Suké. The counsellor had saved him, his family and his house from ruin.

It was by unhappy circumstance that Oishi Kuranosuké had not been at his master's side – there was nothing he could do. Kira had dismissed our master Asano-San from his castle. He was fortunate enough to find lodgings in a decent tavern.

The following day, Asano-San returned to the mansion to apologise to Kira and to present him with gifts purchased that morning. Kira however, went so far as to rebuke him in public. Although Takumi no Kami ignored the taunts and ridicule and submitted himself patiently to Kotsuké no Suké's orders, this only made Kira despise him more.

Asano-San had that morning directed Oishi-San to assemble the thirty Samurai in front of the tavern. By this time, Kira had left his mansion without our esteemed master for the castle of the 'Dog Shogun'. When word of this latest insult reached Asano-San, he lost his temper and with his mounted Samurai close behind, strode into the court of Tokugawa's castle.

At last, Kotsuké no Suké said haughtily "Here, my Lord of Takumi, the ribbon of my sock has come untied. Be so good as to tie it up for me."

Although burning with rage and humiliation at the affront, Asano-san realised that he was still on duty and was bound to obey. He bent down and tied the ribbon of the sock.

Then, turning away from him, Kotsuké no Suké petulantly exclaimed in front of the envoy "Why, how clumsy you are! You cannot so much as tie up the ribbon of a sock properly! Anyone can see that you are a boor from the country and know nothing of the manners of Yedo."

Kira laughed scornfully and moved towards an inner room.

Our master, Asano Takumi no Kami, now lost his patience – this last insult was more than he could bear. He called at Kotsuké no Suké to stop, drew his wakizashi, the short-sword, and wounded Kira on the forehead. He lunged again but the blade skittered off a pillar. Kira, his face bleeding from what was really a small cut, screamed out "Close the gates!" and ran away.

Asano Takumi no Kami was restrained by an officer, Kajikawa Yosobei, who having seen the affray allowed Kira Kotsuké no Suké time to make good his escape.

The castle gates quickly swung shut separating our master from his Samurai. The Shogun's Samurai, armed with bows, swarmed to the top of the walls. Oishi Yoshio leapt from his horse and hammered on the gates to no avail.

There was a great uproar and much confusion. It was reported to us that Takumi no Kami was disarmed and arrested and confined in one of the palace apartments under the care of the censors.

A council decided that the prisoner was to be given over to the safeguard of a daimyo called Tamura Ukiyo no Daibu, who kept him in his own house. It was soon after decided that as Takumi no Kami had committed an outrage - even to draw a weapon in the presence of the Shogun was a very serious matter – and had attacked another man within the precincts of the palace, he would perform *hara-kiri*, ritual suicide by the stomach-cut. His *Han*, the lands, property and livestock, were to be confiscated thus making his former retainers masterless Samurai, or *ronin*. We would be masterless and humiliated, but worst of all, our master's family would be destitute.

A proclamation to this effect was immediately made from the top of the walls. Our master would be under lock and key and we, his loyal Samurai, were ordered out of the city. Many of us wanted to fight it out with the occupants of the castle but, wisely, Oishi-San warned us that this would not be an honourable act against the Shogun. Kira was the one for which justice should be brought to bear.

"Ride out, my warriors," he commanded. "We shall stop outside of the city and discuss our next course of action."

We followed the road back out of the city and continued for an hour until, after checking for signs of pursuers, we felt we were safe enough.

Oishi Yoshio gathered us about him. His anger and sadness were etched deep in his face.

"There is nothing we can do about our master; he is doomed to an honourable death. It is fortunate that he is in the hands of the Shogun and not Kira, who would delight in tormenting him further."

"Death awaits Kira Kotsuké no Suké!" cried my friend, Yoshida Chiuzayémon.

"Yoshida-San, you are quite correct, but now is not the time. We have more pressing matters to attend to. The Han of our master is about to be descended on by the forces of Kira Yoshinaka. They will take everything of value and may even kill those who defend it. We must ride now, stop only when the horses can take us no longer; keep to the road night and day."

A roar of approval erupted from all thirty of us Samurai. We remounted our horses and began the long, hard ride home. Many of us were puzzled at the reason for the haste and, at the end of the first day's ride Oishi-San once again gathered us round to explain.

"We have left sixteen Samurai to protect our Han. They may not be enough. But the primary reason for our haste is that the Asano Han, in common with many other such daimyo, has issued currency notes. Typically, the gold held in the Asano treasury will only cover sixty percent of the note issue. We must have the notes converted to gold coins at this rate. It will enable us to recover something before the confiscation order descends and, of course, deprive the Shogun of a sizable sum of money. From this, we can go on to arrange our revenge in slow-time. The bastard Kira will be expecting us to attack and will be preparing for it. Let us scavenge what we can and ensure the safety of our dependants at Ako. Time to ride."

Ever the practical and logical thinker, Oishi Yoshio proved to us that day that *bushido* may have its duty but the abacus is never far behind the sword. We continued on the road and hurried back to the castle in Ako, covering the one hundred and thirty leagues in five days.

As we arrived at our master's Han in the late afternoon of the fifth day, we could see that the place was in turmoil. The gates were locked and barricaded and a large number of Samurai bearing the symbol of Kira Yoshinaka were striding about in the town streets. They did not make any attempt to stop us. Our own Samurai we had left behind to protect the Han were glad to see us.

"Thanks be to the gods you have arrived," panted Kano Kiyomasa, Oishi-San's lieutenant who commanded the rear-party. "A pack of Samurai and debt collectors arrived just two hours ago to say our master was dead and you all were scattered. They demand the contents of this Han and will kill any of us who oppose. We have one hour to comply."

Oishi-San wasted no time. "Collect all that is of value and load it into your saddle packs. Then make ready to ride. Meanwhile, I shall negotiate safe passage of the women, children, non-combatants and students. Kira's men would not dare harm them; he would lose face if anything untoward happened."

At the top of the wall, Oishi Yoshio introduced himself and demanded to see the leader of the group of Samurai who were besieging the gate of the Han. Safe passage was guaranteed. The non-combatants were led out, each one being carefully scrutinised and searched for valuables. Oishi Yoshio noticed that two or three of the refugees, mainly the teenage students, were taken to one side.

"Now you *Ronin* may leave," shouted the leader, emphasising the new epithet intentionally in order to demean us. "Take nothing of value with you."

Oishi dropped to the ground and mounted his horse. All of the Samurai were mounted and ready.

Quietly he commanded "Open the back gates, as silently as you can."

A woman's or boy's scream came from outside the front gates of the Han. Oishi's head whipped round towards the sound.

"The faithless bastards, what are they doing? I shall remember that leader – I *shall* receive his death"

The screaming stopped. The back gate was now open. At once we forty-seven *Ronin* broke into a trot, then a canter and then into a full gallop. Screaming could be heard again. After an hour in the fading light, the group stopped. Oishi-san directed that they ride into the hills, share the coins they had collected and decide on their strategy.

It was the early hours of the morning before we found an ideal stopping place. All currency notes were handed to Oishi. The gold would be sufficient to last each member of the group for a considerable period of time.

"I can convert much of this paper money in a city," he assured us. "With luck, if I am quick enough I shall be able to do it before news of the confiscation of the Han becomes general knowledge. We shall scatter. Discard your armour; it will only point you out for who you are. Take service with other daimyos if necessary, or become merchants, teachers or craftsmen. I suggest we give the matter time to settle down and meet in the very barracks where we stayed, in Kyoto, on mid-winter's day, not this one coming, but next. I shall use the money to install myself in Kyoto, keep a watch on Kira and start collecting the armour and equipment we need to avenge the treachery that led to the death of our master. Once we have completed our task, there shall be only one course of action left to us: to die with dignity and honour, our duty fulfilled. What say you all?"

As one, we all cried our agreement. Oishi Yoshio placed his hand on each of our shoulders in turn and spoke words of encouragement to us all.

To me he said "Yazama-San, you have learned well, you have a potential to be a legendary warrior. Go with words of appreciation from me. *Sayonara.*"

Within an hour, we had all left the stopping place, each of us making for a place of safety, a haven where we could continue with our learning in secret. I decided that I would make for Kyushu, the main island at the southern end of our country. I had a horse, clothing, my precious weapons: katana, wakizashi and tanto, a considerable amount of money in gold coins and most of all, my courage. I would need more equipment and clothing and probably a pack horse. I had a long journey of probably about three months.

After a week riding west, I turned south to ensure that I put plenty of space between myself and Kyoto.

Eight weeks of riding in all weathers took me to the Straights of Shimonoseki, the barrier of sea between the main island of Honshu and that of Kyushu. I paid a boatman the overpriced sum of five yen for him to take me, my two horses and my equipment across the Straits. He was drunk when I loaded the boat. His wife, a formidable woman with a most unpleasant face, forced his head into a bucket of cold water. The payment was indeed a considerable amount of money; I could have bought a boat for that. I lashed my horses to the boat's side-rail. We cast off into the waters and he pointed the boat to the dark cliffs across the straits.

The weather was worsening and the seas were getting rougher. I tethered my riding horse between the two side-rails at the stern of the boat and was about to do the same with my packhorse when a strong gust of wind whipped the sail at the same time as a wave lifted the bow of the boat. My foot slipped on the wet planks and I crashed to the bottom, falling into unconsciousness.

So there you have it. That is the story of how I became *ronin* – a wave man. But I shall return on the day that has been appointed, to the barracks in Kyoto.

Chapter 2

SILMAR THE GOLDEN

<u>Year Of The Brown Bear</u>

TAMBARHAL'S DAWN, as it was termed by the elves, was passing; that trick of the light, as the sun began its climb towards the horizon in the east, giving the impression that dawn was arriving early. True dawn would begin to appear very soon afterwards. This would be the time that the animals and birds of the forest would abandon some of the caution taken to protect them against the predators of the night. Time to drink from the river's bank and graze in the eaves of the forest before the predators of the day began their hunt. The mountains to the west of the trees held a multitude of predators, some 2-legged, others four-legged, many with even more; some flying – although these vicious predatory monsters were rarely seen during these years of relative peace and prosperity.

As the light slowly grew, the snow-covered tops of the mountains just to the west seemed to glow with a rosy hue while the forest was in relative gloom. The first sign of life was from the song of birds from the wood. After a while a number of deer warily and delicately approached the water's edge, the antlers of the young bucks still stubby at this early time of the year but one magnificently antlered buck led the does. Other beasts timidly came into view while others still watched from within the forest's shadows.

From the cover of the trees, one pair of eyes watched every movement by the riverside in silence, the owner making no sound and no movement. Other pairs of eyes close by were shut, their owners taking their last opportunity for a light sleep – they had been on the move all night.

There was a sudden flurry of movement from the forest not fifty paces away. A hail of arrows arced through the air and buried themselves in and around the most magnificent of the bucks. The stricken animal gave a throaty alarm call and took a few steps into the water before falling in a fountain of spray flecked red with its blood. Three does also fell but one struggled to rise again with an arrow protruding from her neck. All the beasts and birds bolted for the cover of the forest and their panicked movement was heard for many moments until it faded to nothing. Then there was stillness. A short distance away, the sleeping eyes had snapped open but the raised arm of the watcher halted any further movement.

Some minutes passed before the hunters appeared from the forest. They were grotesque to look upon, savage-looking bipeds with short legs, thick arms and foul faces. Their dark faces had large lower jaws from which protruded porcine-like tusks. They were well-armed though; four with crossbows took up a defensive position around the other five bow-men. All had short but heavy scimitars although none had sheaths to put them in. They wore thick leather tabards over which an assortment of armour had been hung. Their coarse guttural language betrayed an aggression which often manifested itself, even amongst themselves.

"Damned *tuskers*!" breathed the watcher from the forest. He made a sweeping signal with his arm to instruct his party to move. They quietly dropped down from the tree branches and crept stealthily through the forest.

The goblins were now quiet as they dragged their prey from the water. They quickly set about removing the antlers, this was looked upon as a prize which would perhaps buy them a human slave, and some fighting broke out among them. A vicious bite from one goblin, larger than the others, settled the argument; he took the antlers for himself. The head was removed and cast into the water – there was little of value there.

Unexpectedly, the faces of the goblins looked up in alarm as a new flurry of arrows flew towards them. Four went down immediately and two others gazed in shock at arrows protruding from their own bodies. The five survivors fumbled for their bows and crossbows but had little opportunity to use them as six grey figures rushed the twenty or so paces from the trees towards them. The goblins were no match for the lithe, fast fighters who confronted them. One by one they were killed until the last, which refused to yield, was finally run through with a longsword. Only one of the attackers had sustained a wound, a long gash which bled profusely until the leader, who had been the watcher, tightly bound it with a clean cloth taken from a belt pouch.

"Watch that wound, it may fester. They do not take care of their weapons as we do," he instructed. "Touch nothing here; let them rot where they lie but chop off their right ears; there will be a bounty for them. The bastards have killed the strongest of this little herd – a damned waste. This herd will take a couple of years to recover before one of the young bucks will doubtless make it strong again."

The others nodded in agreement, their faces grim with anger. They took what meat they would need to sustain them on their two-day journey back home; the remains would provide food for other hungry scavengers. The leader also took the antlers and handed it to one of his companions.

These were High Elves, tall and slim though deceptively strong. Their leader was quite young even for High Elves but when measured in the years of humans, he was older than many of the human elders of the town where he lived. The others however, were younger than him. All elves wore a grey-green cotton tunic over their chain mail and a similarly-coloured hooded cape to enable them to conceal themselves in trees and scrub-land. The only features that distinguished the leader from his companions were the long golden hair worn loose to well below his shoulders, the others wore their hair of a shorter length and tied back for practicality, and the fact he carried two swords, one long and the other a little shorter. They had very few items that would rattle and give away their presence. Only their arrows were white although these were concealed in quivers worn at the waist for speed of withdrawal. The elven band made almost no sound as they moved across the countryside, keeping their profiles below the skyline or in trees to avoid detection.

They were a hunting party; hobgoblins, goblins and trolls were their game. Their tactics were ambush, hit and run; to destroy the enemy and move away before they could themselves be ambushed. There were many such hunting parties during these times. They were necessary to keep the monstrous beasts under control for they were prolific in their breeding. Towns, villages, settlements and farmsteads close to the mountains were always in fear of attack from bands of goblins. Travellers on the roads were generally under threat from ambush by Trolls. Foolish indeed were the travellers and caravan masters who travelled without a well-armed and experienced escort in this area.

The elves were making progress though. For the last ten years attacks were less frequent. The road between Westron Seaport and Northwald City and the area as far east as Gash on the eastern border were safer although travellers were still inclined to attach themselves to caravans for safety. Adventurers were making a small fortune by hiring themselves out as guards to travelling parties.

ѳ ҿ

The bustling, multi-racial little market town of Refuge, on the western fringes of the great but daunting Highforest, nestled close to the eastern foothills of the Spine Wall Mountains. The town straddled a minor route leading north from the Great East Silk Road and into wild lands towards the Highforest. The road through the region was often plagued by troublesome goblins, a few hobgoblins and occasionally ogres, the most ferocious of the monstrous beings. It had been that way for many, many years, in fact. If nothing else, it had provided a valuable training ground for the young elven warriors of the Refuge militia. They had become skilled in the use of a wide variety of weaponry, in ambush and formation attack techniques and in noiseless movement through both mountainous and forested terrain.

High elves were relative newcomers to the region. A turbulent period spanning some decades had followed the collapse of the elven kingdom of Faerhome a few centuries previously. The elves had dispersed and set up communities in many of the lands throughout the Baylea continent generally sharing townships with other races, including human, Halfling and gnome. Dwarven too, but these were rare occasions as dwarves rarely saw eye to eye with elves and Halflings. A large group of High Elves had settled in Refuge and had integrated into the human society, albeit keeping their culture separated from that of what they considered to be disorderly humans.

The protection and safety of Refuge and the area between Spinewall and the peaks to the west had become the responsibility of the highly disciplined elven population. These days, the little-used supply route leading north through by the Highforest and Refuge region was largely safe, with very few incidents from the marauding monstrous goblins, goblins, ogres and trolls. The most difficult times would be during the late summer when goblins came out of the mountains in search of livestock and, if they were lucky, weapons and slaves from poorly guarded wagon trains. At all times though, elven militia from Refuge offered escorted passage, for a fair price, for travellers through the region as well as a safe haven in Refuge itself in times of rare but serious activity from the goblins.

The day had started with light rain during the early hours of morning but the clouds took their heavy load eastwards. The morning was misty but this would soon burn off to leave a bright warm day. A mounted hunting party came in through the town gates and trotted towards the militia muster square. One member handed a fine set of antlers to his leader who proudly held it high.

A collection of young ladies, elven and human, rushed forward, keen to be the recipient of the prize, not necessarily to be the proud owner of the antlers, but more for the attention of the handsome troop leader.

"I shall decide all in good time," laughed the young elf. Cries of disappointment followed from the flock of girls. It was the same every time he returned and they had not really expected anything different this time.

"Hail Silmar!" was the cry of the townsfolk. His return, as well as that of any other leader who returned with all members of his team, was always welcomed on their return to the town. He sent his injured troop member off to the healer's house; the elf's arm was indeed inflamed and had caused him much pain. The Sergeant at Arms strode out from the militia barracks. Silmar handed that leather bag of goblin ears to him.

"Good work. Your report in an hour, Silmar Galadhal. Get yourself and your equipment cleaned up, sort yourself out with a meal from the cook and I want you and your squad on parade at noon. *Move!*"

ॐ ॐ

Silmar Galadhal felt at his most comfortable when wearing tightly-fitting deerskin hose which, it must be said, left little to the imagination of the elven and human maidens in Refuge; it was no surprise that they would try to brush past him in the hope of acquiring a light-handed contact with his muscular buttocks or, for the more daring and perhaps hopeful, with something of a more personal nature. A tightly-knit group of young maidens in the town would swap stories; most of them being just tall tales indeed, of the number of times they had manage to 'accidentally' brush past his most private of areas! Some stories were elevated to description of antics in a hayloft and, on more than one occasion, he had been confronted by a would-be suitor of an aforementioned young lady. At one time, the confrontation involved the furious father of a maiden who, eventually and tearfully, admitted the whole thing had been a just a tall tale made to impress her friends!

But hold! This tale digresses and, perhaps to a reader of sensitive disposition, it may not be to the best of good taste!

To return to the description of his garb then, he also favoured a slightly looser-fitting deerskin shirt over which he wore a grey-green tunic. His sword belt was buckled over this tunic along with another belt to which was fitted his pouches and small packs. Soft light-brown leather boots reached up to just below his knees. He clearly cared much for his attire which was kept in a good state of repair. Apart from being warm in the winter and cool in summer, his clothing assisted him in hiding in forest and plains alike.

On his shoulders he carried an old, shabby and battered, but well-loved, pack. It had also been well-repaired over a number of years for it had once belonged to his father. Inside this he carried his spare clothing, a whetstone, a blanket and his close-woven, waxed, woollen cloak which afforded protection from the wet and cold. Taking up most of the space in his pack and adding much to the weight of it, however, was a corselet of fine chain mail that he liked to wear beneath his tunic when the prospect of battle was likely. Twenty arrows were carefully wrapped in a linen bag and strapped to the outside of the pack. His small pouches carried items of more value; coins, flint and steel, a spoon and knife for eating and an expensive rarity, a bottle of bathing oil, carried on the off-chance that the opportunity for him to bathe (or be bathed!) might arise; in this activity he could be quite fastidious but then he hoped the young maidens might appreciate it! Each of these items was also carefully wrapped in rags to avoid them rattling together when in hiding or waiting in ambush.

Although this young elf gave the impression of a playful and, at times, immature attitude to his learning and fighting skills practice, he actually demonstrated a number of skills which would be of future benefit to him. His rapid progress within the ranks of the militia was in part due to his proficiency with weapons, in particular a double-sword skill which he had learnt over many years from his less-than-patient father and from the militia he had joined when he came of age at his sixtieth birthday. His father never envisaged that the day would come when *he* would be bested in swordplay by the one he considered to be his rather wayward son. It hadn't happened yet but that time was not far away. Skill with blade and bow alone are not sufficient to ensure the value of a warrior. That rapid progress also owed much to his leadership qualities, his knowledge of tactics and his ability to plan a campaign. He treated his team with respect and trained and looked after them well.

As an elfling, Silmar and his friends had dreamt of the day when they would become part of the Refuge militia, the elite fighting force that was sent out into the hills to cull the goblin, troll and ogre numbers. Human warriors were also accepted into the militia ranks and they did indeed make very effective fighters but the elves had qualities of agility, dexterity and acute senses that couldn't be matched by the humans. Men were generally happier when assigned to protect the little town. Once again, Silmar had honed his skills with some other elf-children by practising escape, evasion and creeping up to 'invade' one of their homes. Wooden sticks were their makeshift weapons and bruises and scraped knuckles were their 'battle-wounds'. Furthermore, elves had that advantage of dark-vision ability which manifested itself as they matured. Once he became old enough to train with his father, Silmar quickly developed his incredible agility and his ability to climb rocks, trees and buildings and to hide in trees and undergrowth, moving in silence and, when using his newly-acquired dark-sight, in almost total darkness. This was one aspect which pleased his father.

"He could climb a fifty-foot mirror!" he would proudly boast. "And with a bow, he cannot be bested by anyone in this town. Why, I have seen him on a bare horseback, at the canter, loose off arrows and hit a pumpkin at forty paces three times out of five!"

Other skills however, displeased his father. Silmar could be a practical joker and a trickster. He had the dexterity to perform sleight-of-hand tricks, he would hide coins and make them reappear, do balancing acts, turn somersaults and juggle apples. He had a rather good singing voice too and would sing and play a reed pipe, often imitating bird calls, mostly for the purpose of entertaining the young ladies – of course! These skills had often gotten him into, and out of, trouble on occasions beyond count.

But, the Baylea realms change, people change too and Silmar was beginning to show signs that maturity was at last setting in. He was never happier than when he was on a patrol leading his hunting party. Everything else he did was just to alleviate the boredom he felt when being back in Refuge. At times, the little market town seemed to be getting smaller, too small and at times constricting, and sometimes he would walk alone into the hills nearby although often with friends or perhaps with a young maiden. The outside world seemed to be beckoning to him. Traders, travellers and adventurers passed through with tales of battles, heroism, fame and riches galore. They spoke of Westron Seaport, the famed City of Magnificence; it wasn't that far off, perhaps a tenday-week on foot, but he had never been there. Many stories he took with a pinch of salt, but some were also of hunger, pain, injury, death of comrades, of wild animals, undead and long, cold and wet nights under trees. These interested him as much as tales of treasure and fame. But then, Refuge was still the centre of his life and he couldn't, or wouldn't, envisage a time when he would leave. He was still tied to the militia and there were words being hinted to him that promotion was possible.

His father watched him closely though and considered his future.

◈ ◈

Silmar Galadhal had spent three decades of his youth as a militia cadet developing his skills by tracking and hunting marauders on the mountainous borders of his homeland. The more experienced warriors of the militia would administer the final kill to a troll or orc, the larger of the goblin species. After completing his cadet training, and in the last few years before finally venturing out from his homeland, Silmar gained much experience as a militia member, under instruction, of the town defence. Many years passed before he earned the honour of becoming a member of the hunting party, still more before he earned the distinction of leading one.

At first, his ability in this area was considered by his father, Faramar, as 'disappointing'.

"Teamwork, teamwork, teamwork!" he yelled. "This is essential if the troop is to work together. This is *not* a game! You are *not* a one-man band, Silmar. You will *not* survive on your own, dammit!"

Meanwhile, Silmar had imagined a life of travel, although not necessarily of warfare and battle, of death and destruction. It wasn't that he couldn't use fighting and weapon skills. He was an accomplished swordsman and a more than reasonable bowman. Unusually, he favoured a two-weapon style in hand-to-hand combat having gained expertise through practising hour after hour, day after day and year after year with a longsword in one hand and shortsword in the other. He could hurl a dagger with some accuracy. His ability to move quietly and blend into the shadows was the envy of other young elves. He was very agile, much taken to hiding in ambush within the branches of trees and he coached his party likewise. After all, he had had a good teacher in his father. He had a habit of leading his team much further afield than was advised by his father.

Referred to by the townsfolk of Refuge as *Silmar the Golden* because of his flowing yellow hair, it was his strong, wiry physique and his ice blue eyes that acted as a magnet to young elven maidens, human girls too, who all turned their heads in admiration. His love of poetry and music and his penchant for showing off to these young ladies of the town, was not considered by his father as being in the correct place in Silmar's list of priorities. Faramar was stern at one particular liaison in which Silmar became more than friendly with a young human lady.

"You must *never* become involved with a human woman," he yelled, "not only because they are sometimes unworthy of an elf; I will always consider them inferior as should you. You will no doubt love her and she will love you. She will grow old but you will not. You will see her die while you are still young. You will see your children die of old age before you reach your middle years. And their children too. You will have a life of misery. Similarly, it will be a life of sadness for the woman who will become old and see her husband in the prime of his life. That cannot be fair on you or the woman. Think, damn you! There will be no happiness, only despair. You mark my words well, Silmar." This would be a lesson he would remember for a long time, in the time measured in the years of elves.

His enjoyment of entertainment though, was further enhanced by his ability to demonstrate his sleight-of-hand and to pick pockets or pouches. This also had resulted, more than once, in an irate townsman reporting him to the militia sergeant-at-arms and once being brought before the elven Tribunal of Venerables. On this occasion his exasperated father had used his influence to bail him out of difficulty with payment of restitution and guarantees of good behaviour.

Faramar Galadhal was habitually stern when dealing with his son's indiscretions. He was, after all, a very proud Elven Principal descended from the original House of Galadhal, one of the six minor noble Houses of Faerhome.

"Damn you boy," his father Faramar would shout. "Your tricks will get you into serious trouble one day. You lack self-discipline. When I was your age I was leading my own company of warriors – dammit, I've got the battle scars to prove it!" This was one of a series of oft-repeated phrases, which Silmar had learnt and mouthed in surreptitious synchronisation with his father.

As usual, Silmar's mother tutted and nodded her head in agreement with Faramar. Silmar would listen with rapt attention to the tales from long ago of the beautiful city state of Faerhome, how the gods had warred among themselves in the cataclysmic god-war and the city-state had fallen in the resulting earthquakes. Faerhome was now a ruin inhabited by creatures of foul nature said to have emerged from the depths of the Void.

Faramar placed his arm around his son's shoulder. "You have achieved much over the years and have made me very proud. But our family status will one day require you to take your place on the Elven Council for the defence of the Refuge region, and beyond."

His father continued. "Before you can be trusted with the responsibility for the lives not only of fellow warriors, you will first need to reprioritise your life, discover your own senses of responsibility and duty and further broaden your experience of life. In short, my boy, you need to grow up!"

Silmar could feel a feeling of uncertainty creeping through him.

Faramar sat down on an exquisitely-carved chair and beckoned Silmar to do the same, but on a small, padded stool. "My son, you need to spread your wings and get some experience of the world around us. There is an old friend of mine, a dwarf, Ralmon the One-Sided, who was once an adventurer and who now runs a Tavern in Westron Seaport. He's got two visitors staying with him. It seems that they seek adventure and are looking either to join a party or for people to join them."

Silmar's jaw dropped and his heart lurched. He now knew what was coming next. His mother's hand went to her mouth and her eyes opened wide in shock and fear for her son.

"Husband!" she gasped. "He is still very young and –"

Silmar meanwhile, could hardly contain his excitement. He leapt to hid feet sending the little stool tumbling across the floor. "Father, I didn't think you would ever approve of me leaving the town, let alone leaving you, Mother and the home."

"My son, you've never been able to keep secret your longing to travel. Speak to this Ralmon and these people, but if you do decide to travel with them, ensure they are honourable and of good heart. *Tambarhal* will guide your future decisions providing that you speak to him at times. Do not go off on your travels without first saying goodbye to your Mother and me. I'm afraid you cannot take the weapons and equipment that you train with and bear with you on your patrols; those belong to the militia. I will though, have something for you that will start you on your journey."

"A dwarf, father?" Silmar asked through his excitement and bewilderment. "When did you become friendly with dwarves?"

"He is no ordinary dwarf," his father explained. "We campaigned together and fought side by side many times."

"Any why One-Sided?" gasped Silmar. "What sort of name is –"

"You will understand when you meet him."

Silmar left his home with mixed emotions. The house now seemed both a sanctuary and a cage. Maldor, an old friend, was distraught when he heard the news.

"My father thinks I am immature and need self-discipline," Silmar told him. "He tells me that the caravan of wagons over there leaves for Westron Seaport within the hour and I'm to be on it."

"No room for another to go with you, I suppose?" The request was half-hearted; Maldor would never leave the town on such a hare-brained scheme, as he was to put it later to other friends.

The young elves clasped forearms. "Travel well Silmar, my dear friend, may *Tambarhal* guide and care for you." The final remark, customary for one who was about to embark on a journey, was very comforting for Silmar.

He left his friend standing in the middle of the street. The sun dial in the square showed the time a half an hour before noon.

"By the gods!" he exclaimed! "My report!"

He rushed to the Barracks and swiftly wrote out his report, a reasonable tally but which would do little to earn him praise. His team was already lined up on the square when he strode out. He positioned himself in front of his patrol and brought them to order.

The Sergeant at Arms marched out of the barracks and up to within one double-pace distance from Silmar.

"To order!" he barked. "Absence will not be tolerated, do you hear me?"

Silmar was confused, what was all this about? He had not been tardy.

"Leaving your place of duty without application for leave of absence is a court martial offence," the Sergeant at Arms continued at the team in general. "You can be flogged for less!"

Silmar felt beads of sweat starting to run down his face. All of his team were present; no-one was missing.

"I understand you are about to desert your place of duty, young Galadhal." The Sergeant at Arms was now smiling, a rare sight indeed.

"Under orders from my father, Sergeant," gasped Silmar. The relief he felt was overpowering.

"Sorry to see you go, young 'un. Guess you didn't think anyone else knew about you leaving us but your father spoke to me of this, and the reasons why, the day before yesterday. Can't help but agree with him on that decision. Should make a mature elf of you. And, well, we got together this collection and bought you this."

He brought out a fine dagger from behind his back, removed it from its well-crafted sheath and handed it, hilt first, to Silmar.

The elf took it with trembling hands and tested its weight and balance. The steel of the blade was of very high quality indeed and its hilt was made from ivory; a pea-sized ruby was set into the pommel of the hilt. The dagger, in its engraved leather scabbard, must have cost a lot of money.

He looked from the Sergeant to his patrol. "Sergeant! I can't thank you all as I should. This is beautiful and I shall treasure it for always. It will remind me of my friends that I leave behind when I have times of trouble and loneliness."

"Fall Out!" the Sergeant at Arms commanded. He warmly shook Silmar by the hand and said "I meant it lad, I *will* be sorry to see you go. Over the last year or few you've built yourself up a good team spirit with your squad and they've benefited from it. I'm getting a bit old for this now and my retirement is only a couple of years away; you would have been in line for promotion you know."

"That's not what my father says," moaned Silmar. "He thinks I need self-discipline and experience."

"That's nothing to do with your job, that's your social habits, young 'un. Good luck, travel well and return to us all the better for it. May *Tambarhal* guide and care for you."

Silmar bade his farewells and strolled about the town centre saying more farewells to other friends and more than a few young maidens. He soon ended up in the Tavern by the market square. Being a market day, it was busy inside with many traders and travellers sitting at the tables or standing at the bar. The atmosphere was stifling even though the day was not particularly hot. His eyes smarted at the thick smoke of the pipe-leaf. The noise was loud and somebody was trying to sing in a corner although few were paying much attention. Silmar ordered himself a quart tankard of ale and looked around the taproom at the variety of people. A few curious and analytical eyes looked his way too. He needn't have tried too hard, his bearing and a few small battle scars were testimony to his active life.

After a while, Silmar returned home. He was breathless and excited. "Father, I am now resolved to travel. I have spoken with the wagon master. We leave soon."

"My son, I am already regretting having mentioned the idea to you. Your mother is in tears in the next room. Our blessings go with you but first, take this." He handed his son a small bag.

Silmar opened the bag, surprisingly heavy, to find a large number of gold coins. He had never held in his hand so much money in his life. Also in the bag was a copper disk on a leather thong. He recognised the design on the disk as the symbol of his father's House of Galadhal.

"One hundred and twenty gold crowns and a few silver." He said. "Take this, When you get to your destination, give Ralmon the *One-Sided* my compliments, he will advise you as to which trader will provide you with clothing, weapons, armour and other bits and pieces for you. Choose wisely and listen closely to his advice. Wear the medallion and think of your mother and me from time to time." He then handed his son a sword in a battered scabbard.

"I can't let you go into the world without a sword, Silmar. Take this but when you get to the great city, purchase yourself something better and just sell this in a market. It is an old blade from the militia armoury."

Silmar was unable to speak, being elated and overcome all at the same time.

Faramar hugged his son and continued. "See your mother before you go. Travel well; come back to us safely, my son. May *Tambarhal* guide you and care for you. Send word of your whereabouts when you can."

Half an hour later, with no possessions other than the clothes he stood up in, a few items in his pack and belt-pouch, his precious dagger, sword, coins and his medallion, Silmar left his home and his family.

CHAPTER 3

"*I MUST ADMIT, contrary to all our original opinions, she ends her twelve years here as the best new acolyte Priestess of Neilea that I have ever seen. Observe now her confident manner. Others want to be with her, to be like her. The young trainee men follow her rather than those other new priestesses who are possessed with greater beauty. See how she swings her quarterstaff with an effortless grace and a confident efficiency that will afford her great protection in the years to come. She has warmth about her but she has strength of character too. And what dedication! She puts me in mind of another young girl five decades ago; but I did not have her confidence then. And aye, hahaha! Was I not one for the boys, as were you too Helania, as I remember aright? Did I not also carry out the very same experiment? To this day, she is not aware that we know of it! We shall doubtless hear more of her in the years to come if Our Lady of Kismet protects her – as I have no doubt she will. I would pray that she will return here one day. There was little more we could teach her and always she wanted to learn more. I perceive that she will achieve great things and will be powerful one day. Go, our Daughter of Neilea, with the shining protection of Our Lady of Serendipity. You carry Our Lady's favour, I can sense its strength dwelling within her."*

Simenine Tarathtelle,
Matriarchal High Priestess of the
Temple of Neilea
Year of the Plentiful Harvest

༉ ༉

FOR MANY years now, in fact from the age of five years, Taura Windwalker had been studying in the hope of becoming a novitiate priestess of Neilea – the Arcane Scientist, the Goddess of Magical Knowledge and Destiny. It had been hard for Taura and a wrench for her parents too, for her to be given over to the Temple by her family on the insistent say-so of the local Priestesses who claimed to have seen a potential in the little dark-haired girl. Life had been hard for the family. Taura's mother had also been a Priestess of Neilea until a disease had left her partially blind. The offer of their daughter to be brought up and taught by the Temple would ensure that she wouldn't share in the times of hardship and even starvation that constantly threatened.

The weeks of journeying in wet, windy and cold weather from Lopastor to the Temple of Arcane and Divine Learning in Karne were now only a faint memory. The years that followed had been tough at first but they eased noticeably as she grew older and as younger girls, and on the rare occasion boys too, came in as little students to fill the space as older students moved on. She had cried herself to sleep every night for two years. Now at last, she was trained sufficiently to serve the lands of Baylea in the name of her beloved goddess.

Apart from her mother, her family was virtually illiterate and had kept progressively less contact with her until it eventually stopped altogether. There was no explanation for it ceasing and they were too far away for her to travel to see them. Having lived near to Casparsport in the country of Lopastor, a lawless land of continual upheaval and disquiet, there were any number of reasons why she no longer heard from them. She had vague memories of an ocean and a high rocky promontory upon which stood a tall stone tower that was surrounded by a high stone wall. It was not her family home, she knew, but it was quite close by, but something about the memory disturbed her. Perhaps one day, once her learning was at an end, she would try to find her mother, father and two younger brothers. This mystery of their disappearance from her life plagued her mind for some years until she lost the memories of what they looked like. But now, after lying dormant for so long, the memories, such as they were, resurfaced and became significant once again.

Taura was quite short in stature and, when dressed in a travelling cloak, tended to appear slightly plump. When her cloak was cast off though, her true build was plainer to see. She was stocky and had clearly spent much time in physical exercise. She boasted that she had been able to outrun every other novitiate in the Temple of Learning over a measured mile. Her quarterstaff skills could not be matched by other students either. By the time she was fourteen years of age, she was participating in the town games and was besting the boys of her age with quarterstaff and at wrestling. In fact, by the time she completed her twelve years of studies, she had developed her muscular stature to a point unexpected of a young woman. The senior lecturers had hoped to encourage her to stay on after her studies so that she could teach fitness and the use of a quarterstaff to the newer students. It was not to be however. She had promised herself that she would travel through the realms of Baylea.

She was not considered particularly beautiful. She didn't even consider herself attractive in any way but to others, she was. Her large brown eyes shone and sparkled, particularly when she smiled and even more so when she laughed. She had full lips and dark eyebrows that only enhanced her appearance. The day before leaving the Temple, she cut short her luxuriant long black hair so that it now barely reached her shoulders; she didn't miss it one bit. Her slightly tanned skin and her nose just a little wide, were not the product of time spent in sunlight and accidents when wrestling. Her lineage could be traced to Qoratt, the *Land of the Burning Sand,* far to the south, where the peoples were of a darker complexion. When a smile broke out on her oval face though, she looked very attractive; she did smile often and laugh at the least excuse. She was not in the least proud of her figure, considering herself to be too wide at the waist and thick in the legs – *apple stampers* she called them, much to the protestations of her friends. She also disliked her breasts; she thought them too large although her male friends insisted that that was a matter of opinion and that to complain about them was like slapping their beloved deity, Neilea, in the face!

In one aspect though, she had excelled. She had worked extremely hard at her studies over the last three years after having shown the signs at an early age that she would one day make a very proficient Priestess of Neilea. She certainly had the favour of The Lady of Serendipity because a promising destiny followed her throughout her years at the Temple. She had been popular with her peer group mainly because of her zest for life and sense of fun.

There had been two instances though, which had got her into trouble and each time they had involved dalliances with young boys in the village. "You have more to lose than they have, you foolish girl!" thundered the Matriarchal High Priestess. "Do you realise that the longer you retain your virginity then the more potent will be your gift of divine magic and prayer spells from Her Gracious Lady!" She bowed her head in reverence at mentioning one of the many titles bestowed on the Goddess of Destiny, Neilea. "All they lose is a spoonful of bodily fluid! You will lose infinitely more! You may be called upon to protect others and heal them. You will be hampered if you lose that other gift. Cogitate on this in your cell until the morning feast."

Try as she might, she couldn't shake the image of a spoon of fluid out of her mind!

Even on that day, Taura had doubts that her magic potency would be depleted were she to lose her virginity, certainly not by a significant measure. She discovered, at the age of fourteen, that a couple of the very few trainee male priests of Neilea had not appeared to lose their powers after she and a few other young novitiate priestesses, at her instigation, had witnessed them shed their seed the evening before – all in the name of research of course, as they convinced each other! As her reward to the boys for taking part in the experiment, she had allowed one of them, tall and handsome but rather spotty, to explore the parts of her upper body beneath her tunic. She had also conducted a little exploration of her own and he gasped as she touched him. She watched with curiosity and then laughed lightly as her hand caused him to shed his seed for his second time! This was her first tactile experience and although exciting, the young man had nervously fumbled and one of his fingernails had scratched her breast next to a sensitive and delicate point – that ended the fortunate lad's reward!

The next couple of incidents were to result in those severe warnings from the Matriarchal High Priestess. She had been accused of having scant regard for the authority of her tutors. Chastened, she dived headlong into her studies and completed her training without further incident - or *without being caught* she would boast but she refused to elaborate and the rest was sheer speculation!

Her studies had taken on a new importance at this stage but as the last days of learning approached, she knew she wanted more. She was not averse to asking questions of her tutors. But she would learn little more here, not now; perhaps later. Certainly not while the breadth and depth of her study would be restricted by the controls imposed by the hierarchy at the Temple.

Now, finally, she would soon be free to pursue her destiny. She decided she would travel west to the great city of Westron Seaport on the Landsdrop Coast.

Perhaps the great libraries here or those of Norovir in the far-off eastern realm of Cascant would enable her to peruse the great tomes, scrolls and books of divine magic. But at what price? She had very little money and may need to find work. Meanwhile a wide world continued to beckon her. And she was urgently ready to heed its call. But on the morrow, after early prayers and a celebratory dawn feast, she would be presented with her silver holy symbol; she only wished her family could be there to witness the occasion – would they be proud? She cried herself to sleep that night for the first time in almost ten years.

CHAPTER 4

SILMAR CAUGHT his breath as the caravan crossed over the high pass on the brow of the hills to the east of the city of Westron Seaport; an amazing sight lay before him. The massive city was spread below but even the description 'massive' seemed inadequate to Silmar. Not even in his wildest imaginations could he ever have visualised the city with the great sea glinting beyond. The caravan master, who had seen all this before, grinned at the expression on the elf's face.

"Impressed, young 'un?"

"By the gods!" Silmar gasped. "How can this enormity support itself? And the ocean! Look – I can see the sea!"

Everyone within earshot laughed at his look of wonderment.

"You wait until you get inside those walls, kid. You've seen sod all yet!"

What walls they were. As far as Silmar could make out, because of a mist, the city was in the shape of slightly more than a semi-circle, with its flat side facing the sea. The sandstone walls were very high with watch-towers topped with wooden turrets at regular intervals. The road before them stretched to the city where it led through a great arched gateway. Even from this distance of maybe two leagues or more, the elf, with his keen eyesight, could only just see that the gates were open and that traffic was entering and leaving through it. Within the city he could see towers, minarets, domes and palaces. Some of the domes were painted, he assumed, in gold and these shone brightly in the misty sunlight.

A huge ditch encircled the walls and the elf was certain that it contained water. A great wooden bridge spanned the moat.

The drover confirmed his thoughts. "Aye, it does that but you wouldn't be wantin' ter fall in cos yer wouldn't drown; it's too thick. Gods know what diseases yer would be gettin' b'cos it's full've shit an' dead things. Don't be askin' me what dead things b'cos it ain't jus' animals an' stuff, iff'n yer know what I means."

Another sight grabbed his attention. The walls had been built long ago but the city had continued to grow in size since then. It had been only a matter of time before there was no room left to build inside the walls. Many buildings had been erected slightly beyond the moat at first, then spreading outwards further and wider until the city almost doubled in size.

There were sheep pens and corrals with cattle, horses and camels outside the city that were, in the main, run by honest dealers, according to the wagon master. Also, there were grain stores and warehouses built of both timber and stone.

"A thousand of your puny towns could hide in this city and still leave room for the gentry to become rich on the pickings," said the wagon master. In his wisdom, he had warned Silmar not to stray too far from centres of activity, not to enter establishments promising the excitement of ladies of ill repute and to get himself properly armed straight away. He warned that a rough sort frequented the dock area, always on the lookout for easy prey, but the city watchmen were generally patrolling.

"I have lived not a tenday week's travel from this city and in almost a century of my life I have not seen this – this – oh, this wondrous sight!"

"A century? So you're just a kid, young elf, eh?"

"Aye, but we elves can live up to four hundred and fifty, even five hundred years. I didn't come of age until I was sixty. My father thought I was very immature and sent me to join the militia. I was hunting goblins by the time I was eighty and have been a hunting party leader since I was eighty-five. And he still thinks I'm immature!"

"Ye gods!" cried a wagonneer. "Hey men, we've been travelling with my grandfather!"

Good-natured laughter erupted from the drovers. Even Silmar couldn't help but chuckle. But respect was clearly evident on their faces, particularly as they had seen him practising with his weapons on many occasions.

While heading westwards, they had passed many other caravans travelling in an easterly direction, each of them heavily laden with cargoes. So this was where they had all been travelling from. The caravan continued on its journey and in less than two hours they were approaching the gates. It would soon be evident that many of those living outside the walls did not enjoy the privileges and standards of living of those on the inside. There was much deprivation and squalor among the hovels; beggars lined the road leading towards the gates. The sight of drovers wielding whips was enough to keep child beggars from crawling all over the wagons.

The sight and smell of cooking fires, manure, human waste and the squalor around the huts and hovels was an assault on the senses of Silmar, as well as those of the drovers.

There were other sights however, that were even more distasteful. An area to the right hand side of the road, up against the city wall, had been set aside for criminals to be hung on gibbets and in small, metal cages. There they stayed until long after death and their flesh had been picked clean by carrion birds, only then were the remains removed and cast into the sea. Silmar was appalled at what, to him, seemed like an act of barbarism. Six bodies, one of whom was still alive and appealing for water to children gathered close by, were hanging from beams or in cages. The master drover observed Silmar's revulsion and explained the reality of the situation.

"You must understand, young Silmar, that these are not just thieves and burglars. These are murderers, rapists, spies, arsonists, child molesters and persistent criminals. There is no room for these bastards in this society. It is not fair on any society to expect them to spend money to keep these criminals in a prison cell and, to be quite frank, their crimes are too severe for them to be trusted to be, er, enlisted into the militia. And this does act as a deterrent to visitors to the city to encourage them to be on their best behaviour. You'll find other areas like this at the North and South gates. And near the quayside, there are gibbets from which hang many pirates and buccaneers. Don't feel sympathy for these pieces of shit, they're not worth it."

Although he could appreciate the drover's point of view, Silmar knew that he would never approve of the practice. The wagons continued to the gates where, after a brief discussion with the gate watch, they made their way into the city. Thus began Silmar's introduction to the life within the mighty city of Westron Seaport.

The road surface inside the city gate was paved or cobbled and very smooth. Here, they encountered a different type of beggar; these were offering trinkets, flowers, fruit and other wares for copper coins.

"Ignore them, boy," gruffly warned the wagon master as he observed Silmar reaching for his money bag. "Encourage one and the other shits will swarm all over us like locusts!"

Silmar's hand dropped away and the stern face of the wagon master and drovers' whips were sufficient to deter the beggars.

The wagons skirted around an open area with lawns and flowerbeds. Well-dressed couples, families and children were leisurely walking through the park. It seemed to Silmar to be an incongruous sight so close to the poverty outside the gates. He looked about him, at the buildings, homes and palaces and realised that this was indeed a very rich and opulent district of the city. Carriages, with well-dressed passengers attended by liveried servants, being drawn by well cared-for ponies and horses, were a common sight in this area of the city.

After a long while the caravan turned to the left and continued past shops, store houses, inns, taverns, livery stables and blacksmiths, and even a great amphitheatre. The wagon master explained that these arenas were in common use for the enjoyment of the public with displays of martial arts, battle re-enactments, archery, swordsmanship and spear-throwing skills and horse-racing.

He went on to explain further. "There are also amphitheatres for the arts such as music, theatrical plays, poetry and comedy. You can watch juggling, sleight of hand and gymnastic skills. They got a few places like that in the city. For a silver piece, you can watch a variety of entertainment all day. Have to watch out for cutpurses and pickpockets though. Get lots of them in the crowds at the arena or amphitheatre."

They eventually arrived at an open square and it was evident that the rich houses and palaces had been left behind and the business classes of peoples were now more commonplace. Broad paved or cobbled streets, with raised walkways at the sides, had been evident in the more opulent centres; they were now trundling along rutted dirt roads strewn with litter, or worse, and seemed to be the best that could be found in these poorer districts. The wagon master had said that the streets around the docks area would mainly be cobbled because these would have to carry the weight of loaded wagons to and from the warehouses of the quays. There were not so many beggars to be seen but street tinkers had boxes of wares for sale; their voices cried out to attract attention.

A woman approached the lead wagon and, baring her chest, called to Silmar. "A silver piece, 'andsome elf, and you'll 'ave a memory of me to treasure for ever!" She erupted into a screeching laugh but backed away as the wagon master raised his whip.

"Your loss, then," she retorted with a sour face, covering herself up again.

"What was all that about?" enquired a confused and embarrassed Silmar.

"Eh? Are you serious?" answered the wagon master. "She's a lady of horizontal pleasure!"

Silmar's expression showed he was still confused.

"Er, well, a street walker!" the man persisted.

Silmar was still confused.

The wagon drover turned back and looked at Silmar with a toothless grin. "Look, she gives sexual favours then takes all your money and runs for it while you're pulling your hose up!"

"Oh, by the gods, I see!" replied a flustered Silmar. "That's not allowed in Refuge."

"There are places in this city called brothels, bordellos and bawdy houses, lots of 'em in the dockyard district. Watch out there 'cos you'll come away with a lot more than you went in with if you're not careful!"

Silmar was still confused.

"Pox, crabs, knob-rot! – Gods save us! You don't know much for an elf of your age, do you?"

Silmar gave a shy grin; he was learning the ways of the city very quickly indeed.

They passed down a broad street where rows of shops and dealer's establishments lined each side. Some dealers immediately caught Silmar's eye. These were selling weapons, from inexpensive, poorly-made to those of the highest quality, said to be imbued with magical or even god-given properties, if that could be believed. Many different types of armour were also displayed, much of which had seen action and some of which were new, exotic and, occasionally, impractical or even useless! Burly toughs stood outside the establishments to discourage thieves and looters.

In between some of the shop-fronts were eating houses serving food and drink from many countries. The strong smell of spices and cooking reminded Silmar that he had not eaten a meal for a few hours. He didn't particularly care; there was so much to see here in this busy, bustling city that it took his mind off his growling stomach. There were inns and taverns with well cared-for fronts and stables for horses and wagons. Again, the smells of food and ale from these were very inviting. Silmar was quite partial to a quart of ale from time to time; more than one if he was in the mood! Other buildings with signs showing coins and playing tiles were described to the elf as establishments for games and gambling.

"Keep away from them young 'un," advised the wagon master. "They'll take your money off you and leave you destitute in minutes."

Silmar didn't bother explaining that he was renowned as the canniest gambler in Refuge. But then this was a vast city and perhaps he would find himself out of his depth.

The wagon master reminded him that the inns and taverns close to the dockyard district would be more basic, in fact somewhat rougher, than these in the city centre.

Silmar was filled with a sense of foreboding but as his father had recommended *The Ship's Prow* and its owner, a dwarf called Ralmon the One-Sided, it must be of a very high standard indeed.

They passed by a large building that had a sign outside it showing two water jugs, one of which was tilting and water was pictured pouring from it into a large tub.

"What's that?" the elf enquired.

"It's a bath house!" replied the wagon master. "People go there to, well, er. Bath houses are where men can relax for cleansing, massages or to meet their mistresses or whores."

Silmar now understood these descriptions although he had until now thought that the term *mistress* merely meant a woman of high status or a female employer. He was soon put right. He had noticed temples in every district in the city. He already knew that these were dedicated to a wide variety of gods from the Pantheon. They offered solace, rest, prayer, healing and counselling.

The caravan now turned right down a long curving street, somewhat narrower than the others they had travelled down before. It soon opened into a large square and slowly skirted the biggest market that Silmar had ever seen. There were hundreds of stalls selling cloths, spices, wines, cheeses, meats, fruits and vegetables, leathers, weapons of all sorts, boots and sandals, clothing, tools for farming and craftsmanship, horses and ponies, dogs, cattle and sheep, reptiles, hawks, falcons and parrots, exotic fish and medicines and healers' packs. The elf even noticed stalls providing services, at a price, from mages and priests.

Silmar resolved to visit the market if time allowed.

Beggars were, once again, everywhere. Many of them were ex-soldiers or sailors carrying scars or with missing limbs from countless battles, children born with deformities or disease and ageing whores unable to scrape a living with their bodies but still trying to ensnare the desperate or poor into parting with a couple of copper coins. One of them, a particularly unkempt hag with missing teeth and a black eye, offered to use her hand to provide some 'relief' to Silmar for a copper coin. While the others chortled, he almost gagged.

Another turn down to the left brought the wagons outside the front of a large inn. It looked somewhat dilapidated, needing a coat of paint. The bow of a small boat was attached somehow to the front of the building and the sign swinging gently from a small beam read "Shippes Prowe".

"Your destination, friend Silmar," shouted the wagon master. He jumped down from the wagon and Silmar leapt down to join him. "I've enjoyed your company, young elf. Look, you take care in this city. It's a hard place and this district is about the most worsest part and you gotta take care. I'll be back in Refuge in three weeks and I'll tell your pappy that you got here safely."

The other drovers gathered round and shook Silmar by the arm. The elf was quite moved and thanked them profusely for having looked after him and he handed over a written message for his father. Silmar had actually written this some days before. He would be back one day, he had promised, and forwarded his love to his mother.

Sailors, mercenaries and adventurers from every corner of the Baylean continent wandered about, individually and in small groups. Silmar turned and noticed that the street had its name scrawled in charcoal on the corner of a wooden building – *Odd Strete*.

The buildings along this street were in slightly better condition than most of those close to the waterfront and docks. A few paces down the street a board showing a symbol of a stick-man in a large water-tub with a pitcher of water being poured by a semi-naked woman, hanging on the front of one building clearly indicated its function – a bath-house. This was archetypal in city areas such as this because very few people outside of the mercantile and opulent city areas were able to read and write and what written signs existed were poorly scribed.

The wagons trundled off and Silmar was left in front of the inn with just his weapons and back-pack of belongings. As he turned towards the door to the inn, it crashed open and a large human flew out head first.

"And choddin' stay out!" shouted a gruff, booming voice. Framed in the doorway was a dwarf who paused briefly to observe Silmar suspiciously and then went back inside pulling the door shut behind him. The large human slowly picked himself up from the cobbles and staggered to a hitching rail. Bending over, he vomited, straightened up, wiped his mouth on his sleeve and staggered off.

Silmar picked up his pack, took a deep breath and went inside. As his eyes swiftly adjusted to the gloomy light and smoky atmosphere, he noted that the interior of the tavern was divided into two areas. The bar, and a kitchen beyond, was on the upper floor area with the bar itself on the left hand side. The tables on the lower level were merely rough-hewn wooden planks nailed across upturned barrels. Wooden benches were arranged either side. Each table had a thick, greasy candle stub that was mounted on an ever growing mound of old wax but during the day, with the window shutters open, the candles were not lit. A number of battered metal spoons were attached on each table by an arm's-length piece of chain. In common with many other lower-class ale-houses, it would be the responsibility of the user to wipe the spoon clean before use. Silmar shuddered at the sight of it. The floor was grubby and strewn with spilt beer, dropped food, vomit and pipe-leaf.

A flight of stairs led from the right-hand side of the bar up to the next floor. Up here, he assumed, were the bedchambers.

Four steps led to the upper level which was divided into booths, each being separated by four foot-high wooden partitions. Each booth had a round wooden table on which were similarly-mounted candle stubs. Individual chairs were placed about the tables. This was obviously the area set aside for the more discerning clientele or those who required a little privacy.

Both the lower and upper levels were lit by a dozen or so spluttering candles arranged, on dripping mounds of greasy wax, around wagon wheels suspended from the ceiling. These wheels would be raised and lowered by chains hooked on the taproom walls.

An overpowering smell of stale ale, vomit and pipe-weed assailed Silmar's nostrils as he took in the sight. He had been in better places than this. No doubt though, there were far worse places too.

A small number of people were seated around the lower taproom. The place did not appear well looked after by any means, surprisingly, but then it was quite early in the day. A one-armed, heavily-bearded man stood behind the bar; but Silmar had been told to expect a one-armed dwarf. The barman came out around the bar with a cloth, obviously to clean the tables, and dropped down three low steps. So he was a dwarf after all and one who had been standing on a ramp behind his bar.

"You layabouts get to cleaning this place up!" he bellowed at two barmen who were engaged in chatting to a scantily-clad woman at the end of the bar. "An' you can 'elp as well, ya strumpet!" he added. "I was outa here for a couple've hours an' I comes back to a shit-heap! I wants this place clean an' gleamin', the shutters wide open and this place smellin' like a tart's bedchamber! Get to it!"

Noticing Silmar's gape, the dwarf's expression became suspicious again. "Ah, what's this in mah tavern? An elf!" he exclaimed. "Don't see many of your sort 'ere! What yer gawpin' at, eh? Ah, me platform?"

Silmar nodded.

"If you don't fit the world, you have to make the world fit you!" explained the dwarf. "Well, come in, elf stranger, what can I do for you? Oh, I s'pose I better tell you, yer lucky I don't mind pointy-ears like you in mah place! Not that I get many."

It was midday; Silmar had worked up a mighty thirst on his dusty journey and was more than a little hungry.

"Ale, if you please." He felt, rather than heard, his stomach rumble. "And may I trouble you for a meal?"

"Aye. Not seen yer in 'ere afore. I'm Ralmon Cleaverblade. They calls me *Ralmon the One-Sided* – can't think why. Heh heh! An' who're you?"

"I am Silmar, of the house of Galadhal in Refuge. My father sends his compliments and hopes that you are well and that business is good."

"What? Who? Hah! Well, bugger me with a toasting fork! You'll be Faramar's lad then" laughed Ralmon, reaching across the bar with his hand. "Hahaha, it's been many years since I campaigned with him, the old bushwhacker. I can provide you with a pottage, that's a vegetable stew, a chunk of bread – mah own bread mind you, none of the bakery rubbish that's only good for a doorstop! Need a bed?"

Silmar replied that pottage would be fine and a bedchamber would very much be needed. He cast his gaze around the taproom. A young woman, probably a cleric, Silmar couldn't see the holy symbol, sat at a table in a corner, her slightly well used quarterstaff leaning against the table beside her. A gnome sat chatting to her from the other side of the table but his gaze repeatedly took in Silmar. Four other drinkers sat at another table, smoking pipes and deep in quiet conversation. The rings of ale on their table from the bottom of their tankards suggested they had been there for some time although they didn't seem the worst for wear from much drinking. Occasional raucous laughter erupted from their table as they recounted lewd tales. The daringly-clad woman sat at one end of the bar eyeing up the young elf. After a while, one of Ralmon's barmen sidled over to her and started talking to her while ogling her breasts.

"Get to cleaning, I tol' ye!" roared Ralmon.

Later on, once he had finished his meal, Silmar engaged Ralmon in conversation while drinking his ale. The grizzled dwarf was keen to relive some old experiences and Silmar was an enthusiastic listener.

"Lost this arm in a skirmish when I was with yer pappy in Lopastor. An uprising by some damned religious sect. We was underground. Would 'ave lost the other bugger had yer dad not waded in an' kept the bastards off me. Well, that was the end o' me as an adventurer, I can tell ye. But I 'ad gotten meself enough of a fortune in me adventures to set up this 'ere business. Still 'ave a bit put by for when I retire; plan on going to Refuge in a few years an' live out the last o' me days with me memories an' a glass or five of elven fire-wine with your old pappy."

Silmar asked if Ralmon could suggest a reputable, but not too costly, dealer for weapons and clothing. "I need a cloak, another pair of boots and a pair of swords."

"Just a few doors away from 'ere, turn right outside the door an' it's up a little way on the right. Can't miss it, choddin' great big stuffed bear in the window. Tell Jaspar I sent yeh an' he won't overcharge yeh." He looked at the barman. "Hey! Get to work yous! I don't hire you to chat to, er, an' touch up the whores!" This latest outburst was directed at the barman who was still talking to the woman; his hand was inside the top of her blouse and they were both laughing. "And you, yer strumpet, put them teats away an' get some drawers on an' make yerself useful! Else yer out of here!"

"Frack you!" she retorted but went out into the kitchen.

"You already done that an' yer couldn't walk proper for days, yer hussy!" His reply brought a laugh from her and from everyone else in the taproom.

Ralmon was quite accurate in his description of Jaspar's shop. Almost 60 gold crowns later, Silmar had a rapier, a shortsword and a hunting knife, as well as boots, a couple of leather belt-pouches, a spare deerskin tunic and hose, a new whetstone, flint and steel and some miscellaneous items.

One requested item though, raised an eyebrow of Jaspar, "You won't buy something like that over the counter of any shop. Thieve's lock-picks aren't really legal, you know. Seein' as you're acquainted wiv me mate Ralmon we'll say no more about it. However, a friendly word of advice, if you want something like that then Ralmon's the one to ask, he's had a use for that sort of thing in his past, see? I don't want to get involved with that. If the watchmen catch you wiv 'em they'll lock you up! Keep quiet about it, don't want nobody getting' the wrong idea, right?"

Silmar agreed, paid the account and strapped on his weapons. He carried his equipment back to the Ship's Prow. It was beginning to get dark outside. Lamplighters were lighting small braziers that hung from metal lamp posts up and down *Odd Strete*.

On his return, he went up the stairs to the bedchamber allocated to him by Ralmon and dropped off his sack of equipment and swords. He decided to leave his knives strapped onto his belt – to get used to wearing them, naturally! A celebratory quart tankard of ale seemed an attractive proposition.

Although it was early evening, it was late in the day and the inn was still unusually quiet. He presumed people would still be working. Two of the four drinkers had gone but the cleric and gnome were still there. Two well-to-do men, most likely traders, were just settling themselves in one of the booths on the upper taproom floor. All of the patrons turned their heads to watch Silmar as he sauntered over and stood once again at the bar. Ralmon was busy changing a barrel and teasing in the tap with a mattock.

Silmar was more than halfway through his ale at the bar when the gnome came up beside him and plonked his tankard down on the surface. "'Nother two, Ralmon, if yer please, and one for master elf if he don' mind drinking with a gnome."

"Glad to, Master Gnome, if you will allow me to buy the next" said Silmar. The response was the standard interchange between two strangers at a bar that were striking up a new conversation.

The gnome chuckled. He stood about four and a half feet in height and although a little thick around the waist he looked unusually muscular. His skin colouring was orange, although tanned and leathery beneath his long red hair, and was typical of his race. He was dressed in an opulent dark-blue, hooded, silken gown that dropped to just below his knees. A beautifully-crafted belt, on which a large number of small packs and a pair of daggers were hung, was buckled around his middle. Unusually for a gnome, he wore a well cared-for pair of travelling boots of the highest quality rather than the normally-favoured sandals.

"Aye, young 'un, that sounds good to me but I suspects that the young lady over there would argue that I've 'ad enough, but sod it, a couple more can't do someone no harm, can it? Allow me to introduce meself. Called by some as Billit, on account that humans can't get their mouth round my proper name, at your service."

"Silmar Galadhal, at yours," he replied, offering his hand and being given a firm shake of the wrist. "And I am no human, as you know."

"Over 'ere," indicated Billit with an extravagant wave of his arm, "is one of Neilea's finest, name of Taura

Windwalker." He dropped his voice to a whisper. "She would probably be considered quite lovely by humans but for the life of me I can't see it meself!"

Surprisingly, the Priestess of Neilea offered an even firmer handshake. Taura was much tanned, quite stocky, with short dark hair and dressed almost entirely in light blue. A slightly darker-blue travelling cape was draped over an adjacent chair and she wore dark brown riding boots. Silmar couldn't help but notice that she was buxom and quite attractive, for a human of course.

"Well met, Silmar," she purred with a voice like honey. "Sit yourself on the bench over here next to me. What brings you to Westron Seaport?" Her silver holy symbol dangled from a chain around her neck; it featured two spinning coins, one the obverse face with the eagle-head representation of the Father God, Amae, and the other the reverse face with the representation of the Goddess of Kismet and Magical Knowledge, Neilea.

"Ah, well," he started, settling onto one of the adapted barrels serving as a seat at Taura's table. "My father thinks I need to travel, get experience of the world. He seems to think I'll be important one day. I can't think what as though. What about you two?"

Ralmon brought over a tray holding four tankards of ale, no mean feat for a halfling with one arm. "Mind if I join yer all? Couldn't 'elp but overhear, these first ones is on the 'ouse."

The ales were starting to go to Silmar's head already. Rarely had he had more than two or three ales at any one time; they always seemed to go straight to his head and then starting to affect his speech and actions soon after. He knew it would soon go to his bladder too. He wasn't sure if he could manage another – it would be rude to refuse though!

Billit scratched his head as if working out what to say so Taura spoke first. "I've spent some years in my clerical training," she began, "and it's now time for me to start spreading the word and doctrine of Neilea, my Lady of Kismet, Magic and Serendipity, referred to by some as the *Arcane Scientist*." She bowed her head slightly as she spoke her deity's name.

"Well, me now, I've been under trainin' too," said Billit. "Between you, me an' these tankards of ale, I've learned skills to enable me to travel too, and this is what I intend to do. A user of the powers gifted to us by Lady Neilea through the sun's power am I, just starting out, you may say. Don't let on to too many people though, there seems to be a sort of mistrust of mages and wizards in this city, can't think why!"

"Where do you travel, then?" asked Silmar. "Do you have any plans?" He sensed an opportunity here.

"None as such!" replied Taura.

"Me neither!" answered Billit just as Taura was about to speak.

She took her chance now though. "Look, Silmar, Billit and I arrived here together. We spoke with Ralmon to ask his advice on adventuring. After a while he said he had an idea but it would take a couple of tenday-weeks to arrange. So we waited and you turned up. Ralmon said you would be ideal to travel with us. We have no real plans. What about you?"

"Well, nor me!" replied Silmar, answering his own question. "My father hinted that there were people here who were hoping to strike out as adventurers and that I should offer my assistance. Obviously he was referring to you two."

"Aye, it was them," Ralmon responded before either of the other two could get a word in. "I sent a message to yer pappy near on a month back."

"Does that mean you have been waiting here all this time then?" Silmar asked incredulously.

"Aye, we 'ave," answered the gnome, "an' it don't seem a day over six months!" He winked at the elf.

"Cheeky chod!" retorted Ralmon. "Bin lookin' after yous both fer two months an' all I get is yer cheek. Well, now that you met, I feel a deep, meaningful an' profound plan comin' on. Done some adventurin' o' me own, you know. Like I was saying to Faramar's little lad 'ere, that's 'ow I lost this!" He raised the stump of his missing arm. "In fact, when I were a youngling, me own skills was more in line wi' somebody who might be tempted to remove things from their original owner, if you is understandin' my meaning, but o' course, only to make sure they didn't fall into the wrong 'ands."

Silmar put his ale onto the table. "Ah, I've done a small bit of that myself you know, but only in jest. I must admit to getting myself into one or two difficult scrapes when people took me too seriously."

"Oh, right, er, aye. Well, I never took nothin' from them what didn't deserve it, an' *never* from the poor, o' course," growled Ralmon, none to convincingly. "But o' the future, we must now parley."

The conversation paused for a few seconds as if everybody was trying to work out how to say what was forming in his or her mind.

"We could travel together, mebbe," said Billit, changing the subject and the sombre mood that had descended onto the party. "Sort of see how things go?"

After a few minutes of ideas being passed across the table, but no clear objective being suggested, Ralmon interrupted.

"Yer all goin' round in circles with no clear plan. Look, I got me an idea," he said excitedly. "It's like this. I need a job doing. M' brother, Jasper, he's got an inn up north, called the Wagon Wheel, town of Nor'wald City. It's way, way up north, and this time o' year I always sends 'im up some goods in a wagon. It's choddin' expensive hirin' a drover to take my wagon, and all. Gotta pay for a two-way journey, see, an' a couple o' outriders for protection. If you can do this for me I'll pay yous an' it'll give yous an intro into *real* adventuring. What do yer think? Can yer do it? Eh, eh?"

His enthusiasm must have seemed infectious. Taura, Billit and Silmar readily agreed without even having heard how much he was to pay them.

Billit soon asked the question though. "Hey, wait a bit! How much will you pay?"

"I'll give you twenty five gold. How's that?"

Everybody nodded, delighted happy, after all, this was more money than many hard-working labourers would earn in a year.

"Which of you can drive a wagon?" he continued.

They looked at each other hopefully.

The dwarf sighed. "Ooh! Thought things was goin' too good fer a minute," he grumbled, scratching at his beard. "Look, if yous meet outside the city south gates, not tomorrow but the nex' day, at 'bout an hour after sun-up, there'll be someone waitin' outside with a wagon and a couple o' 'orses. Don't be late, that's when the gates open an' because the wagon's gotta be on the road later in the day. Drover's name is Harald. Oh aye, seein' as yer working fer me now, dinner and rooms are on the 'ouse 'til you go."

This was good news indeed. "Another round of drinks then" said Taura.

"Yer can pay for that yerselves!" replied Ralmon gruffly. "I'll 'ave no choddin' freeloaders!"

Soon after, Silmar wandered over to Ralmon and asked "I'm after a special item which I can't buy from a dealer and wondered if you could give me some advice on where to get it."

"Tell me what it is and I'll see what I can arrange, provided it won't get you, or more importantly, *me*, into any trouble."

"It's a set of lockpicks," whispered Silmar.

"What? Shit, elfling! What yer needin' them for? You get caught wi' them on yer an' you can say farewell to yer freedom for a year or so."

"I need them just in case!"

"Ahhh! Right. Look, I might be able to call in a favour from an ole pal. Leave it to me an' I'll see you 'bout it tomorrow. These might cost ya anythin' up to thirty gold crowns. Er, at a rough guess, o' course, not that I knows anythin' about such things, yer understand. But I might be able to get 'em a bit cheaper. I'll get back to yer."

CHAPTER 5

A STONE'S THROW from the harbourmaster's post stood a large, pitch-blackened, wooden building. Its walls and roof were completely given to tar which gave the structure its blackness protecting it and its contents against the ravages from the occasional storms which plagued the Landsdrop Coast. No sign adorned the building, not even by the double doors which indicated the building as being a warehouse. Although the city was at its busiest time of the day, no movement showed that the building was occupied. Meanwhile, from the grimy, cracked window of another partly-derelict building opposite, a pair of eyes watched the black warehouse. The owner of those eyes had been in hiding there for two days having arrived undetected during the dead of night.

The afternoon became evening as the sun dipped below the horizon across the sea. As darkness fell and the general hustle and bustle died down, figures approached the building through a side door in an alleyway. Each figure was observed by the patient watcher who took in every detail: race and weaponry particularly.

As darkness fell, the watcher moved away from the window and silently roused other figures.

∽ ∾

The merchant was of middle-years but his mighty girth made him appear much older. His waddling gait suggested that he resisted any need to exercise but not the need to eat. He was lavishly dressed and had a white silk turban upon his head. A red conical adornment, almost a hand's length in height, sprouted from the centre of the turban at the top and upon the front there glistened a ruby the size of a pigeon's egg that was set into a gold filigree mount. A wide sash of gold, silken cloth, into which was tucked an ornate curved dagger in a golden sheath, was wrapped about his enormous belly. He breathed with some difficulty as he walked into his room in the black warehouse and carefully lowered himself onto his sofa. His bulk caused the furniture to emit creaks and groans of protest, hence the necessity for him to sit carefully. A recent incident that had caused him to descend hard onto a sofa had reduced it little more than firewood under his considerable bulk. Without doubt the overpriced piece of furniture had been poorly manufactured.

He reached across a small, gilt inlaid table to a crystal pitcher of elven blood-wine and poured himself a generous measure into a silver goblet. *Ah, to relax after a particularly gruelling day,* he thought to himself. An opportunity for an acquisition of almost unbelievable importance was presenting itself. He just needed to separate the item from its owner; he had retainers who would take care of that part of the business. He reached back across the table to replace the pitcher and carefully placed it on the table. As he drew his hand away, a dark-skinned hand grabbed his wrist firmly. It had appeared suddenly, silently and out of nowhere.

"Wha – what?" the merchant exclaimed. His gaze rose up the arm and shoulder and came to rest on the ebony face of a Darkling! "No! You!"

Darkling, known as shadow-elves or black-elves, were the dreaded and evil elves from places hidden deep below ground. Small, wiry but immensely strong, they were the cause of nightmares and of stories told to unruly children in order to encourage good behaviour. "Do as you are told or the Darkling will steal you in the night," the children would hear.

One Darkling stood before him, still gripping his wrist in a vice-like hold. Behind, in the shadows, stood three others; two armed warriors and the third that was tall, unarmed, hooded and menacingly silent – *a priest or mage?* The figures exuded a sharp, acrid, unclean odour.

With an impassive expression, the Darkling said "We have business, human!" His voice sounded thin and reedy but the threat from it was palpable. The way he said the word *human* clearly marked his contempt for the merchant's race.

"Business? What business?" the merchant whined. "We always have business. I have paid you in alchemical substances and weapons for the opportunities you have given me and I have similarly given you information for your profit." He was sweating freely and the Darkling released his wrist.

"You humans disgust me," he spat, wiping his hand on the merchant's sofa. "How I despise you all." He raised his hand to his nose. "Yeesh! You stink like auroch dung." The two Darkling warriors laughed quietly but humourlessly; the fourth Darkling remained silent.

The hooded Darkling spoke with a coarse whisper. "You are about to enter into the business of, shall we say, procuring an artefact from a traveller. Do not insult my intelligence with denial, this much we know. Speak, merchant!"

The merchant wiped his brow with his sleeve and then winced as pain shot up his arm from his aching wrist. "There are many who come this way with artefacts religious, magical and regal. I negotiate to purchase them, of course. How many times have I invited you to make me an offer on some of the items that come my way? Your patronage has been profitable at times for us both but I continue to be successful with or without it."

The first Darkling leaned forward until his grey eyes were but inches from those of the terrified merchant. "Some? Some? You tub of goose fat! You pick at the cream of your crop and offer us those items for which you have little use. Not this time. I will have you know that without our patronage you would *have* nothing, you would *be* nothing! I enabled you to build this business and I can cause it to fall!"

Hearing a commotion in the passage outside his room, the merchant found a morsel of courage deeply buried within him. He rose to his feet and towered over the Darkling.

"Do not presume that you can threaten me – one shout will bring the host of armed men at my command to my aid."

Stepping forward, the cloaked Darkling pulled back the hood – *a woman!*

Her smile was cold and without emotion. Her hands moved in a complex, circular motion and then her right hand closed like a fist around empty air; her thin, cruel lips formed a single word, barely audible.

With a gasp, the merchant felt his chest tighten such that he was unable to breathe or even speak. The pain in his lungs was excruciating. He desperately needed to bring his forearms across his chest in the manner of protection but he could not; his arms were pinioned at his side by an unseen force. He couldn't lift his foot and was unable even to turn his head or move his jaw. A hammering came from the door to the room accompanied by shouts of "*Master, master!*" He hadn't locked the door; the Darkling had not even been by it! *Was that also held immobile by force of magic?*

The first Darkling speaker withdrew a slim dagger and idly used it to pick at his black fingernails. "My companion can have you held thus and then I could slit your throat. You will not even be able to cry out. Do not dare to offer threats to Darkling. Not now, not ever."

The mage spoke. "Where is the priest?" Her voice was dry and threatening. Although she might have been a strikingly beautiful woman, her face was granite-hard. She moved one hand and uttered another word. As if a puppet with the strings cut from above, the merchant slumped to the floor released from the magical bonds that had held him immobile. His lungs wheezed as he gasped deeply for air.

"Answer the question, human!" urged the first Darkling.

The merchant held his hands imploringly in front of him and the words tumbled from his lips. "He comes tonight an hour before midnight to meet with me in the Street of The Moon in an alleyway between the rope-maker and the cattle-shed on the right-hand side. Bring him to me and I shall give you a fair price for it."

The hammering and shouting at the door continued but the Darkling elves were ignoring it, showing no concern whatsoever.

This time it was the female Darkling who spoke. "It is *I* that shall determine what is to be done with the artefact. You can thank whatever of your inferior gods you waste words with that you yet live. But, human, if you lie, you die!

Lay on your belly on the floor, fat worm, *now*!" The snarling woman was clearly the leader and not the first warrior as the merchant had construed.

With stained wheezing and grunting, the merchant turned himself from his side to his front as instructed. The room was in silence except for the continued hammering at the door. With a crash, the door burst open and the merchant's retainers and guards burst in. They were astounded to see their master struggling to his knees. Apart from him there was no other person in the room.

"Fools!" screamed the merchant, his belly and jowls quivering with rage and with sweat dripping from his face. "There were Darkling elves here, only four of them but I beat them off!" He was now almost apoplectic with rage and fright. "Where were you? Where were you? Why do I pay you? Get me on my feet! Do I have to do everything myself?" He climbed with immense effort up onto his knees. "Two of you – yes, you and you – stay here. The rest of you get about your business. Begone!"

Sweat continued to run down his face and he staggered towards a stout, padded chair. He collapsed into the cushions but despite the solidity of the chair, it groaned under his corpulent obesity. It was many moments before his composure started to return and his breathing slowed down.

"Post guards outside the building; I want them there all night. Bring me food, blood-wine and, ah yes, one of those dusky maidens from Gorador. No, no! Bring me both of them. I want them stripped when you get them in here! Move, toads!"

CHAPTER 6

THE GROUP relaxed in the Ship's Prow tavern and were enjoying themselves and getting increasingly merry as one drink followed another. Except, that is, for Silmar who generally took pleasure in a quart tankard or two, was happy just to watch his companions deteriorating as they consumed more ale. He took perverse pleasure in observing his new friends losing their self control. There was so much to see in this City of Magnificence that was new and exciting to him and there was so much more that he wanted to see during the short time he would be here. He decided he would take a walk around the neighbourhood, perhaps down towards the docks.

He made his excuses amidst calls of warnings from his comrades. Assuring them that he would be cautious and remain aware and that he armed with his old sword and his new dagger, he quietly left the inn through the side door. Even though it was now approaching midnight, the road outside was full of people. Many were drunk; some were even throwing up in the gutters or pissing in passages to either side of the street. Beggars were still about and pleading for coppers from revellers and late-night traders.

The street was filthy with horse and cattle dung, and worse, strewn everywhere. Silmar could not believe that children ran about and played among it all.

Silmar's senses were at their highest state of alert. He sensed, rather than felt, a hand at his money-pouch on his belt. With lightning reflexes, his hand whipped to his side and caught the wrist of a girl, probably of no more than fourteen or so years of age. She winced with pain as his hand twisted her wrist and locked her arm behind her. She had a mane of long dark hair and was extraordinarily pretty.

"Be off, child" he growled and released her. She spat an obscenity, ran off into the crowd and was gone from sight in seconds. A shout of alarm was soon raised however, and he could hear calls of *"Stop thief!"* Perhaps she had relieved somebody from the burden of carrying a money-bag as she ran through the throng. This was a good opportunity for him to untie his money-bag from his belt and tuck it deeply inside his vest and jerkin. He continued along *Odd Strete*, making his way through the crowds. He did not rise to calls of 'pointy-eared git!' and similar from drunken dwarves – he had been warned about this before leaving the Ship's Prow.

The crowds were thinning out as he wandered onwards towards the docks. He decided to take a turn to the left. There were a number of store fronts here, all closed, which sold mainly work clothes, tools and fishing accessories. There were one or two weapons dealers but the standard of swords looked to him to be mediocre at best. This street was virtually deserted and soon he was passing by sheds and small warehouses on the left and approaching a stockyard full of large, long-horned cattle on the right. The cattle had not been well cared for and the smell was quite overpowering. There were some decrepit residential buildings and a few people were drinking from jugs and smoking pipes on doorsteps. They looked at him with suspicion as he strode by. He continued on but decided that he would soon turn back. It was very dark down here and he was beginning to feel vulnerable on his own.

He passed by the stockyard and its adjoining shed on his right-hand side. The passage between the shed and the next building was dark but his keen eyesight caught some movement a few yards down. He heard a gasp followed by the sound of a struggle. His elven dark-vision came into use and clearly showed a standing, darkly-clad figure looming over another that seemed to be on its knees. The reflection of starlight on a blade forced Silmar to act and he stood in the shadow beneath the eaves of the cattle shed.

"Ho there!" he cried.

There was a blur of movement and Silmar moved slightly away from the building. A short dagger thudded into the woodwork where his chest had been a second before. Silmar drew his sword and, with a yell, he launched himself at the assailant. The dark figure straightened up and drew a short scimitar – a typical assassin's blade, short enough to enable mobility but heavy enough to kill with a single strike if wielded well. The dark one stepped forward to meet Silmar head-on and with the grace and poise of a dancer, easily parried Silmar's first attack.

Now that he was up close to the swordsman, Silmar tried to look into the eyes of the assailant but could see nothing. The dark figure was dressed fully in black, it seemed. Boots, hose and hooded tunic were all in black and the face, which must surely have been veiled, was black too.

Silmar regained his own poise and, bringing his own training to the fore, circled about with the dark figure. His enemy made a slashing, downward, oblique cut from Silmar's left shoulder to his right hip but the young elf easily stepped back with his right foot. As the scimitar's blade whistled past him, he stepped forward again and executed an upwards slash from the dark one's left hip to right ribcage. Silmar was more fortunate in that he opened the black tunic and felt the little bit of resistance that came with inflicting a light flesh wound.

No sound came from the dark figure; instead he kicked with his right boot catching Silmar's left knee. The young elf staggered back, barely managing to retain his balance, and he crashed against the warehouse to his left. By the time he had regained his balance, the dark figure had nimbly swung up the side of the cattle shed and was disappearing into the dark. All was now still but the elf could hear the laboured breathing coming from the figure now lying on the ground.

Silmar put away his blade and crouched down next to the figure. "Are you wounded?" he asked.

"He has killed me! I am dying," replied the figure amid coughs and splutters. "Stabbed … chest! Aaahhh!" *Cough!*

Silmar was taken aback. In the dark, he still had his enhanced elven dark-sight and could see the spreading stain of blood beneath the man's cloak. He screwed up a ball of the cloak and pressed it to the stab-wound. The man cried out in pain but Silmar still held it there.

"Are you –" *Cough!* "– a man of good –" *Cough!* "– good heart?"

"I am an elf; I am Silmar, known as *The Golden*, son of Faramar Galadhal of Refuge."

The figure's hand clutched at Silmar's jerkin. "Oh, by the Gods!" *Cough, cough!* "– I am to die! Aaiii! The Lord Clamberhan help me –" *Cough!*"

"No, I shall fetch help!"

"Listen elf." *Cough!* "Beware the Darkling! He wants this –" *Cough, cough!* "– Aaahh! Take it, guard it –" *Cough!*

Darkling! That was a word very familiar to Silmar. The young elf could now see frothy blood appearing on the lips of the dying man. As the stricken man reached inside his leather jerkin, a polished wooden medallion on a metal chain swung into view. It looked to Silmar like a divine badge of office, a holy symbol, but not one that he was familiar with. The end of a wrapped package appeared to but the man's hand fell away. He reached for it once more.

"Take it –" *Cough!* "– please take this – *aaahh!* Feel cold!" The poor man was stricken in pain but he continued to grip the package tightly.

"What must I do with it? Who can I take it to?"

"Take –" *Cough!* "– take to Carrick Cliffs, east to Kam –" *Cough!* "– Kamambia –" *Cough!*

"Do not fear, it shall be done, I swear it. What is your name?"

"No matter –" *Cough!* "– give to Gallan – *aaahh!* – Gallan Arran –" *Cough!* "– Priest –" *Cough, cough!* "– vital stop evil. Ohh Clamberhan, I failed you! I come to you –" *Cough!* "– in shame!"

There, that name again. Clamberhan! It sounded familiar. Of course – He is the God of Learning and Knowledge. "No! No! You go to him with honour and courage! Gallan Arran at Carrick Cliffs, I shall not let you down, I swear it!"

The man's body stiffened and a stream of hot blood issued from his mouth onto Silmar's left sleeve. He was dead; his hand fell away from the package. The elf reached inside the man's tunic and grasped it. Immediately, pain flashed behind his eyes and a wave of nausea coursed through him; he was close to bringing up the contents of his stomach. He released the package and the feeling passed. There was no other choice left to him except to take the package and bear the discomfort. As he did so the feeling appeared once more. Gritting his teeth he thrust the package inside his tunic and rose to his feet.

He whispered a few words to his own God, Tambarhal, over the body, asking Him to beseech the dead man's own god, Clamberhan, to watch for the spirit of his subject. The feeling of nausea reduced a little. *Hmm, that is interesting* he thought. He also removed a wooden priestly symbol that hung from a chain around the dead man's neck; although it may help identify the dead man to the City Watch but he didn't want to leave it for the assassin to remove should he return.

As he turned to make his way back he heard a creaking sound from above and, once again, ducked just in time as a throwing star embedded itself in the woodwork behind him. He saw the dark shape of the assassin on the roof as it turned to dart away. *Hah! I'm going to follow that piece of shit!*

The young elf relied on his dexterity to easily swing easily up onto the roof. Using his elven dark-sight he easily spotted the figure as it leapt across from the cattle shed roof to another shed behind the stockyard. The assassin was moving fast and, probably because he was not expecting to be pursued, took little or no notice behind him. Silmar followed silently, years of hunting goblins in the forests and mountains serving him well. The pursuit carried on from rooftop to rooftop and finally the figure dropped down to street level. Noiselessly, Silmar turned to the right and dropped down to an adjacent street. He moved towards the corner of the building and carefully peered down the alleyway. He recognised that he was only a few hundred yards away from *Odd Strete*; there were still a lot of people about, he could hear them in the distance, laughing, singing, carousing, shouting, blissfully unaware of the death and danger only a few streets away.

There he is!

The figure had rapped on the doorway of a black warehouse and the door opened allowing light to pour out. The brightness almost blinded Silmar and he realised he was still using his dark-sight. He turned his head to one side and blinked his eyes, reverted back to normal sight and looked once again down the alley.

Although he could see the killer more clearly in the light and he could also see a man in the doorway, there were boxes and barrels in the way that were making it difficult to see properly. He crept around the corner and silently edged over towards the warehouse, keeping the boxes and barrels in between himself and the figures.

"Do you have it?" the figure in the doorway asked. He was obviously wealthy; he had a cape edged in white fur and a turban of white cloth with a conical projection at the top on his head. Similarly, he wore a wide sash of gold silken cloth about his huge belly. The man was immensely fat and huge jowls hung from his fat face.

"The priest was there waiting as you said he would be. I killed him; I was interrupted before I could find and take the artefact. A damned fool white-elf. He was armed and almost as good with a blade as I. I had to get out of there. I think he now has the artefact."

Silmar edged forward further.

"Damn. *She* will not be pleased, you know that. I suggest that you get it back. I shall send out the lads and see if we can spot him. Describe him to me."

The dark one hesitated. "He was tall, golden-haired."

"Hmmph! Most elves are and many humans."

Silmar moved again but this time his foot caught a pebble and it rattled against a barrel.

"*Have a care, we are seen!*" the fat man exclaimed in a shrill voice.

The assassin whirled around. "There! It's him! He's mine!"

Silmar looked up. There was a gantry above him from which hung a rope through a pulley. By it was an opening into the building. He leapt up and started to climb just as another throwing star thudded into the building where he had been standing. He swung in through the opening and pulled the rope in behind him. Running through the hayloft, he found he was inside a stable. He didn't wait however, but ran through the building and out through an opening onto another roof. He kept running over three more buildings, leapt across a narrow passageway and carried on until he was able to hide behind a small structure. He could see no sign of a follower but to be sure, he waited for many moments. He could hear the busy streets below him and eventually he decided to move.

Keeping low, he crept to the edge of a roof he looked about him for signs of the assassin. Nothing! He swung down and made his way to the main street – he was on Odd Strete once more!

He looked for large groups of people and tucked himself inside them. Eventually he arrived back at the Ship's Prow. Entering in through the side door he stepped into the bar-room. He waited and glanced about him. There were now very few drinkers in the inn. Of his new companions, there was no sign.

One of Ralmon's bar men looked across at him and then bent down to whisper in Ralmon's ear. The dwarf looked across at Silmar and hurried over.

"Ye Gods!" he exclaimed. "What has happened to you? Look at that blood! Are you badly wounded?"

"No, not at all, I think," the elf answered.

"Get yerself out back into me kitchen and sit down! Come down to my height, you pointy-eared elf! What's that?" Ralmon indicated the package that Silmar carried.

"Don't touch it," the elf warned. "It has a curse on it or something. It is making me feel quite ill. Can you call my friends down?"

"They're all pissed an' sleepin'! Best leave 'em there an' we'll sort 'em out tomorrow. Tell me what 'appened, all of it mind!"

Silmar recounted the events and took out the wooden medallion. He repeated the names he had heard and then laid the package onto the table. Once again, the influence he had felt while carrying the package passed from him and he sighed with relief. Ralmon took up the medallion and studied the symbol engraved upon it.

"This is the 'oly symbol o' the God Clamberhan, look, it's a bound book with a hammer on the cover," he said. "This is the god o' wisdom an' learnin'. Thought you would've known that, elf. The dead man must've been 'is priest. Didn't you say that the assassin said somethin' about killing the priest?"

Silmar nodded.

Ralmon laid his hand upon the package, his face paled and he withdrew quickly. "Eugh! Now I understand," he gasped. "I'm gonna call the local Watch Commander in. You 'ad better tell this to 'im, I think. But for now, leave out the bit about the package. An' don't open it, neither.

I'm gonna call in another old friend o' mine first thing in the morning. Stay 'ere, I'll be back in a short while. Clean yourself up else they'll think you did the murder!"

The dwarf went out into the taproom and Silmar removed his tunic. The blood washed off easily in a bucket of cold water and he hung it over the ovens to dry. Ralmon came back in after a while and stated that he had sent one of his barmen off to find the Watch Commander. He had a canvas bag into which Silmar could put the package.

"Wanna eat somethin'?" he asked. "Parsnip stew's gone cold now."

He offered Silmar a chunk of bread, some cheese and a quart of ale. By the time the elf had finished these, his tunic was dry enough to put back on. At that moment, one of the barmen came into the kitchen to tell them that the Watch Commander and a couple of his men were in the taproom.

Strangely, or perhaps not, the taproom cleared of drinkers within a few moments of the City Watch entering. It was just as well because Ralmon did not want all and sundry listening in to the conversations. The Commander, looking and acting very imperiously in his smart uniform, demanded to know what he had been called in for. Silmar gave him the full details of what had occurred while omitting the references to the package and the names: Gallan Arran and Carrick Cliffs. *This business may be better left to Ralmon's friend, whoever he is*, he thought.

The Commander sent his two men out to search for the body and to look at the area where the murder had occurred. "Right then, um, Silmar is it? I want you to tell me again what happened, but slowly so that I can write it down."

Silmar dictated clearly and slowly and after a while completed his tale. One of the watchmen came back into the inn and whispered into his commander's ear.

"My thanks, Tasken," he responded. "The body is still there, just as you said, Silmar. I suggest you stay around here for the next day or two. I may need your evidence again but if you don't hear from me by tomorrow evening then you can consider your part in the matter as closed."

The Commander gave Silmar his appreciation and Ralmon led him and his men out of the inn door. When the dwarf returned, he told Silmar that he would be happy to put his belongings in another, bigger, oh yes, and more comfortable room with Taura and Billit and hoped the elf wouldn't mind. Silmar shook his head saying that he preferred to sleep on his own and that generally, he slept in his blanket on the floor.

"A cot is too soft and I wake up with aches," he added.

"Last door on the left, back o' the tavern," Ralmon directed.

Silmar collected the package and his weapons from the kitchen and climbed the stairs to the bedchamber. When he went in he bumped into Billit at the door to his chamber.

The gnome beckoned him in. "Come in 'ere, Silmar. Where in the seven hells of the Void have you been? I was worried you had been killed dead."

"I nearly was, Billit," replied Silmar. "But I'm fine. I'll tell you all about it in the morning."

"Is it morning?" murmured a sleepy-eyed Taura as she propped herself up in bed. The blanket had fallen away to reveal more of her than she might have intended.

"Not for hours yet, and cover yourself up, yuh hussy!" replied a flushed Billit. "Not very shy, is she?"

Taura huffed. "You are such a prude, Billit. Have you not seen breasts before?"

"Er, um, aye, I did once. Just not yours!"

Silmar chuckled, shook his head and stepped out into the passageway and into his bedchamber. He closed his door, propped a chair behind it and checked the window was secure, the normal action that would be carried out by anyone staying in inns in the rougher or remote parts. Within minutes he was asleep.

CHAPTER 7

DAWN WAS an hour away when the companions woke up. Silmar had been awake for ages with the names echoing around his head: Clamberhan the God of Learning, Gallan Arran the priest from Carrick Cliffs. Names he must not forget. The Darkling. What Darkling? He knew that these were the evil shadow elves of the deep, ancient mines of the Dragon's Teeth Mountains to the north of Northwald City.

He was now very curious as questions echoed around his head. *Was the assassin a Darkling?* The killer seemed to think that he, Silmar, was a good swordsman. *Was that a compliment from a man or a Darkling?* The poise and grace of the assassin was an indication of a very fine swordsman indeed; Silmar considered himself to be accomplished with a sword but there were many elves in Refuge who were far better than he. The killer was someone who spoke the *universal* language but the voice sounded sharp somehow. *Do the Darklings speak their own language, or universal or both?* He did not know. *Ralmon may know.*

He stood up from his blankets on the floor beside the cot and stepped over to the window. The shutter was closed so he opened it. Other thoughts came to him and he crossed back over to his bed. *Who is the fat man? He seemed very rich from the way he was dressed. Who was Ralmon's mysterious friend who was going to meet him this morning?* These thoughts had kept sleep at bay for ages but Silmar was too excited to be curious.

A hammering at the doors brought all of them to their senses. Silmar could hear movement in the adjacent bedchamber.

"Get up you lazy chods," yelled Ralmon.

Silmar pulled back the chair from his door and opened it to find Ralmon standing outside.

"Good morning, elf, or it was when I got up," the one-armed dwarf said. "Got a visitor comin' to chat to you in 'alf an hour an' I got a morning feast laid out on the table downstairs."

"Thanks Ralmon, we're on our way," called Billit from behind a partly open door. "Madame girlie priestess ain't up yet an' she tells me I 'ave to avert me eyes so I can't see. She weren't so shy last night, was she, showin' 'er wobblies? You best come in an' make sure you don't look."

Taura groaned and covered her head with a pillow. Billit pulled it back off and told her to get up and drink a quart of water.

"I'll bring it up again," moaned Taura. "Gods, my head!"

"Then drink some more!" the gnome insisted.

They made their way downstairs, Silmar with his package in the canvas bag; it was the only way he could carry it without feeling too ill. Bread, eggs, cheese and fruit were laid out on a table. Flagons of water and tankards were lined up behind the food. The companions and Ralmon tucked in. A hammering at the door was answered by a young scullery maid aged barely sixteen years of age. Silmar rose half-way from his chair – she blushed when she saw him and dropped her head downwards; she was the very girl who had attempted to lift his money pouch the previous evening. After a moment she looked up at him again. The elf winked at her and put his finger to his lips to signify silence.

She smiled, dipped a curtsey, blushed again and opened the door.

A man stepped in.

He was tall with closely-cropped, dark brown, curly hair. He was dressed in a cowl of grey and purple beneath his travelling cloak with a sword belt around his middle and wearing a medallion around his neck. His cloak was long and white and he carried weapons of quality the like of which they had not seen. A large morning-star hung across his back on a large loop of leather. A smaller but very ornate mace was tucked into a beautifully-crafted leather sheath on his belt. A similarly ornate but very functional longsword hung from a fine-looking scabbard, also at his belt. These weapons had seen action, nonetheless. A number of pouches were attached to his belt too. He moved with athletic grace and the width of his shoulders bespoke a great physical strength.

But it was the man's eyes that took their attention. Apart from the pupils, they were completely black. Was he blind? He seemed to be able to move between the tables and chairs effortlessly. He looked at them all in turn and smiled when he looked towards Taura. She flushed immediately and dropped her gaze; the effects of her hangover did not seem so significant now. Billit nudged Silmar who tried not to laugh.

The new arrival warmly shook hands with Ralmon and they embraced each other.

"Let me introduce you to each other," Ralmon smiled. "Taura Windwalker, the Priestess of Neilea. Niebillettin a

Chthonic gnome mage, and this is Silmar, son of Faramar Galadhal of Refuge. This is Halorun Tann, High Knight Commander, Priest of Tarne the Just God."

Halorun Tann bowed to Taura and said "Blessings, dear lady, from the House of Tarne be upon you." He reached for her hand and kissed the back of her fingers.

"Oh, my!" she whispered. "And, er, oh, aye, blessings be upon you, dear sir, from the House of Neilea." She bowed in return. She was now scarlet and her heart hammered.

Oh, he is so handsome, she thought, *and those eyes – he can see right through me, I am certain!*

"My eyes as you see them, dear lady, are a gift from my God," he said, as if he had read Taura's mind. "I see in the near-dark as you do, Master Galadhal. And that is also a gift from my very own God; a story for another time, perhaps."

Halorun warmly shook the arms of Billit and Silmar and bade them all to sit around a table. He removed his cloak, hanging it across a nearby chair, and sat down.

"I believe that you, Silmar, have much to discuss with me," he continued. "I have met your father on more than one occasion and respect him greatly, counting him as a friend. I am honoured to meet the son of the leader from one of the great houses of the old elven Kingdom of Faerhome. Tell me what occurred last night and what you have to show me."

Silmar once again recounted his story. Everyone, except for Ralmon, was surprised to hear what had happened with the elf during the night. This time he told the whole story and included the parts of it that he had omitted when he was interviewed by the Watch Commander the previous evening.

"An evening walk crowded with incident," said Halorun. "The time has come for me to be shown the content of this package that you carry, and also that medallion that you took from the murdered man. Bring them forth, Silmar, so we may all see them."

The elf reached for the canvas sack and upturned it onto the table. The package rolled out and thumped onto the table top. It was about two feet in length and the thickness of a man's upper arm. The object, whatever it was, had been wrapped in a rough cloth and then tied with cord.

"It is not pleasant to hold," murmured Silmar. "It made me feel very nauseated and my head ached severely."

Billit reached across and put his hand around the middle of the package, and promptly threw up over the floor. "Ye Gods!" he exclaimed. "I enjoyed that morning feast too! Suppose I had better wipe that up then!"

The Dwark shook his head. "I'll get the scullery maid onto it; she's used to doing that. *Sheena*!" he yelled.

The young maid came out of the kitchen and Ralmon told her what was wanted. She appeared with a wooden bucket and rags and, flashing a nervous look towards Silmar, proceeded to clear up the mess. Once finished, she glanced again at Silmar, who smiled and winked back, and disappeared back into the kitchen.

The elf reached for the package and, with a shudder, untied the strings and peeled back the wrappings. He was feeling the effect of the package quite badly now and it was all he could do to avoid emptying the contents of *his* stomach. Finally, the artefact was uncovered. The group seated around the table looked on wide-eyed.

Here, laid before them, was the most ornate dagger any of them had ever seen.

The hilt, guard and blade were crafted entirely of a rich gold. Rubies, diamonds, amethysts and a multitude of other precious stones were set into the hilt and blade. One ruby, the size of pigeon's egg, was set into the pommel of the hilt. The cross-guard was beautifully and exquisitely crafted in a filigree design and set with clear crystals. Beautiful designs were etched into the blade but one had been quite crudely erased, similarly on the reverse side of the blade. A new design had been etched, also quite crudely, of a scorpion. However, the beauty of the dagger took everybody's breath away. There was no sheath for the dagger; it had never been intended for use as a weapon to be carried into battle for its edge was quite dull. This artefact was special, perhaps ceremonial.

"I have seen this before!" exclaimed Halorun. "But not as we see it now."

The companions were silent; even Ralmon was lost for words. But everybody could feel the influence emanating from the dagger.

Taura gasped "Is it cursed?"

"That I'm not sure but I can find out; it can wait for a little while though. You see that scorpion design?" They all nodded. "That is an emblem of the Scorpion Queen, Adelenis. She is worshipped by the Darkling elves and by assassins! Adelenis had brought scorpions into the world long ago. I understand that she enslaved elves, poisoned them and corrupted them so they themselves became Darklings. There, embittered, they shunned the light. This was many, many thousands of years ago.

"She lurks in hiding in the darkness of the Void and of late her followers appear to be collecting powerful magical and divine artefacts of which this may be one. Perhaps she has aspirations of becoming a greater god than the mere demigod that she is and may be using artefacts to develop greater powers and strength."

The group gathered around the table were in a state of silence. They looked at each other and down at the dagger.

Taura was the first to speak. "You said that you have seen this dagger before. Where? When?"

Halorun leaned back, clasped his hands behind his head and his gaze seemed to become lost as if far away, merely emphasising what might have been construed by others as blindness. "I was once a member of an adventuring party," he began. "We were like you, new to campaigning. We travelled north through Cascant into Kamambia and came to the small town of Carrick Cliffs. This town was overrun by Hoshite troops who had set up a garrison there. The townsfolk were very much oppressed and the churches and temples were sacked and looted. Those priests who were not able to escape in time were killed. A suit of armour said to have once been worn by the god Tarne himself had been stolen by the half-human, half-hobgoblin renegade Rolv Hebbern, had been taken to Carrick Cliffs as a gift to Adelenis. I was ordered by my Temple to recapture the armour and execute Hebbern. We organised the towns-folk and drove out the Hoshites."

At this, both Silmar and Billit sat up straight and their jaws dropped.

"But this is the story of the song of the *Freemen of Carrick Cliffs*!" cried Silmar. "Does this mean..?"

"Yes, I am one of those adventurers, one of the *Freemen of Carrick Cliffs!* I carried out my mission successfully and recaptured the precious armour. To this day, I believe, the town of Carrick Cliffs is free of oppression. I hope so anyway but seeing this dagger here puts me in grave doubt."

"But, Halorun, what of this dagger?" cried Taura. "What are we to do with it?"

"This is, I mean was, the ceremonial dagger which is precious to the Church of Clamberhan. This is of unique religious significance. I last saw it when we re-established Clamberhan's church in the town. The Temple is a centre of learning and wisdom and boasts a great library. The wooden medallion is that of a Cleric of Clamberhan. The murdered man will have been a Clamberhan Cleric himself, of that there is little doubt. I did not recognise his face when I investigated the scene of the murder early this morning and looked at the body. He had been stabbed twice through the lungs by a very narrow blade, a typical assassin's blade."

"So what is to be done now?" asked Ralmon. "We 'ave this dagger and there is a tale of horror behind it. Will the assassin be looking for it?"

As if to emphasise his next words, Halorun leaned forward in his chair and placed his hands on the table. "Oh yes, he will want it. I know the identity of the fat man; he is Menahim Begim-Bey. He is a trader from the southern land of Qoratt and will be involved somehow with this plot. It is suspected that he is implicated in kidnapping and slavery as well as the collecting of magical and religious artefacts for sale to the highest bidder. It is also suspected that he has links with people from extremely low places. What he is doing in supporting Adelenis I have yet to find out but if he is then Darkling may be involved too. But he will have some profitable reason for doing so, I have no doubt whatsoever. He seems to have gone to ground but I shall find him, sooner or later."

Taura's hand flew to her mouth. "But the assassin has seen you, Silmar," she cried, "and will surely be looking for you."

Silmar nodded slowly. "Aye, and if that dagger is of some importance, he will not stop looking for me either," he replied. "But the odd thing is, he seems to find it necessary to hide his features. I wonder if he is Darkling! All indications point to him being so because he was small in stature but moved like a cat. He may not be alone either."

The companions gasped. This was terrible news and it would doubtlessly put Silmar, perhaps all of them, in danger. Halorun sensed their concern and gave words of comfort and advice.

"He will not risk being seen during the day. Assuming he is Darkling, he cannot afford to be recognised and wearing a face mask will arouse suspicion. He will hide up during daylight and will hunt during the night."

"I must leave, and alone," gasped Silmar. "I cannot risk the lives of my new friends in this. I shall return to Refuge straight away."

In one voice, each of the friends rejected this and vowed that they would face this hazard together.

"Well, we was talking about campaigning, wasn't we?" Billit asked. "A bit of adventuring? Well then, this is the ideal start for us. What d'yer think?" The little Gnome mage gave a wide grin across his rugged features.

"Aye, your friends are right, Silmar," responded Ralmon. "They are, aren't they, Halorun?"

"I would say so," the Priest of Tarne confirmed. "For one thing, if you are considering riding back to Refuge, he may come on you in the dark of the night. He *will* be looking for you, Silmar. Although it was dark when you fought him he will have been able to see your features, so you will need to disguise them."

"What should I do?" enquired the elf.

"Nothing drastic. Colour your hair and tie it back. Wear a large cap or a hood that will cover your hair and ears.

Darken your skin a little with a skin dye, just enough to last for a few days. I think Ralmon will help you with all that."

The dwarf nodded in agreement. "Aye, I done this sort o' thing afore. You 'ave no idea 'ow difficult it can be to make a dwarf look taller! But yer tall enough already so it ain't a problem!" The group laughed.

Halorun leaned back in his chair. "The time has come for me to find out what this power is that binds the dagger. To do this I need to be left alone with it for a while. Ralmon will see to your disguise and the rest of you can help him. I shall call you when I am finished."

The companions rose up from the table and Ralmon led them into the kitchen. Sheena, the scullery maid, looked embarrassed when they entered. She had tied back her long hair and her grey blouse sleeves were rolled up. Silmar took her arm and led her aside.

"I shall say nothing," he said softly, "providing that you thieve no more. And if you behave, I shall bring you back a gift on my return. What do you say?"

"I mean no harm to anyone, sir," she replied timidly, clutching at his arm. "I looked after my brother 'til he died last month and all my money, five coppers a day, goes on giving me shelter in a shed behind the blacksmith's shop. There's just me now and this work does not pay enough for anything better. My mother died to give birth to him and my father is in gaol. I only work in the mornings and I am lucky enough to have this. I can't survive on such little money and I refuse to sell my body for more. The blacksmith's boy keeps trying to have his way with me, too. What is to be done?"

Silmar scratched his head. "How old are you girl?"

"About sixteen I think."

"Many girls are wed at your age, with children of their own. Look, leave it to me, Sheena. I shall ask Ralmon for a favour and see if he can help in some way. No promises though."

꩜   ꩜

Together, Taura, Billit and Sheena applied colouring to Silmar's hair, face and hands. Ralmon provided a large woollen cap that would cover the elf's head and ears. With different clothing he would be almost unrecognisable. As an elf, Silmar had no facial hair so he would be unable to grow a beard. Elven features were quite distinctive compared to those of humans and would be difficult to alter.

Taura observed Sheena watching Silmar's transformation with interest. The young scullery maid giggled bashfully as Silmar stripped to the waist. Eventually, Billit and Taura went back out into the taproom. Silmar spoke quietly with Ralmon by the door. At first the dwarf shook his head vigorously but soon he was nodding in agreement.

The elf rejoined his companions and they stood back to watch Halorun Tann as he continued with his examination of the dagger. The Priest of Tarne was sweating heavily and chanting softly. While his body was gently rocking back and forth, his hands weaved a complex series of movements over the artefact. The words being chanted seemed muffled and distorted, as though the companions were being deliberately prevented from understanding the divine spell or prayer that Halorun was uttering. Only Taura, being a priestess, could see the faint blue glow that surrounded the dagger and Halorun's hands. The chanting finished with a sudden shout and gesture and the Priest of Tarne slumped back in his chair. His face was drenched in sweat but he had a calm and triumphant look to his face.

Halorun used the corner of his cloak to wipe the perspiration from his face. "I had to invoke all of my powers and strength of will to establish the nature of the artefact and with help from Tarne I have established what it is that it has been imbued with. It is not a curse; that I now know. It is, however, altogether evil and I believe it has been used to murder or execute a victim, probably as a sacrifice and most likely a priest of Clamberhan. It was never intended for this purpose. The use of it in this way, together with the foul symbol being etched upon it, has imbued it with the evil that we can all feel."

Silence descended on the taproom.

"I did ask earlier what we should do with it," stated Taura, "and you did not answer."

Halorun had by now regained his composure. "Then this is my answer," he replied. "It must either be destroyed or preferably, have the evil it contains removed by the High Abbot of the Temple of Clamberhan, Gallan Arran, if he still lives. The murdered priest seems certain the High Abbot still lives so he may be in hiding somewhere. He must be located and brought to Carrick Cliffs to meet with you and the dagger. This really must occur at the place at which the atrocity happened. It would be a great advantage if the one who carried out the execution, could be brought along with it. I know it sounds very hard to bear but proving the guilt of a killer and then his execution will go a long way to removing that evil."

"Will you not be able to travel with us, Halorun?" enquired Billit. "Your experience would be of such benefit to us."

"Unfortunately, no," he replied. "I have some trials to conduct and then investigations to carry out relating to this plot. I have to try to find this Menahim Begim-Bey, then try to find others who may be able to help. I some trials to give judgement on in the Barony of Bocaster. Oh, I also have a particularly nasty criminal to apprehend in Grappina. I shall, hopefully, be able to meet you though before you arrive at Carrick Cliffs. I may have some support with me, too, all going well."

"You mean *we* are to travel to Carrick Cliffs?" gasped Silmar. "We hoped you would take this dagger with you today. But we are so inexperienced and new to this. What are we to do?"

Halorun laughed. "You, Silmar, son of Faramar, have experience in battle; look at your scars. You have the beginnings of a team and I predict your team will grow as you travel onwards. Don't ask me how I know, I just feel this. Together, you will have the strength both of will and for this campaign. Take the dagger, guard it well and tell nobody of its existence from the time you leave this inn. Keep it a secret and keep it hidden well away. I can help you with that. First though, I must have some water, I have such a thirst."

Billit shouted for Ralmon, who was still in the kitchen. He appeared with a very tearful Sheena in tow. As Billit asked the dwarf for water, Sheena threw her arms around Silmar's neck and burst into tears. A few eyebrows raised and questions were hovering on everybody's lips. There was a story to be told too, but that would wait its turn.

"Get us some water, girl," called Ralmon, and out she ran. "She's got a new job with me, thanks to your pointy-eared, choddin' elf pokin' 'is nose into other people's choddin' business!"

"Looks like you have a very pretty new friend, Silmar," laughed Taura.

"It rather does, it seems," he replied. "Perhaps she likes my new hair colour."

"I think it is your muscular hairless chest," she replied with a chuckle.

Silmar posed by puffing out his chest and flexing his arms.

Halorun cleared his throat to get their attention. "I would recommend you travel north out of this city and head for Northwald City, a full seventy leagues but it is a very good road and very busy. That will take you seven or eight days by horseback but double that if you have a wagon. The roads to the east of here will more than likely be watched as this would be the logical route for the bearers of the artefact to take. Once at Northwald, you could take a path from the East Gate, following the road eastwards round the mountains and find your way back towards Gash, perhaps a twenty-day ride." Halorun smiled at this point even though he admitted that the road, although minor, was good providing the weather stayed dry but the mountains were treacherous and alive with goblins and trolls.

"Oh how wonderful!" exclaimed Taura. "Goblins and trolls, my favourite!"

Silmar shook his head. "There are very few of them these days. They just have small hunting parties of half a dozen. You can smell them before you see them. If we pick up a merchant's caravan we shall be quite safe."

"You will pick up the Great East Silk Road below Gash that will eventually would lead eastwards through the Shordrun capital city of Nasteed and the pass through the Dragon's Teeth Mountains and into Polduman. The road swings down; make sure you follow it and not the old road.

You will eventually reach the coast. Take the ferry to The Wildings, a lawless region. Be on your guard there. Make for south Cascant and the city of Norovir. Your journey will then take you eastwards though the Brash Mountains and into Kamambia. The road north will then take you to Carrick Cliffs. I estimate that your journey is about seven to eight hundred leagues which, all going well, would take forty to fifty days, perhaps more."

"How shall we remember all that?" enquired Billit. "I shall need to pen it 'cos we'll not remember that."

"Fear not," laughed Halorun. "I shall draw a nice picture for you."

When Silmar asked how they would meet up with Halorun, he simply replied that he would know where and when.

"I can help you solve the difficult burden of carrying the dagger too," he explained. "I'll need a box that will take the dagger."

"I 'as the very thing," cried Ralmon and he rushed over to his bar. He returned with an oaken box with a hinged lid and metal clasp. "This is a box used fer bottles o' dwarf liquor," he announced. "Don't need it no more, I drunk the liquor!"

The group laughed. Dwarf liquor was very strong and few were the elves and men who were able to drink it.

"I will want some sort of lead powder or grains, or thin lead sheeting, for the dagger to be bedded into or wrapped in," the priest continued. "Perhaps a window-fitter can provide that."

Ralmon nodded. "I knows jus' the man; 'e drinks in 'ere all the time. I'll haul 'is arse outa 'is cot." He walked out of the door of the inn. Sheena had reappeared with water and gave Silmar a huge smile and returned to the kitchen.

"I just helped her out, that's all!" he protested as all eyes turned to him.

Taura laughed. "I think she wants your body next to hers since she saw you with your top clothes off!" she said.

They drank some water and helped themselves to some of the dawn meal that was still laid out on the table. Halorun told them a couple of tales from his adventuring days and told them a little about the other members of the Freemen of Carrick Cliffs. Most of them were still in the local area and now had businesses of their own. He spoke of his wife, Sharness, and they were astounded to hear that she was a Darkling. She was surprisingly a Priestess of Tambarhal, the god worshipped by surface elves, but not of course, by the Darkling themselves. Although she lived with Halorun and their son, Halness, at the new Temple of Tarne-In-The-West, she spent weeks at a time spreading the word of her own god and giving aid to travellers of all races. She had long become accustomed to living on the surface and was well-known and trusted across the Home Territories.

An hour after he left, Ralmon returned with a heavy sack over his shoulder. He opened the sack and folded the edges down so they could see its contents. It was full of lead – powder, small pieces and thin sheets.

"Perfect!" said Halorun.

"Sost me a choddin' fortune," Ralmon mumbled.

Halorun part-filled the casket with the lead fragments and he laid a small, thin sheet of it on the table. Silmar took a deep breath and lifted the dreadful artefact. He winced as pain shot across his temples. With a gasp, he lowered it onto the sheet. Placing another sheet over the top of it, Halorun tightly wrapped the artefact without coming into contact with it. He placed the package on top of the bed of lead granules and then loaded the casket with more until it was full. The priest closed the box and fastened the clasp.

Silmar picked up the box and could barely feel any evil influence at all. "It's very heavy," he observed.

Halorun continued, "I have just one more task to fulfil." He placed his hands over the casket and mumbled a chant. The companions could not understand any of the words except for *Tarne* a couple of times. When he finished Billit, being a mage, could see a faint blue glow around the box.

"I have placed upon it the blessing of Tarne," he said. "And you, my dear Lady of Neilea, can do the same when the burden on Silmar becomes too much to bear. Offer the blessing of the Lady of Kismet." He bowed with each mention of the Goddess, Neilea. It was always a matter of etiquette amongst the priests of various deities when they speak to another. Taura bowed in return and was lost for words, even more so when Halorun stepped close and kissed her on the cheek. He clasped arms with each companion and lastly with Ralmon. He bade a final farewell and went to the door. They all followed him into the street and marvelled at his great white warhorse. A junior Cleric of Tarne had been outside tending to his own and Halorun's mounts all the while. The pair rode off and the group returned inside the inn.

"Well, there we 'ave it," sighed Billit. "We have a quest, a mission."

"I was hoping we would be able to start with something straightforward, a bit easier, like saving a damsel in distress from an evil knight, or something," said Silmar. "Now it seems we have to take on the Darkling! Maybe more than one."

"Perhaps not," replied Taura. "All we have to do is get the thing back to its original home. We have to avoid being found but we do have skills. We have another advantage in that your appearance has changed, Silmar. He may not now recognise you. It is a pity you would not let us cut your hair. He also does not know that you now travel with friends. We will protect each other and you can rely on us to be there for you."

Billit nodded in agreement. "Halorun predicted we would find other companions, too. We gotta take care though. You never know who it is who'll offer to join us."

"How does he know?" asked Taura.

"Some sort o' scrying, prob'ly," answered Ralmon. He had been listening to their conversation. "I got some advice 'bout adventuring, so listen close. I'm pleased ter 'ear you're using yer common sense. You're all startin' to think like profesh'nal adventurers. You must all feel free ter talk 'bout yer ideas or problems with each other. All ideas must be listened to an' considered, no matter 'ow good, or bad, they may be. One idea will spawn another. No idea must be ridiculed. Trust each other but beware of all outsiders. Halorun was right; keep all knowledge of the *burden* that Silmar carries a secret 'tween the three of yer only. Never mention it by name and never mention where you are going an' why. Keep to yerselves the name of the person you seek in the far-east. Other people won't be able to tell yer secrets and pass on information. And remember to keep yer disguise, Silmar. You can darken yer 'air an' skin with berry juices like you saw me doin' earlier. You 'ave a couple o' days now to prepare an' ask me questions. Remember, any questions yer like. I'll 'elp an' advise yer where I can."

The companions looked at each other in silence and all of them took a deep breath. Silmar suddenly realised that this was a world away from goblin-hunting that had been his life before. He now felt as if he were an amateur which perhaps, it could be argued, he was. He had confidence in his weapon skills even though he knew there were many who were better than he. This Darkling assassin, he considered, was probably a better swordsman. If he was in fact a Darkling, then he may well have the same, or better, dark-sight ability; he would, after all, be living in the darkness of the underground cities – miles of tunnels and mines. The female dark elves were the most vicious and powerful with their magical skills given to them by their Scorpion Queen goddess, Adelenis. Normally, only the male warriors ever climbed to the surface to spread the evil and mischief of the Darkling. This knowledge was commonly taught amongst the elven race in Refuge and probably other communities too. Silmar shared his knowledge with his companions and saw real concern on their faces.

It was now time for lessons in driving a wagon.

∽ ∾

The sun was still quite low in the morning sky and the shadows were long as the gates of the city were opening just as Silmar, Taura and Billit arrived on foot. They found a surly, hard-looking drover standing by a wagon with a pair of horses that had obviously seen better days. The man was tall with broad shoulders and a long, bushy, brown beard. He carried a coiled whip tucked into his belt.

He looked at them with disdain and shook his head slowly. "Is yous all Ralmon's victims, er, I mean wagoneers?" he said with a wry grin. He should not have displayed his teeth – they were badly stained, some missing and others broken.

Taura said they were the candidates for the training in wagon-driving.

The man's mouth worked its way around Taura's words and then he nodded. "I'm Harald. You're late; bad start. Right then. Who's the driver? Who's done it afore?"

"None of us," replied Billit.

"By the dancin' gods, looks like I got me a right bunch of amateurs. One girlie, one gnome and, what are you? An elf?"

"Some elvish blood," replied Silmar. His woollen cap covered his long, newly darkened hair and, thankfully, his ears. Obviously, his facial features still marked him as elf-kin.

Although none of them responded to the wagoneer's last jibe, their expression said they were all new to wagon-driving.

"Well, which of you sorry specimens is first then?"

So the day went on. Harald seemed to be enjoying the struggling of the trainee wagoneers. Silmar showed absolutely no aptitude for wagon driving at all. Billit demonstrated some promise but it was Taura, having never tried before in her life, who took to it as if she had been doing it for years.

"You've been havin' me on, young lady. You've done this before. Don't piss me about or you'll feel the end of my whip."

Taura straightened up, looked him in the eye and glared at him with a ferocious expression. "Do not try it, Harald!" she warned. "I haven't, if you must know, but it's hardly difficult is it? I mean, if a man can do it, well, for the love of the gods, anyone can."

The drover had a face like thunder for the rest of the morning.

They returned to the inn for a hearty lunch and more ale. Driving a wagon was dusty, thirsty work and Ralmon's ale was sufficiently good, providing he served them with that which had not been watered down. The one-armed dwarf had apparently heard of the difficulties and couldn't resist the occasional leg-pull. The trio decided to take a walk down to the docks, more for Silmar's benefit because he had not seen the sea before and the large ships would be an interesting diversion to take their minds off their forthcoming journey.

He kept his cap pulled well down.

CHAPTER 8

YAZAMA JIUTARÔ'S ARRIVAL

DREADFUL DREAMS echoed inside his head. This was nothing unusual but this time his dreams were accompanied by a severe headache.

The screams of the dying man back at the *Han* in the Harima province town of Ako gradually turned into the shrieks of seagulls circling and swooping overhead.

Oh how my head aches! Jiutarô slowly returned to consciousness in his boat. He pulled himself up onto the rail. *It is daylight; no clouds. The storm must have passed.*

He shook his head to clear the fuzziness and immediately regretted it. There was a sharp ache in his fingers. He looked down and saw that the little finger of his left hand was in agony – broken. It was bent backwards, grotesquely, at the second knuckle. He plunged the hand over the side of the boat into the sea to cool it down; he was surprised that the sea was warm. *Never is it warm in the Straits of Shimonoseki.*

Gritting his teeth, he closed his right hand around the broken finger and yanked it back into place. Pain coursed through his hand and a wave of nausea rose in his throat; he grimaced but uttered no sound; the nausea passed quickly. He put his right hand onto the left side of his forehead, it came away bloodied but some dryness showed that the wound, the size of a one-yen gold coin, was already scabbing over.

The sail was badly torn and hung partly in tatters from the broken spar. The drunken, bad-tempered boatman was gone, presumably washed overboard during the storm. *He has probably managed to swim ashore; either that or his body will be washed up somewhere.*

His riding-horse remained tethered between both side-rails at the stern and seemed unharmed but of his pack-pony there was no sign. The remains of its harness lay in the scuppers. His horse must have been panicking during the storm; many of the deck planks were damaged and there were cuts and scratches on its front legs. His precious weapons and armour were all in the bottom of the boat, thank the stars! *Damn, my food and most of my spare clothing were on that pony!*

He looked for the familiar landmarks of the Straits, the black rocky cliffs topped by clumps of dark forest – nothing! He could see land no more than a mile off. The low skyline in front of him showed cliffs but not as high as would have been expected at the Straits. The sun was at his back and was quite high in the sky. *It must be past midday but the sun should not be that high, it is winter; it is far too warm, damn, it's hot! The storm must have carried me far to the South but this looks like nothing in my home country, as far as I know.*

A huge walled city stood a little back from the shoreline. Not even Edo was that big. The walls were of stone of a light brown colour, as if made of a particular type of sandstone. They must have been sixty or even eighty feet high. There were towers and minarets, the like of which he had never seen before. A long harbour, with many large ships moored, filled much of the shoreline to the right hand half of the city walls and, even from this distance, Jiutarô could clearly see movement and bustle on the dockside.

Not knowing where he was concerned him deeply. He retrieved his weapons, he may have need of them particularly if he had drifted somewhere off the coast of Korea. Nippon and Korea had been at war on and off for decades, if not centuries. He had heard tales of Korea from battle-scarred warrior veterans who had been garrisoned there. The people there were primitive, cruel, with no culture. He did not know where Korea was or what it looked like but he was sure that this did not resemble a primitive land.

There was enough sail left on his little craft to catch some wind and, using the single oar and what scant knowledge he had of sailing a craft, he slowly but steadily made for what appeared to be the quieter right-hand end of the docks. The sea was very calm, thankfully, but he was not happy, nor confident, on water, particularly when alone. His horse was skittish and its chaotic movements caused the boat to rock unpredictably.

Gulls shrieked and wheeled around his boat but soon lost interest and flew off, some of them swooping at prey on, or just below, the surface of the sea. He slowly got closer to the docks.

৽ ৵

It took an hour, if not a little more, for the craft to arrive at the docks. A jetty, probably forty paces in length, stretched out from the harbour. It was untidily covered in barrels, sacks, ropes, buckets and seagulls. Panishak, the task-master, led his team of four labourers along the platform and started them on clearing up. He'd had his share of warfare, it seemed. He was once broad and very muscular but much of this was turning to fat. He was still mighty however, swarthy with deeply-tanned skin from years on the ocean. Many of his teeth were missing and those that he still had were turning bad; perhaps this partly explained his generally unpleasant temper. He wore a greasy black silk scarf tied around his pock-marked head; a long and heavy dagger hung in a battered leather scabbard at his belt. The bottom half of his right ear was torn, or cut, away but in his other was a large gold-coloured ear-ring. Whatever had taken that piece of ear had also left a vicious scar on his right cheek. He liked to boast that the ear-ring was gold and would challenge any man to take it from him. Nobody had ever succeeded in nearly twenty years. A successful challenger would have been disappointed, it was brass!

One of the labourers, a small half-goblin with short, bowed legs and skin as dark as coal, gave a frantic shout. "Mashter, come quickly!"

The task-master was standing a barrel up onto its end. It looked like a rum barrel and it felt full. And it was now his! He looked up from the barrel to see the labourer hopping from one foot to another and pointing out into the harbour. "Wadya want, pig-face?" he growled.

"A boat comesh, mashter," came the reply.

"It's a piggin' harbour, you thick git!" bellowed Panishak, clearly becoming very annoyed. "It's a tossing boat park!" He was deep in thought on figuring out how he was going to get the barrel from the jetty up to his meagre home. The pained look of anguish on the face of the half-goblin led to laughter from the other human labourers prompting Panishak to berate them for being lazy bastards.

"Mashter," pleaded the labourer. "Come and look, pleashe mashter!"

Panishak gave an expletive, of the sort never used in higher society or even in some of the lower sort. He lowered the barrel and strode over, a face like thunder. The labourer pointed. "Shee mashter! A boat."

The task-master saw the battered craft, a small fabric-covered shelter and a badly-torn triangular sail showing that it had come through some fierce weather. *Strange looking boat, not seen nothin' like that 'round here. Odd, look at the state of it, there ain't been a storm on these waters for soddin' months.* A figure stood in the bow, holding a length of rope to tie up the craft as it moored at the jetty. He had a sword and matching dagger tucked into his sash around his waist and he had an unusual-looking longbow propped up against the shelter. A fine large horse stood in the stern. Panishak was thinking in gold crowns now.

"Listen you," called Panishak in an aggressive and officious tone, his hands on his hips. "Tie up here and state your name and business. You 'ave to pay to tie up here, a silver piece! To me." He looked over to his group of men and winked. They laughed, that would be ale for each one of them in the tavern.

There was no reply from the figure in the boat, just a blank uncomprehending expression. The strange looking man was dressed in loose-fitting grey leggings over which a black and grey silk gown was wrapped. Across the wide collar were unusual symbols embroidered in gold thread. A broad, blue, silk sash was coiled around the man's waist and knotted at his right hip. Apart from the beautiful black scabbard of a long sword was its shorter matching pair. His features were also strange to Panishak. The man's skin colour was pale and his eyes narrow, like slits. The front of his head had been shaven but his remaining hair was well oiled and formed into a tail which was then folded forward on the head, then back again, and tied in place. The man seemed young, probably no more than twenty-five summers.

"I said, tie up and state your name and business here," he shouted, even louder.

Again, there was no reply from the strange occupant.

"Gods, he's a piggin' outlander!" grumbled the task master. "Gannack, take his rope and tie the bastard's boat to the jetty."

The little labourer gingerly strode to the edge of the jetty. The virtually-expressionless face of the sailor had just a hint of a confident and menacing look. Gannack nervously motioned for the rope and the figure tossed it over. The half-goblin tied the craft securely to the mooring post. Panishak used a hand signal to beckon the figure from the craft. "Out you! Come on, move it!!"

Again, there was neither reply nor reaction.

The task-master tried once more, emphasising each word with a corresponding hand signal. "Out of the boat now, onto the jetty! Oh gods, he's as thick as crap!"

"Careful mashter, he hash weaponsh," whined Gannack. Panishak wasn't worried about this small newcomer. He liked the look of the black and shiny sword scabbard though and imagined it hanging from his own belt.

The figure stepped from the craft and stood confidently on the jetty with his legs slightly apart and arms loosely crossed in front of him. Panishak was not going to be humiliated by this calm-looking slanty-eyed foreigner. "I'm taking you to the harbour's watch patrol," he said. He moved forward to pin the figure's arms.

"Take his weapons men!" he ordered. As he moved in towards the foreigner, there was a blur of movement and Panishak suddenly found that his right wrist had been forced up between his shoulder blades, the small *wakisashi* short-sword had been whipped from the scabbard in the sash and was now positioned across his throat. The foreigner was behind him and Panishak couldn't, in fact did not dare, move. A small trickle of blood indicated to all those who were starting to congregate around the scene that it would take the smallest movement for Panishak to be sent to meet his forefathers. Nobody had ever seen Panishak bested in an altercation, particularly not in this manner.

Everything went quiet. Nobody moved a muscle. The foreigner's dark eyes took in the complete scene but there was no expression of fear or concern on his face. A trickle of blood ran down the left side of the foreigner's face from the reopened wound on his head.

❧ ❧

Jiutarô was, in fact *very* concerned. He would not show it. He was not afraid because he knew that if fear rose within him then his mind would be numbed. His years of training were serving him well. These people were indeed primitive. The one who had taken the rope from him was the ugliest human being he had ever seen. It had *tusks* and smelt foul; its faeces encrusted the backs of its legs. *Ughh!!* This huge human smelt foul too. *This place must be what the Jesuits called hell.* The city walls were behind him and he could see the harbour bay to his front.

A shout came from the dock to Jiutarô's right. The sound of marching feet approached and the growing number of onlookers gave way to allow more room for the newcomers. They wore a uniform, of sorts; black hose, a red tunic and armoured breastplates. They wore small helms upon their heads. Their weapons were varied but each had a short-sword. The leader of this militia had a dark tanned

116

face with a short pointed beard. Jiutarô had seen similar before, the Portuguese Jesuit missionaries were everywhere in Nippon these days and they all seemed to favour these little beards. Perhaps he was in *their* country, not in *hell* after all. He hadn't heard rumour of tusked men though. *Perhaps this is really just a bad dream; maybe I am still unconscious in the boat.*

Words were being said by the militia leader; Jiutarô did not understand and did not respond. The leader was getting more and more agitated and an apprehensive expression briefly appeared on his face as he took in the weaponry carried by the stranger. The man barked a command; all six of militia drew their short-swords and circled around Jiutarô and his prisoner who, by this time, was in tears.

Jiutarô was convinced the pathetic man had pissed himself.

He used his training well. Hooking his right leg about that of his prisoner, he gave a firm push and sent the hapless man sprawling on top of the militia leader. Both fell to the ground in a tangled heap. With a controlled sweeping motion, Jiutarô withdrew his *katana* long-sword with his right hand, disarmed one attacker and cut straight through the short-swords of three others. One man only was left with his sword in his hand but he had no intention of fighting; the point of Jiutarô's *wakisashi*, held in his left hand, was at the man's throat. Jiutarô's complete action had taken less than a second. As before, his face was impassive as he once again took in the scene around him. Not one person had been hurt in the fight, except perhaps for the militia leader who had the full weight of Panishak on top of him.

≈ ≈

The militia was in fact a detachment of the Westron Seaport City Watch. Harmon, its leader, was no fool. As he pulled himself out from underneath Panishak, he knew immediately that the stranger could easily have killed them all. He had never in his life seen swordplay like it. The ability to pin Panishak's arm while remaining so calm indicated a fighter with uncanny ability. A different approach was needed here.

"Panishak," he instructed. "Get your men out of here. Squad, put what remains of your swords away and form up over there, two ranks, smart now!" He pointed to an area near to the jetty.

Panishak and his men sloped off, although he did continue to look longingly at that barrel. The Watch had formed two ranks and stood easy. Panishak couldn't get close enough to the barrel to pick it up. He hoped it would still be there later. A small group of people, adventurers by the look of them, stood close by; a tall, athletic fighter wearing a woollen hat, a young female priestess and a gnomish monk by his garb. One could never tell with gnomes.

The stranger remained with his blades at the ready but Harmon gave him a signal that he should put his weapon back into its scabbard. The stranger did not respond.

"Oh shit!" said Harmon.

"May we be of help here?" came a call from the small group of adventurers. The female priestess strode confidently over with a smile.

"He's an outlander, can't get him to understand me," replied the Watch leader. "You can have a go if you like."

"Alright, let's try then!" She stepped over to the stranger and offered her arm in greeting. He looked down and slowly lowered his katana and wakisashi but didn't return the greeting. The blades were the most beautiful she had ever seen. She had noticed, as had her companions, how the blade had cut right though the weapons of three Watch Men in one sweep.

She placed her hand upon her chest and said "Taura!"

The stranger raised his eyebrows and gave a look of comprehension. "Yazama Jiutarô," he replied with a small bow of his head. His countenance remained stern notwithstanding her kindliness.

She blushed and beckoned her companions over one at a time. The tall athletic figure strode over with confidence.

"Silmar," said Taura. "He calls himself Yazaa Juto, or something."

"Yazama Jiutarô" repeated the stranger as he cast a curious gaze over the elf's features.

The gnome stepped over and Jiutarô's gaze was one of complete amazement at the short but muscular figure with orange skin.

"And this is Billit," she introduced with a chuckle as she observed the stranger's expression.

The gnome growled "Not bloody funny, young lady! Hey, is this outlander taking the pi-"

"I gather that you are going to take control of this stranger then," interrupted Harmon. He hoped she would accept; it was quite possible that this stranger could cause problems. He was fortunate because she replied with a nod. "Make sure he behaves himself or we'll have to run him in – if we can!" He marched over to his squad, brought them to the alert and marched them off.

"He'd better bring plenty of guards then!" sighed Silmar. "After all that, it looks like we have another companion, even if we can't talk with him!"

"That might be to our advantage," replied a sullen Billit. The other two laughed. "Let's get his kit off the boat then."

Jiutarô collected his weapons, armour and his belongings that remained on the little craft and put them on his magnificent horse. With gentle persuasion, they all managed to move the nervous horse off the boat and onto the jetty.

Silmar glanced at the horse as it stepped onto the jetty and immediately noticed the wounds on its forelegs. "They'll go bad if we don't clean them up" he recommended. "Can you do anything about them Taura?" Although priests were generally well-trained in healing people, regardless of their race, it was often a different matter when attending to animals.

"Well, I'll try," she replied. "Don't expect too much from me, I'm not very experienced." She rummaged inside a bag hanging on her belt. From it she took a small bottle of fluid that looked as if it contained water.

"What's that?" asked Billit.

"It is water! Very clean water with a plant extract to help wounds heal better. I'm going use some on Jeti, er, Juto's face too."

Using a cloth and the fluid, she cleaned up the horse's leg wounds and expertly bandaged the worst cut. Jiutarô looked on appreciatively. Taura then turned to Jiutarô himself who reluctantly allowed her to treat the wound on his head. She started to quietly chant words while placing her hand over, but not touching, the injury. After a few moments, Jiutarô felt a warm glow followed by a tingling sensation on the side of his face. This went on for some minutes then she said "You'll live, Yazza Juto!"

"Yazama Jiutarô!" corrected Jiutarô. He put his hand to the side of his head and was surprised to feel that it no longer bled copiously. He looked at his fingertips, no wet blood, only dried scab.

"Aii!" he called. "Domo! Domo Arrigato!" and he laughed.

"Don't they do that in his land then? Hey, what's in the barrel?" asked Billit. "Have a look, young elf."

"Shhh! I'm not an elf, remember?" Silmar stepped over to inspect the barrel, turning it and sniffing around the bung.

"It's *rumm!*" he announced with a whoop.

They lifted it up onto the horse and he tied it securely, covering it with a cloak.

Five minutes later, as they rounded the corner of a small timber shed, they almost bumped into the task-master and his group of labourers. Panishak took a step towards Jiutarô with a face full of fury.

Jiutarô withdrew his curved *katana* and, with a cry of "Kii-ai", swept it in a perfect circle and replaced it back into its scabbard, all in a heartbeat.

Panishak shrank back and called "Back to the jetty men".

They were gone in a trice. The little group of adventurers gasped at the incredible, hitherto unseen, display of swordsmanship.

"I know what the fat slob is after!" laughed Billit. They all laughed, even Jiutarô, whose hand was still going up to his now completely closed wound, just the scabbed-over red swelling that still irritated him.

Twenty minutes later, it was late afternoon and they were back in the Tavern. Ralmon was laughing too; he was now the proud owner of a barrel of rumm, a rare commodity in these lands towards the north of Baylea. Not only were the adventurers now staying at the inn at no cost but they seemed to be consuming endless ale, mead or wine. Now there was a fourth member of their group. The rumm however, more than covered his losses.

Jiutarô was devouring a mutton stew and his second quart tankard of ale. His weapons and armour and his belongings, such as they were, were neatly stacked beside his table. The group looked at the bow and armour with curiosity.

"Ale!" called Jiutarô, in the universal language, as he slammed the empty pot down onto the table.

"He's learnin' choddin' fast, that one," grumbled Ralmon. There was more laughter from the group as an impolite belch burst from a nonchalant Yazama Jiutarô.

"I do believe we now number four," murmured Silmar to nobody in particular.

❧   ☙

During the evening, Jiutarô was quite drunk and Billit wasn't far behind him. Ralmon beckoned Silmar over to the bar and glanced about the taproom furtively.

"'Ere, elf," he murmured, "take these." He passed Silmar three items.

"First, young elf," he said. "This is your pay in advance for getting' me wagon up the road to Nor'wald. Go on, open it up."

Silmar took hold of a small leather pouch and pulled on the drawstring. Inside a large number of gold crowns glistened!

"Twenny-five!" whispered the one-armed dwarf. That was a considerable sum. "Right, now," he continued. "This is a map o' your journey up to Nor'wald City. I'll come over an' speak with you all when I'm not so busy. Also, Halorun Tann got one of 'is acolyte priests to leave you a list and a rough map so you knows where you is goin'."

Silmar looked at it and was surprised at the detail. There was much writing on the map but he couldn't read it in the dim light of the tavern. Ralmon then handed him a package rolled in cloth. The elf was about to unroll it when Ralmon slapped his hand over the top.

"Gods boy!" he gasped in a coarse whisper. "Keep this 'idden away, young 'un. It's that special thing you asked for. If yer gets caught with it on yer person, you didn't get it off've me."

"I'll give you something for these now," said Silmar, reaching into his pouch to give Ralmon the payment.

"No, ain't necess'ry," said Ralmon. "They ain't new; the feller I got 'em from 'as adapted 'em for some of them modern locks that are comin' out o' Cascant these days. As I said, I called in a favour. No charge, just tuck 'em away inside your tunic, lad, quick now!"

"I cannot thank you enough, Ralmon. Well, in that case, quarts of ales for us all and one for yourself as well."

"Done!" The dwarf scratched at his thick beard for a moment. "Hey, 'ang on – you ain't payin' for 'em anyways!"

Silmar sat down with the quart pots.

"Ale!" cried Jiutarô once again. "Domo!" The others laughed.

"I suppose *domo* means thanks in his speak," observed Billit. "I'm gonna try to educate him in speaking proper."

"You and Ralmon were deep in conversation," said Taura. "Anything for us?"

"Aye," said Silmar, brandishing the moneybag and map. "Twenty five gold for our payment and a couple of maps. He's coming over later to chat about our road north."

"Don't like the look of this area here," said Taura with a worried frown. "It is a symbol of a grinning skull. On a map drawn by a temple it usually means that there is undead in that area."

"Well," replied Billit, "it's clearly not a new map. Mebbe it's not a dangerous area now. Mebbe Ralmon can explain the route. Mebbe it's guarded. Mebbe –"

"Maybe there's liches, zombies or skeletons!" suggested a pessimistic Taura. "Or all of them – ugh!"

"Maybe you won't be going on your journey alone," said Ralmon. They all jumped as he crept up behind Silmar from behind a wide pillar. "Heehee. Heh heh!"

"Very amusin'," muttered Billit. "Didn't think dwarves were renowned for moving with stealth."

"The road will be fairly busy," warned Ralmon. "I've 'ad a word with a caravan master. His name's Kassall and 'is wagons leave from outside the North Gate an hour after sunup tomorrow. There's a couple of things to remember though."

He leaned forward as if they were discussing a conspiracy. "Although they are travelling as a caravan, you can't travel as part of it 'cos if you do then he has to take responsibility fer you an' that could cost 'im extra in tolls and stuff. Keep fairly close an' they'll 'elp look after you. At night, camp close to 'em but not as part of 'em an' they'll give you what protection they can. If trouble comes to 'em though, you'll be expected to 'elp. Any questions?"

The friends all shook their head, it all seemed perfectly clear.

"I'll be out back in mah courtyard after yer morning feast tomorrer; I'll provide you with plenty o' food, water, some blankets an' stuff an' two ponies. Just make sure that my bruvver Jasper 'as it all when you get there. Best yer get an early night; I'll be callin' yous for yer morning feast afore dawn."

On that, the four went up to their rooms and settled down for the night. Silmar was just about to settle onto his bed when there was a knock at his door. Ralmon stood there with a backpack in his hand.

"Look, young elf. I got this huge debt o' gratitude for yer pappy; like I told yer, 'e saved me life once or twice durin' our days together. There was no judgement fer me bein' a dwarf an' all. I'd be 'onoured if you'd take this 'ere ol' backpack o' mine. Couldn't help but notice all yer gear in that sack earlier. Well, that's no choddin' good is it? Put yer bundle in this. It's well worn in and you 'ardly feel its weight when the waist strap is tightly done up. I'll be 'appy knowing it's back in use again by the son of an old campaigning partner. Go on."

Silmar took it with gratitude, saying he hoped to return it some time in the future when the world was a safer place, if it ever would be.

Ralmon bade him goodnight and left. Silmar closed the door and propped a chair up behind it, for security as always, and settled down to sleep. Some moments later there was another knock on his door but lighter this time. He climbed up off the floor, sighed, removed the chair and opened the door. The caller was invited in and remained there for the rest of the night.

❧ ❧

CHAPTER 9

THE DARKLING slayer of the Priest of Clamberhan in that lightless passage off the Street of the Moon in Westron Seaport now lurked in a disused shed behind a stockyard. His skin was as black as pitch but his hair as white as the snow on the caps of mountains. He could never show himself to the people who lived on the surface; he was safer underground. Not that he couldn't protect himself though, he was a weapons-master without equal in Dannakanonn, the Darkling city of the deep below the western end of the Dragon's Teeth Mountains. The hue and cry that would result, however, would seriously jeopardise the mission on which he had been sent. He moved only at night, kept clear of the highways but always keeping them within sight.

He had a troop of comrades waiting for him in a cavern at the north of the Spinewall Mountains. He preferred being alone; a group of riders were more noticeable but he was not given the option this time. *She* saw to that.

During the day he shunned the light, covering his head in a sheer dark brown cloth through which he could see but not be seen or recognised. His clothing was of a blue so dark as to be almost black; this would make him almost invisible in the night, wherever he was. A hood attached to his tunic could be pulled so far forward as to hide his head and face, covered or no.

This servant of the Goddess Adelenis was furious. The foolish elf had interfered with his mission and taken the very artefact that was much desired by his mistress – *she* who thrived on killing and torture. He dare not fail. He would hunt for the *high elf* that may have been able to identify him, who may alert the Tarne priesthood to his existence and who carried the prize. The white elf would feel the full power of the dagger; he would need guidance from a priest with power and knowledge – hah! Perhaps the meddlesome Tann himself.

The Darkling knew of the dogged determination of the Priesthood of Tarne and that one in particular, Halorun Tann, was the most feared and resolute warrior-priest of them all. Tann, of the black eyes, who was said to be able to see into the very soul of a man, Darkling, white elf or dwarf. He both founded, and presided over, the newest and largest temple on the West Coast yet to have been dedicated to the God of Justice, the head of the Pantheon of the Greater Gods. Tarne it was, so it is said, who intended to dispense justice to Adelenis, the Scorpion Queen, after a trial in her absence which left her a fugitive in hiding. Her surface-bound devotees and her most loyal of followers, the Hoshites, had been confused and leaderless for some centuries but with clandestine guidance from the Darklings, they rallied and were slowly beginning to spread westwards from the far side of the East Brash mountain range.

The assassin considered the most likely course of action that the surface-dwellers would take. The precious dagger would be taken away by Tann's lackeys, that was clear. Tann, or perhaps even the Magelords, would not tolerate the *thing* remaining in the city, let alone his own temple. It would surely be be moved on the road but which way? West? No, not to the sea. South to the land of the burning sand? Unlikely. East through Shordrun and Polduman towards the Kamambia from whence it came? Very possible indeed; logical too. North towards Icedge? That was also very possible, albeit unlikely.

Where to wait then? East by the Great East Silk Road to watch the travellers, pick them off those that seemed to be the likely ones. Give him two days, maybe three, and if the white elf did not appear, he would ride north and overtake him in the night. Yes, watch for that elf then take both his life and the dagger. Or *with* the dagger; hah, a fitting use for it!

Yes, the Scorpion Queen, mused the Darkling. *A fanatical but naïve Goddess too big for her boots! But her fanatical emissary from Dannakanonn, an impatient fool but* nasty. Adelenis should be more careful whom she chooses as her agent. The Darkling female mage-priest chosen specifically by the Scorpion Queen, it was said, was devious and calculating. Adelenis' matriarchal High Priestesses would continue to send out Hoshite agents and spies, hatch plots and collect more artefacts of power. She would bide her time and when she had amassed sufficient power and resources, her armies of Darkling would strike swiftly and simultaneously at the very hearts of the power bases of the Landsdrop Coast, Shordrun, Cascant, Kamambia and other countries on the continent of Baylea. But she couldn't do this alone; she needed allies. Who better than those of the *Shadow World* beneath the Dragon's Teeth mountains? The mighty Darkling would gather and lead the vicious Grullien Shade Dwarves and the expendable Kobolds. The Hoshites, though, would need to be paid and would never accept the majesty of the Scorpion Queen.

But the Great Adelenis would lead and in the end even the Hoshites were expendable.

He smiled as he pictured the face of his God, her spiteful and bitter beauty; the pure whiteness of her face, although she had been Darkling once; Her bulbous, round crustacean-like body with its long thin barbed tail; her desire to feed on living flesh, human or even better, elven – but not Darkling. A Priest of Tarne was said to be her favourite delicacy. Hmm, a pity he could not feed her Halorun Tann! Perhaps one day.

Meanwhile there was that stupid bastard of a yellow-haired elf to find. And kill. Slowly.

CHAPTER 10

THIS IS NOT real! Perhaps I am dead and in one of those absurd Jesuit hells. Perhaps it is a nightmare. Am I still unconscious in the bottom of the boat? Shall I awaken and find myself back in the boat with my two horses and that drunken boatman? I hope so, this place is bizarre! I have seen a bestial man with tusks, an orange-skinned, red-haired midget, a one-armed long-bearded dwarf and many other strange beings. I am in a city where chaos reigns. This cannot be real therefore I am not really here. Is a god, Buddha perhaps, punishing me for my past transgression by putting me in this nightmare? It cannot be real therefore I refuse to believe it. If it is not real I cannot die. I shall awaken sometime and all will be well. It is strange that the pain in my hand did not wake me up. My destiny is to die beside my forty-six comrades after having avenged my dead master. I must be there, I cannot let them down. My face wound was healed with a touch and a whispered prayer or mantra – surely this cannot happen; it does not happen; it is not real. These people have been kind to me, they have offered friendship. I shall remain with them while I am in this nightmare and, if necessary, fight alongside them provided they are just in their actions. I have my weapons and my skills. I shall follow the stream as it flows; although its course constantly changes, it always reaches its destination. Then I am sure I shall awaken. It will all have been a bad dream. It cannot be real.

I refuse to believe it.

☙ ❧

It was still dark when Ralmon banged on their doors, typically showing little respect for his other slumbering guests. Silmar had slept in his separate bedchamber; accepting the offer to share with his new companions the previous night would not been conducive to a good night's sleep. Well, that was the excuse he had given them the previous evening! However, they weren't fooled.

Morning feast was good once again and afterwards, they collected their equipment and met with Ralmon in the courtyard. A fully loaded wagon, with the same two tired-looking horses they had seen the previous day, waited for them. A fit-looking pony and Jiutarô's horse were tethered to the rear of the wagon.

"Don't look so worried," he said. "Them cart 'orses may look like plodders but they're strong enough an' will go all day. Make sure that you're 'appy with the wagon. There's barrels o' mead an' wine aboard look, but this small one 'ere," he said pointing to a smaller barrel tucked in a front corner of the wagon, "contains a special brew, elven blood-wine."

Silmar's eyebrows shot up, this was a valuable cargo indeed. "But this is worth a small fortune!" he exclaimed excitedly.

"Just make sure that Jasper gets it *all*. He gets special clients, see! Right then, Kassall is waiting for yer outside the gates, yer need to be there in an 'alf-hour." He pointed to their supplies and blankets and continued. "Yer all lookin' like folks who can look after yerselves but may the gods protect you on the journey. When yer gets to the town of Nor'wald City, get yerselves some warm clothing, furs and the like. It gets cold up north."

There was a cry and Sheena ran out into the courtyard. She glanced around until her gaze locked on Silmar. Then she rushed across and flung her arms around his neck and kissed him full on the lips. He made no effort to resist. Then, in tears but without another sound, she turned and rushed back inside.

Taura chuckled and made a face at Silmar who stood there with a bewildered expression. "Is she the reason you slept in your own bedchamber last night? She is very pretty and I'm *so* jealous of her figure! You did, didn't you? None of us were fooled you know and she wasn't all that discrete during the night."

Silmar didn't reply immediately but beneath the dark facial colouring his cheeks flushed and he looked down at his feet. "Look," he began. "I only –"

"What are you up to with mah new cook?" demanded Ralmon. "She's 'alf asleep this mornin' an' I got lots of work for 'er to do."

Silmar took the dwarf to one side. "You will look after her for me, won't you?"

"Aye, I will, elf. But think well about this and the implications. You knows what I mean, don't you?"

Silmar knew what he meant. His father had nagged him for years over this. Unions between elves and humans were generally doomed because of the long lives of elves compared to those of humans. The tragedy came when an elf would outlive his or her spouse, children and grandchildren. But, although these unions were not common, there was usually happiness and success but these were tinged with tragedy.

While the strange swordsman, Jiutarô, made ready his horse, Taura checked the tackle but stepped back with a frown. "This isn't done up the same as it was yesterday."

Billit came over to the wagon. "What's different, girlie?"

"Well, the yoke traces are the other way round and this buckle's joined up to that strap instead of this one." She indicated the differences.

The others looked on uncomprehendingly.

"Can you still drive the horses with the different way it's strapped up?" asked Silmar. "It may not be important."

She looked at the traces and rubbed the back of her head. "Well, aye, I think I can. It may be done that way to help the horses pull up hills better. I'll have to see. If there's a problem, I'll have to see if I can retackle the ponies."

Silmar and Billit nodded knowingly, while not understanding a word of what she was saying, but also impressed with her newly found knowledge of the terminology.

Billit, being too short in stature to ride in a saddle, climbed up onto the wagon's seat. Silmar indicated to Jiutarô that they were about to ride off and they both climbed onto their mounts.

With final farewell from Ralmon, they rode out of the courtyard and on through the city to the North Gate. After a while they passed out of the still, quiet city through a large gate and spotted the caravan in an area by the left-hand side of the road.

Kassall was waiting for them. He introduced himself. "We're off in a few moments," he explained. "Keep close, by all means but if anyone asks, you're not part of my caravan."

Taura nodded to indicate that they understood the terms. Soon, the caravan pulled out and Taura positioned the wagon at the rear, although a good fifty yards back. Silmar rode in silence with his wide, woollen cap pulled low over his face, his watchful eyes hiding the fact that he was deep in the thoughts of his night with little sleep.

As the journey progressed the group found that they were beginning to lag behind. The road surface was good and there were few slopes. By midday however, they were almost a mile behind. Although the horses did not appear to be labouring, it was clear that they were not able to go at a faster speed than they were already travelling.

"We must stop to give the horses a break," advised Silmar. The others readily agreed. The horses were given water and food and the trio fed on some of the food that Ralmon had provided.

"P'raps it's the way the nags are strapped up," ventured Billit.

"I think not," answered Taura, "but I'll look at the straps later when we stop for the evening."

The journey was resumed after a half-hour and the caravan was spotted about a mile ahead. At this distance, the friends could see that outriders from the caravan were halting to observe their progress.

Although having no understanding of the language, Jiutarô had settled into the journey well, having ridden out on the flank or in front to keep an eye on the safety of the little group. When he did ride close in, he listened avidly to the exchanges of conversation between Billit and Taura. The gnome spent much of the journey speaking words and phrases which the Samurai echoed back.

Finally, evening came and the concerns of the trio were growing. "We'll have to stop soon," Taura advised. They all agreed.

"Let's go on awhile," said Billit. "P'raps we'll catch 'em."

As darkness descended further, the glow of cooking fires could be seen in the distance.

"That's probably no more than a mile ahead," Silmar called from thirty yards up the road. "It shouldn't take that long to get there."

He was right, fifteen minutes later they arrived at the edge of the caravan's camping area.

Kassall strode over with a relieved expression. "We were worried about you!" he exclaimed. "Thank the gods you're here safely. I was about to despatch one of my riders to see where you were."

"We are grateful for your concern, Goodman Kassall," replied Taura. "Are you happy that we take this spot for our camp?"

"Aye, this is fine. We'll be mounting a guard but I suggest you do the same. Unlikely to be any trouble in these parts but you don't always know what's come out of the mountains to the north."

"We're here if you need us," offered Silmar.

"Likewise. G'night," said Kassall.

The companions tended to their ponies and horses and lit a small fire. Billit cooked a meal of three rabbits from the six that Ralmon had thoughtfully provided. Being a mage required Billit to take as much sleep as he could during the night but he took the first watch regardless. He woke Jiutarô soon after midnight and, using sign language of sorts, indicated that the man should take over the watch.

❧ ❧

Silmar volunteered to take the *graveyard watch*; that being the period leading up to dawn when everything appeared grey until the sun's first light shone over the horizon. It had taken a long time for him to get to sleep before that. The previous night, Sheena had come to his room soon after everybody had retired to their quarters. The elf had opened his door when he heard the light tap and when she had reached to touch his hand; he took hold of hers and had gently led her into his room. She had stayed there with him all night and they were still wrapped up together when Ralmon had knocked loudly on the door in the morning.

❧ ❧

Happily, there were no incidents during the night and the friends had a reasonable night's sleep. They awoke at dawn and finished off the cooked rabbit with some bread. The sun's first light did not appear as bright this morning as it had the previous day. In fact, the heavy clouds threatened rain. The caravan was still preparing to move off by the time the friends had hitched the horses to the wagon and mounted their ponies.

The ride continued although the countryside was now more undulating than before. The snow-capped summits of the mountains some leagues to the east seemed a little closer than they had appeared the day before. Fortuitously, the rain passed them by to the south. Within a couple of hours the caravan was once again a good half-mile ahead. Billit and Silmar agreed that, with Jiutarô, they should all act as scouts to ensure the safekeeping of themselves and the wagon.

"Don't get out of sight of each other, or the wagon," requested Taura. Billit tried to explain to Jiutarô.

They nodded their agreement.

The sound of horses galloping towards them caught their attention soon afterwards. Their hands hovered very close to their weapons. Two riders from the caravan approached.

"Kassall sent us," one rider explained. "We're some way ahead now and it will be difficult for us to lend you our protection, but we have these whistles. They are very loud. If you need us, use these."

With that, they turned and spurred their horses away, eager to be back to provide, as well as to receive, protection of their caravan.

"Thank–" called Silmar towards their rapidly disappearing backs. The little group gained a measure of comfort knowing they had a means by which help could be summoned if necessity arose.

An hour later, a sudden, piercing yell like a war cry emitted from beyond a low hill to their right. Silmar immediately reined in his mount, turned it about and galloped back to the wagon, much to Taura's relief. A moment later Jiutarô's horse, with him upon it wielding his unusual bow over his head, thundered over a low rise. Without slowing his horse's pace, his right hand flashed over his shoulder and drew an arrow. He turned in his saddle to release the arrow behind him. He yelled something unintelligible as he approached the wagon.

ഴ ഺ

CHAPTER 11

A MASSIVE FIGURE abruptly appeared over the low rise from which Jiutarô had ridden. It rushed straight towards them though it was still some way off. Silmar recognised it immediately although it was the first he had ever seen.

Jiutarô watched with an incredulous expression, another arrow at the ready and then released it at the figure just as his horse reared. He thought the arrow passed between the thing's legs.

"An ogre! An ogre, by the gods!" Silmar screamed. "Arm yourselves, make ready."

He leapt down from his horse and hitched it to the rear of the wagon. He drew both of his swords for the first time.

Jiutarô threw his bow to the grass and dropped from his saddle, leaving the reins trailing. He slid his katana from its scabbard and stood with both hands on the hilt.

Billit remained on the wagon, to give himself the advantage of extra height. He began to chant in a singsong voice and his hands weaved an intricate pattern before him.

They were all unmistakably nervous at what could be their first encounter.

The ogre was huge, fully eight feet in height, probably more. It had an animal-skin cloth stretched across its bulbous midriff. Its muscle-bound body was covered in short, dark hair but the head was completely hairless. It was obviously male. It was unarmed but its muscular physique made weapons seem pointless. The ogre roared as it ran towards them, its arms flailing. Then, unexpectedly, it turned away to their right in a direction that took it away from them.

Suddenly, there was another call, a war cry, but this time not from the ogre. Immediately, two monstrous beasts rushed out at high speed from around the base of the same hill. None of them, not even Silmar who seemed knowledgeable on beasts and monstrosities, had seen creatures of this kind before. They could only be described as crab-like but with the head of a humanoid – bulbous and bald but with elongated canine teeth. These were huge monstrosities beyond belief, being twice the height of a man. They scuttled partly upright on six legs and had two large pincers.

They were heading directly for the wagon and the group.

৯৪ ৶

Taura's horses stamped and reared in panic. With Taura struggling, the traces and reins barely held them under control.

Once again, Jiutarô watched them in disbelief and horror. His mouth hung open but then his horse began to rear in panic. He stepped over and grabbed the reins with a free hand and fought to pacify the terrified beast. He dropped the reins and stamped his foot on the trailing ends. He swiftly sheathed his sword and grabbed at his bow once again.

"Taura!" yelled Silmar. "Get the wagon away, fast!"

Amongst the sound of thrashing reins were yells of rage from Taura as she fought to control the wagon and horses and to get them moving. Billit slumped down onto the seat as the wagon lurched forwards. Silmar took out the whistle and blew hard, repeatedly. Its sound reverberated around the hills.

"Help will surely soon be on its way," he cried, his voice high-pitched from both anxiety and excitement. In the past he'd had the protection of many other elves, all of whom he knew and trusted, in a potential battle situation; now, he had his own wits together with the unknown capabilities of his three new comrades – their first real test.

Jiutarô loosed off an arrow at one of the crab-like abominations but it flew harmlessly between its gangling limbs. It seemed not to notice.

The two beasts suddenly veered to follow the ogre, whether as a result of Billit's spell or because the ogre was in reality their quarry they couldn't tell. But soon it became clear that the two beasts were now chasing after the ogre.

The battle-cry sounded once more but it was not from the crab-like abominations. Another figure, this time on horseback, burst out at full gallop from around the hill. A man, bare-chested and with long, straw-coloured, flowing hair, chased out after the two monstrous beasts and proved to be the originator of the battle cry. He carried a long, wooden javelin in the manner of a lance.

By now, Taura and the wagon were fifty yards along the road with Jiutarô, back on his horse, riding alongside in defence. His bow was over his shoulder and his katana was in his hand. The two others took up defensive positions but neither the galloping horseman, the *crab-men* or the ogre, appeared to be taking any interest in them.

Billit's chanting fell to a whisper while confusion as to what was going on set in. Silmar's sword arms dropped a little.

Taura slowed the wagon and, with Jiutarô helping by tugging the bridle of one of the horses, started to bring it about to return to the point where Silmar was positioned; she was not going to be left out of the action!

The *crab-men* were onto the ogre in an instant; one of them chopped its front limb at the ogre's legs and it went down with a roar of pain and terror. Their crab-like pincers held its arms and their mouths hovered just inches away from its head and upper body.

The horseman, a barbarian of some kind, was large and quite pale of skin although it was tanned by prolonged exposure to the sun. He was dressed only in a loincloth and what appeared to be goatskin boots. He reined in a few paces from the *crab-men* and climbed out of the saddle. He signalled to them, with his hand, to eat. The monsters continued to wait, though.

The look of terror on the face of the ogre raised some sympathy from Silmar despite the fact that ogres showed no mercy whatsoever with a humanoid captive. He shuddered inwardly as he thought of what would inevitably occur soon. He could hear the *crab-men* chattering to each other.

With Billit on the seat beside her and Jiutarô riding close by, Taura pulled the wagon up alongside the elf. "Wasn't going off to let you have all the fun," she called. Her face became grim as she looked across at the crab-men and their prey.

The barbarian strode slowly towards them. He was at least seven-feet tall and very muscular. They raised their weapons. He looked at the weapons seemingly with little concern. They noticed that as he walked forward his horse followed him less than a pace behind. The barbarian did not make any threatening gestures.

He stopped five paces from the companions.

"Are you the master of these beasts?" asked Silmar.

The barbarian didn't answer but continued to look at them with a quizzical expression.

"Are the beasts yours?" repeated Silmar.

"Perhaps he don't understand," offered Billit. The barbarian continued to look at them without speaking.

Billit placed his hand on his chest and said "I am Niebellittin, er, Billit."

The barbarian echoed "Billit, gnome." He placed his hand on his own chest and replied "Makkadan."

Silmar pointed to himself and said "Silmar."

Falcon echoed "Silmar, the elf," and then added "I am Makkadan, man-name Falcon, a goblin-slayer. From the north." He pointed to the wagon.

"She is Taura, er, and Juto," answered Billit.

"Jiutarô!" corrected Jiutarô.

Falcon again echoed the names.

By the god's, thought Billit, *this is 'ard work, just like getting Jiutarô to understand the other day!*

The monsters chittered again. Silmar jerked his head up; he was certain he could make out the word *Hunger!*

"Eat all!" exclaimed Falcon. "The beasts are not mine. We shared my meat and then I brought them to this hunting ground. They eat ogre, goblin and troll. They will leave soon. They will eat the ogre first but waited to see if I wished to share. I did not."

Immediately, the *crab-men* set about their prey, rending the ogre limb from limb and feeding as if they were starving. The sight was gruesome to the group but Falcon seemed unmoved by the sight and sound of the carnage. Jiutarô grimaced and turned his head away from the grisly scene.

"Oh damn it!" cried Silmar. "I called for help from the caravan. Somebody will be here in a moment." He rode off up the road and reined in after about a hundred yards or so. He could hear the approach of horses already. They were probably only a moment away.

Meanwhile, the *crab-men* were chittering excitedly. Falcon answered back in a manner that was difficult for the others to follow – a combination of words and hand signals.

Jiutarô looked at Billit and fought to find the word. "Aii, um, bad," he said. He grinned triumphantly.

Billit nodded. "Aye, bad," he agreed.

"They go now," explained Falcon. The *crab-men* scuttled away in the direction from which they had appeared.

Up the road, Silmar welcomed the four riders from the caravan with a look of some embarrassment and explained the situation. The riders could clearly see the two *crab-men* in the distance heading away from the road but, on the insistence of Silmar, made no attempt to follow.

"What in the hells of the Void were those things?" asked one of them.

"I have no idea," he responded and then went on to describe the last few moments.

They were somewhat amused by Silmar's explanation although they fully understood the difficulty the group had thought they were in. With a cheery wave, the riders rode off towards the caravan. Silmar returned to the others.

Taura advised the group that they continue their journey. "We're miles behind them now," she warned.

Falcon was invited to travel with them awhile. He shrugged and looked about the hills but then nodded.

The midday rest came and went and their journey progressed. Rare were the times now when the group spotted the caravan. It was probably more than two miles ahead of them, by now far out of range of the sound of the whistle were the need to arise. Falcon spoke the Universal language haltingly but as time progressed during the afternoon he showed his willingness to learn from them all.

The afternoon passed quietly and once again thoughts turned towards catching up with the caravan by nightfall. The glow from the campfires was spotted while the group was still some distance away and it was fully-dark by the time that they came within sight of the caravan camp. The guards patrolling the perimeter of the camp showed obvious relief once again. One mentioned that there was an abundance of rabbit in the area and that with the half-moon it was not too dark to hunt.

"We have one coney left," Taura told them, holding the rabbit before her. "Not nearly enough for us all tonight."

"Then I shall hunt," replied Falcon.

"I would like to join you," Silmar stated. "I can use a bow, but I have never seen one such as yours."

The barbarian's bow was unusual. It was short, probably no longer than four feet from tip to tip. The bow appeared to be made of wood, horn and sinew and looked very powerful, albeit unsightly.

"You may come," answered Falcon, with his impassive expression.

Do you ever smile? Taura thought. "We'll get a cooking fire going and keep watch then shall we?" she asked with more than a hint of sarcasm in her voice. "Then you boys can go out playing!"

"We guard," said Billit to Jiutarô, while tapping his dagger and pointing to his eyes.

"*Hai*, guard," replied Jiutarô. He strode off to the periphery of their campsite, watching Silmar and Falcon as they walked off over the nearest hill.

Silmar and Falcon searched for sign and soon found a rabbit run. Droppings were scattered everywhere. In the darkness the rabbits had come out of their burrows and were grazing out in the open, well within an arrow's distance. Falcon withdrew a pair of flint-tipped arrows, held one in his teeth, readied the other and fired at the group of rabbits. He hit one but the others scattered before he could make ready his second arrow. Retrieving the rabbit, and the arrow, he made a signal for them to move on.

"You move quietly, it is good!" the Barbarian quietly pronounced to Silmar.

The elf was pleased with the compliment and explained that he had some experience in this kind of movement. "I have also hunted goblins near the lands of my kinsmen," he stated.

Now fully dark, Silmar used his dark-sight, an ability of all elves to see a short distance in almost total darkness. Dwarves had the gift too, evidently, although Silmar had in the past cared little for these beings despite the fact that his home town had a very small dwarven community. This attitude was quickly changing since meeting Ralmon in the Ship's Prow tavern. "I see well in the dark," he explained.

"I know this," answered Falcon. He obviously had some knowledge of elves.

Falcon offered Silmar his bow and an arrow, similarly flint-tipped. He pointed out a rabbit less than fifty yards away and Silmar took aim and fired but the arrow went wide by inches. The weapon felt heavy and ungainly in his hands. Falcon seemed impressed though. Once again, the rabbits scattered. They waited patiently and quietly but it was quite

145

a while before the rabbits reappeared. Shooting their arrows simultaneously, they brought down two more. It was time to return to the campsite.

The first rabbit was stewed by the time the pair returned and Falcon, Silmar and Jiutarô went to work preparing the other three.

The group followed the caravan this way for another five days. Each evening they arrived at the caravan's camp an hour or so after sundown. Billit would sit beside Jiutarô for a couple of hours each evening teaching him some of the Universal language – the *Samurai*, as he referred to himself, picked some of the phrases up quite quickly. Taura would do the same with Falcon.

On the fourth day they were too far behind the caravan to even consider catching up with it. Kassall sent a pair of his outriders to them to say that the caravan would not expect them to catch up and that he could no longer wait. He had wished them a safe journey. The riders waved and rode away.

∽ ∾

CHAPTER 12

A MOTHER SOBBED over the loss of her son who had died from a disease a week ago; influenza the wise woman had informed her. Why, oh why, had she not taken advantage of opportunities to leave this village behind and journey with her son either north to the city of Northwald or south to the huge city of Westron Seaport? Either city might have given her opportunities for work. She was still young, only in her mid-twenties as far as she could reckon. She was very intelligent and extremely nimble with her fingers. Her husband had been dead these last six years and she had scratched out a living on the little plot of land. It provided her with enough money to keep her hut clean, her son and herself clothed and fed; but precious little else. The opportunities didn't seem to come these days; was she losing her looks? Her hair was long and dark and her figure was one to be proud of; she needn't have been concerned about that. The trouble was that there was nobody there to tell her that; only the occasional traveller on the road.

She heard the sound of hoof-beats and looked out of the window. It was a man, or so it appeared, sitting on a small black horse. The hazy sunshine seemed to make the rider's costume look a deep blue; so deep as to almost make it appear black although road dust had made it scruffy. It was always a hazy sunshine here; something to do with the nearby saltwater swamp, the men said. She couldn't see the rider's face, the hood was pulled so far forward that the face remained hidden. He carried very little baggage on his horse except for whatever may have been rolled up in his dark-grey blanket, but she did notice a black sheath as he wheeled his horse to look about him. She suddenly felt uncomfortable and an ice-cold shiver went down her spine.

The dark rider had stopped his horse to address an elderly man who was sitting, with a smoke-weed pipe in his hand, on the porch of his little hut. "I seek a traveller, an elf," the rider rasped in a thin, reedy voice. "Long golden hair. He travels this way. He may be with others. When did he ride through?"

The old man coughed on his smoke and spat onto the road. "Nay. Not seen no-one like that, not today," came the response.

"Yesterday, the day before, or before that?"

"Nah. Not in a ten-day week."

The rider was becoming impatient. "You see every traveller who comes through?"

"Got nuttin' else to do," he old man wheezed.

"If you lie, I shall be back," growled the rider. He spurred his horse and galloped through the village, pausing for a moment at the little square to replenish his waterskin while his horse drank from the stone trough. He considered his options and then rode eastwards along a little-used road towards the small mountains to the east. The old man puffed on his pipe, shrugged his shoulders and shook his head.

The woman, still watching from her window, held her hand to her thumping chest. *He seeks that young man that rode through here yester-eve with his friends, I'll be bound. Silmar was his name but there was something elvish about him.* That rider did not seem to be one who Silmar would call his friend. She would have to warn him when, or if, he came back. She sat on her wicker chair and rocked back and forth clutching a piece of her son's clothing, crying softly.

Two hours later, a heavily-laden wagon pulled by two massive, long-horned oxen slowly creaked its way into the village. Two men sat on its high board and an armed rider followed closely behind. The drover jumped down and called to the old man. "Is there a priest in this village?"

"In Nor'wald City, why?"

"My son has been murdered in the night. He did nothing wrong, he was only fourteen summers." The man's face was tear-streaked. "A rider in black came into our camp, next thing we know he's riding out again. There was my son lying dead on the ground. Is there a provost or thief-taker here?"

The old man shuffled over and pulled back the blanket. The boy's neck had been slashed. His long blond hair was matted with blood.

The grieving mother had stepped out of her hut and now rushed to the wagon and what she saw made her gasp with horror, her hand flying up to her mouth. The elderly villager replaced the blanket and shuffled away puffing on his pipe. He sat on his porch and shook his head sombrely.

The woman immediately took the initiative. "My name is Janna," she declared. "Send your outrider onwards. A wagon with two on the board and three riders will be no more than half a day ahead. They have a Priest. Speak with them. They may know what to do."

ও ৶

The wagon, in fact, was no more than a league along the road. They had stopped at the little community of Dange Marsh the previous evening but, because of the lack of a tavern, they had camped in the little square. They left at dawn but within the hour one of their cart-horses had thrown a shoe. Although Taura had swopped the horse with Jiutarô's mount, it was a far from adequate solution – the horses were badly-mismatched and Jiutarô's mount was resistant. They decided to return to the little village.

Taura still drove the wagon but Jiutarô had to coax his horse into performing a task to which it was unsuited and unfamiliar.

"This is going to take ages," complained Billit. "We'll never catch up with Kassall. We are on our own an' we got that scary undead area to ride through in a week or so, ain't we?"

They had barely travelled a mile when Silmar alerted them. "Rider coming up fast from the village," he warned them. "Keep your weapons handy."

The rider was upon them within moments. He reined in thirty yards or so from them and leapt down from the saddle. He kept his hands well clear of his short-sword, as was the custom when approaching other travellers on the road.

"Greetings," he hailed. "I seek holy assistance for my master back in the village. I am informed by the village woman, Janna, you have a cleric among you. But I expected you to be travelling northwards, not south. Are you those that I seek?"

Silmar eased his horse forwards while constantly scanning their surroundings. "Aye," he replied. "You have found us. One of the horses pulling our wagon has thrown a shoe. We are returning to the village to see if they have a smithy. What is the problem that makes you require our cleric so urgently?"

The rider looked more intently at Silmar. "Murder, Goodsir. My master's son was cruelly killed in the night. Am I right? Would your cleric provide comfort for the bereaved family and speed the boy's soul on its final journey?"

"Boy?" Taura called. "Lead us on."

It was an hour later, just after midday, when the wagon trundled into the hamlet of Dange Marsh with Silmar, Jiutarô and the gigantic Falcon in the lead. The guard spurred his horse and galloped into the village ahead of them. The group had been on the road for only five hours but Taura was already tired from the strain of coping with mismatched horses. They drew up in the little square and were immediately met by Janna.

"Come with me, all of you," she beckoned as she turned towards the great wagon and the small group that stood by it.

"There was a murder on the road in the night," she gasped. "A young boy had his throat slashed ear to ear by a rider in a long, black cloak. The boy was just fourteen years old and had long, blond hair. Oh, I had better warn you that there has been a rider here this morning wearing a black cloak and I think he is looking for an elf with blond hair, long like yours but not so dark," she indicated to Silmar. "The man was small though, not much taller than a dwarf I would guess."

The adventurers looked at each other. Taura gives a deep sigh. "It's him, isn't it?" she whispered. "You are being hunted, Silmar."

"No doubt about it, I think," mumbled Billit. "But a Darklin' though, up on the surface and on a killing spree?"

"Darkling? Oh, may the gods save us!" Janna wailed. "We are in mortal danger!" She turned and walked over to the merchant with Taura close behind.

The group watched from a distance as Taura sang *Neilea's Lament for the Dead* by the wagon. They could see that the body was covered in a blood-soaked sheet of canvas. The merchant and his two companions stood beside Taura as she ended the lament and chanted verses to which they gave short responses.

Silmar led the carthorse to the edge of the village and requested the blacksmith to reshoe the horse.

"I'll have a look at your other nag, if you want," he offered. "Be best if I do, you never know." The man was heavily-muscled and barrel-chested. Although his head was bald, it was more than adequately compensated by his great brown beard.

Silmar accepted. It was just as well that he did.

"Your nags would have lost a couple more shoes if I hadn't checked," the smith advised in his deep, booming voice.

స్ కు

"We had better be on our way," Silmar called an hour later. He leaned against the side of the wagon and rubbed his forehead with his left hand.

Janna had provided them all with a meagre meal but the merchant declared that he was staying in the village an extra day while the body of his son was laid to rest close by. Janna had watched him closely as he fought back his emotions.

"You feelin' tired, elf?" enquired Billit. He had seen Silmar swaying and gripping the side of the wagon.

"Aye, I think so. I can still faintly feel the influence of that damned ceremonial knife in my back-pack even though it is cased in lead and wrapped up in the bottom of my pack. Its weight chafes my shoulders."

Jiutarô was beginning to get a fairly good understanding of some words of the *Universal* tongue and Taura slowly explained to him what had occurred.

The Samurai squared up, tapped the hilt of the katana tucked into his *obi* sash and, with effort, said "We, um, to fight! Hai?"

"Hai!" they all said in unison; the *Samurai's* word for *Yes* was now in occasional use by all in the party. With grim faces, though, they hitched the horses to the wagon, under Taura's direction, and prepared to leave. Out of habit, they checked their weapons, marvelling once again at the beauty and quality of the matching blades carried by Jiutarô.

Despite the language limitations, he was gradually becoming an important and valuable member of the group. His fighting skills were extraordinary; his swordplay when practising was fearsome and without equal, his bow-skill was awe-inspiring and far excelled that of Silmar. He referred to himself as a *Samurai* and they could only surmise that this was his term for a warrior. He had recently demonstrated his bow-skill and horsemanship by putting three arrows into a tree-stump at a slow gallop. He had throwing stars that he called *shuriken* and could hurl these with uncanny accuracy, even while running at full speed. Although he had two matching blades which he kept in black lacquered scabbards, a long-sword he called a *katana* and a short-sword he called a *wakisashi*, There was a third dagger-like knife, a *tanto*, also matching, in the pack on his horse. He cared for these lovingly and with total respect, often chanting a verse in his obscure language, as he cleaned and oiled the blades. Taura wondered if he was intoning a magic spell. All members of the group would eventually see how the katana could cut clean through not only the sword-blades of those he fought, but also straight through the body of a foe as though it were made of straw.

The Samurai's armour was the most unusual any of then had ever seen. The helmet, with its curved side pieces, high crown and its neck guard, looked heavy and cumbersome. But they had all donned the helmet during the early part of the journey and found it easy to wear, light and surprisingly comfortable. The burly Samurai was using more and more words in the *Universal* tongue, with encouragement from Billit. He seemed to be a quick learner.

Together, they discussed the new precautions they would need to take on their journey in light of the potential threat from the Darkling. The party still had some way to go before they reached Northwald City, perhaps a seven-day short week or even a ten-day full week; the map was not accurate.

With a wave, the band of adventurers slowly rode out of the village. Janna went back towards her cabin. On a little table, near to where the gnome Billit had been standing earlier, were twenty silver coins. *So much money!* She rushed out of the hut and stood on the road but the wagon and riders had gone. This money would keep her in food for months. Once more, she cried.

The merchant found her a moment later and placed a comforting arm around her shoulders. She looked up and saw his sad but kindly face and put her head on his chest.

❧ ❧

The Darkling spurred his horse to a quicker pace. Killing the boy had achieved nothing, except to soften his frustration at not having discovered his prey. It was a mistake that could draw attention both to himself and his mission. Somewhere up ahead was his intended victim, and the sacred dagger that he bore. He dare not return to Adelenis' High Priestess without the artefact but perhaps there was another way. If he couldn't find the elf, whose name he did not know, then perhaps he *could* cause the elf to find him. He would have to rely on the fact that the elf would *want* to find him, would need to find him. A plan was forming.

It took six days for the Darkling to reach the gates of Northwald City. He arrived just as dusk descended. Fully cloaked and hooded, as if against the cold, he was not challenged as he entered through the city gates, people rarely were during these peaceful days. Only at nights, after dark, were the gates closed. Within an hour of entering the city, he had found a stable, paying the stable-boy enough money to enable him to care for himself and his horse without questions being asked. He did not look particularly out of place with his cloak wrapped around him; most people were dressed that way as protection against the bitter cold winds this far north; colder still as the sun sank below the horizon. He watched the city gate from a safe distance and started carrying out his plan.

CHAPTER 13

TEN DAYS AFTER leaving the village Dange Marsh, the party arrived at Northwald City. Strangely, to regular visitors, all people leaving and entering were now being challenged. In truth, the city was little more than a large town. It boasted a large square, a little more than a few minute's ride from the gate, around which were almost a dozen inns and taverns as well as a few gambling establishments and whorehouses. Just inside the city gates however, was an array of stockyards, livestock pens and livery stables. This was clearly a market town.

This was not the first thing that focused their attention though.

A hue and cry was evident. City watchmen, aided by the local militia, were everywhere. Visitors to the city were constantly observed by sharp-eyed, uniformed pairs of guards that were stationed on virtually every street corner.

Taura called over a youngster who was sitting astride a corral fence. "What has happened here?" she asked.

The lad looked at her suspiciously until she tossed him a copper coin.

"A kid, well, a bit more'n a boy really, 'ad been viciously murdered, mistress," he replied. "Throat was cut. I think he was 'bout fifteen years of age and was of the northern barbarian tribes."

"What did he look like?" asked Silmar. "Was he short with black hair?"

"Nah, 'e wasn't," replied the youngster. "You wasn't list'ning to me, was yer? Northern tribes, 'e was. A barbarian. That means tall with long blond hair."

A shiver ran down Silmar's back as he asked for more information. This could cause an incident by enraging the tribesmen who were camped outside the city walls. They were there for the annual horse fair and had a number of fine horses for sale. The city watch was trying to calm the situation down and allocating much of their resources to hunt the killer.

All of the companions exchanged worried looks.

Taura pulled the brake lever on the wagon and leaned over towards Silmar. Her face was stern as she whispered "It's him again, isn't it? That gods-damned Darkling. He's looking for you and that wretched dagger, isn't he? He's probably here in the city still and may even be watching us right now. He may know you have changed your hair colour by now, Silmar. What in the name of the gods have you got us into?"

"There ain't no point in gettin' angry with the elf, Taura," replied Billit. "We knew what we were letting ourselves in fer when we took up this challenge, so instead of layin' the blame, let's see what we're gonna do to sort this out. An' there's no call fer you to be apologisin' fer it, young elf!"

Falcon eased his great horse over to them. "The Darkling?" he asked. "That one you told me about, huh? He is here?"

"We do not know," answered Silmar. "He may be. I have to be vigilant."

"Us watch!" said Jiutarô. Due to his limited knowledge of the *Universal* tongue, he spoke rarely. "Um, Darkling, hai?" He patted the hilt of his sword.

"We had better find Jasper's tavern, the Wagon Wheel, and speak to him about it," the elf mumbled with a worried frown. "You are right, Jiutarô. We will all have to be extra vigilant now. Keep together, everything we do."

"Watch, tavern, night, just one, hai?" Jiutarô struggled.

"Good speaking, Jiutarô," said Billit with a rare smile. "Hai?"

"Hai!" they all responded in agreement, smiling and taking heart from the *Samurai's* confident manner. His proficiency with his *yumi* longbow, a very unusual weapon that had a short lower limb and a much longer upper limb, was almost supernatural. The arrows were longer than normal but Jiutarô would draw one back so that its flights were adjacent to his right ear. Very bizarre.

Their enquiries soon led them to the Wagon Wheel tavern and on entering they found the dwarf behind the bar cleaning the jugs and tankards. The dwarf blanched momentarily when he saw the elf standing at his bar but almost immediately recovered his composure. He had immediately recognised Silmar for what he was despite his disguise.

Silmar introduced himself and then the others to Jasper and he shook their arms warmly.

"Yous is friends o' me brother?" Jasper boomed. "Haha! How is the old chod? Must be goin' soft in the head if he is friends with an elf."

"He is good and he sends you his warmest regards," replied an indignant Silmar. "He was friends with my father, Faramar Galadhal, many years ago."

"Ah, I knows that name an' the one who bears it. An elf, but a damned good 'un. Hey, what is that giant with the big beard holdin' on 'is shoulder?"

Jasper was delighted to receive the barrels of mead and wine from his brother, even more delighted with the little barrel of elven blood-wine, and asked many questions about his brother, Ralmon, the City of Westron Seaport and the road to Northwald City.

"I knows o' the murder o' the barbarian kid but what was all that I 'eard o' the killing o' the other young boy on the north road? Sounds like someone 'as a hatred of young kids with long 'air."

He looked around the bar as if to check he wasn't being watched and opened a small trapdoor on the floor behind the bar. Beneath it he placed the little barrel of the elven blood-wine. He closed the trapdoor and wiped his hands on his leather jerkin.

"I can offer yous all one room but that's all I got," he said. "It's got six cots in it an' a stack o' blankets. They all got straw bolsters fer yer 'eads too, 'cos I know how soft you humans are, heh heh! No disrespect to the gnome intended, o' course! Oh, fer now, you can stow yer equipment 'ere in my taproom."

Falcon towered above every other person in the taproom. People skittered nervously out of his way when he passed by. But it was the Samurai who attracted most of the interest for a while because of his arrogant demeanour and his strange appearance. However, by keeping quiet and sitting together in a dimly lit corner, the companions eventually became almost unnoticed.

The tavern was very busy and as the evening wore on the revellers became more and more boisterous. Two scantily-clad whores were walking around the tap-room and attracted much lewd behaviour from many men. At one point, this started to spiral out of control and one or two fights occurred. Jasper waded in with a wooden mallet and put a stop to one of the fights but one disruption was too much for even him. He was laid out cold by a punch from a tattooed muscle-bound fighter and he crashed to the floor stunned.

"Hey, we got trouble!" Billit cried.

The party rose to their feet immediately and went to the dwarf's aid. Jiutarô was a blur of movement. He took a leg from a broken table and, using it with phenomenal skill, managed to clear a space around the hapless bartender. The tattooed fighter was unconscious on the floor so quickly that nobody was sure how it happened.

Meanwhile, Silmar was tackled from behind by two assailants, one of whom had his arm around the elf's neck and the other was lifting him up by the legs. Despite his struggles, he was being unceremoniously carried towards the door. Suddenly, all three of them collapsed to the floor and were completely still.

Taura was using her staff to restore the peace with some success and Billit was standing on a chair in a corner with his hands weaving a complicated series of movements.

The trouble stopped as quickly as it began and some of the people left the tavern. Others sat down and resumed their drinking as if nothing had happened. Jasper was sitting on the floor nursing a swollen forehead. Falcon was holding one man aloft by a single leg while the man swung a spittoon at him. The barbarian strode through the tavern door and then returned without the man.

Billit stepped off the chair and rushed over to Silmar and his two attackers; they were all still unconscious. The gnome seemed very pleased with himself.

Taura strode over. "What has happened here?" she enquired.

"Silmar was being carried out by these two," the little mage explained. "The best I could think of was a spell to knock 'em all out." He gave a sardonic grin. "They'll all wake up in a minute or two."

Jasper stepped across to them with a wet cloth held against his head. "What in the hells of the Void was all this about?" he gasped.

Jiutarô haltingly answered. "Wait, Silmar wake, um, mans gone."

"Nearly time to shut the place anyway," he mumbled then yelled at the top of his voice. "Sod off, you lot! Time to go to yer choddin' hovels an' give the wife somethin' she'll remember for an hour or so, if yous can raise yer wherewithal!" Then he raised a hand to his head and regretted having shouted. He looked about him at the unconscious bodies and damaged furniture.

"Right then," he stated, a little quieter. "Let's get these two chods out into the street afore they wakes up."

With the help of a few revellers, they dropped Silmar's two attackers outside without ceremony. By the time they all re-entered the tavern, Silmar was coming to.

The spittoon that Falcon's assailant had used on him had rolled under a table. Falcon picked it up and replaced it next to the bar. "I likes a good fight in bar," he laughed, "but I never ends up on me floor!"

"What happened to me?" Silmar asked with a look of puzzlement on his face. "I remember being carried out of the tavern by a pair of toughs and then I woke up."

Taura explained about the fight and Billit admitted how he was the one to cause Silmar to become unconscious, along with the two attackers. The little gnome looked very guilty but this expression lifted when Silmar burst into laughter.

"We 'ad better talk," said Jasper. "What's goin' on? I needs ter know. This fight weren't right. Some chod organised it."

The bar-room was soon cleared and Jasper locked the front and back doors and secured the window shutters. Two of Jasper's barmen, one a human and the other a dwarf, both having also taken an active part in the fight, were clearing the tables and the debris. Jasper assured the companions that his barmen were totally trustworthy. They sat round a table, each with a leather tankard of ale, and Silmar described the events starting with their experiences in Westron Seaport, the journey on the North Road and their arrival in Northwald City.

"I think it's clear what happened 'ere tonight," the dwarf explained. "This fight was planned to take attention away from yer young elf while 'e was bein' carried off. You'd better check your baggage in the back o' me tap-room."

Taura and Silmar rushed over and were relieved to discover Silmar's pack had been undisturbed. The *burden*, as he had started referring to it, was still there; they recoiled at the sensation that emitted from it. The overwhelming feeling of nausea still ran through the elf as his hand closed on the casket containing the dagger. It felt ice cold! He removed his hand as though it had been stung.

They returned to the table. Silmar sighed. "*He* knows we're here now and may attempt to take the artefact during the night."

"Take all yer gear up to the bedchamber," instructed Jasper. "We'll mount a watch during the night. One o' you on watch upstairs at all times an' me an' my men will take turns down 'ere."

They agreed to Jasper's proposal. After ten days and nights of continuous watch out on the road, they were extremely tired.

♦ ♦

They had all remained vigilant during the next three days, not venturing out into the city at all, and each taking turns to watch at night; two of them at a time. Billit spent hour after hour teaching Jiutarô the Universal tongue and the ways and customs of the various realms.

They were sitting in a corner of the taproom at the end of the night's revelries. Jasper came out from behind the bar with six quart mugs of ale.

"This reminds me o' the old days when I was campaignin' with me brother, an' yer pappy, young elf," stated the dwarf. "Aye, I remembers 'im well. A tough un, yer dad. Saved me brother's life a couple o' times. In fact, I remembers me brother savin' '*is* life once, too. That was underground durin' the Goblin Wars in far-off Cascant."

Although Silmar wanted to stay and listen, the others had made it clear that they needed some sleep. Suddenly, there was a knocking at the tavern door. Jasper went to the door and, without opening it, asked who it was at this late hour.

"Janniff, City Watch," came the reply. "Need to talk to you, Jasper."

The others in the party stood by, fully alerted. Billit, meanwhile, had rushed over to their equipment and tossed each of the party their main weapons. Jasper opened the door a little, checked the visitor was who he said he was, and then let him in.

"We're questioning all the tavern landlords," said Janniff. "Want to check your visitors, Good-dwarf Jasper. May I come in? I have two men with me."

"Aye, Cityman Janniff. Bring yerselves in." Jasper opened the door wide and three uniformed watchmen marched in. Jasper offered the men a mulled wine to ward off the night's cill but Janniff declined.

"There have been two more killings this evening," Janniff began. "An elf this time. His throat was slashed from ear to ear. Then a rider, in black, forced one of the city gate-wardens at sword-point to open one of the gates to let him out. The bastard killed the gate-man too, for no reason. He's got a family, poor man. One of my men saw it happen but was too far away to raise the alarm. I need to know if your visitors know anything about this or have had any dealings with someone dressed in black."

They all shook their heads, each one knowing that if they owned up to being involved in the dealings of this Darkling killer, they would all be forced to answer questions and bring attention to the artefact. It would also impose delays that they could ill afford.

"We shall be collecting some monies for the gate-warden's family," Janniff stated. "May we ask for a donation from your tavern?"

"Aye. Aye, o' course," answered Jasper. "Return on the morrow. I'll get some coins out o' my regulars."

Janniff was satisfied, bade them a good night and left.

"The Darkling is taunting us now with these killings," said Silmar. "He knows where I am. He's trying to draw me out."

"Let's do it then, let's find him," said Taura.

"If we leave this place, Darkling will follow," suggested Falcon.

"Hai, kill Darkling in wild place," said Jiutarô. "Hai?"

All the others agreed. They decided to leave in the morning. The watches were mounted and the night passed without incident.

ໆ ໙

CHAPTER 14

THEY WERE roused just before dawn by one of Jasper's barmen. Yawning and with bleary eyes, they took their baggage and weapons down into the taproom. Jasper had laid on a morning feast of cold mutton, bread, cheese, eggs and fruit. He pointed over to another pile of baggage and weapons next to the bar.

In response to Taura's quizzical stare he beamed. "That's mine, I'd like to come with yer all."

Despite their reservations, he waved them aside and explained. "Look, my men can run this place. I'm tough, I ain't old yet an' I got all me faculties. I got lots o' experience with this sort o' thing which I reckons will be sort've 'andy fer yous. Me weapons are in good order an' I've cared for 'em over the years. See this battleaxe?"

They looked at the blade; it had a high quality and a wondrous shimmer.

"Well," he continued. "It's got these qualities what makes it special, see. Sort o' magical, you might say."

He was beginning to win them over by now, so he offered his best argument. "'E's Darkling, right?"

They nodded.

"Where will 'e feel most at 'ome if 'e wants a confrontation?"

They looked vague.

Jasper pointed downwards. "Under the ground, right? The Shadow World! Said to be in the west parts o' the Dragon's Teeth Mountains."

Silmar and Taura paled; Billit gasped. Jiutarô shook his head and shrugged his shoulders, not understanding the implications. Falcon sighed and looked downwards.

"Anyway, me, bein' a dwarf in case yer didn't yet notice," he grinned. "Well, I'm at 'ome underground an', if I ain't mistaken, young elf, we both can see in the dark, can't we?"

Silmar nodded.

Billit said "I can too, but just a few paces."

"I've been in the Shadow World," continued Jasper. "Thousands o' years ago, dwarves an' gnomes mined deep fer gold, silver an' precious stones. You prob'ly know 'bout this too, Billit. They mined fer coal too. An' when the mines run dry they closed 'em down. But other bein's moved in. Black Elves, what we know as Darkling, an' Dark Dwarves – nasty bastards. There's spiteful Deep Gnomes, Grullien, who kill yer an' eat yer. They file their teeth into points. It's terrifying. But not all them what live there are evil. Aye, there are creatures who will want ter eat you! There's creatures that *you* will need to eat to survive. There's water, if you knows where to find it, but not all water is drinkable. There's other food sources too. I can 'elp with all o' this. And I'm a choddin' good fighter! Well, I was once. Aye, I know I got knocked on the breadbasket last night but 'e was a chodding great big muscled chunk o' beef an' 'e crept up behind me, unexpected like!"

They all laughed but somewhat half-heartedly. Billit patiently explained to Jiutarô what was being discussed. The Samurai looked very concerned.

"Now, look at these. I'll be takin' these leather tubes too – they're kinda special!" He refused to say any more about them. Each of the leather tubes resembled a narrow scroll case, sealed at one end, and each had a leather cap to close the other end.

The group was quiet for a moment and they looked at each other.

Silmar broke the silence. "Aye, join us. You'll be more than welcome if everyone else agrees," he stated. "But where do we go?"

"I think I may know the answer to that one," offered Jasper.

❧   ❧

The road from the North Gate of Northwald City was not as busy as that of the South. The long road led northwards, inland a few leagues from the coast, to the town of Icedge, aptly named for the sea ice would approach the north coast during the depths of winter. The climate there was generally cold, even during the summer months, but it was bitterly cold during the long winter. Nevertheless, snow was a rarity on the lower ground. The proximity of mountains to the north and east of the town and the direction of the prevailing wind off the sea, gave total protection from the winter snowstorms.

The Darkling travelled on a route parallel to this road. He no longer had a need to hunt; he knew now that he was the prey. This suited him perfectly. He would be waiting. He would be completely at home in the Shadow World. He had his dark-sight. That gave him, and all of his kind, the ability to use his eyes to see in the darkness; it was far more effective than that of the surface elves. Theirs was inferior and relied upon there being a vestige of light thay could be enhanced. Admittedly, there was occasionally some light down there, that given off by the mould growing on the walls, for instance. It was the Darkling's ability to see differences in temperature of whatever was down there and thus make out shapes that made his dark vision so much the superior. As far as he was aware, the white-eye elves had lost this ability because they did not live under the ground. He did know that dwarves and gnomes had a limited ability but the bastard elf did not have a dwarf in his party. The race of men was pathetically weak, poor at swordsmanship and no capability to see in the darkness. They would need to carry light to travel through the Shadow World but the use of flaming torches was cumbersome and a torch only lasted an hour or so. They would need to carry scores of torches to see where they were going and these were slow to light and extinguish.

I will be invulnerable in the Shadow World. Hah! I positively relished a potential confrontation.

They had a human priest – what god she worshipped he couldn't tell - and a gnomish mage. Both were young and would be inexperienced. The large Barbarian was the greatest threat and would have to be the first to be taken down.

The white-eye elf will be the last to die, his ragtag band of misfits will be no match for me and I shall pick them off one at a time if necessary. Eventually, there would just be the white-eyed elf and myself – a Darkling. The sacred ceremonial dagger would then be mine.

❧ ☙

CHAPTER 15

"What do you mean by saying that you can help with where we go next?" asked Silmar.

"I think I knows where the Darkling wants yer to go. 'E'll leave a trail o' dead bodies for us to follow 'til we gets to the very entrance to the Shadow World. Y'know? Like breadcrumbs."

The party listened carefully, hanging on every word spoken by the Dwarf.

"'E prob'ly assumes that none o' you knows where this entrance is," continued the dwarf.

"He's right there," answered Taura. "We haven't a clue where it is."

"Aye, but 'ere's the rub – I does," said Jasper, the look of triumph crossing his face partly obscured by his bushy brown beard. "I been down there with yer dad, young elf."

"What?" exclaimed a shocked Silmar. "My father never told me about the Shadow World or said that he had been there. By the Gods!"

"Aye, lad. Scary as shit, eh? Believe me, it is. But *I'll* go there again with you. Don't make the mistake o' thinking we'll all get out, though. That's where me brother lost 'is arm."

The group exchanged apprehensive looks with each other amid murmurings.

Jasper continued. "Now, pin back yer ears. There's many rules that we gotta consider when we are down there." He spoke slowly and carefully making sure that Jiutarô understood and that each point was driven home with each of them.

"It will be totally an' completely dark down there. Silmar, me an' Billit can see a little in the dark, the elf best of all, sod yer, but there 'as to be some source o' light down there. If you shine a light or light a torch then we will be blinded for quite a few moments, an' it 'urts. And so will the Darklin', don't forget. 'E will almost totally rely on 'is dark-seeing but 'e don't need no light down there to 'elp 'im. Oh no! If a torch needs to be lit then we must use a codeword or give a warnin' or somethin'. Or if you're gonna shine a light you gotta give a warnin' with that codeword. A codeword is best 'cos the Darklin' won't know what yer talking about. Does yer know whay I mean?"

Apart from Jiutarô, they all nodded with understanding.

"Good. Now, this is important. We gotta stay together," Jasper emphasised. "Even when we needs to relieve ourselves! No-one can be left behind, 'less they're dead an' the survivors *all* agrees on it. Taura 'as got wonderful 'ealing abilities, so I'm told, and I got a couple of potions that relieve pain an' 'elps recovery. Use it all but use 'em careful, partic'ly the potions, them's gotta be the last resort. Don't touch anythin' that you don't recognise, it may try to do you 'arm. If in doubt, ask me. There will be deep pits and crev – crevasses an' in some places, we'll 'ave to jump some wide gaps. I suggest we ropes ourselves together to do that."

"What about other races or peoples down there?" enquired Billit. "Are they all out to kill us?"

"Surprisingly, there's quite a variety," answered Jasper. "Darklings ain't very common an' they tend to stay within the confines of their cities like Dannakanonn. That's way off. But there's the Grey Dwarves, nasty bastards who roam about in small war-bands lookin' for surface folk who wander down there to do mining. These are the sworn enemies o' my peoples and are 'ard, spiteful fighters. I came up on them down there all those years ago. There are hundreds of them and they still mine for silver. The Kobolds are known to be there somewhere; these are sort of small, dog-like little buggers who go about on two legs an' carry barbed javelins. They are small but fight in big groups to overwhelm their enemy. Aye, they fights 'ard 'cos of their large numbers but aren't all that good at fighting individually and a couple o' dozen of 'em will run at the sight of a few humans, elves an' dwarves. They don't 'ave no armour. If their javelin gets stuck inside you the only way to get it out is to cut it out or push it straight through. Nasty little buggers, they are!"

They all shuddered at the thought.

"But Kobolds? They are totally ruthless little shits," Jasper continued. "They talk with a barkin' sort o' language with our words scattered in it. I seem to remember that their god is the same one that the Darklin's worship - Adelenis!" He whispered the last word. The group shuddered at the mention of that name. "Worse of all though, are the Grullien, the Shade Gnomes. Nasty, 'ard an' full o' spite. They 'ates the Grey Dwarves with a passion, yer might say. They wander around with war-bands too. Might find 'em near to the end o' the mines."

"What about friendly races?" asked Billit, hoping to hear something encouraging. "Are there any?"

"Funny it should be *you* to ask that o' me," replied Jasper. "There's a couple o' colonies of Gnomes, not much diff'rent to you, Billit. They've learned the art of evading detection an' concealin' their whereabouts now for cent'ries. They mine for precious stones, mainly rubies, sapphires an' emeralds which, I think, are only found beneath the western Dragon's Teeth Mountains. They are the only race of the Shadow World who comes up to the surface to trade. I think they 'ave their own entrances down to the Shadow World tho' I don't know 'em. The Dark Dwarves though, they trade *their* silver with some o' the criminal human gangs on the surface."

By this time it was approaching mid-morning and they were all ready to travel. Jasper suggested they should ride their horses and ponies to the hamlet of Burrak, about a seven-day week's ride northwards. There they would leave their mounts and continue their journey on foot. Jasper looked uneasy and was scratching his chin and looking unusually worried.

"What is it?" enquired Taura. "What worries you so?"

The dwarf turned away from her and cleared his throat. He then slowly turned back to face her. "Well, it's sorta like this," he said softly. "The people of Burrak locks their doors an' secures their shutters at night. It's only a little village, prob'ly only twenty or so dwellings, an' a trading post that doubles as an inn. Bin there afore, many years ago, an' just rode straight through. Oh, they was scared o' somethin' an' din't like to talk about it. Somethin' or someone takes a victim from their village. Usually at night, always after dark. Not often but occasionally."

"Wait, I know something about this!" Silmar exclaimed. "There have been rumours like this for years."

"Best avoid this area, I reckon," said Falcon, his deep voice sounding strangely calming in the tense atmosphere.

"Best it, um, avoid us!" added Jiutarô. He had been listening attentively and was picking up some of the details as the others spoke slowly. They nodded in agreement. "Hai, we strong even with, um, evil!" He patted his blades. "We show this; we fight well."

These were probably the most heartening words that the Samurai had strung together since they had known him. However, nervous glances continued to be exchanged from one to another.

"Aye, listen well to him. We are powerful," Falcon emphasised. "You make magic. We can all fight? We are strong, not weak and afraid!"

"Aye," answered Silmar. "Mayhap you are right. Look, we are all about to go into the Shadow World, right? We are putting our lives at risk to bring a killer to justice. Perhaps there is a lunatic or monster at large. If there is something we can do to help, well, it's what we do, right?"

Laughter erupted from Jasper. "That's yer dad talking. By the gods, Silmar, yer is just like 'im. But, tread carefully, all o' you. You don't know what yer gonna meet. Whatever's out there 'as been around fer ages and we're prob'ly not the first to go lookin' fer it. Let's 'ope we don't have to."

"Aye, but we must fight to help others," stated Falcon. "That is the honourable way. So it is with my peoples."

"Ye gods!" muttered Jasper. "What 'ave I got meself into? A right bunch o' idiots who wanna save the world!"

෨ ෮

The party set out from the little corral behind the Wagon Wheel an hour before dawn. Northwald City was already bustling with people pushing handcarts, herding geese, goats or sheep, and setting up stalls in preparation for another day's trading. They passed through the East Gate as soon as it opened and rode in a north-easterly direction towards the village of Burrack. The weather was overcast and the ground very frosty. After a while however, the sun shone for an hour or two and the frost had disappeared. Now that they no longer had the wagon, they were able to move much faster.

The track was well-defined and clearly well-travelled although they met few other travellers in either direction during their ride.

They continued for six days; each rider remained very quiet, lost in their own thoughts of the challenges that lay ahead but constantly remaining vigilant. A couple of hours after dawn on the seventh day, the group reined in by a junction in the tracks. They could see a small wagon ahead but with no horses or oxen. Three people, one of them a boy, were huddled around a little fire. The sounds of a woman wailing could clearly be heard. As they drew close they dismounted and showed their hands to prove they had not drawn their weapons.

A man came over cautiously towards them. He looked distraught, almost panic-stricken. He started to babble incoherently and Taura handed her horse's reins to Falcon. She took the man by the shoulders, looked him in the eye and calmed him down.

"Now start again," she said softly. "I am Taura Windwalker, a Priestess of Neilea." She gave her customary light bow at the mention of her deity's name.

"I am Tor Angle," he wailed. "Someone came into our camp in the night. We were sleeping. When we woke up we could not move. He, or they, drove off our two horses that were hitched up to the tree just there, he took our lovely daughter, Tassie, an' made off with her into the night."

Taura took him gently by the shoulders once again. "Tor, you said *they*, now you say *he*. What was it?"

"It was probably just one. We saw only one but it didn't walk properly – it sort of floated."

Taura and Silmar exchanged a glance. Both had noticed the man said *it* and not just *he* or *him*.

"Describe him to me."

"He was dressed in dark with a black cape and hood. Expensive clothes like a lord or baron or someone. Dark hair, white skin – very white. A pointed beard. Our horses were terrified. He used a sort of magic to make us keep still."

Silmar quietly whispered in Taura's ear. "Not Darkling then."

"Where were you going, Tor?"

"We were leaving Burrak. Look, it's become too dangerous to stay with people going missing for so long. Now our pride and joy has been taken from us, not three hours ago. Oh my Tassie! We should have stayed, but all I wanted was a better life, a safer life, for my family. We left too late in the day. The wagon and horses were too slow, we didn't get away far enough!"

Taura called over Falcon and Jiutarô. "See if you can find the horses, would you?"

After looking about for tracks they galloped off, following the sign on the ground.

Tor Angle was visibly frightened and shaking violently.

Taura continued. "What is it that does this? You know, don't you?" She had her own suspicions.

"Oh, do not ask me, mistress! I cannot say. It is too terrible."

"Tell me, perhaps we can help but you must tell me."

"Very well, but you will not believe me, nobody ever believes us villagers. We have suspected for years but people from the outside laugh at us. Look now, we're serious about this. We think it's a *vampyre*, or some sort of horror! Oh gods preserve us!"

The friends glanced at each other with doubt and misgiving etched on their faces, apart from Taura who was eager to know more.

"What makes you think that?" she questioned.

Tor trembled with fear and despair. "Many years ago," he explained, "before we suspected what lay behind this, people were being attacked in their own homes. Their throats were torn out and an unholy mess was made. We thought some attackers were bringing dogs with them but we neither heard nor saw any other sign of these. Then the little temple of Clamberhan here was broken into and the priest was killed. He was tied up on his own altar and his neck was cruelly ripped out. His temple was desecrated and much of it was destroyed by fire. We sent a rider to Nor'wald City to find a priest, any priest of any god, to come and advise us. As luck would have it a Priest of Tarne was visiting, a young lad name of Halorun Tann, and he recognised the signs of a vampyre immediately. He made a search of the local area but found no sign and it all went quiet for a few years. We thought he had chased the monster away. Now the troubles are on us again but it's only occasionally. Oh gods, my poor Tassie, my lovely daughter. Gone from us for ever!"

"I am convinced that you are correct, Tor Angle," murmured Taura. "It is a vampyre indeed."

She turned aside from Tor, an immensely distressed man, and spoke quietly to her comrades. "I studied the characteristics of undead during my years of training and this seems to be typical of a vampyre. I must say though, that vampyres generally feed off their victim's blood and although most of the poor people die horribly, every so often one victim is selected by the *master* to become a vampyre too. This does not at the moment seem to be the case here. Well, as far as we know."

"What do we do now then?" asked Billit. He looked ashen-faced, the idea of something as foul as this monster, a vampyre, having its place on this world being absurd to him.

Jiutarô appeared blissfully unaware of their predicament.

"We could end this once and for all," replied Silmar. "My home town of Refuge is across those mountains there but this horror was never defined as a vampyre. We have heard vague rumours of a fiend of some sort that lurks this side of the mountains. It was intended that sometime in the future my father would send out a party to investigate this. With so much activity from goblins, hobgoblins, ogres and trolls in the mountains, we never got around to it. I was hoping that my father would let me lead the expedition but he was going to let it be the last mission of our Master-at-Arms before he retired."

"So you seriously think that there is something in all this then?" asked Billit.

"We now have a good idea of what is out there and it needs to be ended, as you say Silmar," replied Taura. Turning back to the man, she asked "Do you know where this vampyre lives, Tor?"

"No. No, well, um–!"

"You do, or you think you do," persisted Taura. "Out with it, man, if only for the sake of your daughter!"

"In the mountains there's an old track that leads down towards the town of Refuge."

"Aye, I know of it," responded Silmar. "It is many leagues."

"Ah, well, we used to trade with them during the summer, years ago when I was a lad. That all stopped with this vampyre. The track leads from near to Burrack, our village. It will be rough and poorly maintained because we have had no need to use it. It's about four or five hours by horse from there, I believe, most likely six or so on foot. Well, up the track a way and then turning left up a paved roadway, so I was told way back in my youth, there's this old stone keep, on a grassy plateau. The keep was built long ago by a noble who is long forgotten, to protect this side of the mountains from attacks by war-bands of hobgoblins and goblins. Rumour says that it's in there where you'll find it, the monster."

A few minutes later Jiutarô and Falcon returned with two horses in tow.

"See to your family, Tor," Silmar advised, "Let's get you all back to the village. We shall see if we can get your daughter back for you. What say you all?"

Without exception, they all agreed albeit with apprehension.

Tor scattered the embers of his little fire and loaded his wailing wife and son onto the wagon. A few moments later the wagon was ready to move out, this time with Taura at the reins. It was an hour before midday when the party arrived at the village. The gates were opened but manned by ill-equipped guards, little more than farm workers holding the tools of their trade. Silmar and Jiutarô shook their heads at the inadequacy of their defences.

Silmar suggested they waste no time in the village but get on their way immediately. "It is past noon and it gets dark early in these mountains," he explained. "And it may take a while to get there because we shall be going on foot."

179

"Why not horse?" Jiutarô asked. The others voiced in their support of him.

"Because we may not be able to get the horses close enough to the vampyre's keep if they sense that there is something nasty lurking. They can be very sensitive to threats like that and they may bolt."

One of the gate guards offered to guid them to the start of the track but would go no further; he turned about and rushed back to the village as fast as his legs would take him.

The track was quite steep and was clearly not in regular use but there were some signs that it had been recently used. Scratch marks from a horse's hoof on a rock here, a tiny piece of tattered and faded torn cloth on a thorn there. There was hard frost on the grass and bushes, giving an almost ghostly effect which did little to maintain courage amongst the group, and as they climbed higher there were signs of recent snow-fall. It took almost six hours before they arrived at a junction in the track. The path to the left wound up a steep hill where they could just see the crenellations of a stone tower through the dark coniferous treetops. With trepidation gnawing at their hearts, they bunched together and took the path, walking softly through the powdery snow until the steep path flattened onto a lightly snow-covered grassy plateau. The grass had not been attended to for a long, long time, being tall and full of weeds.

The keep was built almost up against a rocky cliff face and was partly encircled by a defensive wall. Each end of the wall butted up against the cliff face and in the centre of it was a pair of entry gates mounted between two gate-towers. In the shadow of the tall cliff, the keep looked dark and foreboding. The gloomy effect was augmented by the late afternoon sun beginning having dipped below the hills.

Without a word, they simultaneously withdrew their weapons, even Taura held her dagger in her left hand and her staff in her right. Their approach to the keep was extremely tense and they all felt fear rise inside them. A Darkling was one danger that they understood, to a point, but undead, a vampyre, was an unknown foe that was completely different.

"Taura, how do we kill it?" asked Silmar. The burden in his pack was weighing more heavily on his shoulders and an ache was growing in intensity behind his eyes. He felt that it wouldn't take much for him to throw up the dried meat that they had gnawed on the walk up the mountain path.

"A strong fire will burn it," she answered. "A wooden stake through its heart or cutting off its head will destroy it too. Choose any one but try them all! Chopping the bastard to bits will work too! It looks like there's only one way in to the keep, and there it is, the main door."

Darkness was descending very quickly and every nerve was jangling. The walk to the keep's door was interminably slow and every sound only served to increase their fear. The sound of a calling vixen from the trees behind them put the fear of the gods into every one of them, Taura almost dropped her staff.

The door opened with a push from Falcon's bow. He stepped in, closely followed by the others.

ॐ ॐ

Unexpectedly, burning torches were mounted in sconces on the walls. The party members spread out and looked towards the flight of curving stairs at the back of the entrance hall. It was bitterly cold in the hall and their breath was clouding in front of their faces. Great tapestries hung on the walls and they seemed to be in immaculate condition, depicting hunting and mountain scenes. There were some pieces of elaborate furniture about the hall: chairs and tables, padded sofas and gilded cabinets. On tables and cabinets were items of value including ornaments made of the finest porcelain and even silver and gold candelabras, plates, ewers and bowls.

"Welcome!"

A resonant, pleasant-sounding, baritone voice spoke from above. "I expect you have come here in the vain expectation of destroying me. You are on a fool's errand. It has been tried before and no doubt will be attempted again in the future. It has, and will always, end in failure."

On a gallery, some way up the rear wall of the hall, they saw the dark figure of a man, tall and distinguished. The facial features were hidden in the shadow of the gallery balustrade.

"Do not be so sure of yourself," replied Taura. "You have taken someone we want back. Someone of value to those who love her."

"Ah yes, the pretty young girl, Tassie. I make no apology when I say that you will have to return without her, if I deign to let you, or some of you, survive. She will stay here, but I promise to bury her remains with care and dignity. I always do." His voice was seductive, smooth and compelling and completely void of emotion.

"Very touching," Taura chuckled, "but we are prepared to take her from you by force and destroy you in the meantime."

"You are a very cock-sure young lady. Ahh, a Priestess of Neilea, I see. With a gnome mage, an elf warrior, a dwarf, a barbarian fighter and, what's this? Another warrior, but I do not recognise your origin. Full of confidence, each of you. Have you fought anything yet? Are you ready for me? Hah,

I doubt it very much. The last threat to me was a young Priest of Tarne. I played with his mind and clouded it from seeing this place. But *he* arrived in the night when I was at my strongest. Fortunately for him I let him live; there was a certain strength about him that would have been wasted otherwise."

Silmar motioned to Falcon, Jasper and Billit and together, they rushed up the staircase.

The figure on the gallery vanished from sight in an instant.

Slowly and quietly, Jiutarô and Taura climbed the stairs. The priestess was in deep concentration while chanting a prayer-spell and her hands were weaving a complex pattern of movements.

At the top of the first flight of stairs, Falcon, closely followed by Silmar, Jasper and then Billit, rushed into a large chamber through a partly-open door. They were immediately overcome by a wave of total immobility. They slumped onto the floor, totally oblivious to their surroundings.

Jiutarô entered the chamber and immediately succumbed. Taura stood at the doorway a few moments after. Her heart thumped as the dark figure stepped over to the five inert bodies and bent forward to look at them.

"There is great evil on this one," he murmured, with his eyes on Silmar.

Taura's voice sounded out to him. "So you think you have them at your mercy?"

The vampyre whipped round but the Priestess was not there. For once, he felt vulnerable. He took a sharp intake of breath as his head turned from side to side searching for her.

"Where are you, priestess?" called the vampyre. "Come out so I can see you."

"I can already see *you*," she answered confidently, "and as foul a creature to behold I have never seen, not even in the filthiest gutters or swamps."

"I can appreciate how you feel about me, young priestess," he responded. "Many decades ago I would have felt the same abhorrence. I did not choose to become what I am but it happened to me nonetheless. I loved the sun and the feel of warmth on my skin. Now, it would destroy me." He paused as if for dramatic effect. "And we really cannot have that now, can we?"

Taura had quietly moved while he had been talking. She had studied his face and features. He was tall and slim. His hair was a rich dark brown, almost black, but his skin was a deathly white. His Hair was cut and perfectly arranged and his beard was trimmed to a point. Unusually, as if from a style popular decades in the past, his moustaches were long and drooping well below his jaw-line. His clothing had been made for a man of great wealth and rank and was of the best silks and linen. He wore black breeches which came to just below his knees and here they were tied with black silk tapes. He had white stockings and the shoes were of soft, black leather with a large buckle atop them. His white shirt was also silk with a wide ruffled collar and loose in the arm. To look at, his face had a distinguished appearance. A normal man with this almost fastidious appearance would be considered very handsome. His voice however, had a richness to it which, together with his refined speech, was pleasurable to hear.

Notwithstanding this, the odour of ancient death and decay hung in the air. Taura almost retched and just managed to stifle a cough.

"I consider that to be an ideal option," she replied after a slow, silent breath.

Once again, he whipped around to face the direction from which her voice now came.

"Don't play games with me, young lady. So, you are invisible; a clever conjuring trick for which I compliment you. You elven friend carries an item of immense power; I shall take it and study it at my leisure once you and your companions are dead."

"You think so, do you? Tell me, how did you become a vampyre?" Her voice came from behind his ear and he jumped forward, turning again.

"Do not for one moment begin to consider that this is an existence that is pleasurable to me, mistress priest! I was once mortal; I still have human feelings and emotions, when I allow them during my hours of solace in the night. These things do not change with undeath. I feel loneliness and have the propensity to hate but never to love. I did love once and she made me like this. She started me on the wave of destruction and killings for that was the only way we could survive. When she attacked the village temple of Clamberhan, she killed the cleric so violently and desecrated the temple so wantonly, I could stand it no more and I destroyed her on the mountain path. But as a parting gift, she cursed me. Yes! Even a vampyre can feel revulsion."

Taura paused. "I don't believe you, vampyre. You seek to escape just retribution of your destruction with a tale of heroism."

"No, priestess!" he barked. "I was made thus by her, I shall forever be thus. I am dead but I am destined to live an undead existence for eternity. I am destined to feed on the blood of humanoid men, women, children, and sometimes worse, for eternity with a constant and unbearable hunger. Eternity is a long time, I can assure you of this."

"So end it, step into the sunlight in the morning dawn. I shall accompany you."

Taura was thinking at a furious pace now. At the far end of the room to the door, she became visible. She had used a *Conceal from Undead* prayer-spell, the most potent spell she had ever used. It had worked perfectly but had exhausted her; she would offer prayers of sincere gratitude to Neilea if she was to survive the night.

"Do you think I could if I wanted to?" His voice had risen almost to shouting and its echo reverberated from the stone walls around them. "I am cursed to continue like this. I am cursed to forever protect myself from intentional destruction. I do not have the will to end my own non-life. So I have to protect my miserable existence by feeding off what I can. If I am able to feed from the animal world then I do so otherwise I have no other option than to take men, elves and dwarves, usually whatever comes within my reach. If I was able to, I would feed from the goblins and orcs that infest these hills but their blood is tainted with an unsuitable foulness – believe me, I have tried on numerous occasions when the need is great. I shall be forced to take your lives too now that you have blundered your way into my home."

"Wait!" she exclaimed. An idea began to form in her mind. "You live in misery? Explain!"

His voice became calm now. "For more than a century I have hunted to survive and survived to hunt. I am cursed to this existence and cannot wilfully end it. There is no future other than to hunt and be hunted. There will be no restful peace for me."

"Cursed? But what if we were to end this misery for you? An honourable ending with the curse lifted; an opportunity for you to live at peace in death."

"You can do this? You would do this? Ah, a stupid question; of course you would."

"I can lift the curse but it will tax me to the limit. Your end will be swift and without discomfort. It would be honourable and the gods, in their understanding, wisdom and compassion, may offer you a life after death particularly if you atone for your misdeeds."

The vampyre stood at the top of the curving stairs. "I cannot deny that I desire this ending," he stated after pausing for a few moments. He paused once again as he paced from side to side wringing his hands. "Dear mistress, I am compelled now to accept although the words do not pass my lips with ease. When it is done, search my keep, and yes, it was always mine from the days before I became thus. You will find many treasures and wonders. I leave them to you and your friends. Use it to give the village down there some comfort. They have lost much at my hands. Give me this ending and everything shall be yours. Burn and bury my remains. Say a prayer to your god, Neilea, that she may judge me favourably. You shall also find, in the chamber yonder, the young lady you seek. She is unharmed but I have left a trauma upon her that she will find it hard to recover from promptly. It is fortunate I was not hungry; I had just feasted on foul goblin blood. That is not a pleasant dish but I could not feed constantly on the villagers. There are not enough of them, you understand! One of your comrades, the mysterious warrior, is awakening. The others shall soon."

Taura wanted to vomit and it took considerable will-power to avoid doing so. Jiutarô shuffled unsteadily to his feet and stood there, now inside the door to the room, with an impassive face and with his katana at the ready. The others were all still comatose.

"Shall we proceed?" she asked.

187

The vampyre dropped to one knee. "Yes, do so. Please dear lady. But first, I would like to know your name."

"I am Taura Windwalker, Priestess of Neilea."

"I was once the Baron Armid Harcuthnut. May my own blood wash away my terrible misdeeds, Taura Windwalker, Priestess of Neilea."

She motioned Jiutarô to take up position. He had been able, just, to keep up with the conversation and knew now what would be required of him.

She explained slowly. "Jiutarô, I shall give you a sign when you are to, er! You know?"

"Hai, I know this."

"Please kneel; I shall too," she instructed the vampyre. As he dropped his other knee to the floor, she asked him "Do you regret and atone for the terrible transgressions of the past in and trust fully to the judgement of the godly Pantheon?"

"Mistress Taura Windwalker, I do indeed."

Taura's chanting began and her voice rose in intensity. She had not performed a *Curse Reversal* prayer-spell before and, although she knew the routine and wording, she understood that it would be difficult to perform due to her inexperience, and she was already drained. Many moments passed and she was getting drenched in he own sweat. Jiutarô watched her intently, waiting for the sign. Taura's shoulders became hunched and fatigue was clearly evident upon her. With a sudden gesture to the Samurai, she fell forward onto her face away from the dreadful Baron Harcuthnut and Jiutarô swung his katana. The vampyre Baron's head was cleaved from his shoulders and the body fell forward to the floor. No blood flowed to soak the richly-patterned carpet. All went quiet.

The four members of the party who, for so long, had been immobile slowly regained their consciousness and looked around themselves in surprise.

At that moment, a slightly warmer draught of air moved through the keep, tainted slightly by the smell of flowers and mild spices. The remains of the vampyre aged before them. A sound of whispered laughter, which had probably not been heard in the keep for many, many decades, rose and then fell again to silence. Taura was exhausted. Falcon helped her to a sitting position and she smiled at her friends.

"It is over," she sighed. "He agreed his own destruction, I removed his curse and Jiutarô destroyed him. It all seemed very much civilised but also a little sad, I think. He endured misery and sadness at his plight for so many decades and was forced by a curse to exist as he did. He tried to make it more bearable by attacking the goblins in the mountains and what animals he could snare to avoid too much destruction to the villagers and travellers. But there were times he must have been desperate and had no choice. He has gone but we must burn and then bury the remains with dignity – it was his request but his remains are now harmless. Tassie is in that chamber over there."

The atmosphere in the keep had changed. A little warmth gradually filled the hallway; not the warmth of a fire, or of hot food on a cold day. This was the notion of warmth that had for decades been rejected by the evil.

"By the Gods! I no longer feel the weight and influence of the burden now," gasped Silmar. "It has passed but, oh, my head did ache. Let's find the young girl."

They entered the adjoining room and found the young girl huddled in a ball on the bed. Her eyes were wild with fright and she was shivering violently. She was otherwise unharmed. Billit took a blanket from the bottom of the bed and gently wrapped it around her.

The gnome gave words of comfort. "Come, little one, you have had such a difficult time. Let us go back to your family. They are waiting for you." Silmar was surprised to hear words with so much compassion from the Gnome. This was a side of Billit that had not been seen before.

"Who's the little one that he's referring to?" whispered Silmar with a broad grim.

"Sod off, fool of an elf!" retorted Jasper.

With Falcon's help Taura was back on her feet. She held Tassie's arm and took over the care of the girl.

Jasper suggested that they look around the keep and collect what valuables were around and lock them away. It took most of the night with each of them taking it in turns to sleep, eat, drink and work. Fires were lit and the keep gradually regained physical warmth. By the morning, the group were staggered at the wealth of furnishings, money, gems, jewellery, weapons and armour that were in the keep.

Silmar gathered the others around him. "I would suggest that this keep belongs to us now," he stated. "I say we can use it for the good and benefit of the village and for our futures. What say you all?"

"What can we do with it?" asked Falcon. "We travel."

Taura answered before Silmar took the opportunity. "We have the vast majority of the goods now locked in a cellar chamber. Perhaps a chest-full of coins can be set aside to rebuild the village and bring prosperity to its people, if they would be prepared to take it."

"I think they will," Silmar replied, "especially if we tell them the story of the last occupant of the keep and the sadness that went with it. A new temple to Clamberhan, and perhaps one to Trangath too, for this is a farming community. A new trading post in the village may bring people and trade here. There is so much good this money can do. There is much set aside for our own futures too, I would say."

The keys to the keep were found in a drawer in an ornate desk and as the party, with Tassie, made ready to leave, Silmar locked the great door to the keep and placed the key in a side pocket of his pack.

Many hours later, the party entered the village through the gate. Tassie was greeted among tears and laughter and the companions were welcomed and treated as heroes.

"What of the vampyre?" a village elder asked them.

"Destroyed!" replied Jasper. "For all time!"

There was a massive cheer and people clasped each other amid tears and laughter. For them, this was unexpected but wonderful news nonetheless. The people in of Burrak had only ever known life under the threat of the horror lurking in the mountains. Now the threat, and with it the constant danger, would become history and eventually a distant memory.

"Can we gather the village elders together?" requested Silmar. "We have something of importance to discuss."

By early afternoon, the small trading post, which doubled as the village inn, filled with people, more than just the village elders. The adventurers stood together and the noise soon hushed.

The story was told of the vampyre, once the Baron Armid Harcuthnut, and how it existed in despair up until its destruction the previous evening. Taura explained that the keep was now the property of the adventuring party but they had brought down a treasure to help the village to recover and rebuild its community. It would give the village an opportunity for growth, trade and prosperity for everyone.

"How can we take this treasure? It has the blood of our people on it!" called one villager.

Another voice raised the same objections but many more were raised to agree that the money should be used, not for any one individual or family, but as a business investment for the good of the whole village.

"We can build a new wall, higher and stronger, with larger and heavier gates. We can build it out from the village to allow room for us to grow larger."

"Aye, and temples with new clerics and for the success of our wellbeing, our farms, our produce and tools."

"And store sheds for our produce."

"Aye, and a new trading post, well stocked. And a new tavern."

"Aye, also well stocked!" shouted a villager. Much laughter erupted.

"And set up our old trading agreements with Refuge, Gash and Westron Seaport. We can buy new wagons and horses, and farm tools. And perhaps the gnomes from the mines will trade here with their opals and rubies. Does anyone remember when they were last here? Many years ago now. Why, I were just a lad!"

"We must give our thanks and praise to our new friends! Our saviours!"

Suddenly, everyone in the village wanted to embrace and shake the forearms of their new heroes. The bar was opened and ale flowed as if it were water, while it lasted. People offered their beds to the party members for the night. They were fed and looked after and their horses were well cared for. They did not make any mention of it to the villagers, but very soon they would be entering the Shadow World.

But tonight, they might get a little drunk.

∽ ∾

That night they all got very drunk indeed. Jasper and Billit consumed ale, lots of it. Each tried to out-drink the other and both eventually collapsed onto the floor. They were left where they lay. Only Taura kept her drinking under control. Oh, how she would make them all suffer in the morning.

Jiutarô sang songs from his own land, unintelligible to those around him because of his strange language; even if he had been able to sing in the Universal tongue, the songs would still have been unintelligible. Then he stopped singing and swayed forward until his head landed on the table, and he fell asleep.

Falcon seemed totally immune from the effects of the ale and his drinking continued well into the night. Finally, some time after midnight, he was the last one drinking. He finished his quart tankard, stood up, and fell flat onto the floor.

Silmar didn't even attempt to get into heavy drinking. He found a quiet corner and, with his quart pot of ale and his pack with the burden buried deep inside it, settled down to relax. He was given a second, and a third, quart of ale and proceeded to drink these too, albeit slowly.

❧ ❧

The crash of chairs! The scrape of tables! The clatter of weapons, armour and baggage.

The yell of "Wake up! Wake up you lazy goats!"

Taura had found a whistle that she blew and blew. She laughed until her sides ached. Five very tired and hung-over adventurers groaned and complained and cursed. Five villagers, each with a pitcher of water, emptied the contents over each of the recumbent forms. Then they ran!

Jasper did not react well and, rolling to his feet with a chair in his hand, looked for the cowardly enemy who had tried to drown him. He did calm down when he spied

Taura laughing loudly. The rest of them clambered to their feet with groans and grunts. There were some really serious headaches amongst them.

"Good morning, my friends," she cooed. "You've had a wash and the kind villagers have left you some morn-feast. You'd better eat it all up like good little boys because Momma is taking you all for a nice walk into some mines soon, mayhap today if we are fortunate!"

"Momma going to get her arse slapped inna moment!" moaned Falcon and made as if to leap at her. Taura squealed and jumped back.

The best any of the rest of them could reply was with a grunt although Silmar was sitting on a chair laughing. The morning feast disappeared as if it were a carcass being devoured by a pack of ravenous hyenas, with the same sort of noise too.

Within an hour the companions had eaten, drunk a lot of water and began preparations for the next part of their journey. Jasper called the companions together and they sat round a large table to talk about what was to come.

"There ain't much else I can say right now," the dwarf said. "We just 'ave to get on with it an' work together. We'll be fine if we take care an' take no risks at all. There's a lot of evil down there but there is some good too. You'll see."

"It may not mean much," responded Silmar. "But I feel the effects of the burden when we get near something evil. You know, the headaches and nausea. It acts as a warning and goes when the evil has gone. It was very strong in the presence of the vampyre. I could feel it even before we entered the keep. It lifted when he was destroyed."

"That's understandable," answered Taura. "Vampyres are evil because they are created by evil to be evil. Simple really."

"So I should feel its effect when we get close to the Darkling, then."

"You not sick on me, hai?" ventured Jiutarô.

"Hai!" answered Silmar with a face simulating throwing up in Jiutarô's direction.

"You're like choddin' children!" groaned Jasper. "I think I can remember near where the entrance to the Shadow World is, just takes a bit o' searchin' for, that's all. Time to get goin'. Let's load up and go. It's a few hours away, we'll be getting there on foot. Like I said, there ain't no point in taking the 'orses so we'll 'ave to carry everythin' we need. From 'ere we should get there by midday I reckon."

Fifty gold coins ensured their horses and some of their belongings would be taken to the Ship's Prow in Westron Seaport. A few villagers clamoured to be the ones selected to take them.

With sombre faces, the companions strode out of the village. A small crowd of people waved them out, knowing nothing of where they were going.

The weather had turned very dismal and a cold rain had been steadily falling but the leaden skies showed that much heavier rain threatened. By the time that the downpour arrived, Jasper had led them into a shallow cave. For him, it was routine that caves, and similar places, were checked for undesirable occupants. Fortunately, in this case, there were none. That they were here at all was most unfortunate indeed.

♥ ♥

PART 2
SHADOW WORLD

CHAPTER 16

JASPER INDICATED a rocky rise. "It's up there," he said gruffly.

Although, from a distance, the entrance to the cavern was well-concealed among tall pillars of rock, the faintest of tracks made by the rare visitors to the tunnel indicated its presence only to a skilled searcher with a keen eye. Moreover, it only became noticeable to the group the closer they came to the entrance. They entered the narrow fissure warily and, even though the day was very cloudy and dismal, it took their eyes a few moments to adjust to the darkness. A doorway, deep within the cave, was almost concealed between two natural rocky columns. The door itself was constructed from very heavy oak and reinforced with four rusting iron bands. It was framed in a stone archway with ancient runes and symbols engraved around the entrance. The door was closed. Falcon, stepped over to open it but Jasper stopped him with a stocky restraining arm across the mighty Barbarian's midriff.

"Wait!" the dwarf commanded with a gravelly voice. "The door may be warded. Well, it may not be but if it is, you might be 'it by a powerful magic spell or somethink.

'Ear me well, all of yous, and mark my words wi' care. I 'ave been 'ere before, an' other fell places too. Girlie, what can you find out for us?"

Taura was irked and was not slow in showing it. "Girlie?" she retorted. "Cheeky bastard! Who made *him* king, anyway? If it is a magical warding, Billit is the one to ask, surely."

"That is not a very pious way of speaking with your bestest friends now, is it? Move aside, let me see," grunted the gnome.

Billit, a few inches shorter than the dwarf, pushed himself through nonetheless, stood back from the doorway and started a soft chanting. None of the group could understand his words; as always when he was voicing a spell, they all felt as if they could not focus their hearing onto his chanting. He waved his hands in a wide arc and a very faint blue glow that only he could see illuminated the doorway. He slowly dropped his hands, relaxed and reached into his pouch. He scattered some powder that looked like shiny sand over the doorway with a smile on his face. Beads of perspiration lined his forehead. "Well, there's no magical ward apparent 'ere," he stated with confidence.

"Well, there may still be a booby-trap o' some kind," persisted Jasper as he peered around the doorway. "Think about where we are. These doorways ain't meant to be easy for just anyone to enter, you know. And I don't trust that dark elf; 'e wouldn't miss an opportunity to do us some damage. Can *you* check to see if 'e laid a trap for us, Silmar?"

The dour elf replied that it really was not something he was well suited for and cautiously stepped over towards the door. As he placed a foot down, there was a click!

"Oh shit!" breathed Silmar. "It's under my right foot, whatever it is!"

Jasper rubbed his face with his right hand. "Um, aye. Oh right, don't lift yer foot, yer dumb elf, keep it there, nothin's happened yet but it may do when you lift yer foot off. Now take care all o' you, watch where you put yer feet. Clumsy choddin' elf! I'm gonna show you what these leather tubes are for. Need yer 'elp, Billit, nothin' hard, just a magic spell."

The dwarf took a gold coin out of his money pouch and handed it to Billit. "Nice o' you, Jasper but you don't have to pay me for a spell," gasped the gnome as he flashed a nervous glance across to Silmar.

The dwarf was about to stomp in frustration but, glancing down at the floor, he suddenly froze on the spot. "Aye, funny choddin' gnome, ha, ha, choddin' ha! I want you to put a *Glow* spell on it so it shines real bright in the dark. Can yer do it? Iannus, my old associate could do it. She was a wizard, choddin' good 'un, too. Dead now. Shame really, she 'ad a lovely chest!" He let out a sigh tinged with sadness.

"Aye, I can do this, but if you want one for everybody then I can't; magic *is* a bit taxing 'specially when I've not eaten for a couple of hours, you know!"

Jasper glowered at him.

Billit held out his two hands in front of his, his staff leaning against his shoulder. "Steady, I'm just fooling Jasper," Billit chuckled. "Heh heh! Serious though, I can do one now and then a couple more in a few hours. To use a spell, I have practice the words first; don't wanna get the spell wrong an' the gold coin turns to dust or somethin'. You didn't tell me you wanted this spell so I need to think 'ow it goes."

The dwarf was growing impatient. He glowered at Billit. "Well, get on with it then!" he roared

Billit hopped backwards but regained his balance and composure. He flexed his voice to produce the required, almost musical, intonation. He placed the coin in his left hand and moved his right hand in a circular motion above it. As he began uttering some words in a tongue, unintelligible to the others, the coin started emitting a white glow between his fingers. It steadily became brighter and brighter until its light became almost too bright to look at directly.

"Done!" the gnome muttered. "That shine, it won't wear out for weeks." He handed the brightened coin back to the dwarf.

Jasper replied "I 'ear that it don't work so well on a silver coin an' 'ardly at all on a copper one, does it?"

"'S righr," the gnome mage agreed. "You wanna see what it does to a diamond though; it looks like the sun!"

The dwarf pushed the coin deep inside the leather tube and pointed it at the door. A beam of light shone out and the door was bathed in a white light while all other parts of the cave remained in the gloom. "An' when I wanna cover the light, I do this," he said and put the leather cover over the tube. The light was gone – completely.

"Ha, not bad for an old dwarf, eh! I've got five o' these tubes with covers an' with the 'elp of the gnome most of us should get one. Event'ally."

He removed the cover again and handed the light tube to Silmar. "See what the trap might be, elf."

"At last," Silmar sighed. "I thought you had forgotten me. My leg is beginning to tremble."

There was total silence from the companions. Silmar slowly moved the beam over the door and the archway. "Nothing," he whispered. He started looking around the walls of the cave adjacent to the doorway. He took his time; he was the one at risk of something terrible happening. His right leg was aching and a small tremble was building up in his knee. "Oh Gods, I really do want to move my leg!" he whispered.

"Don't you choddin' dare!" growled Jasper.

Jiutarô, Taura and Falcon quietly stood out of the way, apprehensively looking on.

"Wait, what's that over there?" Silmar pointed to what appeared at first to be a small crack in the cave wall about three feet up from the floor. Jiutarô was the closest and he started to move towards the wall.

"Jiutarô, take this light thing," Silmar instructed. He was sweating profusely. "Check the floor before you go over, there may be more traps."

The Samurai dropped to his knees and started to examine the floor, moving slowly closer to the wall. He stood and pointed the light tube at the crack in the wall. "Hole! Stick, look out at you," he warned Silmar. "Pass big rock, Falcon."

Falcon lifted what for him was a fist-sized rock from the ground and passed it to Jiutarô who held it over the hole but at an angle which would deflect the apparent missile out of harm's way.

"Foot up, Silmar," instructed the Samurai.

Silamr did so.

Another click sounded and immediately there was a loud *crack* as the missile struck the boulder. A dart, the length of a man's forearm and the thickness of a thumb, clattered off the cave roof and dropped down onto the ground.

"Feel like wiping yer arse now, elf?" asked Jasper. Everyone laughed this time, including Silmar, who thought it best not to admit that Jasper was not that far from the truth with that question.

The dwarf looked down at the mechanism that Silmar had stepped on and called Billit across. "Take a look at this, gnome. How do you think it works?"

Gnomes were renowned for their natural aptitude with mechanical devices and Billit often showed curiosity with locks and unusual objects. "A floor plate, with a length of cord connected to it, by the looks of it. Aye, the line's buried under the dust and rubble but it looks like a very recent addition. Clean as your mother's bonnet, this cord! It goes up behind this rock pillar and, ahhh, hmmm." He studied the rock face near to the doorway. "Aye! Ahhh right, aye!"

"What, yer chod? What? Tell me!" yelled the dwarf. He was hopping from one foot to another in frustration.

"It goes through this gap and connects up to this little lever. When Silmar stepped off the plate, the lever released the spring retainer and shoots the dart out. Simple really! I could make a few improvements here."

"Not now, gnome! Yer don't wanna improve it, yer want to break it!"

"Right, er, no, then. Another time p'raps. Lovely bit of cord this, feels like silk. I'm keepin' this." He pulled on the cord and it came free with the lever assembly attached. He cut the device off with his small dagger and coiled the cord around his hand.

Meanwhile, Silmar picked up the dart. It seemed to be made of bone. He looked at the point and noticed a slight discolouration. "I think this is a poison or venom on here," he warned.

Jiutarô struggled to find the words. "I put in wet dirt, make safe," he suggested and he took it from Silmar. He was back in a few moments and the company turned as one towards the door.

"By the way, where did you find wet dirt, Jiutarô?" Taura asked him.

"I piss!"

She would have chuckled but tenseness grew among the group.

They drew a collective breath knowing it was time to enter the Shadow World. All of them were anxious about entering, and some more so than others. Jasper was the least apprehensive of all of them and even he was edgy. What waited for them the other side of that door? Would they all make it through the ancient mines and back out safely? Would Jasper's skills in the ancient mines be sufficient to keep them all alive or would his age and memory let them down? His new friends were all amateurs but together, their fighting and magical skills were awe-inspiring. Yet they trusted him completely.

The ageing dwarf looked at each of them in turn, perhaps in an attempt to gauge their feelings but also to offer some encouragement and comfort. Taura was the most visibly nervous and he put an arm around her waist – he could barely reach her shoulders! "Fear not, m'lady, we shall care fer one another an' protect each other down there, eh?"

Jiutarô handed him back the light tube and the dwarf replaced the cover.

"I think I need to relieve meself afore we enter," mumbled Billit.

"Best yer have yer crap out 'ere," grunted Jasper. "The stink will warn all the beasties that we're on our way!"

"It's a stand up, not a sit down, ya fool of a dwarf!"

"Just tryin' to cheer us up, that's all. You feelin' alright, missy?"

The Priestess of Neilea nodded and gave a half-hearted smile. "I'll be fine," she replied, but she was trembling.

The barbarian, however, looked quite comfortable but his knuckles were white with his grip on the handle of his warhammer. Jasper glanced up at him.

"Watch yer 'ead down there, yer big lummox!" the dwarf advised sombrely. "The tunnel roof can be very 'igh one minute and barely 'igh enough for me the next." He patted his weapons and with a deep breath. "Keep yer 'ands close to yer weaponry. Are we ready?" he asked.

"Aye!" they all replied.

"Hai!" replied Jiutarô softly. "Am ready."

"Hmmm, try it once more with a bit more feelin' all've yers? Nay, p'raps not. Let's do it then!"

He placed his shoulder against the door and pushed hard. He needn't have, the door opened easily.

But loudly, the hinges hadn't ever been oiled, it seemed.

"Shit, sod it, bugger it!" Jasper could be coarse, even for a dwarf! He earned a *Shush!* from Taura.

The echoes of the door being opened came back at them for many heartbeats.

And they were heard by other ears.

❧ ☙

The Darkling had waited impatiently for too long. Their first test would be the trap by the doorway. He had known it was there, of course. There had been other traps laid there by the ancients but time had ruined most of them. He had repaired the one that looked the most promising. The chain linkage from the floor-plate to the firing spring had rusted and he had carried out a repair with the silken cord that he carried. He was loath to part with such a valuable length of twine but perhaps the followers wouldn't spot the trap in the gloom of the cave and they would lose one of their number.

Two days, he'd estimated. *That's how long I have waited for these weaklings.* Being much more at home in the darkness of the ancient mines, he, like others of his race, had developed an accurate body clock but it failed him on the surface. The headaches plagued him constantly during the daylight hours. *Oh those damnable headaches!* He mumbled regardless of the precautions he had taken to protect himself from the daylight's glare. He felt some relief already now that he was in the mine's tunnel and could concentrate on the passing of time. It was said that subtle changes in the rock were felt with the rotation of the sun and moon around the world of Amæus and this effect was felt in the bodies of Darkling. So it was alleged by the old sages and this knowledge was now claimed by the depraved female Darkling mages and the priesthood, who rigidly governed the Darkling race, as their own.

He carried a small bow barely two and a half feet in length. It was ideal for the narrow confines of the Shadow World. His arrows were short such that he was unable to draw the bowstring back to his chin; it did not matter, he wouldn't need a long range down here. It was more usual for Shadow Elves to be armed with a small crossbow. Although very light and unlikely to cause much damage, the crossbow bolt's head would be coated in a powerful and fast acting venom milked, predictably, from scorpions. Unless treated, death would come quickly and excrutiatingly. He did not favour the crossbow – it was cumbersome, unpredictable and inaccurate – he favoured the short bow.

Now his mind wandered while he waited for the arrival of the fools from the surface. He reflected on the matriarchal society he had left behind. Their female mages and clerics chose chaos, trickery, evil and destruction for their oft inexplicable causes. The clerics wielded an awesome and terrible arcane power in the name of Adelenis, the evil Scorpion Queen goddess; *Her* with *Her* foul army of *adelonnes*, the huge white scorpions that they farmed, fed, trained and milked. Even the Darkling mages and warriors feared and despised them!

Ah yes! The *adelonnes*! He had seen one in Dannakanonn, the grand Shadow World city of the Darkling that he had left behind on this challenging errand to recover the artefact, a ceremonial dagger that had been touched by the very hand of Adelenis, so it was said by the Esteemed Priestess who had sent him and a troop of warriors on the mission. He quietly harboured doubts; to express them would have meant death as a heretic, because it was rumoured that Adelenis was in hiding from Tarne – temporarily, of course.

His home was far to the north-east, deep beneath the Dragon's Teeth Mountains. *Adelonnes* were hated and feared by most Darkling and regarded as an aberration. The priestesses venerated them however. These beasts were fearsome, bloodthirsty creatures created by Adelenis herself, so her priestesses lectured, from male Darkling who had failed to complete the sacred tasks set by Her, through her priestesses of course. Yes, loathsome they were to look upon, the body and tail of a gigantic, white scorpion. The one he had seen, long ago, was caged and tormented. It had eventually broken out from its cage and had been slaughtered in the main marketplace, but not before it had killed some Darkling and even more Dwarven slaves, worthless surface scum that they were. The full length of the carcass was estimated at eighteen feet, ten of these being the barbed tail.

It was said that Adelenis Herself took the form of a great, white scorpion but with a darkling head, startlingly beautiful in its appearance. It was also said that she was not dark at all but white-skinned like the surface elves.

She was normally illustrated in the temples as a beautiful, dark-skinned woman, resplendent in her nakedness, with a typical scorpion tail with its huge poison sac and barb at its tip. Priestesses taught that She did not yet inhabit the Outer Planes, where resided the Pantheon of the Gods, as did the other senior gods of evil persuasion, including Killik and Terene. Rather, She had *chosen* to remain closer to her followers from whom She took her powers and Her strength; so it was said.

It was also said, albeit quietly, that She did not have the strength to rise to the greatness accorded to those older and greater gods in the Outer Planes because She was in hiding and too weak at this time. It was being said that She needed these artefacts of power to develop the power so that She could emerge to face Her nemesis, Tarne, and match Him strength for strength and to oppose Him with His moralistic and judgemental attitudes, that so-called *superior* god with his benevolent countenance and whose name he, the Darkling in the service of his *Exalted Mistress*, the Esteemed Priestess from Dannakanonn, dared not utter.

And then his thoughts were broken. There came to his ears the sound of the door being opened. The sound was faint because of the distance, but not too faint for his keen ears to perceive. This was the sound he had waited for. *Two days!* Those hinges called out their warning that the fools were on their way.

He sniggered quietly to himself and shook his head. *Amateurs. Hah!* One at a time, he would pick them off. *But not yet, let those other aberrations that inhabit the Shadow World have their fun first.*

He rose to his feet and slowly strode away.

❧ ❧

CHAPTER 17

IT WAS WITH fear and trepidation that they entered this place of dread, the unknown realm of the Shadow World. A place rumoured to be swarming with foul, bloodthirsty creatures, and with undead too. Parents in villages on the surface would tell stories of creatures from the Shadow World to scare their children into behaving or to ensure that they returned home well before dark. Children would suffer nightmares, some adults too. Unexplained occurrences were often attributed to the terrors from the Shadow World. People went missing; for sacrifices it was rumoured.

The Shadow World – that cold, damp place crawling not only with the rats and great spider but with the very beasts and devils of the abyss.

"Better shut the door, I guess!" grunted Jasper. He signalled for Jiutarô to close the door but as the Samurai turned, the door noisily swung itself shut with a faint *boom* and the group was in total pitch black darkness. It wasn't just darkness; it was the total absence of light.

A cold chill had crawled up Jiutarô's spine. "I touch it not," he gasped. "Close itself."

"Spooky, huh?" whispered Billit. And louder he cried "Whoo-ooo!"

"Idiot!" cried Taura. She swung her staff and caught the gnome on his leg. He let out a yelp.

It was now quiet. There was very little sound of their breathing – almost all of them were holding their breath. One of them was panting – Taura, was it?

Silmar listened to the beating of his heart; he was certain that his companions could hear it above the sound of their own. He was fearful that his dark-vision had let him down until he realised he had not enabled it. He did so now but it did little to aid him; he saw the faint outlines of his companions but little else.

"Quite warm down here, ain't it," whispered Billit after what seemed an age. His eyes flitted from side to side, and from roof to floor. He saw very little with his dark vision.

"Dark too," replied Falcon. He could see nothing and felt totally disoriented as the sounds of their voices echoed back.

"A quart of foaming ale in a lively tavern would be far better, right now," said Silmar softly. Even then, his words seemed as a bellow. His dark vision, although generally very good on the surface above, was limited because he needed a little light in order to magnify it. Down here, there was little of it, usually none.

"And a nice comfortable bed in the Ship's Prow in Westron Seaport," responded Taura, her voice quivering with fear. Falcon had his arm round her shoulder and she felt somewhat safer. Truth be told, he felt vulnerable too but would never admit to it, particularly in front of Taura.

"Behave! I think I'll risk a little light 'ere," hissed Jasper. Although a whisper, it seemed incredibly loud in the darkness. "Got a light tube; shield your eyes. Ready? Three, two, one. On!"

They all gasped as a beam of light shot up towards the roof of the tunnel. It was a very uneven rock ceiling that loomed above them. It was high enough for Falcon to stand fully upright. The dwarf shone the beam to either side. The group had enough room in the tunnel to walk side-by-side in pairs. They could clearly see the deep scores on the walls where they had been worked by miners long ago. The tunnel stretched out in front of them far beyond the reach of the light beam. The floor was generally flat and even and few obstacles littered the path although in places there were signs of loose rocks and boulders from roof falls. Decayed remnants of lanterns, shovels and picks were stacked to one side.

Niblit's voice, confident compared to those of the others, except perhaps for Jasper, sounded startlingly loud. "I reckon we should keep light on, or torches," he said. "That will put anything, or any creature, at a disadvantage, don't you think?"

"Sounds good," Silmar agreed slowly. "We only 'ave a few torches, though, and will need to use 'em sparingly."

"Hey now, we should limit our talking to just whispers," advised the dwarf. "We'll keep the light tube on but it may make us a target for the dark 'un. Let's go."

They started forward, very slowly at first as they became accustomed to their environment. The sound of Jasper's whispers echoed from the walls but the sound itself seemed dead, as if it was being absorbed by the tunnel about them. Because of the echoing, the members of the group were able to speak to each other only in hushed voices. This was to the best advantage because they would not want their voices to carry along the tunnel.

They had been expecting a rank smell of damp and decay. But the atmosphere was quite fresh, not unpleasant, at all. Nor was the air as stale as would have been expected; they discerned a faint movement of air on their faces or in their hair. The tunnel was surprisingly dry; from time to time though, they could hear the dripping of water though. Here and there were some muddy areas as trickles of water found their way into the dust and rubble on the floor. As they marched on slowly and cautiously, they passed by a few puddles and occasional pools, some of which were very deep. In the larger pools the water was always extremely cold. Jasper explained that the pools would often provide a good source of drinking water but it was advisable to check it first.

"Yer don't know it somethin's pissed in it so smell it first," he advised. "Then put a bit on yer lips, then on yer tongue an' spit it out an' then try a mouthful an' spit that out."

As time crawled on, the mine changed from a low and narrow tunnel to massive, wide, cathedral-like chambers where the roof disappeared from even the reach of the beam of Jasper's light tube. There were times that the bright beam from the light tube could not even find the width of the tunnel. Their path was always clearly defined however, but the mine tunnel became narrower the further they progressed. Stalactites hung down from the ceiling in many places, often in ones and twos but occasionally in clusters. Generally, stalagmites reached up from the floor towards them. Some stalactites and stalagmites met to produce a pillar.

Time had no way of being measured when there was no light from the sun, the moon and stars. There was no change in the level of darkness, no change of temperature.

At the very start, Jasper had said "We eats when we're 'ungry, we sleeps when we're tired, otherwise we walk an' we 'unt Darkling. An' we stay alive."

They already felt that they had been walking for some hours and some of the group felt they were in need of a rest with some food and water. The pathway was now becoming narrower and an order of march was discussed by Silmar and Jasper.

Silmar leaned forward to whisper to the dwarf. "Look Jasper, you are comfortable down here, I am not. You have dark-vision, do you not?"

The dwarf nodded. "Aye, 'bout ten, mebbe fifteen paces or so. Why?"

"So it makes sense for you to lead the party. I'll take up position at the back of the group so I can protect our rear. Taura is terrified but she is taking much comfort from Falcon. He really is looking after her but he is very much afraid of being here. He doesn't show it but I can see it in his eyes and his voice wavers. I think he takes as much comfort by being with Taura as she does with him. They should be in the centre of the group."

Jasper whispered his agreement and took over the discussion. "Billit is quite 'appy here, 'e is reasonably confident in tunnels. 'E says 'is limited dark-vision allows 'im to make out shapes an' heat-sources up to about twenty paces away. 'Is cheerful manner encourages us all, me included. 'E could take up position next to you, mebbe. Jiutarô is a strange one though, don't yer think? He's picked up the Universal tongue so quickly. 'E seems 'fraid of nothin' an' you say that 'e told you that this is not real for 'im? Like it's a dream. It's real enough fer me, I can tell you. I'd like 'im behind me with that strange bow of 'is. I can't believe that 'e can loose off three arrows in as many heartbeats and each one can take the eye out of a rabbit at a 'undred paces! I never seen nothing like it."

"I agree, and it's the same with that sword of his," mused Silmar. "He calls it a *dai-katana* and handles it both one and two-handed. It's so fast that he can take it out of his scabbard, swing it once and replace it again. And in that time two people are dead. It is truly awesome. And that blade cuts through all other swords. I would love one like it. He truly is a weapons-master."

"What say you about our order o' march then, elf?"

Silmar nodded his head in full agreement. "Aye, 'tis good. Let's let everyone know."

"Aye, well," murmured Billit. "I gotta sort out some more o' them light tubes. Taura is givin' me a hard time 'bout 'em. I need a couple o' gold crowns though. Ain't usin' me own!"

Silmar flipped him two coins, the gnome mage sat on the ground and began chanting over one of the coins, making circular motions with his hand above the coin. Many moments passed before a very bright white light emanated from it. Billit had cast a *Glow* spell on the coin. Jasper thrust the coin deep inside another of the leather tubes and placed the cover on it. He passed it to Taura.

"There, girlie," he grunted. "That is for you."

Billit repeated the process for the second coin and passed it to Silmar. The mage was bathed in sweat. "Choddin' 'ard work, that was. 'Ain't brought no more tubes so can't really do another one. Hey, you wanna see the light that comes when I do it on a gemstone. Awesome!"

"Lookit now," Jasper advised. "We 'ave a few o' these light tubes, we must 'ave a spoken code word that could be called by any one of us if the need arises, to both cover the beams an' to open 'em. If me, Billit or Silmar are using our

215

dark-vision an' one o' these light tubes is uncovered, we'll be blinded fer ages an' won't be able to see to fight if we need to."

"What do you suggest?" asked Falcon.

A couple of suggestions came from the others but Jasper held up his hands and shook his head.

"Keep it simple," advised Jasper. "I suggest we use the words '*lightson*' an' '*lightsout*'. If fer some reason it ain't convenient fer the lights to be covered up or uncovered, then someone 'as to call '*nochange*'. Or something like that. What say you all to that?"

Silmar recommended that they all try to get used to relying on the three members of the party who had dark-sight and move in darkness through the tunnel. "The advantage is that if we come across something down here, or someone, who is used to being in total darkness, if we uncover our light tubes on a '*lightson*' word, they'll be more blinded that us."

"He's not just a handsome face," remarked Taura.

"He's a choddin' elf, so he's not *even* a handsome face!" replied Jasper. "Time to move on. Let's try it in darkness."

Both Silmar and Jasper had noticed that Taura and Falcon had been sitting together hand-in-hand and the dwarf winked. Silmar smiled. Billit produced the silken cord that he had recently acquired. It was decided that this would be useful in keeping Jiutarô, Taura and Falcon together. The others wouldn't need it.

Progress was extremely slow for a long time and almost every pebble, rock or uneven surface on the tunnel floor seemed to be a significant obstacle. The path turned and twisted, climbed and fell. Sometimes they had to climb up slopes on all fours or slide down other slopes. As time went on, Jasper and Silmar were able to whisper warnings and progress became slightly faster. After some hours their speed was almost the same as it had been when they had the light tube uncovered. Signs of ancient mine workings were everywhere. To each side were narrow openings with piles of detritus.

"What did the old mine workers do with all the rock they dug out?" asked Taura.

Jasper shrugged his shoulders but it was an action that went unseen by Taura, Jiutarô and Jasper. "I would reckon it got took up to the surface," he surmised. "Never thought 'bout it really."

A very unusual and unexpected thing happened to Taura, Jiutarô and Falcon after a while. They could see, very faintly, the walls of the tunnel and its floor. A faint yellow-green glow seemed to emanate from the rocks. Jasper stopped the party and they all took the opportunity to sit down.

He whispered "I wondered who would notice it first. It's got somethin' to do with the mould that grows down 'ere in the Shadow World. It glows an' you can see a little. Sometimes it's lots brighter than this. This could go on for ages now. *Lightson!* I wanna see the mould."

The party began to rise to their feet. As Jasper stepped off, he tripped and fell to the floor. There was a swishing sound as an arrow flew into the group. Two more quickly followed. Jiutarô gave a cry and staggered to the floor, an arrow protruded from his upper left thigh. Falcon raised his left arm; an arrow had embedded itself just above his wrist. Both of them were groaning with the pain. A third arrow had passed harmlessly through Jiutarô's loose-fitting hose.

"Another trap, an' I didn't see it!" called Jasper. "I'm a choddin' idiot." He had got his foot caught up in a thin chain which led to a pile of rocks a few paces in front of them and luckily for him, had fallen to the ground. "Choddin' Darkling been up to 'is mischief again, huh?"

Jiutarô was in considerable pain and was mumbling in his own obscure language. Billit was attending to him and had his hand on the shaft of the arrow. The gnome slapped the Samurai's face hard with his other hand and then, in one movement, pulled the arrow free. Jiutarô gasped out in surprise and agony.

"Why did yer slap him?" asked Jasper.

"To distract 'im from me pulling the arrow out, o' course. Good idea, ain't it?"

"So how do you know it wasn't barbed?" asked Silmar.

"'Cos the arrow sticking through Falcon's arm isn't!"

"Ah, aye. I see. The Darkling may have used venom though so take care."

"Let us hope not," gasped Taura. "I can help to heal. As you know, The Lady Neilea has given me some healer's skills. I shall stop the bleeding and then ask Her if She will help with the healing."

She knelt on the ground beside Jiutarô and pulled out a small bag from her pack. She set some of the contents on the ground. She took a bandage from the scattered contents and picked out a glass jar which she opened. She scooped a little of the jar's glutinous contents and smeared it across a bandage which she folded and then tightly wrapped around Jiutarô's shoulder wound. Then placing her hands, without touching, over Jiutarô's wound, she chanted words which, in her sing-song voice, became impossible for the others to understand. It took about three or four minutes before she finished her incantations. Although the bandage was bloodstained, the wound no longer appeared to be bleeding heavily.

Jiutarô was astounded. "How you do this?" he asked. "Magic? Aiii, strange powers."

"You have magic in your world, don't you?" asked Billit. "Your priests and mages do healing and stuff?"

Jiutarô shook his head. "No magic. See none; never." He flexed his shoulder and winced as dull pain shot through it.

She gathered up her paraphernalia, replaced it in her bag and attended to Falcon next. He had pulled the arrow out himself by quickly cutting off the flight end with his hunting knife and removing the remaining portion by tugging it out. They hadn't even been aware of him doing it. He grimaced at Taura as she sat next to him with her bag.

His wound was bleeding but not liberally. He was using his other hand to press against the wound on either side of his wrist to stop the bleeding. His wrist and fingers were blood-soaked, nonetheless. Without using a bandage she started her chant to Neilea once again. A few minutes passed and the wound no longer bled. She used her substance on a bandage once again and wrapped it tightly around Falcon's wrist.

Falcon raised his hand to Taura's cheek and looked onto her eyes. She leaned over and kissed him on the mouth, hard. It was a few minutes before anybody interrupted.

"Time to sort ourselves out, I think," Jasper said softly. "Come along my little lovebirds! What was the stuff yer put on the bandage? Something 'oly?"

"Very much so," replied Taura. "Very holy indeed. It was honey. Just honey. It helps cure many ills and wounds and prevents infection."

Jasper and Silmar had looked around to check for any other unwanted distractions. They had found none. They studied the trap. It did not appear to have been freshly set;

clearly their quarry may not even have noticed the existence of it because there were no fresh signs around it.

Silmar breathed a sigh of relief. "I thought the Darkling had left us another hazard in the hope of reducing our number. We were most fortunate that he had not set it himself for he would surely have used venom. Will the next trap take its first victim? We must try to be careful."

Jasper was quiet but then he spoke, uncharacteristically softly. "I feel so choddin' stupid, elf. I think it's better that you lead fer a while. That trap may 'ave killed one of us an' I didn't even see it there. You may stand a better chance o' spotting something' as we go on. I'll take up the rear position with Jiutarô and Billit will 'elp me. A gnome bein' of a minin' tribe will be very 'elpful to me. Falcon an' Taura can stay in the middle; holdin' 'ands."

"You're just jealous," responded Taura and stuck out her tongue at him.

"Why would he want to hold Falcon's hand?" answered Silmar. They all laughed but once again, they earned a *shush* from Taura.

Billit had puffed out his chest at being told he would be of value in the group. It was generally in the nature of gnomes that they were ignored, being small of stature and easily forgotten.

Silmar emphasised that they all keep as quiet as possible from now so that he could concentrate better. "And we don't want to let the Darkling know that we are behind him.

Once again the group resumed their march. Silmar felt the weight of responsibility heavily on his shoulders. What if *he* failed to spot the next one? If one of his friends were to die, it would be his own fault. Would they blame him? Traps were designed and made so as not to be seen, obviously. Progress would be a little slower now because the elf would be checking to each side and ahead. The faint light from the tunnel walls seemed to increase a little although there were places where it gave out completely. Their eyes were growing accustomed to its faint glow and it did help Silmar with his dark-sight. The dripping of water through the mines was incessant and annoying. Within the silence, they occasionally heard the sounds of tiny skittering feet, probably rodents or similar, rushing away as the group passed.

There were still a number of little caverns and openings in the walls of the tunnels. Often, they passed these with care and silence. Sometimes, they entered them to find nothing, except perhaps the putrid or desiccated remains of a raw meal eaten by some sort of animal. Once, the remains appeared to be human. It was not recent however; scraps of clothing fell to shreds as Billit pulled upon it to investigate. There was a coin, probably silver, on the floor though; the symbols upon it were unknown. The gnome put it in one of his pouches.

For many hours, it seemed, they had been on the march. They were all hungry, thirsty and very tired. Jasper finally called for a halt. They went into a little cavern which, except for some dry droppings, appeared uninhabited. Small droppings were not unusual here in the Shadow World; they weren't everywhere but they were noticeable from time to time.

"How long we walk?" asked Jiutarô.

"'Alf a day," replied Jasper. "'Bout two leagues I would say."

They lit no fires, having agreed that they wouldn't be needed and, of course, it would affect the dark-vision of those that had it. They ate whatever they had brought with them, mainly dried meat, nuts and dried fruit. A little of this would provide enough energy to march for many hours and there seemed a plentiful supply of water from pools in the tunnels.

Taura, Jiutarô and Falcon were not expected to stand guard during the rest periods. There was no point; they didn't have the dark-vision and heightened senses of the dwarf, elf and gnome. Billit would need to practice the words of the spells he thought he might need and then get enough sleep to be able to use his concentration to cast them. Similarly, Taura would need to sleep to be able to beseech Neilea for her aid through prayer-spells.

Billit was voicing some words of a spell when there was a flash of searing light and a whoosh of power.

A cry of protest and an oath from Jasper was followed by a sincere apology from the gnome.

"I can't see a choddin' thing, you – you chod!" the dwarf groaned. "What in the seven hells of the Void did you do?" He sat rocking back and forth while rubbing his eyes with his hands.

The others had woken up.

"What was that?" Silmar gasped. His eyes, too, were clearly affected although not as much as those of the dwarf because he had been dozing.

"I 'adn't done this spell afore," the gnome whined. "It was a, er, an *Energy Blast* spell I was practising the words for but it worked too well."

Indeed, out through the doorway of their chamber and across the tunnel, the beam from Taura's light tube showed a darkened, smoking patch on the wall.

Billit wilted under the withering glares from his companions. No further words were necessary.

༄ ༄

CHAPTER 18

THEY MOVE like a herd of aurochs, the Darkling thought. He was appalled by their careless attitudes when navigating the mines. *So, they have light. Their need for it emphasises their human weakness. I must be wary in the event they use them while I am relying on my dark-sight.*

He reflected momentarily on the flash he had seen earlier. There had been a slight *whoomph* sound from its source back along the tunnel in the direction of the white-skinned surface elf and his accomplices.

Magic surely! So, they must have a mage with them with formidable power. Again, I must be wary, devious in fact.

He considered revising his plan. Perhaps a strike and run tactic. Take one of them out and run while the rest of them were confused and frightened in the darkness. An arrow here, a trap there, although it appeared they had been alerted by another trap that he had missed and were now cautious. The arrow-trap some hours ago had taken casualties, he was certain.

He had used the last of his phial of scorpion venom on the trap by the entrance but without success. This had angered him because his *Exalted Mistress* had provided little of what amounted to a very valuable resource.

She expected success. She would not tolerate failure.

He rose off the gravel floor, hefted his pack, grabbed his weapons and sauntered quietly along the tunnel.

ॐ ॐ

They resumed their march but were forced to rely on their light tubes because the dim light from the fungus had waned. It was just as well they had their own light sources because they almost immediately began to find chasms across the floor of the mine tunnels. Many of these were no more than a foot or two in width but some made it necessary for them to need to leap across. These had once had wooden bridges across them but over the long years these had disintegrated or were too fragile to trust. All chasms appeared bottomless.

"I wonder how deep these are," murmured Silmar.

"Deep! Choddin' deep!" replied Jasper in an irritated manner. "It don't choddin' matter! Don't drop anything down there; you don't know if it is in'abited by somethin' that will come and get us."

At length, they came to a point where the path seemed to end. A vast chasm, many yards across, barred their way. As they approached, it was evident that sometime in the distant past, an ancient civilisation had carved a ledge on the left side of the chasm; the marks of picks and chisels were clearly evident. It was barely wide enough for them to pass and a lot of care would have to be taken if they were to get to the other side. There were also remnants of a bridge. Two short pillars, approximately three feet in height and a foot in girth, stood a couple of yards back from the lip of the chasm. Rusted remnants of an old chain hung from the top of one of the pillars.

The drop appeared interminably deep; the beam from the light tube did not show the bottom of the pit.

Although the majority of the party, being quite small in stature, easily managed to find their way along the ledge, two of them had difficulties. Jasper was the first to cross and, being wide of girth as were most dwarves, he did find it a complication to get to the other side. At one point, about half way across, he had to drop to his hands and knees to avoid what he thought to be the certainty of falling to his death.

Silmar crossed with ease but as he sat down to wait for the others a small ache lanced through his head. *Probably tiredness*, he thought.

He should have recognised the warning sign.

၆ ၄

The mighty Falcon did not fare quite so well. Billit had to take himself and his own equipment across and then return twice to take across the barbarian's weapons and equipment. Once the great barbarian started to cross, it was clear that he was terrified. At one point he froze and could not move. At that moment, an arrow whistled over Silmar's head and clattered off the rock an inch away from Falcon's head. The great man's right foot slipped from the ledge and he stumbled.

"No!" Taura screamed. "Hold on, Falcon!"

Silmar turned and, with his bow readied, searched for the one who had sent the arrow. Jiutarô had already loosed an arrow across the chasm and he pointed and called "There! Arrow hit, I know it!"

The elf applied his dark-vision and saw a dark shape dart from behind cover, disappearing into the distance. He did not pursue it.

Billit shuffled back along the ledge to where Falcon was hanging on for dear life by his arms and one leg and helped him back up onto the ledge. A weeping Taura was already shuffling along the ledge to give her help as best she could and, together, she and the gnome encouraged the barbarian to the far side.

"That sneaky bastard again!" growled Silmar. "I felt this sharp headache but thought I was tired. It must have been the dagger reacting to that evil piece of shit."

Falcon sat on the floor, shaking like a leaf, and Taura was hugging him tightly and showering him with kisses.

"Not happy in this place," he moaned. "Kill the Darkling and get us out of here!"

"I give Darkling sword lesson, hai?" replied Jiutarô, with a menacing face that none of them had seen before.

"I think we'll queue up to cut bits off 'im," snarled Billit. "Oh, a very brave bastard to attack from a place of ambush!" He had yelled the last comment.

"No point in trying to keep quiet," Silmar pondered. "He is more than likely fully aware of where we are. What worries me is that he may be watching us or laying in wait again. We must remain vigilant."

"Aye," agreed Jasper, "an' 'e is wounded, 'opefully, with Jiutarô's arrow. Hey, 'e might also be dyin' down 'ere."

They continued once again and fortunately, there were no other wide chasms and no further sign of the Darkling. They marched, albeit slowly, for an hour or so. The tunnel once again opened up into a mighty cavern and they agreed to risk using the light tubes to look about them.

"Ready?" whispered Jasper. "Three; two; one; lightson."

The light tubes were uncovered in unison. By habit, they crouched low or behind what scant cover was available, expecting at any moment the whoosh of an arrow.

Their light showed where ancient peoples had engraved a number of tall stone pillars to support the cavern roof. Some of them showed engravings of runes and symbols but these were not recognised by any of the comrades.

This vast hall showed no indication that it had recently been used. They carried out a quick search with some surprising results. Signs indicated that this area of the mines had been used as a city by the ancient civilisations. Apart from the pillars, there were arches, doorways and stairways leading upwards and down. There were also remnants of ancient battles with scattered bones and heavily-rusted remains of weapons and armour. There was nothing that could be salvaged and the group decided there was no reason to remain.

"We should rest," suggested Jasper. He was clearly fatigued. "Forgotten 'ow unused to campaigning I've become. I'm choddin' tired."

Silmar shrugged his shoulders. "I really don't think it would be a good idea rest here," he said. "It is too difficult to defend."

Silmar followed the path through the great hall and led the group through to the far end and back into the mine tunnel. The floor was very uneven now and sharp-edged rocks made progress difficult. This did not last for long however, and the path once again became easier to navigate. As before, there were a few caverns in the sides of the tunnel. The group halted to eat and sleep. A sentry schedule was set once again and the party settled down to sleep.

৯ ৶

Not very far ahead along the passage, the Darkling attended to his wound. That unusual warrior, the one with the strange shining sword and the extraordinary bow, had sent an arrow quicker than sight. It had unerringly found its target – entering the side of his stomach just above his hip but fortune decreed it hadn't seemed to puncture his intestines or any organs. *Ach, the pain though!* This warrior would be one to reckon with. This was twice now that he had received an injury while down in the Shadow World. He had twisted his knee in a poor landing from having leapt across a chasm with insufficient care. It was not supposed to be like this.

Although he was always confident in his ability to survive in hostile environments, he fully expected to feel invulnerable in the Shadow World. He was beginning to recognise the fact that he was vulnerable after all. He felt exhausted. Being alone meant that he could only semi-sleep for short periods. There were races down here that would be happy to tear apart the group that followed him limb by limb. Some of these races would also tear him apart too, given the opportunity. He probably had as many potential enemies down here as did the surface-rats. They might even have friends. But not him.

He would lead them towards the *City of Shade* and let *them* deal with the fools. He would be there to collect the artefact from the elf's dead body. Then the *Grullien* should be satisfied with any gold or precious stones they could get from the bodies.

The *Grullien!* These were the ancient race of *Shade Gnomes* who inhabited an area of the Shadow World that they guarded with a viciousness bordering on frenzy. The Darkling thought about what he knew of this malicious race. He knew that they would give him some aid but only if they could profit from it. They were still some distance away and would rarely venture far from their holes. Their shamans had some basic magical powers granted to them although they would be no match for a priest and a mage from the surface world. The Grullien were fierce and relentless warriors but they were armed just with basic weapons such as metal darts, no more than spear blades, and throwing nets; but they were still fearsome nonetheless. They had a deep hatred for the races of peoples who live on the surface. *Well, we have something in common there then*, he thought. They also had a fear and hatred of the sunlight, their skin and eyes being too sensitive to endure it. Their fanatical devotion to their Rock Mother Goddess, Grull, made them a target for derision among the races of the Shadow World. It was debatable whether Grull actually existed.

Let the Grullien have the fools, he considered. *Hah, they might even use, or sell, the surviving surface rats for slavery*. A faint smile briefly showed on his dark, bitter, face.

Once more his mind wandered off as he attended to his wound. This would undoubtedly slow him down for a while. There were Grey Dwarves down here too but it was rumoured that some were renegades who shunned the ways of the Dwarves of the Shadow World and their god, *Killik was it?* and embraced the more traditional surface-Dwarven pantheon. These renegades were outcasts, tattooed and treated as criminals by the Grey Dwarves and would almost certainly be killed if they were to return to the depths. He was in as much danger from them as from the Grey Dwarves.

There were renegade Darkling too, particularly to the east – they were generally nomadic surface-dwellers in The Wildings, the lawless lands in between the Dragon's Back peaks and Cascant far to the east. They also honoured the gods of the surface world and in turn found that they were able to bear the ravages of the sunshine.

My mind wanders; I must focus.

CHAPTER 19

THANKFULLY, their break passed without danger and they were all roused by Silmar. Once again, their long, slow trek resumed. They marched now for many hours without incident. The nature of the tunnel changed constantly; they climbed up long slopes which showed grooves made by wagons in millennia past. Old rock-falls were commonplace with heaps of boulders littering the tunnel floor. Everywhere they looked they could clearly see, or feel, the ancient marks of picks and shovels. They came to a very long flight of steps which climbed hundreds of feet upwards. Alongside it was a slope where the old wagons would have been winched up or down.

They moved as quietly as they were able and spoke rarely. Progress was interminably slow while they risked using their light tubes only occasionally.

Once again, a dim glow came from mould-growth on the tunnel walls and eventually, the damp mould provided sufficient light for them not to have to rely on their light tubes.

"How far have we marched?" Taura asked during one of their short breaks.

Jasper paused for a few moments while he rubbed at his hairy chin. "I reckon it's been three days now," he pondered quietly. "That'd be about six leagues. We need to be extra watchful from now, not just 'cos of the Darkling but we might run into other, er, undesirables."

"Like what?" queried Falcon.

"What I told yer about. Like Grey Dwarves, the choddin' bastards, or them Grullien Gnomes. Whatever, watch yer arses. If I remember aright, we're more than 'alfway through by now. Time to walk. Keep quiet now."

For a roughly-estimated half a day they trudged on. Jasper had the strangest feeling they were being watched at times, but then he knew there was much down here that was alive, and dead. He did mention it to his friends, however. Surprisingly, Silmar quietly admitted to having the same feelings. They kept silent and moved as noiselessly as they were able. No more traps had been set for them, as far as they were aware, and there were no dangerous encounters.

Their fortune was about to change though.

Food was starting to run low. Drinkable water would never be a problem down here; much of the water they discovered was not fit to drink but some of it was, provided it was flowing. Jasper had warned them there were very few food sources in the Shadow World. Fish was occasionally plentiful in some of the deep pools but not all were easy to catch or good to eat. There were many different kinds of beast in the tunnels and some of these, if they could be caught, would be a providential source of food. Their problem was that this source of food would have needed to be cooked and there was very little material available to light a fire with. Edible fungus was identified, some of which would have provided an accompaniment to other food but alone, it would not be very nourishing.

"Yer use up more energy lookin' fer it an' tryin' ter find a way of cookin' an' eatin' it than you would get from it," he advised. "It ain't worth the trouble unless yer starvin'. We got 'nuff food fer a day or two so don't fret 'bout it."

Taura thought she knew a prayer spell that would provide water but it probably wouldn't be needed here. Besides, they had nothing handy to collect it in.

Without warning, Silmar staggered to the wall of the tunnel, leaned against it and retched onto the ground. Some of them recognised the symptom immediately.

"It your burden, isn't it," whispered Taura.

"Aye, Taura, it is I am sure of it. Urghh! But it usually only happens when we are in the proximity of something evil. Oh, my head!"

Then they heard a piercing scream of terror.

☙ ❧

Silmar straightened up, all thoughts of his discomfort put to one side. He raised a hand and hissed a *shhh*.

The scream sounded again, this time accompanied by much shouting. It seemed to derive from a passage off to the left hand side, a narrow opening in the tunnel wall.

They froze in their tracks. Silmar motioned with his hand and they moved to stand in two groups; one each side of the tunnel entrance. They all slowly and quietly withdrew their weapons and listened for further clues as to what it may have been that made that terrible scream. Once again the scream came but this time it was muffled as if the person making the sound had been gagged.

"Sounds like a woman," whispered Silmar. "Let's go!"

Jasper stepped forward. "Aye," he agreed with a nod. "I'm not 'avin' none o' that, even if she's an elf woman!"

Taura glared at him but he merely winked back.

They cautiously eased forwards along the narrow tunnel. Jasper led with Silmar and Jiutarô close behind. Billit followed with Taura and Falcon a few paces behind but stopped as Silmar raised a hand and the other three moved onwards. It had not been easy for any of them because their way was partially blocked by various items of ancient mining detritus and some boulders that had accumulated there for a long time. A bright glow from ahead gave them sufficient light for them not to need their light tubes and to make dark-sight unnecessary.

The screams had now subsided into pitiful sobbing. Quietly, they eased forward. The leading trio cautiously made there way around a bend and about twenty yards in front of them was the entrance into a chamber that appeared to be brightly lit by flaming torches. Silmar again motioned to the others to keep back while he, Jasper and Jiutarô used what cover there was to get as close to the chamber as possible.

The noise was quite loud now. One voice seemed to rise above the rest but it was in a language that Silmar did not recognise. A single word seemed to be often repeated though – "Kalanisha! Kalanisha!"

The trio stood slightly back from the entry into the chamber and Silmar risked a cautious look inside. The sight that greeted him was grim. He signalled Jiutarô to look and the expression on the Samurai's face was pure anger.

A group of six men dressed in the black and scarlet robes of clerics, together with about a dozen worshippers of an unknown cult, were in a state of some sort of frantic trance; they swayed and held their hands above their head. There was no music which may have explained this rhythmic movement, but merely the chanting of "Kalanisha!

Kalanisha!" This was occasionally interrupted by shouts from a man who seemed to be a High Priest or shaman. The whole area was lit by flaming torches held in sconces on the cave walls. There was an overpowering stench, Silmar recognised it immediately – stale blood!

The High Priest stood next to a large stone altar. On this alter was bound a naked female human, she was conscious and struggling against the bonds that held her. A wad of grey cloth had been stuffed into her mouth. Her hair was jet black and very long. She was very pretty although blood ran from the side of her face.

Silmar and Jiutarô backed away from the cavern. "Get the others!" said the elf. Jiutarô quietly left.

"Kalanisha! Kalanisha!"

The others carefully made their way forwards to where Silmar and Jasper watched the cavern. They all moved to a position where they could take in the details of the scene. A crudely-drawn symbol of a skull with a dagger embedded in the top of it adorned a rock wall. The Altar was heavily stained with, Silmar assumed, blood. It appeared that it was either used for sacrifices or as a place for butchering animal carcasses.

"Kalanisha! Kalanisha!"

A large metal cage stood in a corner of the temple, inside was a beast of some kind. The High Priest and his attendants were grouped at one side of the altar. The leader removed his hood. His hair was caked in dry blood, so it appeared because it was matted and his hair was spiked to give him a grotesque appearance. His face was covered in swirling tattoos. The other priests were bald but their heads were similarly covered in the thick dark blood. The leader started a rhythmic chanting, interspersed with the word *Kalanisha* again.

234

Silmar's companions were now standing behind him. Jiutarô grunted "We go in?" His faces was grim.

Silmar replied "Ready?"

They all nodded.

The elf turned back to the scene before him just as the high priest removed his robe and stood naked by the feet of the female tied to the altar. In his hand was a large stone dagger. The terror on the woman's face was palpable. A part of the High Priest's anatomy made his first intentions quite obvious. An assistant passed a large iron chalice to him and he swallowed a mouthful of the dark liquid inside. It seemed to have an immediate effect. Passing it to one of the worshippers, he became almost manic, as did the worshippers as they drank, each of them going into a frenzied gyration. He was just about to climb up onto the altar when a yell came from the tunnel.

"Charge!" Silmar yelled. "Stop their madness!"

With yells and war-cries, the companions rushed together into the cavern. There was total surprise and the cultists were thrown into a state of confusion. Jiutarô tried to make his way to the High Priest but he lost his footing on a pool of the liquid from the chalice. Silmar also tried to get to the altar before the High Priest had a chance to slay his victim. The elf was too late; the naked priest plunged the stone dagger through her chest. She was most certainly dead.

Silmar became embroiled in a battle with the assistant priests and although he was far better armed, there were many of them. Jiutarô, having recovered his balance leapt around the altar and with a mighty two-handed swing of his katana, cut through the panic-stricken High Priest from right shoulder to left hip. The two parts of the body separated and fell to the floor. The Samurai cried out in pain from his previous shoulder injury and almost dropped his katana but he recovered and leapt to Silmar's aid. The elf was bleeding from a slash to his right thigh and was almost engulfed by the priests.

Meanwhile, the other members of the party were engaging the worshippers. Once again, these were poorly armed, having short blades and staves, mainly. With a short arcane word, Billit fired a flurry of magical fire darts with great effect; these were bright points of flame that crackled as they left his hand. Falcon's war-hammer felled two with a mighty stroke.

None of the cultists escaped. Billit blocked an exit from the cavern with a magical wall of energy but received a brutal blow from a priest's staff. This man's head was crushed with a blow from Jasper's battleaxe.

Eventually, every cultist was killed, not one escaped such was the fury of the companions' attack. The battle ended and silence fell. Taura rushed over to Billit but the gnome bade her see to Silmar first. The elf was now slumped onto the floor and there was quite a lot of his blood pooling beneath him. She immediately went to his aid. With Jiutarô pressing a wad of cloth from a cultist's cloak to the elf's wound, she began the sing-song chanting to enlist Neilea's divine aid in giving healing to the wound. It seemed to work because the bleeding slowed and then stopped.

"How did that happen?" she asked Silmar.

"I kicked the man in his tender place and the bastard stabbed me with his dagger. You should have seen what I did to him!"

"Well, you are fortunate because your injury looks worse than it is. You will be dancing with your young lady again in no time!"

"I hope so," he replied. His wound was still painful and he would probably have a limp for a few days.

Billit's injury was not serious and Taura liked to believe that another prayer to Neilea had helped the gnome's healing. The injury was small enough for the little mage to not be too encumbered by it.

As the last cultist had died, Silmar had felt the nausea and head pain start to dissipate. It did not fade away altogether though. Taura explained that it was probably the residual evil of the temple itself. The bodies of the fallen cultists were everywhere. Jiutarô used the discarded robe of the high priest to cover up the body of the victim. He removed the filthy wad of cloth that was still stuffed in her mouth. She hadn't been very old; probably no more than about sixteen years of age.

"Break it; destroy it," called Jiutarô, still showing the anger he had felt at first seeing this scene. He now held a large chunk of rock in his hand.

Both Falcon and Billit leapt to their feet and started to smash the wooden benches that were arranged in rows in front of the altar. Jiutarô placed his chunk of rock on the altar, carefully lifted the body of the young girl from it and laid her down on the ground next to the far passage. He then returned to the altar, picked up the rock and started to beat it down onto the surface. Falcon joined him and used his massive warhammer with more success. Within five minutes the altar slab was broken into pieces which were scattered about. The altar mount was hollow! Inside were ornate and plain weapons, gold and silver ornaments and candelabra, and a vast amount of coins.

"Look here," called Falcon. "Treasure!"

They were all on their feet now and came over to peer inside.

"A fortune!" gasped Jasper. "Some of these coins are old, look. These gold pieces haven't been in use for a century. These are from Cascant. There is a likeness of King Dar-Cascan the First."

Silmar was shocked. "Looks like these bastards were collecting and stashing away a fortune for years and years. Perhaps we can put much of this to some good. I'm going into that passage to see where it goes. Looks like some stairs there and, if I'm not mistaken, there is some mud and grass at the bottom. It may be a way back up!"

"We've still got a Darkling killer to find, don't forget," Taura reminded them.

"And finish off," added Billit. "We 'ad best form an orderly queue when we get to him! Let's destroy that symbol on the wall there. Anyone recognise it?"

Nobody did. Taura considered it was just a symbol used as an excuse for a killing spree, raping and sacrificing some poor victims and amassing a fortune. Falcon made short work of smashing the engraved symbol.

Jiutarô stepped over and around the bodies to make his way over to the cage. By it were some large barrels of oil or pitch. These were used to dip the burning torches so they would stay lit for some time.

Help?

Jiutarô spun around and held his hands up to his temples. He faced the cage.

It was made of iron and was partly covered in a sheet of canvas but he could distinctly hear movement from within. It wasn't a spoken word; it was almost as if it had been implanted in his mind.

Free? There once again, an unspoken thought in his head. He lifted up the canvas and stood back.

Inside the cage was a beast that resembled a miniature dragon and it looked Jiutarô straight in the eye. The Samurai was astounded. He staggered back a couple of paces, dropping the canvas over the cage. He shook his head as if to clear away the subliminal thoughts and cautiously moved back to the cage. He lifted the canvas once more.

A creature surely born of myth, known to him only in tales and theatrical performances in his own home country, his own world, had sprung into the reality of this new and strange land.

Free? Nuts? Drink?

Again, there were no audible words spoken but Jiutarô instinctively knew the beast had communicated with him. In fact, the messages seemed to be more like an idea or notion implanted into his consciousness rather than a word of any kind. Its light red-brown body was about the size of a medium dog but it had bat-like wings and a very long tail that had a large curved barb on the tip.

Silmar stepped across. "What is this? A fire-drake? If so, beware!" He leaned forward to get a better look at the creature. "Oh no!" he exclaimed. "A *Cleret-wing dragon!* If one gets to like you they can be a lot of trouble. Deadly in a fight though!"

"It attack?" the Samurai asked. "It talk me here!" He indicated his head.

Friend! Free?

"It talks to you? Then you are indeed privileged, friend Jiutarô! I have heard many tales that should one bond with an elf or a human then it will be a faithful companion and would be able to talk through the mind, you would see what it can see. Should be fine! Let it out but it may just fly like mad for the passage up there."

"Then it be free."

Jiutarô opened the cage door and the beast slowly came out. It sniffed Jiutarô's outstretched hand and leapt up onto the top of the cage.

Friend! Nuts?

"Friend!" answered Jiutarô. The claret-wing dragon climbed off the cage and onto his shoulder. There was a strangled cry from Taura who was standing by the altar.

Kill! Immediately, the cleret-wing dragon leapt off and flew across towards her.

"No!" called Silmar. "It's going for Taura!"

But Taura was struggling against another attacker. One of the priests that they assumed had been killed had risen up behind her and was trying to strangle her with a cord. His face was covered in blood and he had a malicious expression of hatred and pain on his face.

The cleret-wing dragon flew round behind the priest and there was a cracking sound as it whipped its tail and caught the priest on the side of the neck. He was dying before he hit the ground, his hands clawing at his neck as poison coursed through his veins.

Taura slumped to the ground next to the dying priest who choking and gasping for breath. Then he stopped. The cleret-wing dragon returned and lightly landed on Jiutarô's shoulder. Silmar went over to the body and inspected the neck-wound.

"The little beast has poisoned him with its tail. By the gods, the poison worked fast! I didn't think they were able to kill a humanoid that quickly."

Jasper looked at the dead priest. "The barb went straight through the priest's skin into his artery, pumping the venom into the brain! Ughh!"

"It's earned its keep already," said a smiling Billit.

Jiutarô reached for his pack and pulled out a canvas bag of nuts and dried fruit. He emptied a pile into his hand and offered it to the cleret-wing dragon. It was soon eaten, as were the next three handfuls. He took off his light helmet and poured some water from his water-skin into it. The cleret-wing dragon drank greedily until it was all gone.

"You have name?" asked the Samurai as he lifted his pack up onto his shoulders.

Name? echoed the cleret-wing dragon into Jiutarô's mind.

"You are Sushi! Friend!"

The little dragonlike creature responded to Jiutarô with subliminal word-like thoughts. *Sushi. Friend Sushi.* It glided to the floor, chattered and playfully skipped around his feet and then flew up and curled itself around his shoulders once again. The Samurai stroked its neck and Sushi purred like a cat. It was surprisingly light.

Jasper was deep in thought. "Lookit," he said. "We gotta get out o' here but we can't take all the gold an' stuff. We should bury it someplace safe. Just take what we can. An' we still gotta destroy this place so it can't be used again. An' we oughta get that dead girl back up to the surface. Mebbe she got family."

Together, they piled the wood from the broken benches by the altar. With time and effort they piled the dead bodies on top. Using a couple of blood-stained robes from the priests, they loaded all of the treasure into them. The hundreds of precious and semi-precious stones and about two hundred gold pieces they divided between them.

Falcon carried the dead body of the girl in his arms and Jasper emptied all of the barrels of oil over the pile of dead bodies. Silmar picked up one of the sacks of treasure and, with difficulty because of his new and recent injuries, started to climb the stairs. He counted more than sixty before he emerged exhausted into a cave. There was no door, just a pile of boulders to conceal the passage. He whistled and all of the others, except for Billit, came up to the top.

Jasper called down a signal to Billit and they all stepped back from the passage entrance. They heard the pattering feet of Billit running up the stairs and then there was a flash and a *whoomph* from down the stairway. They were all concerned and they called down to the gnome.

A moment later, his smiling face emerged through the smoke at the entrance. His sparse hair was smouldering and he was covered in bits of ash. Otherwise he seemed unharmed.

"That was a bit bigger than I expected," he gasped. "Must've been the barrels of oil. Can I have some water?"

The entrance to the stairway was many paces away from the entrance to the cave. They looked out but there was only the darkness of the night sky.

Falcon reverently placed the wrapped body of the girl on the ground. His left forearm continued to ache badly from his injury.

"I wonder where we are," said Taura.

"We been walking eastwards and a little south since we was in the mine tunnel," stated a confident Billit.

"More like east," corrected Jasper, just as confident.

"About four days?" asked Taura.

"Five and a half," replied Jasper and Billit together.

"Oh, aye! That is about right!" Taura answered with an air of confidence. Nobody was convinced.

"So I reckon that we are somewhere north-west of Gash then," suggested Silmar. "The foothills near the market town of Dalcutta Trading Post. A lawless place if there ever was one. Full of miners! And dwarves!"

Jasper was irritated by Silmar's barbed jibe. "Got a problem with that, have yer? Pointy-eared elves too high and mighty fer Dalcutta, are they?"

"Leave each other alone or I'll bang your heads together," growled Taura. The pair had been annoying and jibing each other on and off since they had first entered the Shadow World.

"You'll have to cut 'im off at the knees first," muttered the dwarf.

Silmar wisely ignored the barbed comment.

Now that their eyes were growing accustomed once again to the darkness, they could see some mountains and hills. To their right was a long valley which they could just discern when the clouds passed and the moon shone.

"Lights!" called Jiutarô. "Village? Far away." Sushi could sense the Samurai's anticipation of civilisation and stretched her head to improve her view.

Sure enough, they could see the tiny twinkling of lights in the distance and decided to make their way down at first light. They slept in the cave that night, some of them taking turns once again to guard their position.

∾ ∽

The next morning they awoke to a brightening dawn. After days in the Shadow World they were cheered to hear the birdsong and to see the oncoming daylight. Sushi had curled up next to Jiutarô and when she awoke she played around the Samurai's feet until he also awoke and petted her. She seemed to like a lot of that.

"What I do with Sushi?" Jiutarô asked Silmar. He still struggled to find the right words; intensive coaching in the Universal tongue by Billit was paying off but the Samurai followed conversation between the companions with great effort.

"You have taken a lot of responsibility there," explained the elf slowly.

The Samurai frowned. "Not know talk," he replied.

"These are hard work to look after," Silmar explained slowly. "Let me tell you about them." He proceeded to tell the Samurai all he knew about claret-wing-dragon. There was much to know.

These miniature reddish-brown dragons were playful and benign. They were said to have simple magical powers. If it chose a humaoid companion, as was the case with *Sushi* and Jiutarô, the cleret-wing dragon could communicate thoughts by telepathy, transmitting an image of what it saw and heard short distances. It could blend in with its surroundings by using a chameleon-like ability and had dark-sight which enabled it to see quite long distances.

The cleret-wing dragon liked to be perched on top of its human companion's head or curled around the shoulders and upper back. It liked to be well fed and would eat almost anything. It would love to be pampered and groomed and to receive lots of attention and, in this, it would be very demanding. If it was made to feel very important, then it would perform well for its companion. It would not tolerate mistreatment, neglect or cruelty by its companion nor would it tolerate a human who would rather be a master to it than a companion. In combat, it could deliver a vicious bite with its small dragon-like jaws and would rake its claws to tear the clothing or flesh of its adversary. But its main weapon was its barbed tail which carried a powerful poison. It could whip its tail with astonishing speed which could render the victim unconscious for many days. It could, if angry, inject sufficient poison to cause the victim to die slowly or even immediately, although it was not in the nature of claret-wing dragons to inflict this except in times of need. In addition to its telepathic communication, it could vocalise animal noises such as a rasping purr for pleasure, a feline hiss for an unpleasant surprise, a birdlike chirp for desire or a canine growl to show anger.

"So you will have a good friend but never an obedient pet. You must care for it and it will also care for you. It will be a friend to us all in time."

Although he had some difficulty in understanding everything that Silmar told him, Jiutarô made sure that the elf repeated or rephrased anything he had trouble with. He felt content that he had found a creature such as this. In his home country, Nippon, there were myths and old stories regarding dragons of all sorts; some of them bad and troublesome and others that were wise and benevolent. Now one had adopted him as a friend and he felt a sense of honour in having been selected.

Jasper paced over to Billit and asked him why there had been such a huge explosion in the temple below.

"Ah, well, er. Aye, it's like this. There was oil everywhere and I thought it might not catch properly if I tossed a torch on it so I went up a few steps and blasted off a small *fire-blast* spell. Well, you see, it's only a small temple and even a fire-blast is quite big and it blasted me upwards about ten steps and burnt my backside. Have ya seen what it's done to me 'air? Look!" His curly red hair was noticeably singed shorter in some places but his skin did not appear damaged.

It took about ten minutes before the group could stop laughing! They were still chuckling as they started their march down towards the village. Even Sushi was chirruping with happiness; it was as if she understood. Alone, Falcon remained sombre. He carried the body of the young girl, struggling at times over the uneven ground. It took over two hours for them to reach the village and its gates were still closed when they got there. Taura used her staff to bang on the gates. Eventually one was opened by a worried-looking villager. He looked even more concerned when he saw the heavily-armed strangers standing there.

"What's your business here this early in the morning?"

"I am named Lord Silmar the Golden, son of Faramar Galadhal and Prince of the town and district of Refuge, on the edge of the Highforest by the eastern foothills of the Spine Wall Mountains in the Home Territories. I have come by perilous ways from the Landsdrop Coast with my companions to speak with a village leader here. It is a matter of immense importance. We are peaceful and bring no trouble but we have left trouble behind us. Bring a village leader swiftly. We have much to speak of that is urgent and our time is pressing."

The companions looked open-mouthed at each other as the elf introduced himself. There would be much for them to speak of later.

A tall middle-aged man with long, greying hair and an eye-patch on his right eye arrived at the gate and Silmar repeated his introduction. The man introduced himself as Finnucchi, the leader of the village.

"Finn?" cried Jasper from the back of the group. "Is that you, you old bushwhacker?"

"Jasper! It cannot be, after all these years. You old rascal! Come here so I can see you!"

They clasped wrists and it was clear they were old friends from long ago.

"We campaigned together fer many years, *Lord* Silmar," explained Jasper. "We was with yer dad in the Shadow World, were we not Finn?"

"Silmar, son of my old friend Faramar Galadhal once of Faerhome?" The man clasped the young elf's hand and cried "Well met. Welcome to Dalcutta. You have your father's features but your hair is darker!"

"That is because I had to colour it. We hunt a Darkling that is hunting us, or me really! I darkened my hair to change my features but it has not seemed to work. He knows we hunt him. He kills time and time again to lure me in."

"Now we hunt him in the Shadow World," continued Taura.

Finn shuddered. "Never again! That's where I lost my eye and it was the end of my campaigning. That's how I ended up here after Faramar and Jasper got me out of that place and left me here. I recovered and have a family and a small farm and I am now the village leader. Come with me to the village meeting hall. So, Faramar's son, eh? Lord Silmar the Golden you are called? A grand soubriquet indeed. We shall prepare a meal and somewhere for you to sleep a proper nights rest. You all look like you need it. The village shall look after you tonight."

"I saw very little farm-land here," said Silmar. "What is it you do for trade in the village?"

Finn lifted the bottom of his eye patch and scratched beneath it. "Ah, we trade in lamp-oil and pitch. We have a well not far from here that was made for us by the Chthonic gnomes."

At this, Billit's head spun round and he gave his full attention to Finn's account.

"We pump the well and bring up oil. It is thick and black when it comes up but we have a process which allows us to filter and refine it and make a lamp oil that we sell to towns and villages in the Home Territories and Lopastor. We have stores within the walls but they are kept away from the houses in case of fire – these wouldn't just burn, they would explode in a huge ball of flame! We buy flasks from Icedge and we fill these with the oil. Tell me, what is it your big friend carries?"

Jasper explained about the cultists and the death of a captive. He spoke of how the cultists were all destroyed along with their evil temple.

"The Kalanisha cult?" asked an astonished Finn. "You've killed them all? But we have wanted to do that for years. We have never found out where they hide to do their evil deeds. That is good! But let me see the body."

He stepped over to Falcon and lifted the robe to see the girl's face.

His face paled as he looked at the body. "Oh, no! By the gods!" he exclaimed. "It's Junkett's daughter. She didn't return home from the farm two nights past. We hoped she would be with friends but she must have been taken as she was on her way back. We instigated a search yesterday but found nothing. The village folk are out again shortly. I shall have to be off to inform her family. She was to be wed soon." He shook his head and strode off into the village.

The gateman led the group to the meeting hall and they sat around a large table. The body of the girl was reverently laid on one end of the table and Taura carefully adjusted the robe. A while later, Finn arrived closely followed by a tall, lean man and stout woman. The woman held a pinafore to her face and the man wrung his hands; the couple were in tears. They went to the body and the man tentatively lifted the end of the robe.

"It's her, our Kattia," the man whispered. Louder he demanded "Who did this?"

"The cultists," answered Finn.

"Kalanisha! Those blood-soaked, murdering bastards!"

"Goodman Junkett, they have all been destroyed by this group of adventurers," stated Finn as he placed a hand on the farmer's shoulder.

"Every one? Then may the gods bless you, visitors. Anything in my house is yours." He placed his arm around the shoulder of his sobbing wife. "We shall take our daughter and prepare her for her final journey. I would be grateful if your lady priestess would give my wife some words of comfort." He carefully picked up the body of their daughter and made his way out of the hall followed by his wailing wife.

The group sat quietly for a a few moments while Finn busied himself with a sheaf of parchments.

"Finn, what can you tell us about this cult?" Taura asked.

He sighed and shook his head. "There is little known of them but what we do know is of a brutal and violent gang of cutthroats. Many of the villages, farms and even towns in this area have lost men, women and children to this Kalanisha. Wagon trains have been raided in the night and many people slain. Survivors talk of a black-skinned giant who leads a group they call the *Blade Riders*. It is said that they are mainly deserters from the militia or escaped convicts. The giant is a cruel man to his victims and even cruel to his men. There is no law in the region like you have on the Landsdrop Coast. We make are own laws here and generally there is peace in Shordrun but not here in the west of the country. But perhaps now there will be at last and we have you to thank for it my friends. How many did you kill? Was one of them a huge man with black skin?"

"We slew 'bout fifteen priests and followers but not the man you describe," replied Jasper.

Finn smiled. "Well, perhaps this thing is ended. It is doubtful whether there actually is a deity by the name of Kalanisha. Just ask and anything will be yours."

"We need little," explained Silmar. "But there is a cave up in the hills up the valley. Outside it you will find two trees. In between them is buried a stash of treasure. Use it for this village to grow and expand. Strengthen your laws and defences. We have kept a little of it for ourselves but the vast majority of it is still there. The cave is an entrance to the Shadow World. We have to go back in there but after we do, it may be a good idea to seal up the passage and perhaps the cave too."

Finn agreed to do this. The group decided that they would have a day's rest and continue with their journey at first light next morning. Jiutarô's new companion encouraged much attention with the children of the village. Sushi rather enjoyed the petting and delighted them by flying over their heads and making noises. Some of the mothers were not quite so keen though. It did look ferocious with those rows of small sharp teeth and that tail looked positively dangerous.

Later that afternoon, while Jiutarô was standing by the village gates, Sushi took herself off for a flight. She came back after a long while and, although exhausted from her flight, she chattered excitedly to Jiutarô. He fed her some strips of raw goat and she settled happily around his shoulders. Within two minutes she was fast asleep and purring gently. Jiutarô was now very concerned, but not for Sushi.

CHAPTER 20

"Well, speak!" demanded the warrior curtly. "Where is he?"

The man was black-skinned, very tall, heavily built and mounted on a great black warhorse. He had a long, bushy, matted, black beard that hung down to the bottom of his chest. His black hair was also long and filthy. He was constantly scratching at his scalp and his grimy fingertips would occasionally come away with smears of blood on them. He was dressed in black furs and leather. He wore heavy riding boots that were much dilapidated. He carried only one weapon, a great pick. The handle of it was more than three feet in length and at one end was a large curved and pointed, black, steel horn sticking out at right angles and a full foot in length. Black feathers and strips of brown hide adorned the handle. It was said by the other warriors that the pieces of hide were taken off the bodies of those slain by the pick's owner.

"He issa dead anda de temple destroyed is, my Lord Saddiq. Alla his faithful issa destroyed him with." The mounted speaker was dressed in a dark red robe, similar to those worn by the clerics in the temple. He had a bald, tattooed head and was armed with a chipped and rusted shortsword.

The warrior dismounted and slapped his horse on the rump to encourage it to move aside. "The treasure?" he boomed. "Where is the fracking treasure?"

"Issa taken, my lord."

"Taken!" he roared. "I give your puny sect our protection! We even find you hostages to sacrifice, or eat, or whatever it is you do. I trust you with the care of my treasure. You live well from me!" The black horseman strode up and down, waving his arms in frustration. To his lieutenant at his side, he said, quietly "Kill him!"

The lieutenant signalled to a mounted archer and an arrow streaked into the cleric's chest. The cleric fell from his horse onto the ground stone dead.

The other priests, all on foot, were now shuffling very nervously. The black leader pointed to one who began to quiver uncontrollably. "Who did this and where did they go?"

"My Lord! It-it is n-not known who did this b-b-but their tracks go to the vil – er – village of Dal – Dalcutta by the eastern end of the White Peaks.

"I know where Dalcutta is, idiot." He nodded to his lieutenant. Another arrow found its mark and another cleric lay dead.

He pointed to a third priest. A spreading wet stain showed on the front of this one's robe.

"How many were there?"

"Six, my lord."

"You live, for now! My Blade-Riders! Come! We ride to Dalcutta now! You so-called clerics shall ride with me and use your puny god to give me a victory this night! Death shall betide you all if your god or any one of you should fail me!"

The large band rode northwards, their huge leader to the forefront. They would get there just before dark. The spared priest wept with relief. His companions kept their distance from him; he was a man marked for death.

The robed men knew they had a problem; they were not priests. Well, some of them had been, once upon a time. But now they were followers of a cult that enjoyed the thrill of a sacrifice, the orgy that preceded it if there were women, or girls, or whatever took their fancy. They had no divine spells available to them. The few cult followers that were with them were ex-fighters of sorts who kept watch over the treasure. Many of them were once Saddiq's men but were now advanced in years or disabled through having taken part in one battle too many.

The band of fighters and priests did not know they were being watched.

♋ ♋

Jiutarô rejoined his friends in the meeting hall. Most of them were dozing on straw mattresses. Billit was learning spells from a small bound book he carried in his pack. Taura was conversing quietly to her god; her hand tightly clutched her holy symbol, a polished wooden pendant with the design of a pair of spinning coins.

Silmar woke up as Jiutarô approached and he asked the Samurai if all was well. The Samurai replied that he was worried, Sushi had flown back towards the cave and returned with important news.

"Red priests, horses go cave." Jiutarô still struggled to find the right words. "Sushi see. Many priests. Um –"He

253

held up his hands with his fingers outstretched and then did it again. "Hey Silmar, that many, hai? How many?"

The elf smiled. "Hai, Jiutarô. That is twenty."

"Hai, twenty; I remember." Jiutarô smiled triumphantly. "Priests little swords; go big lake." He paused while searching for the words. "Big village, many men wait. Sushi say twenty, twenty, twenty. All come here. Leader black skin, big black face hair!" He used his hand to indicate a long beard.

"Ye gods! Darkling? With a beard? Nay, not a Darkling."

Jiutarô shook his head. "No Darkling; big black man, big black hair!" He indicated the head and beard again.

Silmar leapt from his blankets and reached for his weapons. "Tell Sushi that she is wonderful! Wake the others. We must alert the village. Sixty you say? Ye gods!" cried the elf.

The companions were all on their feet within heartbeats and Silmar rushed out of the door, closely followed by Jasper.

They discovered Finnucchi standing with a small group of men and women by a well in the village centre. The man saw their haste and walked over to meet them.

"You have need of speed?" the village leader asked. "There is concern in your eyes! What is it?"

"Ho Finn, there ya are," called Jasper. "We may 'ave ended one problem but started another!" replied Jasper. "Tell, 'im, Silmar!"

"Jiutarô's cleret-wing dragon flew off towards the cave, saw a group of red-robed priests and followed them to a large river or lake at the foot of the mountains. There was a band of fighters not far from a large village. The gang was led by a huge black man. They are coming this way, about sixty of them!"

Finnucchi looked horrified. "Oh, my gods! We cannot manage this alone! What are we to do? It is too late to get help. Will you aid us? They will be here by dusk."

Jasper took over. "Right! We 'ave two hours an' maybe, if they're riding 'ard, they'll be tired when they arrive so we must allow 'em no chance of rest. Get everyone 'ere who can fight, with all o' the weapons they own, but 'ide the women and children who cannot fight. You got just ten minutes. Go!"

The remainder of the companions waited in the village centre. They were fully armed and looked ready for battle. Between them they had carried all of Silmar's and Jiutarô's weapons while the pair had sped out to locate Finnucchi. They looked round the village perimeter.

"This wall is too weak," observed Falcon. "And the gates are thin. Difficult to defend against a small army." The huge barbarian shook his head in despair.

"But this is just a village," countered Taura. "They don't usually have to defend themselves against anything more than raiding goblins or kobolds."

The wall completely encircled the village, fortunately, and was constructed from thick wooden planks that were arranged upright on a sturdy framework. It was probably fifteen feet high with a rampart all the way round along which a guard, or number of guards, could walk. Although quite strong, a few good kicks from a horse might dislodge some of the planks. The gates, when opened, gave access just wide enough for a large wagon. They were very strong and were barred on the inside with two stout planks.

Villagers started to arrive in ones and twos at first but then in groups. Most of them were men, of all ages from sixteen to sixty. Remarkably, there were also a number of women including two tall, quite young ladies who carried bows and many arrows. They looked identical. Finn saw the quizzical expression on Silmar's face.

"These are the two Caspan sisters," Finnucchi explaines. "They are twins and the best archers in the Dalcutta region. No-one has bested them with a bow for five years. They practice every day! Just look at their broad shoulders! We have four other archers in the village too; they are arriving now."

"We shall have need of all of them this evening, Finn," said Silmar with a broad grin. "With myself and Jiutarô, and the twins, perhaps we shall be able pick a few of the raiders off at the start."

Jasper took Finn's arm and quietly led him aside. They spoke together for a few minutes and then Jasper returned to the others while Finn, in turn, spoke to a handful of villagers.

"What was all that about," asked Taura. "Secrets, Jasper?"

"Nah, not secrets, just a little plan I've thought up. I'll tell you all 'bout it soon!"

Jasper and Silmar spoke with the villagers of their plans for the defences of the village. Very few villagers had been in the militia or used weapons in anger. Apart from Finnucchi, only one other man had been an adventurer. He was a middle-aged muscular man who carried a broadsword and a round shield. He was taking a few practice swings with his sword and seemed quite competent and confident.

It was agreed that the archers would be arranged three each side of the gates but were to keep their heads below the top of the rampart when the *Blade Riders* arrived. If the village was to show that it had archers, the enemy may decide to stay out of range. Billit and Taura would also join the archers. The villagers armed with swords, axes and other cutting or crushing weapons, would wait in two or three groups in the village. All together, there were fifty villagers, almost all of them men-folk, who were armed and ready to fight. Finnucchi spoke to them all and encouraged them to fight to defend their families, their homes, their livelihoods and the village. The villagers responded with a rousing cheer.

Meanwhile, Taura arrived with about thirty women, the majority of whom were as determined as their men-folk to defend the village with their lives. Each of them carried a large wooden box and a cooking pot of burning coals taken from their own homes. These women were stationed around the village walls.

"What's all that about then?" asked Billit.

Jasper chuckled. "They got oil grenades! Yer gonna get a, er, demon-stra-tion in a little while. Wait and see!" He was very pleased with himself that he had been able to use a big word like that! Well, he would have admitted Finn had helped with it if anyone would have asked!

Finn introduced his wife Linette to the companions. She was a large, busty, pleasant lady with a permanent smile. "Show them, my sweet!" he stated, "the grenades that is, not your charms!"

A call went out to the villagers and they gathered to watch. From her box she took a bottle of liquid. Around the neck was tied a piece of cloth. She removed the cork and sloshed some of the liquid out of the bottle. Dipping the cloth into her pot of coals, she lit it then launched the bottle hard towards a rock. The bottle smashed and with a *whoomph!* there was an eruption of fire which totally engulfed the rock. The blast of heat was felt by almost everyone in the village. Any person caught in it would have been incinerated. A loud cheer went up.

The sun was now starting to dip behind the hills to the west and Finn told the villagers to make ready. Within a few minutes the village was quiet. Just the barking of a couple of dogs and the calling of crows broke the silence.

Finn ordered the gates to be closed and barred.

The village waited.

☙ ❧

"Who are you and what is your business?" Finnucchi used the officious tone that the gateman had used when the companions had first arrived at the village that morning.

"You don't know who I am?" came the reply in a deep, booming tone. Coarse laughter came from his riders. "You soon will. I am the Lord Saddiq." The speaker indicated himself with a grand flourish. He then indicated behind him. "These are my Blade Riders. We are hungry and thirsty. You will open the gates and let me and my men in so we can feast, rest and enjoy ourselves."

"I cannot do that. It is late. We do not have enough food, ale or room for you all in my village."

"I know for a fact that you are a wealthy village; my men have told me this. Your Cleric of Diette, one Orban Hilger, came to me and was one of my own trusted priests, that is until he fell off his horse today. He said how your villagers wanted for nothing."

"We had a hard winter," responded Finn. "Now we live frugally."

"I tire of these games. I wish to speak with your leader." The voice was uncouth and adamant.

"I represent the leader," Finnucchi replied. "You may converse with me."

"Very well then, I shall get to the point. You have something of mine."

Finnucchi laughed. "And what is that? Have you lost something?"

"Don't play games with me! I already told you that. You know what I seek."

Finnucchi grinned and pointed to Silmar who was standing beside Finn.

"Trinkets? Copper coins?" Silmar called. "I have seen them but they are not here, they were not worth taking so we left them underneath the bodies to burn."

"Ah! So, it was you and your villagers who destroyed that temple," roared Saddiq. "I care not a whit for those that died in it. But you lie, there was a treasure. I left it there for safekeeping. So, it is mine by right, you see? You have it. Let me in right now or I shall shatter the gates, burn your homes, take your women and girls for my own amusement and later for the amusement of my men, and slaughter everyone else here."

A small cheer came from his riders but a glare from Saddiq silenced them.

This time Jasper responded. "There was no treasure in that tunnel, just trinkets an' copper, an' very fat priests with expensive gowns, perfumes and silk clothes. Speak to those who kept it for you."

Saddiq considered those words for a moment, then spun his horse away and, with his lieutenants, rode over to the priests.

Silmar was impressed. "Good words, Jasper. He will be furious! I think some heads will hit the ground. That was a neat little line!"

The exchange between Saddiq and the priests couldn't be heard at the village walls but soon, they heard some shouting and screaming and those on the ramparts reported a commotion and a flurry of whirling swords.

Saddiq returned with three lieutenants each bearing two blood-soaked shaven heads. Six more priests had lost their lives.

"Now I *know* you lie, the priests would have confessed to me in their terror and fear of me. You *do* have the treasure and I have come to get it back. You have to the count of one hundred to open the gates and let me in."

His men were milling around on their horses, taunting and shouting obscenities at Finnucchi, and they were very close to the village gates.

Finnucchi turned slightly and called "Now!"

All of the eight archers leapt to their feet from behind the ramparts and began pouring arrows into the throng of warriors below. The blade riders were caught by surprise in the trap. Not one arrow hit Saddiq but twelve of his men went down in the first few seconds. Only two of them were still moving. A few crossbow bolts were returned but only one came close to finding its target; it glanced off Finnucchi's helmet and into a thatched roof beyond. By the time the horsemen had ridden out of range, they had lost another eight, two of whom limped away with arrow wounds while two more screamed in agony in addition to the first two on the ground. A loud cheer erupted from the village at the sight of Saddiq having lost a quarter of his men. Of the remaining red-robed priests, there was no sign. They were either hiding or had made good their escape from the tyrant while he was under attack from the archers.

Saddiq threw his head back, roared in anger and strode towards the village followed a few paces behind, by his remaining thirty or forty men. They were all on foot now and held their shields in front of them. At his command, they rushed towards the gate.

Finn gave another command. "Now!"

Twenty women, stooping low on the ramparts, simultaneously rose to their feet and hurled their bottles of oil towards the fighters below. Every bottle had a burning rag tied to it and all were uncorked to enable them to smash. Most of the bottles shattered on the road below and flames engulfed many of the men. Even those that did not smash had the oil pouring from them so they soon burst into flame anyway and could not be thrown back. Screams of anguish sounded and a few burning bodies staggered about soon to collapse on the ground. The archers found a few easy targets and after a couple of minutes only Saddiq and about twelve of his men were left to fight. His clothing was smouldering and smoke streamed from his mass of hair and his beard. He frantically brushed at the smouldering hair and roared with anger.

He knew he had allowed himself to become complacent with the result that the attack on the village went disastrously badly for him. He now did not have the strength of force necessary to retrieve his treasure. They were backing off again out of range using whatever cover they could, even each other, and didn't stop until they were almost two hundred yards away. Meanwhile, at least eight wounded men were scattered in front of the village walls screaming in agony.

"I shall return for my treasure!" he roared. "Send me your best fighter for a duel. I shall show you what a real warrior can do. If he bests me, my Blade Riders will leave, for now! If I win, I take your women and girls for my pleasure and the village is mine. You see, I am a fair man." He stood there with his hands on his hips with an expression of arrogance and confidence and then strode out of bowshot.

Silmar called Jiutarô and asked him "Can you kill him with an arrow from here? It is a long way, probably three hundred paces, and it is getting very dark."

Jiutarô nodded slowly. "Hai! I try. But I go down fight him! He slow; eyes show moves early."

"Now is not the time for his games. You cannot trust him and he may hold you hostage to exchange you for the treasure. He's not so stupid really. He knows he can't now beat us by force. It is time to finish this."

Jiutarô shrugged but studied each arrow in turn before selecting the right one; he looked along the shaft and at its fletchings. He then fitted it to his bowstring. Both of the female twin archers agreed that the shot could not possibly hit the target at this distance.

The Samurai smiled at them, dropped a little dust from his fingers to measure the breeze and lifted his bow. "From here? Pah! Easy! Watch!"

He used the traditional Samurai method of bringing the arrow back past his right ear and sighting along it. Adjusting for the distance, air movement and the difference in height between himself on the ramparts and his target, he loosed the arrow. It flew too fast for it to be seen in the evening gloom.

Nothing happened for about five heartbeats. The remaining light was just sufficient for the defenders on the ramparts to see Saddiq fall backwards. The gates of the village were flung open and the armed defenders yelled and shrieked as they charged towards the few remaining *Blade Riders*. It was a long way and by the time the villagers reached the point at which they hoped to do battle, the riders had mounted their horses and ridden off hard.

Saddiq lay dead with an arrow through his left eye. Jiutarô later insisted he had been aiming at his right eye! The Samurai was a hero! The two young lady archers certainly thought so; they showed their appreciation for some hours that evening. Sushi enjoyed the affection of all three of them but later, she flew off and didn't return until soon after dawn. Jiutarô had been awake for a couple of hours fretting for the claret-wing dragon.

The news from Sushi was that the remaining riders had ridden eastwards. They wouldn't be coming back, that was certain. Sushi spent the day playing with the children of the village. She learned to use her tail to hit a ball to the children. It was just as well she was occupied because Jiutarô was very busy with his two new friends. All day! He did check on her from time to time though – she *was* very important to him!

The companions decided to spend the rest of the day in the village resting. They would return to the Shadow World, with some of the villagers, that evening.

ᤥ ᤣ

CHAPTER 21

THEY RE-ENTERED the mines through the destroyed Temple of Kalanisha. Billit's *fire-blast* had virtually rendered the bodies of the so-called priests and their followers to ashes. The walls were blackened and all signs of what the chamber had once been were obliterated. Even Billit was surprised at the way in which the destruction had been so total. Silmar looked over at Taura but, apart from a small smile, her face was expressionless. The elf shook his head and decided to say nothing.

The villagers had assured them that would do as much as they could to destroy the entrance to the cavern and, if they could, would attempt to seal the cave as well. Many of the villagers had escorted the companions and Sushi had flown over to ensure that the area and the cave were deserted. A wagon and horses had been brought along to take the treasure back to the village and two men set about digging it up while others looked on. The shock on their faces and the stunned silence that came with it as they removed the bloodstained robes from the precious items was a sight that the companions would remember and talk about for years after. There were no long goodbyes, except for Jiutarô and his two young ladies. The village would prosper and grow; that was a certainty.

The companions were back in the dreaded tunnels, well rested and fed but still not feeling as if they were sufficiently prepared for what might come. The sound of rocks and boulders being pushed into the stairway from above was very loud in the tunnels. There was no going back.

"That's the way of it down 'ere," said Jasper. "You'll never feel that yer ready fer this shit-'ole!"

There was no natural glow from fungus down here at this time. They used their light-tubes to show them the way now. Sushi was not settled in the Shadow World and she gripped Jiutarô's shoulder with her talons until he was sore. After a couple of hours, she did relax a little but her little body and tail was tightly wrapped around his neck and shoulders. The floor was now flat but quite dusty and some tracks were visible in the beams from the light tubes. Many of them seemed to be of small rodents but from time to time, they noticed larger footprints.

"Stop!" whispered Silmar from the front. He went down onto his haunches and studied the ground in front of him. "Look at this," he murmured. His fingers pointed to a footprint, or rather a boot-print.

"This looks fresh, the edges are sharp an' it's smaller than human," responded Jasper. "It's that choddin' Darkling, bet yer life on that!"

"That is why we here," growled Falcon. He rarely spoke. "We here to kill the bastard Darkling!"

"Kill him? You take 'is head off and I'll shit down his neck!" grunted Billit.

Taura gave a mock expression of horror. The depth of loathing by the group had not receded even though they had had no contact with the Darkling for a couple of days or more. None of them had forgotten the victims that they had encountered on their way from Westron Seaport to Northwald City and beyond and then on to the entrance to the Shadow World.

"We make careful," said Jiutarô. "Maybe he, ah, waiting. Sushi say to me if smell him. Aii, she got good ears, hear, um, mouse make fart at fifty steps!"

They all laughed so much that Jasper had to get them to quieten down.

"Yer still all a bunch o' childish fools," he mumbled. "Prob'ly a good thing Sushi's with us though! Let's be off again."

Taura remained very close to Falcon while in the Shadow World even though their own fear of being down in the mines was not as great as it had been. They stopped to rest, eat and drink after some hours. Once again, they decided to try and move in the dark so that their skills at doing this wouldn't be lost. Billit's silken cord, as before, was loosely tied between Jiutarô, Taura and Falcon. They came upon small areas of a dull glow from the fungus, but only occasionally. They set off once again and, although the pace was slower, they felt a little safer.

At one point, Sushi gave a hiss and the group stopped. Her claws dug into Jiutarô's shoulder and he imagined the word *beast* in his mind. He whispered this to his companions. In the darkness, their other senses sharpened, particularly their hearing. Only Billit could hear a faint and fast snuffling sound. Soon, it was accompanied by a skittering sound of little footsteps.

"Lightson!" said Silmar. "Three; two; one; on!" The beams were uncovered and their brightness momentarily blinded them all. There was a squeak and a creature resembling a large rat bounded off into the darkness.

"What was that?" asked Taura, a hint of panic in her voice.

"Dunno! A sort o' rodent I think," replied Jasper. "I only seen it as it buggered off down the tunnel! Keep going, it won't get ya! If it does, it won't eat much of ya! Heeheehee!"

He continued to snigger as his own joke for the next few minutes. The light-tubes were covered up and, after a short while they were on their way again. They would hear the sounds of snuffling and skittering many times during their walk along the tunnel. After a while they began to ignore them.

The Shadow World did not seem to vary much in width and height along this section. It was ten to twelve feet in width and six to ten feet in height and quite straight, as far as they could tell. It caused more of a problem for Falcon who had to march with his hand in front of his head. There were few obstacles and no crevasses across the path but the marks of picks and other tooling was evident along its entire length. It was as if the way had been kept clear through regular use. Every time they uncovered the light-tubes they could clearly see the tracks of a pair of boots, small in size, in the dust and fine rubble.

Occasional caverns were seen on each side of the tunnel and they investigated many of these. Only rarely were there signs of them having been mined but that would have happened long ago. They saw rusted mining tools, wheeled trolleys, tatters of clothing and perished leather belts and pouches. No weapons of any sort were seen and no coins or items of value. Jasper recommended that they should rest, eat and sleep in one of the caverns. They set up a sentry roster.

Fortunately, there was no disturbance of any sort during their rest period. The following 'day' they continued along the tunnel, in total darkness mostly. The mine was getting wider now; about twenty feet across in some places with concave pillars supporting the roof and the sometimes disturbing knowledge that there was a massive amount of rock above them.

At one stop, Sushi gave a loud hiss which made them all stop instantly. They trusted her instincts completely. Jiutarô once again felt a word in his mind; this time it was *people*! He whispered this to his friends.

They all moved across to either side of the tunnel and crouched down. They could hear voices coming towards them – they were the voices of dwarves! They could hear their own heartbeats thudding inside their chests.

Jasper whispered "Grey Dwarves! Lots! Be silent! Get lights ready!"

Probably only Silmar, Jasper and Billit had any idea of what, or who, the Grey Dwarves were. They were known to inhabit the deep tunnels and mines of the lands but not necessarily just the Shadow World itself. They did, however, send the occasional hunting or reconnaissance party along the tunnels of the Shadow World and were known to be ferocious killers who would slaughter the unwary traveller in the subterranean tunnels without mercy.

Jasper, Silmar and Billit were understandably nervous; they knew that if it came to a fight, it would be hard and bitter and they would very likely sustain casualties. It would all depend on just how many Grey Dwarves there were. At this time, none of them could tell.

The voices were getting closer and the sound of their heavy boots was now much louder on the dusty, rocky floor.

Fifteen? thought Jasper. *Twenty? About that.*

The tunnel just ahead of them had a slight bend which would be of an advantage to the waiting companions. They were barely breathing now. Jiutarô could feel Sushi's claws digging into his shoulder and the pain made him wince; he did not cry out though.

Taura felt a dusty irritation well up in her throat. It was all she could do to resist the need to cough.

The footsteps and voices were now coming round the curve and would soon be only paces from them.

"*Lightson!*" murmured Jasper.

At that moment, three light tubes were uncovered and all the hells of the Void broke loose. The Grey Dwarves, who had all been using their dark-vision, were caught in the startling glare of the light tubes. All were blinded and were grasping and fumbling for their weapons. The companions however, were already armed, prepared and, apart from a momentary blindness, could see everything clearly. The dwarves had two prisoners; these were Chthonic gnomes. Each was securely and painstakingly tied, hand and foot, to a pole that was being carried by a pair of Grey Dwarves, one at each end. The blinded dwarves dropped the poles and the gasping grunts that followed indicated that the gnomes were still alive.

Jiutarô, without Sushi on his shoulder, charged forward with his sword held high. With him were Jasper, Falcon and Silmar. They all waded into the group of Grey Dwarves with blades and weapons whirling.

The Samurai caught two Grey Dwarves with one sweep of his katana and both fell heavily to the floor. The mighty barbarian crushed the head, complete with its helmet, of another which also crashed to the ground. Silmar kicked one in the stomach, thrust his shortsword through the throat of a second and then returned to the first to finish him off. He was too late, this Dwarf, although blinded, swung a hand-axe and tried to embed it in the elf's left thigh; fortunately for Silmar it was the back of the blade that caught him. Even so, Silmar lurched against the tunnel wall, pushed himself off it and swung his weapon to open up the dwarf's chest. Falcon was roaring and swinging his massive warhammer catching many a Grey Dwarf. Blood sprayed about the tunnel as two more fell and would not rise again.

Taura brought her staff down heavily onto the helmet of one and judging by the deep dent the damage to its wearer was fatal. Jiutarô leapt over three bodies and swung his sword in a horizontal sweep that passed straight through the midriff of a Grey Dwarf. The two separate sections splattered to the floor spraying more blood, this time over the supine figures of the two gnomes.

The surviving Grey Dwarves were starting to recover their sight and now were fighting back. Two of them, seeing that the elf appeared wounded, came at him from two sides. The hair of one of them though, burst into flames as fiery magical darts hammered into him. Within seconds, his head was a mass of fire and he screamed and reeled along the passage. He fell shrieking to the ground as the flames overwhelmed his head and upper body.

One Grey Dwarf was fighting off an attack from Sushi. She was far too quick for him and her tail whipped with a *snap* as the barb embedded itself in the side of his neck. Screaming, he went down immediately and shuddered in his painful death throes. She spun away to find another prey.

Billit had three Grey Dwarves circling about him and for a time seemed vulnerable. Taura, however, waded in with her staff, swinging it with all her weight behind it. Its tip caught one Grey Dwarf on the side of his iron helmet, denting it so badly that its wearer spun sideways and crashed onto the tunnel floor, probably unconscious. She moved her hands to the centre of the staff and made it whirl faster than the eye could follow. One tip of it crashed down onto the Grey Dwarf's helm just as Sushi's razor-sharp claws raked the face and eyes.

Silmar risked a quick glance about him and in the dim light he could see that Jasper lay unmoving on the tunnel floor. He pushed through the swirling melee.

Billit however, was still under attack from the third dwarf and had blood streaming into his eyes from an injury to his forehead. Just as Taura turned her staff towards this dwarf he began to chant a magical spell. Suddenly, a long, dark dagger buried itself in the Dark Dwarf's back and he fell stiffly, face down to the ground.

Silmar meanwhile, was down on one knee with blood pouring from his nose. He persistently jabbed with his sword to keep an attacker at bay but it would only be a matter of time before his attempts would fail. Another Grey Dwarf, seeing an elf in difficulty, yelled in triumph and joined in the melee.

Jiutarô was besieged by three Grey Dwarves and his katana was scoring hits with each swing but they were now keeping out of range of his blade. As he swung one way, so a dwarf would charge in from the other side with axe and shortsword. He had been hit two or three times. He was getting wise to this tactic nonetheless. He feinted to the left and as he turned his body to the right an attacker came in. The Samurai continued his circular swing and brought his blade back around to take the head from its shoulders. With the same swing, this time powerfully executing the fearsome *butterfly* stroke, he took one, then another attacker, obliquely across both of their chests and stomachs.

Two Grey Dwarves remained to threaten Silmar and they were not about to give up the fight; it was not in their nature to do so. They knew they would be given no quarter; no mercy.

"Someone help Silmar!" cried a voice. It was Taura.

She commenced battle with one of the dwarves and stunned him with a swing from her staff as he was about to launch a frenzied attack on Silmar. The elf had backed against the tunnel wall and was kneeling on the ground with his lower face covered in blood. Jiutarô leapt into action and, his katana dripping blood from his previous encounters, swung it two-handed vertically upwards and removed an arm from one of the two dwarves. The Samurai reversed his swing and cleaved the stricken dwarf's head in two. Silmar's remaining adversary made the mistake of glancing over at his collaborator. This was just the opportunity that the elf needed to thrust his sword under the dwarf's left arm-pit and into his heart.

The fight was over. There were body parts, dead Grey Dwarves and blood everywhere. The walls and floor were running with it and most of the group had been injured.

Billit sat on the floor cursing. "I couldn't do no magic," he moaned. "Face bloody 'urts! I couldn't concentrate on me spells."

Silmar was half sitting against the tunnel wall with his leg stretched out in front of him and wiping blood from his chin with his sleeve. Jiutarô had a bloody wound to his right hip and right arm and blood oozing from a deep scratch on his chest; he was also sitting on the floor. Falcon seemed unharmed apart from a graze to his left cheek; he apparently received this when he collided with the tunnel wall during the battle.

Jasper stirred and tried to rise from the floor. He fell again. He had a small dent in his helmet and was looking very dazed. He sat down on the ground and took his helmet off, rubbed his head and swooned. Sushi had received a stab wound on her back leg causing her to lick at the blood that welled from it. Whining, she dragged herself over to Jiutarô who held his hand to the injury to try to stop the bleeding.

Taura was the only one who was completely unharmed but she was desperately exhausted. "So many injuries!" she wailed. "Oh, Neilea give me strength! They are all injured!" She knew she wouldn't be able to treat them all.

Falcon advised that she treat Silmar first. "He will quickly die if you do not and then see to Nib–"

"Wait!" a thin, high-pitched voice commanded. "We shall help you! Do not fear us! We shall help!"

In the glow of the light tubes, a line of gnomes stretched across the width of the tunnel. They were garbed and armed as if for war.

∽ ≈

Taura gestured and called out to them in a despondent wail. "Come, help! Please!"

The gnome leader barked a command. A handful of gnomes rushed over and started attending to the injured, rummaging in their packs for materials, potions and salves. Two cloaked figures pushed through the throng of gnomes and arcane glows lit up the tunnel. Unlike Billit, who had wispy red hair, all of these gnomes were completely bald apart from short, sparse, white beards. With a cry, four of them rushed over to where the two captive gnomes were still trussed up on the poles and started cutting them free. They seemed unharmed apart from bruises and small cuts. Once they had wrapped the worst of the injuries to the companions, the leader came across and stated that they would escort the party to a place of refuge close by.

Billit was by now unconscious and had to be carried; Jasper was concussed and was barely aware of what was going on; he mumbled incoherently. Jiutarô was able to walk and he carried the whining Sushi in his arms. Falcon helped Silmar to walk because of his loss of blood. This battle had left most of them severely battered and with combat wounds.

The gnomes gathered up the various weapons and equipment that the party had dropped and took them a few hundred yards back along the tunnel in the direction that the group had come from and then stopped in front of the tunnel wall.

"Behold, the haven of the Chthonic peoples," stated the leader.

"What?" exclaimed Taura. "I see nothing here!"

"Of course, a good camouflage is it not?"

With the Chthonic Gnomes ensuring they were not being overlooked, the leader uttered a series of gnomish words and waved his hand in an arc across the wall. A section of rock the size of a small, narrow doorway seemed to dissolve and an entrance to a tunnel appeared before them. The gnomes immediately filed in through the entrance and Falcon squeezed in behind them while supporting Silmar; the Barbarian was almost bent double as he went in through the opening but was able to stand almost upright once inside.

The entry was closed behind them and they were led, or taken, along a lengthy, straight passage. Silmar was starting to regain consciousness and was moaning with the pain of his injuries, old and new. Billit was also coming to and tried to sit up on the makeshift stretcher made from two staffs and a cape. His face was still covered in drying blood and he wasn't able to see through it.

"I'm blind, ohhh, I cannot see!" be moaned, more in dread. He was told assertively to keep still.

The march continued for what seemed like an hour, but which was probably considerably less, when the passage opened up into a dimly-lit hallway. The leader called out *"Teaccasia"* and a number of Chthonic gnomes appeared through one of the many arches cut into the walls of the hall.

"Take them to the healing caverns!" called the leader.

The companions were led and taken away and the gnomes disappeared through other arches. Once more, the hall was silent.

৯ ৶

"We are the Chthonic gnomes. I see you travel with one of our surface kinsmen. Although he is distantly related to our tribe, he is not known to us. He is a mage! Interesting! Is he useful to your party? Gnomish mages rarely aspire to much more than simple conjurers in our domain!"

Taura and Falcon were resting on straw palliasses laid out on the floor in a rocky chamber separated from the others. They had been left there when their comrades were taken elsewhere for treatment. A single candle guttered in a dish. Taura had slept, she did not know for how long. Falcon, because of his size, was on two beds. He had dozed fitfully. They were both awakened by the gnome leader coming into their chamber. He carried an oil lamp that gave a little more light.

Without preamble, he continued "Tell me of your mage."

"He is a bold, courageous and valuable member of the party and is a powerful wizard," Taura spoke with a firm voice. "Well, he will be one day; of that I have little doubt. He studies constantly when we have a peaceful rest."

Although of small stature, the Chthonic gnomes leader had a presence that indicated a position of influence in his tribe. He nodded and moved over to a wooden bench and sat down.

"The elf carries an item of power," he continued. "One of us has felt its influence and believes it to be evil. I do not believe you or your mage are evil, nor perhaps, are those others with whom you travel. I wish to know what this item is that you have with you and whether it poses any danger to us in our haven." His statement was neither a question nor a command. But Taura felt that she was being given no option but to speak of it.

She took a deep breath and exhaled slowly. "You are right," she replied nodding her head. "It is a holy artefact that has been made wholly evil. But we are not. We are taking it somewhere to destroy its evil. We have been given a task by a Priest of Haeman, one Halorun Tann, and must see it through."

The gnome snapped his head up sharply. "Halorun Tann! Hmm, that name is well known to me. I shall consult my Assembly and discuss this. Very well, for now I shall ask no further questions of this and we shall continue to provide your group aid and succour where we can."

Taura persisted. "But the task itself is beset by evil. We are hunting a foul creature that desires the artefact. At the same time, he hunts us, or rather, he hunts Silmar, seeking revenge as well as the artefact."

"You speak of the Darkling." It was a statement, not a question.

"You know of him?"

"We have been tracking him for a couple surface-days. He is two days ahead of you although he waits and listens from time to time. I expect therefore, he indeed waits for you. We have disabled many traps that he has left."

"But, but we have seen nothing!" gasped Taura.

"Nay, we do things properly down here! We have been tracking you since Kalanisha. You destroyed an evil which has endured there for thirty years! That is impressive! We left it for it posed us no threat. You have much power and inner strength. Halorun Tann was right to entrust this quest to you."

"So why you not destroyed the Darkling?" asked Falcon.

"Because we do not know whether he is the herald of a greater force that is to follow. Or there may be those who await his coming. Either way, we may create a difficulty for ourselves if we intercede now. We are content to watch and wait and avoid the risk."

"He has no following army and travels alone," stated Taura. "He killed many innocent victims to force us into following him. He may well be meeting others down here but that is pure conjecture."

"It certainly won't be the Grey Dwarves, although there will be a fearful anger when they come searching for whomsoever carried out the destruction of their patrol. Another worthy battle your group has fought! The Grey Dwarves will think nothing of killing the Darkling. Perhaps we shall leave sign that their deaths were caused by the Darkling. The Grey Dwarves have no regard for one of his kin. No, I believe the Darkling most likely intends to meet up with the Grullien, the Shade Gnomes, our bitterest enemy, rather than the Grey Dwarves! He will give them promises of treasures and slaves to work their silver mines. If I do point the finger of suspicion at the Darkling, this stretch of the tunnel will be far too dangerous for you to travel. We shall guide you by a parallel path."

"Where are the Grullien?" asked the barbarian.

"They are at the extreme end of this mine."

Taura continued. "The Shadow World mines are huge, far bigger than I ever imagined they could be!"

"Do you reall believe that this is all of the Shadow World? If so, you are mistaken. There are many tunnels linking mines, chasms, underground rivers and even cities to the Shadow World and they spread like a spider's web throughout the lands of Amæus. Far, far away is the mighty Darkling city of Dannakanonn. But even that can be reached from the mine tunnel you have travelled without ever having to go back up to the surface. You have met and destroyed so-called priests in a temple; you have destroyed a small Grey Dwarf hunting party. Darkling are rare in this area and the one you seek is the first I have known during my lifetime."

Taura looked across at Falcon but his eyes were looking down at his feet. "When we have adequately recovered, we shall have urgency to continue our task," she explained. "I would assume that our quarry is far ahead of us by now. Can you warn us of what we can expect on the way ahead?"

"There is far more than just a Darkling down here," the Gnome continued. "*He* will be in as much danger from threats as you are, probably more so because he is alone. I warn you however, to beware! Think about this carefully. I shall leave you to rest once again. Food and drink will be brought to you soon and I shall have news of your friends, oh, and of the captives you freed! You have done extraordinarily well and have our immense gratitude."

Taura watched the gnome leader, she still did not know his name, leave the room and she settled down to sleep.

Falcon had already descended into slumber. Food and drink arrived some time later. She was surprised to see that there were nuts, berries and meat on the tray as well as hunks of bread and warmed honey. She woke the barbarian and together they ate the meal. She then spent a long period of time in praying to her god, The Lady Neilea, for guidance and good fortune. She fervently hoped that The Lady could still hear her prayers and entreaties despite the vast amount of rock that was above her. After a while she was rewarded with a wave of warmth – although this may have been her imagination brought on by fatigue.

⧏ ⧐

Falcon and Taura may have slept for many hours for she was stiff about her hips and shoulders when she awoke but they both felt somewhat refreshed. Surprisingly, her head was on his shoulder and his arm was around her with his hand clasping her bottom. Although another meal had been left for then, along with water to wash with and cloths to dry themselves, they had no idea how long they had been left in the cavern.

Within an hour a young gnome politely coughed by their doorway and asked for them to accompany him. He led them down a long passage and into a large chamber. There, sitting on low benches, were Jasper, Silmar, Billit and Jiutarô. Sushi was sitting up on a pile of cushions looking very playful and, as Taura and Falcon came over to embrace their friends, the little dragon chittered and purred happily. All of them looked fairly well recovered from their wounds although bandages were wrapped around heads and arms; it was obvious that Chthonic gnomes healers had used considerable healing skills.

Sitting on a bench on a raised dais in front of the companions were five gnomes. They were dressed in their normal costumes of leather hose and boots and canvas jerkins; but each also wore a fine gown.

The stern-faced leader was clearly a gnome of dignity and influence; he sat in the centre of the group and the others had risen to their feet as he came over to sit. He began the discussion.

"It is time for introductions." His voice was gruff but not unpleasant. "I am the Lord Cephod, the leader of this community. This is our mining area and we are able to do this without being detected by other species and races that live down here. Oh, do not misunderstand me; our presence is known of. Both the Grey Dwarves and the Grullien are aware that we are here, somewhere. The biggest threat is from the Grey Dwarves, we have lost some of our people to them, both as captives for ransom or killed in battles.

"You see, they are greedy for that which we mine – crystal-silver, valuable and harder than elven steel, and rubies of immense purity. They had only just caught my son and his guard. On my right here is Cephal. He was the one caught and trussed up like a lizard for the spit!" Cephod had spoken with a raised voice and was clearly enraged with his son who sat there with a dejected and embarrassed expression. "If your group hadn't come along when you did, the rescue party would not have been there in time. For that alone you have my immense gratitude and that of the community otherwise we should not have allowed you into our haven, despite your predicament. You see, my son had talked his two personal guards into stepping out into the main tunnel and within moments they had blundered into the Grey Dwarves. One guard was able to escape and warn me but these two were taken hostage. It would have cost us dearly to get them back and may well have compromised our secrecy here.

"We Chthonic gnomes have a trade arrangement with certain communities on the surface above. We have our own access to the surface and, through some acquaintances of ours, have trading posts in towns as far away as Gash on the Landsdrop Coast and Nasteed in Shordrun. Here we have wagons and horses to take our wares to cities."

At this Jasper interjected. "Pardon me, my Lord Cephod. We have recently been to the village of Dalcutta. They are now growing and would be delighted to have a trading post there, I am certain!"

"Hmm, we shall look into this as a future opportunity," said Cephod, looking at the gnome seated on the far right. This gnome nodded but remained silent. "This is Merwian, who manages the mining operation and the trading businesses. He is also my Master at Arms and takes responsibility for the safety and security of our community.

"Here on my right is Trefannwe, she is our healer and Priestess of Clambarhan, the God of learning, artifice and invention, and wielder of the great warhammer: *Craftmaster*!"

Both Cephod and Trefannwe bowed slightly. Taura, taking the hint, also bowed her head in respect in response to mention of the God. "We also have a mage in our haven and that is Cerianath. I understand that he would like to speak afterwards with you, er, Billit, who we welcome into our haven as a brother. I do not believe Billit to be your real name but we shall leave that for later. It is always a pleasure to greet one of our kin-folk. But, although we rarely open our halls to peaceful travellers in the tunnels, you are all welcome here.

"I and my Assembly gathered before you, have expressed concern over that which the elf carries. But before you satisfy our curiosity, as I sincerely hope that you will, I should like you all to introduce yourselves. We keep a journal of our history in this community here. On the rare occasion that we gather with other clans of Chthonic gnomes, we tell stories of our exploits and occurrences. I think this will one day become a magnificent story for us to tell. Perhaps the Priestess of Neilea would like to begin. Please, go on."

The adventurers looked at each other and Taura rose to her feet to begin her introduction. "Erm, I am Taura Windwalker and I come from Casparsport in Lopastor. I was one of six daughters and the youngest. I also had two brothers. I was studious when my sisters were playing games so my mother encouraged me to study in the Temple of Neilea in Casparsport. It is a city of much vice and gambling so Neilea has many followers there and the temple is one of the biggest in the city. So there I stayed for nine years. But I saw nothing of the world and listened long to the stories told by visiting adventurers when they stopped by for a blessing on their way to the gambling house. That was the fee I charged them you see – instead of a silver piece, I asked them for stories. That is why I am here today. I have no regrets about my decision."

"No doubt you are now collecting stories of your own, young Priestess of the Lady of Magic and Serendipity," said Trefannwe, bowing once again. "I hope you shall tell us some of them before you leave."

"It will be my pleasure, my lady!"

"And such courtesy too!"

Taura sat down, relieved that her story was over.

"Er, me next Lord Cephod?" began Billit. "Obviously, this name is only an epithet that some humans gave me because they couldn't get their lazy tongues round me real name! I'm Niebillettin, originally from a mining community in them Brash Mount'ns to the east of Triosande. We *rock-jumpers*, as the 'umans name us, like you are Chthonic Gnomes, well, we've traded there for centuries. If I'm not mistaken, I wouldn't be surprised if your tribe was originally from that area too, M'Lord."

Cephod frowned briefly and nodded. "You are quite correct, Niebillettin. This community was set up two centuries ago, when my forefathers decided that the Chthonic gnomes were becoming too numerous to be able to support themselves in one place. Then, of course, the goblins and ogres flooded into north Cascant and the whole tribe was driven out. Continue."

"Well, I was the only child of Af-Niebillettin but I, too, was studious. I didn't wanta be, oh no! Not at first. I wanted to get out with the lads and fight and play games. But my father goes and decides I should study. By the time I was eleven year old I could read! Well, that was it! Off I was sent to the College Tower o' Magic in Norovir. Hah, a tower! It was three stories of a badly built wooden structure run by Evialannais, a fat, drunken ex-battle-wizard who, it was said, had been asked to leave the Royal Palace o' King Barsani Dar-Cascan VII in Norovir by none other than the Royal Magician, Barganisseroi, hisself. Oh Aye. The royal family, with many o' the Corps of Foresters, the elite soldiers o' Cascant, are in exile in the west while Barganisseroi and the Corps o' Battle-Wizards defend the south o' Cascant from Norovir. Anyway, me and the two other trainees virtually 'ad to teach ourselves from magic books because Evialannais couldn't keep off the rough wine and was considered too unreliable. He 'ad taught me the basics, mind you, but the rest I taught myself by spending hours and hours with his old books o' spells and his alchemicals that I, um, borrowed when he slept. I knew I was doing well when I blew the front door off his library! He was livid; he thought I was trying to burn down his tower!"

The Assembly did not give any indication that they were amused by Billit's story.

Consequently, Billit's smile dropped away. "Aye, well, it was time for me to go when I reckoned I knew more than 'e could teach me, so I got a ride on a mule train. I went from one mule train to another until I ended up in the *Ship's Prow* at Westron Seaport!"

Puzzlement appeared on the faces of the Council. "Oh, that's a tavern in Westron Seaport!" explained Billit. "So, anyway, here am I too with this sorry-looking bunch!"

"You tell an interesting and amusing story, mage Niebillettin," said Cephod. "I should like to discuss more with you, perhaps later, alone!"

Chthonic Gnomes from the surface, known as *rock-dwellers*, were ever the storytellers. They would go into great detail of their stories of bravery and exploits with enthusiasm and with much waving of arms and falling about. It was as if the retelling of great events would make a little folk appear larger. But here in the roots of the mountains, the Chthonic gnomes did not seem well disposed to hearing one of their own tell a humorous tale. Everything about them was sullen and withdrawn. Not once had a member of the council given the faintest glimmer of a smile.

Silmar started to speak but the wave of a hand from Cephod silenced him. "I would like your story to be the last to be told, warrior-elf. I should like to hear of the giant human."

"You want I speak now, Lord?" offered Falcon.

Falcon was not used to speaking more than a few words at any one time. The Universal tongue was not his first language and he did struggle with it at times. But, taking a deep breath, he began to speak, slowly at first. The group of adventurers listened avidly because he had told them nothing of his background.

"I am Falcon-Hawk Makkadan from Livuria. I travel far; two winters. Wytch Queen and her wytches banish me, their magic take away my, er, my war-rage. I kill wytch's champion in challenge. They do not forgive. They hunt me if I return but here I am far from their reach."

"So there is some truth in the legend that your warriors are *ragers*?" enquired Merwian, the master at arms.

"Ragers, aye. Not me! Not now." Falcon looked sullen. "Not even with Livuri *fire-berry* wine! Now I am on *wanderlust*."

Once again, puzzled frowns showed on the faces of the council members.

"Explain," said Cephod.

"Wanderlust, I travel to see Amæus. I meet new friends here and now we fight together!"

"Perhaps your rage is better left beyond your reach!" responded Cephod. "It is uncontrollable, as much a risk to your friends as it is to your enemies. Do not look for something that may occur naturally in time of great need."

Falcon dropped his face dejectedly as if in silent repose. His sadness was plain to see so Cephod said no more to the Barbarian. He turned instead to Jasper.

"I should like to hear your story; surface dwarves have ever been friends to the Chthonic gnomes and are trusted here. There is something about you that stirs old memories from within me. Have you been here before? I know not your name."

"Hrrrm, yes! I'm known as Jasper but me real name is Harval Cleaverblade. Soon after me an' m' brother, Ralmon, first passed through yer realm, 'is arm was taken from 'im in battle. Aye, many years ago, with this 'ere elf's father, Faramar Galadhal, the *Spirit Panther* as 'e was known to 'is friends an' enemies alike."

At this, Silmar's eyebrows rose in surprise – he had not heard this before!

"It was 'e what saved me brother's life but could not save the arm!" exclaimed Jasper.

"The Spirit Panther indeed!" exclaimed Cephod. "A name I remember well, we were there when the enemy was vanquished! He was unconscious; his shattered arm lay twisted beneath him. He must have lost all but a cupful of blood by the time Faramar applied wadding to his wound and tied a cord around to stop the flow. This undoubtedly kept death at arm's length, if you excuse the term; I apologise if you consider it to be in bad taste. But it was our sister, Trefannwe, who asked Clambarhan to intervene and save the life of one of the two dwarven heroes who were prepared to sacrifice their all for the fight."

Jasper's jaw dropped with surprise. "M-My lady! I didn't know of this!" he stammered. "B-Blessings on you and, er, an' to the Lord Clambarhan."

He prostrated himself at the feet of the Priestess but she placed her hand on his shoulder saying "Rise Harval Cleaverblade, friend of the Chthonic gnomes, be thou not at my feet."

The dwarf rose and returned alongside his friends. He muttered "My brother 'as taken the name HalfJasper 'cos of 'avin' just the one arm." For the first time a slight smile quickly manifested itself on the face of Cephod. But, just as quickly, it faded.

The gnome lord continued. "Clearly, you are still campaigning. Have you not retired from this life? What life have you given yourself now?"

"Well, aye! I got this inn in Nor'wald City. The priest Halorun Tann pays me a visit every once in a while. Halfsatg's got a tavern as well, but in Westron Seaport. He calls it the Ship's Prow 'cos it's near the docks and it keeps 'im comfortable, if yer knows what I mean. I met this sorry bunch of adventurers when they called at me place with a barrel of bloodwine from me brother. And that's 'ow we got into this mess in the first place!"

"A sorry bunch?" gasped Cephod. "Nay. It seems to me that they have achieved more than would be expected even for an experienced group such as yourselves."

"Well, er, actually it's our first campaign!" exclaimed Taura.

Now it was Cephod's turn to display surprise on his stern face. "What? Impossible! Such a small and very inexperienced band of warriors! I salute you all! You certainly have achieved much."

Merwian, the Master at Arms, Trefannwe, Priestess of Clambarhan, and the mage Cerianath similarly looked at each other and at Cephod. Lord Cephod's son, Cephal, who had been sullen and quiet during the story-telling, looked surprised at the group of adventurers sitting on the benches before him.

"I wish to hear more from your companions. I see someone from the race of men that I have no knowledge of. The features I do not recognise and the garb is strange but he carries himself with a self-assuredness and dignity the like of which I have never seen before, even in the race of men. Something tells me that he is a warrior from a far off land. Your little companion is very attached to you. A cleret-wing dragon, I believe."

Sushi had been wrapped around Jiutarô's shoulder throughout their time in the haven. She raised her head as the eyes of the Assembly turned towards her and Jiutarô. The Samurai, however, looked with some incomprehension.

At this, Trefannwe rose to her feet and looked straight into the eyes of Jiutarô. She signalled with her right hand for him to approach and he stood before her. Standing on the dais, she was able to reach towards him and she placed her right hand on the side of his head. Sushi's claws tightened on his shoulders momentarily and she gave a little hiss but a quick look from the mage seemed to settle her. The Samurai stood rock still and did not flinch nor even blink his eye. She maintained that link for many moments and then she let her hand fall away.

"Nay, Lord," spoke the mage. Her expression was one of sadness. "I can let it be known that he comes not from any land on Amæus but from across the skies; a world amongst the stars; a land in turmoil as those in power exploit those who serve. I read it in the sadness and confusion that surrounds him. One of forty-seven is he. Return he shall, to face his doom. Each of that number shall share the doom of his comrades. Know that his honour shall have its rewards. Search him not for answers to those puzzles and doubts that he himself will not understand. His courage and loyalty are without question."

The members of the party looked at their comrade with puzzlement but theirs was nothing compared to that of the Samurai. A period of silence followed and Trefannwe said no more as she returned to her seat. Her words had been confusing and none understood all that she had said.

Cephod broke the silence. "No doubt all will become clear in time," he stated. "The elf has much to tell us about himself and in particular the burden he carries. I have spoken of it and the evil it imbued with but evil is not in the group that escorts it. Please tell us more, elf Silmar Galadhal, son of Faramar, the Spirit Panther."

Silmar took a deep breath. He had been turning his story over and over in his mind, fully aware that he would have to explain in detail everything that had happened. Once he started talking however, the story flowed easily from his lips. He recounted his early years as a patrol leader, how he had started his journey, his arrival in Westron Seaport and meeting with his new companions. He carefully told of his encounter with the Darkling assassin and the discovery of the artefact on the dying Priest of Clambarhan. He explained how Halorun Tann had given them much advice and prepared them for their quest.

Cephod interrupted continuously, asking for clarification or more details. At times, Trefannwe also asked him to repeat or explain further some of the details. A full hour passed in the telling and retelling of Silmar's story. At the end of it, Cephod refused the offer to examine the artefact.

"It is not necessary for me to see that which is evil, I have no doubt that it is there. I can feel its influence as can we all, none more than Trefannwe. We shall now take the time for you to rest, eat and sleep. You shall be returned to the quarters where you slept and recovered earlier. In some hours we shall escort you by some paths that are known only to us. Once we come close to the main tunnel, with your agreement and for your and our safety, we shall blindfold you so that you will be unable to disclose our secret ways even though you may be compelled, physically or magically, to do so. Are you in agreement?"

The companions looked at each other and all nodded their agreement.

"Good, then let it be so. Niebillettin, I request that you remain with the Assembly here for a while. I wish to speak with you further."

Trefannwe added "We have known that none of you are evil from the start."

To her surprise, Taura replied "Yes, I am aware that you cast a *Detection of Evil* across us. I felt it and also did the same to you! Did you not know?"

"You are a cunning young human, Taura Windwalker. I felt it not! I trust that the response you felt was to your satisfaction. Accept my apologies, please. I was acting in the best interests of my community. I hope you understand. A thing of evil would normally be carried by a person of similar evil, do you not agree?"

Taura nodded and said "Apologies are not necessary, Holy Mother Artificer. But I do offer mine in return. I would have done the same to ensure our safety. If you are happy, we shall speak no more of it and remain as friends in the eyes of our Gods."

The two priestesses bowed and parted. Two Chthonic Gnome warriors escorted the party to their quarters.

ഈ   ഹ

Apart from Cephal, who sat at the end of the dais, the Gnome Lord and Billit were alone in the meeting hall.

"By birth, you are a Rock-Dweller, a Chthonic Gnome. How long is it since you were in the darkness with your kinfolk, cousin Niebillettin?"

"Not since childhood have I been below the surface, lord."

"Are you not aware of your innate capabilities commensurate with your race, then?"

"I do not understand. I am strong, fast and seem to be able to hide behind a pebble, an advantage for being small of stature. I feel confident and not to out-of-place or frightened in the Shadow World. I have some skills as a mage and these are growing quite well since I started on this campaign. But if that is what you mean as innate capabilities, I am no different to any other Rock-Dweller, I think."

"You are indeed a mage of swiftly developing powers, according to Trefannwe. As a priestess, she herself has powers beyond my understanding but she also has a gift of farsight. She can look into the distant past or the future merely by a touch on the person and applying her mind's strength. That is how she knew of your strange warrior. As both sage and priestess she is both wise and powerful. But she is not a mage. That power could well be yours in years to come, she tells me. She says it is not a god-given power nor is it magically-learned but rather a skill that comes from exercising the mind as one might train one's muscles to develop physical fitness. By Clambarhan, she can implant thoughts into the mind of others! She can even move objects by the power of thought. Who then, cousin, do you consider as being your most hated foe?"

The sudden change in direction in Cephod's conversation caught Billit unawares for a few moments, having been so wrapped up in the apparent skills of Trefannwe. "Ah, that's simple," he said, "anyone who is a threat to me or my comrades at that particular time. But if I must select a race or species then it would probably be Darkling. They're the most evil of all those we have met so far."

"And what of those you have never met, or perhaps are yet to meet?"

"It's strange really my Lord, but there is somethin' that sends a shiver down my spine when I hear them mentioned.

I don't understand why. I've never encountered 'em but heard 'em mentioned a couple o' times over the last few days. It may just be something I remember from many years ago."

The Lord Cephod had been sitting upright in his chair and now he leaned forward towards the mage. "Tell me who it is."

Billit scratched at a drying scab in the sparse hair on his chin. He looked at the piece that had lodged under his fingernail and flicked it away. "There are a couple really," he said slowly. "Kobolds, because their threat is understated, and although they are very small they have such great numbers that they can overwhelm you. And those damned Grullien! The Shade-Gnomes. When I think of 'em, I imagine a foul smell in my nostrils and a rasping voice yet I am certain I haven't seen 'em during my lifetime."

"It is not so strange that you should mention them. The enmity that exists between the Chthonic gnomes and the Grullien has been so for countless generations. Ever have they sought to destroy us or take captive our people for food, trade or slavery. Yes, they are known to eat their captives as do the Grey Dwarves. Ever have we sought to destroy them, our most deadly of foes. They are not so intelligent but they are cunning. We are miners and can move from one place to another in our own tunnels in complete secrecy. We hear and see much that occurs in this Shadow World. You have dark-vision, cousin, do you not?"

"Er, aye. I do my Lord. I can see quite a long way but it's not very clear, a bit fuzzy-like. The dwarf and the elf, now, they can really see well. At least, that's what they tell me."

"Good, but you have been too long on the surface, cousin. For clear dark-vision you would need to spend your life in these tunnels. But you have made your choices in life and you must accept the consequences. As a mage, you have knowledge of spells that you have had to learn, and relearn no doubt. Would it surprise you to know that you also have other magical abilities that you have no need to learn? Magic that comes naturally to you when in the darkness of the tunnels?"

Billit looked dazed. "What? Really? Nay!" He shook his head doubtfully. "What are they? How do I start 'em up? What can they do? Can I blast my enemies asunder?"

Cephod chuckled. "Calm cousin. It may be better for another to explain." The Lord Cephod closed his eyes for a moment and then opened them again. A few heartbeats later a distortion in the air appeared as if it were a large bubble in water. Through it stepped Cerianath and she stood before them. The distortion disappeared.

"Merely a portal from my chamber to this Assembly chamber, cousin Niebillettin," explained Cerianath. "You summoned me, my Lord?"

"Thank you for your promptness, Cerianath. I wish you to explain to our cousin the innate abilities of magic that he has, in addition to those he acquired. Surprisingly, or perhaps not, he has no knowledge of this."

"By your command, my Lord. It should be no surprise that you have no knowledge of these gnomish abilities, Niebillettin. Long have you been estranged from your kinfolk. Who, then, would school you and encourage you? There are simple abilities which, after much patience, come naturally to a mature Chthonic Gnome. I can spend some time with you, if you and your friends can spare that time, to instruct you in these ways. There are two skills. Use them wisely. You can use them with your other magical abilities without detriment. The effect of these skills is only temporary when cast on the target. Depending on your power with these, the effects will last longer the better practised you are. *Black blindness* is one. Casting this will cause a black disk to appear in the line of vision so that the victim cannot see before him. *Hazed sight* is the other. The receiver cannot clearly see friend from foe and this confusion will either cause him to attack any who stand before him, should he be of a ruthless nature, or force him to withdraw from battle. Use them both wisely. I shall council you with the use of these. Being a mage, you should quickly learn these, I am sure."

The expression on Billit's face clearly showed his astonishment at having learned of these new powers.

"There is one more," Cerianath continued, "however, that you will always find useful. It is a *Hide from sight* spell."

Cephod spoke next. "This spell we use constantly should we be in the main tunnel of the Shadow World." Looking towards Cephal, his son, he added "Foolish indeed is the gnome who does not use this ability to protect himself. But, perhaps I am unfair. In this case, my son still achieves maturity and the innate magical powers still develop within him. Take no notice of a concerned father, my son; I was sure that you were lost. My heart soars to see you returned to me."

At this last remark, the morose expression finally lifted from the young gnome and he rose to his feet, bowed to his father and left the Assembly chamber.

"What is this *Hide from sight* spell, Lord?" asked Billit.

"You are probably aware that we have the advantage of being able to move with stealth and can be difficult to observe, let alone catch! Did you not yourself say that you can hide behind a pebble? Well, the *Hide from sight* spell will allow you to pass unseen and not be detected by any magical charm. It will hide you from the cunning eyes of a mage of any power less than that of a demi-god. Consider the potential, cousin."

Cephod rose to his feet and addressed Cerianath. "Take our cousin and school him in the new arts, Lord. Advise him in the best way for him to free his mind to release the new powers. I shall now speak with the elf warrior, meanwhile allowing the remainder of our guests to rest and gather their strength for they have more tests to overcome. One of these causes me grave concern – even with our numbers, we dread to walk that path and avoid it completely." With that, he was gone.

Cerianath motioned to Billit and said "Follow me!" With a flick of his wrist and a muffled word, another portal appeared before him. He stepped into it and was gone from view. With a nervous sigh, Billit followed.

৯ ৵

Silmar was led by a gnome messenger along a short passageway and into an austere chamber. Cephod and Trefannwe sat on two simple chairs and gestured for him to be seated on a somewhat larger wooden bench.

The two gnomes exchange a brief glance at each other before Cephod looked at Silmar directly in the eye. Trefannwe sat with her eyes closed and her hands clasped in front of her face.

"Have you brought it here with you?" he asked curtly and without preamble.

"I have," the elf replied. "It is in my pack."

There was silence for a considerable time until Trefannwe opened her eyes suddenly and took a deep breath in.

"It is an aberration!" she cried out. "A travesty. How can its presence be tolerable?"

"Undoubtedly, it cannot be," the gnome lord stated brusquely. "What can you tell us about its provenance, elf warrior?"

Silmar explained in much detail about how he had taken the artefact from the dying cleric of Clambarhan and that Halorun Tann had informed him that the dagger was of unique religious significance to the Church of Clamberhan. It had been stolen by the followers of Adelenis, corrupted by them and then stolen back by the cleric carrying it who had been slain by the very Darkling that skulked in the mine tunnels.

"We intend to return it by the long road east to Carrick Cliffs in Kamambia and then to the Temple of Clambarhan so that it can be restored once again. We are all resolved to do this no matter what the risks will be. We have come far and we have much further to go."

"No matter how that foul thing makes you feel," interjected Trefannwe.

Silmar paused before answering. "Aye, but it has been of some benefit to me, somewhat surprisingly. You must understand that by its nature, it knows when an evil presence draws close to it and, in some strange way that is unexplainable to me, it seems to call to them. It is that influence that affects me in such a way that also warns me to the approaching danger. By misfortune, that warning manifests itself by a wave of nauseous, and occasionally painful, reaction. At other times it gives out a coldness which produces frost inside and outside of my pack. I bear the artefact with fortitude. The burden, as I call it, is inside a box resting in a bed of lead powder otherwise the reaction would be much worse I am told."

The discussion concluded soon afterwards.

"Where do you think he is?" A sleepy-eyed Taura was starting to show concern for their little friend Billit. They had been led back to the chamber where they had began recovery from their wounds and had eaten and drunk. They had been advised to get what sleep they could to complete their recovery and prepare for their remaining journey.

Like all of the other chambers, the Assembly chamber and the tunnels, the floor, walls and ceilings were smoothly carved into the rock and there was little sign of the tooling marks that had originally fashioned them.

Some hours had passed and there was still no sign of Billit. Silmar had been whisked away some time ago for an audience with Lord Cephod. He had taken his back-pack containing the burden with him. Falcon had risen from his bed and, with his head held low, was now pacing back and forth across the dimply-lit chamber. A gemstone set high into the wall seemed to give off the dim light. Falcon resumed sitting on his two straw palliasses. The height of the room had made it impossible for him to stand upright. Taura also sat on his palliasses, leaning against the barbarian as he placed his arm protectively around her shoulders. His fingers soon strayed down to her breast and she made no effort to remove it.

Jiutarô was sleeping with his arm over his head to block out the rumbling snores coming from a deeply-sleeping Jasper. It was unusual for the dwarf to snore but he often did so only when in a safe environment. Sushi slept beside the Samurai.

"He probably talks with his long-lost kin," replied the Barbarian. "We are well treated so I am sure he is too. Do not worry unduly about him. But should one of our hosts come in, I shall ask."

More time passed and eventually a Gnome messenger entered the room, he made a sound as if clearing is throat and the party slowly awoke.

"Have you lost this?" he eventually asked as the group climbed to their feet.

Into the archway stepped Billit, his little face smiling broadly.

❧ ❨

"Up you lazybones all," he exclaimed. "We are going soon. Eat, drink and then off on our travels once again."

Behind him, next to the messenger, stood Silmar.

They spent time checking their packs and weapons. Billit stood grasping something close to his chest. It appeared to be a book.

"Look at this," he proudly boasted. "He gave it to me! It is indeed priceless and he gave it to me! Cerianath!"

"A book!" said Jiutarô. "Just book."

"Nay, not just a book! It is a magical spell-book. It contains spells that are more powerful and 'e says they will be within my skills soon. I read some and I think I may be able to do some of 'em." He carefully wrapped the book in a blanket and placed it in his pack.

Once again, they were taken to the Assembly chamber where Lord Cephod and the rest of the Assembly were standing.

"The time has come for you to take your leave of this haven," he said. "We have benefited from your being here as much as we hope you have. We now have another trade opportunity and you have regained your fitness and your strength to face your next difficulties. You shall be led through the tunnels of our haven, as aforesaid, we must ask you to wear blindfolds, and we shall lead you out into the Shadow World. You shall be led a short way still wearing blindfolds but these will be removed. You will be quite safe. We shall leave shortly but there is something else we need to do. Merwian?"

"My Lord," replied the Master-at-Arms and he passed to Cephod a small linen bag.

"The council wishes you to accept these as a token of our friendship. As we are not likely to meet within the tunnels of this haven again we would like to present you with small gifts that will enable you to keep in your memories the friendships we have made this day. There is one for each of you." To each he presented a carved and polished ruby. Although the size of a pigeon's egg, each gem was crafted into the shape of an apple. Its surface was perfectly round and smooth.

Each of the adventurers gazed at the gems with wonder.

"My Lord," exclaimed Silmar. "This shall be treasured. The story of its presentation to me shall be told and retold and never forgotten. I am honoured. I am sure I speak similarly for my friends too."

Each member of the group nodded and spoke in agreement.

Trefannwe reached out towards Taura. "Take these, Lady of Neilea." In her hands she held three glass phials. "A dark poison may afflict some of you. This will be needed. You will know when. Take also this sack. Within are items belonging to Grey Dwarves. These will aid you at the right time. You will know that time."

Jasper opened the large, heavy-looking sack and looked inside. "There's a helm, a hand-axe, some arrows and two swords, one of which is broken. He looked puzzled and gave a questioning look to the sooth-sayer. She said nothing more. Falcon took up the sack and swung it over his shoulder.

Cephod turned to them all and said "It is now time to leave."

৵ ৶

CHAPTER 22

THEY STOOD together once again in the Shadow World mine tunnel. The Chthonic Gnomes had removed the blindfolds and without a single word had melted into the darkness. No sound from them was heard, not even the scurry of their small feet.

After a long moment, Taura nervously reached around her in the pitch darkness. She could hear her own heartbeats hammering in her chest. Her hand collided with clothing.

"It is I, Taura," murmured Jiutarô.

She whispered into the darkness. "We are back. It is almost as if it didn't happen at all."

There was a wave of relief as she heard Jasper's reply. "It did, we're all together, I 'ope so, anyway! Are we all 'ere?" Softly-spoken responses from each of them confirmed that they were all together once again.

Surprisingly, each of them quickly grew accustomed to the darkness. They could make out pebbles and rocks that littered the floor. There was a vestige of light they recognised as being from fungus and mould that aided Silmar with his dark-vision.

"I believe we are quite safe here for the moment," he said confidently.

The passage was very wide here, probably just enough for them all to walk in line abreast. Large rocks, the size of a crouching man or smaller, were scattered about on the floor. Pieces of wood, cloth and leather, all in various stages of decay were also strewn about. A rusting helm, too small for a human or elven head, lay by a boulder. There was no sign of its original wearer.

Taura kicked it gently; it clattered across the floor and its chin-guard fell off it.

"Oo was that?" growled Jasper.

"Sorry," Taura squeaked.

"That was choddin' stupid. It might 'ave been joined to a trap an' the sound of it can carry for miles along 'ere. Don't do it again!"

They had been walking for a few hours and they agreed to stop for a while to take a little water and food in the darkness. They then continued on for another considerable length of time.

They passed many openings on either side which had been hewn through the rock long ago. These were generally narrow. One however, appeared in the wall to their left; it was both wide and tall enough for them all to enter side-by-side in pairs should they need to, but it was full of rusting mining tools, handcarts and detritus. Rather than look through it they decided to continue on. The main tunnel however, started to narrow considerably from then on until it was no more than two paces across. It bent sharply to the left and suddenly came to a stop at a great chasm across the floor. It must have been at least thirty feet across. There was no bridge or means to cross it and no ledge to climb around. The walls to each side were smooth and sheer and the bottom could not be seen by the members of the group blessed with dark-sight. The continuing tunnel could be seen stretching on from the far side of the chasm.

"Tunnel on side," called Jiutarô. "Small it is."

"Lightson," warned Silmar. "Three; two; one. Now!"

Three beams of light cut through the gloom. In the dim light, Jiutarô had seen the black opening of a tunnel to the right side, half-hidden behind large boulders.

"How did you see that, Jiutarô?" asked Silmar.

"I feel air."

"We can't cross the gulf," said Jasper. "No other choice. 'Ow about you lead, elf? Then if there's a nasty accident we won't lose nobody important. Heh heh!"

The dwarf always managed to make the title *elf* sound like an insult. Silmar was learning quickly to ignore the taunt.

The narrow tunnel led off to the right and they followed it with the light beams scanning the floor and walls. The beams flitted across the ugly, pale faces of Grullien, the dreaded Shade Gnomes.

❧ ❧

"Where are they, godsdammn!"

The Darkling assassin had plodded for a long time and there had been no sight or sound of his quarry. He knew that noise could carry a long way through these mines but he had heard nothing. He was worried that they had given up the chase and had gained the surface once again. He couldn't let that happen. He must have that artefact or it would be his neck on the altar and his blood running into the vessels.

He was now deciding whether or not to backtrack the way he had come but the difficulties that would present would be immense. The leg-wound from the arrow a few days ago had been serious and he had not enough healing concoction to treat the burn after he had used most of it on the arrow wound, to little benefit. He had resorted to using a needle and thread to do his own repair to his leg and the stitches pulled as he walked. Still the wound bled but, for now, it was not life-threatening.

He had found a niche in the tunnel and had taken some badly-needed rest. He hoped the sound of their approach would arouse him if he lapsed into a deeper sleep than he intended.

Sometime later, he awoke to the sound of shouts and a battle, it seemed. He knew from experience that any noise of battle being fought in tunnels and mines would sound much worse, or closer, than it actually was. It was likely that some members of the following group of surface fools were meeting their doom, after all, they were few in number. They had started the journey two humans, one gnome and a bastard elf? But they had picked up some extra help on the way, a huge human and a dwarf!

He waited.

The sound of the battle continued but after a while grew less and less. Then there was silence. Had an enemy defeated them all? He just needed to get back there to observe. He rose to his feet and left his niche. Quietly limping back up the tunnel, he approached the source of the noise. *Godsdamn*! He could see no bodies of his prey or any other beings. Not a single one of them had perished out here. He carefully and quietly turned off the main passageway listening to the muted conversation of his enemies. They were discussing destroying something! Were none of them defeated? It seemed he was underestimating his enemy! He had left many traps but they had not worked. He had tried to ambush them but he had been the one to be injured.

They get stronger while I get weaker. I'll have him though! Soon! In the deep city! Hah! My brothers-in-arms will be there waiting for me.

The Darkling turned away and limped back along the passage and into the main tunnel. He had gone no more than a hundred paces when he heard a hiss. A sequence of clicks followed and he made some clicks of his own.

"Brother! Are you *The One*?"

"It is I," he responded.

"Long have we waited. Too long. *Her* patience wears thin. Two of us there are here. Four more wait in the city beyond and four again at the surface. Do you have it?"

"I do not!"

"What? Your life will be forfeit, brother, if you do not present it. Where is it?"

"Do not presume that you may castigate me, you low-born scum! Listen to what I have to say and bite back your tongue."

The Darkling assassin briefly told of his difficulties and of the group that pursued him through the mine tunnels. He explained how he had left traps and danger in his wake and he said how the group still survived to follow him still.

"We shall proceed straight to the City of Shade then," stated one of the other two Darkling. The assassin hid his displeasure at being told what to do by these underlings. A thin blade between the ribs would silence that one's attitude soon enough.

The second Darkling however, was more respectful. "Perhaps we could spring our own trap, or ambush. Not far ahead, but beyond the razor-rocks, is a great pillared hall. Were we to spread ourselves across the hall, we may be able to have better success and turn our, er, problem into a success."

That idea was much more to the liking of the assassin.

The trio marched on in the darkness in total silence for many hours. Eventually they came across a change in the tunnel floor. The flat surface abruptly changed into razor-edged rocks that were difficult to walk across.

"She anticipated the need," one of the assassins whispered, "and furnished us with these gifts."

The two Darkling had arrived suitably prepared. A potion was administered to each of them and, although encumbered with weapons and packs, they were nevertheless able to float above the surface of the tunnel. Using their hands to guide their weightless bodies over the razor-sharp rocks and against the walls and ceiling, they soon made their way to the far end of the obstacle, a distance of about two hundred paces. It was many more minutes before the effect of the potions wore off but it was not instantaneous when it happened and they gently sank to the smooth floor.

Will the fools behind me be so well prepared? mused the assassin.

∽ ∽

"Look at this boot-print!" indicated Silmar. "It's his for sure."

The fight with the six Grullien had been short. They were bald-headed and their eyes large and dark. Their mouths were wide and their teeth pointed, including their abnormally long canines. They wore armour of thick, rigid leather on their chests and backs and were armed with short-swords and picks with long, sharp spikes. Billit destroyed two with a *Storm-Bolt* spell and Jiutarô sliced through one with his katana. Meanwhile, Jasper pummelled another with his war-hammer, smashing his skull. Silmar and Jasper engaged the remaining two in a bitter melee, the Grullien proving to be relentless in their ferocity. Taura used her staff to batter Jasper's foe on the back of its neck and was rewarded with the sound of breaking bones. She finished it off with a thrust onto it bald head. Jasper and Silmar joined forces to slay the last Dark Gnome. The companions stood back to survey their handiwork.

"Nasty little buggers, weren't they," observed Jasper. "Wouldn't want ter meet loads of 'em."

Leaving the bodies of six Grullien behind them, the group marched on and from time to time had used the beams from their light-tubes to find their way. In this way, they had seen much more sign of ancient occupation of the mine tunnels. There were remains of wooden boxes, pieces of rusting armour and helms, broken shields and weapons too. There were the complete skeletons of humans and dwarves, as well of others that were not so easily identified. In some cases, the bones were scattered about is if more recent travelling groups had callously kicked them about.

Jasper even picked up one or two copper coins that had been caught by chance in the light-beams. They were coated with the green patina of age. He rubbed one vigorously with his thumb and studied their surfaces. The ancient designs embossed upon them were unknown to him. As an innkeeper, he was familiar with coins from many of the kingdoms on Amæhome, but these coins were very old from long-forgotten realms. Some of these he pocketed; they would still have some value. If not, he would mount them on the beams of his tavern in Northwald City.

The tunnel became quite narrow at one point, being no wider than would allow two people to walk side-by-side.

After a while though, it widened again but Billit, who was now leading them, pulled them up.

"'Ow in the seven 'ells of the Void do we go on from here?" he asked.

Ahead of then the floor was carpeted with upright razor-sharp stones.

Jasper replied "This is choddin' bad. The floor 'as gone and these rocks are damned sharp. We won't easily be able ter walk across 'ere. My legs is too short an' so is yours, Billit"

"We have no choice. We'll need to go on. How far does it go?" asked Silmar.

"Sushi look for us?" asked Jiutarô.

The cleret-wing dragon purred and perched on his shoulder. "Look for me?" whispered Jiutarô. "Nuts and fruit for you? Fly, friend!"

The little creature launched herself away and Jiutarô closed his eyes. Within a few dozen heartbeats, Sushi was back. She returned to her favourite spot on Jiutarô's shoulders and twittered in his ear.

"My eyes see Sushi eyes," he explained.

The meaning was unclear at first. Then Billit laughed gently. "'E means that what Sushi sees, 'e can see through his eyes."

"He's sorta mentioned this afore," murmured Jasper. "But I weren't sure what 'e meant. A 'andy trick."

"Aye," replied Silmar. "'Tis true for I have heard it mentioned by our loremasters. It takes a while and the two of them must be closely-bonded for it to happen but, when the cleret-wing dragon allows it, she can enable her human partner see images through her eyes."

"Rocks go, um, two-hundred walks, er, walks?"

"Paces?" asked Falcon.

"Hai, paces. Hai!" The Samurai was feeding the promised nuts and fruit to Sushi.

"That's a choddin' long choddin' way! I been 'ere before and they weren't 'ere then! What do we choddin' do about it? Some o' yer longshanks can walk through it but not me 'n' the gnome."

"Hey! I might 'ave an answer to that," said an excited Billit. "Wait a bit. A couple o' you can take all the packs across an' come back for me an' Jasper. What d'yer think, eh?"

"Can you not try a magical spell," asked Taura.

"Dunno one like that," the gnome admitted.

"I shall carry them," Falcon volunteered.

His last passenger was not such a straightforward task. Jasper was deceptively heavy. By the time Falcon had carried the dwarf to the smooth floor of the passage, his short goatskin leggings were badly torn from scraping twice with the jagged rocks, he had many gashes and deep scratches on his legs and arms from the jagged rocks of the floor. Taura spent a long time with him, longer than was really necessary, healing the worst of his injuries and then curled up in his arms.

They agreed that they should rest, eat and sleep. Taura felt a strong need to converse with her God and Falcon badly needed sleep.

Silmar couldn't help but wonder how the Darkling managed to cross the razor-rocks, if he indeed had done so.

In the darkness, the Darkling waited. The ambush was set. It was foolproof. *We shall finish these fools and put to an end whatever quest they thought they were on. And that damned white elf! He's mine! He shall know pain before he dies at my hands!*

From their vantage points, each of the assassin's companions, using their well-developed dark-vision, they could clearly see the archway through which the group would enter. Unlike the surface-dwelling elf, the Darkling needed no faint vestige of light-source in order to see in the darkness. Generations of Darkling beyond reckoning had dwelt in the dark, low places of Amæus and their vision had developed such that differences in temperature of every material, be it rock, wood or flesh, enabled their shapes to be clearly defined.

The assassin had refused the offer of one of his two companions to rush the short distance to the City of Shade to bring the four brothers-in-arms to the assassin's aid.

The two Darkling warriors sat apart from each other with their light-crossbows and throwing-knives at the ready. The assassin waited to one side, away from his companions with his sword and daggers loosened in their scabbards. He reflected on the wisdom of declining that offer. The surface scum had proven themselves to be tenacious, having survived his numerous attempts to entrap them.

CHAPTER 23

THE COMPANIONS had rested on the floor of the tunnel, Falcon was sleeping and Taura was deep in meditation. Jasper reckoned that some hours had passed but sleep did not come to him. Silmar, Falcon, Jasper and Jiutarô had taken turns in keeping watch over the sleeping group. The elf stood in silence, his eyes straining to see the merest speck of light in the deep blackness for without it he had no dark-vision. His keen hearing detected no sounds at all from the darkness ahead of them but, of course, this was no guarantee of safety. So many lessons had been learned during their perilous journey in the mines of the Shadow World. Danger might have come from almost anything that walked, flew, slithered, burrowed or ate its way through the mines. It wasn't just from Darkling, the Grey Elves, the Grullien or even undead that were rumoured to infest areas of the deep. The very walls of the tunnel seemed almost alive with hazard and even death. They could be under scrutiny now, from eyes unseen. But there was good here too. For many years the disparate races had endured the Shadow World and they had adapted to survive in its hazardous and treacherous darkness.

The elf had roused Billit first and the gnome was now huddled beneath a blanket, with a light tube, studying and learning spells. This was a necessary activity because the mage, like any other mage, could not cast a spell unless he or she had taken the time to study the vocal nuances and gestures required so that the spell, when cast, would be successful.

After a while, Silmar roused the rest of the party. Water was getting very low. They had perhaps the equivalent of a wineskin's worth between them. It would not last a day's march. It had been a long time since they had come across a source of drinkable, clear, flowing water.

Within a few moments, they were walking again without light beams. Jasper led this time, with Silmar to one side and slightly behind him. They moved in the pitch darkness and, anxious that the floor might be hazardous, were all linked with lengths of rope; but the going was miserably slow.

The dwarf was confident, however. "I think this tunnel is getting wider," he whispered. "Can we risk some light, do you think?"

Although he was whispering, all of the group could hear him more clearly than was comfortable.

"I think so," replied Silmar. "Move to the sides of the tunnel just in case. Ready? *Lightson!* Three; two; one. Now!"

Three beams of light lanced out before them from the leather tubes in Jasper's, Silmar's and Taura's hands. They squinted their eyes for a few moments until they became accustomed to the brightness and could see the tunnel stretch out before and behind them. It curved to the right within a few dozen paces and the floor and walls seemed smooth and solid. With surprise, they noticed that the floor was littered with crumbling bones, decaying cloth and leather, and rusting armour and weapons. In anger tinged with frustration Jasper kicked at a helmet and out of it rolled a dwarf skull.

Taura recoiled in horror into Falcon's protective arms. "You told me not too –" she began to admonish him.

"It's a Grey Dwarf helm so I don't care! Old battle, long ago. *Lightsoff!* Move quietly now," mumbled the dwarf angrily and the beams were extinguished. The darkness closed around them and the group of friends felt vulnerable once more.

They moved forward, using the tunnel wall on their right-hand side as a guide.

ରୁ ଛ

Where are they? The assassin was getting very impatient. He badly needed to relieve himself despite not having drunk water for a very long time. His mouth was dry and his head ached from dehydration. Damn, he should have taken some water off one of the other two but he felt, in his arrogance, that this would have shown a flaw on his part.

Have they found another route? How can they? There is no other way, I am certain of it.

He could hear the faint rustlings coming from his two companions and a muted cough.

Damned undisciplined fools!

There was a faint *clink!* as a Darkling blade gently struck a rock and a shuffle as the malefactor shifted position.

I shall skin them if they have alerted the surface rats!

ରୁ ଛ

Both Silmar and Jasper stopped and stiffened at the sound. A faint chitter came from Sushi and her claws dug gently into Jiutarô's shoulder.

"Metal!" breathed the elf into the dwarf's ear.

"Darkling?" replied the elf.

"Aye, gotta be."

Silmar gathered the group around him. "Darkling ahead, maybe. Total silence now. Billit, can you make magical light?"

"Aye!"

"Immediate?"

"'Ow 'bout this? I can make ready the *Radiance* spell 'n' hold it 'til you say *Lightson*!"

"Good. Ready everyone?"

Each of them reached instinctively for their weapons, slowly withdrawing them to avoid any scraping sound. They crept forward at a snail's pace in silence, still using the wall as a guide and taking care not to scuff the ground. Unfortunately, this was made almost impossible due to the scattering of old armour and bones.

There was a whistling sound. Falcon grunted and the party stopped.

"Lightson!" yelled Silmar.

A small ball of light appeared in Billit's hand and momentarily, the group was illuminated. He flung it in front and it hovered above the scene. They saw two Darklings, one to the left, the other to the right, huddled behind pillars of hewn rock.

Silmar heard rather than saw the light crossbows in the hands of the Darkling warriors as bolts were released almost by instinct rather than aimed purposefully. *They've hit Falcon! But, where is the assassin?*

But the giant Barbarian was on his feet, apparently unhurt. He had been hit, a bolt jutted out from his left hip. Seeing the pair of Dark Elves, he charged. But not at the Darkling; he collided with the pillar itself and struck it hard with his right shoulder. Some debris fell from the top of the pillar as it moved, grating against the ceiling. He pushed again with all his strength and more movement was evident as one of the great stone sections slid a little to one side. With an ear-splitting yell, the barbarian took his great war-hammer and struck the displaced stone with all of his might. It shattered to small pieces. The top sections of the pillar crashed down, followed by massive boulders from the roof of the chamber. The two Darklings squinted upwards in the glare in horror. One of them leapt to the side but the other had no chance to escape as the rocks struck him and crushed him to pulp.

Billit and Jiutarô rushed forward looking for an enemy but all they saw was Falcon falling, retching and twitching, to his knees. Jiutarô dropped beside the warrior just as the man fell to his side. There was no sign of the claret-wing dragon. He looked over and saw Silmar circling the Darkling that had survived the rock fall, each wielding a drawn sword. Neither was making any attempt to open with an attack.

Taura moved around to find better target, her lips moved as she chanted a prayer. There was no sign of the Darkling assassin.

With a lunge, Silmar drove the point of his rapier at the Darkling's chest. The dark elf avoided the attack by a whisker's width and countered with a swing at Silmar's neck.

The elf was ready for this and deflected the attack with the cross-guard of his weapon. Instead of replying with another swing or lunge from his blade, Silmar kicked out with his foot, connecting it with the Darkling's kneecap. The Darkling flinched with pain but did not cry out. There was a flash of movement and the Darkling dropped to the ground with Sushi's tail wrapped about his head. The little dragon had released the stricken Darkling by the time he hit the ground and she glided back towards Jiutarô. The Darkling was clearly dying, albeit slowly and in acute agony, while twitching and clutching at his neck. He expired almost immediately.

"You have something I want, white elf!"

The voice was harsh and bitter. Silmar looked to his left. The Darkling assassin stood just behind Taura, his scimitar across her throat and his hand clutching a handful of her hair. A trickle of blood ran down her neck where the blade had made contact. Her staff clattered to the ground.

"Give it to me immediately, now! No counting to three or any other dramatic action to give you time."

Silmar knew he had no time to bluff or try to rescue the Priestess.

Suddenly, Taura disappeared from sight! The Darkling's face showed surprise, but that expression turned to shock as he looked down to where a small dagger jutted out from his right thigh.

With a grunt, the Darkling took hold of the dagger and pulled it out, and threw it towards Silmar.

The elf easily dodged it.

A smiling Taura was standing right behind him. "What did he do with my dagger?" she asked.

Billit's conjured light began to fade. Under cover of the deepening darkness the assassin staggered behind pillars and rubble and was gone!

"Damn, He's gone. What did you do, Taura?" asked Silmar.

"Ah, well, that was easy. I could say I let myself get captured by him on purpose but that would be a small lie and Neilea would not be happy with me. He was behind me but I drew my dagger and stabbed him in the leg. But then something else happened and I changed places somehow."

"That was me doing a *Secret Jump* spell on you, girlie," called Billit. "I was looking at that one when after I got woke up earlier! I didn't think I could do it yet! Taura, come and 'ave a look at this Barbarian, will you? I think he got poisoned by this bolt."

"Falcon!" she cried and rushed to his side.

Sushi sat atop the Barbarian's prone form and licked at his face but then took off from his chest. Almost immediately she gave a shrill cry and settled back down onto the ground next to him. Falcon was lying there with two small crossbow bolts sticking out the side of his chest next to his left armpit. Silmar listened carefully to the Barbarian's breathing. It was very shallow indeed.

Then Billit called out excitedly. "Falcon is still breathing. It might be venom. What did my cousin gnome Sage say about venom?"

"I have it!" replied Taura. With a little rummaging inside a small pack on her belt, she held aloft the three glass phials.

Billit held out his hand. "Trickle some down Falcon's thro—"

"I know what to do," replied Taura sharply.

Within a while, Falcon's breathing was improving.

The Priestess of Neilea went over to Billit and kissed him on top of his head. "I'm sorry," she said. "I was very worried. He has been saved from a probable painful death."

"It's alright," the gnome replied. "I do understand."

Taura looked pensive. "How did she know?" she pondered. "The Chthonic Gnome soothsayer, I mean."

Silmar smiled. "Amazing, isn't it?" he replied. "She's a sage, how can the likes of us explain this?"

"I expect Falcon will be asleep for a long time while the poison leaves his body."

"We are now stuck between Grey Dwarves on one side and the Darkling on the other," said Silmar. "I don't know where the Grullien are but they are probably ahead of us somewhere. May the god's help us if a force of either one of them comes this way. The Grullien patrol around the tunnels looking for slaves from Chthonic Gnomes and Grey Dwarves."

"What do they use slaves for, anyway?"

"Aye, yer right about the Grullien bein' ahead of us," admitted Jasper. "They use 'em to dig their own mines fer the silver that they crave. That bastard Darkling may've gone off to the Grulliens. That light spell of Billit's was ideal; it really blinded those Darkling. We may be able to use that against the Grullien too. Should imagine they don't like bright light either. The Chthonic gnomes say you can smell their City of Shade long afore you get there. Real bad too! Trouble is that we 'ave to go through the Grullien city to get to the end o' this tunnel."

It was a long time before Falcon woke up. For what seemed like ages, he was drenched in sweat but eventually he shivered. He had thrashed about for a while suffering from nightmares. When he did awaken, he was still cold.

Taura walked over to Silmar and whispered something in his ear. The elf nodded and spoke quietly to the others. They went a few paces down the passage, leaving Taura alone with a recovering Falcon.

In the dark, Taura slipped beneath the blanket and cuddled Falcon in her arms to give him the warmth of her body. She gasped as his coldness touched her warmth for, under blankets, he was naked, and soon after so was she. Long after, when both of them were warm, he awakened.

"What do you think they are up to?" whispered an exhausted Jasper.

"Use your imagination," laughed Silmar, also quietly. "I'll keep watch for a while. You and Sushi next, Jiutarô?"

"Hai! You wake me. *Domo arrigato!* Um, thanking of you."

A smiling Silmar stood guard in silence, thinking of a very beautiful young human lady in Westron Seaport, not for the first time, either. He was fully aware of the warnings his father had given him over the years. For an elf to have a relationship with a human there would be consequences to consider. These could be bitter-sweet; wonderfully joyous and then tragic. The human partner would grow old and die while the elf would still be relatively young. Offspring would, of course, be half-elven but while their features would show the signs of both races, their traits would favour only one and, should that be human which was most likely, the day would come when the elven parent would be the one to bury their partner and, eventually, their own offspring. Many elves had found this hard to bear in the past. Silmar was resolved to take this in his stride and see what would happen.

Sometime later the companions were roused and they moved on, again in silence. Nothing was said to either Falcon or Taura.

๛   ๛

They continued walking for a few hours. For the most of it, there was some dim light emanating once again from the mould-growth on the smooth walls of the tunnel. There was a smell of dampness now, which they had not really perceived before. Having tried the water which had settled in pools in some places, it was found to be bitter and undrinkable; they now had almost none to share and were urgently looking to fill up their empty water-skins.

After trekking for another hour in silence, Billit gave a sniff and said "Choddin' reeks down 'ere now, like something crawled 'ere an' died!"

It was a powerful, pungent, smell of decaying matter.

"Silence!" whispered Silmar. "Hide!"

There was insufficient cover; nowhere for them all to hide. Billit seemed to disappear from Silmar's dark-vision. Within a few heartbeats, they could clearly hear the sounds of shuffling & rattling.

It was too late. Before them, in the dim light from the mould on the walls, they could see Shade Gnomes, the dreaded, cruel, Grullien; probably almost twenty of them not thirty paces away from the group of adventurers and every one of them armed and ready to fight. They spotted the companions straight away.

Inevitably, accompanied by much yelling, the war-band of Grullien moved to engage the companions. Each of them felt a warm glow envelop their bodies. *Very strange*, thought the elf.

"Ready light-tubes," Jasper yelled. "*Lightson*, now!"

Three beams of light streaked into the Grullien and many of them surged about blindly. A couple of them dropped their short-swords; they clattered to the rock floor.

The Shade Gnomes were horrible to look upon being virtually identical to the six they had vanquished earlier. Arrows streaked from both Jiutarô and Silmar and immediately three Grullien fell to the floor. Billit reappeared to the right side of the tunnel with a blindingly white glow on his hand and he yelled "Hit the Floor!"

They needed no further prompting and, as one, they dived, head-first, to the ground. There was a very loud *Whoomph! A Fire-Blast* cast by the little mage immolated many of the Grullien. The companions felt the heat from the blast as it seared across the backs of the heads and necks. When they lifted their heads, the majority of the Grullien were dead. Billit leapt about in triumph, laughing at the top of his voice.

Jiutarô and Silmar were the first to leap to their feet. The surviving Grullien were totally disorientated by the blast and it looked like all of them were suffering from effects from the heat and flame. Wisps of smoke curled up from many of them, including that of the largest one of the Shade-Gnomes who stamped forward shaking his barbed spear and yelling orders at the top of his voice. His face was badly seared by the flame but it did little to reduce his ferocity.

Arrows from Jiutarô & Silmar continued to streak into the survivors, including the leader, and two more of them fell. The leader, however, stumbled forward with two arrows protruding from his body but did not fall.

A voice tore through the dimness – it was Billit again calling arcane phrases. A moment later, a very bright ball of light, centred on the Grullien leader; it lit up the tunnel. The surviving Grullien, about eight in all, were once again completely blinded for a few seconds. Even the companions blinked against the brightness of Billit's latest magical spell. This was all the time that Sushi needed to play her part in the battle. She darted forward and attacked the Grullien leader with her deadly tail sting and with bites from her needle sharp teeth. The leader slumped to the floor with his throat torn out, his life-blood ebbing away and did not move again.

"Forward, my friends!" shouted Jasper. He, together with Silmar and Jiutarô, charged forward and took the fight, hand-to-hand, to the remaining Grullien. Swords, spears and an axe whirled in a confusion of movement in the now brightly-lit tunnel. Jiutarô found himself besieged by two Grullien but a flurry of sword-swings cut through their weapons and despatched them before they could score a single strike with their barbed spears and short-swords.

The great Barbarian, who limped as he stepped between two Grullien, whirled his great warhammer with a single hand and both fell at his feet. He immediately fell to his knees in pain but using his warhammer as a crutch he slowly pulled himself up again. Taura rushed over to him.

The fight over in less than two minutes; all of the Grullien were dead and there were no injuries to the companions. Falcon still moved stiffly from his previous injuries and he examined one of the deep cuts that had torn its stitches. Taura was quickly giving him attention.

"Was that warm feeling we had something to do with you, Taura?" asked Silmar.

"Aha, I asked Neilea to hold you all in her favour and give you all strength!" she replied. "I am pleased that you noticed it."

"Well, that sure 'elped me, I was buzzin'," replied Jasper.

"What in the hells of the Void are we going to do with this little lot?" she asked. "If another force of Grullien stumble on these bodies, we may have a complete city of them after us."

"Wait a moment!" exclaimed Jasper. "Look! I got it! Trefanwe! She told us what to do! The dark dwarf weapons an' armour that she told us to bring. Drop 'em 'ere! Haha! It'll make it look like they done it."

"Hai!" exclaimed Jiutarô. "I have idea!"

He haltingly described a plan which, despite his language difficulty, seemed absurdly simple.

For a little while they looked at each other and one or two additional ideas were put forward. Although impractical, one idea led to another and then another.

"Lookit!" said Billit. "We need to work out 'ow to do it? Cephod told me that I can move with some measure of invisibility. I thought I was just clever at 'iding and blendin' in but it looks like that is what it's all about with us Chthonic Gnomes. We're really good at doing it, that's all. So it makes sense if someone needs to go forward and yell swear-words at the tooth-gits, then it's gotta be me! Well, 'ow far is it to their city?"

"I have these Grey Dwarf arrows," said Falcon. "They might be helpful. What is Grey Dwarf word for *run*?" suggested Falcon.

"Grey Dwarf word for run is *kra'kth!*" said Jasper.

"Krakth," echoed Billit.

"No, yer chod! Try it again. Krak'th! ***Krak'th!***" The last word was almost a shout until Silmar shushed him.

"*Krrrak'th!*" tried Billit.

"Oh, shitty hells! That'll do, ya choddin' fool!"

"Look everyone," called Taura softly from a little way along the tunnel. "No wonder it smells so bad. There's all sorts of dead bodies dumped in this big chamber here. It's like a tomb. Ugh!"

Once more, the companions strode forward along the tunnel. The smell was intolerable for a while. They were totally silent now and, for once, even the young, giant Barbarian's footfalls were gentle.

The smell became slightly more bearable quite quickly but the air remained stale - there was no ventilation. They had been walking for a while and were aware of dull sounds of life ahead.

"We must be getting close to the city," whispered Silmar. "We need to find a hiding place."

They had noticed a few suitable places on the way, mainly small chambers and ledges. One ledge, however, caught Silmar's eye. A raised projection on the left side of the mine tunnel was at a height a little above Falcon's head and looked ideal. The elf nimbly leapt, caught the edge of the ledge and easily swung himself up.

"Come," he whispered. "I'll help you up."

Soon, all except Billit had climbed, or been hoisted, up onto the ledge and the elf jumped back down. In his hand he held two black arrows that had been taken from the Grey Dwarves. Silmar and Billit silently walked along the tunnel towards the City of Shade, the lair of the Grullien.

A little while later, Silmar returned alone to the ledge with his companions.

❧ ❧

"Lightoff, now Billit!" hissed Silmar. "Crouch. Weapons ready!"

They could hear the faint sounds of voices and movement ahead. Once their eyes grew accustomed to the pitch darkness, they could both detect an increase in the light level ahead of them. It seemed to indicate that they were close to a centre of life, perhaps even the City of Shade itself. Silmar and Billit crept forward silently until a narrow opening allowed them to see the entry into the city. It was wide enough for three large men to walk side by side and as tall as a hill giant.

The pair could plainly see three Shade Gnomes, dreaded Grullien armed with barbed spears, short-swords and picks. They were standing guard a few paces beyond the opening. Flanking the arched doorway were two wide pillars and the entry itself was framed by a plain carved arch. The guards appeared to be taking little interest in the archway but were talking amongst themselves.

But that is the nature of guards everywhere, thought Silmar, particularly when they would have been standing guard day after day for years or even decades.

Carefully, they inched a little closer to the entrance. Silmar wielded his bow and held in his right hand the two arrows taken from the Grey Dwarves earlier. The pair now had a slightly clearer view of the city. Although dimly lit, they could make out small, circular huts that appeared to be made of stone slabs. Each structure had a roughly hewn wooden door and an open window but there was no roof on any of them. It would hardly be necessary underground. The road from the tunnel led straight through the city but they were not able to see much further than a few hundred paces or so.

Silently, Silmar nodded to Billit who nodded back. The elf nocked an arrow, shorter than he was used to, into his bow, aimed it and released it. The second arrow quickly followed the first. There was a loud scream followed by an unintelligible word of alarm. With an evil-looking grin the elf nodded again at his companion.

The gnome mage winked back and shouted, at the top of his gravelly voice, a harsh *"Krak'th! Krak'th!"*

Then the pair took to their heels and bolted back down the tunnel.

They almost ran straight past their companions' hiding place, a ledge on the right-hand side of the tunnel. Jasper hissed "Here, you chods!"

Silmar hoisted the gnome up towards the ledge and Falcon lifted him the rest of the way. Before they had a chance to offer a lift to the elf, he had already nimbly climbed up unaided.

Nothing happened for a long time then gradually a noise cane from the direction of the Grullien city. It grew louder and louder.

They were coming in great numbers.

❧ ❧

"Keep still," whispered the little gnome mage. "Wanna try something!" He mumbled and his hands weaved a series of complex moves. A faint blue glow flared and then died down. "Guess what; we are now invisible."

Perhaps sensing a magical field, the cleret-wing dragon nervously chattered. Jiutarô gently held his hand over her snout to calm her down. Within a few heartbeats a group of about a hundred or more Grullien, all of them heavily armed, rushed by along the tunnel, their feet clunking loudly on the rock floor.

"Hee hee! Now the fun begins!" whispered Billit.

"Wait a while, some of them will come back in a bit," replied Jasper.

"And they will be more than a bit pissed!" added Silmar.

"Oh do shut up, you silly men!" hissed Taura.

"Er, I'm a gnome!"

"And I'm an elf!"

"Oh aye, an' I'm a choddin' dwarf! You mind who you is callin' men!"

Taura was puzzled. "So what?"

"It's like this, human girlie! We're not men!" replied the dwarf with a chuckle.

"Well, you're all bloody males! So just shut up!"

The three males all went "Hmmmph!" in unison.

After a long period of silence, they heard a commotion along the tunnel. There were shouts of alarm and anger.

"Ooh, they find bodies!" hissed Jiutarô.

A while later, five Shade Dwarves rushed by the hiding-place heading back towards the city.

This plan's developing very well, thought Jasper. "The big bunch of 'em will be along in a while," he whispered.

"Er, oh shit! Our hiding spell's worn off now," moaned Billit. "Couldn't hold it any longer. Not done it before. I'm quite, er, pleased with myself that I done it!"

"Can you do it again for when the main force comes along?" asked Silmar. "They might have mages with them, or priests. We must be hidden."

"Well, aye. But I must 'ave time to prepare for it. I can't just turn on an *Invisibility Cloak* spell over six people and a miniature dragon like a, a water pump, you know!"

It must have been a full hour before the approach of a massive force of Grullien could be heard advancing from the city. Billit had just had enough time to prepare for, and cast, the *Invisibility Cloak* spell. So large was the force that it took almost an hour for it to march past.

The leading Grullien had been bristling with weaponry and anger was deeply etched on their faces. In the lead had been what seemed to be larger and more heavily-armed fighters of the species. These wore a variety of armour parts and wielded a collection of spears, swords and picks, and each of them held a round, battered shield. At the rear of the vanguard followed what seemed to be their battle-wizards or clerics. These were dressed in cloaks and each held a staff.

The main force though, was not so well protected. As they marched, their voices were raised in unintelligible war-chanting and the leaders were beating their shields with their spears in rhythm. More clerics followed the last of the army. As they passed, one of the cloaked Grullien glanced up at the ledge upon which the companions were hiding. The Shade Gnome then looked away, seemingly satisfied.

The companions could now breathe a little easier.

Silmar puffed the air out of his lungs. "The city must have emptied itself of Grullien," he whispered.

"Hey, that was too easy!" whispered Billit. "I have to dismiss the invisibility now. I'm worn out!" With a single word and a brief flick of his hand, Billit dispelled his *Invisibility Cloak* spell. He was clearly shattered and running with sweat.

"It has served its purpose, Billit," replied Taura. "Well done. My heart was in my mouth when that mage, or whatever it was, looked up."

Suddenly, the beating and chanting stopped. The Shade Gnome army had reached the dead bodies. Suddenly there were new shouts of fury. "*Gabbrabba! Gabbrabba!*"

"Any idea what they are saying, Jasper?" Silmar asked.

"Not sure," he replied. "Think it might mean kill, kill, or somethin'."

The sound of the army disappeared after quite a long time. The companions waited but there were no more shouts from the direction the Grullienn army had taken, nor any sounds from the direction of the city.

The group dropped off the ledge and carefully made their way towards the City of Shade.

❧ ❦

They walked along the tunnel in complete darkness. There was a vestige of light here and there from little pockets of mould growth on the walls but to the humans, it was not enough to see by. The companions still needed to hold onto those blessed with dark vision. After a while the light grew. They were approaching the arched entrance to the city.

With weapons drawn, they inched towards the opening. At the arch, Jasper, Billit and Silmar, each using as much cover as they could, glanced in. Not ten paces away stood two Grullien guards. The bodies of the two killed earlier lay where they fell, each with a dark dwarf arrow protruding from their body. Twenty paces beyond them was a narrow bridge crossing what appeared to be a deep chasm. Two more guards stood on the bridge.

In a low voice, Silmar described what he could see to the others

Judging by the waving of arms and coarse voices, these two were arguing over something.

The portal at which the three now stooped was at the top of a slope that gradually dropped as it crossed the bridge. From their vantage point they could see across much of the city although, because of the dimness, it was difficult to see detail. Light throughout the city was provided by glowing globes placed atop poles across the city. Although termed a city, it covered little more than an area no larger than that of an average market township up on the surface but the small, round structures were densely packed. These appeared to be constructed from bricks that were roughly laid in circular rows. The Grullien guarding the tunnel entrance and those at the bridge had yet to notice the companions, who, by now, were making little attempt at using the cover and darkness of the tunnel mouth.

The attention of the Shade Gnomes was centred on the few goings on across the city and they were gruffly babbling away in their own language. The city itself seemed almost deserted. There were very few Grullien about, except for a group in the city centre. There was no sign at all of the slaves that were reputed to be in the city.

"By the smaller gods!" whispered Jasper. "The city is nearly deserted but there's still too many fer us to fight."

"No, look!" breathed Taura. "Most of them are unarmed. Mind you, that group in the centre there look like they may have weapons. They're too far away for me to see. What do you think, Silmar?"

"There are about twenty of them and they *are* all armed," replied the elf. "One of them is huge, for a gnome; about the same size as you, Jasper."

"Eh? What you sayin'? I'm fat or somethin'? I'll 'ave you know –"

"There is another one though," continued Silmar. "He looks like a mage or something. Wait! That group. Maybe they're the females."

"Them guards are young, sort of children," whispered Billit as he peered through squinted eyes. "Look at how they 'old their weapons."

"We still won't manage 'em all on our own," whispered Jasper. "We could use an army; there may be more hidin' in the huts." He patted his war-axe. "C'mon, let's get out there an' see how it goes!" he growled. "Are you ready?"

They stepped out of the tunnel and made their way straight towards the two Grullienn guards. The Shade Gnomes turned and, with their mouths agape, dropped their weapons in terror as the strange shapes approached them. They fled shrieking across the bridge. The other two bridge guards saw the two approaching and did the same, this time taking their weapons with them.

Laughing, the companions stopped at the bridge and looked across the city. They could see it all a little clearer now. It stood at a crossing where each road led to four tunnels that opened into the city. As with the entrance through which they had come, the other three portals were each flanked by two pillars that held a carved lintel. At the centre, where the four roads met, was an amphitheatre around which were rows of benches, roughly hewn from rock. Its surface, however, was polished smooth by countless years of use, or probably by Grullien artisans and their slaves. The chasm, across which the bridge spanned, stretched from one side of the city to the other. There was just the single bridge across it.

The area to the side of the chasm at which they had entered the city was narrow, probably no more than thirty paces at its widest place but it stretched two or three hundred paces each side. Amazingly, the roof over the city's cavern was not supported by pillar or any other means. The entire city was on the far side of the bridge, the area of which was divided into four quadrants by the roads. The nearest quadrants to their left and right each had a large number of circular but roofless huts, each with its narrow doorway. It appeared that the two quadrants furthest away from them also just had the huts but there were also some significantly larger structures.

"Where are slaves kept then?" called Falcon.

"Behind – you look!" replied Jiutarô.

Sure enough, the cavern wall to the left of the tunnel entrance had dozens of cells hewn from the rock. Across these had been fitted crude, but strong, iron bars and doors. Grim faces peered at them through the bars.

"There's our army!" said Silmar.

"Then let's get the poor sods out!" growled Jasper.

"Look what I can see!" yelled Taura. She was rattling a gate, about five feet in height and three wide, that had bars too close even for them to stretch an arm through. She shone her light tube through the gaps. "This chamber is full of Grullien weapons and shields! It's locked, though, and I can't get in."

"Can't get these cells open to release the captives, either," called Billit. He had trotted over to one of the cells.

"Wait," called Silmar. He dropped his pack off his shoulders, opened it and rummaged inside. "I knew these would come in handy one day," he said with a grin. In his hand, he held up a number of long, thin keys on a ring.

"Lock picks!" exclaimed the dwarf. "You little devil, elf!"

While Silmar started work on the crude locks, Falcon used his considerable strength to lift the gate of the weapon store right off its hinges. His muscles bulged with the strain and he also succeeded in tearing open the wound in his leg. With a screech of tearing metal, the gate came away and the store was open. He flung the gate to one side. By this time, the elf had opened the first cell and a dozen captives gingerly poked their heads out of the cell.

Silmar pulled open the cell door. "You are free, come out and take up arms against these Shade Gnomes!" called Silmar. "It is time to avenge yourselves."

The captives were gaunt and clearly undernourished. They were also filthy and covered in body-waste. Looking into the cell, Billit noticed one figure hunched in a corner. He went inside and prodded the figure. It did not move. He prodded it again and the body toppled to the side. Leaning forward, the little mage knew that the figure would never move again.

Having opened the first cell, Silmar opened the other two very quickly. One had two dead inside, one of them having died some time previously. All the captives shuffled out of the cells and gathered together. The stink was overpowering.

Twenty-seven men and seven Chthonic Gnomes were offered arms and, although willing to fight, some would not be capable of battle such was their poor condition. Two Grey Dwarves stepped out from behind other captives. Jasper immediately readied his battleaxe but Falcon steadied his hand. The Grey Dwarves asked for weapons and swore a promise to Jasper that they would fight providing that they be allowed to leave afterwards. Their own condition was enough to show that they would not be too much of a threat to Jasper or anyone else if they reneged on their promise. The Chthonic gnomes looked at the armed Grey Dwarves with suspicion and contempt.

Suddenly, six well-armed Grullien stormed across the bridge. Nobody had seen them coming. Immediately the freed captives, under the command of one of them, rushed to meet them. Weeks and months of captivity, slavery and mistreatment had build up dormant ferocity in them which exploded in a whirl of frantic fury. The Shade Gnomes were quickly despatched by the freed slaves but at a cost. By the end of the fight, two men and a gnome lay dead. The weapons wielded by the dead Grullien were of a better quality than many of those that some of the freed captives held. Some of the rusty spears and swords were cast aside to be replaced by the better ones.

A shout came from further along the cavern wall. Arms reached out from behind another cell door that had been concealed around a slight corner. Silmar rushed across. After some effort Silmar finally opened the last cell and was astonished to find twenty stronger and fitter captives. These were clearly recent additions to the slave numbers. They were mainly human, a few Gnomes. Most were given weapons.

A large number of Grullien, most of them armed, stood a hundred paces back from the far side of the bridge. They could clearly see that their captives were now freed and armed and were becoming extremely agitated. A group of Grullien was still standing together in the amphitheatre a few hundred paces away.

"I think we are ready to confront them," called Silmar. "We are not after wiping them out or harming their females and young. We seek Darkling!"

"Darkling?" called an ex-captive, spitting the word as if it was vitriol. He was the one who had led the others in the fight against the six guards. "We saw damned Darkling here earlier; about eight or ten of them. They mocked and taunted us and encouraged the Shade Gnomes to treat us badly. Many of us have been beaten on the orders of Darkling. One passed through a few hours ago. Not seen him before but he was in a fury. I wanna tell you that these bastard gnomes take the occasional captive away and eat them so I have no problem in wiping out the whole bloody lot of 'em."

Other voices were raised in anger against the Shade Gnomes. Silmar and Jasper silenced them.

"We want to leave these tunnels and you will want to come with us," Silmar called.

The two Grey Dwarves shook their heads and made to move away. "Grullien go to attack our community," said one. His voice was thickly accented as he struggled with the Universal tongue. "We go now to help our kin. We want to find why they make war."

"Aye, go forth and fight your enemy," said Jasper who turned to wink at the others.

With that, the Grey Dwarves turned back and disappeared through the entrance to the tunnel.

Jasper grinned. "We're better off without 'em anyway!" he muttered.

"Down to the amphitheatre, then," called Silmar. "Do not attack the unarmed Grullien unless they attack you first. We do not attack unarmed, females and the young. If we do then we are as bad as they are."

As they filed across the bridge, they prepared to do battle with the large group of Shade Gnome warriors on the other side but these gnomes rushed back to take up a defence of the amphitheatre. The companions and their new forty-strong army made straight for the circle in the centre of the city. There was no longer and need for stealth and hiding. They marched along the road towards the central arena. Unarmed Grullien, presumably females and adolescents, although it was difficult to ascertain, were standing away from the amphitheatre in between a cluster of huts. They backed away in terror as the group passed. A few armed individuals fled to the arena as the band approached.

Without warning, a band of two dozen Grullien charged out from amongst the huts on the right. The group of captives unleashed their fury as the Shade Gnomes charged in amongst them.

The six companions also set to with their weapons and skills. Although the captives fought hard, ages of captivity, mistreatment and malnourishment had weakened them dreadfully. Spears jabbed and blades crashed together and the roadway became slick with blood and dismembered limbs and heads. Nine men and two Chthonic gnomes died almost immediately but the Grullien were quickly overwhelmed by the companions and the remaining freed captives. Not one was left alive, such was the ferocity of the revenge of the captives.

Silmar and Jasper, followed by their companions, led the remaining thirty-three men and four gnomes straight to the amphitheatre. As they arrived, the group of Grullien drew together in a tight group. Meanwhile, more bands of armed Grullien who had dared to resist the companions' small army either bolted, not to be seen again, or were quickly dealt with by the released captives.

There was a sound of marching feet on the rock floor as they approached. An individual marched before them. Arrayed behind him was a force of twenty Grullien guards, larger than those they had seen. By the look of the weapons and armour, they were the elite of the city. The shortest of them stood at about five feet tall, a full foot taller than the average Shade Gnome. One standing amid the group however, was no warrior. He looked elderly, wore a long cloak of a shiny black material and carried a black staff upon which he leant heavily. However, one individual standing alone before them was the Darkling assassin. He was dressed fully in black although his light yellow hair looked incongruous across his shoulders.

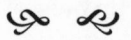

CHAPTER 24

"Once again, we meet. You thought that you could evade me by colouring your hair, you white-eyed, surface rat elf!" He spat on the road. "So, it was easy for me to get you to follow me instead of me hunting you. The outcome of either is clear. You have something that belongs to me, white elf. You will give it to me immediately."

"Come and take it if you dare!" replies Silmar. "I do not parley with a child-killer."

The Darkling chuckled drily. "Bah! Mere humans! What care I for them? And you? Oh, a simpleton, weak surface rat!"

He nodded slightly. Without warning, a blast of hot energy erupted from the old Grullien's staff. Silmar was blown off his feet and lay on the floor with a singed chest. Amazingly, he staggered back onto his feet brushing off the singed tunic. The old mage looked amazed. So did Silmar, truth be told.

He repeated the spell. Once again, Silmar was blown backwards and once again, he regained his feet and his composure. This time though, his head was badly bleeding from a deep wound above his left ear, clearly from his fall. He was obviously very dazed.

For a third time, the mage prepared to hurl the spell at Silmar. With a shout, Taura hurled a large fist-sized rock and caught the mage squarely on the nose. The old Grullien howled in agony, dropped his staff and fell to his knees.

"Thought he would hurl a blast of heat or something like that?" chuckled Billit. "No imagination, these Grullien! I just blocked it dead easy!" He strode over towards the Grullienn mage and kicked away the staff. "You are a very naughty Shade Gnome!" he added at the top of his voice.

Taura knelt beside Silmar and tended his injury.

"So, the white elf is wounded," spat the Darkling. "And he has a pet to help make him feel better. Such a pity as I had hoped to do sport with him. Is there no-one to play sword-fighting with me? It is time now, for you to give me what is mine." He gave a signal and the twenty guards fanned out across the amphitheatre.

A figure stepped forwards from among the companions.

"I play sword with you," responded Jiutarô in a very calm voice. His dead-pan face, with its dark, slanting, slitted eyes, gave nothing away to the Darkling. "You black devil! You give *me* something. I *shall* receive your death!"

"You? I think not. You may have a nice collection of pretty blades in your pretty sash and you may be quite good with that odd little bow, but with a sword? I doubt you even know which end to hold it! I shall teach you tricks with the sword for you to take with you to your grave!"

Jiutarô withdrew his katana but, this time, without the usual confident flourish. He grasped the hilt with both hands and with the blade extended over the top of his head towards the head, not the weapon, of his foe in the classic

Samurai position of readiness. This gesture, of course, was totally lost on the Darkling.

The Darkling immediately attacked with a flurry of circular swings. Jiutarô met each of these with apparent clumsiness and took a number of small steps back.

"Jiutarô!" cried Taura in desperation.

Encouraged, the grinning Darkling repeated his attack with greater ferocity behind each stroke. A swing to Jiutarô's right flank was quickly followed by another to his left. Each was again blocked but without a counter stroke.

The Darkling was now laughing. "You are now just moments away from death. You use the sword like a novice! Hah!"

Another set of co-ordinated swings, with deft footwork and an obvious mastery for the blade was resisted by Jiutarô. This time though, Jiutarô was much faster with the blocks, meeting each stroke at the top of its swing and each thrust with fresh air. He turned aside as a perfectly-executed lunge passed him by a hair's breadth.

For the first time, the Darkling's face showed some concern. *He toys with me, this strange-looking swordsman. Have I underestimated him?*

The dark elf took a step back and he recomposed himself. His last attacks had been too unco-ordinated, culminating in what he had hoped would be the killing stroke. The expression on the strange one's face had not changed. The assassin's breathing was deeper now because of the brutality of his opening attacks and he now wished he had been more cautious, more disciplined, more controlled.

Jiutarô turned his upper body to the right to stand sideways on to his enemy and he raised his katana horizontally at head height, the blade-tip still pointing at his foe's eyes. Puzzled by this apparent disregard for protecting the lower body, the Darkling made a sweeping attack to the Samurai's hip and belly. But the swing was in the opposite direction to that which a right-handed swordsman would naturally take and therefore lacked proper strength and control he might otherwise have had. Jiutarô countered easily with a block just below the Darkling's sword's guard. He followed it up with a swift kick to the Darkling's knee.

The Darkling stepped back sharply.

Jiutarô locked his gaze on his opponent. His foe took on a wide stance with the sword held up and to the right. The assassin looked deeply into Jiutarô's eyes but the Samurai exhaled sharply and charged forward.

As he perfectly executed each attack, he screamed the name of each one. '*Shomen Uchi*'; '*Kiri Age*'; '*Migi Kesa Giri*'; '*Hidari Kesa Giri*'; many more besides. Years of dedicated, rigid training and experience, and the ancient code of *Bushido*, the way of the warrior, all but obliterated any creativity that his consciousness might have initiated.

His opponent barely managed to deflect or block each successive attack, dancing it seemed in a travesty of the deft footwork of the Samurai. He was almost unaware that he was now fencing defensively.

Jiutarô's attacks, meanwhile, were purely a means to gauge the proficiencies and limitations of his opponent. At this moment he was collecting information of the best way of killing the Darkling. In moments he knew he had discovered that weakness, the dropping of the shoulder that opened the Darkling to a finish. But the assassin stepped backwards out of danger and delivered an impulsive, audacious attack, his sword circling that Jiutarô barely managed to avoid.

There it was again – the dropping shoulder.

The Samurai's blade whipped faster than sight and dark blood welled from a cut to the assassin's forehead. A pull-stroke brought blood to the Darkling's right shoulder. A similar stroke, made on the opposite side deeply bit into the left shoulder.

A look of panic crossed the Darkling's face and he launched a desperate swing towards Jiutarô's head.

Jiutarô's sword whirled faster than before as he achieved the pure state of *Bushido*, the way of the Samurai warrior. He easily deflected a weak attack, stepped forward and removed the Darkling's head in a series of swings that were too fast for the onlookers to see. The headless body dropped to the ground and shuddered as the head bounced across the ground.

Jiutarô closed his eyes and dragged his mind and spirit back together, bringing himself back to the reality of the present. He exhaled sharply, swung his katana in a circle to rid it of the dark blood and, with his customary flourish, re-sheathed his sword.

Silence descended on the gathering as the black-garbed body fell to the floor. It was many heartbeats before anyone moved or spoke. Suddenly, the remaining Grullien guards made ready with their weapons just as their mage regained his feet. As one, the companions and freed slaves brandished their weapons and stepped forwards. Faced with this, the guards flung down their weapons and gabbled away incoherently.

Jasper gestured to them with his arm and shouted "Go!" More quietly, he added "While you can, you bastards!"

The guards wasted no time in rushing out of the amphitheatre.

Nobody noticed as four other dark, lithe figures very quickly disappeared through an archway in the cavern walls at the top of a slope at the far side of the city.

❦

"Your swordplay is amazing, Jiutarô," said Taura. "Unconventional, I must say."

"The murderous Darkling swine has been defeated in great style," said a slightly dazed Silmar. "Hopefully, this is the end of the danger to us. All that is left is to get us all out of this place, out of the damned Shadow World, into the world above and off to the east."

"Aye," replied Jasper. "With thanks to our released captives fer their aid. Oh, an' we still need to fill up our waterskins. My mouth is as dry as a snake's testicles!"

One of the captives pointed to a raised pool. "Over there," he said.

Their *army* of thirty-three men and three Chthonic Gnomes offered to show the way back to the surface world. One of the men had stepped forward as a leader. "It's less than a day's march and the floor surface is good. But a force of Grullien guards the way to the surface. It may be a tough fight."

The remaining Grullien guards and citizens were clustered in a single frightened group. They made no move to take up the discarded weapons but stood there with much spitting and hissing in a last act of bravado. But they merely cowered and whimpered with terror when the newly-armed and freed captives made as if to step forward to attack them.

"We need some answers here," growled Jasper. "We need to get the bastards talking." He strode over to a Shade Gnome who, from the quality of his clothing, was clearly the leader. He grabbed hold of the terrified Grullien's collars. "Why was the Darkling 'ere? What was he doin'? Why did he wait?"

There was no answer from the terrified Grullien.

Jasper continued. "Was 'e meetin' someone? Who? Where are they?"

There was still no response.

"Perhaps they don't speak Universal," suggested Taura.

"Aye, he does," replied one of the freed captives. "That piece of sheep dung has spent a month threatening me and the men. He speaks it good."

"So you understand me, do you? Well answer me or I'll fillet you!" He pulled out his dagger and waved it in front of the Shade Gnome's face.

Questioning and threatening the Grullien leader had no response. The gnome jerked his head up and hissed in a sneering way, baring his filed teeth.

"So you refuse to talk, won't speak in Universal," growled Jasper who held his sleeve to his nose. "By the Gods, 'e stinks!"

"He pissed himself!" exclaimed Falcon.

Billit stepped forward. "Watch this!"

The little gnome mage mumbled, made a series of hand gestures and fired a streak of lightening onto a group of dead Grullien. A loud crack sounded and a metallic smell hung in the air. The bodies of the Grullien had jerked as if some vestige of life remained. The Shade Gnomes jumped in fear, as did some of the ex-captives.

"Yiz, human. I spik, I tell you," grated the leader in his guttural way. "There izza more Darkling, four go when you little group attack zity. You not be brave iffa my, ah, warband here iz!"

"Get on with it, shit-face!" growled Jasper.

"Darkling zeek zpezzal artfact, izza great power and, um, potenzee. It izza holy. One of you have. It bring-a small god, make her big god! Zhe zit by our god. Then all humanz die, all-a elvez zuffer and die, all 'Thonic Gnomes die. Darkling and-a they alliez on-a top world will be toolz of your deztruction!"

"Allies?" shouted an angry Silmar. "Who?"

But the Grullien, in particular their leader, were by now far too terrified and refused to answer any more questions.

Taura stepped in front of the group. "We must leave. The Grullien army will come back, if any left the battle alive! Which way is it?"

"Where is way out?" roared Falcon, completely startling the Grullien, the captives and the group alike.

The trembling leader pointed a shaking hand, indicating a doorway at the top of a slope behind a pair of pillars. His expression was one as if glad to be rid of troublesome relatives. The freed slaves agreed this was the entrance through which they were brought in as captives.

A call from the side of the city through which they had entered gathereed their attention. For a second they thought perhaps the Grullien war-band had returned but, to their astonishment, a large force of Chthonic gnomes was rushing across the city to the amphitheatre.

Within a couple of minutes the gnomes arrived, shaking their heads in wonderment.

"It is good that you are still here," the Lord Cephod gave a rare smile. "We have seen much of your progress after your visit to us. Your ruse has had a large effect in these mines. Know you that the battle has brought many losses to both the Grey Dwarves and the Grullien? But a large number of Grullien return now with their dead and wounded. Together, we would be enough to fight them but under the circumstances, Trefannwe tells me that it is the will of Clambarhan that we spare the Grullien. It is advisable that we all take our leave of this foul-smelling place. We shall return to our haven by using paths hidden to others. We rejoice that you have reunited us with some of our lost ones. We grieve for those who will not return but offer you our heartfelt thanks once again for what has been achieved at this time."

Trefannwe pushed back the hood of her cloak and bowed respectfully to Taura. "Take with you these ropes. You will need them."

She spoke no further words of advice. The band of Chthonic Gnomes turned and made their way back out of the city.

Jasper addressed the surviving Grullien. "You would do well to return to your homes. We have no wish to fight you or kill you. We shall leave now. Do not follow because we shall fight you and kill you. Our gnome's powerful magic will destroy you."

The Shade Gnomes made no move to comply so Jasper shrugged and led the group towards the tunnel entrance.

The companions, with their small army, made their way up the slope, out through the pillars and into the arched doorway, leaving behind them the City of Shade. They also left behind them the small and bewildered group of Grullien.

⚮ ⚭

The Grullien picked up their fallen weapons and, with much spitting and hissing, shook them at the backs of the freed prisoners in a final act of bravado. This only served to raise laughs from the band. The Grullien looked at each other and towards the tunnel entrance at the other end of the city, wondering if their war-band would return but knowing that if they did not, or if only a few should return, the hard work of rebuilding their city would have to be done by themselves until they could capture more slaves. Should none or few of them return to the city, the population would take generations to recover. What would happen then? How vulnerable they would be, forever at the mercy of those terrible, foul Grey Dwarves, even the cruel, mysterious 'Thonic Gnomes who, it was said, could walk through rock as if it were smoke with their strange and powerful magic.

One Shade Gnome, the apparent leader, pushed his way forward to address the few that stood there. The Grullien language was guttural and coarse to the ear of any other race. Few spoke the Universal tongue except sufficient to taunt and insult the slaves. "Did not some of the freed slaves threaten to return to kill the young and the females? Does this not show how barbaric the humans are? So, they make war on the defenceless? Why do they complain if we make war on their young and females? Check our females, our young. If they have been harmed the humans will pay!"

"How, you old fool?" replied another. "There are scarce enough of us to mount an attack on a wagon, let alone a village!"

"Our war-band will return, then shall we decide the future," shouted yet another.

"Calm yourselves, the defenceless are unharmed," spoke a female from a nearby hut. "We shall grow strong again."

৶ ৶

CHAPTER 25

WITH JASPER and Silmar in the lead, the band progressed through the passage. Both the elf and the dwarf carried their light-tubes and searched about them for traps and obstacles. With so many in the group now, and with the Darkling assassin killed, they had little fear of attack. The freed slaves were in high spirits and the chatter between them grew in intensity, becoming louder than the companions were comfortable with.

After a while, the mighty Falcon growled "Be silent! We have met many foul beings in this tunnel and would rather not meet any more! From now you whisper."

This had an immediate and long-lasting effect. Taura moved in closer to the Barbarian in an admiration of his strength and confidence.

After an hour or so, an awful smell became overpowering. The companions looked inside some of the small chambers on either side of the tunnel and found putrid waste products from the Grullien thrown into pits and long-dead Grullien laid in heaps. Other caverns contained only a single body, but with armour & weapons. There was very little else of value.

"These must be kings or leaders or priests or high-ranking Grullien," surmised Silmar. Some weapons were taken from these bodies by the freed captives but what armour there was to be found was useless for the humans.

Once the group had passed the chambers, they came upon a large cavern where the roof was held aloft by many pillars. They decided to rest for a short while and took the opportunity to pass round the waterskins.

"I ain't very 'appy about things right now," said Jasper. "Been thinking. What if the Grullien war-band returns an' sets out after us? We got these farmers at our back an' things may turn out nasty. Mayhap they will follow us to avenge the trick we played on 'em or they could warn others who may in turn come along 'ere after us! We will be in the deep an' sticky cack!"

Silmar nodded in agreement. "We don't know what else is down here. They said something about Darkling and their allies. We may get out of the mines and feel safe. Some of these farmers may split away and make their way back to their farms or communities. The problem may not just be with the Grullien. What if the Grey Dwarves annihilated them and start looking for revenge? How can we stop them? The answer is simple – we can't!"

"Hai. Stop them easy!" replied Jiutarô. "I learn much. Block tunnel. Bring it fall down. Big rock falling!"

"Hey yes!" said Taura. "But how?"

"Well, if you want my suggestion," said Billit. "We could try to pull down part of tunnel to slow them up for a few days. But the problem is how?"

"The rope!" cried Falcon, then he laughed. "*That* was Trefannwe's idea. We use rope and many arms to pull these pillars! By the gods! Magic will not work but muscle-power will. We have enough people and enough rope? Aye, because

Chthonic Gnome sage said to take some! How did she know? Pull down some pillars?"

"But we will need to pull down many pillars to make the tunnel blocked enough," said Silmar.

"Now look," said Billit. "If you want a solution to this problem then think back to your childhood. Did any of you ever play the bones? You know, where you match up the ends and try to use up all your bones before your opponent?"

They all nodded but were still puzzled.

"Well then. What else did you do with the bones?"

They looked at each other still puzzled.

"Gods! You are all hopeless! Look. You stood 'em all up side by side…"

"And you pushed the end one to knock them all down!" finished Silmar. "That's what we can do to these pillars! One falls onto the next and knocks it down onto the third and so on! Hah!"

Billit, having a better understanding of the task, took charge. Three long lengths of rope were tied at points up a pillar furthest away from the doorway out of the chamber. The pillar appeared to be in four sections. The top was out of reach for the upper rope but Billit did not seem to think that mattered. He was sure that when pulled, the pillar would collide with the next nearest causing them to collapse in a direction towards the escape route. Hopefully, the roof of the chamber would crash to the floor. The gnome arranged for men to take the ropes, instructing them to release the ropes once the pillar started to collapse.

"Start running as soon as pillar starts to collapse! Start to pull!"

It too quite a while and much tugging before the sections of the pillar started to show signs of movement. At first, dust floated down from the top, then pieces of rubble.

"Easy lads," called Billit. "Rest a bit."

The men dropped the rope and wiped the dust from their faces. This was not as easy as they had thought it might be.

"Once more then. Pull!"

This time, the men put everything into it. The top section didn't move but the next did. The lower three sections of the pillar started to slide and then lean outwards. One more pull and it began its fall.

"Run!" screamed Billit. "Run for your lives! Get outa here!"

The men didn't need telling twice. They ran as the first pillar crashed into the second. For a couple of heartbeats, nothing happened. Then the top section crashed down onto the pieces below it and the second pillar leaned towards the third. By this time all of the men had run out of the chamber into the tunnel and they all kept going.

"Run. Don't stop here! Run on!" screamed Billit.

They heard a deep rumbling and the ground beneath their feet trembled as massive amounts of rock fell downwards, not only in the chamber but along the tunnel behind them. Fortunately the companions and their army were well clear of the falling rock.

There was a loud cheer as a cloud of dust poured along the tunnel. After what seemed a long time the crashing and rumbling ceased. There was so much dust that, even using the light-tubes, they could see very little. But there were no casualties. There was a lot of coughing and spluttering until the dust settled.

Silmar eventually found Billit and embraced him. "Well done, my friend. You did well."

Billit beamed with pride, especially when Taura kissed him on his forehead. Luckily, in the gloom nobody could see him blush.

Waterskins, now full, were passed around again and the group were soon on their way.

❦ ❧

They had been walking in the tunnel for a few hours when Silmar softly called "Stop! Stop!"

"What is it?" whispered Billit.

"Have you found somethin'?" breathed Jasper.

"Oh aye, by the gods!" gasped Silmar. "Boot prints, unless I'm much mistaken. Look! It's the damned Darkling! There are many tracks here. There's Grullien, lots of them, look! Here's some human prints heading towards the Grullien city. Probably captives. One of these men here hopefully. A few other prints I don't recognise. They are all quite old. These boot prints are fresh and going in the same direction as us. There look! Some more. See how the edges are so sharp! There are more Darkling out here somewhere. That Shade Gnome mentioned four of them."

Billit humphed. "I thought he was bein' full o' shit," he said.

The men being led out by the companions were now visibly nervous. These were not soldiers although some had been in the past, but in general they were farmers and young lads. A few of the older ones were ill with emaciation having been half-starved, beaten and badly treated for a long time. Although all were armed to some degree but few, perhaps six or eight at the most, had any experience with using weapons in anger. The adventurers knew that should battle occur, they would only be able to rely on limited support from the men.

The band moved forward in silence. From time to time, Silmar moved a short distance forward to examine the path ahead of them. The hours passed by and water was once again getting scarce. There had been no subterranean springs, waterfalls or pools from which to refill their water-skins. Some of the men were grumbling but a warning from Falcon kept them silent.

After a while one of them started to complain. "Hasn't yer got any water? I'm spitting feathers 'ere. We always had water back there with *them*!"

"Then choddin' well go back, idiot!" grated Jasper. "Else shut it and we'll find yer some soon."

The group walked on for another hour by which time there was no water left. Taura asked Silmar to stop the group. She stood at his shoulder for while and they talked in silence. She then moved away and, with a light beam, looked at the path, the rocks and into cracks and pits.

"Found one!" she called.

Taura reached inside her tunic and brought out her sacred symbol of Neilea. Her hands weaved a complicated pattern around it, she called out a stream of complex words that no other could understand and she spat on the ground. The others slowly started to move towards her out of curiosity. As they approached they could see a pit in the rock the size of a small barrel, filling with water.

"Your drink!" she called. "Use it sparingly. I cannot do this again; it taxes me too much."

The men eagerly crowded around it. Minutes later, using just their hands they had drunk a little each but there was still more than enough to fill three water-skins.

"Don't suppose you can magic up some bread!" one of the men called out.

"Don't push your luck!" replied Taura. "I am not a cook-house."

Jiutarô called out to Silmar and Jasper. "Sushi she fly to check path. Not far. Dead Grullien there. No Darkling." The Samurai and the cleret-wing dragon stooped at the water source to get at the last drop.

"Let's do it then. Time to get out of this hell-hole!" whispered Silmar.

"Well, I like it here!" responded Jasper.

"You would, you contrary git!" retorted Billit.

"Shut mouth all you!" answered Jiutarô in a rare example of joining in a conversation.

"Hai!" replied Silmar, Jasper, Billit, Taura and Falcon in unison. Then they laughed.

The large group walked on with more confidence. It had been many hours since they had left the stinking Grullien city and they were now all hungry and tired. They had no idea of the time of day, or even of the day itself, nor even where they would be when they reached the surface world. They would not know what weather they could expect or whether there would be anyone waiting outside when they emerged. But every one of them was eager to step outside of the Shadow World no matter what awaited them.

The dwarf walked beside Silmar. "In all the excitement I forgot to ask. 'Ow's the burden? Have yer felt anythin' of it? I assume it's still there!"

"I can always feel its presence, Jasper. I feel the nasty taste of vomit in my mouth all the time. It's a bit like it's trying to remind me that it's still there. I've not had any nausea or headaches since we confronted the Darkling assassin and the Grullien so that's a good thing. At least I know if an evil *nasty* is close. I felt quite sick when the Darkling was fighting against Jiutarô and, well, it was strange really. As soon as Jiutarô killed him the feeling went away and the Grullien were no real threat. So it has its uses really. I did check that the box was there a while ago, before the Grullien city and touching the box made me gag a bit. Oh, look out!"

The tunnel came to an abrupt stop. In front of them was a rock wall. There was no door or portal of any kind. Sushi gave a chitter and launched herself off Jiutarô's shoulder. To their left was a natural pillar of stone and around it flew the cleret-wing dragon. Jiutarô followed next and behind him the rest of the companions and the men.

"Stairs!" called Jiutarô.

"Where do they go?" asked Jasper.

"They go up!" replied Silmar. "Where do you think they go?"

"Just choddin' askin'! No need for cheek! Mighta gone down. You goin' first, Jiutarô?"

"Hai."

Jiutarô followed Sushi up the stairs. She was crawling upwards, catlike, nervously keeping her profile very low to the steps. At the top was a circular boulder, rather like a very large grinding wheel, the width across it as great a man's outstretched arms. It had been rolled back to allow room for people to pass through a portal one at a time. However, in the space lay the body of a Grullien guard. It had evidently been killed by a single thrust of a narrow blade in the throat. Jiutarô stepped to the side to allow Silmar to see.

"Killed by Darkling do you think?" asked Silmar.

"Could be," responded Falcon. The giant put his shoulder against the wheel and pushed it back a little further. He pulled the small body aside. Silmar bent down to examine the body, saying "He hasn't been dead that long. The skin's cold, but then it would be anyway but it's still soft. They go all hard after a few hours. Watch out for Darkling. Or for anything, I suppose!"

Jiutarô, with Sushi now back on his shoulder, squeezed past the stone and out into a large dark cavern. Behind him emerged the others, one at a time. It took quite a while for all of the freed men to file out.

"There's five more bodies here," said Silmar softly. "They're all Grullien. There's been quite a fight but no other bodies. "Better tell you that there's a lot more footprints here. Darkling! Probably eight to ten of them. They kept horses in here too. There's dung and some oats somewhere, I can smell it. Be alert, they may still be around."

"I can smell it too, now you mention it," called Billit.

"Roll the stone back and close off the entrance," advised Jasper.

"We can't," replied one of the men. "You can only do it from the other side of the opening. It's behind this rock."

Falcon strode over to the stone and spat on his hands but, even with his great strength, he could move it no further than a hand's width. "Can you use magic?" he asked.

"Too heavy I think," Billit replied.

"Leave it, let's see where the cave entrance is," advised the dwarf.

The band made their way with Silmar and the group in the lead. The light grew stronger and some distance ahead the mouth of the cave was clearly outlined.

❧ ❧

PART 3
SHADOW WORLD

CHAPTER 26

THE SURFACE was in darkness but after the blackness of the Shadow World the night was a welcome relief to them. How clear, fresh and so, so sweet was the air. They felt the cool vesper of air movement on their faces even in the depth of the cave and sighed with pleasure. There was no moon or stars and as they walked towards the opening they heard torrential rain falling.

Silmar crouched and examined the cavern floor. "Hoof marks here, but few boot prints," he murmured. "They rode their horses out of here." He studied the tracks carefully, tracing the outline of one of them with a fingertip. "This is interesting," he said quietly. "The horseshoes are unusual. They aren't as rounded as usual; they come to a point almost, do you see? And there is a notch at the point."

"It should make 'em recognisable," Jasper mumbled. "Let's 'ope the bastards 'ave buggered off! We might as well get some sleep. It's too wet to go out right now an' we won't see where we're goin' anyway. Oh, we need to make ready to fill our water-skins."

Five men ambled over to the group of companions and one asked if they could parley.

"In a moment," Silmar replied. "First though, I think we should try to build a fire using some of this wood that's scattered around here. Can somebody round up a few men to gather some water outside? With that rain there should be lots of clear pools somewhere." He passed over the six empty water-skins.

With a little magical help from Billit a number of fires were quickly burning and groups of freed captives were warming themselves. The companions and the five men sat around their fire.

The leader of five men returned back to the companions. "Look," he said. "We five have been fighters in the past. Soldiers and adventurers, haven't we lads?"

The others nodded in agreement.

The leader continued. "All the others over there have decided they want to peel away and go back to their homes. Well, us five reckon that if it's good by you, we would like to join you and travel with you awhile. If you don't mind, that is. We heard you were going east and that's the way we're going. We're handy in a fight and not bad with decent weapons. It wasn't us what complained about the water, we're better than that. What do you say?"

Silmar and Jasper looked at each other and paused in thought. Finally, it was Silmar who broke the silence.

"Look, we aren't looking to make our group any bigger than it already is. We're adventurers of a sort but we're not in it for making a vast fortune."

"Aye, but hold it just there, Silmar," interrupted Taura. She had been on the edge of sleep. "We're not looking to *ignore* gold or gems or anything else we might find. With the task we have to do, it wouldn't do us any harm to take extra support. It seems a good idea to me."

"Aye, then," the man continued, "it's no secret you were hunting Darkling but now you've seen there's more of 'em out there somewhere and you've maybe got some problems. All I'm saying is that we're happy to join in and help if you want it. We're not too bothered about equal shares of the treasure with you, but we would be happy to be your escort, night watch, fighters, or whatever, for a fair pay. What do you say?"

Jasper spoke up straight away. "I say aye to that but the rest of our group needs to agree." He looked at Taura, Silmar and Billit and they nodded in agreement. Jiutarô and Falcon were both sound asleep. "We can pay yer but only if we collect gold on our travels. You'll need to buy yerselves some decent weapons an' stuff when we get to a town. If we can afford it there'll be a bonus when you do battle or show a quality. 'Appy with that?"

The man nodded keenly. "That will be great. Really great! If it weren't for you all coming and rescuing is we would have all been dead soon for sure. Some women captives were taken away one at a time. We think the Grullien wanted tender meat. We just hope it was quick for them; we heard no screams. Like I say, we all have some soldiering and campaigning experience and a couple of us are skilled with tracking, hunting and foraging for food."

Billit spoke wearily for the first time. "It will free up some time too," he said. "This would give me some time me to study my new spells and Taura to chat with her god. You know who we are, guess you'd better introduce yourselves to us."

Their leader was tall, muscular, and broad-shouldered with a ready smile. He kept his fair hair tied back with a cord and his beard trimmed short although it was somewhat unkempt since he had been held captive. He smiled broadly as he brandished the battered short-sword he had been given in the Grullien city. "Well, I'm Varengo, I like a long-sword I can hold with two hands if I can get one; this little pigsticker will do for now. I can ride well on horseback; we all can."

He introduced the first of his four friends. The man was slim and of medium height. His long, black hair was tied back but his beard had once been trimmed quite short; hacked short would have been a more apt description. "This is Vallio the hunter. Best tracker I ever knew. He's expert with a bow and will be more than happy with that old short-sword. We must get you a bow, buddy."

"Aye," responded Vallio, "or I can make one if we can get a bowstring. Arrows I can make dead easy."

Varengo indicated the next man; short but athletic with unkempt long, brown hair and beard. "This here is Jassio, he doesn't stop smiling even in combat. He can ride horses better than any man I've ever seen but you were once a horse-thief weren't you, Jassio?"

Jassio grinned back and shrugged. "I never got caught though so nobody could prove a thing!"

"But he can make a short-sword sing," Varengo continued, "and he can throw a dagger and split a bee at twenty paces."

Varengo then pointed to a man squatting next to the fire. He was short but very stocky with sandy-coloured hair and beard, all cropped very short. Tattoos adorned his arms, chest and the top of his head. "Morendo here, he is the crazy man; another hunter and swordsman. He was a horse-thief along with Jassio and has this amazing way of calming down a skittish horse. Lastly, but not leastwise, Yoriando." He indicated the last man, tall, broad-shouldered and athletic with long, wavy, black hair and a long, pointed beard. He waved his left hand showing where he had lost the little finger and half of his index finger. "Yori and me have fought together for many years, since we were young," he explained. "He can find a way through impossible terrain; very handy sometimes. Good with a sword, amazing with hand-axes and throwing daggers but you want to see what he can do with bolas and an ensnaring net. Well, were going to grab a bit of sleep ready for dawn if that is good with you."

෨ ෭

The six companions were seated or laying around a small fire a little way back from the cave's mouth. Their five new comrades were either resting or collecting what weapons and scraps of food and water they could find in the cavern. They took the time to bid farewell to their fellow captives who had decided, against the advice given by their liberators, to leave the cave straight away now that the rain was abating. The countryside outside of the cave was their homeland; they knew the best ways back to their farms and villages. They were many, well-armed, although with crude weapons, and still harbouring the anger that would sustain them during their travel and would encourage the weaker ones if need be.

Being the one with decades of experience, Jasper gave words of caution for everyone in the cave.

"Before yer goes off, if yer been captive for some time, 'ware the sun on your skin – it will burn you. When the sun comes up, 'ware your eyes in the bright light, yer ain't used to it. Keep together, work together an' share the chores."

The sight, smell and touch of the ground gave the large group of ex-captives all the encouragement they needed for their forthcoming march. Without waiting, but with words of gratitude and a cheery wave to their saviours, they started on their march towards the south-east. Although they didn't all know where they were, they were determined to find their homes and families, their villages and farms.

The dishevelled bunch was soon out of sight. The dwarf picked up his blanket and pack. Scratching his head, he asked "Where are we, anyway?"

Silmar watched the faint glow of the rising sun to the east as it appeared through a pass in the very tall, rocky hills. His keen eyesight carefully scanned the countryside before the cave. No threats were visible, fortunately, but he knew that this would be no guarantee of their safety. The fresh air was a welcome relief. Elves were not comfortable below ground. The fading moon and stars were now barely discernible in the sky.

"We are at the northeast point of the Spine Wall peaks. Ye gods! That means we must have done about twenty-five leagues through the mines."

The companions and their five new comrades strode out into the meadow and looked down at grass under their feet.

"I never thought I would see this again," said Varengo. "It makes me feel like ripping all my clothes off and running arse-naked through the grass!"

"Please don't," Yoriando gasped. "It won't be a pretty sight!"

"Oh, I don't know!" mused Taura.

The others roared with laughter.

As the sun rose above the peaks to their east, the group of adventurers silently and grimly filed out of the cave's mouth.

"Where we go from here?" asked Falcon, eager to be out of the cave and under the skies once more.

"East, towards Cascant," replied Silmar. "But I want to look at the tracks of the Darkling riders first." It wasn't difficult; the hoof prints were plain enough to follow in the soft ground. "Aye, they are heading straight for that range of hills way off to the east there. Now we have the added risk of them ambushing us."

"Does that mean we are following them?" asked Varengo.

The elf considered this for a moment and then rummaged inside his pack. He grimaced as his hand came into contact with the box holding the burden. It was freezing. Swallowing hard, he pulled out a roll of vellum. "I don't believe we do," he replied as he rolled out the vellum on the ground. "This is Halorun Tann's drawing. Somewhere, probably a few leagues to the south, is a track that should take us to the city of Gash. If we find it we should get to Gash quite quickly and then we can use the busy road eastwards. But we could also go straight across the plain to Nasteed."

Jasper leaned forward to get a better view of the map.

"From Gash we go eastwards to Nasteed," Jasper suggested, "through the Dragon's Teeth, across Polduman, through the Brash Mountains, into Kamambia and then up to Carrick Cliffs. This is a long and perilous journey an' we shall 'ave to start it on foot. I think we need to see what Varengo says 'cos 'e might know these lands. We 'ave far to go and will need 'orses or ponies. Or a cart. The gods know that I do not like to ride them beasts. They are cruel and vicious!"

"What?" exclaimed Taura. "Nonsense!"

"It's choddin' true, girlie! They bites yer at the front end, kick yer at the back end. And while you are nursin' that damage, they swishes yer with a tail that's half full of shi-, er, dung!"

They all laughed, as did their new comrades; it was good to hear mirth and humour again after so long.

The recent rains had left pools of clear water in crevices in the rocks just outside the cave entrance. With some encouragement from Taura, the five men were soon washing off weeks, or months, of grime and filth from their bodies. The companions used this opportunity to talk quietly amongst themselves.

Silmar explained how he had been feeling the influence from the artefact, or the burden as they referred to it, throughout the whole of their journey through the Shadow World.

"You kept that quiet," Taura observed.

"Aye, I know that but we had enough to worry about. My head ached almost constantly. I was sure I could sometimes feel the nearby presence of the Darkling but it may just have been my sixth sense which rarely lets me down. I do think we must keep the artefact secret from our new friends for now. What they don't know, they can't reveal to others."

They all agreed readily. Taura suggested that the Darkling, or any other being with arcane ability, might also be able to feel the burden's energy or evil. "What do you imagine would happen if they could? Would it draw an enemy to us? Would an evil cleric feel it and understand its presence? It could be the best way of saying *Here we are, come and get it!* that there could be."

"Probably," conceded Silmar. "What about you though. Can you feel its influence?"

She shook her head slowly. "Nay," she replied. "But then, I don't consider myself and evil cleric. I can be bad at times, though, when the mood takes me!" She looked up at Falcon and gave a wicked grin.

"Then I don't think we need to worry unduly about anyone else sensing its presence."

They agreed quietly not to inform their five new allies about it. "The least they know," said Silmar, "the better for themselves and for us. Any signs shown by me of its effect could be attributed to other excuses. I need to wash!"

After a while, Varengo and his men returned. Their clothing was wet but they looked, and smelt, much more presentable.

"I think I know roughly where we are," murmured Varengo. "Gash is less than forty leagues directly south and the Great East Silk Road runs about eighty leagues eastwards towards Nasteed. That is a tidy way. I would say that if we were to walk south-east direct to Nasteed there are very few roads and a great big marsh and it will take a few ten-day weeks because the land is rough. I reckon we go south to Gash and see if we can buy ourselves a wagon and ponies. What do you say?"

Silmar considered this for a moment. "I daresay you're right," he said. "A ten-day week to get there, maybe less if the weather stays good. There are farmsteads in that area with tracks for the farmers to move their cattle and crops to the city."

"I reckons the roads will be watched," replied Jasper, "'specially as at least eight Darkling are still out there somewhere."

"But what if there are more or they split up into groups?" responded Billit. "Prob'ly means they can watch more roads an' they got horses or ponies too!"

"Aye. There were at least eight ponies, but most likely a few more," answered Silmar. "I should have looked at the tracks more carefully."

Varengo spoke up again. "Aye, but, remember, the assassin and two Darkling were killed in the tunnels and it is likely that there were ponies for them too. So there may be many but probably not more than six to eight."

"Still a formidable force, even with our party of eleven," mumbled Jasper.

"The Darkling may well rest up during the day and only travel during the dark," suggested Taura. "They are not suited to moving in sunlight, are they?"

"Assassin did!" Jiutarô reminded them. He had been playing tug with Sushi, using a piece of black rag that had been lying on the ground.

Silmar sighed. "We can't assume anything here. We must remain on our guard but even more so during the night."

"Aye, keep watch for their tracks," Jasper advised them. "They won't risk fire so there won't be smoke." He was poking at the fire with a small stick and sparks flew up towards the top of the cave. "We must keep *our* fires low."

Falcon spoke up. "I know some of these lands, too. I been here before in my *wanderlust*. Best keep off the roads, they not safe, use small tracks where we can. That way we do best to avoid trouble."

ဟ ၻ

Varengo led the group out from the cave into the dawn's light. The day was already very warm, in stark contrast to the occasional numbing cold they had experienced during their march up the coast road towards Northwald City, so many tenday-weeks before but clouds rushed in to hide the sun. The ground here was different too. The soil was poor and dry at higher levels, despite the recent heavy rain, and very sandy. Gorse, blackthorn and hawthorn bushes grew in clumps and a tall, coarse grass waved in the soft breeze.

As the party moved through valleys and into low ground they found that they had to wade sometimes ankle deep in waterlogged soil. The skies remained overcast but the rain held off. As the first day wore on so gaps appeared in the cloud and the sun shone warmly upon them. The cleret-wing dragon spent a little time flying above the group but, having been underground for such a long time, she found that she tired quickly.

Water had been plentiful and their water-skins were full. Food was another matter, however. Stomachs were growling particularly now the food they had been eating was no longer quite so palatable to them in the open air. Jasper's warning to the other group of freed slaves had been well founded. By the end of the first day, Taura was treating sunburned noses with a salve from her bag of healing paraphernalia.

There had been no sign of other travellers during that first day. They did see remnants of old stone huts, their roofs having long been lost. There were stone walls that had once encircled small enclosures. Most of the walls had collapsed and were little more than piles of rock. The travellers found it difficult to avoid tracks because of obstacles that were hidden in the overgrown grass. They were relieved to have seen no sign of the Darkling group's pony tracks. Silmar had said that he would know them if he saw them. As late afternoon approached, Varengo suggested they find a suitable spot for a camp.

"Sushi help look," suggested Jiutarô. He looked quietly into her eyes, no words were spoken, and she flew off. The Samurai moved off to one side and sat with his hands over his eyes. Within a few moments, the cleret-wing dragon returned and perched on his shoulder. She was exhausted and panting deeply. The Samurai led the party between two low hills to a narrow, steep-sided valley. Stunted trees and bushes lined each side of the valley and a narrow stream flowed over a stony bed. A stone hut was perched on a small plateau that was edged with a tumbled stone wall. It had no roof whatsoever.

Jasper was pleased with the cover provided by the valley. "This is ideal, Jiutarô," he complimented. "Sushi 'as done well. This is good water too. We need somethin' to eat though. Me choddin' stomach is flappin' against me backbone. Who's a huntin'?"

Jiutarô and Morendo followed the stream up the slope to find food. It was getting quite dark when they returned with a small mountain goat and a sack that wriggled.

"He's a damned good bowman!" exclaimed the Morendo. "He killed a rabbit, a long way off too, with a single arrow."

"I may be wrong but it looks uncannily like a goat to me," Taura laughed. "Where is the rabbit then?"

"Stolen!"

Taura looked incredulous. "What?" she gasped. "Stolen? By whom, may I ask?"

Jiutarô laughed but Morendo looked hurt. "A buzzard took it! Hah!" he huffed. "But I brought down a young wild-hog alive as well."

With a watch set by the warriors in the party, the group settled down to sleep at around midnight. The lack of blankets for the five men was going to be a problem. The skies were clear and the moon, although just above the eastern horizon, provided a lot of light. The valley, accordingly, was cold that night.

❦ ❧

CHAPTER 27

THE GROUP HAD been walking along what appeared to be the best, and safest, route for a few days. The last couple of days had been grey and overcast but what rain fell was light and short-lived.

"Yer reckon we're back into the 'Ome Territories?" muttered Jasper. "There ain't much in the way o' game fer us to catch. I'm so 'ungry I could eat a rotten dog!"

"Aye, the border with Shordrun is some leagues to the east although it passes almost through the centre of Gash. We know these lands, don't we, Yori?" Varengo stated.

Yoriando nodded in agreement but his expression was not one of good cheer. "Aye, we battled here years ago and lost a few good men on the way. They called the area the Wild Lands then. But we helped tame them before we went back east, didn't we? But now, if we continue southwards and are fortunate enough to find a better way without encountering the giants, wargs, goblins and dragons, we should reach Gash in a few days."

The track would occasionally disappear without warning. The group stumbled through long grass following the remnants of old tracks and even watercourses when they could. Snakes were a constant worry since Billit uttered a shriek when he almost stepped on one. At about six feet long, coloured orange with black bands around its body, it was almost sure to be poisonous. Whether it was or not was something they would not leave to chance.

"Make a lotta noise as you walk," advised Vallio. "Snakes will move outa the way."

They suddenly emerged from the long grass and onto a narrow road which curved towards them from the west. It looked as though it was still in occasional use because of the fresh-looking wheel ruts and cattle-hoof prints. They followed it southwards.

"Now we need to keep a watch out for riders," advised Silmar. "I think this is the old road from Northwald City that passes around the top of the Spine Wall Peaks and goes down to Gash. If it is, it fell out of common use when goblins started moving into the northern part of the peaks. But these tracks show that some farming folk are still using it."

"The way I see it, we need to march south on this track 'til we reach Gash and the Silk Road," suggested Yoriando. "Where are the towns or settlements?"

Varengo marked the map with an indentation on the trade route that ran south from Nasteed. He indicated Harrick, a hundred leagues or so south of the great city. "This is a stopping place for caravans and traders," he explained. "The town elder is a Hoshite sympathiser who does not tolerate adventurers. Now, if I remember aright, there is a minor road that runs from about twenty leagues east of Gash, on the Silk Road, across the moors straight to Harrik."

"Aye, you got it right," said Yoriando. "The trade road from Nasteed is well-travelled by Hoshite soldiers as well as by merchant caravans. The district government in Nasteed is believed to use them as mercenaries to provide a measure of rule in eastern and southern Shordrun but as yet they don't have much authority in the city itself. As you cross into Polduman the Hoshites do not take kindly to adventuring parties like us and they won't just stop us, they'll search us and take what they want, including money, weapons and horses. We may even find ourselves in a pitch-battle if they are a big force and we try to resist. Adventurers are seen as a threat to the Hosh authorities in Harrik."

"The Hoshites seem to have come a long way west," murmured Silmar. "They must be hundreds and hundreds of leagues from West Hosh."

"Aye, you're right," said Varengo. "But with the Polduman State not having the manpower to provide a military force west of the Dragons Teeth Mountains, they have an arrangement with Hosh and now the soldiers are oozing westwards like a mud slide into Shordrun, reason being that they come cheap. Trouble is that they've brought corruption with them and they are bleeding the caravans dry with their tolls and fines. It is likely that Hosh agents watch the caravans as they set out from Nasteed so the patrols and checkpoints know what is being transported. As for us, we'll need to keep clear of the Great East Silk Road and the Hoshites may even have agents watching the moor road down to Harrick too. They are said to be as thick as fleas on a goblin's balls!"

"Tell us about the Great Moor," said Billit.

"Oh aye, as if the Spine Wall peaks aren't bad enough, you have the dangers of the Great Moor, with its infestation of gnolls and orcs and ogres."

"Gnolls and orcs I know," said the gnome, his voice gruff. "Not so sure 'bout ogres."

"Oh shit!" grumbled a very grumpy Jasper. "What sort o' lands are we travellin' in 'ere? We could not 'ave left the mine tunnels in a more desolate and dangerous place! Well, obviously we can't all go onto the trade road and into Harrik. We'll stick out like a sore coc–"

"Jasper!" snapped Taura. "Your language is far from universal."

"Grumpy girlies! I woulda said it were completely universal. Look, I got an idea. It's another three-day walk to Gash, we reckons. We need some money, right? So we need to get a ride on a caravan towards 'Arrik, offer our services as protection an' earn a bit o' gold too. Might even be able to shake off some o' them Hoshites down there."

"Then what are we waiting for?" prompted Varengo. "Let's get on with it!"

❧ ☙

They trudged ponderously towards the city of Gash for three more days. A torrential downpour on the second day had turned the sandy surface of the track into a quagmire. The two hours of rain had taken two days to dry out. During this time, Jasper had continuously complained about the mud filling his short, heavy, iron-shod boots. The others had tolerated his whingeing and grumbling until the morning of the third day.

Taura was the first to break. She rounded on the dwarf with uncharacteristic fury. "Will you stop your *chodding* whining, Jasper?" she yelled. "It rained! It is muddy! Your boots are full! There is nothing to be done about it. We're all the same. Take your boots off once in a while. When did the sun last see your feet?"

"Mah feet ain't s'posed to come outa mah boots, girlie!" the dwarf retorted loudly. "If they was, we wouldn't 'ave boots, would we?"

"So, how do you–?" she began but ended her question with a shrug of her shoulders. "Just stop complaining and whining and protesting and whingeing and –. Just stop, that's all."

"What did I do?" the dwarf asked nobody in particular with a shrug of his shoulders.

The others wisely kept quiet with their eyes looking straight in front or cast down on the road surface. Jasper mumbled incoherently for a short while but then became quiet for the rest of the day. By the next morning, after having spent half the night on watch, he was his usual chatty self and continued to be for the following day encouraged, no doubt, by the improving track condition. They kept a continuous and meticulous watch around them. Although there were clusters of shrubbery and patches of foliage and heather, there was very little which would provide protective cover in the event of an attack by Darkling or other undesirables.

Finally, before midday on the third day and from the vantage point of a rise, they saw the great trading city of Gash sprawling below them. The air above the city shimmered in a dusty haze and wisps of smoke from countless cooking fires trailed vertically into the air. Spires, domes, minarets and towers rose up from various places inside the city walls.

"Those are the back gates of the city," Varengo pointed out to them. "They keep 'em closed. All entry and exit is done through the front gates round the other side. It's probably another six or seven-hour trudge before we get there I reckon."

"Aye, that is good," chuckled Jasper. "Ales would be choddin' nice."

"There is a road of sorts," Yoriando indicated. "Not a very good one though. It seems to cross over the ditch around the outside of the city walls and if I'm judging it arightl, it will stink of all the worst wastes that the city discards – there's dead things thrown in it. We might be better circling around through these surrounding hills."

Varengo nodded. "In that case we will probably be camping out here this night," he said. "It would be well past sundown when we get there and the gates will have been closed."

They climbed through the hills taking advantage of animal trails. From time to time they walked through meadows where goats scattered at their approach and sheepherders grazed their flocks. Hunters passed them and glared at them with surly expressions, refusing any exchange of greeting.

At dusk they crested a low hill and gazed down at the city of Gash. From their viewpoint, they could see its tall, near-white mud-brick walls with its guards, dressed in light brown garb, patrolling the ramparts. They could also see figures maintaining watch from the tall gate towers seemingly on both the outside of the city walls and the inside.

Queues of traders and merchants filled the approach roads for almost half a mile. To the right-hand side of the great roadway, large and small corrals were filled with cattle, horses, sheep, swine and goats. Great mounds of straw and hay bales were placed at strategic points. To the other side of the great roadway, scores of caravans were grouped together in tight clusters.

Suddenly, there was a loud *boom* followed by shouts from those gathered before them.

"They've closed the gates!" Silmar hissed. "I see a lot of very unhappy traders down there who now have to spend the night outside the gates."

"They should be used to that," replied Taura. "They've been on the road to get here, haven't they?"

"Aye, they have," Varengo answered. "But they won't sleep tonight because they know that thieves will be swarming over the wagons and pack-mules like locusts if they close their eyes for just a second. They have killings down there sometimes."

"Where city guards?" Jiutarô asked.

"They stay in the city when the gates are shut," Vallio responded.

"Bah! No rule," Jiutarô commented.

"We need a campsite," Falcon reminded them. "How much food have we got?" He rummaged through a hemp pack that hung from his belt and pulled out an unappetising hunk of dried meat.

Jasper raised his hands in an exaggerated shrug. "Hmmph! Not enough," he complained. "I do need to rest mah achin' bones though. I ain't as young as I was."

Silmar was about to comment when Taura interrupted him. "Over there!" she hissed, indicating a gap in a stand of coniferous trees.

They all immediately reached for their weapons.

"Where? What?" whispered Silmar, his senses alert. He peered towards the tree-line but could see nothing. He turned back to Taura.

"The gap," Taura laughed. "Ideal for sleeping tonight!"

❧ ❧

The companions woke before dawn. Falcon kicked sand and soil over the fire and they made ready with their kit.

Jasper rubbed his aching posterior. "I'm getting to old for this campaignin'" he moaned.

"Hah, you grew fat in your tavern and now you are weak!" teased Silmar. He had taken the graveyard watch, the period of time just before dawn that was unpopular with most people, soldiers and adventurers alike. He had rubbed his own aching muscles while everyone else was sleeping so nobody would notice.

They walked in small groups along the road towards the city gates and took in the sights and smells. The odour of the livestock was similar to that of most cities outside the walls. The spaces within all city enclosures were permanently limited by the very walls themselves requiring the growth of shanty towns, livestock corrals and pens and storage sheds outside the walls. But there were other effects too. Poverty and crime was commonplace but city authorities kept these separated from normal life within the city confines.

The sun was still low in the eastern sky and already the cattle pens were busy. The noises of protest from the cattle drowned out all other sounds although the barking of dogs and yells and whistles of the stockmen could occasionally be heard. The livestock smells were unusually overpowering here and the road was almost totally covered in horse and cattle dung.

"What they?" Jiutarô pointed to two very large groups of strange beasts; his expression was one of awe.

Tall and narrow beasts with oddly-humped backs and long necks, the animals stood apart from the groups of pack-mules and wagons. Figures, dressed in long, loosely-flowing robes and headdresses and armed with wide-bladed weapons, strolled around them.

"Oh those?" replied Morendo. "These are camels from the far south. They are used as beasts of burden and can carry great loads. The humps are fatty and allow the beasts to travel great distances with little need for water. They can feed just on the spiny grass of the deserts and if need be, can travel between water holes that can be a hundred leagues apart. Horses would need regular stops but it is not quite so with camels. Their feet are wide and allow them to walk on soft sand. They do have nasty tempers though and will remember any mistreatment for a long time, often biting a man who had once whipped it many years after."

"I have seen merchant caravans with many hundred camels," added Jassio. "They come from the southern lands with spices, silks, semi-precious jewellery and other wondrous goods and then return with gold, iron, copper, fabrics and minerals. The merchants are well-protected too."

They joined the long queue of travellers, farmers, merchants and traders on the approach to the gates.

A row of gate-guards blocked the entrance as the group of bedraggled but well-armed travellers approached the gates.

Silmar shouldered his way past Varengo, Vallio and Falcon. Jiutarô, with the little dragon, Sushi, on his shoulders and his unusual garb, attracted suspicious glares from the guards.

"What is your business in our city?" one sentry asked, his lip curling as he looked at the shabbiness of some of the group.

"We are here to enlist as caravan guards," replied Silmar. "Who do we speak with?"

"An elf," the guard responded with disdain. "A dwarf too, and a gnome. I'm half expecting to see a goblin with you. And what is this one here?" He clearly referred to

Jiutarô; with his unusual features, clothing and weaponry, and the cleret-wing dragon, rarely seen in the lands of Baylea and usually known only in folklore.

Silmar squared his shoulders and glared at the guard. The mighty Falcon stood close behind him. "He is our companion and friend and comes from a distant land," he retorted. "As are all members of this group. I ask you again, who do we speak with?"

The gate-sentry suggested they go to Guild of Merchants and Traders. "Go down Street of Ropemakers, yonder. Quarter mile down on the right. Big wall 'round it. Wooden gates; they'll be opening shortly. Enter the city but cause no trouble; we come down hard on rabble-rousers here. I would suggest soaking yourselves in a horse-trough first."

Silmar said nothing but nodded to the guard in acquiescence. "Let's go," he said to the others.

"We wanna eat first!" Jasper grunted and grimaced as he anticipated an objection from the others. Surprisingly, none was forthcoming.

"For once I agree with *stumpy*!" Silmar responded. "Let's see if there's a tavern open."

"Stumpy?" roared Jasper. "Yer pointy-eared chod!"

"Hey!" one of the gate-guards yelled. "What did we tell you? No trouble or we'll kick the lot of you out of the city!"

"'E can choddin' well try," retorted Jasper.

An hour later, they were all marching towards the Guild of Merchants and Traders.

"I am happy to do the talking," suggested Varengo. "We know these folk and some of their ways. Are you happy with that?"

"That's fine by me," replied Silmar. "Everyone else?"

There were choruses of "Aye".

"Only 'cos it keeps pointy-ears quiet."

"Will you two children behave?" yelled Taura. "Is that the Guild? It looks very grand."

They could see through the open gate the Guild, a large, two-storey, stone-built building set within a white-walled palisade. On the wall, to the right hand side of the door, was a red, circular badge. The emblem on it was a black representation of a foot-trader; a travelling tinker with a wide, flat cap, a smock coat and a large pack on his back.

The group joined the back of the short queue. Two armed guards stood at the gates accosting each visitor as they approached.

"What is your business here at the Guild?" The gate warden was a huge, heavily-bearded and long-haired man; muscle-bound although carrying a lot of fat. His uniform of black pantaloons and tan smock, once smart, was stretched tightly across his belly and none too clean.

Varengo stepped forward. "We are a company that provides a guard service for the larger merchant caravans," explained Varengo. "We wish to speak with someone who can provide us with employment."

The wardens looked them up and down. "Aye, well, you can come in. Leave your swords, bows and knives on the tables outside the entrance to the guild, just over there. They will be cared for and quite safe."

Jasper grunted and gave a scowl. "Not 'appy 'bout that," he complained.

Jiutarô also looked doubtful. "I not put swords," he gasped. "My sword and me not parted." Sushi changed her position on his shoulders and hissed at the warden, her barbed tail waving provocatively.

Startled, the man stepped back but quickly regained his composure. It would not be right to show fear or weakness in front of his men or these visitors. He straightened up and brandished his pike across his body. To the companions, he gave the impression that he knew how to use it. "Then, dwarf, you don't go in!" the man exclaimed.

Falcon stepped forwards and placed a massive hand on the dwarf's shoulder. "My great hammer will keep your axe company, Jasper; and your swords too, Jiutarô."

Jasper was clearly unhappy and he stamped his feet and slapped his hand on the haft of his axe. "Bah! Very well."

Jiutarô, however, was not so compliant. "I stay out with my swords," he declared. "Not go in. Never leave katana."

"We shall have to speak for you in there," stated Varengo.

There was a gentle clearing of a throat. "Er, 'scuse me," called Billit. "What about my staff?"

The guard looked confused but then seemed to come to a decision. "You can take it with you, gnome," he said. "Guess you can't do a lot of harm with that."

Silmar gave a wry smile. He was only too aware of the damage that Billit could do with that relatively short staff.

The warden let loose a shrill whistle and an ageing guard, similarly attired, stepped out from behind the wall where he had obviously been relieving himself. A wet dribble ran down the front of his pantaloons.

"You can take these people over to the tables and look after their weapons until they come out," the guard instructed. "I think that one will stay by the table. Beware his beast; it is ferocious and a danger; of that I am certain!"

Once inside the compound they laughed at the warden's attitude towards Jiutarô's little companion. They looked at the Guild building. Its ground floor was of stone with many narrow windows either side of the central entrance. The upper storey was of timber with larger windows that were barred. The main entrance was covered by a portico that was framed by two tall pillars; a stone canopy was supported on their capitals. In between the pillars stood two uniformed wardens. They were smartly-dressed in the same black pantaloons and tan smocks but over this they wore gleaming breastplates. Their light helms were also shining but held tall, red plumes. The wardens held long pikes, the blades of which also gleamed in the early-morning sun.

They piled their weapons on the wooden trestle table except for Jiutarô who sat rigidly on a bench. Sushi floated to the ground and played with a leaf that fluttered across the gravel. The elderly guard looked at her suspiciously for a moment but decided she was harmless. He took something out of a belt pack, crouched down and offered it to her. Jiutarô gave him a withering stare.

The old man paled and his hand froze. "A piece of dried meat, 'tis all," he said.

Jiutarô nodded curtly and then, sitting bolt upright on the bench and his hands placed on his knees, looked straight ahead. The little dragon moved forward gingerly and sniffed at the man's hand. Her long, black tongue shot out and whipped the meat from his hand. The old man sat on the ground and very nearly fell backwards in surprise. He wheezed and pushed himself up onto his feet with considerable effort. He sat down at the opposite end of the bench to Jiutarô, looking ahead impassively.

੭ ੭

CHAPTER 28

WHILE JIUTARÔ waited outside with Sushi and the weapons, the rest of the party stood in a loose group before the Guild official who sat on a tall stool behind a high, narrow desk. The lobby was wide with rows of doors along the back wall. In the centre, a wide staircase led up to the next floor and beneath it, another stairway led down towards the basement or cellars. Sounds of talking and laughter drifted out from behind some of the closed doors. A few grim fighters stood in small groups or sat individually with smoking pipes.

The overweight, balding official was dressed in a flamboyant doublet and hose with a black cotton cummerbund separating the two. The doublet was made of white silk with a wide collar but it had seen better days; its stitching was beginning to come apart and the cuffs were fraying. He rummaged through sheaves of open scrolls, looking myopically at them one at a time and ignoring the group that stood before him.

Jasper was about to shoulder his way past Varengo but Silmar placed a hand on his chest and brought him to a stop. Varengo cleared his throat needlessly loudly. The official looked up with an irritated glare and just as he dropped his gaze back down to his documents Yoriando dropped his hand palm-down on top of them.

"How long do you intend to keep us waiting?" growled Varengo. "We are here to talk business and I am sure that you riffling through those scrolls can wait until we're through. Now, who are you?"

The official leaned back nervously. "I, er, I am Guildsman Affett. What is it *you* want?"

"We are a caravan protection team," explained Varengo. "We wish to provide our services to a merchant or trading organisation. What do we need to do?"

Affett had regained his composure. "Of course, trading caravans are always requiring protection and will pay well, particularly if the team is well-disciplined, well-armed and professional. Teams have to be registered before they can offer their services. Are you registered as a protection team?"

"Nay, we are not," replied Varengo. "What do we have to do?"

"I, ah, we, er, I cannot do anything until you are tagged. I advise you to register with the City Assizes as a security trading company otherwise when you cross into Polduman the Hoshites *will* detain you. This will cause unnecessary expense and delays to the caravan."

"Tagged?" queried Taura. "What is this tagging?"

Varengo flashed a scathing look towards her. "You know," he said, "it's the medallion of registration that we usually wear."

"Ah, aye. Of course," she murmured. "We had better go to the Assizes then."

Affett gave them directions and they filed out of the Guild.

They didn't have to walk far. After collecting their weapons from the table they trudged along the dusty road through lines of gaping onlookers. Jiutarô drew the majority of stares and hushed comments not only because of his outlandish and distinctive garb and weaponry but also the strange winged, dragon-like beast that curled around his shoulders.

The city Assizes was housed in a typically austere, single storey, grey stone building with a pillared entrance. Small, barred windows, no more than a foot in height and width, were set along the front wall a little above the ground. The three guards at the entrance were more practically equipped than those at the Guild, with swords and cudgels. There was no uniform as such; they wore a variety of clothes with only a thick, black leather weskit and leather helm for protection. Pairs of armed guards patrolled the perimeter of the building. More guards, armed with crossbows, were posted on the building roof.

"This place is a fortress," observed Silmar. "Look there!" He pointed towards a group of six prisoners chained together. "Some of them are just youngsters."

A single gaoler, a huge brute with a large belly, an unkempt beard and armed with a stiff whip, goaded the wretched group towards piles of wood and straw. Each prisoner carried a piece of sacking. The gaoler wasted no opportunity to use his whip on the backs of the prisoners.

"Nasty bastard," breathed Falcon. Taura gripped his arm with her face a mask of fury.

"They are just boys," she whispered.

Varengo shook his head. "Boys, aye, they are that," he said. "But you must ask yourselves what it is they may have done. A boy is capable of dealing misery to others, or even death. Do not be hasty to show sympathy to them until you know they deserve it."

"But they are still boys," she persisted.

"Ask their victims," offered Billit. "P'raps we oughta go inside."

Once inside, the Assize official, dressed in black cotton shirt and narrow hose, the uniform of Assize officials everywhere, looked imperiously at Silmar and Varengo, not surprisingly because the pair looked grim and dishevelled. His gaze lingered on Silmar, probably because elves were uncommon in these lands; Silmar fervently hoped that was the reason. This elf looked back at him with a dour expression intended to make the official feel uneasy. The man peered at the others of the group who crowded behind them. Like everyone, he looked suspiciously at the little dragon perched on Jiutarô's shoulders.

"What is it about officials?" whispered Morendo to Jasper.

"Arrogant bunch o' buggers," the dwarf replied.

"How many of you?" the Official requested. He didn't offer to introduce himself.

"Eleven," answered Varengo.

"I shall need all of your names listed on this parchment. What is the name of your group?"

Varengo looked vague. "Er, I –"

Taura stepped forward. "We are the Windwalker Caravan Protection Company," she stated before anyone else had the chance to respond. The others looked at each other in bemusement.

Billit, being better versed in the art of penmanship than most, took the parchment and began scribing the names.

The official rose to his feet from the leather-covered stool behind his wide, darkwood desk. It wasn't that much of an effort for him; he was quite short in stature. He still managed to convey a domineering personality. "There is a bronze token that each of you must wear about your necks. It will identify you as officially registered protectors of the merchant caravans that you are employed to protect regardless of their realm of origin. There is, of course, a charge levied for each individual member of your company."

"How much?" asked Silmar.

A faint smile crossed the man's face. "That will be twenty gold crowns per person. I shall write up an brief account for your, er, gnome to sign. Your tokens will be etched and given to you momentarily." He stepped towards a closed door behind him, called a name and strode back to his desk. A young lad rushed through the door and took the list of names from the official. Then he was gone again.

The official tersely gestured to a row of benches and group ambled across to them.

"Two 'undred and twenty gold!" gasped Billit.

"Aye," answered Silmar. "That is a big slice of the money that we have. I hope this is worthwhile."

"What other choice do we have?" asked Taura. "We need the money we can earn from protecting caravans."

"If we can get employed by one of the big caravans, it can be very lucrative," Varengo assured them. "We shall have to encourage the Guild to find us a trading caravan going in the direction we need."

"Hey, Taura, just what is this Windwalker Caravan Protection Company?" asked Billit. "When did we agree that one, girlie?"

"You need to be quicker than me if you want a quick decision," she replied with a grimace.

An hour passed before the official summoned them back to his desk. They were each given a bronze token bearing their name and stamped with the company name, Windwalker, to be hung on a leather cord about their necks. The man took a sheet of parchment and began to write.

From where he stood, Silmar used his keen eyesight to try to read the official's script. He frowned and slowly shook his head but said nothing.

The man completed the document and handed it to Varengo for him to make his mark. Without warning, Silmar took it and read through it slowly.

"Wait a moment," Silmar said slowly. "You have said that we have been charged a sum of money but you have not specified just how much. And here, you have written 'the sum of', then a space and then 'gold crowns'. I want that filled in properly before we give you the money."

The official took a sharp deep breath and paled visibly. "I can assure you that the sum will be entered once you give, I mean pay, me the money," he said. There was a tremor in his voice, however.

"I would like to see the senior man here," ordered Varengo, his voice raised so that it echoed along the hallway.

"I assure you that –"

"Right now, or I shall become very unpleasant!" exclaimed Varengo. He placed a hand on the hilt of his sword.

The official backed away in a panic, his eyes flitting from left to right and back at the group again. A door opened behind the desk and a figure strode out. A woman, dressed in a dark blue military-style uniform with silver braiding and epaulets, and with a similarly dark blue cape strode purposefully towards them. The official, now panting furiously, leaned against his desk.

"What is going on here, Abranath?" her commanding voice called. She was tall, with her black hair arranged in a chignon.

"Nothing, ma'am!" the man replied. His voice shook with fear. "We are just discussing their registration as a caravan protection company."

"Then why the commotion?"

"If I may just say something, m'lady," Varengo stated, his voice now rich with charm.

She turned to face him. "Well?"

"Your man here is charging each of us twenty gold crowns for us to register as a caravan protection company. That is two hundred and –"

Her face scanned across the companions. "I can count!" she responded, irritation sounding in her voice. "Two hundred and twenty. Right."

She took a whistle from her pocket, raised it to her lips and blew it. A shrill tone emitted. A moment later, doors crashed open and a number of armed guards flooded into the hall.

"What is this?" snarled Falcon, his warhammer suddenly appearing in his hand.

ふ ふ

The companions reached for their weapons. There was a period of silence as the approaching guards skidded to a halt.

The woman raised one hand towards the guards and the other towards the companions. "Stay your hands!" she cried. "My guards are not here for you. Seargeant-at-Arms! Arrest Abranath and take him to the cells. Search his chamber and tell me what you find."

"Why?" Abranath protested. He whimpered as he was led away between two of the guards.

She turned to the companions. "I am Captain General Larissa Brawth. Now, to your business. Have you your tokens?"

Varengo gave a broad smile. "We do indeed ma'am. May I compliment you on your –"

"Spare the charm, I have no need of it. Now, take yourselves out of here before I remember that I forgot to take your fifty-five gold crowns."

Outside, they could hear the cries of protest emanating from one of the cell windows. A voice yelled "Shut yer godsdamned mouth, thief!" and then a cry of pain.

"Ooh! He'll end up in chains and no doubt will get his share of whippings too," said Silmar. "Let's get back to the Guild."

"No sympathy for 'im," growled Jasper. "That bastard tried ter make, 'ow much gold from us?"

"One hundred and sixty five," answered Silmar. "Question is whether that Captain General will find any more gold that's been taken from other protectors. A man can get rich quickly doing something like that."

Varengo gave a laugh. "Mmm, that is one very tough lady," he muttered. "I wouldn't mind getting to know her better! By the gods, she was a beauty."

"You will need to bathe first," Taura snapped. "You still stink after having been in the cells in those mines."

Varengo bristled. "If you remember, young lady, we crossed through that stream just the other day and that river-crossing we did a week or so ago."

Taura huffed. "That's twice in how many years?"

Laughter rippled through the group.

"Hmmph!" muttered Falcon. "I thought we'd need ter fight our way out. It didn't look good for us."

"No, not hardly," agreed Yoriando.

✤ ✤

Guildsman Affett was sitting at his high desk when they filed into the Guild. Once again, Jiutarô sat outside with Sushi, his weapons and those of his comrades.

Affett's face fell as Silmar and Varengo stood at his desk. He immediately pushed aside his parchments and scrolls.

"Gentlemen," he declared. "Do you –"

"And lady!"

The Guildsman's head shot up. He looked perplexed. "What?"

Taura stepped to the front. "I'm no gentlemen!" she announced. "But then, neither are half of these boys with me!"

"Erm, aye. Er. Lady and gentlemen." He wiped his hand down his face, partly to hide his awkwardness. "I see you have your tokens. That is good, ah, aye. Good! So what is it I can help you with?"

Silmar asked if a trading caravan would be leaving for Harrik in the near future.

Affett wrung his hands together and smiled ingratiatingly. "Ah, it's fortuitous that you ask right now," he said. "A string of fifteen or so waggons drawn by heavy horses belonging to the Silver Hand Trading Company leaves in six days and they could use all eleven of you. However, there is a smaller oxen-drawn caravan leaving beforehand if you need to be on your way but they are not likely to arrive at Harrik until a couple of days after the Silver Hand, and they will not need all of you."

"I think it's best to wait for the Silver Hand caravan," suggested Varengo. "How much will they pay?"

The Guildsman rubbed his bristly chin. "The usual payment, I expect, which is two gold for each person each day. It is normal for a bonus to be paid if the caravan is attacked and successfully defended."

"How many days?" asked Yoriando, just beating Varengo who was about to ask the same question.

"If the weather stays good, about thirty. That will get you –"

Varengo bristled. "Aye, I know. Six hundred and sixty." *Condescending bastard*, he thought.

"Give or take. Aye. Suggest you go see Amaric Hand tomorrow morning; he runs the company. I shall send word to him to expect you at the Silver Hand Corral."

Varengo nodded succinctly and led the companions out of the Guild building.

"I wanted to slap the arrogant fool," muttered Yoriando as they stepped out into the courtyard.

Jasper spat onto the gravel. "I wanted ter kick my boot right up 'is ar–"

"Jasper!" exclaimed Taura.

"What?" the dwarf retorted as he raised his hands in a gesture of innocence. "I was a-gonna say *armpit*, so I was!"

They slept in the hayloft of a tavern stable that night.

❧ ☙

The companions had gathered by the open gateway leading into a very large corral. A large wooden board showing a silver hand was attached to the fence railings. Three large wooden sheds, covered in black pitch, stood at the far end of the corral. The doors of one of them were wide open and teams of labourers were ferrying crates and barrels across the corral. A dozen or more great waggons were arranged in a line and many men, and quite a few youths, were loading goods upon two of them from numerous smaller carts that had been led inside the corral. The remaining waggons had already been loaded with their cargoes. As yet, there was no sign of the horses that would draw the massive waggons.

"There's horse shit everywhere," observed Taura as she scraped a chunk of it off her boot onto the railings. The smell was overpowering. "I'm surprised they don't clean it up; it's worth a few coppers to the farmers."

As if her words had been heard by others in the corral, a voice boomed. "Get those boys to cleaning up the dung. It's getting everywhere."

"He must have heard me!"

A pair of men strode towards them. One, a large, towering, brute of a man with wide shoulders, a large belly and massive black beard with streaks of grey, had been the one who shouted the orders. He was dressed in a worn, black hose that was tucked into scruffy leather riding boots, a black shirt that had seen better days that was stretched tightly across his large chest and belly and a brown leather jerkin. The other man, shorter and squat and dressed more ostentatiously in wide, brightly-coloured silk pantaloons, a loose, white shirt and a light blue turban, led the pair as they strode directly up to the companions. His hair was totally obscured by his turban but his beard, black with specks of grey was closely clipped. Both men looked suspiciously at Jiutarô and the little dragon. The flamboyantly-dressed man introduced himself as Amaric Hand.

"I am the owner and proprietor of this business," he announced outspokenly with a pronounced accent typical of the realms to the far south. "This is my caravan manager, Silass. Am I correct in saying that you are the, er, Windwalker Caravan Protection Company?"

Nobody said anything until Taura pushed herself forwards. "Aye, we are!" she replied confidently with a scathing glare at Varengo, Silmar and Yoriando.

"Good. I was told to expect you. Who is the leader of your company?"

"Ah, aye," Taura said a little uncertainly. "I am Taura Windwalker so I suppose that will be me, er, sort of."

Hand gave her a puzzled look. "Do you have your own horses?" he enquired.

"Nay, we lost them some leagues to the north-east of Nor'wald City," explained Silmar. "Well, not lost exactly but left in the care of the people of a village. You see, where we travelled, our horses would have found difficulty. We moved across the peaks on foot."

"Ah, mountains can be treacherous this time of year particularly after the snowmelt," Amaric Hand agreed. "Now then, I can afford to hire six horses for your company from the Gash city livery corral. I'll pay for that but the cost of saddles and bridles will have to come out of your payment. They won't hire them out with the horses; they have to be bought."

Varengo looked across at Silmar and then at Taura. "That will cost us over a hundred gold," he stated. "Most of the money we have. It will leave us nothing to buy better weapons with."

"That is not all," added Hand. "Once we do get to Harrik we would have to get the six horses returned to Gash. More cost."

Varengo looked puzzled. "Goodman Hand, what if you were to buy the horses outright here in Gash, along with the saddles and everything, and then sell 'em when we get to Harrik?"

Hand laughed and nodded slowly. "Perhaps you are right. I shall make a deal with you. My deputy here, Silass, and another person from my company will go with you to the city livery corral. You see if you can purchase six mounts and everything you need to go with them at a bargain cost. When I sell them at Harrik you pay any losses from your bounty or you get any profit. What say you, Mistress Windwalker?"

"It is acceptable," she replied. "What will you pay us for our services?"

"Two gold crowns for each of you every day. You will get a bonus if there is trouble and you successfully protect us without us losing goods or dray-horses. If any of you are lost in battle, full payment will be earned up to the time of death which will be for his, or her, family. Um, you will also earn five silvers for each troll, ogre, orc or goblin ear you bring back to me."

It was traditional for these ears to be collected after a conflict. The fronts of many homes and the bars of some taverns were decorated with them.

Once again, Taura nodded her agreement.

"What are the cargoes?" she asked.

The merchant shook his head. "You do not need to know. Suffice to say it is the business of me and my drovers."

Taura bristled. "If me and my company are willing to put our lives at risk to protect you, your drovers and your waggons, I strongly insist that we have a right to know."

Silass took a step forward. "Now look here –" he began.

The merchant held a hand across to stop him.

"I agree," he said. "It is hardwood timber, coal, oil, calico and other trade goods. More than half of the waggons are loaded with this. The rest of them carry all of the water, food and supplies that we and our horses will need for our journey. There, are you content?"

Taura nodded once more and offered her hand for the clasp. Amaric Hand took hers and instead of clasping it he kissed the back of her fingers. "We shall be ready to move at dawn five days from now. Five of you shall ride on board my waggons. Silass will tell you which ones. Ah, a note of advice. There has been some thieving among my drovers. I respectfully request that you think twice about making it worse but I also request that if you find out anything then come to me or Silass here." He bowed slightly, smiled, turned away from Taura's blushes and strode away leaving Silass with the companions.

∽ ∾

Silass was a man with an attitude. He was a disagreeable character who considered himself having been unfairly treated by fate, he now believed he was to be nothing more than a nursemaid to this ragtag bunch of would-be adventurers as well as the caravan owner. What were they? Little more than a diverse collection of misfits? One of them, in strange clothing more suited to an aristocratic female with his flamboyant silk and a wide sash through which were thrust what appeared to be little more than toy swords. *Weird,* he thought, *little more than a fop with a strange pet.* He didn't like the look of the dragon thing that wrapped itself around the shoulders of the fop. It eyed him closely, its lips curling to show rows of razor-sharp teeth. The tail was odd with a bulbous hook at its tip.

He had looked at the group of five fighters, that stood separate from the others, each approaching middle-age; they moved athletically, could prove formidable and had the look of ex-soldiers about them. The huge barbarian was the one he would have to watch out for if things were to come to a confrontation. The elf-boy, the gnome and the old dwarf he discounted as little more than nuisance-value in spite of the weapons they carried.

Silass' main attention however, was on the young lady; apparently the leader of this bunch. A priestess of sorts, he figured. She was quite short and stocky, not particularly beautiful but with something attractive about her that he couldn't put his finger on. She also moved with an athletic grace that gave her a femininity that he liked. He had fixed his eyes on the shape of the generous breasts beneath her robe, but she had caught his leer and given him a look of repulsion. He didn't care; he would soon wipe that sneer off her face.

"Mornin', tomorrow, a hoor afeter sunup," Silass directed with a forced smile. He flashed a quick glance towards Taura and barely avoided casting his gaze down to her chest.

Those teats will be mine for playing, he mused. *In time. I can wait.*

༄ ༅

"He likes you, Taura!" chortled Varengo.

She gave a look of total revulsion. "You mean he likes my chest!" she growled. "I'm watching him. If he tries anything –"

"We all like your – mmmph!" gasped Jasper as a huge hand closed over his mouth. "A joke!" he spluttered in between Falcon's fingers.

Silmar chuckled with the rest of them. "Look, we need somewhere to stay for the next few days," he advised, changing the subject so as to avoid an altercation.

After enquiring in half a dozen inns, and sampling ales from some of them, they were directed to the Gash

City General Boarding House for Merchants and Traders, a large, pitch-covered shed close to the city gate.

"Oh, I thought that was some sort of store shed," murmured Vallio. Most of the companions agreed.

Two burly ruffians, armed with cudgels, lounged by the entrance and two more were strolling together around the building's perimeter.

A signboard, to one side, read:

> *Tarriffe -*
> *Cotte 3s for nite StaBel for nite 1s*
> *NeW StraW beds evry munthe*
> *HorSe inne stabel 2s inne corale 1s*
> *Ale 5c for quarte Wine or meade 2s for quarTe*
> *Meale withe meTe 3s not withe mete 1s*
> *Bredde + chees 5c*
> *Rools -*
> *No SpittiNg or piSSing insiDe*
> *Pipes nOt to bE nokked oute on tHe cOtts*
> *Bootes Not be on The cottes*
> *TakiNge sPurs off at The door*
> *Keep Wepons under cOttes*
> *Monkeys to be Kepte on ledes after sundowne*
> *Parottes be kepte in cages*
> *No Noisie carrYinges Onne bye menne and ladyes*

"It don't say nuffin' 'bout yer dragon," observed Billit.

Jiutarô scratched his head. "Not cost maybe?"

Jasper peered over at the board. "What's it, er, what's it say?"

"Read it for yourself, stumpy!" called Silmar. "Or is the sign too high up for you?" The elf laughed but Taura's angered expression quickly stopped him.

"I choddin' can't read it, can I?" the dwarf responded at the top of his voice. "I only does numbers, don't I!" Billit read it for him.

Taura looked concerned. "Can we afford this for us all?" she asked Silmar.

"Aye, just about," replied Silmar. "I reckon it'll be about four hundred silver, or forty gold, for the lot of us for the six days."

"Forty choddin' gold?" cried Jasper. "That's a choddin' fortune! But we gotta keep the elf on a lead after sundown – heh heh!"

Everyone laughed, except for Silmar.

"You deserved that one, Silmar," said Taura.

Silmar shrugged his shoulders. "Aye, I concede that just this once. But I did say that this cost is for all of us for six days including the sleeping cots and food. It would cost a lot more in a tavern especially with the amount of ale the dwarf drinks!"

"I'll knock your foolish heads together, you two," Taura warned them again.

"We did save fifty-five gold at the Assizes," Jassio reminded them.

The boarding house was vast inside and in the dim light they could see a maze of small bays enclosed by low wooden walls at a foot or so above head height, for the average human. Long timber beams that supported the great roof were themselves supported by wooden pillars. There was a little light provided by oil lamps that hung from the beams. These were just sufficient to light the width and length of the shed. Privacy was adequate to maintain dignity even though the doorways to each bay being little more than thick canvas sheets. The air was thick with pipe smoke even with every shutter on the outside walls being wide open but there was little breeze to freshen the air inside.

A large number of men, and a few women, walked between bays or stood chatting idly in small groups. There were a few women, obviously whores, who flitted from bay to bay touting for business, their scant clothing clearly marking them for what they were.

The companions were shown to a group of six bays, each of which had two cots. These were little more than oblong frames across which were stretched sheets of hessian with poorly-maintained straw-filled canvas paliasses placed on top.

Both Taura and Jiutarô turned up their noses at the stained bedding and myriad of unpleasant, stale smells. The noxious stink of sweat and body waste mixed with pipe smoke were the overriding odours.

"Do we *have* to stay here," the priestess moaned. "We were better off under the trees and stars two nights back. Backaches are surely preferable to this."

Sounds of revelry came from the far end of the shed. Raucous laughter and singing suddenly erupted.

"We could make this a little more agreeable," suggested Varengo. "I suggest we buy horse blankets to put over the top of these. We'll need something to keep bug-bites to a minimum."

They chose their bays but it was with a moment of awkwardness that Falcon stood at the flap to one of them.

Taura gave a *huff*, grabbed Falcon by the front of his tunic and thrust him backwards into the bay.

Jasper chuckled. "Aye, yer a strumpet, lass." He leapt out of the way just as Taura's staff arced towards him with a resounding *whoosh*.

ඉ ෴

CHAPTER 29

NEXT MORNING, soon after dawn, Silmar, Taura, Varengo and Yoriando waited in the corral by the largest of the three wooden sheds.

Amaric Hand emerged from the door almost immediately with Silass and a third man close behind. He whispered something to the latter and stayed by the building as the other two made their way forwards towards the four companions. The third man was a short, almost weasel-like character with a thin face and a long, narrow beak of a nose. He walked with a limp and leaned heavily on an ornately-carved staff. Unusually, he was almost totally bald except for small tufts of hair that grew randomly on his head. He was dressed in a long, plain, brown cloth gown about which was wound a plaited leather rope. He appeared to carry no weapons but had a large leather pack that hung from the rope belt. Additionally, he carried a small sack suspended from a strap over one shoulder. As they approached, the companions could see scars that criss-crossed his face. He was flanked by Silass who was now armed with a massive, vicious-looking, curved and wide-bladed scimitar that he supported over one shoulder.

The huge man looked contemptuously at the group but his eyes settled lasciviously upon Taura. Jiutarô stepped in front of her and stared directly into the man's eyes.

For the first time, Silass felt uneasy. This strange-looking man was thick-set, broad-shouldered and, notwithstanding the miniature dragon watching him closely with its lips drawn back, he appeared very confident in his demeanour.

Billit nudged Silmar surreptitiously. "This one is a mage, I am sure of it," he whispered. "Watch 'im. An' I don't trust that Silass one bit."

"Oh I don't trust either of them," Silmar whispered back. "The big one has an unhealthy attraction towards Taura. Look at Jiutarô facing down that monster."

The weasel-like man stopped in front of Jiutarô. "I wish to address the leader of your, er, company; one Mistress Windwalker." He looked past Jiutarô at Taura. "I assume that is you. My name is Emageer Namast. I am the, shall we say, counsellor to Amaric Hand. My employer has charged me with providing you with funds to procure six horses with saddles and whatever you require to ride them. My associate here has here a satchel containing one thousand gold crowns. My employer has decreed that you should use this but at the end of your task of escorting us you are to return that same sum back to him. Any profit you make on that sum may be retained by yourselves. Do you agree to that?"

Taura stepped around Jiutarô and stood next to Varengo. "Aye, that is acceptable," she replied without looking at Varengo for his approval. "Amaric Hand is very trusting with such a vast sum of money. Why is that?"

"I must warn you that failure to return that sum in full, for instance, if you were to ride off in the night, will have repercussions. Amaric Hand's influence and reach is long indeed and once his word is circulated, there will be no place where you can hide. I am certain it shall not come to that. In the meantime, Goodman Silass shall accompany you as you procure your mounts and equipment and then you shall bring them here where they remain the property of Goodsir Hand."

Taura's heart sank. She now resigned herself to spending the whole day with Silass continuously leering at her while the companions were buying horses. She could feel her heart beating furiously, her cheeks flushing and her hands shaking. She fought to control herself.

Varengo smiled reassuringly at her. "If you wish I shall take the man aside and warn him to keep away from you," he offered. "He should be told that he will not be able to catch the attention of Mistress Windwalker."

"Be careful," she warned, "he is probably hot-headed and unpredictable. I can handle him in ways that he will not expect. Besides, if you confront him we may have problems with Amaric Hand and Emageer Namast. We need this work. Just stay close to me."

"Aye, I shall."

Silass led them out through the city gate. Once again queues of people lined the road leading to the city. A small group of raucous traders had gathered around a pair of men who, with their hands gripping each other's shoulders, were taking turns to kick each other's shins. Blood ran down their legs until one of them uttered a cry of pain and collapsed to the ground. Coins changed hands amid laughter as the men drifted away.

From the top of the slope the companions could see four large corrals. Each of them had a large number of horses, mules and donkeys. Wranglers, some aged no more than twelve summers, moved through the herds rubbing the beasts down with straw while older men went from one to another to pick out individual beasts for potential purchasers.

"We have to haggle with them to buy horses," advised Varengo. "Have you done any of that?" He looked at the sea of blank faces arrayed around him.

In truth, many goods were bought by haggling in the Home Territories but these were generally limited to previously-owned weapons, armour and clothing. With livestock it was different; one would simply move from one trader to another looking for the best horse at the best price.

He sighed. "You'd best leave it to me and Yori then," he said. He led the group past each of the corrals, finally settling on one.

A dealer dressed in leather hose and jerkin strode over to them and nodded at Varengo. He glanced nervously at Silass and then, with curiosity, at Jiutarô and Sushi.

Varengo nodded back. "How much for one horse?" he asked nonchalantly.

"But we want six!" whispered Taura.

Yoriando placed a finger over his lips. "Shhh! He knows what he's doing. Listen!"

"Two 'undred. Are you buyin'?"

Varengo gave an expression of shock. "Two hundred? I can get one for half that over there."

The dealer shrugged and waved an arm. "Go over there then! Does it take all've you to buy one 'orse?"

"Aye, it does. Seventy Five. Not a bit more."

The trader now looked hurt. "You tryin' to rob me? You'll put me outa business. Look, I feel gen'rous today. Most've these are fresh in and well fed and were rubbed down this morning. One-fifty. It's a bargain!"

Varengo chuckled but shook his head. "Eighty, that's a fair price."

"Fair?" the man asked incredulously. "Ask yer friends 'ere an' see if they'll stump up another thirty. If they can, the 'orse is yours. Now *that's* fair!"

Varengo persisted. "One-ten if you throw in saddle, bit, bridle and blanket."

"One-ten? You're 'aving a joke with me, are you?"

Varengo turned as if to to go. The dealer stepped after him. "Hey! Look, I'll make a good deal wiv you. One-twenty an' everythin' thrown in. He spat on his hand and offered it to Varengo.

Varengo ignored it. The dealer raised his eyes upwards in exasperation.

"Give me that and five more mounts, with saddles and everything, for six hundred and fifty, in gold coins right now, and you have a deal."

The dealer moved his lips as he calculated the cost. "You wanted six all along? You gotta piggin' good bargain out me there!" His shoulders sagged a little but he held out his hand once more. This time Varengo spat in his own hand and they shook on it. Yoriando checked each of the mounts thoroughly, including teeth, eyes, legs and hooves, and nodded approvingly. Varengo counted out the coins as the man looked greedily at the satchel.

Later, as they led the mounts back towards the corral, Varengo laughed. "I would have been prepared to pay seven hundred and fifty for 'em. They're worth it; they're good mounts and the saddles are fair quality. And we still have three hundred and fifty gold left. So if we give that back to Amaric Hand we'll only need to pay him back the six hundred and fifty for the horses. Then we shall see if we can drive a better bargain than that idiot in the corrals outside."

Yori and Jiutarô made a point of keeping themselves in between Silass and Taura, mush to Silass' vexation.

∽ ∾

The evening before Amaric Hand's waggon caravan was due to begin its long trip, the companions stood around the corral in small groups watching the drovers making their final preparations.

A breathless Billit hurried up to Varengo, Taura and Silmar. The three of them were deep in conversation.

"Listen," the gnome mage puffed. Either they had intentionally ignored him or they hadn't heard him. "LISTEN!" he yelled.

"Did somebody hear something?" murmured Taura. "Anyway, what were you saying, Varengo?"

By now Billit was hopping from one foot to another. "Oi, you lot! That was me, you dozy fools! Open yer ears. We got a problem so listen before I start throwing idiocy spells around. Not that I would need to; you're already there."

"Just teasing you, Billit," Varengo admitted. "What have you found?"

"Look, I was walking past your 'orses when I came over all strange, like a buzzin' in my 'ead. So I stopped and, well, it felt like the 'orses was under a spell. I've felt something like it before."

"Do you mean the horses have been enchanted?" asked Silmar. His face had a sceptical expression.

Billit shrugged his shoulders. "Can't be sure. Wouldn't surprise me if that Emageer Namast has placed a spell on the mounts, or more likely on the saddles, so the 'orses can be traced in case you decide to ride off in 'em. Mayhap they'll burn our arses if we try to ride them away."

Varengo looked doubtful but Taura was clearly concerned. "Can he do that?" she gasped. "I mean, won't it have a bad effect on the horses?"

"Could do. I don't recognise the spell at all, not even what sort of spell it is. It's not a magic that I understand; like it's some sort of old sorcery, I think, 'cos I don't understand it at all. It's deep and, look, I can't dispel it, whatever it is."

"Then we must have it out with Amaric Hand," growled Varengo. "The bastard obviously doesn't trust us."

"Aye but we need those horses for this employment," explained Silmar. "Six hundred and fifty gold is a lot of money to trust us with. Also, if we ended up being attacked and lost a horse, its value would make it difficult for us to make up when we have to pay the money back to Amaric Hand. Rather than go shouting and yelling to the man, perhaps we should just approach him and make him aware that we know what's happening."

"He'll prob'ly deny it anyway," mumbled Billit.

"Then we should find out right now," Taura responded. "Don't say anything to the others just yet; let us see how this plays out."

They strode side by side towards the large shed. As they approached, the door opened and Silass stepped out.

"Whatta you want?" he asked, his eyes finally settling on Taura's chest. Varengo stepped in front of her.

"We want to see Goodsir Hand," Silmar stated. "Right now would be good."

Silass puffed out his chest and looked aggressively at Silmar. "He'm busy, elf. Come you back later."

A voice sounded from inside the shed. "What is it, Silass?"

"Nothin', Goodsir Hand. It'sa they protectors wantin' to intrudin' on your time. Tolda them you was too busy righta now."

The door was wrenched open and Hand's face appeared.

"Check out the water barrels, would you, Silass," he instructed. Silass backed inside the shed. "Ah, Mistress Windwalker. What can I do for you?"

Taura stepped around Varengo. "Why did you arrange for our mounts to be given a magical charm?" she asked.

The merchant looked confused. "A magical charm? I'm not sure I understand."

"We have detected a powerful magical charm on our six horses. I consider that to be a sign that we are not to be trusted."

"Er, dear lady, I can assure you that I have not requested a magical charm. I shall speak to my, erm –"

"To Emageer Namast?" Taura offered.

"To, ah, Namast. Leave this with me, dear lady. I offer you my most profound apologies. Return here prior to sunrise and I assure you that this misunderstanding will have been put right." He turned and re-entered the shed.

As they strode out of the corral, Silmar turned to Billit. "I really believe he had no knowledge of the magic spells on the horses. What do you think?"

"I put a small spell of my own on him to test if he was telling the truth," said Taura. "I'm certain he was. Namast was working on his own with that one."

"Gonna 'ave to watch 'im," suggested Billit. "I think 'e's dangerous. Silass too. We made an enemy there, I reckon. Prob'ly two. We'll all need to watch out for each other. Are we goin' through all this shit just to get some 'orses, or money, or what?"

"Nay!" replied Silmar. "We spoke about this. We need to get to Nasteed and Harrik and we also need the money."

"Aye, we should have taken more money from that vampire's keep, eh?" Taura admitted.

"Aye, we should have done really. It was ours to do with what we could after all. We have hidden a great amount for our future."

� �

Varengo, Vallio, Morendo, Yoriando, Jassio and Falcon had already been selected to be the six outriders for the caravan.

"Always stay within sight or at least within yelling distance of the caravan," Varengo had advised, "particularly in wooded or hilly countryside. Oh, aye, also to keep an eye on Silass and that mystery mage, what's his name?"

"Namast, 'es near the back," offered Billit. "I checked round yer 'orses too. I couldn't trace any enchantment on 'em but o' course, that don't mean there ain't any."

"Not a problem," laughed Morendo. "We don't plan to cut and run, do we? Needing the gold anyways."

Silmar, Jiutarô, Taura, Billit and Jasper took their places amongst the thirty-odd waggons.

Taura sat beside a drover on a waggon in the middle of the caravan. Jiutarô's was directly behind hers, his bow, arrows and swords laid across the tarpaulin behind him within easy reach.

One of two covered wagons, each of which was hauled by two heavy dray-horses, was driven by the thin-faced, hawk-nosed, balding sorcerer towards the back of the caravan. He wore a black, hooded cloak pulled tightly around him to ward off the early-morning chill. He had glared at Taura and Billit as they walked past. Beside his wagon, mounted on a great, black warhorse, rode Silass. Despite the cold, he wore a sleeveless leather jerkin, his grey-streaked, black beard now flanked by two braids tied off with cords.

He hadn't planned for the strange-looking warrior to be situated so close to the waggon upon which the priestess rode but for some obscure reason, Hand had insisted on it. Probably something to do with its cargo, whatever that was. *What in the hells of the Void are those weapons anyhow?* he asked himself. *The boss rarely confided in him. That strange bow surely cannot work properly, the arrows are too long. The sword thing looks like a child's toy or something that would decorate the hall of a lord's manor; it is too light and flimsy. My blade will shatter it on the first clash.*

Silass called the six riders over to him. "When we gettin' outa da city and into da open countary, I want you be providin' da wide cover for da caravan. Dat way we is gettin' early warn if dere are nasties outa dere. I don't wantin' to see anyone closer dan a hundered yard fromma da waggons. Iffa de roads quiet is an' de countery is open, I wantin' two to ridin' outa front and one behind. When we stoppin' over de night I expectin' at least three offa you awaked an' patrol all de times. Issa dat clear?"

Aye, is that to see some of us cut down so you can get closer to Taura? Silmar asked himself. *We'll be watching you and we're not easily downed.*

Every one of the companions was aware that Silass posed a threat to Taura even though they were less confident than she was that she could hold him off by using one of her divine spells.

Varengo hid his annoyance. "We are professionals, Silass," he growled. "We know what to do!"

The companions nodded having already agreed between them that they would use this tactic. Silass hesitated as if he had expected a dispute from the riders.

Whips cracked, the drovers bellowed and whistled while men on foot cajoled the teams of horses with long, thin whips. The horses strained against the stout wooden yokes and the mass of waggons gradually creaked and groaned into movement.

For a few days Silass would draw his horse up alongside the waggon on which Taura rode. The drover cowered under the withering gaze of the huge horseman and held his own gaze forwards towards the horses.

The first time that Silass ogled her, Taura flashed a quick glance at her drover. The man was middle-aged, probably no younger than forty years of age. *He'll be of no help to me if I need some muscle,* the young priestess thought to herself, *but I have Jiutarô just behind me, thank the gods, and a couple of tricks of my own.*

She turned on her seat for reassurance, gave a little wave to Jiutarô who gave a wink of encouragement and nodded back in response. Taura felt relieved knowing what he was capable of. His daily sword practice was still awe inspiring to every member of the group of companions as his blade whirled and slashed in circles about the Samurai's head and body. Even the way in which he returned his curved blade back into its black lacquered scabbard was a deliberately efficient and long-practised move.

Each time the brutish caravan manager was met with an impassive silence from Taura. *The arrogant bitch acts so cold but she will not be so stony-faced soon when she writhes beneath me,* he promised himself.

❧ ❧

CHAPTER 30

It was late in the afternoon of the fifth day when Jassio casually reined in his horse by the lead waggon. His unkempt brown hair and bushy beard gave him an almost wild appearance. Silmar, seated beside the jovial woman drover, leaned towards his mounted comrade.

"In the hills to our right," Jassio whispered to him. "Three men dressed in loin-skins and armed with javelins and wide-blades."

"Are they keeping abreast of us?" Silmar murmured back.

The drover looked across to him, a fearful expression etched on her face.

"Aye, looks like it," Jassio replied. "Faint tracks in the long grass shows their passage. We seen 'em for a while now. They're keeping a low profile behind the hills but they're not that good at keepin' hid. Vallio wants to get up in the hills to track 'em but it will look too obvious if there is an empty horse."

"Send him back here, I'll take over on his horse and he can get up into the hills."

❧ ❧

A short while later, Silass rode up. "What going 'on?" he asked of the drover. "Where dat snooty elf?"

The drover, an ageing, stocky woman with a stained smoke-weed pipe clenched between her similarly-stained teeth, looked at the man from beneath her wide-brimmed hat with barely-concealed contempt. "'E ain't 'ere," she answered tersely, looking forward again to her four horses, a far nicer view than the ignorant caravan leader was. "Got on a horse and is up ahead somewhere."

"Den where –" he began but then he thought better of it. With an exasperated grunt he spurred his mount forward.

Silmar and Falcon were a couple of hundred yards ahead as Silass' horse thundered along the road towards them. The elf turned Vallio's horse to meet him and Falcon continued slowly onwards down the road.

"What's goin' on?" the caravan leader asked loudly, gruffly.

"What do you mean, Silass?" Silmar replied with an innocent air.

"Don'ta you givin' me shit, elf!" Silass exclaimed loudly. "Why you is ridin' now an' where de black-hair man who usual is ridin' dis horse?"

Silmar hesitated knowing it would aggravate the brute. The caravan manager was obviously impatient and the elf's attitude was something he could not tolerate. Silass gritted his teeth; once he had given the priest wench what he felt she needed, he would deal next with the elf.

"Well, where he, elf?" persisted the brute.

"He has gone into the hills on foot," Silmar replied. "Your caravan is being followed, Silass. Best you inform your employer quickly. My friend is an accomplished tracker and is out there looking to see what is following us."

Anger grew on Silass' face. His beard jutted forwards. "Why you not toldin' me earlier?"

"We are *toldin'* you now and are perfectly capable of handling this. Your employer has entrusted us to take care of the safety of the caravan. Once we have something positive to tell you, you shall be informed."

"Makin' it sure I am." Silass whirled his horse about and thundered back up the road towards the caravan.

Falcon trotted back and rejoined Silmar. "He does not look happy with what you had to say, friend Silmar," he commented.

"He is losing his self control, I am sure of it," mused the elf. "It's hard work listening to him talking but he is beginning to rave."

"Aye, that he is. If he comes anywhere near Taura I shall gut him." The great barbarian's hand strayed towards the hilt of the large hunting knife that hung from his belt.

"Jiutarô is watching closely, as is Billit. We shall all have to form a queue behind you, my friend."

❧　☙

Every few miles along the road, clearings to the side had been worn by countless previous caravans to act as overnight stops. It was common for these to be situated near to sources of water: a stream, spring or even a river, where possible. This night, however, the caravan would have to rely on the water carried on one of the waggons. Much of it could be used up in a couple of days, being used by people and horses alike. It meant that sometime very soon it would all have to be replenished – half a day's back-breaking work.

It took almost two hours for the caravan to form up. Silass was in his element, yelling and gesticulating from the saddle as the waggons lined up in rows.

"Maka da tent," he yelled at the top of his voice, "getta da fires lightin' up, getta da water for da horses and den getta water for yous."

Everywhere, there were drovers and caravan footmen shaking their heads and muttering. They didn't need telling; they knew the routine. They also knew that it didn't do to complain.

Varengo, Jassio and Yoriando stood the first watch. After a couple of hours they were relieved by Jasper, Falcon and Morendo. Varengo strode over to Silmar, Taura and Jiutarô, his expression one of concern. A small fire had been lit alongside Taura's waggon.

"There's no sign of Vallio," he said. "Surely he would have been back by now. I fear for his wellbeing."

"There is little we can do right now," Silmar replied. "It is pitch dark out there and he could be anywhere. I could probably –"

Before he could finish his statement, Amaric Hand stepped out from behind a waggon. A few paces behind him was Silass. There was no sign of the merchant's so-called advisor, the sorcerer Namast.

"Mistress Windwalker," boomed the merchant. He took her hand and brushed the back of it with the bottom of his chin. "I understand from Silass here that we have some suspicious characters following our caravan. What is that about do you think? Is it likely that we are in any danger?"

"Obviously, I cannot say one way or the other," she answered him. "We did send a skilled tracker out to investigate but he is yet to return. It concerns us greatly, of course. I would suggest that the whole caravan is kept at a state of alert and request that some of the drovers and walkers assist with watching tonight."

Silass pushed past the merchant, much to the latter's annoyance. "Yous is paid to makin' the guard watch. I says that yous –"

"I totally agree with you, mistress!" Hand interrupted. "I shall inform my people imminently. I should like you to advise them all accordingly and –"

"Boss-sir!" Silass interjected. "*I* is the managing for the caravan."

"Let us leave it to the experts, Silass. Mistress Windwalker, what will your team do in the meantime?"

"We have a plan to discuss between us, Goodsir. We shall keep you informed of –"

Shouts came from the right-most edge of the caravan. They observed Falcon striding up to them carrying something in his arms.

"Gods!" exclaimed Silmar. "He has Vallio. Falcon, bring him here, close to the fire. What has happened?"

"He is sorely wounded," responded the barbarian as he approached. "He lurched up the road towards us. He has an arrow wound in his leg and looks to have lost a finger. His hand is a mass of blood. He also bleeds plentifully from his head. He needs Taura's aid."

The priestess had already cleared a space close to the fire and Falcon carefully placed Vallio down.

The tracker tried to sit up but Taura held him flat on the ground. "I can sit, surely!" he argued. "I am not that badly hurt. Ooh my head aches though!" He stopped his resistance as she placed her hand flat on his forehead. A gentle, wordless song came from her lips and Vallio fell into a stupor.

Silass sat brooding on his horse blanket beneath the tarpaulin he had stretched on a rope between two wagons. "Bastards!" he muttered. Even Amaric Hand was treating him as little more than a serving man, a messenger.

He rummaged inside his saddlebags until his hand closed around an earthenware flask. He removed the stopper and raised the flask to his lips. He almost gagged on the acrid fluid that poured into his mouth. Its warming effect quickly calmed him though. He coughed and spluttered and then raised it to his mouth once more. Within half an hour he had emptied the flask. He dozed for a while, unsure as to how long, but was woken up by the noise from around the waggons. He tried to stand up, staggered as his head came into contact with the tarpaulin and collapsed rump-first back down onto his blanket.

"Shit!" he exclaimed. He still held the empty flask in his left hand. He threw it against the side of one of the waggons, intending it to shatter but it just bounced off and rolled beneath the waggon. He couldn't even get that right. He swore again.

His liquor-befuddled mind tried to reassert itself. His authority was steadily being eroded in favour of those damned *caravan protectors*. He was beginning to notice that the caravan drovers were taking him less seriously. They had always resented him but his massive size had always been sufficient to ensure they all complied with his authority.

But now. *Bah,* now he was becoming a laughing stock; he saw how the drovers continued to resent him and how they even now whispered behind his back. In fact, not always behind his back; he had recently needed to take punitive action against one man, little more than a boy really, for openly criticising an order he had given. He had beaten the boy senseless with his bare fists and it was only by the caravan owner's intervention that the boy had not been killed. *Aye, I was careless,* he thought. *I should have done it in the night, away from the caravan. Next time, godsdammit!*

But now, he had another task to do. Perhaps in the early hours once the moon had dipped behind the hills. He lay back down on the blanket and dozed.

ॐ ॐ

Silmar and Jasper prepared to leave. Amaric Hand was now taking personal interest in the tasks his team of protectors was undertaking.

"Why are you doing this?" he had enquired. "Why do you intend to leave the confines and the safety of this caravan?"

"Ain't nobody's gonna sleep good with them stalkers out there," Jasper had explained. "The elf an' me, we can see better in the dark than you humans and prob'ly better than 'oever is out there. Vallio got hisself too close in the dark and they jumped 'im. They won't find us so easy; I can tell you that fer nuthin'. Might even get some payback for Vallio, y'know, chop a finger off here or there, heh heh!"

"We need to find out if there are just a few of them or if they are part of a larger force," Silmar explained. "We should not be that long. We will return well before dawn."

ॐ ॐ

The moon was little more than a narrow sliver that was slowly sinking towards the horizon when the elf and the dwarf crept away from the camp.

Using every available bush, scrub and boulder as cover and keeping to the shadows where possible, their progress was quite slow. They did, however, have one very important advantage: dark-vision. This was an innate ability gifted, it was said, by their respective gods to dwarves, elves and some species of gnomes which enabled them to use the natural light provided by the moon and stars, as well as any residual light from dawn or dusk, and enhance it to allow them to see better in near darkness up to a distance of thirty to forty paces.

Darklings and Grey Dwarves, the evil races that inhabited the mines and tunnels of the Shadow World also shared this phenomenon although it was believed that they had no need for the residual light on which the surface-dwellers relied. The companions' experience in the mines confirmed this.

They now used this dark-vision to aid them with their trek through the hills. Surprisingly, Jasper could move almost silently when need arose. Apart from his wheezing and the occasional kicked stone, he was almost as silent as the elf. This did not stop Silmar from wincing each time a clatter cut through the quietness of the night but he said nothing to Jasper.

The elf was in his natural element, doing what he did best and thoroughly enjoying himself..

ॐ ॐ

Jiutarô slept lightly as he always did. With Sushi either on his shoulders or scampering on the ground by his side, he had completed his first watch having finished by patrolling the perimeter of the camp site. On his way back to his shelter he had paused by Taura's own refuge beneath the waggon on which she travelled. Satisfied that she was safe and comfortable, he crept away.

He was unaware that he was being observed.

❧   ❧

Keeping themselves as low to the ground as possible, they crested a scrub-covered rise, skirted a small hill and headed towards a stand of trees. They had walked in silence for almost a mile taking a circuitous route around the caravan's night camp. A small cloud had been shielding the moon but it briefly moved to one side. It soon hid the moon once again.

"Shh – down!" hissed Jasper as he raised a hand against the elf's chest. "Voices, yonder!" He pointed towards the trees.

Slowly, cautiously, they crept forward once again.

❧   ❧

Taura dozed fitfully at first. The camp had been quite noisy but she had eventually become accustomed to the hubbub and settled down to a deeper slumber.

She didn't hear the footfall at first. When she did, it was too late.

One huge hand clamped over her mouth. The other tore at her gown. She smelt the breath made foul by strong liquor.

❧   ❧

Jiutarô was woken by Sushi's snout as she snuffled in his ear. Uncharacteristically, she mewed insistently and nuzzled the side of his neck.

"What is it, little one?" he asked in a whisper. Immediately, he detected a subliminal image of Taura in his mind. The little dragon hissed, spun about and shot out from beneath the shelter.

∞ ∾

A small orange glow shimmered amongst the trees. Silmar moved noiselessly through the scrub to get a better look at the figures seated around a small fire. Six men, dressed in an assortment of skins, were laughing and drinking out of stone jugs.

A pile of animal hides, deer mostly looking at the markings in flickering firelight, had been loaded on a small, two-wheeled handcart.

From the descriptions that Vallio had provided, these were the very same men that had appeared to be following the caravan. Silmar listened in to their conversation. From snippets of information he gathered from their fireside talk, he guessed that the sound of movement of the caravan flushed out the wildlife from their places of concealment during the daylight hours. *Logical, I suppose,* he thought to himself. *But why the attack on Vallio?*

"How's your hand, boy?" one of the hunters asked.

"Fraggin' painful!" a youth responded. "I might've broke my thumb on 'im. It really hurts."

"I think we was a bit 'ard on that man though," another stated. "I hit 'is 'and and think I cut it bad."

"Don't yer start feeling bad for 'im," the first man said. "He was after our skins, I'm sure of it. 'E got back to the caravan so it's their problem now. We lost a couple of arrers on 'im. Let's drink up and forget it."

Silmar watched for a few moments more, then edged quietly away and slipped through the undergrowth to where Jasper waited impatiently.

"Oh, at last!" the dwarf exclaimed. "Thought I might 'ave to come an' rescue you. What did you find?"

"They are hunters and trappers," Silmar explained. "They were the ones who attacked Vallio but they think he was after their animal hides. The noise of the passing caravans flush out the deer and other animals and they shoot them down."

"So you reckons they're no threat to the caravan then?"

"No, there's not enough of them anyway. We better get back."

⚓ ⚓

She struggled erratically at first while her mind overcame the numbing shock of the attack. She focussed and drew one leg beneath her. She bucked hard causing him to lose his balance. He released his hand from her ripped gown and placed it on the ground to steady himself.

She had played through this scenario countless times over the last few days and had drawn on her old memories from her wrestling skills. Using all the force she could muster, she rammed her elbow into Silass' wrist.

The man cried out in pain. "Bitch!"

She tried to bite the hand and succeeded in catching the web of skin between his thumb and forefinger. The grip across her mouth loosened and she managed a faint cry of despair. Using his loss of control she managed to open up a gap between them. Her left arm reached for his collar and she gripped firmly. She brought up her right leg and jabbed her knee into the inside of his thigh, lifting her leg upwards while pulling his neck downwards and to her left. His right hand released from her face and she screamed out again, louder this time.

Suddenly, a hand appeared from behind his head and gripped his beard. Silass' weight lifted completely off her. Her shelter had disappeared. Two faces hovered above Silass' expanse of dark hair.

A deep, gruff voice called "Bastard!"

Another grunted "Hold him!"

A wave of relief surged through Taura and she fought against her tears. It was Falcon. With him was Jiutarô. She heard a hissing. Sushi?

Silass began struggling violently. His foot stepped on Taura's chest. She bit his leg hard and almost gagged at its bitter taste and the coarse hairs. The leg lifted and the brute crashed to the ground with Falcon on top of him. A flailing foot caught Taura on the side of her chest making her gasp in pain.

A flurry of blows rained down on to Silass' head. He stopped struggling.

"I could have had him then," Taura gasped. "I was winning!" She held her torn gown tightly beneath her chin.

"'E sure didn't 'ave it all 'is own way though, did 'e?" growled Billit from behind the others.

Amaric Hand's head pushed through the throng. "I have seen enough," he said. "Bind him and bring him to me! Mistress Windwalker, I cannot apologise enough."

"It was not unexpected," she replied as Falcon placed a cloak around her shoulders. "He had been an annoyance to me since we introduced ourselves to you."

"Silass! Is this true? If so, we shall hand you over to the authorities in Harrick."

"No, wait!" wailed Silass. "Not the Hoshites! Look boss, I wasn't going to –; I did not intend –"

He struggled violently in a desperate attempt to escape from his captors. Jiutarô thrust his foot into the back of the man's knees causing him to collapse to the ground once again. Rough hands bound his arms and wrists. Even then he tried to kick and bite his captors, catching one of them, a drover, with such a vicious bite that it bled profusely. Jiutarô launched a backhanded blow that caught Silass on the side of his jaw, rocking him such that he had to be held up by two other drovers.

"Any more of that and you shall be gagged," Falcon said. "We should kill you now for what you have done."

Silass cursed the Barbarian and spat at him but Falcon merely wiped it from his cheek without reacting. Together, they dragged him and lashed him to a waggon wheel. Silass' incessant cursing and foul language served only to encourage Amaric Hand to order a thick gag to be placed around the brute's head.

Under Hand's order, Yoriando and Varengo searched Silass' saddlebags. Many items, including coins, three whetstones, tinderboxes, some with a flint and steel inside, a hunting knife in a brown leather sheath, a small leather bag with something inside and a small, highly-polished wooden box the lid of which was covered in complex engravings. They brought the items to the merchant.

Amaric Hand studied the items. "These are probably the items reported as having been stolen from around the caravan during our journey from Nasteed up to Gash last month. What is this box? I don't remember anything about this."

Despite the hinges and a clasp being obvious, they could find no means to open the box.

Emageer Namast limped over from his wagon, using his staff to knock others aside. He had his customary cocksure arrogance about him that unsettled Billit and his companions. "I would hazard a guess that the box is magically closed," the sorcerer stated. "I shall very quickly overcome that. Stand aside!"

Everybody moved back a few paces. Billit was agitated. "We wanna move back a bit further," he quietly advised the companions. "I don't like the look of that engraving on the lid. Get well back, lads."

The sorcerer moved his hood back, lifted the box and peered all over it before replacing it on the table. His hands passed over the box and he began to chant.

Taura nudged Billit. "What's he doing?" she asked quietly.

The little gnome shrugged. "Dunno," he whispered. "Don't unnerstan' a word of it. It's not a magic I know anythin' about. It's weird stuff. I ain't 'appy with it, neither." He shuffled back another step with Taura following him.

Namast's voice rose as his chanting became more insistent. His hands weaved a complex pattern and very soon a bright crimson glow grew. A buzzing noise as of a thousand great bees sounded from around the box but the sorcerer did not falter.

"Back, more," Billit insisted. "This ain't good!" He gripped Taura's gown and they moved back a few paces.

The crimson glow brightened in its intensity until it was impossible to look into it directly. Only now did Namast hesitate with an expression of dread but it was too late. There was an ear-splitting *crack*. The piercing light seemed to shatter and Namast was lost in the centre of it. The smell of burnt metal filled the air around him.

By the time the onlookers had restored their vision, Namast was laying on his back on the ground. The table on which the box had rested had shattered into fragments but the box, slightly burnt but still appearing whole, lay on its side amongst the shards.

"Wait!" called Billit as the onlookers began to edge forwards towards the sorcerer. "Let me. There may still be danger here. Keep back!"

He stepped forward very slowly, holding his staff horizontally towards the centre of the magical conflagration. As he approached the supine form of Emageer Namast, he moved around it in a complete circle. He seemed satisfied and knelt by Namast's side. Billit nodded and lifted the man's head.

"He lives!" the little gnome mage announced. "He 'as lost much skin from 'is face and 'ands. Oh damn, he 'as a ruined eye, too. Taura, this is work for a priestess. It is safe 'ere now. There's no trace of 'is staff; burnt away I 'spect. Oh dear, how sad!" The little gnome did not look sad however.

Billit cautiously picked up the box, dusted it down and took it across to an ashen-faced Amaric hand. "It's perfectly safe," the little mage assured him.

"Can I open it?" Hand enquired with a trembling voice as he took one faltering step back.

"Yer want me to?"

"Ah, er, aye if you don't mind."

Billit flipped open the lid. The box was empty except for a piece of parchment. He took it out gingerly and handed it to Amaric Hand. The merchant looked at the writing that was neatly scribed on one side but shook his head.

"I cannot read this," he said. "Not only is the writing tiny and my feeble eyes unable to read it all, but I do not recognise the symbols that I can see." He passed it back to Billit.

"Ah, that's because it is penned in an ancient arcane script known only to those in what is termed the *esoteric fraternity*."

"The what?"

"Those with the knowledge of the arcane sciences; you know, magic."

"Ah, I understand. So you can read it?"

Billit gave a haughty expression. "Aye, I can but I shall 'ave to study it first in case somethin' else nasty 'appens."

Hand nodded in appreciation. "Er, ah, I see. Another magical blast, you mean."

"What is it likely to be, Billit?" Taura asked. "I mean, the parchment."

"You'll 'ave to wait an' see, girlie. Give me a bit o' space in case somethin' goes wrong."

Silmar and Jasper had returned to the caravan just in time to witness the aftermath of the incident.

Amaric Hand spoke with them to one side and then nodded with a satisfied look.

It was an hour or more before Billit strode across to Amaric Hand's wagon. He was laughing to himself and shaking his head.

"It says '*You are fortunate indede if you are reading this, my ultimate missive. Be in noe doubt that were you to have bene a lesser mortal, your inquisitiveness mighte have ledde to your ruin. You have evidently proven your worthe unless the charme was triggered by another unfortunate soul. Therefore, I implore you that you learne from this. The spelle is my last and will rightly see me dedde. I was once the Archmage Garabor Mandabar of Faerhome and I shalle have met an appropriate ende. Long live the descendants of the house of Oten'Galadhal.*'"

"An elven magician?" Hand asked incredulously. "A rarity indeed."

Silmar stepped in front. "That is correct indeed," he confirmed. "The practice of magic had been forbidden long ago in Faerhome in all but the royal court. It was whispered that perhaps if the elven kingdom had been able to practice the magic arts widely, they may have been better able to defend themselves against the monstrous hordes that had overrun their homeland some centuries earlier." He pondered for a moment. "I do not recognise the name," he said slowly. "No doubt he was the sovereign's personal warmage. Nobody else was allowed to perform magic."

"That don't make no sense," interrupted Jasper. "If 'e got killed, 'oo else would be able to do magic fer the king?"

Silmar rubbed his chin. Unlike all of the other males in the party, his was the only chin that remained hairless. "No idea," he replied. "I can only guess that he would have had an apprentice. As I say, I do not recognise the name of the Archmage, but of Oten'Galadhal now. That is another matter entirely. I shall have to speak with my father about that sometime. May I have the box, Goodsir?"

Amaric Hand passed it to him. The elf tucked it down the side of his pack, shuddering as he inadvertently touched the wrapped casket containing the cursed dagger. The pack and the clothing around it felt slightly damp from the ice-cold object. Apart from regularly checking it was still safely packed, he had given the *burden* little thought over recent tenday week and had felt little effect from it. He was never more than arm's reach away from his backpack.

As they strode back to their waggons, Billit was almost hopping from one foot to another. "But you're of that 'ouse, Silmar!" the gnome mage exclaimed breathlessly. "Does that mean you're heir to the throne of Faerhome?"

"Nay!" he chuckled. "*Oten* means the High family dynasty, the royal line. My father and I are descended from a minor house of the Galadhal family line. A branch or offshoot, you might say. I shall let him have the box and its parchment. If nothing else, it may serve to explain an event in the history of Faerhome."

Taura joined them a while later. "The sorcerer has lost his mind and will not survive long," she said with little emotion and no regret.

"Oh dear, that's choddin' sad!" deliberated Jasper. "We're all gonna miss 'im, ain't we?"

"Say it once more but with some feelin' behind it," laughed Billit. "The idiot was stupid enough to believe 'e could break that charm. 'E didn't even take the time to find out what it was. No sympathy, me. What's 'appened to Silass?"

"He's tied up in the back of the sorcerer's little wagon," Varengo answered. "One of Hand's walkers is driving it. Kandur I think he's called. You should have heard the foul language the thug was using. It doesn't matter much because Kandur speaks very little Universal. He just laughs a lot, nods when folk talk to 'im!"

Two days later, as the caravan burst into life an hour before dawn, shouting erupted from towards the rear of the caravan. The companions rushed over.

Amaric Hand was already there, panting from the exertion. "What is this clamour?" he cried.

A drover excitedly ran over to him. "It is Silass, boss!" he called. "He has escaped and has killed Kandur dead. Slit his throat, he did. He's stolen the horse he used to ride and rode off during the night with no saddle. He's gone, boss."

Falcon arrived quickly and confirmed that he had heard a galloping horse during the night. "I could not chase after the rider in the dark," he explained. "I knew not that it was Silass so I did not check the wagon."

Hand gave a look of exasperation. "We can just hope he causes no more mischief. Let us continue."

Later that day, despite Taura's ministrations, Namast the sorcerer expired. He was buried in a shallow grave by the roadside with only a few words spoken by Taura.

The caravan crossed the border into west Polduman forty days later.

∽ ∾

The route through the Great Moors to the east of the Spine Wall Mountains had been ponderous to say the least. Even the usually tolerant elf was becoming frustrated with the slow progress. Hard rains had caused the marsh road to become a quagmire in some places. The heavy horses were barely able to drag the waggons through the swamps and there were times when horse teams had to be doubled-up to heave the waggons through to drier ground. During these days the caravan might make no more than between three and five miles.

Flies, midges and mosquitoes were a constant nuisance. Often the only defence they had was to cake mud over their exposed skin but once it dried and cracked, the mosquitoes would find their way through it. Pipe smoke, for those who indulged in it, warded off the worst of them. Jasper and Billit ignored the insects and Silmar seemed unaffected by them.

When they finally reached drier and rockier ground, snakes and scorpions became the next challenge for a few days. Very rarely did anybody walk and during the night people slept on top of the waggons.

At midday they reached the rolling hills that indicated they were about to leave the kingdom of Shordrun. The border post was manned by a small troop of men dressed in voluminous black trousers tucked into black riding boots, a brown leather jerkin over which was hung a chainmail corselet and a light helm fitted with a neck and chin guard.

"Damned Hoshites!" growled Varengo. "Expect them to be into everything. Make sure you flash your Protector's tokens otherwise they will fine us heavily."

Ten armed Hoshite troopers stood in a line across the road. There were others lounging close by armed with heavy crossbows. Nonetheless, faced with such a large caravan with a similarly large contingent of professional-looking protectors, the Hoshite leader looked somewhat anxious as the great horse-drawn waggon trundled towards him. He held up a single hand and the lead waggon, with the ageing, stocky woman drover, her stained smoke-weed pipe clenched between her teeth and accompanied by the grim-looking elf, stopped just inches in front of him. He was by now somewhat apprehensive. He had noticed the gleaming token that Silmar hung on the outside of his tunic so he made no demands to see those of any of the other protectors.

After payment of an extortionate toll, the caravan rolled forward.

Varengo rode alongside the lead waggon. "Six or seven leagues to Harrik," he shouted. "About two days from here. The roads are safe, so I'm advised by that fool of a Hoshite. Mind you, it's a dangerous job being a highway robber in this country. Thieves are strung up where they are caught in this country. You see them dangling in the trees from time to time."

Later in the day, just as Silmar and Varengo mounted the first watch, a riderless horse wandered into the camp.

"It's Silass' mount, surely," suggested Varengo. "Wonder what has become of him."

"We will probably never know unless he comes back looking for trouble," replied Silmar.

"I really don't much care," muttered Taura.

"And you a cleric!" laughed Billit.

For the next two days the riders rode their mounts closer-in to the waggons. Occasionally, mounted Hoshite troops would ride past them, glaring suspiciously at the Protectors and sometimes demanding to see their tokens. They were relieved to see the smoke from the cooking fires and the haze above the town of Harrik a league ahead of them.

༚ ༚

CHAPTER 31

THE CARAVAN trundled through the town. This was most likely to be the largest caravan that the inhabitants would see during the year. It was the town's opportunity for a festival. Crowds lined the streets, whores waved at the drovers and displayed their breasts, bards played lutes and flutes, tumblers performed acrobatics and vagrants and children begged for coppers. Dogs barked excitedly and snarled at the legs of the horses; drovers cracked their whips to scare them away, some of whom yelped as the whips struck their backs.

The woman drover, her grimy pipe firmly gripped between her teeth as usual, led the caravan to a large corral inside which were two large sheds and half a dozen smaller ones. A few youths, armed with cudgels, had dragged the great gates open and stood as if on guard at the wide opening.

One by one, the great waggons entered, drew round in a great arc and began to line up. The horses, weary after weeks of hard work, were unhitched and led to another large corral. The work of unloading the waggons would last for many more days to come.

The companions took the opportunity to make for a nearby tavern except for Taura, Silmar and Varengo.

Amaric Hand sank gratefully into a large padded chair in a private chamber. "Enter!" he called in response to a knock on his door. Taura led her two companions inside.

"Ah, sit down." He waved nonchalantly at a row of chairs to one side of the chamber. "Time to recover and settle our dues?"

"Aye, now is as good a time as any," Taura answered.

"A couple of tenday weeks ago, Mistress Windwalker," he began, "my man Silass did something treacherous and did you a foul injustice. It has been on my conscience since then. I trust you are fully recovered?"

"Aye, I am. I was more angry than frightened and he caused me no physical harm. It is the memory that is slow to fade."

"A difficult time for you, I am sure. Now, forty-five days works out at nine hundred gold crowns, a tidy sum. But we have an issue over the horses. I asked for return of the monies, er, six hundred gold crowns I believe, on the completion of your duties with my caravan. By way of compensation, however, you may keep Silass' mount. What say you?"

"That is most generous of you. May I suggest an alternative?"

Hand nodded.

"Pay us five hundred and we keep Silass' mount and three of the horses."

The merchant was silent for a few moments, his face expressionless. Then he laughed, softly at first but then burst into a roar of mirth. "Mistress, you should bargain on my behalf. Ah, you have reached a deal. Return within an hour and your money shall be paid to you; the horses, all four of them, shall be yours." He continued to chuckle as Taura, Silmar and Varengo left his chamber.

$$\text{\textnormal{\textcyrillic{}} \qquad}$$

"We needin' some more of us *own* 'orses," complained Jasper, "even though I can't abide the beasts. Stupid choddin' animals! Mah feet is sore an' even mah boots got blisters, I'm certain of it. Four 'orses 'mong eleven o' us ain't enough. We'll be walkin' ferever."

They had walked south from Harrik for many days now. The road was quite busy but poorly-maintained in places. It was customary for merchant caravans to patch holes in the road as they slowly travelled along although it rarely happened. Consequently, the surface was badly-rutted where poor weather had taken its toll. This type of surface could potentially cause broken wheels or axles, particularly now that it had been baked hard by the sun. Where conditions allowed, they rode and walked along the verge of the road.

The countryside here was sparsely populated and with very little tree cover. The ground was too arid to support farming except in the few river valleys. Far off to the east, tall, misty, grey mountains, some snow-capped, reached into the clouds. They looked somewhat mysterious in the mist. The companions took turns in riding although Jasper and Billit, being short of stature, were very unaccustomed to being on horseback and preferred to be on foot. Taura rode most of the time with Falcon striding along beside her.

"*Our* own horses, Jasper," Taura forcefully corrected the dwarf. "*Our* own, not *us* own!"

The dwarf muttered something incomprehensible under his breath.

"You're right about all of us needing mounts," laughed Silmar. "We don't have sufficient money to buy enough for all of us. We all needed our new boots and clothing, some better weapons and decent armour and now we're down to just about five hundred gold between eleven of us; a tidy sum I grant you."

Jasper and Falcon had been tasked with caring for the gold coins.

A few moments later, Varengo sidled across to Silmar and pulled him to one side. "I'm a bit concerned about the attention we got at that village last night," he said quietly, scratching at his brown beard.

Silmar looked across at him and nodded. "Aye, I did notice. The Hoshites are keeping an unhealthy watch on us. I would be willing to bet that they sent a rider out on the road ahead of us once we'd all settled down. I've been keeping an open eye on the countryside today. Have you said anything to the others?"

Varengo shook his head. "Nay, not yet. Mori is a sharp one though. He was curious about the Hoshite's interest in us and brought my attention to it. They're probably wondering why a well-armed group of us are walking through east Polduman."

The elf gave a sardonic smile. "They haven't stopped us yet though. That is most likely because we are such a large group and the Hosh patrols number just a handful of men. My greatest concern at the moment is that without enough horses we are vulnerable."

Varengo scratched at his beard again. A small rash had appeared that was beginning to bleed. "Damn!" he growled. "I shall have to ask Mistress Taura for a salve for this. To matters; I have little compunction about, er, borrowing some horses, on a permanent basis you understand, from the Hosh. What say you?"

"This could well bring down a greater force of Hoshites upon our heads," Silmar warned. "Let me ponder on that a moment."

At that moment Taura rode up to join them. As always, Falcon was by her side. "I am a bit concerned," she said in a low voice. "You may not have noticed but I think the Hoshites were watching us."

"Aye, they were!" Varengo interrupted as Silmar was about to reply. "We have discussed this just a moment ago."

"Were you going to say anything to the group? You should, you know. Jasper and Vallio were talking. Word will spread."

Silmar took a loose grip on her horse's bridle. "I shall speak when we stop in a while."

With a nod and a smile she dropped back.

The group waited off the road while a line of traders' wagons trundle past on their way north towards Harrik. Varengo and Silmar walked in silence for about an hour. Occasionally, the fighter glanced at the elf until finally, he could contain himself no longer.

"Have you given my idea some thought, Silmar?" he questioned. "Come now, this is most vexing!"

The elf chuckled. "Aye, Varengo. I have thought. It is an interesting plan which grows on me rather like an untended wart! However, I see no reason why we should not give it some thought and then some meticulous planning. You might need to help us out there with a plan of sorts, my friend. Look, it is past midday and we should all take a rest."

While they all gathered around a small fire, Silmar spoke with them of their concerns regarding the scrutiny by the Hoshites and mentioned the idea of obtaining horses from the Hoshite force at the next trading post. He half expected some objections from the gathering but apart from some raucous laughter and a few heads bobbing in agreement, it seemed to go down better than he expected.

Meanwhile, Varengo stood aside from the companions deep in thought. He strode to and fro, rubbing his bearded chin in contemplation and sometimes looking to see if his rash was still weeping.

Finally he turned to the group. "I have an idea but you will need to trust us with a load of our money. Now, us five lads can blend in and if we don't carry too many weapons we won't be accused of being adventurers. Half a day south of here, where the road fords a river, will be a good place to meet. At the ford is the Broken Wheel tavern and trading post. We'll go there to buy horses. It's a stopping place for caravans and horse-traders who compete to sell their animals. There will be Hoshites in the tavern so I suggest the rest of you don't wait too close. What Yori says about Hosh agents watching the road is right so you had better hide well off the road. Look, there's an old quarry that the ancients used to dig up in the hills just to the south of the ford, maybe we can meet you there with the horses. What do you say?"

Jasper and Silmar looked at each other and then at their companions.

"Agreed," said the dwarf. "It's a fine idea, better'n we can come up with. But just take care, that's all. I ain't just thinking 'bout the money, neither. We oughta then leave the road an' go south. Prob'ly the safest route. But 'ow are the five of yous gonna leave the post with seven 'orses? You're bound to be questioned."

"That'll be easy," said Varengo. "We say we're buying nags for the new Hosh cavalry troop setting up a post by the

Claw Mountain at the southern end of this road. We should get a good price for them with a story like that. I'll need all the gold we have though. Price of horses around here can be sixty to eighty Gold Crowns each. But Yoriando here knows his horse-flesh; the best horse-haggler I've ever met."

The band continued on their walk for a few hours but it was almost midday before they saw the trading post with its tavern straddling the road below them. They were still high up in the hills but the village was not far off; they were close enough to see the black and brown uniforms of Hoshite troops and the more colourful blue and white uniforms of the Polduman militia. Beyond the village glistened a river. It wasn't particularly wide but its flow was fast, judging by the white water in places.

Jasper held out two money-bags and Falcon held two more.

"Take this 'ere gold," stated the dwarf. "I'm trustin' yer now, lads. Split it between yers. What profit yer make yous can keep. Sayin' that yer buyin' for Hosh soldiers may cause unwelcome interest from the other Polduman militia at the tavern. Best try not to let on about that unless you 'ave to. Watch that yer not followed when yer ride out to meet us."

❧ ❧

Once Varengo and his four men had ridden down to the village, with Vallio and Morendo mounted on a single horse, the remaining companions had followed a small merchants' caravan past the post and across the ford. The bored-looking Hoshites had hardly given them a second glance, enough only to take a toll of silver coin per person. A mile or so further on they climbed up an old track and settled on a ledge near the top of an old and long-abandoned stone quarry. Although the old workings were in the hills they weren't particularly high up. From his lonely vantage point, a little higher in the hills, Silmar had enough of a view of the road to see a few miles in either direction. To the north, the trading post was clearly visible, despite the heat haze. A large forest was also visible to the west through a cleft in the hills. Below him were the ford and the huddle of buildings, now tiny because of the distance. It would take only a few minutes for the companions to be at the foot of the hills to meet the riders and their horses.

It was about two hours before a cloud of dust appeared from the huddle of buildings by the river. The elf took a mouthful of water from his skin and re-attached it to his belt. The pace of the riders, each leading one or two horses, was casual but quickened as they gradually increased the distance between themselves and the tavern and the trading post.

Silmar gave a high-pitched whistle. "It's them. They are coming," he called to the others below. "Uh-oh! Another cloud of dust. Riders are following them. Riding hard, too. I hope Varengo has seen. Aye, by the Gods! Varengo's men are riding harder. Let's get down there and give them some help!"

༄ ༅

Varengo was anxious. The horse-trader was suspicious. The man had clearly been displeased when Yoriando had walked over to another trader to commence business with the *filthy Bocastrian*.

"Hey, no, c'mon!" yelled the fat and greasy wrangler. Yori glanced at him. "I'll do ya a deal, right? Five war-'orses, two ponies and a pack-'orse for six-fifty, right? They're all well broke-in. All healthy, right? Ya seen their teeth, ears and hooves, ain't ya? Good coats, right? These don't have the mange."

Yoriando continued to chat with the Bocastrian dealer. The man was ageing and with a wracking cough.

"Six hundred," the wrangler yelled. "Don't listen to that idiot *Boke* over there. You seen mine. Hey, they're worth nine hundred or more if you buy 'em in the city. C'mon!"

There was no response from Yoriando although he did give a quick glance at the wrangler.

"What's the *Boke* tellin; ya?" the fat wrangler yelled furiously. "I'll take five-fifty. Yours for five-fifty with saddles, bridles, blankets an' a pack saddle fer yer mule."

The fat wrangler was becoming more agitated as Yori continued to speak with the elderly Bocastrian. "The *Boke* won't let yer 'ave saddles and bridles for that price, and no pack frame either," he protested. "My last offer, four 'undred an' fifty gold 'uns if yer can give it me in coins right now. One 'undred fer all the tack."

The warrior glanced back at the wrangler. "I'll take your horses, ponies and a mule for four hundred and fifty," he said. "Not your saddles and stuff though. I got them from this man." He handed eighty gold Crowns over to the very satisfied Bocastrian trader. But the deal had aroused interest from a group of ten Hoshite soldiers. Varengo had quietly observed everything from a doorway by the side of the tavern while Yori conducted his business.

As the wrangler and Yori spat on their palms to shake on the deal, Varengo and his other men made their way over to join them. They handed over the payment for the mounts and then crossed over the Bocastrian to complete the deal with him, much to the fury of the wrangler.

"You bastards are robbing me," the greasy horse-trader grumbled as he strode away.

While his men saddled the horses, Varengo watched as one of the soldiers slinked away. After a while, the Hoshite soldier returned accompanied by another man, a black-robed figure, all the time suspiciously watching the horse-buyers.

A few minutes later, however, group rode away with their new mounts.

"Take it steady lads," warned Varengo. "We don't want to arouse suspicion and we don't want to tire the mounts."

The horses were led and ridden at a trot but the pace quickened to a canter after they crossed over the ford.

It was a sharp-eyed Vallio who raised the alarm. "Varengo! Riders behind! Coming up on us fast!"

"Move it lads, but keep together." *Hope our friends in the hills can see this happening!*

༄ ༄

The companions were well-concealed behind boulders and scrub as Varengo and his men approached. Although they were travelling very fast on their mounts, the Hoshite soldiers were gradually gaining on them.

Silmar gave a shrill whistle to catch the man's attention, wove his arms and yelled "Keep going, keep going!"

The riders needed no further encouragement. Barely a minute passed before the pursuers approached.

"Oh, they have a mage with them by the look of it," the elf cried out to his companions. "No weapons but he grasps a carven staff."

As the pursuers approached, Taura and Billit leapt into action.

"Well met, you bastards!" grunted Jasper as both the priestess and the gnome mage began chanting and weaving their magical semantics. Billit flung forth what looked like a handful of water and immediately a fog cloud formed just in front of the galloping Hoshites.

The pursuers were powerless to stop their horses and were swallowed up, it seemed, by the fog.

Simultaneously, Taura held aloft her hands and yelled words of prayer to Neilea. Thin streaks of light sprang from her fingertips and from inside the fog there were sounds of loud cracking and bangs, the like of which few of the companions had ever heard before.

From the fog burst three horses. Two were rider-less but the other dragged its rider, who had the unfortunate luck to have had his right foot caught in his stirrup, along the ground. He was screaming in an attempt to stop his mount but the horse, terrified by the *Firecrack* prayer spell, bolted. The screams stopped after a hundred yards.

"Where are they? Let us see them" snarled Jiutarô, in a rare expression of ferocity. He held his bow at the ready. Three more horses bolted from the fog and headed back at full gallop in the direction of the Broken Wheel tavern. One thrown rider charged out of the fog on foot, yelling and waving his sword. He was followed by another. Jasper stood up from behind a boulder, yelling curses at them, and the Hoshites charged up the slope towards him. Two arrows streaked from the hillside and the two men pitched forward to the ground.

Abruptly, the fog cleared away and there were the remaining eight Hoshites and four mounts. The mage stood with his staff held aloft. From his chanting and cackles, he had obviously used a counter-spell to lift the fog. His black cape billowed and beneath it the companions could see his black chainmail armour with its terrible symbol – a black globe, with a streak of lightning through it, held in the skeletal dragon's claw and mounted within a red disc. This was the symbol of the infamous Hoshite *Black Dragon* magical cult.

Billit reacted immediately. Three magical fire darts streaked down to the mage but they seemed to have little or no effect.

Taura, meanwhile, held up her sacred symbol of Neilea. With words of prayer she seemed to make pushing and grasping motions with her hands. Nothing happened. She continued with her chanting and hand motions. After some tense heartbeats, Silmar, who had been shooting arrow after arrow at the other soldiers, noticed the Hoshite mage look down at his black chainmail. He put his hand upon it only to withdraw it as if he had been burned by the metal.

"By the holy gods!" gasped the elf. "She is burning the metal of his armour. I have heard of this but never witnessed it. This is truly awesome!"

The Hoshite mage was now in a state of panic. Smoke could be seen emanating from his chest. The mage tore at the chainmail straps and bindings in an uncontrolled panic. He screamed in agony.

Still Taura chanted her god-given prayer spell. Small flames flickered from beneath the chain links and leather straps. The terrified mage flung away his cape and tried in vain to put out the flickering flames. Taura swayed and dropped her hands and fell to the ground, gasping for breath. Her *Iron-Sear* prayer spell had drained her to exhaustion.

Jiutarô ended the agonies of the Hoshite mage with a well-placed arrow in the man's neck. This wasn't bloodlust; he saw no honour or glory in allowing an enemy to die in agony. One of the horses was lying on the ground, kicking out but unable to rise. Its foreleg was broken. The three surviving Hoshites, who had been trying to calm their horses, now almost panic-stricken, mounted them and turned to retreat back towards the tavern. They were gone in a cloud of road dust.

The sounds of Taura's opening magical pyrotechnics had caused Varengo and his men to turn their mounts and return to the fray but by the time they got there the surviving Hoshites had gone.

Jiutarô ran to the stricken horse and, with his *wakisashi*, the shortsword that perfectly matched his katana, put an end to its suffering.

The companions grimly gathered together and were joined by Varengo and his men.

"What in the seven hells happened there in the town?" asked Jasper.

Varengo, panting from the exertion of the ride, managed a chuckle. "The buggers took an interest when we handed the money over," he said. "They probably thought they could take the horses back off us."

"They are good mounts," said Falcon. "Good saddles. Good price?"

Varengo laughed again. "The wrangler was a slimy Poldumanian. He was gonna try to swindle us so Yori here spoke with another dealer, a Bocastrian, to haggle over saddles and stuff and the wrangler thought he was dealing for horses. So the greasy Poldumanian kept dropping his prices. Wouldn't be surprised if he had something to do with setting the Hoshites after us to get the horses back and keep the money."

"They ain't got the money, boss!" a voice spoke out.

Varengo turned and looked at the smiling faces of Jassio and Vallio. Jassio held up two money bags.

"I was having this quiet chat with this oily Poldumanian," said Jassio in a matter-of-fact manner. "Gods, he stank! Told him we would be coming back for more horses and while we talked, Vallio here, eased up behind him and grabbed the moneybags."

"What?" gasped Silmar.

"Aye, and I left two bags of small stones in their place. We got out o' there fast, din't we? Just as well really."

"We got us five more war-horses," explained Yoriando. "They're not too fast but they'll go all day. There's two riding ponies for the little 'uns – no offence intended. All of them've got saddles and tack and saddlebags too. The pack-mule has a pack-frame on it with a sheet of tarp and loads of rope. We done well, aye?"

"You did very well," replied Silmar. "But we may have a problem now. The Hosh scum has ridden back to the tavern. They could be back here in a short while with reinforcements."

"Not likely, leastways not for a few days," replied Varengo. "There weren't many more Hoshite mounts in the corral and we didn't see many more soldiers there. It will be a quite a while before they come back this way with reinforcements from Harrik. We should use this opportunity to get some space between them and us."

Taura sat on the ground and leaned against a rock. She looked exhausted and hung her head wearily. Using divine magic always taxed her resources. Falcon held a waterskin ready for her.

"Can yer ride, girlie?" Billit asked her.

"A little water and a short rest and I shall be ready," she panted.

They selected their mounts and were soon riding their horses and ponies at a steady trot. Most of them felt a little awkward at first. It had been many a ten-day week since the dwarf and gnome had last ridden, much longer for a couple of the others, and they knew that legs, groins and hips would be aching later.

While they were riding, Sushi would occasionally fly off and take herself in the direction from which the group had come. Each time, after having been away for increasingly longer periods, she would return and Jiutarô would quickly know that there was no sign of pursuers.

Next day, the little cleret-wing dragon flew off at dawn and she did not reappear until the hazy midday sun was at its highest point in the sky. Jiutarô had been worried for some time and his relief at seeing her was obvious.

"Followers come," warned Jiutarô. "A day behind us. Trackers follow. Wear black. Number, ahh, as of fingers and toes together. This what Sushi say, not me. I can count, hai? One, two, three, five, four. This is, aii, twenty men. Not move fast but may just keep to come until find us. Hai?"

"Nay, sixteen," Varengo corrected. "Look at her claws. We just gotta keep going until they either give up or we go where they can't. Maybe like Cascant. One day, eh? They might move at night too."

"Aye, yer right there," agreed Jasper. "Cascant don't tolerate the Hoshites one bit. 'Less, o' course, they cast off their uniforms an' armour an' travel as ord'nary folk, they'll 'ave to stop eventually. A group that big will 'rouse a lot of suspicion."

"A group our size will arouse suspicion too," said Yoriando. "But at least we have the benefit of our Caravan escorts' tokens."

"Aye, but we're now in West Polduman," explained Varengo. "There's no towns, few villages or farms. Folk don't live here. They're bad lands. Nobody wants to claim these lands as their own, that's why they call South Polduman the *Unclaimed Lands*. It's just too damned dangerous for travellers and for people to live in. Look at this soil. It's just sand, rock, pumice and dry shit. Nothing will grow here. Hardly any water; it don't rain much here. Things that live here may want to eat us or just kill us for the fun of it. It's lucky for us that we're a big, well-armed party else we would just attract trouble. It's all the same a few days to the south except there are swamps and sinking sand too. It's not clean water for drinking; it's foul, rancid and deadly to all but the worst of beasts that crawl or slither. It's all gonna be like this 'til we get to the pass taking us east through the Dragon's Tail Mountains, I'm reckoning for a seven-day week 'til we get within the shadows of Claw Mountain, less if we move quicker."

"Hmm. We 'ad better load up with as much water as we can carry while we can," Jasper mused.

Before dawn the next day, they were travelling south at a steady trot. The road was little more than a faint, little-used track following the Wyrm's Tail Stream, a trickling watercourse that occasionally disappeared beneath rocks and impenetrable thickets of gorse. It provided an ideal route to follow and provided them with some water. Most of the party were distinctly unimpressed when Taura said she would not travel with any of them who refused to bathe in the stream. She had no choice but to relent when Jasper stolidly declined.

"I ain't wettin' mah body!" he yelled at her. "Look girly, Mah skin ain't used to it. I don't take mah clo'es off fer no-one. You don't wanna travel wi' me? Fine, I'm goin' back to mah tavern."

By this time, most of the group were sitting in the stream. Jiutarô had moved upstream a short distance and was busy with washing himself. Only Jassio and Morendo also resisted Taura's demand.

She threw her arms up in disgust and walked along the stream until she was out of sight of the others.

A short while later they resumed their ride but Taura rode alone and in silence.

There had been no sign of followers or of any other travellers. Neither had they seen creatures that may have offered them any serious danger. As expected, there were no signs of villages or farmsteads and few well-defined and well-used tracks. They felt quite secure as they travelled these lands but they kept a careful vigilance to the hills on the left, the plains to the west and on the road behind, which stretched almost arrow-straight.

❧ ❧

The Hoshite sergeant-at-arms was in a dilemma. His troop was mounted on horses that were only suitable for pulling wagons, he was certain of it. He led an ill-disciplined rabble of thugs, as far as he was concerned. The further he led them away from their outpost near Harrik, the more likely they would be to abscond. Their post was lucrative; a lot of money was collected from travellers and merchants although this time of year, the hot season, was not so good for them. Caravans were infrequent, traders did not travel alone but occasional groups of adventurers and campaigners were a source of gold, a healthy percentage of which passed into his money pouch.

The horse dealers, however, had offered a reward for the return of the horses and for the gold that had been stolen. It was relatively paltry by comparison with the tolls they took in the cooler seasons.

"Carrib!" he called. One of his riders rode forward. "Call the scouts back. We're returning to the post."

"What, now?"

"What now, *sergeant!* Aye, right now. This is a fool's errand. There's too many of them for us to handle and it ain't worth it."

Two pairs of eyes watched from the hillside as the Hoshites turned about and rode northwards.

ॐ ॐ

CHAPTER 32

SILMAR AWOKE with a start. Varengo was gently shaking him by the shoulder.

"Two figures, down the valley." The man's whispers were urgent. "Very tall. Jasper is watching them. Thought you would want to know. There may be more."

Silmar shook his head, his long hair in disarray, but was immediately alert. "Aye, er. Thank you. Good. Quietly wake everyone else. Tell them to stay in the camp. Is the fire out?"

"Aye. Done that. Jasper is by that brush down there."

"Get someone to watch upstream too."

Silmar crept forward, keeping his profile low to the ground. As he approached Jasper, the dwarf turned his head towards him and raised his finger to his lips.

"Two 'undred paces. They've not seen us yet. Trolls I think."

"They look big," whispered the elf. "They're not trolls, some sort of ogre by the looks of them. They carry spears and one has a sword."

"Oh shit!"

One of the ogres lunged with his spear into the stream and something small was impaled on the tip. A few heartbeats later the other troll did the same with his sword and another catch was made, long and dark, but narrow.

The dwarf gave an exasperated growl. "Jus' fishin'. Wish I could do it that easy! Damn, they're comin' up 'ere. Be ready."

The ogres slowly walked uphill towards the group's campsite, apparently unaware that it was there. At about fifty paces distance they stopped, looking ahead and clearly sniffing.

"Greet travellersh," came a harsh and guttural call.

Silmar stepped out from behind the bush, his hands held palms forward towards the figures. "We greet fellow hunters," he replied.

"You elf, a-yes? You-a number eleven peoples. We-a know this. We-a peaceful. Share food a-yes?"

Silmar's heart thudded as he glanced at Jasper, who nodded. "You are welcome to our camp. Come in." Turning to Jasper he whispered "Half-ogres, part human. Be wary, they tolerate humans but you and me maybe not."

As the ogres approached, Silmar whispered to Jasper "I have killed every ogre I have ever encountered. They have always tried to kill me. It's not like them to be peaceful."

"Stay alert, we may 'ave to do it yet," replied the dwarf. "By Trangath's holy skirts, these bastards reek!"

By now, every member of the party was standing by the camp except for Varengo. The half-ogres approached with caution but stopped in mid-stride when they saw the Samurai and the alert cleret-wing dragon astride his shoulders. Sushi hissed and her lips were drawn back aggressively.

To look at, these beasts were massive humanoids, towering head and shoulders above even the mighty Falcon. They were dark-skinned; their teeth and fingernails looked quite dark in the dim moonlight, perhaps a deep-orange hue to their skin but it was difficult to discern in the gloom, and they appeared somewhat rounded at the shoulders. They were muscular although not heavily built. Their skin was covered, as far as the companions could tell, in dark, matted body hair. Both of them were dressed in skins and with a heavy fur loin-cloth. Their hair was long and tied back in a tail. One had steel shoulder plate attached to the skins he was wearing but it was doubtful as to whether it would serve any protective purpose. Their spears were fully eight feet in length and were metallic over their full length. Tufts of hair hung from their belts.

Silmar was revolted. *Scalps?* he thought.

Yoriando and Vallio rebuilt the fire. Jasper motioned for the ogres to be seated and produced a cooked leg of the deer the companions had started feasting on that evening. The visitors sat down but their weapons remained within easy reach. The smell emanating from them was foul. One of them broke wind without as much as a change in his expression.

"Everyone sit down for the gods' sake!" Jasper growled. The ogres sniffed suspiciously at the meat and muttered in their language. They ate greedily. All the time, their gaze was firmly, but uneasily, fixed on the cleret-wing dragon. Jiutarô winced as Sushi's claws dug into his shoulder. One visitor glanced briefly at Taura.

"You-a burn meat! Spoil taste," one stated. "Eat-a this! Better!" He handed Silmar a large frog and a long, black, snake-like thing that twisted itself around the half-ogre's wrist. Silmar judged it to be an eel.

Silmar almost retched. "Can you eat this?" he asked, handing the frog to Jasper.

"I choddin' knowed you would give this to me! Aye, I've eaten worse! I bet you get the snake-fish! I just knows it!"

Silmar slowly withdrew his dagger and set about peeling the skin off the eel. He cut the skin all the way around the neck, just behind the gills, and then slit its belly down to the vent. He lifted a corner of the skin with his dagger, gripped it between his teeth and pulled the skin completely off in a single smooth movement. He spat the reeking grease off his lips and wiped his arm across his mouth. The half-ogres watched with expressions of puzzlement and suspicion. Silmar took a bite at the eel and handed it to Falcon, who did the same. He then gave it to Taura who took a small nibble. One at a time, each member of the group ate a piece from the eel. Each of them was determined not to pull a face.

"It is good," Jiutarô and he handed a piece to Sushi.

"Good," said the half-ogre. "We-a go now." *Belch!* "Travel in peace. We-a be friends now with-a no trouble from us and-a you."

"No trouble. Travel in peace and safety."

The half-ogres left and were out of sight in moments.

"By the gods, Silmar!" Varengo exclaimed. "What was all that about? Do you think they were sizing us up for an attack in the night?"

The elf considered his response before answering. "I do not think so," he replied. "I believe they were just hungry."

"I detected no ill will from them," Taura offered, "but I do think one of them knew I was scrutinising them."

"I can still smell 'em!" Yoriando gasped. "I will do for a tenday week."

The party was on full alert for the rest of the night and they slept poorly. Next morning, they were roused early and fed on more of the cooked venison. The remainder was left to dry out over the campfire.

"I puked the frog up just after the ogres left," grumbled Jasper. "It was all I could do to keep it down while they was 'ere. Half of it I hid up mah sleeve while they was looking at Sushi. I'm a bit curious there. They took a lot of interest in 'er."

"Not surprising really," replied Silmar. "You don't get Cleret-wing dragons in this part of the lands. They come from further south, around the forests of Faerhome and east Polduman. I was wondering how she ended up locked in a cage in the Shadow World."

Jasper stepped forward. "Captured for trade, I bet," he suggested. "Prob'ly get lots o' gold for a pet like that."

Silmar couldn't resist an opportunity to tease the dwarf. "Try telling Jiutarô that. He'll bend down and slice your head off! Ha ha!"

As always, the dwarf reacted predictably. "Bend down? Yer cheeky pointy-eared chod!"

They returned to the narrow animal track they had been following the day before. Knowing that they had been watched by the ogres the previous evening, they kept a cautious watch of the hills and plains around them. The threat from the following Hoshites was a constant concern although Jiutarô seemed confident with the little dragon's subliminal messages that the followers had gone. Silmar and Jasper were impressed by Varengo's professionalism. He had proved to be a good leader of his group and his experience was an asset to the group.

Then, as they entered a small valley, a heard a sound that chilled the blood in their veins to ice.

❧ ❧

Three pairs of eyes watched keenly from amongst the rocks and crags high about the group of travellers on the track.

The owners gave mirthless grins as the horses below became skittish and struggled against their ties. One of the figures hissed a word and the three of them moved along the skyline although out of sight of the group below.

Little did they know that they were also being observed.

∽ ∾

The first sign of any menace was when Sushi raised herself up on Jiutarô's shoulders and became alert, her claws digging into his upper arm. The little dragon gave a throaty growl. The Samurai hissed out a warning to his comrades. The group stopped, reining in their mounts and dismounting.

Then, barely a dozen heartbeats later, a wolf-like howling echoed from further up the valley. This was followed by the howling of more beasts.

Immediately, all of the companions made ready their weapons. Taura intoned softly, instilling a sense of calm amongst the comrades while Billit chanted mystical phrases, the words unintelligible the others.

"Wolves!" called Jasper, thinking with clarity and taking the initiative. "Make ready. There is no point in running. If they come, we gotta fight 'em off. Come, you all, close in together now. We need to build up the fire. Protect the mage and the priestess."

Sushi leapt from Jiutarô's shoulders and flew up into the air.

They led their mounts shoulder-to-shoulder in a ring with Billit and Taura in the middle. Aword blades glinted in the sunlight as they prepared to fight. Bows were readied.

Then the first beast appeared.

It was huge, grey and menacing, fully eight feet from snout to tail-root. Its massive jaws open, saliva dripping from its teeth and tongue; its yellow eyes glaring at the group not forty yards from them.

Then another appeared, and another. They kept gathering.

"Worg wolves!" cried Silmar. "Do not despair. Do not be fearful. There are enough for us all to fight and destroy!" He suddenly felt the effect of his burden, the foul ceremonial dagger that nestled in its casket at the bottom of his pack, starting to overwhelm him. Pain coursed through his head, behind his eyes. He felt nauseous. There was indeed evil in there. He wouldn't have believed that these beasts were so evil until now. He fought to keep the influence under control. He expected that worg wolves do what wolves do, that is to eat to survive and survive to eat.

There were nine in all. Each was fully grown; a huge, fearless, ravenous, growling killer.

The wolves advanced almost leisurely to gather to within ten paces or so of the companions and then slowly circled them, looking for a weakness in the defence. There was no immediate obvious intent to attack but most of the companions knew it would come soon without the need to be told and without warning.

One wolf in particular, was obviously the leader. It had nudged and goaded the others into moving round and round the group in the centre.

"Watch its hackles," warned Jasper. "When they rise, it will be a signal to the others. They will attack." The dwarf was ready with his great axe, swinging it in well-practised moves.

"Look up there, on the hill!" growled Falcon. "Recognise them?"

Three hooded figures, somewhat small in stature and dressed in dark cloaks, called in an unknown language.

"The choddin' Darkling!" snarled Jasper. "Well, I'll be gods-damned. That probably explains these worgs! 'Ow did they conjure them up? Bastards!"

The elf nodded. "Aye, they're up there shouting encouragement to the wolves, of that I am certain."

At a sharp high-pitched cry from the Darkling, the hackles rose. Suddenly there was a yap from the lead worg-wolf and at once the beasts turned towards the group and charged in. Two arrows and a flurry of magical fire-darts slammed into the leader and, with a yelp of pain, it fell to the ground. Its movements showed that it wasn't dead, however, as its jaws and back paws scratched at the injuries.

One worg leapt high, over the heads of the fighters. Avoiding the blades of Morendo and Vallio, but was slashed by Billit who was now wielding a sword of bright flame. The worg was dead before it hit the ground, its entrails showering the little gnome and his pony with gore that glistened in the hazy sunlight.

Falcon pushed his mount forward a step to enable him to swing his mighty battle-hammer at another brute that advanced to meet him. The hammer struck the worg-wolf at the shoulder. Although badly bludgeoned, the worg spun and its great jaws took Falcon's left lower-arm in a vice-like grip and tried to drag him backwards. Despite the agony, the barbarian continually slammed the beast's back with his battle-hammer until it fell, its spine shattered. Falcon's badly ripped arm was bleeding profusely, bone showing through the damaged flesh, and he fell to his knees.

Silmar and Jiutarô were firing arrows at two worgs. Although all arrows found their mark, they did not seem to slow down the movement of the beasts. Jiutarô threw down his bow and, with incredible speed, whipped out his katana and slashed one beast from neck to stomach as it reared up. The worg was dead immediately.

One of Varengo's men was down, blood pouring from a neck wound. Was it Jassio? His horse had panicked, knocked him off his feet, and tried to bolt. A worg-wolf immediately leapt upon the horse and brought it to the ground. The stricken man's comrade, Morendo, was still astride his horse, standing in his stirrups above him, hacking furiously at a worg. The beast moved backwards and to the side looking to strike. A huge spear appeared from nowhere and slammed into its flanks. The beast fell and moved no more. The fighter immediately dropped to the ground to attend to his friend.

Shrill yells still came from the hillside as the Darklings directed the attacks.

Another flurry of magical fire-darts hit the beast which had already had a taste of this form if attack. It howled as its fur singed and the flesh beneath it sizzled. The smell of burning was acrid to those close by. Although it struggled to rise to its feet, it gave a final howl as yet another group of fire-darts struck its head and neck, melting one of its eyes.

Jasper was slamming his great-axe at a beast that circled him cautiously. As the dwarf lifted his weapon over his head to deliver a massive blow, the beast lunged forward with it jaws open wide. It then crashed down upon him lifeless. A huge iron spear had passed through its body, narrowly missing the dwarf as he lay pinned beneath it. Slaver dripped from the dead wolf-worg onto Jasper's face. *Urrgh! Gods, does it stink! Where did that choddin' spear come from?*

Yet another beast was felled with a spear thrown from above. The two surviving wolf-worgs, one which was badly injured, fled yapping back up the valley.

"Get me out from under here, you chods!" yelled Jasper.

"Falcon is down. So is my man!" called Varengo.

Falcon was sitting on the ground cradling his damaged arm in his other. Despite the pain he was obviously feeling, he uttered not a sound, merely rocked to and fro with his face screwed up with the agony. Taura rushed over to him and looked at his arm. The barbarian stuttered "See to Varengo's man first, I shall be fine for while."

Reluctantly, she moved across to the man in time to see a tearful Varengo close his friend's eyes. "It is too late for Jassio. He died bravely. I am very proud of him."

Taura put a hand on his shoulder and mouthed a silent word of comfort, or it may have been a blessing, and returned to Falcon's side and immediately started working on his arm.

"Jassio is dead," she whispered. "I must reset your bone before I start the healing process. I need to pull your wrist. Can you bear it? Can you help me, Jasper?"

The young barbarian started singing. Loud and strong was his voice. The language of the words was unknown to the others around him but his voice was clear and tuneful. As he sang, the priestess gripped his wrist and, with a slight twist, stretched it to straighten the broken bone fragments. Falcon gave out a yell and slumped forward to the ground.

Meanwhile, four half-ogres stepped out from behind the large bushes on the sides of the valley. Silmar walked over to them with his hand raised in salute. "You have saved us!"

"You-a welcomed us. Others do not. We-a gave each other friendship. Help is-a what friends do."

The elf extended his hands and offered his arm to the half-ogre speaker. Puzzlement briefly showed on the ogre's face but then understanding dawned. The half-ogre took the wrist and shook it.

"Black elves gone fast on-a horses! You now travel in-a safety. We-a go to setting sun. Where you-a travel?"

"To the rising sun. Travel in peace and safety."

Another half-ogre had recovered the spears and yet another hefted the carcass of a dead worg over his shoulders. With a salutation, they marched away.

Holding her holy symbol over the barbarian's broken and heavily-bound arm, Taura had begun her chants. After a few dozen heartbeats, a faint blue glow enveloped the arm. Sweat poured from her face as she continued to chant, rocking back and forth much the same as Falcon had when he had been pain-wracked. It was a great many moments before she stopped to check on her progress.

"It is working! My blessed Holy Mother Neilea is curing him of his breaks and his pain!" She continued with her chanting, but at a more relaxed pace now. Many more moments passed and at last she stopped. Falcon was breathing deeply and sleeping soundly. "His bones should come together very quickly. Leave him for a while then he must have his arm bound tightly again but with splints. Does anyone else have injuries?"

"So the bastard Darkling 'ave bravely buggered off then, 'ave they?" asked the dwarf, at the top of his voice. "I don't think we've seen the last of 'em. I would guess that this attack was set up by them to test our strength."

"You are probably right," replied Silmar. "Also to reduce our numbers." He dropped his head in sadness.

"Well, I 'ope you're impressed!" yelled the dwarf again at the top of his voice. "It will be your turn soon, you bastards!"

His words echoed off the valley walls. Jassio's horse had perished, its throat torn out. A mass of blood soaked the gravel of the road. The beast that had caused this devastation had turned tail and run.

Jasper stood before his comrades. "We was lucky that the 'alf-ogres turned up when they did. Our injuries would 'ave been worse and p'raps more of us would 'ave died. But everybody fought well. That magic was wonderful. Hey, Billit, that fiery sword was good! Can you magic one up for me? Heh heh!" His laugh was forced however. His expression turned to one of sadness and he struggled to retain his composure. "But let us remember our fallen comrade-in-arms. Jassio will be missed. 'E was a good fighter an' shall be buried with honour. Yer right, Varengo, 'e fought well. Taura shall say words to 'elp speed him to the afterlife. Is that alright, girlie? He 'as earned his place next to 'is ancestors and shall sit aside 'em with pride. 'E shall show the exalted ones 'ow he can make 'is shortsword sing, I'll be damned if 'e won't! Oh, b—by the gods!" He turned away from his companions for a few heartbeats of private contemplation. He had forgotten over the recent decades the pain of losing a fellow fighter.

Varengo bowed his head for his fallen friend. A deep hollow was scooped out in the hill to one side of the valley and Jassio's corpse was placed there with his heavily bloodstained sword resting on his chest. Soil and gravel was heaped over the body and then rocks, collected from the stream's bed, were placed on top. Taura spoke words to her beloved Goddess, Neilea. When she finished, the group slowly walked away.

"Thank you for those words, Jasper," said Varengo. "Aye, he would have been proud to have heard them."

"Perhaps 'e did, Varengo, just afore Taura 'elped show 'im the way with 'er words! Aye lad, I reckons 'e would 'ave." The dwarf clapped his hand onto Varengo's shoulder and they walked off together to join the others.

Falcon had recovered from his many hours of sleep and Taura checked the condition of his left arm. The flesh was still very red around the scabs of the larger injuries and the elbow and wrist were extremely swollen and stiff, but the divine healing had been effective and the Barbarian poured out his thanks to Taura while she bound his arm. She used some of the arrows from Jassio's quiver wrapped tightly within the bindings.

"You will not be able to use your arm properly for a few tendays," she explained. "Care for it. I shall look at it from time to time. When the pain makes you uncomfortable, chew on this willow bark until its bitter taste has gone, not too often, mark you. I only have a few pieces of bark and shall try to find more but you must use it sparingly."

They sat together for many minutes until the time came for Jasper and Silmar to tell them to continue with their journey.

Silmar spoke to them all. "The bastard Darkling know where we are. Perhaps we should find a new track to walk."

"Aye, or we go on this way an' hunt the bastards an' stick 'em!" growled Jasper.

The little dragon had returned and Jiutarô was able to report that the Darkling, numbering four, had ridden hard into the foothills of the mountain range to the east.

"They may well try to find us when we get there," suggested Silmar, "or wait in ambush."

"Cheerful, that pointy-eared git," the dwarf snapped.

❧   ❧

CHAPTER 33

SILMAR SHIELDED his eyes from the sun's fierce glare. "Is that a river far to the south of us?" he asked.

They had endured many days of riding, slowing only to walk beside their tiring horses and ponies. A few other travellers and merchants had reported that the roads ahead were in good condition and that they had seen no sign of brigands. Water had been scarce now that the Wyrm's Tail Stream was little more than mud. They had dug down through the damp gravel to find sufficient water for themselves and their mounts. Few of the companions were familiar with these lands. It was just as well that Varengo and his men had joined them. Falcon had endured long periods of intense pain in his arm to the point that Taura had no more willow bark to offer him.

Although the others peered with their hands raised they could barely see through the shimmering air.

"Buggered if I can see anythin', elf," Jasper murmured. "It's a choddin' mirage, pointy-ears!"

Silmar chose to ignore the jibe as Varengo moved his mount closer.

"Ah, Land's Wash it is called," the grizzled warrior confirmed. "For much of its length it flows through a deep gully as it turns south and west. People say where it's at its widest it's too thick to drink and too thin to plough. It's not easy to cross because it's deep and fast-flowing in some places and thick, deep mud in others. We'll need to look for tracks to see where other travellers cross."

"If I remember aright, there may be a town on the way south," suggested Morendo, "but not for a long way. There's little water once we turn away from the Wyrm's Tail, well, that is except for the river but that is a few days off. Apart from that it's quite, er, pleasant!"

Next morning, the group turned south-east away from Wyrm's Tail Stream. Although Silmar, with his keen eyes, had scoured the lands around them, there had been no sign of the Hoshite pursuers or the Darkling.

"I'm surprised at that," exclaimed Jasper. "I wouldn't have expected the 'Shites to give up so easy. Them losing 'orses so easy won't sit well with their big bosses."

"Maybe they didn't give up the chase," responded Varengo. "They may have gone a different way, maybe to intercept us somewhere. We will have to press on and hope we avoid them."

Jiutarô, who had been leading the group, was noticeably irritated, turned in his saddle. "I said to you, Sushi tell me they *not* follow, they gone. Bah! Where is trust? Aii!" He turned forwards once again and spurred his horse on. It would be a few days before he spoke with the others again.

"Aye, 'e was right, there," added Jasper. "We best get on with it then." He shrugged his shoulders and shook his head.

Three days later, in the late afternoon, they came to the wide river, the Land's Wash. It was the flat lands that caused the river to wind hither and yon, carrying much mud from the higher slopes of the mountainous regions to the east. In the distance, many miles to the west, they could clearly see the dark spread of a large forest. Varengo admitted that neither he nor his men had any familiarity with these lands.

"That's not exactly right, boss," admitted Morendo. "I've been in this area during my old days with a group of raiders." Shaking his head he sighed "Jassio was with me for a short while. Bad days, aye, but lucrative. Oh aye, that distant wood is vast, known as Wyrmlair. The giant redwoods in the low lands and thick pines on the high plateaus are said to be home to great dragons. They sleep long but can be bastards when they wake up. A bit like my wife really! Hahaha! She's passed on now."

"Oh, sorry to hear she's dead," responded Silmar.

"Nay. She's not dead. She passed on to my friend Garro, the poor bugger! Anyway, the Forest of Wyrms is a place to be avoided. Fortunately we won't come close to the forest. And over there, see, to the east that lone peak, tall and conical? Well, that's Claw Mount, also known as the Hill of Lost Souls. Don't know why. Just a name I guess. Never wanted to find out 'cos the word is that it's haunted. We shouldn't go anywhere near the godsforsaken place. You know the lands too, don't you Vallio?"

"Well, not as well as you, old friend. But let's see what I can remember. Beyond the Wyrmlair forest is a tall range of hills many leagues in length. You can make them out quite well from here. Let's go up onto this higher ground and you'll see all the better."

From a low rise they could see the gloom of a vast dark forest that in the distant south.

"The great Tyben Forest," sighed Vallio. "A fearful place!" He shuddered but continued with his speech. "Many miles to their south, the River Tyben flows into the Tyben

Woods – the haunt of centaurs, satyr druids and other strange creatures. Centaurs were not a threat but, like many reclusive creatures, they did like to be left alone. They're like a hive of bees, you upset them and they'll sting. A satyr druid, like any other druid, will only let you enter the forest if it wanted you to do so."

"I have heard about Tyben," murmured Silmar.

It was the morning of the following day that they managed to cross the Land's Wash River. Fording the river proved more difficult than they had perceived. After many hours of searching the previous day along miles of very deep and sometimes fast-flowing, murky water, they found a wide, sweeping curve. Even so, it was mid-morning before they were safely on the opposite bank. It was only then that they realised how fortunate they had been.

Not far along the bank lay a few large alligators basking in the sun.

By late afternoon on the following day, they had found a road stretching east and west. It was busy with many travellers. To the east, just a league away, they were surprised to see a town. It was large and sprawling and a vain attempt had been made to construct an encircling wall. However, it was soon evident that a large amount of the wooden stakes had been removed from it to build huts and corrals. As they approached the town's edge, a sign had been crudely painted on a piece of wood – Claw Drift. Caravans were occasionally using the road through the town and the group was surprised to see many Hoshites, both soldiers and travellers, amongst the caravans.

Claw Drift was a typically lawless frontier town like so many others throughout the lands of Baylea. This town was a magnet for brigands, adventurers and deserters who congregated in all the bars. Even in the early evening there were fights, duels and brawls. Drunken men were staggering from tavern to tavern and leering lecherously at the scantily-clad strumpets. One man had taken a street-wench into a side alley where he had lifted her skirts and was taking full advantage of her services. Others were laying in the filthy street lost in their drunken stupors.

Yoriando winked at one of the whores. She walked seductively over to him, thrusting her bare breasts at him. "Wanna spend some time with these, soldier?"

"Maybe later, sweetlips," he replied, with another wink and a huge grin. This turned into a grimace as he looked at the front of one of the taverns.

A body had been suspended in a crude metal cage from a hastily-constructed gibbet. The victim had long since expired, the head having been picked clean by the rooks still bickering for morsels that were not still covered by the tattered clothing.

"Wonder what his crime was," muttered Varengo.

"Prob'ly didn't pay the whore," laughed Jasper. "No more'n food for the corvids now."

Yoriando snorted. "Yeah, right. Funny. Bloody funny! By the gods, this place stinks of rotting fleash. Hey! What's going on there?"

A roar of voices erupted from down the street. One man, naked, heavily bleeding and screaming obscenities, was being led on the end of a rope out the doorway of an inn. The crowd gathered around him pushed and jostled him and he stumbled to the ground many times. The rope, tightly tying his wrists behind his back, was used to roughly yank him to his feet. Another rope was being carried by a loudly-screeching woman. She was short but stout in stature with a face that looked as though it had experienced much hardship. A smoke-weed pipe was clenched between her teeth except when she took it out to bellow more obscenities.

"Over here with the bastard!" screeched the woman, while using the rope to lash his back. "String 'im up over here!"

Her rope was thrown aloft to a high beam extending from the front of a livery stable and was secured by a young man sitting astride it. The suspending end of it had been fashioned into a simple loop with a slip knot.

Silmar was appalled. *By the gods, they are going to hang the man!*

The unfortunate victim, blood pouring from a smashed nose and ripped lips and yelling out his innocence, was cajoled onto the back of a wagon.

Within ten heartbeats the wagon lurched forward and the man swung from side to side, hanging by his neck. His cries of anguish were cut off by the constriction to his throat and his legs thrashed wildly in the air. As he hung there with his wrists bound behind him, the woman, now sobbing, beat his head and body with a cudgel. With each vicious blow, she screamed an obscenity. A sign; upon which were crude writings, was brought out of the nearby inn and placed around his neck.

"Oh for the love of bread, honey and fine wine!" Vallio croaked. "What in the seven hells does that say?" The execution was too far away for the sign to be understood but Silmar, with his keen eyesight, could quite clearly read it.

He turned to look at the others. "It says *Child Killer!*"

"Let the bastard rot then!" said Taura with surprising uncharacteristic bitterness. "Let's get what we need and ride on out of Claw bloody Drift."

By the time they had replenished their food supplies at the little market the mob had dispersed. Only the fierce woman remained by the bloodied and battered remains of the now dead man. Exhausted, she sat below his feet with the bloodsoaked cudgel across her lap. Blood dripped from the hanging body onto her hair but she appeared unmoved by it. She even raised a hand half-heartedly as the group rode past. Only Taura responded, with a gesture her companions recognised as a blessing.

Silmar had been surprised to see half-orcs, and even a half-Darkling, amongst one small band of adventurers as he led the group westwards out of the town. Sushi had drawn some unwelcome attention from one member of the band but the man turned his heavily-tattooed head away when he received a ferocious glare from Jiutarô. The Samurai rode with Sushi on his shoulder and his hand on the hilt of his katana. That expression was enough to deter all.

The mighty Falcon rode a little more comfortably now; he flexed his arm and squeezed his hand around a wad of cloth. As always, Taura fussed around him at every opportunity. He didn't appear to complain. She now had a good supply of fresh willow bark.

The sun was sinking low in the western sky when, two days later and having continued eastwards on the road, they arrived at a sign that read "hiLLs eDge". Any person with the ability to read the simple sign could have been forgiven for expecting to see a small village or farming community but when they rode through the surprisingly stout gates they were confronted by a small, sprawling town inhabited by dwarves, gnomes, halflings and a few humans.

Although many curious faces turned their way as they rode along the main street, there was little in the way of suspicion or fear. In fact, after the lawlessness of Claw Drift, they were surprised at the cleanliness and neatness of the street. Indeed, in common with any city, town or village, there were inebriates, mostly human, sitting slumped on the stoops in front of the taverns; there were voices raised in argument and threatening gestures between drunken louts; there were revellers leering at street-walking scantily-clad whores, there were shrieking children and barking dogs; there were even dung-sweepers and street cleaners. But the atmosphere was not as threatening as it had been two days earlier at Claw Drift.

There was poverty here, however. Disfigured and limbless ex-soldiers and adventurers, mainly humans but among them, one or two Halflings and dwarves, begged outside taverns for enough coins to buy an ale or a meal. Many travellers and traders passing through the little town ignored the beggars although one or two threw coppers in the dust and laughed as the beggars crawled and jostled to retrieve them. The travellers would then laugh again and ride or stride on.

The group led their mounts and pack horse into a corral beside an inn and left them in the charge of a couple of young lads. Unusually for a tavern, a number of trestles and benches were arrayed outside in front of the tavern and the group wearily settled down on these. The little town was busy, despite the oppressive residual heat of the early evening. The dust of the road and the tiredness of the group gave them a grimness that implied a tough demeanour. That one of them had a miniature dragon on his shoulder and a fearsome expression, and that there was a gigantic barbarian with them, and that they were all armed to the teeth, only added to the apparent robustness of the band. Very few people dared to openly stare in their direction, except perhaps for the young boys, and a few young ladies too, and some not so young.

Very few words were exchanged between the members of the group as they sat on the boards and stretched their legs. An elderly dwarven barman came out of the doors and nervously took their order. He reappeared a few minutes later with empty, battered pewter tankards. With him was another younger dwarf with pitchers of ale and wine. Jasper ascertained from the barmen that there was little accommodation to be had in any of the taverns but they would be welcome to find bed-space in amongst the stalls in the stables at no cost provided they paid for the care of their mounts and pack-pony and took a meal in the tavern. This they all readily agreed to.

Nevertheless, one pair of eyes watched them carefully through a grimy window of the tavern. After a few minutes, he replaced the dagger he had been using to scrape his fingernails back into its belt-sheath and ambled out through a side-door of the tavern.

ᔆ ᕒ

They tucked in hungrily to their thick soup and crusty bread. They had travelled long and hard and they were irritable, tired, stiff and saddle-sore. The prospect of sleeping on beds of hay and straw was too good to miss.

More pitchers of ale and wine arrived unexpectedly. Standing beside the barman was a greying human of middle years. He was tall, bearded, and was dressed in quite opulent finery. He wore a black silk shirt tucked into loose-fitting black leather hose. His knee-length boots were well-polished and their buckles on the insteps were of gleaming silver. He carried an ornate but fully-functional rapier sheathed on his left hip. It was not his garb or his weapons that caught an onlooker's gaze, however. His ruggedly handsome face showed the disfigurements of battle, as did his left hand which was missing its two smaller fingers. Despite walking with a slight limp, favouring his left leg, he had a commanding air about him. His frame showed signs of considerable physical strength.

"Lady; gentlemen," he began. His baritone voice had a commanding confidence with a slight accent. "Allow me to introduce myself," he began. "I am Borgan Drogarn, the baron-lord of this town."

The group shuffled from their seats to their feet and Silmar bowed slightly. "Silmar Galadhal, Prince of Refuge in the North, above the Home Territories."

"A prince? Well, this is indeed an honour. Elven nobility in my humble town."

"I never stand on ceremony, Lord. My father is no king but his line goes back to the days of the Realm of Faerhome beyond the Dragon's Back peaks."

"Is that so? Faerhome is now a place of sheer evil which, fortunately, the Dragon's Back and the Dragon's Tail mountains contain to a certain extent. But enough, this you know already. Where do you all sleep this night? This tavern? The stables? But I cannot allow it!"

The travellers looked at each other in a confused bewilderment but Drogarn continued. "I apologise, I did not say that well. I mean, you shall spend the night in my humble dwelling. You are a travelling adventuring band, which is plain to see. It is also plain to see that your weapons have seen action. The cuts and slashes to your clothing are testimony to that. There has been some rumour of a large band such as yours riding south and east towards us. Little is secret here. We place watches and listen to the tales of other travellers.. We must know when to protect ourselves. These are dangerous times, Prince Silmar. The Hoshites spy on us and we spy on them. It is the expected way. There are recent rumours also of Darkling. We would hope that they confine themselves to the dark forests and deep tunnels to the north but nay, it appears they are now probing abroad. I shall, of course be asking questions of you, because one does not get something for nothing in the lands of Baylea. And I do, of course, offer you my hospitality."

The lord's eyes studied each of them as he spoke and, although Taura used some of her God-given powers to detect anything amiss, she could sense no malice or evil in this man. That did not, of course, guarantee their safety from him; a person competent in arcane or divine arts could probably hide any evil or malicious intent. Furthermore, Drogarn gave no sign that he had felt the priestess's mind probing.

As darkness fell, the party were shown to a large chamber in which a dozen beds were arrayed. There were tables at one end with a row of bowl and water pitchers and there were hooks on the walls for hanging their packs and clothing. They lit the oil lamps which hung around the walls of the chamber and most of them immediately laid down on the beds.

Meanwhile, at a request from Drogarn, Silmar and Jasper were invited to join him in the dining chamber. He called a manservant who brought in a pitcher of ale and a small silver jug. The jug he passed direct to Jasper who, on examination of its contents, exclaimed "*Bloodwine*, by Trangath's silver skirts!"

For the next hour or so, Drogarn spoke in conversation with the two adventurers. "I am somewhat surprised to see the two of you travelling together," he began. "Rare, not unknown but unusual, nonetheless."

Silmar leaned back in his chair, unsure of what to say.

Jasper, however, leaned forward. With a fleeting glance towards the elf, he sighed. "We 'as a sorta understandin'," he growled. "Aye, you could say we 'ave a toleration of each other."

Silmar gave a chuckle. "As dwarves go, he's not too unpleasant; he could benefit from being dragged through a river to relieve us from his terrible smell and from sleeping more quietly."

Jasper dragged his fingers through his thick beard. "An' what 'bout you, the 'igh an' mighty prince? Bah!"

Drogarn clapped his hands together and laughed briefly. "I do not believe either of you harbour such a seriously deep distaste otherwise your travels would not have endured." He spoke of the lands thereabouts and of the ever increasing presence of Hoshites; their presence having been at the request of the many Polduman barons that were so disparate, they had been unable to agree on the provision of an established system of internal defence and rule of law. "The Hoshite centre of administration, and its southernmost stronghold is the Landhold fortress, is less than a tenday week's hard-ride north-eastwards.

"We have little here in my town that is of interest to them. But I know they covet it, regardless. We do little to antagonise them but I know that one day they will come to my gates and demand entry to take Hill's Edge over. It is just a matter of time. Now, tell me of the purpose of your travels through this land."

This question was not unexpected and the pair had answers prepared for anyone who asked them of it.

"We travel to Marsaise, the capital city o' Cascant," began Jasper. "We've journeyed fer many, many tendays, developed our skills, found friends an' bought better and better weapons an' 'orses. We lost a good man in a fight with Worg-wolves not a tenday back."

Silmar continued with the tale. "We intend to take part in the annual warrior's tournaments. It is the best opportunity to make our fortunes in the arena. These are rarely fights to the death and, for some of us, it is the dream of a lifetime."

Drogarn sighed. "Ah, long ago now are the days in which I myself took part in those very same tournaments. There was not quite the gallantry in those days. There were, more often, fights to the death and we were warned of the risks of fighting against warriors who cared little for the fate of others. These days though, thanks to the late King Barsani Dar-Cascan VII and his war wizard, Lord Korderndahuhl, not to mention the elite royal bodyguard, the Corps of Foresters, if someone takes the life of another, he could find himself paying a small fortune in *blood money* to the family of the unfortunate. As you no doubt perceive, I bear some scars from those old days."

"The King is dead?" gasped Silmar. "The rumours are true then. It was known that the northern parts of the realm of Cascant was in dire peril but it has been assumed by most in the west that the peril was fought off and the monarchy was strong. This is sad news indeed."

Drogarn nodded. "Obviously then, you know of the darkness that fell across that land not three years ago. Goblins and orcs invaded in great numbers, having been driven to it by an evil winged, magic-draining creature called a hargh-demon. It seemed that Cascant was doomed. A large contingent of the army fought the goblins but defeat came to them. The city of Triosande fell and many of Cascant's nobles treacherously fled the battlefields. Finally, the hargh-demon and king slew each other on the field of battle but by then a great number of the realm's soldiers, warriors, wizards, nobles and officials were lost. The king's daughter, the beautiful but fearsome warrior Crown Princess Laurellien, and her Corps of Foresters, defeated the goblins and reclaimed Triosande but it was only temporary. What became of Kordern-dahuhl at that time remains a mystery. It is spoken that he disappeared along with the boy-king, Barsani Dar-Cascan VIII, his family, nobles and senior retainers, into exile when his country's need was great.

"Since the king's death Laurellien now rules the kingdom and is affectionately known as the *Shield Regent*. She is ably assisted in the matters of diplomacy, by her own battle-mage, the Earl Rameus-dahuhl. Once her young brother, whom she adores it is said, comes of age, he will presumably take over as ruler. She earned the hearts and respect of her peoples for her bravery and strategy in the earlier battles against the orc hordes. Those wars, my friends, are where I received these scars." He indicated the vicious wound-scars across his arms and slapped at his left leg.

"Do dangers still threaten the Realm of Cascant?" asked Silmar.

"Aye, just as much as they always have. Many of the realm's nobles are trying to ingratiate their way back from the exile they made for themselves after the fall of Triosande. The neighbouring land of Kamambia looks at Cascant with avariced eyes and waits to see how the game plays out. They strengthen their armies on their borders in case the orcs and goblins turn their eyes towards them."

"'Ow safe is it to travel through Cascant?" Jasper asked.

"It is safe enough; traders and merchant caravans still cross the south of the country. The threats are far to the north of the realm. Princess Laurellien has her hands full with the deceit and intrigue that goes on around her, does that feisty, lovely young lady. But she has the skills and loyalty of her peoples to defend her lands against any dangers that may occur. The defences of Cascant are being rebuilt by her. The Foresters are regrouping and have the best weapons, armour, training, discipline and love for their *Shield Regent* that there could ever be. I was once in those ranks. Now though – hah! Age and battle have sapped me of the strength that I once had. But the memories will stay with me until death takes me."

The Lord Drogarn conversed with Silmar and Jasper late into the night, asking questions of them and of the lands they had recently travelled through. Silmar said nothing of the burden he carried. He had noted that there had been no disturbing influence from it at the meeting with this lord and that gave him confidence that they were all safe in his dwelling, which was far from being humble as Drogarn had earlier claimed. They answered his questions with caution, nonetheless, giving away as little about themselves as possible and answering fully only when it seemed prudent to do so. They eventually returned to the sleeping chamber and collapsed onto their beds.

ം ഛ

As they left town the next morning, Drogarn watched them as they took the road south. He turned slightly to speak with a figure standing in the shadows behind him.

"They carry something of great magical or god-given power. I felt it, but I don't recognise that feeling. Despite my questioning, they gave little away about themselves but it was what they didn't say that seemed to convey much. I know the priestess has used her powers to detect my intent. She will have sensed nothing from it. I shall send a message to the *Great One*. They go to the city of Marsaise in Cascant. Wait and watch for them there. Warn our allies on this road as you travel."

He said a few more cryptic words to the man, a tall, lean and battle-scarred, seasoned warrior who then left the town, content that his mission was clear.

❧ ❧

CHAPTER 34

FROM A WINDOW near the top of a tower in the fortified Temple dedicated to the God Tarne, in the little trading and market town of Dillan's Farm, a pair of eyes watched the steady flow of traders and travellers entering and leaving through the North Gate. People arriving through that gate had invariably come through the little town of Hill's Edge, a tenday week's easy ride from the west.

The temple, a large and well-defended fortified centre of prayer, refuge and learning, dominated the town. The town itself was given protection under the eyes of the God Tarne, sometimes known as the *Vigilant Protector*. Sanctuary and protection were offered to any folk, regardless of species or intent, who was unable to protect themselves.

The sun was low in the western sky and shadows were lengthening. One unusually large group of well-armed adventurers riding through the gates caught the observer's eye straight away. He had been chewing on a strip of dried mutton that he had occasionally dipped into a cup of honey. He had been losing the battle against the flies that also had a liking for the honey, causing him to discard the cup to the other end of the window sill; if nothing else, it would now distract the wasps that also plagued him this day. The owner of those eyes watched every move of the band of travellers, taking in their number, race and weaponry. The watcher moved from one window to another to note every move of the riders.

He turned to another saying "It is them; word must be passed at once to the *Great One* at once."

"I daresay he already knows but it will be as well to inform him of their progress. Then can he decide his move. The view to the Hoshite fortress of Landhold is clear today. They did well to pass it without interference. I shall despatch a man to watch them."

The observer nodded slowly. "Perhaps the Hoshites have no interest in this group but if Lord Borgan Drogarn *does* have an interest then it will be for a very good reason. These riders would not have passed by *him* unnoticed."

"The Landhold received visitors today, I am told."

His eyebrows shot up in surprise. "Really? Who was that?"

"A group of twenty riders, with arms and armour and a mage! Is it coincidence that they should call in just as this band of adventurers should be travelling in these lands?"

The observer frowned and pressed a fist onto the window ledge. "We can't risk interference from Landhold. I think a welcome should be arranged should they ride this road."

The observer's companion, a burly man with an unkempt appearance scratched his long dark hair. "I must ride on in the morning. Regardless, I shall need to be on the road before this group leaves."

"There is no need, I understand they are staying for the full day tomorrow and leaving on the morning of the following day."

"You know this so soon?"

"Careful and thorough observation, my friend. Also, word from Hill's Edge informed me of this likelihood before even your arrival. Tell me about them. What do you know of them?"

"Little is known but they are a mixed bunch. Leadership seems shared between an elf and a dwarf."

The watcher frowned in puzzlement. "Unusual that one would tolerate the other…"

"Nevertheless, they do. A gnome mage and a woman priestess of a god; Neilea, I believe. A strangely-garbed man with a matched set of blades and a cleret-wing dragon as a pet is a perplexity. A group of fighters, one of whom is a huge barbarian, are well armed as you can see. As a campaigning party, they look capable of defending themselves. But what their true intentions are have yet to be defined."

"We shall set watch on them; meanwhile you take some rest and be on the road in the morning. Take a force of my men to ensure the road is clear and safe."

∾ ∾

The whole group of adventurers had managed to get two large sleeping-chambers at the back of a run-down tavern, the Boars Head. Locally known as the *Whore's Bed*, the latter summed up the real character of the place. The tavern's owner, Peppi-Beppo, was very chatty and a very pleasant character.

"The temple here looks after us good and proper. Garadog, the high priest who, it is said, fights with a magical singing sword, along with his many followers, protects the town. We're not sure about the sword but it's a very popular story." He went on to describe how the followers of Tarne had strengthened the townspeople's resolve to strongly resist interference by the Hoshites.

The group spent the whole of the next day resting, drinking, gambling and talking. Jasper reminded them that it had been many a tenday week since they had swapped jokes and stories. It had been a long time since they had felt like doing so.

"Hey, I got a story," cried Vallio. "It goes like this."

The others quietened down and craned their necks.

"There was this group of four retired city watchmen and they decide to go up to a retreat in the mountains for some well-deserved retirement relaxation. Well, these places cost a lot of money, 'cos it costs so much to get the food and ale up there, see? What with the wagons and all."

"Oh, gods, get on with it," chucked Taura.

"Aye, anyway. So to save money they decided to sleep two to a bedchamber. But no one wanted to share with Big Doob because he snored so badly. They decided it wasn't fair to make one of them stay with him the whole time, so they voted to take turns. The first man slept in Big Doob's room and comes to dawn-meal the next morning with his hair a mess and his eyes all bloodshot. They said 'Hey, what happened to you?' He said 'Big Doob snored so loud, I just sat up and watched him all night." Vallio started giggling at his own story.

"What's 'e laughin' at?" wheezed Jasper through his pipe-smoke. "'E ain't finished yet!"

"I'm laughing 'cos I know what happens next, you, er, chod!"

The dwarf's face clouded over for an instant but lifted as the jape sunk in. He burst into laughter.

"Anyway, the next night it was a different man's turn. In the morning, same thing: hair all standing up, eyes all bloodshot. They said 'Hey, bad night? You look awful.' He said, 'By the gods, that Big Doob shakes the roof almost right off. I sat up and watched him all night. The next night it's the third man's turn. He was a big, burly ex-wrestler; a real man's man. The next morning he comes down to dawn-feast all bright-eyed and bushy-tailed. 'Good morning!' he says, all cheerful. Well, they couldn't believe it. They said, "Hey, what happened?' and he said 'Well, we got ready for bed. I went and tucked Big Doob into bed and kissed him good night. He sat up and watched me all night! Haha! Hahaha!"

The group dissolved into laughter, particularly when Taura spluttered a mouthful of ale over the table.

Their discussion with Peppi-Beppo continued well into the night and was very informative. Their intention, as described by Varengo, was to take the East Way to cross the Bone Hills and on the first night to make camp in a valley in the tall hills. But the tavern-keeper warned them that the dangers of these lofty hills were not merely from beasts and monsters or from brigands and cutthroats. It was from the occupiers of the Darkhold Fortress. The bleak and forbidding spires and turrets of Hosh's western outpost had, until quite recently, been occupied by one Goran Harmass, a ruthless warlord of the foulest of reputations. His fearsome character had not been enough to save him from a well-deserved execution. It was spoken that his skeletal remains still hung in a rusting iron cage alongside the main gate of the fortress.

Taura gave an exaggerated *humph*. "Barbaric!" she exclaimed. "I have no doubt he deserved to be hung but not for feeding crows."

"Aye, but it is probably done to deter others," said Peppi-Beppo, "or as an example of what people can expect if they lead a life like Harmass."

"Not much of a deterrent if the only ones to see it are the present occupiers of the Darkhold Fortress," mumbled Falcon.

One solitary drinker, an ageing, stocky warrior, had been listening closely to the conversation and, despite their low voices, spoke quietly to them.

"It don't do to discuss those bastards, boys." The drinker had murmured through his thick, curling pipe-weed smoke. "Yez never know who's listening. Take some advice from me though if yez have a care to." He coughed a couple of times on the acrid smoke from his pipe.

"We're listenin', friend," Jasper replied, rising to his feet but then sitting back down. "What news do yer 'ave fer us?"

"Fetch me a quart of ale then. Listen close, friends." He leaned forward, casting his eyes about as if in the midst of a conspiracy. "It is spoken that the manner of Harmass's recent departure has been the cause of some conflict and desertion within the 'Shite forces within the fortress and it's rumoured that the defence has become lax, to say the least. They might have removed the head from this snake but the body is still causing much distress."

"You mean that the warlord's gang is still ravaging these parts?" Falcon asked.

"Nay, not this far south, as far as I know. Now, if you's travelling along the East Way, then the 'Shites will prob'ly just rob yez and, if yez puts up a fight, they'll cut and run or, if there's enough of 'em then they'll leave yer carcasses out to dry in the sun. They're no better than brigands and highway robbers now. That's the word. Yer look tough enough to fight off the buggers but yez wouldn't get me riding that way. Traders 'n' merch'nts travel in very large and well-defended groups now. There is another way east, a game trail used mostly by hunters and those who don't want to attract attention."

"Where is trail?" Jiutarô asked. "How we finding?"

The ageing warrior looked suspiciously at the inscrutable fighter with the little dragon on his shoulders and the unusual clothing.

"Is that beast safe?" the man asked.

"If you mean it do no harm," the Samurai replied.

"Wasn't talking to you; I was asking the dragon!"

Jiutarô scowled. "She tell the same about me but she tell untruth – I am *not* safe."

"I do not doubt it, friend. The trail is easy to find if you know where to look. Two days ride on the East Way and you get to an old ruined farm hut set back a short way from the road on the right side. You'll need to lead your horses round the ruin because it's very overgrown. There's a grove of trees behind it. Take yourselves through it and the trail will be easy found. It is a long road, very long; probably a full hundred leagues. What's that, about two tenday-weeks?"

"Gods!" exclaimed Billit, for once listening in to a conversation instead of sitting aside with his nose buried in his leather-bound tome.

"Aye, friends," the ageing fighter continued. "It'll take that long to ride, that is if you don't meet something 'orrible on the way."

The companions looked at each other and allowed the man's information to sink in a little before Silmar responded. "Appreciated, friend. We shall heed your advice and may well act accordingly." He called to Peppi-Beppo for ales. The solitary drinker spoke no more to them but returned to his pipe, his full ale pot and to his own thoughts.

Varengo leaned across to the tavern owner. "Is this old 'un trustworthy? We don't want to be walking into a trap."

The taverner nodded, saying "Hey, he;s a good man. I've known him for some years. Jabb knows his stuff. You can trust his judgement."

ৡ ৶

It was not yet dawn but the group made ready to leave nonetheless. Silmar had roused them early. Last night, the elf had insisted that they maintain an all-night watch. He explained how, despite the security of being in a well-defended town and within a fairly secure tavern, he had slept poorly during the first night.

"Why is that?" asked a concerned Jasper. "It's very unlike you, elf. Never known anyone sleep so lightly though. Your pointy ears probably heard a cockroach farting during the night!"

Silmar raised his eyes upwards as the dwarf chortled while the others moved in closer.

"I have had a strong feeling of being watched," he said softly. "I had a tingle of warning from my burden a couple of times in the taproom. But it felt different to the usual, rather like a warning of sorts. I am wondering whether or not that helpful old fighter in the tavern was all he seems."

"Are ye sure it wasn't just a mouldy hambone?" asked Jasper. "Heh heh!"

"Peppi-Beppo says he's safe. Er, what burden?" asked Varengo. "What's going on?"

Silmar looked at his companions noting the subtle nod that Billit gave him. "We think you ought to know," he replied, "that we are carrying a religious artefact to Carrick Cliffs. It is totally evil but wasn't always so."

"So why did you not tell us about it earlier?" asked a frowning Yoriando. He stood facing Silmar with his arms crossed. "Did you not trust us enough?"

"Hey, steady on now, Yori," answered Jasper. "It's not like that. Look, lads. We was sent on this, sort of, mission and we was all sworn to secrecy. Ain't that right, Silmar?"

"Aye, that is so. But you have become trustworthy friends and we thought that it is time we owed you an explanation."

"Especially as one of you, Jassio, has already died fighting by our side," said Taura. "We can only apologise if you think we didn't trust you but, well, it is a bit difficult, you see."

"So do you want to tell us what it is or what you intend to do with it?" asked Varengo.

Silmar explained how he had come across the dying priest of Clamberhan in an alleyway in Westron Seaport, the encounter with the Darkling assassin, the meeting with Halorun Tann, the High Priest of Tarne the Just, and their journey on the trail of the Darkling.

"As you know," said the elf, "we caught up with the bastard at the Shade Gnomes' city and Jiutarô defeated him. We know there are more Darkling somewhere about but we must take this thing to Carrick Cliffs and give it to the High Priest of the Temple of Clamberhan, one Gallan Arran."

Morendo scratched at his bushy beard. "You may have a problem there," he said. "The town ain't what it was. It's been taken over by a large group of renegade militiamen, deserters probably, from various realms, and they use it as a base for whatever it is they do. I don't know much more than that except that the townsfolk are under some sort of tight control and don't talk to outsiders. That's it really, all I know."

"I think we are still a few tenday weeks away from the town," said Taura, "so we have a chance to look into it and see what is going on. Then we can decide on a plan to get that artefact delivered."

They looked at each other, silently nodding in agreement.

"Well, we appreciate you telling us," replied Varengo. "I think I speak for me and the lads when I say that you can rely on us to do our part and continue to fight together. Our paths run together all the way to Carrick Cliffs so we shall all make sure that your artefact gets there."

"We 'ad no doubt about that at all," replied Jasper.

"What is this thing, anyway?" asked Vallio.

"It's a dagger," replied Silmar. "It's very ornate with a curved blade and a few precious stones inlaid on the hilt, cross-guard and scabbard. But it has a terrible evil influence which makes one feel a very severe sickness just to put a hand near to it, let alone touch it. It was a holy artefact of the Temple of Clamberhan but it was taken away and had been corrupted by evil. We carry it back to where it should be and hope there is someone who can destroy that evil."

"Where is it?" asked Yoriando.

"Buried in my pack," answered the elf. "It's in a box and covered in lead. It seems to do the trick but sometimes I can feel its foul influence." He shuddered involuntarily. "Especially if we are in the presence of an evil being. It's damnably heavy but I have to admit it has actually been quite fortuitous at times because it has warned me of something nasty that we have gotten close to, or has gotten close to us!"

"By the gods!" exclaimed Varengo. "Well, tell us how we can help and we will! Won't we lads?" Vallio, Yoriando and Morengo nodded enthusiastically.

"You're helping us just by being with us," replied Taura. "And we're glad you are. So then, where do we go from here?"

Now, neither of their options were particularly attractive.

Varengo outlined these to them as they prepared their horses and pack-ponies. "On the one hand, the East Way would provide us with places of rest, water and provisions whereas on the other we will have to live off the land for a long period of time. I have no doubt at all as to our ability to scavenge what we need from the land. We have done it before. Peppi-Beppo has given us sacks of food and we have as many waterskins as we can carry. The only risk we have is putting our trust in the stranger in the tavern."

"Yer right," said Billit. "That man was somewhat free with his assistance, don't you think?"

"True enough," added Varengo. "But he was quite drunk and by the time we went to our chambers, he was sleeping on the floor under the table!"

"Peppi-Beppo swore to me that the man was trustworthy," Varengo assured them.

ço ʻeↄ

The early-morning sun was rising over the low eastern peaks as the party wound their way high up on the narrow, winding track. Far below and a little to the west, the village of Thlottle was clearly visible with its quarry workings a mile or so to the north. A few wagons and travellers were evident entering and leaving the town. Figures, tiny from this distance, could just be seen walking on the street of the town.

Jasper was sulking.

"Dwarvish community," he grunted. "That means a decent tavern, with decent ale, decent bread and choddin' decent company!" His voice grew in intensity as he spoke.

By noon, the heat was almost unbearable. The bright sun in a clear sky beat down upon them with an unchecked ferocity.

"Wait! Get down!" The elf spoke with an urgency that caused the others to pull up short.

While Taura held the reins of his horse, Silmar had been scouting the track a hundred or so paces ahead of them. As they approached the upper slopes of the peaks, the horses had begun to shy at first and then became skittish. Silmar had darted ahead a little way but quickly sprinted back to the group.

"I smell blood, death - a battle has been fought near here. The stink of it is strong in my nostrils. Can you not smell it?"

Both Jasper and Billit sniffed the air. The gnome nodded but the dwarf merely shrugged his shoulders.

"Wait, I ask Sushi look ahead," said Jiutarô. He whispered to the little cleret-wing dragon and she reared into the sky. She has only been gone a few minutes when Jiutarô raised his face to the sky and closed his eyes.

"I see Sushi's eyes," the Samurai murmured. "It in my head I see. Aii - two group dead cover road. See no living people waiting." Whispering, he concluded "Return, little one. You see enough."

Within a few moments Sushi swooped down and lightly landed on the ground in front of the Samurai but then with a beat of her wings she soon found her way back up onto his shoulders.

Carefully and on foot, the party led their horses over the summit of the pass. The sight before them was gruesome.

A number of dead bodies – all Hoshites – lay strewn about the road. A few more bodies lay further along the track, all signs showing that they had all been struck down as they ran. Clouds of flies rose as the members of the group walked their horses through the bodies. Varengo and his three men were lucky enough to find weapons lying among the bodies. Many of these were more suitable for them than those they currently carried. Vallio swapped a pair of blood-spattered boots and Yoriando a back-pack.

Further ahead were more bodies – mainly Hoshites but a couple of what appeared to be brigands, including a half-orc. Two charred bodies lay grotesquely bent and twisted, their blackened faces stretched to show their teeth in a bizarre death grin. The stench of scorched flesh and of the blood-caked wounds on the dead was overpowering.

"The attackers 'ad a mage!" exclaimed Billit. "Look, these 'ave been hit by a magical fireblast. The ground itself 'as been scorched an' the stones hereabouts are still hot."

A few dead horses, Hoshite mounts judging to the livery, lay about the road too. Varengo's men searched each of the bodies – valuables had already been taken, as had many of the weapons. The majority of the deaths were from arrows and every Hosh body had a arrows protruding from them. But many more lay scattered on the ground and those were collected by Vallio. There were no live horses and the dead carcasses did not number the same as the dead men. It was clear that the surviving mounts had been taken by the attackers.

"Lucky we didn't run into this 'ere 'Shite patrol," said Jasper. "Would 'ave been too many fer us. There must've been forty of 'em. Must've been a huge group of brigands, if that was what they was!"

"What do you mean?" asked Taura.

"Well, look at it all. This was a well-planned ambush an' battle, very few attackers killed by the look of it, but, it seems all 'Shites died, includin' them two burned mages, look! See their charred cloaks? I can't see no tracks of 'orses continuin' up the track so I guess they went 'cross the 'ills. Not bad fer brigands, I gotta say."

"May've been army deserters," said Billit.

"Oh c'mon short-ass! Use yer noggin! With an 'alf-orc? Aye, possible I s'pose but unlikely. Oh well, a good Hosh's a dead 'un, whoever done it!"

"Doesn't mean it's safe for us though!" said the elf sombrely.

"Aye, I know that – I ain't got shit fer brains, you know! Hey Varengo! 'Ave the bodies got anythin' useful that was left behind?"

"Loads of arrows, most of them sticking in them, hah! A few coins, mostly silver and copper. Two very nice swords and a few daggers. We're sorting through the boots 'cos ours are near useless! Won't be long, nearly done here."

Following the road, the group crossed over the highest point of the pass fully expecting a long descent down the other side. Only, there was more ascending to come. The hills stretched far ahead of them, rising and falling far into the distance. They could even see the faint narrow line of their track winding through distant hills. Nevertheless, the view before them was breathtaking and dramatic.

After many days, nonetheless, the novelty of this landscape had worn off. Fresh water was scarce and wildlife similarly rare. They were constantly looking out for other riders that might give them news of the road ahead or even cause them a threat.

Silmar rarely showed discontent when travelling but concern was beginning to show on his face. For the last two days Vallio had struck out before dawn in an attempt to find water and game. The first day he had returned with an antelope and the second he had brought back some water that had been too brackish for them to drink although their horses seemed to benefit from it.

"We need a source of fresh water with some urgency," Silmar said to Varengo one morning.

"Hmmph!" retorted Jasper. "We're always lookin' fer choddin' water!"

"I guess we should've asked that old fighter in the tavern," replied Varengo. "Vallio and Morendo have both gone out searching. There is little more we can do for now."

By noon the next day they were all on foot leading their flagging mounts when they saw in the distance, on a rise, two riders gesticulating wildly.

"Ho there! Look ahead!" cried Yoriando. "'Tis Morendo and Vallio, surely."

"It looks encouraging," said Taura. She walked side-by-side with Falcon, as always. "Perhaps they have found water."

"Perhaps they find tavern," drawled Jiutarô, with a faint smile.

The companions led their horses towards their two friends, conscious that their mounts were all but incapable of bearing them.

They did not stop however, as they reached the two beaming horsemen. In the near distance the track sloped down into a narrow verdant valley with an abundance of green grass and small groves of woodland as opposed to the baking-hot, brown, sun-scorched grasslands and scrub of the countryside they were just leaving behind them. In the mid-afternoon, because of the altitude and shade from the peaks, the air was cooler. Some of the taller peaks were capped in a dusting of snow. But in the distance, far to the south and west, were the massive peaks of the Dragon's back mountains. The dark grey snow-topped peaks dwarfed the nearer peaks.

It took them a couple of hours to walk down into the lush grasslands below. By then the sun was sinking beyond the summit they had just crossed and the light would soon fade. The group made camp in a clearing in a small wood and quite close to a stream. The flowing water was clear and refreshingly ice cold. Silmar and Jiutarô quietly searched the wood to the east of their camp while Jasper and Vallio explored the western fringes. Meanwhile Varengo and the others prepared the camp. They had seen no sign of the Darkling for many days but did not relax their vigilance. It was agreed that an overnight watch would be kept with two awake at all times.

ॐ ॐ

Four days later the group began a long descent from the hills into a vast, flat plain. As far as the eye could see there were swamps and marshes, some wreathed in mist but others with the sun reflecting off wide pools of water. In particular, a single vast marsh, a green mass of swamps, fens and dark green vegetation lay to the east. From the lower slopes of the hills, patches of slowly-swirling grey mist covered the marsh.

"Ah, the lovely smell an' the dampness, an' the mists," mused Billit. "Aye, it don't look too misty there right now but I bet it does sometimes, y'know, early in the mornings."

"That's the Marsh of Tash," said Morendo. "Up north is another swamp, the Pallae Marsh. Legend has it that thousands of years ago, a wicked old woman stirred up trouble between two cities that were at the centre of these two lands. They threw loads of magic at each other, destroyed the cities and devastated the lands. Each king had blamed the other, you see, not knowing that this witch had started it all. No idea why she did. Anyway, what we now have is two great big swamps with a narrow strip between them."

"Any beasties?" asked Billit.

"Well, aye, er, probably because it's a swamp. I'd be surprised if there wasn't any. But the biggest thing is the diseases and the very large mosquitoes that spread them. But they stay within the area of the swamp, I think. Hope so, anyway. Provided we keep to the road north we should be quite safe. These Tash Marshes are a refuge for raiders who take on the caravans heading west from Cascant. That's why these caravans are now well-guarded. Trouble is the ranks of raiders are growing to take them on. As we're quite a large group, we should be safe."

"Oh, choddin' lovely," muttered Jasper. He carried a sullen expression at the best of times but now it was deeper than usual as he checked the edge of his war-axe.

"Oh, by the gods!" called Silmar. "Guess what I have just found!" He had been scouting the road ahead of the, as usual. "Horseshoes with a notch at the front edge."

"I think I can guess," replied Taura. "It's them, isn't it? The Darkling! Are you sure about the horseshoes?"

"Yes, there is no doubt. The notch, look. They have turned off to the south towards the mountains. About two or three days ago, I think, but not much more than that. But why? It is strange that we have not noticed the tracks until now. There has been nowhere for them to take shelter during the daylight hours. Do we follow them? Are they taunting us or tempting us to follow them? It's obvious what they are after."

"How many of 'em?" Vallio asked as he scanned the hillsides and peaks to the south.

"It's difficult to say but I reckon about six or eight. The ground is too hard to make them out clearly."

With his knowledge of the terrain hereabouts, Morendo offered an idea. "Look, they have about a two-day head start on us, perhaps more. I can't see 'em riding through the marshes 'cos they won't want to be seen and there's few places for 'em to hide. So they will want to ride round it to the south over the foothills of the mountains. That means, if we're lucky we'll come through the marshes ahead of 'em. They really are going a very long way round."

"We'll take your word for that," replied Silmar. "It's probably not likely that they will lay any kind of ambush for us. What is the road like through the marshes?"

"Er, not very good, it;s…" Morendo hesitated as if unsure of what to say.

"It's what? You don't like it, do you?"

"Nay, I do not. It will mean following this road east, today and tomorrow. Then before daybreak on the next day we move fast, cutting between the two marshes for most of the day. We'll have to cross the river and keep going a while 'til we reach the hills. And we'll need to do all that in a day. We do not want to get caught between the marshes when darkness comes. The biggest, baddest, nastiest beasties probably come out then and they will be hungry."

"And we'll be safer in the hills?" asked Billit.

"Aye, very much so," offered Yoriando. "We'll just need to travel south for a few days and we'll pick up the East Way once again. But this time we'll want to cross it and pick up the Silk Road eastwards."

"And what's the advantage o' goin' that way?" asked Jasper.

"We'll save about two days and should get to the Silk Road just before the Darkling do. Oh, there's a trading post there where we can maybe get some rest and some ales. If they're planning on preparing an ambush for us, they'll wait a couple of days for us to appear but we'll already be a day or so in front of 'em. Good eh?"

They agreed unanimously to follow Varengo's advice.

Turning north-east they took to the road for the rest of the day and all the next. Only once did they encounter others on that road. A train of more than a dozen wagons, with many armed outriders, passed them heading west. Silmar and Jasper spoke for some time to the wagon-master. There was no news of any dangers on the road towards the Stormhorns and Silmar had warned the man of the site of the battle high in the Far Hills many days ahead.

∽ ∾

They all peered towards the east, their eyes squinting in the bright sunlight despite the dark gauze that covered their heads deep inside their hoods.

"They will not follow," said the figure in their own harsh language. "We should continue. There is only one road they will travel by."

"This bright sun burns my skin and blinds my eyes," spoke another. "Even the moon causes me discomfort." His voice was thin and complaining.

"It's not only you that feels this discomfort but the rest of us bear it. But it is always you that whines and complains. A friendly warning, boy – I can put you out of your discomfort! Tempt me not! *My* solution to your discomfort will be PERMANENT!"

The whiner dropped his head. "I apologise, exalted one, I shall bear the pain with fortitude," he replied but his facial expression towards his leader's back contradicted this.

"Keep your eyes wide open and your mouth tightly shut, Ti'thimmon. We shall move on, continuing during darkness as before. We shall ride parallel to the great road for a few nights, cross the border and shelter in the forest that lies just within."

The seven Darkling riders had crossed the little mountain river that flowed northeast-wards into the marshes of Tash and Pallae. Alligators had been basking in the humid heat on the river's banks but had not caused them any threat. An hour later the Darkling climbed further into the foothills and found a hollow suitable to spend the rest of the day to rest, eat and sleep. Once skirting the marshes, they faced a ten-day ride eastwards whereupon they would follow the East Way and cross over the pass leading them into Cascant. Once there, they would have to take utmost care – if word spread that Darkling were travelling that kingdom, they would be hunted.

∽ ∾

CHAPTER 35

THE RIDERS SAT astride their mounts and were arrayed in line abreast. Their gazes were firmly set across the couple of miles of open ground that lay ahead between themselves and the two marshes but they could see little, despite the full moon. Dawn was still some time off and it was still very dark. To the north was the Pallae Marsh and to the south lay the Marsh of Tash. None spoke. Their jaws were tightly closed with apprehension of their forthcoming journey. There was little to be said that had not already been voiced and argued about the previous night.

The mounts clearly sensed the apprehension of their riders, probably the tightness of the grip of the legs in the stirrups and the tension of the grips on the bridles. Perhaps they also sensed the ride ahead of them. They snorted and stamped and a couple of them were difficult to handle. The pack-pony was probably the most difficult to control that morning. It constantly reared and pulled against its lead rope that had been tied to Morendo's saddle.

Once, it had bucked so severely that it had upset its load and the contents had spilt across the ground.

Varengo was furious. "Who tied that godsdamned pack?" he roared. "Get it reloaded damned quickly!" This was out of character for him, evidence of his nervousness.

None had slept well the previous night, except perhaps for Silmar who had managed a couple of hours during the early hours of the night. Typically, for an elf, he showed little sign of sleeping poorly. He could manage adequately on just a few hours each day. The others, though, were bleary-eyed, fatigued and irritable.

Jasper was the only rider to exhibit signs of dread. His grubby knuckles gripped the reins of his pony and his expression was grim. It was not a fear of the unknown in the desolation between the two marshes that gave him so much concern. Like all dwarves, he was not a natural horseman although many years as an adventurer had given him a small degree of proficiency in the saddle. He knew that on a nervous horse, in boggy ground, he would need to use every last ounce of his skills and energy just to stay astride. He did not relish the thought at all.

"I fear this day," murmured Billit to nobody in particular. "What if my 'horse gets frightened? What if I fall off?"

Jiutarô brought his stallion alongside him. "Ride by side of me," he said with a rare smile.

Billit closed his eyes, took a deep breath and nodded.

Dawn showed as a faint hazy glow above the mist that shrouded the marshes. It had been agreed that Morendo would lead the party. His familiarity with the road they were to take, although scant, was better than any other's. Varengo would ride alongside him and the others would follow. Morendo gave his final words of advice followed by the order to advance.

"Keep close up; no stragglers," he began. "Anyone stops, we all stop. No faster than the canter unless the need is great.

Remember, our best defence against any kind of attack by weather, man or monster is to stay together. On no account can we split the party. Watch in front and watch for those behind. Forward! Steady now, at the trot."

Strained, fearful glances were exchanged between most of them as they all kicked their horses forward. No well-used path was there for them to follow in the gloom and although the ground was dry and firm, they expected it to turn boggy quite soon.

⤜ ⤛

From a vantage point quite high up in the hills and far away, a pair of eyes followed the group of riders as they rode into the strip of swampland between the two vast marshes. The owner of those eyes rubbed bristles on his chin and shook his head slowly.

Fools! What has possessed them to take that route? The elf scans the ground as if searching for sign of other travellers. Or perhaps he looks for sign of monsters. But few are those who would ride across that wilderness.

He had done so, a few times in fact, but with the experience and knowledge of the ways of the beasts that inhabited the foul, dangerous and unpredictable place. They had not even taken precautions against the plagues of insects, in particular the mosquitoes that swarmed in the swamps. There were plants, the leaves and roots of which would ward off the worst of the insect attacks when crushed and rubbed across the skin. He knew them. Dis they? He smiled coldly as he reflected that the acrid smells of these plants would probably even fend off a hydra.

Borgan Drogarn of Hill's Edge had tasked him to watch this group and that is just what he would do. It was an undertaking that he was most suited to.

But he had other concerns on his mind than just the threat of monsters and insects. There were other travellers in this dismal corner of Polduman, cloaked and hooded riders that he did not like the look of one bit.

❧ ❦

Morendo proved to be a very able leader on this part of their journey. He kept the horses at a steady trot for a while but then decided to take advantage of the firm ground and he increased the pace to a canter. This way, the riders and horses were able to maintain their energy while making good speed. From time to time, narrow streams or stagnant pools slowed their pace and they were forced to pick their route carefully. The cleret-wing dragon saved them much time by finding their path for them.

The sun slowly climbed above the distant hills but, although it was low in the sky directly in front of them, it did not blind them. The damp mist dimmed the ferocity of the light and calmed its heat. There was virtually no breeze and the mists hung over the marshes like blanket. They plainly heard sounds of movement in the mires to either side of them – the slithering of unknown beasts that caused fear and concern to be deeply etched on their faces as they constantly switched their gaze from one side to the other. The deep croaking of frogs was annoyingly relentless.

Occasionally, Silmar pointed out some faint hoof-prints although these faded as the ground started to become softer and muddier.

"Bah!" exclaimed Varengo. "They are the tracks of the bandits and thieves who roam these bogs and take shelter in the edges of the islands and pools. They count their stolen coins and watch their weapons and armour rust in the dampness. We are too many for them to assail us!"

"We can only hope so," sighed Silmar.

Jasper, who was still gripping is saddle and reins for dear life, flashed a look at Silmar that cast doubt on the opinion of Varengo.

As the sun continued to rise, so its heat became stronger and started to burn off the mists but not nearly enough to clear it away altogether. The limit of their vision was no more than thirty of forty feet at best. As the ground became more waterlogged the mist actually thickened until each of them could barely see the next rider ahead.

Morendo slowed the pace a little but did not stop. "Close in, my friends," he called.

"There's no air movement, and by the gods, what a stink!" exclaimed Taura. The smell of putrid vegetation and stagnant water was foul and Morendo told them to expect worse as they progressed deeper into the swamps.

"Smells like dragon shi-, er, very nasty to me!" gasped Billit. He had hastily changed his choice of words as Taura threw him a look of displeasure. Rarely did the priestess use a profanity unless the situation demanded a phrase for which a polite choice of words was not available in the Universal tongue. The gnome, however, had never been so fussy. "Sort of place yer might expect to see a soddin' great big hydra, if yer ask me."

"Our mounts are struggling," Varengo warned them. Indeed, they gasped and puffed in the fetid air.

"We can ease up when we have better visibility," Morendo replied. "it is not safe right now."

As the sun rose towards its zenith, it was visible through the dense mist and the riders were able to use it to maintain their direction. All of them had enough experience to be able to judge its movement across the sky and adjust their direction accordingly. They could still not see the hills towards which they rode.

With no warning, a massive eruption of water immediately to their left side caused panic amongst the horses and riders. A massive, writhing, snakelike form climbed higher and higher and loomed over the top of the group. Water sprayed over them all as the monstrosity swayed over them as if selecting its prey. A huge mouth opened into a gaping maw that was easily large enough to pluck a rider from the saddle. There was little sound except for thrashing of water. The horses and ponies reared and screamed in panic. The cleret-wing dragon leapt from Jiutarô's shoulder as he fought for control of his own mount.

Varengo roared at the top of his voice – "Ride! Ride on! Keep together!"

The riders, and indeed their mounts, needed little more encouragement. The group fled.

Except for Jasper.

❧ ☙

The group sped in the direction they had been travelling to put in as much distance between themselves and the dreadful monster, whatever it was, as they were able.

Falcon, the mighty barbarian, was the last in the chain of fleeing riders. That is, until a riderless pony slowly overtook him. The dwarf! The loose pony overtook the tail-enders as the barbarian roared at the top of his voice.

"Jasper is down! Wait! Wait!"

He reined in his horse and stopped, turning in his saddle. Taura, Vallio and Jiutarô also turned in their saddles and similarly brought their mounts to a halt. The rest of the group, presumably having been out of earshot, continued onwards, the riderless mount with them, galloping into the fog and out of the sight of the little band. The remaining four turned an, d, without waiting for mutual agreement, anxiously rode back in the direction in which they had come.

Following the course back was relatively easy. The mud and the waterlogged ground had been thoroughly churned by the speeding horses. When they reached the scene of the massive abomination's thrashing, neither it, nor their little comrade, were anywhere to be seen.

ॐ ॐ

Morendo and Varengo rode quickly side-by-side, leading the little group away from danger. Behind them, rode Yoriando then Silmar and Billit together. Silmar was concerned. He was sure he had heard a bellow from behind him but his own panicking horse had fought against him, resisting all his attempts to control it.

By the time the riders slowed down, only a few minutes later, they had probably covered two miles or more. They had managed to keep close together and had assumed the others were close behind. Now, as they stopped, with the horses' chests heaving, Morendo turned to speak.

"Is everyone safe?" he asked. His eyes scanned the little group and grew wide as he noticed that some were missing. "Where are the others?"

The riderless pony abruptly stopped among them. Immediately, concern registered on all their faces as they looked to see who was missing.

"Someone is down!" gasped the elf. "Only half of us are here! Damn!"

"Taura, Falcon, Jasper, Vallio and, er, Jiutarô!" whispered Yoriando. He took up the loose horse's reins. "This is Jasper's mount, is it not? Aye, of course it is."

"Just what we do not need!" growled Varengo. "The group is now split up. The foolish dwarf is now dismounted! We are all now vulnerable. What in the seven hells of shit do we do now?"

Silmar, with a face like thunder, dismounted, turned and stepped up to Varengo. "I may have little regard for dwarves from time to time, human, but speak not of our comrade in such a manner. He is courageous and stalwart and will leap into the fires of the Void to save any one of us, including you. Many times has he distinguished himself in battle and, may the gods allow, let us hope he continues to do so."

The warrior was about to stand up to the slightly shorter stature of the elf but then hung his head in humiliation. "Heed not my words, master elf," he said firmly. "I spoke out of turn in the midst of fear and concern that I have for the safety of those behind us. My words mean no ill will to the dwarf. Please, accept my apologies."

Silmar nodded and dismounted from his horse. The others also dismounted.

"We ain't goin' back for 'em, are we?" asked a doubtful Billit.

"We can't, not with this damned mist and the water covering our tracks," replied Yoriando. "We can't even guess on the direction to take and may get lost trying to find them."

The elf slowly rubbed his horse's nose. "The only choices we really have are to wait here for them in the hope that they will come this way, or close by, or to carry on to the river."

"Either way," suggested Varengo, "they may pass us by unnoticed by us or cross the river in a different place."

For the space of many heartbeats, the little group gazed sullenly at the sodden ground beneath their boots, each considering a logical solution to the problem. The only sound was the shifting of their horses, still unsettled by their recent scare, and the trickling of running water all about them. The mist seemed much thinner here and the warmth of the sun was finally penetrating the mists.

Unexpectedly, a flapping sound overhead caused the warriors to reach for their weapons and Billit to stand with his hands poised ready to spell-cast. Dragon-like wings swooped to block out the sun's light and Silmar breathed a sigh of relief.

"Sushi!" he exclaimed. "Where are they?"

The cleret-wing dragon bent his neck to point his head back in the direction from which the group had ridden.

"Behind us? Back there? Are they in danger?"

Sushi twittered and chirruped like a bird for a few seconds and then gave a loud hiss. Then, with a flapping of her large leathery wings, she launched herself back into the air. In seconds, she was gone.

"She seemed to be telling me something but I do not have the bond with her," said Silmar sadly. "I could not understand."

"So what now?" asked Varengo. "We must decide on what we are to do but we must all be in agreement with it."

Billit was the first to reply. "I say we go to the river. Find a suitable place and wait for as long as we dare and hope that they meet us or the little dragon can find us. Whatcha reckon?"

The group unanimously agreed that this was the best course to take. The elf looked towards the sun and suggested that they were still probably just after mid-day and there were still many miles to cover before they reached the river. Splashing sounds came from the swamp to their right.

"Gods! What was that?" Varengo gasped. "That settles it. We must go now as quietly as we can, and as quickly as we can, to make sure we reach the river by soon after the sun is at its highest. We don't know what we shall meet at its crossing and must make the best of the time that we have. Take Jasper's pony."

Having allowed their horses to drink from the shallow waters, and having taken the opportunity to take water from their skins, they wearily climbed up onto their horses. Morendo led once again and they continued towards the mid-morning sun.

❧ ❧

"This where we stop when horses afraid," whispered Jiutarô. He still had difficulty finding the right words at times but his grasp of the Universal tongue was improving day-by-day under Billit's tutelage. He and Vallio had dismounted and were looking at the ground.

Vallio studied the ground carefully, concentrating on one spot thoroughly. "Aye, here are signs where Jasper fell from his pony. Oh gods, no! Here look, he was pulled across to the edge of this pool. Nothing to show what took him."

They had all dismounted by now. Falcon stood with the horses and, with weapons readied, Taura, Vallio and Jiutarô approached the water's edge. Taura gasped as the marks clearly showed where their friend had been dragged into the water.

"Oh no!" she croaked. "He's gone!"

The pool before them seemed to explode with the huge shower of water and a long tentacle-like shape writhed upwards from it. The three watchers leapt back in alarm, each emitting a cry of fear or alarm. Although he was many paces away from the pool, Falcon still needed all of his strength to hold the four panic-stricken horses.

A familiar voice gave a massive battle-yell and the long, writhing shape slammed to the ground. Wrapped around the head at the end of it was a dark wet shape that had been fortunate enough to be on top when the thing hit the ground.

"That's it! Just stand there gawpin' why don't yer! Don't mind me at all. Me damned axe is jammed in its skull an' I can't get it out. You don't think I was gonnta leave it there while the bastard swam off, do you?" The dwarf's long hair and beard were dripping with water and filthy weed covered almost the whole of his upper body. He stank.

"Jasper!" cried Taura. "You fell off your horse, you numbskull!" she grated. "What happened after that?"

The dwarf sat up on the twitching body of the massive serpent and gave a cough. "Well, I hit the ground sort of 'ead first and must of passed out fer quite a while 'cos the first thing I knew was that I was bein' pulled into the water. That woke me up quick, I can tell yer, but this snake thing was wrapped 'round me an' it took me out into the swamp an' I was in the water, outa the water an' in it again. Then I got mad an' pulled me arms out an' managed to get mah axe an' slam the bastard but then I was under water fer choddin' ages. I was about to start breathin' in shitty water when it shot me out an' there yer all was lookin' dumb an' scratchin' yer arses wondrin' what to do!"

"Well met, dwarf," responded Vallio. "But we now have a problem. Only us came back for you. We lost the rest of the gang and they're probably leagues away from us now."

Jasper looked at the others in turn and laid his axe on the serpent's body. "Er, oh. Right then. Well, yer have me gratitude fer comin' back fer me. Aye, really yer do."

They made their way back to where Falcon held tightly on to the horse's bridles.

"We best get riding on our way," suggested the barbarian. "We lost much time and got to catch up. Or get out of this place."

"Hey, that's if you finished playing with your little snake," retorted Taura.

"Little? Little? I'll have yer know that *little* bugger was fully sixty feet long! An' I'm only five foot high!"

"Four!" called Vallio and Taura, in unison.

"Aye, even more reason why I'm today's 'ero. We better get on our 'orses then. Oh, anyone got mine?" He looked over to Falcon. "Oh, right, obviously not then!" By now, beneath the dirt and grime, his nose and cheeks were very red.

"Here! Climb up behind me," whispered Taura. "Just hold tight round my waist and grip the horse with your legs."

The dwarf reached up for her hand but for all he lacked in height, he more than made up with his great girth. Nor was it all fat. Years of running a tavern in Northwald City had reduced much of his battle-hardened frame to fat but these last few months had started to hone him back towards the muscle-bound body he had once been proud of. Nonetheless, Taura's horse, being taller than his own, was not easy for him to mount, even with the priestess's aid. He finally managed by climbing up onto the great serpent's body and mounted Taura's horse from there.

More great splashes and the movement of beasts from pools quite close now caused them to exercise caution with their speaking. Jiutarô had been quiet for some minutes, covering his eyes or scanning the skies all about them.

"He seeks his little dragon," Vallio whispered to nobody in particular as Jasper eased himself into place behind Taura's saddle.

"She is safer than are we," replied the Barbarian. "Shall I lead us through this mist? We may find sign of the passing of the others."

A sudden thin screeching sound came from somewhere in front of them. Immediately the riders froze and then withdrew their weapons once again.

"It is Sushi, I am sure," hissed Jiutarô. "She calling to me." He placed two fingers into his mouth and a piercing whistle erupted from his lips.

"I tried to do that for years," whispered Taura. "Could never do it. I remember, my father could –". He words caught in her throat and she bowed her head sadly.

Another screech sounded as if in reply, closer this time. Jiutarô answered with a softer whistle. Heartbeats later, the sound of beating wings sounded to their right side, hidden in the swirling mists. The cleret-wing dragon swooped overhead, circled around them and landed perfectly on the Samurai's shoulders. A moment later though, she flew off again.

"She did see the others a little way ahead," Jiutarô assured them. "They seem good. But she not happy. Something great comes."

"We best ride now, maybe another little snake," suggested the barbarian.

"Idiot!" retorted the dwarf, louder than he should.

Without warning, a cacophony of roars as of a group of great monsters sounded only yards behind them and there was a large *whumph!* as of something huge and heavy landing hard on the wet ground.

"Ride on! Quick! Keep together!" roared the Barbarian and, as one, they kicked the flanks of their mounts and leapt forward into a gallop.

Once again, Jasper held on for his life. This time, his arms were locked around Taura's waist such that she could barely breathe. She said nothing; she would do later.

Fortunately, the sound of the roaring and charging of the beasts was soon lost behind them but it was many moments before the group slowed their mounts. Jiutarô passed a hand across his eyes as if to shield them and, after a few moments, lowered it again.

"I see with Sushi's eyes," he murmured. "Another many-head. It stop to feed on Jasper's little snake. Haha! Hahaha!"

"You may be a *sammarray*, or whatever you calls it, but damn yer impudence, sword-master!"

Jiutarô grimaced. "I am *Samurai!*" he yelled.

CHAPTER 36

THE SUN WAS now well-past its zenith and was in the western sky but its blaze still roasted their shoulders as they saw the river's great bend before them. The mists were clearing rapidly now and few sounds emanated from the swamps to either side. As they rode on, all of them took glances behind them in hope of seeing their friends racing along the wetlands to catch them up. But there was no sign of them. Nor was there even of the cleret-wing dragon that had the advantage of being able to soar at a great height and see clearly with her extremely sharp eyesight.

The river was quite wide and from its large bend flowed slowly southwards. Herons and ibis stood lazily in the shallows, patiently waiting for food to swim by. The mists had cleared enough for the band to clearly see the far bank, probably more than two hundred paces away.

"Look! Alligators!" yelled Billit.

On the far bank, basking in the sun's warmth lay three immense grey-green lizards.

"Lovely! More damned monsters!" groaned the gnome mage. "Will this nightmare never end? Why don't we see nice little rabbits or cuddly animals?"

"Remember," explained Morendo patiently. "These swamps were once two great cities, centuries ago. It is said that there is still a residual magic that covers these lands and many of the normal animals were transformed in foul beasts that prey on anything that walks. It is also said that these monsters have roamed the lands and spread across the world of Amæus itself."

Billit thought for a while. "Aye, but these alligators are sort of natural animals, aren't they?"

"But they can still eat us! Well, maybe not you because you're barely a mouthful!"

"Oh very funny!"

"We must cross though," said Silmar thoughtfully. "The only solution is to go for it and try to kill them if they come close."

"Wait a minute!" exclaimed Billit. "I got an idea! Gimme a little while."

The little gnome climbed down from his pony and walked carefully to the water's edge, all the time looking up and down the bank. Reaching inside his pack, he pulled out a large book. Silmar recognised it immediately – the spellbook. The gnome squatted by the water and began to read. After a while, he returned the book to his pack and stood up. Satisfied that there were no other alligators in the shallows, or on the same bank as him, he stepped into the water and waded further out until it came up to his waist and almost immediately started to shout and beat the surface of the water with his hands.

"Billit!" called Silmar. But he ignored him.

One of the alligators lazily lifted a head and then, with a sudden movement, it glided into the river. Immediately, it disappeared below the surface. Within a few heartbeats the other two followed it. Surprised at the effortless speed at which the alligators had moved into the water, Billit gave a yelp of panic and hastily waded back out onto the bank. With both hands held out in front of him, he gave a chant that none of the others could understand. At first, his hands glowed with a blue shimmering light and then, with a loud crackling, he fired a bolt of dazzling energy into the water directly at the first alligator.

For the length of maybe a dozen heartbeats, the stricken alligator thrashed in the water which turned into a muddy, boiling cauldron. Suddenly, the beast split asunder, turning the water into a pink froth, and sank from sight. Although the other two alligators were many yards away from the first, they were severely affected by the energy bolt and were thrashing furiously, the spray virtually hiding them from view.

The spell dissipated. Billit, sweating and utterly exhausted, sank to the ground. The two surviving alligators gathered their wits and, with a gracefulness that contradicted their ferocious nature, glided across to the remains of the dead beast. They immediately tore into the pieces of flesh and, rolling over, they dragged their bloody trophies to the bottom of the river. Some pieces of alligator floated down with the river's current.

"By the gods!" exclaimed Varengo as, open-mouthed, the group sauntered over to where Billit sprawled against his pack. "What in the seven hells of the Void was that?"

"*Storm Bolt* spell," gasped the gnome. He was dripping with sweat. "Another one I didn't try before. Didn't think it would work. It's wiped me out. I really must rest awhile."

It seemed an age before the two surviving but well-fed alligators finally emerged from the river to bask in the sun once again.

"I think we can quite safely cross now," called Varengo from where he was checking his horse. "The depth there doesn't seem that great, perhaps the height of a man."

"Ah, my friends!" called a loud, deep voice from behind them. "Stay here awhile. I insist. You see, you have destroyed one of my most favourite pets. For that, now, you will have to, er, compensate me."

๑ ๑

The little group spun round at the sound of the voice.

There, stepping through the dense, tall gorse and hawthorn bushes emerged a band of a dozen swarthy, stocky, figures. As they fanned out before them, the group could see the diversity of races making up this obviously threatening and fierce-looking band. Humans, not only light-skinned but a couple very dark, from Gorador or Pashunt in the far south probably, who were renowned for their savagery. Two half-orcs were leaning on stout spears and, surprisingly, a Grey Dwarf and a surface-dwarf stood side-by-side. Three other men, dressed in worn and tatty, brown Hoshite uniforms stood behind a huge human who would have been half a foot taller than Falcon.

Deserters or renegades, thought Silmar.

All of the members of this band were heavily armed but many of the weapons were tarnished, even very rusty.

Of course, the damp of the marshes.

Yoriando, who was standing closest to the bandit leader, swiftly reached for his sword. An arrow slammed into the flesh of his upper right arm, felling him to the ground. His sword clattered to the ground beside him but he was no condition to use it. He writhed in agony but no sound issued from his lips.

"A stupid man!" spat the leader, with a heavily accented Universal tongue. In addition to his extraordinary height, the man was heavily-built and muscle-bound. His darkly-tanned face was virtually divided into two by a long, deep scar that ran from his forehead, through his now empty left eye socket and across his nose to the bottom of his right cheek. His thick, dark-brown beard hung down to his chest but was matted with filth and neglect.

Judging by the array of weapons carried by the bandits, they were probably all seasoned fighters. Many of them also wore pieces of plate, leather or mail armour but even these seemed to be very tarnished, the leather fixings also badly perished.

It was the pair of orcs that caught the eye more than any of the other bandits. Their porcine faces showed an almost unnatural cruelty and to make them even worse to look upon, from their belts hung rather small human skulls. Their leather clothing was so badly perished as to be almost non-existent. The tatters of what had once been hose and tunics hung in strips about them.

Silmar looked closer at the skulls. *Oh gods! Children?*

All three Hoshites had arrows nocked onto their bowstrings. One of them had shot the arrow into Yoriando. Billit still lay exhausted on the ground by the river. The others stood in a stunned silence.

The bandit leader swaggered over to where Yoriando lay on the ground. The brute planted his foot on Yoriando's injured shoulder causing him to scream in agony.

"Hah!" shouted the man in triumph. "He does gotta voice then!" He reached down and viciously yanked the arrow from the stricken man's shoulder. Yoriando screamed in pain once again and then fainted. Many of the bandits laughed.

"That was not necessary!" yelled a furious Silmar.

The leader pointed to the elf, calling out in a loud voice "Him too!"

Instantly, another arrow streaked across from one of the Hoshites and embedded itself high up in the elf's right thigh. It was closely followed by another that thudded into Silmar's right shoulder. The elf dropped to the ground. Both of the half-orcs rocked with laughter and waved their spears above their heads.

The leader paced to and fro. "Do *not* told me what is nessary or un-, er unnessary, elf. Next time any of you opening his mouth, he be alligator food – or orc food, mebbe."

The orcs whooped with joy.

"Everything you got is now mine for me. All of it. Horses, good. Hmm, no womans. That a shame. We got urges, don't we boys?" The bandits laughed derisively. "Haha! That a shame. We, er, share them around until them die. Take two days sometimes. But, hey. You are now mine for me to treat as I want. We want workers. But not for long, I promise. Then we release you. No, I just joking. We feed you to my alliga–"

For a few heartbeats, the man seemed to freeze. Then his expression changed to one of shock as he wondered why he suddenly had a metal tongue. An arrowhead protruded forward out of his mouth. His lips closed about it in disbelief. He pitched forward and fell face-down onto the damp ground. There was no movement from anyone. There was no sound except for short painful cries from the stricken leader. The arrow shaft protruded from the side of his neck, its white fletchings fluttering slightly in the gentle breeze.

Under Falcon's confident leadership, the little band rode swiftly but as silently as galloping horses would allow. Every few minutes, he would turn in his saddle and give them a broad grin. But the self-assurance he showed was not what he felt. There had been no sign that the other group had ridden this way. He did not doubt that he was taking them in the right direction – the sun was high and at their back now as was expected at this time of day. The mist was thinning considerably and the peaks of the mountains in front of them were beginning to appear. They could now see clearly up to about fifty paces or more in all directions and, although there were many sounds of movement on either side, they did not see, or sense, any predators stalking them. They had ridden for two hours and Falcon expected to be seeing the river before him very soon.

The cleret-wing dragon had been airborne for more than an hour and Jiutarô was unable to see anything through her eyes. Suddenly, she swooped down and landed awkwardly on the Samurai's shoulders. What she had seen caused him to race ahead and warn Falcon to stop them all immediately.

"This is dire peril," gasped the great barbarian as Jiutarô described what Sushi had seen. "I suggest we creep forward and shower this new evil with arrows. What say you all?"

Abruptly, there was havoc and confusion. Arrows streaked from behind bushes and trees. Almost every one found its mark. A shower of lights streaked from the bushes and slammed into one of the half-orcs and then the other. As they found their marks so they exploded, knocking them to the ground. Despite running for cover, the bandits had nowhere to go. An armed warrior was there to cut off any escape.

Taura was armed with her staff! It was shod at one end with an iron ring. With it, from horseback, she struck down the two panic-stricken dwarves. The shock on their faces as she, a woman with a face full of hate, cleaved their skulls gave her an uncharacteristic satisfaction.

Varengo, who had taken up Silmar's bow and arrows, and Morendo leapt into action and their bows were soon picking off the remaining bandits. Meanwhile, Silmar lay on the ground where he had fallen – he was losing much blood from the two arrow wounds. From where Taura sat in her saddle, over the body of one of the Hoshites, she could clearly see him.

Within a few moments, all of the bandits except for the leader and the two half-orcs, who had been wounded by numerous arrows, were dead. Jasper, Morendo and Billit strode together over to the leader who, defiant despite his painful neck wound, continued to taunt them or curse in an unknown language.

"You nasty, nasty, vicious bastard," growled Jasper. "Death is too good for you. Alligator food, eh? Hey Silmar, do you think alligators like eating shit? I got some for 'em!"

"You don' dare! Hah! Arrgh!" replied the man slowly, coughing on the blood that flowed from his neck and mouth over the arrowhead. "Aghh! I has m—more mans what come now. Dey carve you all up. Let me go an' I tells 'em to make you die quick!"

A back-handed swipe from Jasper's gauntleted hand shut the man up for a while.

Meanwhile, Varengo, Falcon and Vallio squatted by the half-orcs. Taura attended to Silmar and then Yoriando using the divine powers of healing from her deity, Neilea.

As always, this sapped her energy and she wearily rose to her feet and wandered away, stopping a few paces away, her gaze fixed on the small skulls that hung by their hair from the half-orc's belts. Her usually pretty and tanned face was twisted in disgust and hate and it took all of her self-control to refrain from smashing their wounded bodies into oblivion with her staff.

"So, you kill children, do you?" asked Vallio, his voice grating with loathing and disgust.

"Ayeah, an' we eat dem too. Heh! You should try. An der womens. Dem really squeal when we skin 'em! An' den we cook on fire for eat."

Vallio threw up on the ground. Tears welled up in Taura's eyes as she looked once again at the little skulls. She spun around and walked over to the group standing around the bandit leader. A ferocious punch from Falcon had shattered the man's jaw. The Barbarian turned to face the half-orcs.

"You too?" he asked. "You child killer? You woman burner?"

The half-orcs shrank back in fear and said nothing.

An agonised shouting caused Falcon and the others to look towards the spot where Morendo, Jasper and Billit were gathered around the bandit leader. Taura had rejoined them and, surprisingly, she had her foot pressing down heavily at a point on the leader's neck where an arrow had torn into the muscle.

"Aiii! Tell woman stop!" screamed the man.

"Hurts, doesn't it?" said Taura, her face grim. She took her foot off and strode over to Silmar.

"What shall we do with 'em?" asked Varengo.

"Stake the bastards out on the river bank," replied Jasper. He looked over to Falcon who nodded in agreement. Jiutarô, who had been tending the horses and looking after a weary Sushi, merely shrugged his shoulders and turned away.

From where he lay, Silmar called over to them. "Move the dead away from the riverbank. Alligators prefer the freshest of meat."

All of them, except for Jiutarô and Taura, were more than willing to engage in the distasteful job of moving the bodies and securing the three thugs to the stout, deeply-driven stakes that Falcon and Varengo had cut from nearby hawthorn trees.

Within an hour, Silmar and Yoriando were helped up onto their horses and the band rode away, crossing the river. Shouts of curses and pleading followed them as they rode. These they ignored, probably as had the bandits when they heard the pleadings from their victims.

The two surviving alligators raised their heads to follow the movement of the riders and then, having been woken from their reverie, plunged into the cool waters to investigate the sounds and smells drifting over to them from the opposite side.

❧ ☙

The lone rider came across the horrific scene a couple of hours later. The alligators were basking in the sun having fed well.

The marks in the gravel where the great lizards had dragged their prey towards the river were streaked with blood and gore and with bits of clothing. The rider grimaced as he forced down the bile that had risen to his throat.

That is one problem dealt with, he mused. *But what of their own injuries? Surely they must rest.*

He spurred his horse across the river and observed the alligators as they raised their heads to look at the new disturbance to their slumber.

He tarried for a moment as he looked up the dusty track that rose into the hills but decided to veer off to the left and ride across the higher ground.

CHAPTER 37

DARKNESS WAS falling swiftly as the sun set behind distant clouds over the western hills. As the party left the wetlands behind them, so they begin to feel the dry heat of the sun despite the lateness of the day. It had taken them an hour climbing the steep foothills before they found the track that would eventually take them to the East Way and then on towards Cascant. Only then did they gaze back across the desolation that had brought them so close to danger.

Here, high above the flat, humid marshes, there was an abundance of game. They made camp behind some low hills, well away from the road. Jiutarô and Falcon were away from the camp for less than an hour when they reappeared in the darkness with a brace of rabbits and a small mountain goat. Silmar and Yoriando were exhausted and in considerable pain after the ordeal during the day and the jolting from the ride. Taura's attention to their injuries had seemed to significantly reduce their pain and their wounds appeared partly healed but large bruises and swellings were excruciating and the elf walked with a painful limp while Yoriando's arm was strapped tightly across his chest.

Taura was most despondent. "I have not conversed with my deity, the Lady of *Kismet* and *Serendipity*," she wailed. "I have used many of her powers today and I must make some time for her. How is your shoulder, Yori?"

Yoriando stood up and carefully attempted to lift his arm. He winced and gasped. "It pains badly but there is no bleeding. I doubt that I will be able to use my sword in this hand for many days but I shall exercise my shoulder. I can use it in my other fairly well though. Fear not, my lady, I shall be fit soon. Please convey my gratitude to your Lady of Fate."

The priestess was always encouraged by the man's charm and respect when he addressed her. She smiled her appreciation and rose to her feet while Jasper and Varengo prepared the fire and the meal. It was time for prayer.

Silmar lay on his blanket and studied the stars. "In the morning," he muttered, "we head towards the Kingdom of Cascant." He slept fitfully.

The fire was allowed to burn itself out and they settled down for the night. A watch was set, as was their practice. Everything was quiet and the occasional scurrying of night-hunting animals was strangely comforting. Owls calling and responding and the bark of foxes in the little wooded copses that dotted these foothills were a welcome relief. They all knew that while they heard these sounds, and the chirping of the crickets in the grass, then danger would not be close by.

The moon was very low in the sky in the early hours of the morning when they were all quietly roused by a gentle shake and a hand loosely clamped over their mouths.

"Riders! Shhh!" It was Morendo's warning that carefully brought them awake. There was hardly any light. "Listen. Quiet! Billit is watching them."

From where they were laying, they could all hear the sound of hooves on the road, despite the distance. Although faint, they undoubtedly heard an occasional whispered or muttered word or curse.

It was many minutes before anyone dared speak by which time the riders were long gone.

"It's choddin' well them, innit?" whispered Jasper. "Where's that daft gnome?"

"Right behind yer!" replied Billit quietly.

Jasper had almost leapt into the air in surprise.

"You tit! I near on shi-, I mean, you choddin' numbskull!" stammered the dwarf as, once again, Taura's glance of disapproval was cast towards him.

"Amazin' how high the fat dwarf can jump, ain't it?" Billit laughed.

"Typical for a fat, stumpy, tunnel dweller!" retorted Silmar from his bedroll. "Aye, it was them indeed. I felt the effect on the burden in my pack that I rest my head on. Well, what did you see?" He had gritted his teeth as he turned his head to look over to where they crouched in the grass.

Billit took a deep breath. "Seven riders, all dressed in black, all their 'orses look black too. We seen that before, din't we? No guesses there then. Darkling! Definitely! Odd though, one of them was being taunted by a couple of the others. I din't understand what they was saying but I think that one of 'em is a bit of dead wood they are being forced to take along with 'em. I did 'ear 'em say the word *Cascant* though."

"Right then!" sighed Varengo. "We've missed them and lost any chance of catching them in an ambush. I guess we will need to play catch-up when we get to Cascant."

"It's too dark for us to risk the road right now," suggested Taura.

"Aye, yer right there," replied Jasper. "We best get on with our sleep an' try for an early start in the morning."

"Agreed," said Silmar. "And we will have the benefit of tracks to follow, too. It's still about three hours before dawn."

The mighty Falcon offered to take the rest of the night watch despite Silmar's assertions that he could help. "You sleep, elf! We need your skills so you recover. Don't get injuries again; we may leave you behind next time!" The broad grin on the barbarian's face was not an expression they saw very often.

⅌ ⅌

The sun had risen but was still hidden by the eastern peaks when Falcon eventually roused them. Morendo had already produced a warm broth from the leg bones of the mountain goat that they had feasted on the previous evening. Yoriando tried to stretch his painful shoulder and reassured everyone that it felt better.

"It is little improved, is it?" Taura whispered to him.

"It will soon, dear lady. It has only been one day."

"Sit down and I shall try appealing to Neilea once more. Let us see what she can do for us."

While the priestess attended to Yoriando, Silmar struggled to his feet but instantly collapsed to the ground. Varengo rushed to his aid.

"Taura!" he yelled. "Silmar is burning up here. His shoulder has become infected; there is much redness and heat."

"See to the elf, mistress," said Yoriando. "I shall be fine for now."

It was midday before she was able to sit and relax. "Silmar must have more time to recover," she advised. "We need two days at least before we can move away." She was plainly exhausted and her damp hair was stuck to her face.

It was in fact another three days before they were back down on the road. Almost immediately, Vallio spotted the tracks left by the passing Darkling. He called Silmar who gingerly eased his horse over.

"Aye, it was them, most certainly," he confirmed. "Judging by their horses' strides, they were not moving particularly fast in the darkness but they are a few days ahead now. There's that notch in the horse-shoe, look!"

The track was very rough and, in places, badly pitted through neglect and disuse. Damage caused by rock-falls from above and subsidence from below caused them to dismount from time to time and lead their horses or even to leave the road altogether.

"Observe how the Darkling have had to do likewise," explained the elf. "Here are their boot prints. Look how narrow the foot is and how the heel is more suited to walking than riding."

He was right in this. The heel did not have the customary step as it met with the sole, as would have been found on a riding-boot. In this way, a riding-boot would not be so liable to slip through a typical leather and wood stirrup. Darkling may have had have some difficulty in securing their feet to the stirrups unless they dispensed with the stirrups completely.

The road wound higher and higher as the morning wore on. They had a wondrous view westwards across the Marshes now far behind them. The flat and mist-covered plain through which they had travelled the previous days was visible from where they now rode. The river, too, looked almost like a winding strip of glinting silver in the distance. The horrors they had left behind them were still fresh in their minds but none of the group would ever speak of them.

They rode quietly and were surprised to meet a long merchants' caravan moving steadily westwards.

Varengo and Morendo rode forward to meet with the caravan master. There must have been more than four dozen covered wagons hauled by teams of heavy horses. Each wagon had a drover and many of them also carried an armed guard. There were six outriders that the companions could see.

"Goodsir, this is a very bad road," Morendo called. "It is uncared-for and even if you do get through the deep holes it will take you through the dangerous marshes where unspeakable monsters and gangs of vicious cutthroats roam. Why do you come this way?"

"Our two guides recommended this route so as to avoid the Hoshite tolls," the master admitted.

"Where are they?" Varengo asked. "They should know better. Bring them here."

Two horsemen appeared. They were attired in worn leather hose and jerkins similar to the thugs they had encountered by the river and were armed with badly rusted swords and javelins.

Morendo was the first to quietly speak out to the caravan master. "The cutthroats I spoke of were dressed in leather and their weapons, and what little armour they wore, were rusted – similar to your guides. We were fortunate enough to destroy one gang of about a dozen women and child killers. I believe your guides were delivering your caravan right into their hands."

"Take them!" the master yelled.

The guides exchanged glances, one nodded and they spurred their horses.

Jiutarô took up his bow quickly, reached for two arrows, put one between his teeth and nocked the second. As one arrow flew, the other was released. Both found their mark. One of the fleeing riders fell from the saddle and crashed to the ground in a cloud of dust. The other wavered in his saddle but managed to stay upright. Unable to properly control his mount, it came to a stop amongst a confusing series of conflicting commands. It took a few steps to the right, reared and dipped its head causing the wounded rider to pitch forwards over the neck of the horse and headfirst onto the ground.

"Good arrows, Jiutarô," Falcon complimented him. The others agreed.

Both horses had galloped on a few hundred paces and then stopped to graze. Silmar and Taura rode over to the bodies. The priestess dismounted and leaned over the first body.

"This one is dead," she quickly confirmed.

She strode over to the other body and knelt down beside it. From her movements it seemed that she was looking for signs that the man lived. She then rose to her feet.

"This one is dead too."

Silmar gave her a brief expression of curiosity but she gave no indication that she had noticed it.

The caravan master had been shocked by the ease in which he had been duped by the two guides but now faced a new problem.

"Are you certain that we can't get this caravan up this track?" he asked.

"Hai," Jiutarô replied. "Not go that way. There bad things."

"Aye, I seen somethin'," Jasper cried. "A choddin' great snake-like creature that 'ad a mouth big enough to pluck a rider off 'is 'orse. Aye, I killed it but it musta had a ma or pa else 'ow could it get made?"

"Not to mention the sound we heard that must've been a hydra," added Vallio.

"A hydra?" echoed the master. "By the gods! That's it then, I have to get these wagons turned around."

"There is a wide enough area a short way along the track but you'll need to fill in some pits."

"You have my gratitude, all of you," said the caravan master. "Travel safely."

As the party rode away they heard the yelled orders of the caravan master and the cracking whips of his drovers.

ঔ ঙ

The following morning, the group stumbled across the broken remains of a wagon half-hidden in grass and weed. From the weathered state of the timbers, it had been there for some time and much of the wood had been stripped away, probably for use as firewood by passing travellers. No sign was there of its cargo but there were a few broken arrows strewn on the ground in the grass. Whatever had befallen the wagon and its drovers had clearly occurred some months or even years before.

As the group led their horses past the broken wagon, Falcon rode through the grass to the side of the track and soon discovered the remains of three human bodies. The bleached bones lay off the side of the road between a jumble of boulders where the ground fell away steeply. The bones had long since having been stripped of flesh by time and scavengers. Some remnants of clothing lay in tatters about the bones but there was no trace of boots, belts, armour or weapons. Anything of value had been removed presumably by those who had caused the death of these unfortunate people.

"A skull here has been cleaved," Falcon reported. "Another has had a leg chopped away. That one was a woman, I am certain of it."

"Maybe their killers died by us," murmured Jiutarô, his face grim. As if sensing his concerns, the cleret-wing dragon launched herself into the air and soared high into the sky. Although she had flown a couple of times during the morning, she had seen nothing of any other riders on the road except for the caravan.

The Samurai watched her as she floated on the rising air currents. "She hunt Darkling," he said.

"They'll be restin' up a few days ahead somewhere well off the road," said Jasper. "They won't ride durin' the day, I reckons. Sun will burn their eyes."

"That bastard assassin did if you remember," said Falcon, spitting on the ground with uncharacteristic vehemence. "He pulled his hood over his eyes to shield them from the sun."

The little dragon soared to their left and swooped low where the hills dropped away. She very quickly dropped out of sight.

"If Darkling in hills, she seeing them," murmured Jiutarô.

"They could, of course, be waiting in ambush for us to pass by," suggested Vallio.

"They probably don't know that we are behind them," replied Varengo. "Besides, seven Darkling and seven horses will be easy for a cleret-wing dragon to see from a thousand feet up in the air."

Suddenly, Sushi swooped down over an area to the right side of the road. She gave a screech and swooped over the spot again. The Samurai heeled his mount towards the spot.

"Aiii!" he exclaimed. "There only six Darkling now. Observe!"

Well hidden behind a rocky outcropping, lay the body of one of the Darkling. An attempt had been made to cover it with branches and rocks but it had been done with haste. Perched on the chest of the Darkling, as if in triumph, was Sushi. She was hissing and spitting and the barb of her tail hovered less than an inch from the Darkling's neck.

The figure was dressed in tight-fitting doublet and hose over which a finely-woven hooded cape covered much of the body. The riding boots were of a type of soft leather that none could identify. Any weapons that might have been carried had been removed from the body.

"Gods!" gasped the elf as he limped to the scene. "This swine is dead but I can still feel the effect of his malevolence on the burden that I carry. It must have been the swarming flies that Sushi noticed."

"Aye, mayhap you're right," Jasper agreed. "Sharp bugger for an elf, ain't yeh?"

Silmar was not to be drawn in by the terse comment; he was well used to it by now.

"Mayhap the others are close by," whispered Taura. "Beware! Jiutarô?" She indicated the hills with a sweep of her arm.

The master swordsman nodded and murmured quietly to the little dragon.

The others looked up at the hills and Sushi once again launched herself above the hills. Within moments, she was high up once again on the rising currents and circled above them. Then she was gone from sight.

"Is there anything?" Varengo asked.

"No, she too far for me to see from her eyes," muttered the Samurai.

Meanwhile, Taura stooped over the remains of the Darkling and examined his body and clothing. The face was white and very narrow with a beak-like nose. The pointed ears were typical of an elf although somewhat longer. The eyes were closed but the mouth had frozen in an expression of wretched fear. A mass of almost black blood about his jaw, neck and upper chest was swarming with flies.

"Yeesh! Ugly bastard, ain't 'e!" grunted Jasper. "'E's 'ad the shit beat outa 'im by the looks of 'im."

"He's been garrotted," replied the priestess. "Look at his neck! The mark goes all the way around. The wire's cut right through his windpipe and blood vessels. What a mess! Ugh!"

Silmar bent forward to look and gasped at a stab of pain. "I think he was executed by one of his own, or all of them conspired to do it. A wire! It's a typical assassin's trick. Quiet and extremely efficient."

Turning to Billit, Taura asked "Didn't you say that one of them was being taunted by the others? Something about one of them being *dead wood*?"

"Er aye," he replied, pausing as he tried to remember. "Aye, that's right. He was being given a right good bollockin', er, oh sorry, missy! A right good telling-off by one o' the others. Might be that one, eh? They all look the same to me. A charmin' way of encouraging team-work, I must say!"

After circling for a while, Sushi landed close to the Darkling body and then hopped up onto Jiutarô's shoulders with a flap of her wings.

"Are you tired, little one?" asked the Samurai, tickling her soft throat. He rummaged in his bag and fed her with a morsel of dried meat. "She see no Darkling in hills. I trust her."

Tipping a little water into the palm of his hand, he held it up for her to drink. It was soon gone but she wanted no more. He fed her the last of his nuts and dried fruit and she curled up to sleep. After all of her flying, Jiutarô knew she would probably sleep for a couple of hours.

The group made its way back to their horses and, apart from Silmar, resumed their journey on foot to rest their mounts. After a while, Silmar called a halt and spoke to them all.

"Look, everyone," he began. "I'm going to scout ahead for a while. It is folly to travel like this along the road and not see what could be waiting for us around the next bend. If someone can take my horse, I can travel light and quite fast and keep an eye open for Darkling. Or for anything else for that matter."

"What?" shouted Jasper. "On yer own, yer termite? If anythin' was to 'appen to yer up there, then we wouldn't know nothin' 'bout it and wouldn't know where to find yer."

"Thanks for your concern, Jasper," replied the elf.

"Hah! Don't give a badger's bleedin' chuff about you, elf. But I don't plan on mindin' yer 'orse and stuff while yer sittin' on a rock with a broke leg! Take someone with yer, yer bleedin' chod! Elves? They got shit fer brains, the lot of 'em, I reckons. Ev'ryone knows that!"

Almost everyone was rocking with laughter.

"Hey! Just you wait a moment, Silmar," Taura called. She stood in front of him with her hands on her hips. "You have injuries. You are not going. That is my final word. I will not discuss it further. I have not spent time and energy, as well as appeals to The Lady, for you to go and open up your injuries."

"Vallio can go in his stead," said Vaengo. "How about it?"

"Aye, that I can," the small warrior agreed. "Wondered is anyone would think of me. I can do tracking real good, too. You all know it."

"Hah!" retorted the dwarf. "Last time yer done that you came back wi' two fingers less. Taura wrapped her 'and up then, gin't she?"

Jiutarô offered to go with Vallio and was pleased that the offer was accepted.

"I change clothes first," the Samurai called. He carefully lifted Sushi from his shoulders and settled her on the saddle of his horse.

Jiutarô removed his boots, his short trousers and his tunic. Reaching into his backpack, he removed a black bundle that was tied up by a long strip of thick, dark, narrow cloth. In a few minutes he had donned a full-length, single-piece, blue-grey garment that covered the whole of his body, including his head. This hood also completely covered his face except for a slit for his eyes, it being fitted with a mask. The narrow strip of cloth that acted as the belt, or *obi* as he called it, was not fitted with any buckle but instead, was tied with a knot so that the ends hung loosely almost to his knees.

The group looked at him in astonishment. He looked every part the archetypal assassin and in the many tenday weeks they had known him, they had seen nothing of this garb. His *katana* and *wakisahi*, the Samurai longsword and shortsword in their black lacquered scabbards, were tucked into his obi. He slipped two objects into the side-pockets of his garment. He pushed his clothing and riding-boots into his backpack and on his feet he put on a pair of light sandals, or *zori* as he termed them, of the sort that would have been considered by the others better worn inside a house than for scrambling over rocks and hills.

His garb he referred to as his *gi*, but this meant nothing to the group of onlookers and he did not offer to explain. He then gathered up his bow and arrows.

Vallio took only his bow, his shortsword, and his quiver of arrows at his belt. Falcon handed Jiutarô a length of coiled rope that the samurai looped across his neck and round his left shoulder. They were ready to go.

It took barely a dozen heartbeats and the two warriors had disappeared from the sight and hearing of the group, and into the hills high above the road.

"What is that garb?" Taura whispered rhetorically.

Silmar had heard her and offered an explanation. "It will help to conceal him in the rocks I expect."

        ℽ   ✍

The group had waited a while before resuming their journey. Yoriando led Jiutarô's horse, with Sushi sleeping peacefully on the swaying saddle and the backpack hanging from the saddle-ties at one side. The seasoned warrior still had his arm bound to his chest but occasionally he would release it to give it some exercise.

Jasper reluctantly led Vallio's horse and had wasted little time in complaining about the danger the two warriors would face.

Taura had been quick to reply though. "The last person to complain on this road was garrotted!" she growled.

"Person?" answered the dwarf. "What in the seven choddin' hells o' the Void do you mean *person*? Hardly a person! A Darkling is *not* a person!"

"Please do not shout, master dwarf," whispered Varengo. "Especially the name *Darkling*!"

Jasper immediately glanced about, his face a picture of mock fear. "Ooh, er, aye. S'posed ter be terrified, am I?"

By now the sun was well past its highest point. They had been travelling for almost four hours since discovering the body of the Darkling. The group had seen nothing of Vallio and Jiutarô in all that time. Now, they were all scanning the hills and the road ahead in the hope of seeing their two friends. Of them, there was no sign.

ଓ ଏ

With Vallio leading, the pair climbed up or around a couple of small hills and were soon out of sight of the rest of the group on the road. Almost immediately, they knew that finding a route across these hills would be no easy task. Steep climbs or drops and deep gullies made it extremely difficult for them to find their way and they found that the concentration they needed in order to keep their footing distracted them from their task of checking for danger around them.

Once they gained higher ground, however, the terrain became much easier for them to travel over. Some cover was afforded by crags and rocky outcroppings and the extra height gave them much better visibility of the hillsides and the road far below. Despite thorough searching, they caught no sign of the Darkling at first but they eventually they did discover the remains of a small campfire by the side of a small stream. A shallow dip had been scraped in the ground about which a ring of small rocks had been placed. While Jiutarô studied the fire, Vallio noticed the tell-tale hoofprints.

"They rested, fed at this place," mused Jiutarô. "Fire stones cold, it days when they here. They put out fire with piss." This was a common method of extinguishing camp fires employed by most male members of adventuring parties as well as most other travellers.

Vallio was impressed by Jiutarô's hunting and tracking skills. This was the first opportunity for him to travel with the strange Samurai about whom he still knew so little.

"You're right," murmured the tracker. "Three days, maybe less but not by much but we know this from when they passed us on the road."

Encouraged by this find, they ran on. The energy of the Samurai also surprised the tracker. He proved to be very agile when climbing rocks and steep hills and, when hiding in shadows, his grey-blue garb caused him to be almost invisible, despite the bright sunlight. Vallio continued to lead the way and the Samurai was twenty yards to his right while crossing the hill. Once they caught sight of the little dragon circling high above them.

They were just making their way around a large rock face when a blur of movement caught them both by surprise.

৯৯ ৶৶

"Gods!" grunted the dwarf, absently. "Where in the choddin' world are those two mischief-makers?"

All of them had been asking themselves the very same question and deep concerns were now setting in.

"Sushi," called Taura. The cleret-wing dragon raised her head lazily from the saddle and looked at her. "Where are they? Can you find them?"

Sushi just gazed at her uncomprehendingly.

"There is no bond," sighed the priestess dejectedly. "She will not understand."

Silmar stood by smiling and shaking his head.

"Oh, gods-dammit!" exclaimed Billit. "Look, you stupid minitcha dragon – get off yer lazy arse and go find yer master – now!" The mage swung his arm so that his finger pointed up to the top of the hills.

At this, the cleret-wing dragon yawned, lazily stretched her wings and then took off up into the air. The horse shied momentarily at the sudden movement but soon settled again. With a few powerful beats of her wings, Sushi was gone.

Taura and Jasper stood there aghast and mouths open wide in surprise.

"By the..! What did, er…? How...?" stammered Jasper. "Well, I'll be..!"

"Look, you dozy articles," laughed Billit, "if you want somethin' done proper-like, then ask the mage!"

❧ ❧

The mountain cat launched itself off the rock and caught Vallio full on his chest. With the small but powerful beast locked onto him by its claws and its wide jaws just inches from his face, the tracker knew he would not be able to hold the animal off for many more seconds. The pain in his chest was excruciating as the claws dug deeper and he found he couldn't even cry out.

Suddenly, he was on his back and the beast was on top of him. Its hot, stinking breath almost made him gag particularly when its slaver dripped on his face. Then the animal seemed to collapse and its head, with its mouth open, thudded into his own head and, after a momentary shudder, lay still.

In a panic, and using the last of his strength, Vallio rolled to one side and the animal fell to the ground, its claws tearing from his chest. The tracker cried out in agony as the claws ripped free and took shreds of clothing from him. Jiutarô dropped beside him, pulled the dead animal's body out of the way and yanked open the tracker's shirt. Where the mountain lion had grabbed Vallio, there were some very deep flesh wounds that were pumping blood. Opening the top of his costume, the Samurai ripped off his own undershirt. This he tore into pads and strips and quickly bound the deepest of the injuries as best as he could.

Vallio was breathing erratically, uttering a cry with each breath, and his face was very pale. Jiutarô knew he had a difficult decision to make – whether to try to carry the tracker back down to the road or to leave him behind and seek the help of the priestess and her healing magic.

"Help me up, I'll be alright to walk, Jiutarô," panted Vallio, unconvincingly.

"You go no-place, Vallio-san," replied the Samurai as he held his hand across his companion's forhead. "You lay down."

Suddenly, a shriek and a flapping of wings startled them both and Jiutarô turned with a small, star-shaped, object in his hand. It was a *shuriken* throwing star, made from iron and larger than an outstretched hand.

"Sushi!" he called. "You come to me just when I need you." He beamed with relief and delight.

Jiutarô took a small piece of his now wrecked undershirt and smeared it with some of the tracker's blood. He then held it for Sushi to take into her jaws. He ooked into her eyes and unspoken thoughs passed between them.

Then she was gone, soaring up into the air.

Jiutarô stood up and pulled the body of the cat closer so that Vallio could be propped up against it.

"Now you have warm bed," laughed the Samurai.

"What... did you do... to the great... cat?" whispered Vallio then he grimaced as he gave a cough.

"Ah, hai! I throw these!" From his pockets, he withdrew the heavy, star-shaped object that Silmar had seen when Sushi arrived. It had four points each of which was as sharp as a skinning-knife. "My *shuriken*. I have some in *gi* pocket. Great cat have two in head. I take them out now. You keep still, not, er, play!"

Vallio could feel the body of the mountain lion shaking as Jiutarô worked the throwing-stars loose from the animal's skull. The tracker tried to laugh but was overcome by pain.

"I needed company after all," whispered Vallio. "The damned dwarf was right."

"Why elf and dwarf not friends?"

"Well, I think they are really." He wheezed as he spoke in short, measured gasps. "It is a tradition that they argue or call each other names. You see, Jiutarô, many centuries ago, before men arrived in these lands of Baylea, there were wars between elf-kind and dwarf-kind. Then men came with their mages and so came the goblin-kin and orcs, the trolls, ogres and then the undead. So there became an uneasy peace between elves and dwarves and they often needed to stand together to fight for their homes and lands. But they do like to show disrespect and a mutual dislike but it is not always serious – until the ale flows. Do dwarf and elf fight in your world?"

"My world? Homeland far away, I think." Jiutarô also spoke slowly as he searched for the words in the Universal tongue. "Aii, there no elf, no dwarf, no orc, no monsters, no many-heads. This a bad world, Vallio-san. Only man on my world but we have many war. Hai. My land fight land of Korea, we fight neighbours too. Ahhh, Nippon! My land. How I miss it. I must go home." He paused a moment. "I go home to die, Vallio-san." Jiutarô was silent again for another moment. "My friends and me have, ah, what the word? Debt of honour so we will die for the doing of it by own hand. Kira-san must die to avenge dead master, Assano-san."

Vallio's eyes were beginning to flutter as he grew weaker and more tired with each breath. Jiutarô continued to talk though, all the while carefully watching Vallio as the tracker's breathing grew increasingly laboured. He spoke of Kira's treachery and the demise of Assano's *han*. He spoke of his forty-six friends left scattered about his homeland and of the pact they had made to meet once more so that the honour they owed to their dead master would be satisfied. He then spoke of *bushido*, the warrior code of conduct of the Samurai. He explained the act of *seppuku* by *hara-kiri*, ritual suicide by the stomach-cut, the ultimate demonstration of honour and loyalty.

Jiutarô examined Vallio's injuries and, using the pressure of his hand, did his best to staunch the blood flow. Looking up at the sky, he knew that dusk would soon approach them and he also knew that, with his blood-loss and the oncoming cold, Vallio would probably not last the night.

ॐ ॐ

CHAPTER 38

THE SAMURAI was about to rise to his feet when a familiar beating of wings caused him to look up. Sushi landed less than gracefully a few paces from him. In her jaws was a waterskin. With a broad grin, Jiutarô patted the cleret-wing dragon's scaly neck and took the gift.

Some moments later, a crunching of feet on pebbles caused him to look up in alarm but there stood Taura, and behind her, the sandy, short-haired and close-shaven face of Morendo. She was exhausted from her climb but without a word she immediately began to carry out work on healing the tracker.

"These bandages have been well done, Jiutarô," she complimented him. "You would make a good healer. It will be dark soon. We could do with some food, more water and a fire."

Jiutarô went up to Morendo, grasped his hand in appreciation and said "Hunt." Together they gathered their bows and quickly sped off.

It was fully dark by the time that the two hunters returned with a hare and a porcupine. Morendo used his flint and steel to light a fire while Jiutarô carefully skinned the porcupine and prepared the game by skewering them onto a green branch above the fire. While the meal was cooking, the men went out and scavenged for fire-wood.

That evening, Taura spent a long time giving healing to the tracker, so bad were his wounds. At last, she straightened up and took water from the skin. Her hair was soaked in sweat despite the cool evening. She moved close to the fire and took a chunk of meat from the spit.

"Vallio will sleep through the night. I can set up warding spells that will help make us safe during the night but we will still need a watch. I must converse with my God for she has been very generous in her healing powers today. In the morning of the second day he may be ready to move down to the road but not tomorrow. Even then he will need help for he will be very stiff and will have some pain."

"Two days?" gasped Jiutarô.

Morendo, Taura and Jiutarô had little opportunity to sleep that night and took it in turns to take watch. Vallio was restless and cried out in pain many times. The next day was colder but two small fires kept the chill at bay. Taura spent more time with the tracker in an attempt to improve on the healing from the previous day. The effect was minimal but Vallio was now able to breathe without pain.

"The others have not come to find us," sighed Taura. "Can it be they are in danger?"

"Many of them," replied Jiutarô. "Big place look for us."

That evening, the skies cleared and without the blanket of cloud the cold descended. The moon rose in the depths of the night and the three adventurers on watch felt a little easier. They were not disturbed by beast or monster. Or Darkling.

Next morning, after a meal of the remains of their meat, they made an early start for the road. Vallio was moving stiffly at first and slowly, needing much support from Jiutarô and Morendo particularly when the terrain was rough. There, on the road waiting for them and smiling broadly, was the rest of their group.

Jasper's greeting, however, lacked some of the warmth that the others had shown. "The Darklin' are prob'ly five full days ride ahead of us now 'specially since you bin up there playin' with the pussy cats! An' you achieved chod all!"

"Just let it be, dwarf," snarled Silmar. "You have done nothing but complain for the last two days."

Jiutarô stepped across and placed himself in between Jasper and Silmar. He leaned forward and stood nose to nose before the dwarf. His face was a mask of fury. The Samurai was grim and his face was dark. "We *did* find Darkling fire before big cat came," he growled. "It could be happen to you. No more insult. Stop fool words or I get mad! Fight Darkling and crazy night monsters, not we, us! You be like children. No more! Hai? *Hai*?"

The group stood open-mouthed at the Samurai's rage. It was the first time anyone had seen him so assertive. His words cut through the atmosphere like his *katana* through flesh. The dwarf stood there dumbfounded. Jiutarô whirled and strode over to where Sushi sat atop his horse. Within a few moments he had moved to a quiet corner to change back into his normal clothes, muttering in his own language.

Varengo broke the silence. "I suggest we stay together and ride at our best speed up and over the hills to the border crossing. Will you be able to ride, Vallio?"

"Aye, sure I can. One way to find out, eh?"

The others made ready their mounts and stowed their packs and weapons. Jasper, meanwhile, walked over to where an aching Silmar stiffly made ready to climb into his saddle. The dwarf was gesturing with his hands as he whispered something into the elf's ear and then he quickly returned to his own mount. Silmar nodded.

"Aye, time to go," replied Jasper. "We may get news of the Darkling from the border guards. That's if they went that way."

"They have to," said Yoriando. "There's no other way if you're mounted. Now, if they're all on foot, then they might find a way over the hills and peaks but unlikely. Far too dangerous and it would take them a couple of ten-day weeks, I reckon. No, they have to find a way through the border crossing. Only way, especially with horses as I say."

"Then we must be on our way," advised Varengo. "We have a damned long ride to the border."

"'Ow long?" asked Jasper.

"A tenday week all going well. A couple of days to the East Way and then six to eight days when we reach the Silk Road. The road will be busy with a couple of trading posts and taverns."

Falcon stood with his arm around Taura's waist. "Aye, that is one advantage we have that the darkling don't – ale!" The priestess looked up at him and smiled back.

૭ ૦૯

It actually took them eight days to travel the ninety or so leagues. The roads were good and the days long. They were even able to exchange their mounts at a trading post that was not under the close scrutiny of the Hoshite militias. It was opportune; their own mounts were spent with three horses and a pony in urgent need of re-shoeing. As the days progressed, the road steadily climbed into the low mountains before it rose and fell from one summit to another. Very gradually it curved eastwards so that by the end of the day they had left the foothills and the marshes very far behind them.

"The Darkling have made little attempt to hide their tracks," Silmar observed at one of their rest stops. The group had ridden quite hard all day and the new horses were tired. "They have branched off the great road along this track to the south."

"That track is the old road that climbs up over the peaks," Morendo explained. "That way is covered by a small garrison but is probably easier for a group of Darkling to get through, particularly at night."

"We ought to follow this track, I reckon," advised Varengo.

Two days later they had climbed even further into the mountains where the chilly air caused them to don their travelling cloaks.

Varengo pointed up into the mountains ahead of them. They could just make out a narrow gap between two great, grey, snow-capped mountains. This late in the day, the sun shone from the west giving the peaks an orange tint.

"Look yonder," he called. "Just up there in between those peaks and slightly beyond, is the border crossing point. It is very well guarded. The border guards are led by the Cascantean Corps of Foresters. I expect you've heard of them. In no way could six Darkling, even if they themselves are elite, take on that garrison in hand-to-hand fighting."

The reputation of the formidable Corps of Foresters, the highly-trained elite forces of Cascant, was legendary throughout the lands of Baylea. But, apart from their prowess in battle and their almost fanatical dedication to the Dar-Cascan Royal Family, so also was their chivalry and charisma. Some, who listened to their old-fashioned, somewhat charming way of speaking, regarded them as nothing but pompous, strutting fools. But they were far from it.

"The sun will set soon," Taura called. "If we set up camp here for the night before we climb too high into the cold, when shall we get there?"

"About midday tomorrow," replied Morendo. "You think so, Yori?"

Yoriando nodded in agreement, his gaze fixed on the pass ahead. "Just hope those Darkling aren't waiting for us somewhere nearby off the road."

Silmar thought for a while and slowly rubbed his chin. "They can't know we're behind them or even perhaps ahead of them. We've ridden hard and have had longer hours than they in which to do so."

Darkness fell almost instantaneously in the mountains. They moved a little way from the road but there was no suitable place in which to keep out of sight. Earlier that afternoon, the group had been surprised to see a small goat, with a crude bell around its neck, on the hillside above them. Jiutarô had brought it down with a well-placed arrow. Despite the welcome meal cooked above the small fire, the group spent a very cold night huddled close together against the wall of rock that was their only shelter.

At dawn they continued up the long, winding slope but it was late morning before they breasted the summit between the two massive peaks. The tracks of the Darkling were clearly visible for Silmar to see. He was very puzzled. *How in the name of the gods did they manage to go through the border crossing?* After briefly telling the group of his concerns, he began to follow the tracks with more care.

It was almost midday when he suddenly stopped the group. "I smell smoke in the air," he whispered.

Everyone else stopped still and sniffed at the breeze but they smelled nothing.

"Look, meanin' no disrespect, elf," murmured the dwarf, "but are yer sure it ain't last night's cookin' fire in yer clothes? I can't smell a choddin' thing. An' my nose is choddin' keen!"

They travelled on for another hour and once again Silmar raised a hand and stopped the group.

"Here! Look at this!" he exclaimed as he pointed to the ground. "The road here has been churned up by waiting horses. See the hoof marks? They stopped here awhile. Boot prints, too. But not all the Darkling waited here, some have gone away. Aha!"

All of them tried to look at the marks on the road but it was Jiutarô who called them to a place a few yards ahead. "Here!" he exclaimed.

"Well spotted, Jiutarô," complimented Silmar. "The boot prints climb the slope up towards the hills there. Three of them, I would say. And over here, the prints come back down and jump onto the road!"

"I suppose yer wants to see where they went," growled Jasper. "An' after what happened last time two of us went gallivantin' off. Well, don't say I didn't warn yer. Don't come runnin' back to us if yer gets et by a monster!"

"I won't be long. I think I know what this is about," said Silmar and in a few heartbeats he was gone.

❧　❧

Crouching low and ignoring the dull aches of his recent injuries, the elf followed the tracks for what seemed like ages. He crossed two tall hillocks and, with his keen senses soon smelled smoke once more. It was much stronger in his nostrils this time. He leapt across an icy, gurgling brook and climbed up a rocky incline. At the top, he once again crouched low. He could hear voices.

⤎ ⤏

"E's choddin' lost or 'ad a fall," grumbled Jasper. "'E don't choddin' listen. Frackin' fool of an elf!"

"Jasper! That sort of language is unnecessary! He's only been a while," replied Taura. "He'll be back with us in good health this time."

"In short time I ask Sushi go find Silmar," said Jiutarô. "Don't worry."

"Worried? Me worried? Not worried! Nay! I don't waste mah time worryin' 'bout an elf! Where is 'e?"

⤎ ⤏

Below him straddling the road was the border crossing. A stone hut with small windows stood by the roadside. A low, stout gate was closed across the road.

A good horseman could easily clear that gate, thought the elf.

Four armed foot soldiers dressed in leather armour, two of them with bows, stood by the gate. Near to them stood another figure dressed in a green and brown uniform, a steel helm and highly-polished riding boots with a dark green cape over a very shiny breastplate.

Forty paces back from the gatehouse, but on the northern side of the road, had stood two large wooden buildings. But now, just one remained because the other had been virtually destroyed by a recent fire. It still smouldered and many soldiers were busily clearing anything worth salvaging from the remains. The second wooden structure had minor fire damage to its thatched roof. Silmar shook his head at the sight. Four or five soldiers were carrying out a temporary repair to the roof with a tarpaulin sheet. The area between the buildings had obviously been a corral for in it was three wagons, one of which was also destroyed in the conflagration. A large number of horses were tethered to the fence that still remained. A fourth wagon stood close to the gatehouse and on it was two large boxes.

By the gods! Thatched roofs on these buildings - stupid!

Looking back down the road from his vantage point, Silmar could clearly see the group of adventurers awaiting his return. Having seen enough, Silmar made his way back to the road.

❧ ❧

"It appears the three Darkling climbed up there to get a good look at the border crossing below. It must have been almost laughable for them to come up with a plan so easily, so audacious. The guard's quarters have thatched roofs! Unbelievable! The signs show that they spent some time up there, judging by the remnants of food and even a small fire that they let burn out."

Silmar had described what he saw. The others shook their heads in disbelief as he described the guard post.

"Obviously the bastard Darkling started the fire in the compound as a diversion as they rode through at speed in the confusion," growled Jasper. "Prob'y find that there's usually only one or two guards on the gate. Now they got four but too late. What d'ya think was in them two boxes?"

"I believe they were coffins," replied Silmar. "There were probably two guards on the gate last night."

"It may be wise to say nothing of the Darkling when we pass through," suggested Varengo.

"Possibly," answered Silmar. "But then it will seem strange that there would be two parties using the border crossing within a day or two of each other. I would guess that the soldiers up there do not realise that the first group were Darkling."

"So, we could say that we're huntin' a party o' Darkling that 'ave ridden this way," suggested Jasper. "It's true, ain't it?"

"That will leave us wide open to questioning by the Foresters," Taura warned.

"Well, perhaps," replied Varengo. "Then, maybe not. They may be glad to let us through to resume our chase after the mayhem that was caused."

"Only one way to find out. Let's go and see," said Taura.

❧　☙

CHAPTER 39

CAPTAIN FLAMMARD was a seasoned veteran. He wore his slightly battered but highly-polished breastplate as a badge of honour. His recent battles against orcs, trolls and goblins in the southern Brash Mountains near to Triosande had left his face and upper body badly fire-scarred and with only one arm, his right. Being hailed a hero of the Triosande wars was a matter that shot him to fame as a celebrity but now he was no longer physically capable of commanding a fighting company of Corps of Foresters. Instead he was cast aside to this damned border crossing – a mountain pass rarely-used now that the road was virtually impassable due to too many bad winters and the inability, or unwillingness, of the Polduman Council of Barons to carry out repairs to their own roads.

Captain Flammard was tall at six feet four inches – a Forester had to be over six feet – and, because of his facial scars, he was permitted to wear a trimmed beard. It did not grow well though, there were bald patches because of his injuries. Unexpectedly, the ladies had gathered about him at his recent honouring celebrations.

The Corps was the elite military force in Cascant and he was proud to have retained his commission despite his physical condition. Apart from battle-readiness, they were the force assigned to protect the royal family, the Dar-Cascan dynasty, and although their dark green and brown uniforms were well cared for and their armour very ornate and highly polished, they were far from being ceremonial. The steel from which the helms, breastplates, arm-guards and greaves were made was the strongest and finest in the known lands on the world of Amæus. Every breastplate had an embossed tree upon it that was coloured green. Of a hundred recruits who might apply to become members of the Corps of Foresters, probably only between five and ten would be successful, generally having already earned distinction in battle.

Who came by this way these days? Adventuring parties mainly, hoping for riches in far-off lands and using Cascant as a stopping-off point in their travels eastwards to Kamambia, or even to Hosh, or westwards to the fabled riches in the tortured realm of Faerhome.

. Hah! Nobody ever returned alive from *that* hell-hole. There were no longer any stories of the monstrosities that had once been said to inhabit the ruined palaces and gardens of the once beautiful realm of the elves.

Today, his mind wandered. Neither he nor the men under his command had slept the previous night. Events that night had upset him badly. He knew that questions would be asked over his ability to manage the most tedious and trivial of commands that a battle-proven *Forester* officer could be given. Hooded and caped riders had sped towards the barrier in the night and leapt over it, killing the two guards and setting flame to the thatched roofs of the two guard-houses. One building had been totally destroyed.

Fortunately, the weapons, armour, food and stores had been kept in the other, mostly undamaged building. It was providential indeed that nobody else had been killed. His Sergeant-at-Arms had been outside the building answering a call of nature when the riders had stormed through. He had roused the sleeping men and all of them had survived without injury. Much of their personal equipment had also survived. But Flammard would be in deep trouble over this incident.

Command of a border crossing? Bah! He had not welcomed, nor had he deserved, this posting. He had been briefed to prepare for attachment to the Officers' Battle and Arms training barracks in Marsaise. He was devastated when informed that a much younger captain had landed the job. What experience and benefits would the son of the deposed mayor of Triosande bring to warfare training? Particularly at a time that regular incursions deep into Cascant by orcs, trolls and, allegedly, Darkling required the best training that could be offered by experienced and battle-hardened soldiers. And now, of course, there was the ever-present threat of invasion by Kamambia.

Flammard was in a quandary. He poured himself a generous measure of rum into a glass and swallowed half of it in one gulp. *Oh, gods! That's better.* He knew, of course, that a report needed to be sent to Marsaise immediately. *In my day,* he thought, *I would have sent off a patrol to chase these bastards.* But who now did he have under his command? Motley bunch of ageing foot-soldiers and half a dozen *Foresters* who, like himself, carried one too many scars and needed a mundane place of work.

He placed his glass to one side and shifted a small pile of Travellers' Pass forms to one side. These had needed his attention for many days but, somehow, he could never find the motivation. But now they would have to wait for he had a sensitive report to complete.

He had written most of his report and he picked up his glass of rum. His door banged open and there, framed in the entrance, was his Sergeant-at-Arms, "Duck-face" LeDuk.

"'Twould be nice, Sergeant, if for once thou knocked upon my damned door!"

LeDuk took two steps forward and slammed his right foot onto the floor at the attention.

He whipped his right fist across to his left shoulder in a drill-perfect salute.

"At thy ease, Sergeant."

LeDuk relaxed but the change was barely perceptible.

LeDuk was priceless. He was the perfect right-hand man to have with you on the battlefield. And he too was totally unsuited to life on a border crossing but his age was now against him. His concession to standing at ease was to slightly relax his shoulders.

"Visitors, sah!" the man barked loudly. Flammard winced. LeDuk continued. "Calling themselves Darkling Hunters, sah. Wouldst thou prefer that I march them in, sah?"

"Descibe them, Sergeant."

"They number ten, sah. They have mage and priest. They are well-armed. They act peaceably, sah."

"Bring before me no more than four of them. Leaders or those who would seem the most capable. Also I would ask thyself to be present. They are to leave large weapons on the stoop."

প্ত ২

With Silmar and Varengo leading and Taura and Jasper close behind, the ten riders approached the border crossing barrier with slow and easy caution.

At forty paces from the barrier, a foot-soldier called out to them. "Halt! One only to approach and identify thy party."

Keeping his hands well away from his weapons, Silmar rode forward to the barrier and introduced himself. "I am Silmar Galadhal, Prince of Refuge in the Home Territories, Goodsir. I carry with me a Protectors' token issued by the authorities in the city of Gash. Each of my friends carries a similar token. I can vouch for every one of them."

A man dressed in the green cape and armour of a Corps of Foresters Sergeant-at-Arms stepped across and demanded to know the business of the travellers.

"Stand each of you forwards singly, with thy mount, moreover, each of you is to clearly display thy token," shouted the *Forester*.

Leading her horse, Taura walked forward and stood by Silmar's shoulder.

"Mmm mmm, he's rather nice," murmured the priestess, just loud enough for Silmar to hear.

The elf cocked an eyebrow at her but said nothing.

"I know not the nature of a Samurai," said the man, looking at Jiutarô. "Dost that term relate to thy beast draped about thy shoulders?"

Jiutarô looked uncomprehendingly at the *Forester*.

Fortunately, Taura spoke up for him. "Goodsir, he is from a far-off foreign land and knows little of the Universal tongue and even less of your charming rendition of it. I can tell you that he is a true and trustworthy member of our group, as is everybody standing here before you and those who are yet to be called forward."

"Very well. I warn thee that should thy beast cause mayhem in this kingdom, the full weight of our laws shall descend upon it and upon thee. Bring forward and name the remaining members of thy party. Thou hast yet to make clear thy business here in the Kingdom of Cascant."

"Goodsir," stated Silmar. "We hunt fiends who infest the lands hereabouts."

"Fiends? Explain thyself. What are these fiends?"

"They are the ones who paid you a visit last night. We can tell you exactly what they were, how they rode through and the diversion they created that allowed them to do it. We can even tell you how and from where they spied on your garrison to lay their plans."

"And just whom dost thou think it was that burst through into this most fair Kingdom of Cascant in such violent fashion?"

"Six Darkling, possibly with seven 'orses," called Jasper from behind.

"Darkling!" gasped the Sergeant. His face contorted into a mask of horror and revulsion.

"A seventh lies dead in a ditch some forty leagues along the road behind us," added Varengo. "We hunt the remainders."

"My name is LeDuk, I am Sergeant-at-Arms here. Call in the others of thy party and wait here if thou please."

The man turned and marched smartly but quickly to the remaining large wooden building. A minute later he reappeared and barked out another order. "Four of thy party, leaders preferably, this way."

Silmar gestured to Jasper, Taura and Varengo and they made their way towards the building where LeDuk held open the door.

With Taura leading, the four filed into the building in the footsteps of LeDuk. Inside, the structure was quite plain. It was built of stout wooden logs laid horizontally atop each other. The entrance door was of a very heavy studded oak and the windows were little more than narrow arrow-slits.

The thatched roof, which Silmar eyed with misgiving, was supported on a stout wooden frame. *Hmm, a strong building but the roof is weak and vulnerable*, he thought.

They were shown into a curtained-off section that allowed for an office and sleeping area for the garrison commander. The man rose from a chair and stepped over to greet them. He introduced himself as Captain Flammard of the Cascantean Corps of Foresters.

"So, thou hunt Darkling!" It was a statement that Flammard made, not a question.

"We hunt those Darkling who burst through your border crossing last night," replied Taura.

There was a moment of silence as the officer seemed to digest Taura's statement.

"So thou canst confirm that they carried out this debacle last night then." It was another statement. The Captain placed a heavy weight on a piece of parchment to hold it down while he made notes with his one hand. "Tell me more."

"We know where they spied on your post. I found their tracks as some of them left the road to climb into the hills and I followed their marks because we were puzzled as to how they would pass through the border crossing. We knew they would not risk battle with the Corps of Foresters."

Flammard gave a wry smile. "Why dost foul Darkling enter this kingdom?"

Silmar took over the explanation. "They seek an artefact that they wish to take to their lair in Dannakannon. We wish to find it ourselves first and take it to its rightful place in the Temple of Clamberhan in Carrick Cliffs." The elf's earnest expression gave no hint to the fact that he was telling but a half-truth.

Once again the Captain wrote some notes on the parchment. "Dost thou think that thou canst find these six Darkling and destroy them?" he asked, after a few minutes of writing.

"If we do not tarry here for too long, we believe we can," replied Taura. "We have tracked them for some tenday weeks now, from the west of Polduman, through Hill's Edge and over the mountains, and through the desolation between the two great marshes and then to here."

"A perilous journey indeed. You passed by, unscathed, the Landhold fortress? A Hoshite threat lurks there, I am told."

"Battle had been fought close by there before our arrival," replied Silmar, "and the bodies of many Hosh dead were strewn about the mountain pass."

"And thou dost consider thou hast the capability to stop these Darkling wreaking havoc in this Kingdom." Again, it was a statement.

Silmar nodded.

Flammard wrote once more on the parchment and, with a flourish, signed his name at the bottom. With a little difficulty because of his one arm, he rolled the parchment and sealed it with hot wax. With his quill, he wrote on the outside of the rolled parchment a name.

Flammard took a deep breath and stated that he would, in this instance, drop the formal language accorded by Corps of Foresters to all visitors although its use was habitually ingrained. "The use of it has always been obligatory but it seems that younger officers find it too much of a chore these days. I bid thee, continue with thy quest. But I urge thee to take this report to the Duty Officer at the Marsaise Barracks. Explain that it is an important and urgent report. He is to pass it to the officer named on this parchment."

Flammard took up another parchment and started to write with his quill. He asked Taura to state the names of all her companions. After a few minutes he folded but did not seal, the document. "State my name to any militia guard, soldier, *Forester* or official who will demand to know thy business and show to him this pass. It lists all of thy names. It requests in the name of the Princess Regent that thou are given courtesy and, without let or hindrance, freedom to travel these lands to Marsaise for the purpose of the security of this kingdom. Ride now and take with thee my best wishes. Sergeant, if thou please, escort these travellers to their mounts."

Once outside, LeDuk stood by them as they mounted up onto their horses. As they made ready to ride, he gave them his own farewell.

"Thou hast brought much encouragement to my captain in this time of evil tidings. For that I give thee my appreciation for he is a good man. Take care whilst thou ride for I know that Darkling are scheming and cunning. I am told they poison their blades. A terrible death even from a scratch."

The travellers were soon making haste along the road into Cascant. Meanwhile, Flammard sat down at his desk and drank the remainder of his glass of rum. A solution had materialised and he now felt better than he had since the early hours of the morning.

CHAPTER 40

THE TRACKS OF the Darkling were easy to follow. *Too damned easy, thought Silmar. They may as well have laid a trail using bread crusts.*

It was still early in the afternoon but the day had turned very dismal with a heavily overcast sky. A cool wind was blowing in from the east and rain seemed inevitable. The road taking them from the border crossing was in a far better condition than it had been before in that deep wagon wheel ruts had been filled in with rubble topped with fine grit. The roadsides had been edged with white-painted stones every few yards. But now, the road was little-used except for the traffic of relief troops to the border crossing and rare travellers.

Silmar urged his mount to a canter so that he could scout ahead of the party of riders. When out of sight of his companions, he was shadowed either by Sushi or by one or more of the other riders. With the Darkling clearly not hiding their tracks the risk of ambush was greater than they liked.

The road descended steeply from the mountain pass, often switching sharply back and forward to minimise the steepness of the slopes. There were very few trees high up in the pass but as they entered the foothills, small woods of pine trees eventually gave way to larger forests of oak, birch, elm and willow.

By now, Silmar was becoming concerned. For a while, he had seen little, then nothing, of the Darkling tracks since they had ridden into the lower tree-line. He was convinced the Darkling pony's hooves had been wrapped in thick fabric to disguise the sign. He also feared that the companions may have ridden past the Darkling while they were resting in one of the stands of trees higher up in the foothills after their successful surprise breakthrough at the border post.

The road wound through a deep gully between two steep cliffs of rock. Alongside the road gurgled an icy mountain stream from which they refilled their waterskins. In places the rocky track itself had become wet and slippery. Silmar waited for his companions to catch him up and advised that they dismount and walk.

A low whistle from Jiutarô, who had ridden forward a few yards, caught their attention. He called softly. "Broken shoe track here! And look!"

The Samurai leaned forward and picked up a small piece of black fabric that had lain in between two small boulders. A small distance away, clearly shown in the mud, was a hoof print. The notch in the horseshoe told them all they needed to know.

"Hah! Darkling not see he lose cloth," laughed the Samurai. He lifted it to Sushi's nose for her to smell.

"They are still ahead of us but may have rested somewhere ahead," said Varengo. "Probably be a good idea for us to keep quiet and take care. That Samurai is almost as good a tracker as you and Vallio, Silmar!"

"Aye, you're right there. But look," responded Silmar, "See the tracks. Their hooves bite deep; they are riding harder than are we. It seems they are making for the great forest ahead."

From their vantage point high in the eastern slopes of the low peaks, and high above the Kingdom of Cascant, they could see a huge area of dense forest to the south east.

"That is the King's Forest," stated Morendo. "He would hunt there in better days. The Darkling are probably travelling there to make it easier on their eyes."

"And to travel unseen," added Falcon.

"Aii, more monsters?" asked Jiutarô. "Every place we go are monsters. This is mad land!"

"Aye, yer not wrong there, Mishmash," replied Billit. "Yer must be in a really boring world if yer got no monsters in yer forests."

"Boring? What is boring?" answered the Samurai.

"He means quiet and peaceful," responded Taura with a chuckle. "He means you live in a world of butterflies and flowers. Haha!"

"Nay. My homeland, Nippon, is place of war and of, erm, *Ronin* wave men we call. They Samurai with no masters who cast aside *bushido* code and be outlaws."

"But are you not also masterless, Jiutarô?" asked Taura. "You have said that your master was killed."

"Not yet masterless. When my duty, and that of my brothers, to, um, Asano-San is honoured then we become *Ronin*. I must return home to my land first. But I think we not live that far."

"I don't understand," whispered Taura although she had an inkling of what he meant. It was not a thought she felt comfortable with.

But Jiutarô said no more on the matter despite more questioning from the others. He stared morosely at the track ahead of them.

"What other dangers are there in your world of Nippon?" asked Varengo after a short while. He had been totally transfixed by Jiutarô's descriptions of his own world and customs over the last few tenday weeks but rarely was the Samurai prepared to speak much of them.

"We have the *tengu!*" he whispered. "Hai. They wood creatures, like your goblins. A man-bird. We say to our children not stay out in dark or *tengu* will get you! I think it is only a not-true that they are, oh, I know not the word."

"A myth?" replied Taura. "A story?"

"Hai! A story! They speak them in *bunraku.*"

"The what?" chorused most of the group.

"Aii! The bunraku!" Jiutarô was becoming a little exasperated with trying to explain in his limited Universal tongue. "Bunraku it where people give story to people who watch."

"'E means a theatre," called Jasper. "So they have these *tengu* in theatre plays?"

The Samurai look a little confused but nodded in agreement anyway. "They hand people, er, little people move on hand?"

"A puppet theatre?" asked Varengo. "A bunraku is a puppet theatre where they have the tengu?"

"Hahaha! Hai! Hai!" Jiutarô slapped his thigh in triumph. "But we Samurai think these bunraku for *chonin,* er, people of town, them have time for waste."

As they continued their ride down onto the foothills, they continued to chat between each other. Silmar stopped the riders as darkness began to fall. He soon found an ideal place to camp and in the time Varengo had prepared the fire, Morendo and Jiutarô returned from their hunt with a young roe-deer. There would be enough meat to feed them for two days or more.

Once again, Silmar gave sound advice to the party. "We must keep the fire low again during the night, because we don't know where the Darkling are and the glow may be seen from below."

ೲ ೱ

"Fool!" gasped the Darkling captain, Tak'Haerla. "You have lost the wrapping from the hoof. Dhe'Ganlla, unless you wish to share the fate of your brother, you will damn well hide the crack in that shoe or I shall place a similar one in your skull."

That morning, the Darkling group had entered the forest along a seldom-used track. Clearly, it would lead them to somewhere useful but it was necessary that they should do so unobserved. After weeks of travelling in what for them were bright moon and star-lit nights, they all suffered from headaches and nausea and some of their eyes were badly affected.

"You, Dhe'Ganlla," barked Tak'Haerla, "will backtrack and ensure all sign of that hoof is erased."

Dhe'Ganlla cursed under his breath and shot away as ordered; he knew that to object to the great amount of risk he was being placed under would seal his fate. The others dismounted and stretched their aching limbs while their captain continued to speak. All of them had built up an unhealthy hatred of their leader. Quiet words had often been spoken suggesting a blade during the daylight while he slept but that was generally the point where the plotting ended. Not one of them had the courage to do it himself.

"My warriors," started Tak'Haerla. "I am now certain that we have passed that mixed group of riders. I am surprised that I did not sense the damned white elf when we passed by them."

The dark elves looked at each other. *Who does he think he is?* were the thoughts buzzing around their heads. *Son of a minor prince of Dannakanonn he is but with the ego of a demigod.* But he had kept them all alive, well, except for one of them, all the way from the Shadow World lair of the Grey Dwarve's City of Shade.

"But we do know their destination. And we know the route they will take, for there is only one practical way if they are following us. But we now have the difficulty of travelling through this land which will be more hostile to us than any other that we have passed through so far. We must continue our travels in the night but we do need to rest up for two days. I believe this track will take us to an ideal place because all tracks lead to something. Continue to place your trust in me and I shall lead you through. Do not fool yourselves into believing that I do not know of your plotting. Remember that not one of you gathered before me now could lead the rest of you through these lands. And I shall not hesitate to snuff the last breath of life from the body of anyone foolish enough to try to end mine."

Total silence filled the air about the group of Darkling warriors. They shuffled their feet and stole brief glances at one another. Egotistical Tak'Haerla may be but he was also correct in saying that he was the only leader capable of leading them through these dangerous lands with some degree of safety.

Dhe'Ganlla appeared soon after and saw his companions standing silently together.

"Say nothing," said one of them to him.

"Mount up," called Tak'Haerla. "We are moving deeper into this forest. Keep silent and keep a careful watch."

❦ ❧

Jasper woke the comrades before dawn and Varengo relit the fire. All of them were very cold but the sky looked clear and they all hoped for a fine, warm day after so many days of cold winds and icy nights.

They took dawn meal while they rode. It was mid-afternoon when Silmar raised a hand and bade them to stop. The skies had clouded over during the morning and it was now much cooler. Leaden clouds moved eastward, beneath them were grey sheets of rain but they hoped that, with Neilea's fortune, the rain would miss them.

"The hoof prints are very mixed up here," said the elf. "There's a track there on the right but the hoof marks are not easy to follow in the sand. Now, where the track becomes muddy again down there, I can't see the mark of a cloven horseshoe. But there is recent sign of many horses having gone up that track and it's my guess that the Darkling have ridden that way."

"Well, let's check it out then," suggested Taura.

"I was hoping you would say that," replied Silmar. "You and me again, Jiutarô?" To the rest of the companions, he added "We may not be back til after dark so fear not until dawn comes."

Once more, the Samurai changed into his grey-blue *gi* and took up his blades, bow and quiver. Together, they took off down the track on foot keeping to the shadows as best they could. Sushi circled above the trees and kept the two warriors in sight. The rest of the group led their mounts off the road and kept in concealment.

❦   ❧

Once inside the forest, the pair made their way stealthily off to one side of the track and weaved through the trees. In this way their progress was slower than they hoped. They caught sight of the cleret-wing dragon occasionally as she silently soared and wheeled above the trees and once or twice she landed and twittered. Jiutarô confirmed that she had seen nothing. An hour after they left the group, Sushi landed on a low branch and hissed a warning.

"Little way ahead," whispered Jiutarô. "Hut and many horse. Maybe Darkling, she not see. Man dead outside hut, two more dead at side." He puffed in relief at the effort it had taken him to describe the scene.

"We need to get back to the others as quickly as we can," whispered Silmar. "Gods, I can feel the artefact affecting me. It is making my head ache and if I had eaten anything recently I would be looking at it now. We will need some reinforcements!"

They set off at the run and were soon at the road with the others. Varengo agreed with Silmar that half of them should return to watch the cabin. Briefly, they discussed a plan.

❦   ❧

Dusk was beginning to fall when Silmar, Taura, Jiutarô and Vallio trotted along the track into the forest. It was almost dark when the little group crept to the edge of a clearing and dropped to the ground. In the last light the terrible events that had happened became plain to see.

The track through the forest had emerged into the clearing. The small, low log cabin, with its thatched roof, stood in the centre of the glade. The door to the hut was closed and its windows shuttered. To the right hand side of the hut a large wagon had been drawn across the front of a small barn. To its left side was a large corral in which there were many black ponies. A large stack of wood cut into various lengths and widths stood behind the hut. In the fading light, the watchers took in these details in an instant. It was the other sights that drew their gazes.

In front of the hut laid the body of a woodsman although the cause of his death was not obvious. Two more bodies were sprawled by the wagon. One, clearly a woman, was heavily bloodstained. The other body was that of a very young lad, probably no older than ten summers. A dead dog also lay in front of the hut.

"Poor bastards!" mouthed Taura with sadness reflected in her eyes. The others nodded.

They drew back a few yards from the edge of the clearing and waited. It was soon very dark but there was sufficient moonlight filtering through the trees for the watchers to see any movement should it occur. They heard no sound from inside the hut.

But then, after an hour of watching, the door of the hut opened and a dark figure stepped out.

Darkling!

Vallio reached for an arrow but Silmar's hand stopped him.

The figure urinated against the side of the hut and returned inside. Everything was once again quiet.

Silmar whispered to his comrades. "I'm going to scout around the edge of the clearing. I will be some time but do not try to follow me. All will be well. I do still feel nauseous though."

"Don't puke up," Vallio hissed back. "It'll stink and give us away."

Taura snorted stifling a laugh.

The elf silently melted into the darkness.

ക്ക ക്ക

He moved cautiously to the right keeping his profile low to the ground and using every bush and shrub for cover. His enhanced elven dark-sight showed every twig and root that might cause him to make a sound or stumble.

It was not the Darkling he was looking for though. Another figure lurked in the undergrowth at the edge of the clearing.

With one hand on his dagger and the other carefully moving branches and debris out of his path as he moved, he used his dark-sight to look for the position where the mystery watcher lay. *There*! Just twenty short paces away.

Silmar kept very still and waited for about half an hour. The watcher was good; hardly a movement could be seen. The elf's dark-sight showed him that the watcher wore a hooded garment, probably a cloak. There would be little threat from this individual but for now, the elf would not risk any noise caused by apprehending or, if necessary, killing him.

He crept back and signalled to the group to follow him along the track. Silently, they left the clearing behind and walked for a couple of hundred paces.

"We were not the only watchers there," he said softly. "I saw another."

"What?" gasped Taura. "But who? Gods!"

"Mayhap there was someone the Darkling didn't kill," suggested Vallio. "We must maintain a watch on the hut. The Darkling may leave during the night and resume their journey."

"I think not," Silmar replied. "It is well past the middle of the night and it will be getting light in a few hours. They are there to rest, I am certain. They would not have killed the woodsman and his family *and* occupy his hut unless they planned to be there a day or two. No, I think they will stay the night and the coming day and move out at last light. Or maybe even longer."

"So what shall we do then?" asked Vallio.

"I feel awful, the artefact is affecting me badly, but I shall go back to the clearing in a while," replied Silmar. "I want to try and find out what is happening to see who is watching them and think of a plan. You all go back to join the others and when it is light again I shall return to you."

As the others returned to the road, Silmar turned and inched carefully to the edge of the clearing. This time, he saw that the Darkling had posted a sentry outside the hut. At first the Darkling stood and occasionally paced back and forth, his eyes scanning the forest, but after a short while he seemed to get bored with this and sat down on the doorstep instead with his hood pulled low over his face. After an hour, Silmar moved off to a place where he could get a view of both the hut and the mystery watcher.

Two hours passed by and dawn would soon break. There had been two changes of sentry by then and the new one was clearly not interested in doing his job properly. The Darkling promptly dropped his head and dozed.

There was a slight rustle in the bushes five paces in front of Silmar. It was followed by a small sigh. Silmar crouched low. Silently, the figure rose and backed out of the place of concealment.

Straight into Silmar's grasp.

Jiutarô took over the watch from Yoriando just as the first light of dawn began to show. He carefully and silently walked around the perimeter of the campsite to satisfy himself that there was nothing to threaten the safety of the sleeping adventurers. Sushi, suddenly alert, sat upright on his left shoulder. Two figures approached the camp in the grey light of dawn. So silent were they that they had remained unnoticed by Sushi until they were barely fifty yards away. A whisper behind him made him start.

"It's the elf!" hissed Billit. "Hey sorry, Mishmash. I just got up for a piss! Oo's that with 'im?"

Jiutarô slowly let out a breath of relief and he stepped forward to greet the elf. A small figure, dressed in a dark-green, hooded smock that was belted around the waist, stepped forward. The tight-fitting, light-green hose was tucked into soft brown leather boots that rose almost to the knees. An arm reached up to pull back the hood that covered the head.

The face that emerged took Jiutarô completely by surprise such was the beauty that had been revealed. The well-tanned face was framed by a mass of copper-red hair, the curls of which tumbled to her shoulders. The features, however, were more akin to those of an elf despite the uncharacteristic hair. As she turned her head to look at Jiutarô, her ears were confirmation enough of her elven race. She was armed with a slim shortsword, a hunting dagger and a quiver of arrows at her belt. It was her bow though, that caught Jiutarô's attention. Its design was of a type rarely seen, in that the two ends curved forward. Elven bows occasionally had this characteristic which provided additional power behind the arrow.

"Put yer tongue back inside yer head, Mishmash!" murmured Billit.

"Well met, Jiutarô," called Silmar. "I have a guest for our dawn meal. But first she needs to warm herself by the fire, if you would be so kind to escort her."

The Samurai took a deep breath and stepped forward offering his hand. The young lady took it with a nervous smile. Never before had a woman caused Jiutarô's heart to beat as it did now. As she sat by the fire she rubbed her left shoulder and grimaced in pain.

"Is shoulder hurt?" he asked her. "Can I help?"

She eyed the little dragon with curiosity but said nothing. She merely nodded and showed him the painful area. He rubbed his hands briskly together for the space of a few heartbeats and gently rubbed her aching muscle. When he was finished she circled her arm to test her shoulder and gave him a smile of appreciation.

"Much improved. Thank you," she whispered.

Sushi had climbed down from Jiutarô's shoulders while he gave the girl his attention. The cleret-wing dragon now sat in front of her feet and looked into her eyes.

"Does she talk to you?" the girl asked him.

"She does," he replied. "I see what her eyes see."

"You are honoured, you know. It is rare for a human to have such a bond with a cleret-wing dragon. She speaks to me too, she says she loves you. She is fortunate that you are so kind to her."

"I happy she my friend. My future may not so good. Doom hang over my head. I have my *giri*, er, debt to repay. I tell you one day. Or Silmar if you ask of him. What is your name?"

"I am Caeron of the King's Wood. I saw my good friend, DuCote the forester, and his family killed by the Darkling. So I watched and waited while they slept. I did not sleep. Not for more than two days. I knew they would be too many for me but I wanted vengeance. I saw when you and your friends came to watch. Silmar the High Elf saw me but I was glad of it. You see, because I wanted to meet you, friend of the cleret-wing dragon."

"But why? Only because Sushi my friend?"

"Mostly, not just that but it does make you special for a human. It is something, oh! Now I am getting embarrassed! I think perhaps I have said too much. Forgive me. I must sleep. I am so tired."

"Then sleep here, you will be safe. I am Yazama Jiutarô, Samurai of Ako Province and will watch over you as will Sushi."

She yawned. "Ako? I have not heard of this. Is it far?"

"Hai." Jiutarô shrugged but said nothing more. It would not have made a difference if he had, she would not have heard. She lay down by the fire and had immediately drifted off to sleep.

Jiutarô fetched his blanket and spread it over her. With an unspoken message into Sushi's eyes, the cleret-wing dragon curled up beside the sleeping Caeron.

"You have a new friend," laughed Silmar as Jiutarô walked over to him. "She spoke not a word to me from the time that I caught her watching the Darkling but she seems to have taken well to you. She is beautiful, is she not, my friend?"

"I not see woman of such beauty. But make me sad, I know I will, um, desire her. It cannot be for doom to come."

"She is a half-elf, Jiutarô. That is born of a union between one of the race of men and another of elven-kind. I would say she is between fifteen and eighteen summers. She dresses and arms herself like a hunter and carries the best bow I have ever seen. I would love to have one such as that. It looks like one from the old days of Faerhome. She has the strength in her arms and shoulders needed to pull it. Do not be afraid to care for her, Jiutarô, but as long as you make her aware of your predicament. She will then be able to decide for herself the path she will follow. I notice that you cannot take your eyes off her. Sushi also likes her."

"She like Sushi too. Her name is Caeron of King's Wood. Dead family her friends."

As the adventurers rose one-by-one, they all cast curious glances at the sleeping figure beside the fire. Silmar took them away from the fire and, with Jiutarô, explained the situation.

"Oh, aye," added Silmar, "I think that Jiutarô is more than a little captivated by this young lady!"

The Samurai blushed a little and turned away. Surprisingly, the others refrained from teasing him. This, however, was probably more as a result of the stern expression on Taura's face than of any politeness on their part.

The companions busied themselves with looking after their horses, saddles, equipment and weapons for the rest of the morning. The days were much warmer now that they were out of the mountains and much of their filthy clothing was now laid out to dry across rocks or the branches of trees.

At around midday, Caeron stirred. She sat up, her luxurious hair in disarray. "Jiutarô?" she called in a tremulous voice.

He strode across to her and knelt by her side. He placed a reassuring hand on her head and, reaching for her hand, he helped her to her feet. She did not release his hand when she stood up.

"By the gods!" gasped Varengo. "She's lovely!"

"She is indeed," replied Taura, "and it seems she only has eyes for Jiutarô. Stop panting, men, you're using up all the air!"

She suddenly, and unexpectedly, found herself comforted by Falcon's arm as it gently found its way around her waist. There had been little opportunity for them to spend time together since their brief intimacy in the Shadow World. She had even found that she distanced herself from Falcon, perhaps fearing that the effects of her prayers would be lessened at a time of dire need or even that Falcon might place himself or the others in peril when trying to protect her.

"I think we need to come up with a plan for dealing with the Darkling," suggested Varengo.

"Aye, I've been thinking about that," replied Silmar. "I have an idea. Well, you know that we are most vulnerable just before dawn, aye?"

"That's when the watch is called the *graveyard watch*," responded Jasper. "'Cause everything looks grey in the dull light an' we're all tired."

"That's right. So is it correct to assume that the Darkling graveyard shift is at dusk when their eyes can begin to cope with the onset of darkness?"

"Ahh! I do understand," said Varengo.

"A good time for them to die," added Caeron.

୬ ୬

The bodies of the damned forester and his mate and brat are beginning to smell, thought the watching Dhe'Ganlla. *Ach, how my head aches in this sunlight.*

The man had put up a valiant fight while his family looked on and screamed in terror. A bolt shot from Takhaerta's light crossbow silenced the woman. As the boy rushed to his mother's dying body Takhaerta silenced him too, his hands around the boy's neck, squeezing until the bones cracked.

As the horrified face of the forester looked on in shock, a blade had entered his chest from behind and clove through his heart. At the time, Dhe'Ganlla wanted to suggest that the bodies be moved into the forest but it did not do to tell Takhaerta his business. After all, had not Dhe'Ganlla already put himself in enough of a difficult position already? This was why he had earned himself this daylight watch.

He was just moments away from being relived. By Adelenis, he was hungry. His mouth felt dry and tasted as if he had been eating horse shit. And, oh, his aching head! He turned his head towards the door as he heard the latch being lifted. But at the same time he sensed, more than saw, on the periphery of his vision, a movement by the edge of the clearing. His head whipped back but the setting sun glared in his face.

As the door to the hut groaned in its opening, all the hells of the Void seemed to break loose. He did not know whom it was coming out to take his place but a yell from the doorway caused a flurry of movement from inside the hut.

A ball of white-hot fire streaked as fast as an arrow, from the edge of the clearing, narrowly missing Dhe'Ganlla, and shot through the open doorway of the hut.

❧   ☙

"I need to get a little closer," whispered Billit as he lay in the bracken at the edge of the clearing. "I'm too far away and the *fire blast* will explode in front of the hut."

"The next Darkling will come out any moment now," replied Silmar. "How much closer do you need to be?"

"A few paces, that's all."

"Look, you are quite small and the grass should hide you. If it looks like you will be discovered, we will make some sort of diversion. Off you go."

"What? Crawl out on me belly?"

"Aye. Quick! Now!"

Slowly and quietly, Billit crawled through the grass. His small stature and his recently-discovered innate ability to move almost unseen enabled him to easily move close enough for his needs.

The scraping sound of the door latch caught Billit's attention immediately. As the Darkling sentry turned his head to look at his relief, Billit rose to his feet. With a movement of his hands and a muttered phrase, a bright ball of flame the size of his fist was launched directly at the opening door. The emerging Darkling gave a shout of alarm and the bolt of flame shot past his chest into the hut.

There was a mighty *whoomph* as the *fire blast* erupted inside the hut. The open door was blown clean off its leather hinges and catapulted the emerging Darkling way out into the clearing. Flame flared out of the doorway and windows and through the many narrow cracks in the log walls. Tongues of flame and smoke rose from the thatched roof.

Caeron and Silmar simultaneously rose to her feet, each of them bracing their bow with arrow at the ready. Silmar's arrow streaked across the clearing, finding its target; the centre of the chest of the Darkling who had been standing on guard during the late afternoon. The black figure dropped to the ground. Caeron, meanwhile, slowly released her bowstring and replaced the arrow into her quiver. She placed her bow on the ground.

No sounds came from inside the hut amid the conflagration that consumed the interior and the thatched roof. Within seconds, the hut was a great pyre of flames.

The Darkling that had been blown out of the doorway of the hut made feeble attempts to rise up onto his hands and knees. Before anybody could stop her, Caeron ran across to him and, without emotion, plunged her hunting knife straight through the back of his neck and into the depths of his skull. His look of fear and shock as he died had no effect on the girl. As she pulled out the knife, its blade dripping with gore, the dead Darkling pitched forward onto the ground.

"For DuCote and his wife and child," cried Caeron aloud.

The forest was dark by the time that the flames of the burning hut died down. Silmar and Jasper went over to the smouldering remains and looked inside. After a few minutes, they stepped back out to Caeron and Jiutarô who were waiting together.

"There is one missin'," growled Jasper. "We only 'as five bodies in this clearing. We better get back to the others choddin' quick. Where's yer little dragon, Jiutarô?"

∽ ∾

Takhaerta heard the shout from his warrior and immediately feared the worst. With a single fluid movement, he crashed head-first through a rear window just as the hut exploded in a mass of fire.

Pain enveloped his legs and back as the fire engulfed his lower body and he landed on the ground at the rear of the hut. Here the grass was long and he rolled over and over, successfully extinguishing the flames. But still the pain drove rational thought from his brain.

As his mind slowly regained control, he crawled away from the burning hut. The edge of the clearing seemed a vast distance away but the instinct to survive this day pushed him on. A shallow stream barred his way but he rolled his body into it. Oh the sweet relief from the pain!

He lay in the flowing water for a long time during which the glow from the burning hut grew dull. He heard the voices of his accursed attackers. *Damn them, damn the surface rats*! Then there was silence. He closed his eyes against the glare of the daylight but heard a minute rustle nearby.

He raised his head to look towards the centre of the clearing and gazed straight into the eyes of a small dragon-like creature. The creature gave a hiss and bared its teeth at him. He heard a swish and felt a new pain as something sharp embedded itself hard in the side of his neck.

Then his world went slowly cold and dark.

❧ ❧

CHAPTER 41

THEY RODE AND walked northwards in bright sunshine for many days and passed much traffic on the road, a little of which were farmers' wagons carrying farm produce to the capital city of Marsaise. The majority, however, was Corps of Foresters soldiers and squads of militia moving in each direction.

Silmar had felt no effects from his burden since the Darkling party was destroyed but he occasionally checked for its unpleasant but reassuring presence in his pack. Once they emerged from the King's Forest, heading north towards the great capital city of Marsaise, the road was so busy they often had to walk or ride off the road to make progress. Even when on the road, they had to dodge piles of horse and ox dung, all of which were swarming with flies. In the heat, the smell was often quite overpowering. The Cascantan *Foresters* regularly issued challenges for them to identify themselves. The pass provided by Captain Flammard carried much authority and the companions were given polite and prompt passage. The group was repeatedly advised to report to the first major garrison they arrived at to register their movements.

Six days after leaving the King's Forest, they crested a low rise and there before them was the great city of Marsaise. Even from a distance of two or three miles they could clearly see that it was a great walled city of stone buildings, spires, minarets and towers, great houses and palaces. Beyond it was the great inland sea. The Dragonwash, Falcon had said it was called.

They joined the long queue of travellers and traders at the city gate and eventually their Protectors' tokens were checked together with the pass issued by Captain Flammard.

The Corps of Foresters guard called across a number of militia guards and ordered the leaders of the companions to step into the guard hut. Startled, Taura and Silmar did so.

"What's goin' on?" asked Jasper.

"I think I know," Varengo replied.

The Sergeant-at-Arms waved Flammard's pass at the pair. "Thou hast one more member of thy group than is listed therein by Captain Flammard," he explained.

"Ah we can explain –" began Silmar. He was surprised that no other challenge had indicated this omission on their ride from the King's Forest.

A *Forester* officer entered the room.

The Sergeant-at-Arms whipped a salute. "Sir, the names do not fully match –"

"Obviously an oversight on Captain Flammard's part," interrupted a Forester captain. "Allow me to amend the list."

He inscribed Caeron's name on the list and added his personal mark. "When thou show this to another post, there shalt be no further difficulty. Thy weapons are to be peace-bonded. Thou canst continue to carry them because of thy tokens but thou must have them all sealed to their scabbards with peace-bonding cords. Break thou this cord and thou must explain thy reason. Withdraw thy weapon in any place and thou will be subject to the full weight of the laws of the governance of the City of Marsaise and of Her Majesty the Princess Regent. The use of magical or holy spells for malevolent purposes is forbidden. Thy tokens and the document allow us to trust thee. Remember that thy tokens also empower the governance of this City, of any other city, town or community, and of the Kingdom, to call upon thee to act for us in event of times of need. To refuse is not viewed well and may mean that the Kingdom is closed to thee in the future. However, thou may feel free enjoy fully the hospitality of this fair city."

Relieved, Taura gave her thanks.

"I am Captain Breul. My good friend Captain Flammard is highly respected in this city. Take thou this letter to the Barracks, yonder, and a force will be sent to deal with the Darkling party."

"We destroyed them six days back," replied Taura. "Not one remains alive."

"By the great gods!" exclaimed the man. "Do thou as I bid and thou may expect a handsome reward, of this I am certain. My man shall escort thee."

The *Forester* officer saluted the party and bowed respectfully to Taura in recognition of her deity's holy symbol.

"By the god's, they know which way is up in this city, don't they," mumbled Billit as Taura and Silmar rejoined the party.

"Everything is up when it relates to you, hahaha!" joked Jasper.

"Idiot!" replied the gnome. "I'm as tall as you – taller, even! What's all this thee, thou and thy, anyway. That Flammard was the same."

"It's a mark of respect that the Corps of Foresters have to use when conversing with their leaders and with visitors," explained Silmar. "It's tradition. Many High Elves who perhaps have had little exposure to the outside world, speak the same."

It wasn't until they had made their way on foot, walking their mounts and pack-pony through the checkpoint with their escort leading the way, that they could see the city boasted libraries, theatres, street performers, street-markets and even the famed great market and fayre with its annual warrior tournaments.

"It don't stink here like it does in Westron Seaport an' Nor'wald City," observed Jasper. "There's not much shi-, er, I mean open sewers, in the street 'ere. Lots of animal pooh though!"

Taura pointed out where groups of men, all chained together and armed with wooden shovels, were picking up most of the animal dung. Each group they encountered was being guarded by a couple of members of *Foresters*.

"Convict gangs," said Silmar. "What a good idea. Work for your keep and give something back to the community! They should do that everywhere."

The escort led them through a gate in a long wall. On his formal greeting, the gate was opened and the companions were led through.

One pair of eyes followed them with interest. The owner of those eyes put his fingers over his tunic and felt for a small pendant that hung there. The pendant marked him as a member of a secretive society which, if discovered, would place him in great danger.

༄ ༅

"Honoured ladies and gentlemen," called a rich baritone voice behind them.

They had been led into a reception chamber that was richly decorated with ornately-engraved wood panelling, beautiful silk tapestries depicting hunting and battle scenes and great colourful vases and urns. Soft, thick carpets covered the marble floors and glass chandeliers with glowing globes hung from the ceiling spreading a soft light throughout the great room. A sweet smell of flowers filled the room and incense burners spread their richness into the air.

Their escort had led them in but left hurriedly as if not wanting to meet the owner of that room.

They spun around as the deep voice boomed at them from the door.

"I am Kordern-dahuhl. Perhaps you have heard of me?"

There was a gasp as Niblet stepped forwards in front of the group of adventurers. He dropped to one knee. "M-my Lord," he stammered. "I am Niebillettin, Mage, a Chthonic gnome from the Brash Mountains and your obedient servant."

There were few in the whole of Baylea who had not heard of the mighty arch-wizard of Cascant; once second in power only to that of the king-in-exile, Barsani Dar-Cascan VIII. It was suspected that he now acted as advisor to the exiled king's daughter, Laurellien, the crown princess of Cascant, and its Regent. She had now taken on the mantle of protector of the kingdom and had led the forces that held the monstrous hordes at bay in the north. She had earned a reputation for being a tenacious leader and a resourceful war-tactician and was much loved by her followers. Rumours had abounded for a couple of years that Kordern-dahuhl had disappeared, probable with the King-in-exile.

"Oh, get back up. I shall have no mage grovelling before me."

All of the companions suddenly felt insignificant in the presence of this infamously powerful man. The arch-wizard was tall and thin, with a straggly beard that hung down to his breastbone. His hair was unkempt as if he had just climbed out of bed. But the eyes were bright-green and piercing. He wore a light blue silk gown that had seen better days many years before.

Standing behind him was another man, smaller but much smarter in dress. No introduction was given for this man but his appearance and bearing marked him as a person of importance and influence.

"I understand that you have averted a potential incursion by Black Elves," he began. "The Princess Regent has returned to the palace here after having been under much pressure of late, what with the loss of Triosande in recent years and her repetitive attempts to retrieve it. Her vigour is currently low now otherwise I am sure she would have been keen to meet those who have destroyed Darkling. Ah, but you look surprised at the seriousness of how we greet this news. Do not underestimate Darkling; we certainly have learned the hard way not to. We have had little success over the years in tracking, catching and eliminating Darkling who come into this kingdom to spread terror and death. But it seems you have triumphed. Which of you will speak to me of the way in which you vanquished the foe?"

Taura nudged Silmar who stepped forward to explain how they had tracked a Darkling assassin through the Shadow World and destroyed him, only to find themselves on the heels of seven more Darkling riders. He continued with an outline of how they had tracked them for many tenday-weeks until their path through the mountain border post took them to the King's Forest. Not once did the great Kordern-dahuhl or his companion interrupt although the unnamed man scratched with a quill on a sheet of vellum that was mounted on a piece of slate.

"Good! Good! I shall pass this on to Her Majesty momentarily," exclaimed the arch-mage. "Did you get all that, er, erm?" Kordern-dahuhl did not wait for a response. "We must go now. Affairs of state and that sort of thing but my man here will look after you." Without another word, he turned, albeit rather unsteadily, and sped out of the room.

Still no introduction was given by this other man. He was of middle years with a recently clean-shaven face if the numerous cuts and scratches were any guide, and with thick, grey eyebrows that Taura would have liked to take a pair of shears to. He was dressed in a garb typical of a man in the position of a senior administrator with voluminous grey pantaloons, a loose, white silk shirt and a long, black tabard that reached almost to his knees.

"I have here a modest reward for your trouble," the man began. His voice wheezed as he spoke, not surprising as he strongly smelled of pipe-smoke. With a little effort, he handed Silmar a leather bag the size of a man's heart.

"I, er, we thank you, er," he stammered. "But we did not –" He hefted the bag expecting coins to weigh more heavily.

"Never mind that!" he interrupted brusquely. "Take it. It has been hard-earned. You lost a member of your group. You will be accorded the freedom of travel in the kingdom without hindrance. Simply show this scroll to whomsoever you have dealings with and you will be well-treated." He handed Silmar a silver scroll-case.

The man turned and marched out of the door. A few moments later their escort stepped in and bade them to follow him.

Outside the gates the stunned companions gazed at each other in silence. Their escort saluted and made his way back to the city gate.

"Well," said Jasper. "Open it then. What's in the bag? Silver?"

Silmar released the cord and opened the bag.

"Oh! It is not just coins," he whispered. "Gems! Lots of them! Gold coins beneath. Feel how heavy the bag is."

"We better share them out," suggested Varengo, "because a single one of us can't wander around this city with such a fortune in treasure. To a tavern I suggest."

In an inn that went by the name of *The Greased Pig*, each of them gazed at their own share of the gold, ten gold crowns and twenty gems each. For Varengo and his men, it was a fortune the like of which they had never seen before. Caeron's hand shook as she looked at her own pile of treasure, shocked that this much wealth existed – and it was all hers. She looked from the gold coins and gems that lay in her hands to Jiutarô and back again with an expression of amazement.

"What shall I do with all this, Jiutarô?" she whispered.

He srugged his shoulders. "Do good things," he said softly.

"Some of us need new clothes, boots, weapons and armour," suggested Varengo. "We should go to the markets and see what we can find."

Falcon and Taura used their charm to encourage the innkeeper to agree to the group leaving their horses in the inn's corral. Recognising the opportunity to make some money, the innkeeper demanded payment that would normally be considered extortionate.

"It is the city's spring market and fayre, after all," he insisted. "Ye won't get no place no cheaper. I got a sleepin' chamber for all've ye iff'n ye wants it. Eleven o' yer, is it? Fifty-five gold will see you 'n' yer nags cared for this night. Yer will need yer bedrolls though."

"Just one night? Hold the chamber for us," answered Taura. "We shall check on our ponies and horses later."

Falcon drew himself up to his not inconsiderable height. "Make sure they are well cared for," he growled. "Half the payment now, other half when we collect."

The innkeeper nodded vigorously, spat on the palm of his hand and offered it to Falcon to seal the agreement.

The group followed the crowds of travellers, mainly city-folk, traders and tinkers, through the city. Many roadside stalls had been set up providing meats, stews and ales but these were poor in quality. Water carriers made their way through the crowds offering a cup of cool, clear water for a copper coin. Their sing-song cries of *"Coolie, coolie!"* resonated across the streets and squares.

A large grassed area within the walls of the city was covered in brightly coloured tents, covered wagons and stalls. People thronged the spaces as they moved from one seller to another.

"Watch your purses," warned Silmar. "Stay together, do not separate. Watch out for each other."

They had become accustomed to openly wearing their now bulging purses for many weeks. There had been no threat of theft and they had given no thought to keeping their few coins safe. Now though, it was different. The companions discussed what they should now do but agreed not to separate at this time. Their four fighters needed weapons and armour and decided that in a while they would peel off and scour the weapons sellers.

They sauntered past a vast variety of traders. Almost every tent had tables and stalls selling wondrous cloths and silks, semi-precious stones, shells and metals, fur head-wear and cloaks, and boots for riding and for walking. There was old and new armour and weapons of many types. Other stalls exhibited exotic foods, breads, cheeses and fruits, spices and herbs, and ales and wines. Mouth-watering smells of many meats cooking in rich and delicate sauces drew large crowds. Other smells of fish and foods from the great inland sea delicately cooked in wines and sauces also attracted the curious crowds.

Billit stopped at a little tent that had no obvious wares. A symbol on the tent flap must have meant something to him; the others waited until he appeared with a beaming smile.

"Just a few bits 'n' bobs to 'elp me magic," he muttered.

Members of the Corps of Foresters were everywhere in twos and threes. Their skills and reputation were legendary; just their mere presence was enough to deter all but the most desperate and daring of rogues. But they were also gentlemen with strong morals. Children would run to them just to be seen by them or have their hair tousled by them. Young ladies would blush at the merest glance from them. Even young men would look with respect and envy at the high quality of the armour and weaponry carried by the *Foresters* hoping, perhaps, that one day they would enjoy the same status. But woe would betide any rogue who was caught by one of these guards. The cuff on the ear and the lock applied to the arm would not be gentle while they were taken to the most basic of accommodation to be provided by the city.

There were tents and stalls with priests of varying deities giving blessings to pregnant women and babies and providing cures to maladies, illnesses and disease. Some were offering advice to people with fears, woes and worries. Taura bowed to each priest, regardless of their deity, if they made eye contact while she passed. Some gave formal greetings to which she replied. Not all priests, though, worshipped deities to which she would harbour a mutual respect. More than once did Silmar feel a nauseating power emanate from his burden while he walked past a priest's tent.

"Can these bastards feel its effect?" the elf asked Taura.

"Probably," she replied. "But let us hope they do not recognise it for what it is. They may think it's a weapon imbued with an evil magical spell. In a way, I suppose that is exactly what it is. Let us not tarry here. Move on!"

They passed corrals on their left-hand side that were stocked with horses, camels, oxen, and other beasts of burden. On their right, smaller tents had merchants with dogs and puppies for sale. Many envious eyes were on Jiutarô's cleret-wing dragon; after all, these beasts were treated as an extremely valuable commodity. Silmar had advised Jiutarô to take particular care of Sushi, especially as people might attempt to abduct her, even by force.

This being her first visit to a crowded city, Caeron was understandably anxious. She gripped Jiutarô's arm firmly.

Some offers were made to buy Sushi.

"I not sell a friend," responded Jiutarô. "Would you sell yours?"

"Nah, but you can buy mah wife – hahaha!" answered one man.

A *slap* from the man's wife brought shrieks of laughter from onlookers and from Jiutarô as well.

But the stalls attracting much attention were those displaying the wares for which Marsaise was most famous – ivory. Tusks were imported from far-off lands and were diligently worked by artisans to produce exotically crafted and decorated forms.

There were small tents with fortune-tellers and sages promising a future of fortune and longevity. Other tents had whores of varying ages, races and attractiveness, promising horizontal pleasure in exchange for silver. One tent in particular had a queue of six men waiting for their turn to be looked after. Varengo looked at Yoriando who raised a quizzical eyebrow.

"Later," said the fighter. "Not just now, Yori."

As the group moved along the rows of tents and traders, they passed performers blowing great gouts of flame or walking taut ropes, clowns on stilts pulling faces and teasing passers-by and other clowns juggling and giving comic displays to raucous onlookers.

The smells, sights and sounds of the great fayre were wondrous after their months of adventure, travel, danger, injury and death.

The street of traders and merchants opened up into a massive arena. Hand painted posters showed pictures of archery, horse-skills such as races and taming-the-wild-horse, wrestling, rope-pull, spear-throw and feats of strength and power.

"The tournament arena!" shouted Silmar. He could hardly hold back the excitement in his voice. "This arena is hallowed ground indeed. It is sacred!"

"What happens?" asked Taura. "How does someone take part?"

"Simple," Varengo answered. "You approach the table that deals with the activity you want to do and you challenge someone who is there, or they challenge you. You put gold into the dish and they match it. Winner takes it all."

"What shall we do?" asked Taura.

"Join in some tournaments?" asked Falcon. "I do wrestling, maybe!"

"I would love to try my hand at the archery contest," said Vallio. "But I need to buy a good bow first."

"Can you use this one?" asked Silmar. It was a sign of trust indeed for one warrior to offer another his bow.

"Oh! By the gods, Silmar!" exclaimed Vallio. "May I wield it?"

Taking the bow, he strung it and lifted to feel its weight, balance and pull. "It is perfect! May I use it for the contest?"

"What is archery? Is this arrows? No, sword is better," responded Jiutarô. "Or…"

"Ho there, strange one!" called a deep, resonant voice. "*I* shall challenge you for your cleret-wing dragon!"

A tall, heavily-built, seasoned-looking fighter stood before Jiutarô. "Your pretty sword against mine in the arena. What say you?"

൭   ൶

Jiutarô's challenger was tall and broad-shouldered, dressed in light leather armour, a light helm with cheek-guards but open at the face, and a round shield slung on his back. His face was ruddy and scarred. His long brown hair was showing signs of greying beneath his helm but his neatly-clipped beard was still dark albeit with streaks of ginger. His heavy longsword in a battered scabbard at his left hip showed signs of much use as did the matching dagger on his right. Bright blue eyes shone with an ambiguous merriment that suggested his challenge was not serious. But the man's stern, deep voice indicated that his challenge was sincere.

"No, Jiutarô," said Caeron. She grasped his arm tightly. "Please, no."

Jiutarô kissed her on the cheek. "And if I win?" he replied to the warrior.

"Ha ha ha! In the *very* unlikely event of that happening, I will happily *give* you one hundred in gold. Otherwise just sell me the beast now for 50 gold and we shall call the matter closed."

The Samurai shook his head. "I not sell a friend! How is winner to be judged?"

The warrior gave a broad, amiable smile. "That will be decided on the first to yield or perhaps to lose an arm. I have no interest in killing you; I need not prove to anyone that I'm the master. Not in twenty years or more have I been bested. Do you accept my challenge?"

Jiutarô's expression was dour. "My friend does not want to be fought over."

"You mean you have not the courage to fight!" He crossed his arms and gave an air of arrogance.

Jiutarô shrugged. "Take it as you choose, I care not!"

"I challenge you to fight me," the warrior insisted, louder this time. "One hundred gold against your dragon!"

Sushi chattered into Jiutarô's ear. The Samurai's raised his eyebrows in surprise. "My friend she say *yes* to it!"

"You see, the beast knows I am the better man and would prefer my care over yours! Fear not, I swear I shall care for it with kindness when I win."

"Jiutarô, you need not do this," whispered Caeron. "Please!"

"Do not fear, Caeron. He shall not harm me. You have not seen me fight yet, have you?"

She shook her head dolefully.

The protagonists made their way to entrance of arena. The warrior announced the event to an official who asked them their names. The peace-bonds were removed from their weapons by the city official who said to them, in a well-practiced voice "In this arena you are not under the peace-bonding enforced by the crown and governance of the city of Marsaise and the Kingdom of Cascant. When the challenge has been completed you will both return to me to have the peace-bonding remade, provided that one or both of you survive. You will not, nor cause to happen, any act of revenge or violence upon the winner, or loser, of this challenge once you are beyond the confines of this arena. Is that clear?"

Both fighters nodded their agreement while looking at each other squarely in the eye.

Caeron, with tears in her eyes, rushed over to Jiutarô and kissed him fully on the mouth. It was the first time they had done that and Jiutarô gasped with pleasure. His challenger smiled at the sight.

"Take care, my beloved," she called. Jiutarô's look was one of delightful astonishment.

The tournament official raised a speaking funnel against his mouth to announce the forthcoming event to the gathered crowd. "A challenge! A challenge! The great swordsman, Kell of the Vale of Celesta, unbeaten for many years, hereby challenges Mishma, er, Mimsh, er, the stranger, pitting a hundred gold crowns against the, er, cleret-wing dragon! The bout begins in ten minutes. Now is the time to lay your bets."

There was a sudden frenzy of activity as gamblers gathered around and money was placed.

Jiutarô, dressed in his *hakama* over-trousers and his kimono, pulled his katana, in its sheath from his *obi* sash. He passed across his wakisashi to Caeron, pausing briefly to wipe a tear from her lovely face. Calmly, he stood in the arena while his adversary, Kell, removed his shield and then swaggered around waving his arms and showing off to the crowd. Jiutarô spoke to Sushi who then launched herself off his shoulders and landed on the rail next to Caeron.

"I have put a bet on Jiutarô to win," announced Jasper to his companions.

"You are gambling? How much?" asked Taura incredulously.

The dwarf raised his eyes skywards. "Only one 'undred, girlie!"

"H-how much?"

"A hundred!" he yelled. "Are yeh choddin' deaf or somethin'?"

"Gold?"

"Nay! Sausages, you chod! Aye, gold! If I win, I get, er, 'ow much, Falcon?"

"Depends how well Jiutarô does."

"Idiot!" She flounced to the railing with a face like thunder. "It's a lot to lose if this Kell is as good as he thinks he is."

A trumpet blared from beside the official. "Begin!"

The crowd erupted with cheering, and some jeering particularly when Jiutarô stepped into the centre of the arena. The throng shouted and yelled. Virtually all of the encouragement was directed towards the warrior with cries of "Kell! Kell! Kell!"

The tall warrior leapt forward with a huge downward swing of his great sword. Jiutarô, yet to draw his katana from its scabbard, unexpectedly stepped neatly inside the arc of the sword swing and the heavy weapon dug into the ground. Kell lifted the sword and swung it up towards Jiutarô's head. Again, the Samurai stepped forwards, ducked and the blade *whooshed* harmlessly above him.

As the sword carried around to Kell's rear, Jiutarô whipped his sword from its scabbard and whacked the scabbard down onto the warrior's back. In a lightning-fast move, the katana was back inside the scabbard again. The warrior fell forward onto his knees but quickly recovered and turned to face Jiutarô.

There were *oohs* and *aahs* from the crowd. "Come on, Kell. Stick him!" a voice called from the onlookers.

"That was very good!" the warrior complimented. "Now let us try again! Why do you not take out your sword?"

"I do not need it yet!"

Kell's expression was one of uncertainty. "Do not expect that I will not attack."

"I expect nothing, and everything!"

The tall warrior gave a puzzled expression as he took a step backwards and readied his sword once again.

The two circled each other, Kell with his sword in a two-handed grip extended in front of him and Jiutarô with his scabbarded katana clutched gently to his chest with his left hand, his right hand taking a reverse grip on the long hilt. The warrior prodded his sword forward to Jiutarô's chest to test the reaction but, once again, the Samurai side-stepped with ease to avoid it.

Brandishing his sword in a lunge, Kell took a long step forward with his right foot. Jiutarô stepped back with his left foot and, as Kell's leading foot was about to plant itself on the ground, the Samurai used his right foot to sweep the warrior's ankle further forward than was intended. Badly off balance, the warrior staggered and crashed down onto his behind.

Cries of "Ooh!" chorused across the arena.

Once again, with a single lightning-fast action, Jiutarô removed his scabbard from his sword and brought it down hard across the warrior's chest. The watching crowd cheered loudly. Kell coughed but grinned broadly.

"Very good, once again!" Kell stated. "A style of swordsmanship I have never seen before. Shall we continue?"

"If you wish." Jiutarô's face retained its impassive countenance. He stepped to his right more out of curiosity than anything else. He wanted to test his opponent's reaction.

Kell climbed to his feet but stumbled back onto his posterior. The deadpan-faced Samurai reached forward and took the warrior's hand, pulling him back up to his feet. They separated. Once more the fighters circled each other.

Kell was cautious now. He feinted with a short step forward and a small swing of his blade towards Jiutarô's left side but, as the Samurai stepped back, he changed the stroke so his blade slapped Jiutarô's hip. Now it was Jiutarô's turn to smile as the crowd cheered for Kell once again.

"That I did not expect with large blade." It was now Jiutarô's turn to give a compliment.

Kell raised his head in mirth. "Neither did I, ha hah!"

Another lunge from Kell and Jiutarô, once again, attempted to sweep the ankle. As his foot flashed towards it, Kell lifted his leg. Jiutarô's foot failed to connect causing him to be off balance momentarily. Kell brought his hand onto Jiutarô's chest and heaved the Samurai onto his back. The crowd roared again with appreciation.

The warrior reached down to pin Jiutarô's chest with the point of his sword but, in another lightning-fast reaction, the Samurai swept aside the blade with one bare hand and gripped Kell's upper body with his other. Planting his right foot into the Kell's stomach, he threw the warrior over him and rolled to the side. Kell crashed to the ground, landing on his sword and breaking the blade by the cross-guard.

Jiutarô leapt to his feet and rushed to the warrior's side, his blade resting lightly against Kell's throat.

"I yield!" Kell called. He was winded but otherwise unhurt. The relieved Samurai helped him to his feet. The crowd was roaring still.

"I declare, er, Mishma-, er, the stranger as the winner" called the official. Once more, the crowd roared.

"You are a worthy winner," Kell saluted loudly. "And not once did you attack me with your sword. What manner of fighting is this?"

"It is *bushido*, in my land it means the way of the warrior."

"One hundred of my gold crowns are yours." He handed the Samurai a large bag of coins. "I consider it money well spent. What is your name?"

"I am Yazama Jiutarô, Samurai of *han* of my master in Province of Ako in land of Nippon."

"Well met, Yazama Jiutarô. I know nothing this land of Nippon. I am Kell of the Vale of Celesta in the Realm of Kamambia. I hope we shall meet again one day. Where are you bound?"

"East to Carrick Cliffs." Sushi swooped over and landed on the Samurai's shoulder. Kell cautiously reached over to fondle the side of Sushi's face. The cleret-wing dragon flinched and hissed.

"You have nothing to fear from me, little one!" said the warrior softly. "Jiutarô, hearken to my words. Do not go to Carrick Cliffs. The town has succumbed to an evil threat. I have travelled from the Vale and the Count Coldharth has discussed this problem. How many is your party? Why go there?"

Jiutarô considered his response for a moment. "We number eleven. We go to see problem."

"Then may the gods protect you. You will be in dire need of it. Travel well. I must be away now to buy a new sword. Fortunately, my sword was old and of little value to me."

Kell handed Jiutarô a heavy leather pouch and then saluted him. Jiutarô bowed in return. The pair strode to the arena gate where the Samurai had his weapons peace-bonded once more. With a cheerful wave, Kell walked off into the distance whistling tunelessly.

Caeron rushed to him and leapt into his arms, showering his face with kisses. "I was so worried," she gasped breathlessly. "You were unbelievable!"

Jiutarô stared into her eyes and saw an emotion he had not seen before. It was a few heartbeats before he could tear his eyes away.

"How much you win?" Jiutarô asked Jasper. The others crowded around to hear the results.

"Two 'undred an' fifty. I might 'ave won more if you 'ad made it look more difficult at the start. Who's the idiot now, eh Taura?"

"Aye, gloat why don't you!" she replied with a scowl.

"And my hundred gold too!" added the Samurai, emptying some of the gleaming coins into his hand. He handed them to Caeron. "You keep," he said.

Varengo showed some coins in his hand. "Twenty five for me too!" he laughed. "Just as well you won, Jiutarô. The ten gold was from my share that we got today! I shall now be able to buy a good sword also and maybe more besides."

"A very productive day, I think," said Silmar. "We need to find somewhere to deposit our money and gems. We can't walk around here or anywhere with this fortune."

Varengo and his three men separated and moved off together having arranged to meet the others somewhere by the stockyards in a short while. The companions circulated around the corrals and stockyards, looking at the horses, dogs and other animals. They had been there but a few minutes when Sushi hissed and became agitated on Jiutarô's shoulders.

"What is wrong, my little friend?" asked Jiutarô. An expression of concentration crossed his face.

Suddenly, Silmar gave a cry and clutched at his head. His face had become white with the searing pain that lanced through it.

"We are followed," Jiutarô called softly. Caeron clutched again at his arm. "Sushi tell me. Behind us. Two men. They wear black robes and hoods."

"Evil priests or mages pr'aps," replied Billit. "Or Darkling!"

"Ohh shit! My head is painful!" cried the elf. "I think they are probing me with something magical to see what I carry. I feel awful!" He stumbled and Falcon rushed to hold him up.

After a few moments, Taura said "I know that. It's a *Detection* spell but there is something else I don't recognise; something to cause you this pain."

Jasper growled in anger. "I'm not 'avin' that! Cheeky bastards! Who do they think they are? Let's lead 'em somewhere quiet an' see what they're up to. Chat with 'em all nice an' friendly, like!" To emphasise his intent, he punched his right fist into the palm of his left hand.

They casually made their way around the main horse corral as if unaware of the following figures, stopping occasionally to admire a horse or pony. Silmar's searing pain had now begun to subside but he was still white and shaking. Ahead of them were some large wooden structures, two of which were stables adjoining the corral. Moving slowly, they wandered into the alley between the two stables. The passage was quite narrow with just enough room for two people to stand shoulder to shoulder. When they were out of sight of the followers they broke into a trot. At the far end of the alley, on the right-hand side, was a narrow open door into one of the stables.

"All of you in here, quick now," gasped Silmar. "But would you stay out here with me, Taura?"

The priestess looked at him questioningly but nodded. Both of them remained in the passage as two priests, dressed in hooded black robes, appeared around the corner. On their feet were sandals but the features that caught their attention were the total lack of facial hair. The looseness of their hoods showed that they had no hair at all on their heads. Each priest held a short but sturdy wooden rod that was shod at each end with a silver cap.

One of the priests called out in a clear but heavily-accented voice "You vill give us de artefact. You vill not resist!"

The other priest pointed his rod directly at Silmar and Taura.

"Come and take it, if you want it!" called Silmar.

"Fool!" the first priest spat.

Without warning, a blast of white ice erupted from the rod and enveloped the pair. But the blast stopped almost immediately. The elf and the priestess slumped motionless to the ground covered in a thick layer of white frost.

Immediately, the other companions rushed out of the stables but without their weapons drawn. Looking along the passage, they noticed the two priests were lying on the ground, each in a growing pool of their own blood. Standing above them was the warrior, Kell, and a *Forester*.

But Silmar and Taura appeared undamaged as they moved awkwardly and stiffly on the ground.

"Brrr! That was s-so c-cold," gasped Taura while trying to roll onto her knees. Silmar rubbed his legs briskly.

Falcon rush to her and immediately scooped her up into his arms, rubbing her vigorously.

"These two have been a nuisance for a week or more," growled the guard. "I have been waiting and watching them thanks to thee, Kell. They have been preying on travellers and adventurers who carry magical or holy artefacts. If their money won't buy what they want, they have other ways to persuade their victims. It is as well that we caught them in the act this time." To the shivering pair who had now regained their feet and were brushing off the last of the melting frost, he smiled broadly and added "'Tis good thou didst not waylay or retaliate with thy weapons drawn. The penning of my report would have been horrendous! Hahaha!"

"They will bother travellers no more, D'Angmor," called Kell. "Thank you for your forbearance in this matter. Will you need a statement from me?"

"Unnecessary, my old friend. If thee and these adventurers can drag the bodies into a corner of the stable, yonder, I shall ensure that this mess is cleared up from this alley."

They clasped each other's wrist warmly and the member of the Corps of Foresters marched away.

Silmar looked Kell in the eye saying "You followed us. Why?"

"Ah, I shall explain but I would prefer that you and I stand aside from the others."

The pair moved out of the passage towards the corrals. Kell leaned against a corner post and idly watched the great cart-horses that fed from a pile of hay. Silmar followed closely behind him.

"I know who you are and I am aware what it is you carry," the warrior admitted.

CHAPTER 42

"But, how in the seven hells …!" exclaimed Silmar. His hand strayed towards his dagger but Kell raised his hand.

"Fear not. I am here by the command of Count Coldharth of the Vale of Celesta."

"I recognise the name," interrupted Silmar, "but it is a name that I associate with criminal activities, murder and piracy."

"Ah, these are common stories that are frequently put about by the Hoshite and even the corrupt Kamambian authorities that are known to pay a levy to Hosh. This is so as to explain our continued freedom from their tyranny. Piracy indeed, but targeted against the Hoshite vessels that plunder our Vale coastline on a regular basis under the request and direction of the Kamambian regime."

Silmar considered this for a moment. "Perhaps you should be circulating the truth of your activities. However, you mention the Count."

"Aye. On his command I have followed you all the way from Hill's Edge, with the collusion of Borgan Drogarn, whom you have met. What a trail of destruction you have left behind you! Hah! Did you know that the gang you wiped out on the riverbank has terrorised the region for more than twenty years?"

Silmar shook his head and did not reply.

"Aye, Silmar of Refuge, the alligators fed well that day. Now then, Halorun Tann, an old and valued friend of mine, whom you have also met, sent word to Count Coldharth many months ago that you would be expected in the late Summer. I had been trying to track you for many tenday-weeks, with much success for you have left a trail of events and triumphs behind you. Now is the first time you and I have been able to meet. We originally expected a small group of four or five but you are now a small army."

"Ah, we picked up a few extra at the City of Shade," Silmar explained, "and the lovely young half-elven lady in the King's Forest."

"You mean you just walked through the city of the Grullien?" gasped the warrior.

"We created a little diversion first." He smiled at the memory. "Gods! That was so easy. They were so stupid! But it emptied out their city; we freed all the captives and brought down the end of the mine tunnel behind us!"

Kell smiled and shook his head. "Not with an army would I have considered going into that foul place, even if I knew where the entrance could be found. But to bring out the captives too! Five of them you say?"

"Nay, more like forty! Most of them went back to their homes but five stayed with us. Sadly, one perished when the Darkling brought down wolves upon us. Look, the four men are good and faithful but we did not tell them about the artefact for a long time. We thought it best for their own sake as well as ours. What they did not know they could not be made to tell about. But they proved to be resolute and faithful so they had a right to know. Tell me, how is it that you are acquainted with Halorun Tann and Borgan Drogarn."

"It is interesting that you should ask that question." Kell looked about as if confirming that they were not being overheard. "There is a, erm, society of prominent people throughout Baylea who watch as things develop. Halorun is one, Borgan Drogarn is another. Your father, Faramar Galadhal of Refuge, was one of the founders of the clandestine *Society of Sentinels*. This is a network that feeds information to the Count, the Magelords of Westron Seaport and others of high significance."

"What sort of information?"

"Threats to political stability, primarily. Intrigue and movements of the Hoshites. If we were to get wind of activities that might threaten to undermine the safekeeping of the populace of the Home Territories and their neighbouring realms then we find solutions to deal with it."

"Should you be telling me about this, Kell?"

"You are known to us, Prince Silmar Galadhal, son of Faramar Galadhal, Lord of Refuge. Your honesty is considered beyond reproach otherwise I would not have spoken to you so freely of this. I am placing my trust in you but this comes with a word of warning."

Silmar stiffened but nodded slightly.

Kell looked about him once again. "The Vale is now being continually harassed by Darkling and their allies from the Dannakanonn as well as from the Hosh raiding ships. We, of the *Society* are unable to offer you much aid for your quest without leaving ourselves exposed and in peril. I am directed to tell you though, that aid *will* come to you in many guises and at unexpected times. Rely on your own skills and guile but you must be careful in whom you place your trust. Beware of those who still seek you for although you have destroyed the group of Darkling, there may be more. I advise that you do not tarry in this city any longer than you need to provision yourselves and perhaps re-arm." He looked over Silmar's shoulder. "Ah, here comes your little army. I shall leave you now. Get these bodies out of sight and try to cover up the pools of blood. Farewell for the moment and I shall speak again with you in the morning."

Silmar took a deep breath and stepped back to rejoin the others. Varengo and his three warriors had already rejoined the companions and were proudly showing off their new weapons, boots and helms.

"We missed some fun by the looks of things," said Yoriando. "These look like mages or priests. Why are you two wet?"

The bodies were moved and then thoroughly searched. Taura advised that they take care should they find anything unusual as it may be magical. The rods she handed to Billit and they shared out the coins. The companions had earned more money this day than most of them had ever seen in one place.

❧ ❧

"Tell us of the road through the Brash Barrier Peaks, Kell," Silmar asked as the companions prepared to leave the city of Marsaise.

The dawn next morning was unusually overcast but they were in high spirits and keen to be on the road once more. During their stay at the Greased Pig Tavern, they had heard stories of the fall of the city of Triosande far to the north but much of it was old news. It did not concern them overly because they knew that their route would take them

612

east. They had sleepy poorly because of the sounds of revelry that went on long into the early hours of the morning.

"Your road takes you Norovir and on towards the peaks," explained Kell on their second day in Marsaise. "I do not doubt that the high road over the peaks will be somewhat treacherous because of the fell beasts that roam there but I have no doubt that your numbers will be sufficient to deter any monstrosities. It is the nights that you must be cautious. It would be best if you attach yourself to a group of wagons for there is safety in numbers and caravans are plentiful. Merchants will pay well for an additional escort across the high pass but the going will be slow. You have your Protectors' tokens and your group has royal patronage, I understand."

Kell spoke with a sombreness that emphasised the dangers that were to come should they stray from the recommended road.

"You will be met by a small force of Corps of Foresters stationed in the region that will set you in the right direction. The Princess Regent left Marsaise for Norovir last night so you may encounter her. Ensure that you exercise the utmost courtesy because she does not tolerate fools. She is also a formidable warrior and I doubt that even you, Jiutarô, could best her in single combat. She is a hero of many battles and is deeply loved by her subjects. I shall say nothing of her exquisite beauty but her temperament is cold and calculating. But she takes seriously the future of the realm. Nonetheless, she is charming and considerate to travellers. She makes my heart leap when I set my eyes upon her."

"We shall be most courteous if we are fortunate, or unfortunate, enough to meet with her," said Silmar.

Kell sidled over to Silmar and spoke quietly. "She is one of that *Society* that I spoke about but she will not admit to it unless one was to identify themselves as a member also. If you have a care to be an associate then take this medallion and wear it beneath your tunic next to the skin else I urge you to never speak of it again."

Silmar nodded in agreement and took the medallion. The bronze disc was the size of a silver coin and hung from a leather thong. The emblem on one side was a pictogram, its meaning unclear, the reverse was plain.

"I accept," he said softly. "What am I expected to do?"

"In time, you will get to know some others in the society. You know me, of course, Halorun Tann and Borgan Drogarn, your father and the Princess Regent, were you to meet her. They will soon learn that you have joined the Society and when required, they will contact you if information is to be passed on."

"How will I know them for what they are? The Princess Regent for example."

Kell paused while Varengo and Yoriando strode by, then he continued. "In the midst of a conversation she will say 'The mounts are restless; they sense something in the air.' Your response will be 'They are sensitive to unrest, Majesty.' She will say 'Show me' and you produce your medallion. Others will use the same phrases."

ဆာ ‍ ‍ ‍ ‍ ‍ ‍ ‍ ‍ ‍ ‍ ‍ ‍ ‍ ‍ ‍

The party left the city by the south gate in the early hours of the morning. There were few travellers on the road that early in the day but after a while, they met caravans and travellers trundling towards the city. They took advantage of some of the many wayside inns and trading posts along the busy road.

It took them a little more than two tenday-weeks to reach Norovir. The city was bustling but much restoration was being made to buildings that had suffered due to a great fire, allegedly caused by Hoshite or even Livurian agents the previous winter. Taura was determined to visit the Temple of Neilea to see for herself how the High Priestess and Lord of the city, Lady Cirmahl L'halle, had rebuilt the temple that had been totally destroyed. While the companions rested at a tavern in the city, Taura called in at the temple.

"Welcome. Taura Windwalker," said the Lord of the city. "It pleases me that you have visited this humble temple."

Lady Cirmahl L'halle was a tall, stocky lady of middle years. Her once copper-red hair was starting to show signs of grey but her features were still young-looking and very attractive. She wore a plain white gown with a black smock that was open.

Taura bowed deeply. "My lady," she began, "it is I who am pleased to be in such esteemed company. Your dedication to the restoration of this fair city and to the rebuilding of the temple was a matter of discussion at the Temple of Learning before I left there."

"And tell me, Taura, how fares the Matriarchal High Priestess, Simenine Tarathtelle?"

"She is as fierce and daunting as ever, my lady, as far as I know. I have not seen her for many months now."

"And ever was she so," laughed the High Priestess. "Tell me of your travels while we sit and drink for I have taken little rest in a long time."

Taura spoke for a long time detailing many of the encounters of their long journey. She said nothing of the artefact that Silmar carried but the High Priestess was shrewd.

"I sense that there is something of importance that you keep from me. Taura. I shall request nothing of it for I suspect that you keep it close within you for a good reason."

No, my lady. It is not my intention to keep the secret from you. It's just that Halorun Tann, the –"

The Lady Cirmahl gasped and flushed slightly. "Halorun? The High Priest of Haeman in Westron Seaport? My goodness! There is a name I have not heard of for many a year! Is he still handsome? Did his black eyes unnerve you as they once did me? Hahaha! I can tell you stories of him and I that would embarrass you!"

"My lady! Erm, aye. He is very handsome indeed. I must admit to more than a little shyness on my part when I first met him in Westron Seaport. He teased me into thinking he was blind! The rascal!"

The High Priestess threw her head back and laughed. "I still hope that one day he will grow up into a mature adult, may the blessings of Haeman be upon him, haha! I understand his son is even more handsome. I do not expect you to tell me more on this matter. But I would like to speak to you of another issue if you can spare me the time."

The Lady Cirmahl and Taura spoke together in hushed voices for a long while and then they rose to their feet. She showed Taura a fine golden torc and helped to place it around her neck.

"There is something special about you, Taura Windwalker. I sensed it when you came to me. You are favoured by Neilea in a way that very few priestesses are. Wear my gift constantly; it will provide a measure of protection should another priest attempt to use their evil unholy magic against you. No person will be able to take it from you except when you give it to them freely."

Taura thanked her profusely; this was an invaluable artefact indeed. The High Priestess Lord of Norovir bent forward and kissed Taura on the forehead.

As Taura left the temple, she fingered the gold torc around her neck and could already feel the reassuring warmth of its divine influence. She had much to think about while she walked back to the tavern in the torrential rain through the busy streets.

૭ ૨

CHAPTER 43

"What? All of 'em? But we paid a fortune for these mounts."
Jasper was astounded.

The companions looked at each other in disbelief. The officer of the Corps of Foresters was clearly sympathetic but he would not be dissuaded from his task of the compulsory purchase of the horses belonging to the party.

"Thou shalt be given a fair price for them and thou canst keep thy pack-pony."

"But we have a great distance yet to travel," insisted Taura. "And we have been promised the support and protection of the Corps of Forester Knights during our journey past and beyond Marsaise."

The eight-day ride from Norovir towards the high pass through the Brash Barrier Peaks had been rapid despite the poor state of the surface. The road had been busy at first as traders and caravans made the long but lucrative journey west from the copper mines of the southernmost Brash Barrier Peaks and the mahogany-rich forests in the Vale of Celesta. Deep pot-holes caused wheels and axles to shatter but there were many eager artisans on the road that were willing to assist with repairs, generally at an exorbitant price.

It was commonly suspected that the roads were deliberately kept in a shoddy state so that local wheelwrights could make a healthy profit.

But after a few days the oncoming wagons became fewer. They had been within five leagues of the pass over the peaks when they came upon a large troop of Corps of Foresters. Many were wounded, two of them badly. Some had already been buried by the side of the road.

They had been attacked at night by an overwhelming combined force of orcs, trolls and, unusually, ogres. The *Foresters* had fought valiantly and ferociously and had destroyed majority of their attackers, including one of the two ogres. The cost had been high however. Of the forty *Foresters*, eleven had been slain and all of their mounts had been hacked to death or driven off.

"As thou canst see, we have many badly wounded men. Those two will not last the day."

"I can give the healing of Neilea to these two men," said Taura.

"I cannot impose upon thee, my lady," responded the Dragon. "But I insist that I shall still need thy horses."

"It is no imposition. Lay them on the ground and I shall give them healing adequate for the journey ahead of you."

Silmar, Varengo and Jasper moved to one side with the *Forester* captain. It was almost an hour before agreement was reached and by then Taura, looking exhausted, joined them.

"Well? How much did you get?" she asked.

"Eight 'undred and we keeps the pack-pony!" grunted Jasper.

"But we have made a loss there then," said Silmar, a declaration rather than a question.

"A little more than a hundred gold, if my memory serves me right," answered Varengo.

"But we would pay almost that much for a good pack-pony so we did quite well," added Yoriando.

"But now we 'ave a choddin' long choddin' walk!" growled Jasper. "'Twill take us a day by foot."

"We had better get on with it then," said Varengo.

The eighteen surviving *Foresters* rode away westwards on their newly-procured mounts and were soon out of sight. As the companions stood there with their belongings scattered on the ground, they began to feel the tiny spots of rain. The day had turned cloudy and a cold wind started to bring heavier clouds.

"Doesn't look too good, does it," said Silmar as he donned his cloak.

"An elf statin' the choddin' obvious!" grunted the dwarf. "Nothin' new there!" Although unsteady in a saddle, the thought of a long walk up the steep road towards the pass was not appealing to him. Consequently, he was cantankerous. His travelling companions noticed little divergence from his customary temper however.

The others ignored him but donned their cloaks too. Varengo and his three men had bought themselves much clothing, armour and weaponry in Marsaise and were now looking like the warriors that they were supposed to be.

ॐ ॐ

Silmar called for the group to come to a halt. Tired and footsore, they were feeling the effects of trudging on their feet and legs after months of riding and now a full day of marching. By now, it was dark, freezing cold and the rain continued unabated. Few had been the recent days when it did not rain. Their once comfortable boots were now waterlogged, mud-caked and bringing up blisters. Their feet were soaked through, nonetheless, which served to reduce the pain of their blisters. Every stop, they knew, would be welcome and streams and rivers gave a welcome relief to aching feet. The pack-pony carried all but their essential personal equipment Food was plentiful, and water too, but thankfully for more than one reason. Some of their food was hunted during their arduous walk but most was bought from passing traders.

It was fortunate that the *Forester* had allowed them their pack-pony because they had been able to make fairly good progress despite the deep mud that had been churned up by the wagons and horses of other travellers on the road. Their next night stop was to be longer in duration to give them as much rest as they could get. They were fortunate to be able to negotiate with a traders' caravan to allow them to sleep beneath wagons for the night, the price being that they provide additional sentry watch.

Surprisingly, the elf had felt no effects from his burden since they had left Marsaise. He had even looked into his baggage on more than one occasion to check it was still there. Opening the lid of the box that contained the cursed dagger was all the confirmation he needed. The familiar pain quickly coursed through his head and he had to struggle to keep the effects of intense nausea under control.

They crossed the pass in a violent thunderstorm. The weather and road conditions had kept most of the travellers off the road; the only merchants were those using oxen to pull their laden wagons. The rough and lofty peaks towered to the north and south but because of the foul weather and low clouds they were almost totally obscured.

As they progressed eastwards and left the pass behind them, so also did the thunderstorm move westwards. Although the rain continued to make their journey one of misery they were glad to see the back of the storm. The pack-pony had been difficult to control for some days and had it not been for the strength and care given by Falcon, they might have lost much of their equipment.

Morendo had developed a wracking cough that was getting worse by the hour. Varengo was carrying much of the fighter's equipment so that the sick man could lean on his friends for support. Taura promised to do what she could to ease the man's discomfort but as the day wore on she also showed signs of sickness brewing.

The clouds were so heavy and dark this day that they could barely tell night from day. The mountains also served to prevent the day's light. Fierce, crashing storms could be heard echoing through the peaks but they were thankful indeed not to have these directly overhead.

The group stopped and they all faced Silmar. "Aye, I know, there is no need to say anything," he said. "This is ridiculous! We cannot continue like this. Look at Taura and Morendo! We must find shelter as quick as possible."

Morendo was by now very sick and was being helped by his two friends, Vallio and Yoriando. He was doubled up with his coughing.

"We bin looking fer two days, elf," growled Jasper. He had huffed and puffed as he hauled his ageing legs through deep mud and water-filled wheel ruts. "Use some sense – if we can't find shelter 'ere, we gonna 'ave to build one."

"Better to build many small shelters for one or two in each," suggested Falcon. Taura raised her pale face to look up at him. She had felt quite unwell for a couple of days but had kept quiet about it until today. She had begun shaking with cold but her inner clothes were wet with perspiration and rain.

"Hah! He's got a dirty mind!" Varengo laughed despite the rain running down his neck. "But in all seriousness, we should build shelters as far from the road as we can and make sure they, and any fire, are well out of sight. We don't want unwelcome visitors and even if we just have a rock-face, it will give some shelter from wind. Perhaps me and Jiutarô can go look for someplace suitable. What say you all? Jiutarô?"

Only Jiutarô had shown any enthusiasm for the march. He was used to this sort of weather in his own land, far away. "Hai, is good. Sushi help look," he suggested.

Caeron, the lovely young half-elven archer, was constantly at his side and lately, Sushi could often be seen draped across her shoulders. The rain had little effect on Sushi and she often rode quite happily on top of the packs on the pony where the Samurai had loosely tied a piece of tarpaulin to give her some shelter.

Varengo and Jiutarô had been gone for well over an hour. Anxious faces peered in the direction they had gone, hoping they hadn't become disorientated and lost in the foothills of the mountains. Suddenly, Sushi flew over the heads of the group and landed on the grass in front of them.

She turned her body to face the mountains and waddled off. Stopping after a few steps she turned her head back towards the group.

"Hey!" cried Caeron. "She wants us to follow!"

For a mile or more they followed her through low hills and small tree-lined valleys until she led them into a narrow defile in the rocks. There, standing with broad grins, were Jiutarô and Varengo.

"Ideal!" called Silmar with a broad smile.

"I was afraid for you," whispered Caeron into Jiutarô's ear. She kissed him hard on his mouth.

Rare were the times that she spoke and then, only to Jiutarô in a gentle whisper. Taura had tried to engage her in conversation but the girl just smiled, nodded or shook her head when necessary and dropped her gaze to the ground.

The defile gave excellent protection on three sides. The walls were steep and would not enable anyone to raid the camp without making a lot of noise. The entrance through which they had come was about three paces wide and gave little cover to any man or creature trying to sneak up.

It was now past midday and they were all soaked to the skin. It took them the rest of the day to build small simple shelters from wood and grass. Although the huge pile of wood collected for their campfire was waterlogged, Billit was able to use a flame spell to light it and even then it hissed and produced a lot of smoke. A shallow hollow in the rock-face to one side was suggested as the ideal place to build the fire. Their blankets would be able to dry out in there and then their clothes.

Taura was settled into one shelter near to the fire, with Falcon next to her, and Morendo in another. They both slept until darkness fell.

The downpour continued unrelenting for another three days. The sloping rocky ground channelled the rainwater away and, fortunately, was firm enough so as not to turn to mud.

On the fourth day, breaks appeared in the grey cloud and the rain slowed to an occasional gentle drizzle. Silmar was tending the fire and had some oats boiling in a cooking pot. He heard a shuffle behind him and turned to see Taura standing there wrapped in a blanket.

"Gods! Who was up first?" Taura asked. "You or the sun!"

The elf smiled and continued with preparing the simple meal.

The priestess was much improved but Morendo was so ill that he couldn't even take food. He was cold and shaking. Taura sat by him for some hours while sorting through some little packets in her healers' satchel. She mixed these with the porridge that Silmar had made earlier and produced a warm broth of unpleasant-smelling soup.

"You *must* take this, Morendo," she said. He turned his head away, refusing to open his lips. She chided him, saying that he shouldn't be acting like a child. "Everybody is looking at you! Typical of a man to put on an act when he is a little bit poorly!"

Eventually, he took a little off the end of the spoon. It took her a long time to make him take the rest. He slept soundly for another few hours. While he slept, the Priestess rocked back and forth over him and, holding her holy symbol aloft, chanted words known only to her and her beloved deity. Eventually, she returned to her shelter and laid down to rest.

Silmar had been sitting alone for much of the morning. He seemed preoccupied and spoke rarely. Eventually, Jiutarô wandered across and spoke to him. "Caeron sleeps well. You are quiet, my friend. Does something trouble you?"

"Aye Jiutarô. It does. I have had a voice speaking to me since yesterday morning before the sun rose hidden by the clouds. I cannot explain it. In my head it is clear and precise in what it is saying. I do not know who it is but it is telling me to do something. It is telling me that I need to enter the Spiderhome Forest to do something."

"Why and what?" asked Jasper. "Aye, I was listenin' to ya! You should *not* be listenin' though. It bodes ill. Mysterious choddin' crap!"

"I think perhaps not. I feel a calling. It is specific."

"A trap!" said Jiutarô.

The elf hesitated for a moment. "If it is, the burden I carry will tell me."

The dwarf was adamant. "You're choddin' well *not* taking that with you, elf!"

"I have to!"

Jasper crossed his arms. "What's this *I*, Silmar? What about the *we*?"

"Are *we* going in there now then?" Billit asked nervously from the opening in his shelter. "I've heard something about that place and would not even look at it as we walk past. Spiderhome is a forest of dire reputation. If you ask me, the whole place would benefit well from a gigantic forest fire!"

The elf sighed. "I am told I cannot take more than one companion."

Jasper was now indignant. "And choddin' well why not? That settles it! It's a choddin' trap!"

"I think not. There is no malevolence in the message."

"There won't be, will there? But the malevolence is in the Spiderhome itself! For the gods' sake, you elf fool, choddin' great big spiders the size o' donkeys still wander out of these woods to drag away captives, it is said. *Huge* spiders live there, that is known. Evil mages, it is said, go there to look for webs, spider eggs and spider fangs for their foul magic. I am telling you not to go there. Do not go!" The dwarf's voice was now on the edge of panic. Despite his occasional teasing of the elf, there was genuine fear and concern in his objections.

"I must! I would not go if I thought it was perilous. I do need one person to go with me but not if he does not want to go. I would like to take you, Jiutarô – I really do need Sushi's *eyes*. Will you come? I will understand if you would rather not."

Caeron shook her head vigorously, her eyes wide open with fear.

"My love," the Samurai said as she gripped his arm tightly. "I protect him, Sushi protect me." With a reluctant expression, the half-elf nodded slowly dislodging a tear from her eye.

"Hai. I come, Silmar. I shall speak to Sushi. When we leave?"

Silmar looked up at the sky. "In the morning. Very early, before dawn."

"Hey!" cried Taura. "Do you remember when we were down in the mines of the Shadow World? I still have a spider anti-venom phial here. It may still be potent. I would like to say I also think you're a fool. And you too, Jiutarô! You should know better! I thought you had a brain, of sorts!"

By now, nothing anybody could say would sway Silmar's mind; he had made his decision. There was some comfort that the Samurai *swordmaster* would be going too. The evening meal was a quiet affair during which Caeron shed a few tears. Falcon, Varengo, Morendo, Jasper, Vallio and Yoriendo provided the watch during the night so that Jiutarô and Silmar could get the most amount of rest but for Jiutarô, there was little sleep that night.

Both were up well before dawn. The showers had stopped during the night and stars had appeared in the gaps in the clouds.

"A good omen," muttered Jasper. "Me, Vallio and Morendo are coming with yer as far as the eaves o' the forest. Then we'll come back 'ere. No choddin' arguing, yer pointy-eared elf! The decision 'as been made! 'Ow long will yer be in there, do yer think?"

"Probably two or three days. I believe we will be led to where I have to go. I'll know where to go because the path will be shown to me."

"Aye, an' there will be ten Darkling waiting to say *Thanks for the present! You can go once we've chopped yer 'ead off yer stupid shoulders!*"

❧　☙

In contrast to the warmth and bright sun outside of the Spiderhome Forest, the wood itself was dark, dank and overgrown. The trees were black, gnarled and shrouded in creeper-like growth. Almost immediately the air was humid, still and oppressive. Within a hundred paces, a thick, heavy silence had descended on them. No sound of birds or recognisable life could be heard but there were noises of creatures rustling both through thick undergrowth and through the higher branches. The smell of rotting vegetation was overwhelming.

The eyes of the two warriors constantly flitted back and forth, up and down, as each crack, shuffle or rustle took their attention. Sushi's claws dug into Jiutarô's shoulders, such was her fear. No room was there for her to open her wings, let alone fly – the forest was too dense. Constantly she hissed and chittered as her gaze flickered up, down and to each side.

Web-makers! formed in Jiutarô's mind.

"There spiders here now!" whispered the Samurai. "Sushi tell me."

Almost immediately there were visible signs of movement in the thick growth of forest – dark shapes flashed from trunk to trunk and bough to bough but too quickly for even the elf to make out. "I do not fear spiders!" he said, unconvincingly.

Each of them had their blades held out before them ready to meet whatever came at them.

The track they were following was narrow, twisting and very overgrown. However, it was apparent enough for them to follow. No tracks led off to either side, except for those made by animals. After an hour or so, spiders were evident on the trees, mostly on small webs, and a few on the track. They were unusually large, some being larger than Silmar's hand. Larger and thicker webs hung from boughs as they went deeper into the forest, and many were large enough to stretch between the dark boles of the great trees. Several strands of web stretching across the path needed to be cut to allow them to pass through. Great care had to be taken so that their swords would not caught fast in these sticky strands, some of which were as thick as their fingers.

Another hour or two passed when, suddenly, a hiss from above his head caused Silmar to freeze. Looking up, a great spider, its body as great as that of a sheep and its legs the length and girth of a man's arm, darted back into the branches above just as the cleret-wing dragon made a lunge with her strong jaws.

"By the seven hells of the Void!" cried the elf. "What manner of spider was that? But Sushi kept it at bay! But do they come any bigger?"

"Hai!" replied Jiutarô, his voice quavering. "Behind us!"

The elf glanced back down the track and barely twenty paces behind was a monstrosity the like of which they would not have imagined in their darkest nightmares. A spider, its body raised high on its rear legs so that its eyes could see its prey ahead of it, was far bigger than that which they had seen just moments before. From the tips of its legs on one side to those of the other, it was fully twelve feet across. Its mouth was a gaping maw and high on its grotesque body was a great pair black, multi-faceted eyes. It was making no effort to advance towards Silmar and Jiutarô. The cleret-wing dragon, perched across Jiutarô's shoulders, was alert, hissing and chittering at the monster but she made no attempt to move towards it.

"Let us keep walking, Jiutarô."

The great spider did not appear to follow them but Sushi's head repeatedly darted in all directions. She continued to hiss as dark shadows flitted between the trees. Her claws dug so deeply into Jiutarô's shoulders that he grunted with the pain. There were the same sounds of movement from either side and from above that had dogged them for almost the whole duration of their march through the forest. Wisps of mist curled around the trees and this only served to heighten their fears. *Were there other massive spiders such as that which we had seen? Was that one waiting for us?* Strangely, at no time had Silmar felt the effects of his burden, however. He took some little comfort in that because he hoped it meant that there was no evil intent from the foul creatures. That, however, did not serve to make them any the less dangerous.

More time passed as they cautiously made their way along the narrow and winding track. It seemed that they were gradually climbing higher. They left the wispy mists behind them and suddenly found themselves in a small clearing atop a grassy knoll. They sank down on the damp grass and rested their weary legs. Sushi spread her wings and flapped them but then settled down in between the elf and the Samurai. Then she gave a loud hiss, arched her back and raised her barbed tail. Silmar and Jiutarô, trusting the instincts of the cleret-wing dragon, leapt to their feet. Before them, advancing slowly out from the trees, was the huge spider.

This time there was no doubt. It was coming for them!

PART 4

CARRICK CLIFFS

CHAPTER 44

"It has been three days. Where are they?"

Like all the others, Taura was fearful for their friends. Varengo had offered to take the men and march into the forest with swords drawn. Taura, Jasper, Falcon and Billit had, in one voice, forbidden them to do this. Caeron stood staring, moist-eyed and silent, in the direction from which the two warriors should be appearing.

"There's nothin' we can do," Jasper had insisted. "Where would we look in the forest? It's very large, dammit. And damn 'em for their lunacy!"

"Our task will be for nothing if they do not return," said Falcon. "We may as well just go back to Westron Seaport."

"We must stay here for a while longer," said Billit. "There is little else we can do. As you say, where would we look?"

"Perhaps we should give them another couple of days, then?" asked Varengo. "By the task, I assume you mean taking that artefact to the priest in Carrick Cliffs."

"Aye, that is the task."

"But without Silmar and his burden, as he calls it, there is no task, is there. Let us hope your God is looking kindly down upon him and Jiutarô."

"She will be smiling down on our two friends at this time," she murmured.

❧ ❧

The beast was now within two paces of Silmar and Jiutarô. Sushi was flying above the monster and swooping down over its eyes. Ignoring the cleret-wing dragon, the thing rose up on its front legs to prepare its strike. The elf and the samurai leapt into action and attacked simultaneously. With Silmar's two blades whirling and Jiutarô's katana slashing, the spider backed away a little. Sushi swooped once more, this time clawing at its eyes. Gore splashed about the spider's body and it reared up high before ducking down in an attempt to catch one or both of the humanoids.

The beast's long forelegs waved frantically in the air and once more it raised itself high. Acting on sheer instinct, the great, partly-blinded spider jumped forwards. Without any warning, a streak of white hot energy blasted noisily into its underside and the thing was thrown back to the trees. It struggled to regain its feet and another blast destroyed its mouth and face. This time the monster gave a shudder and then moved no more except for its legs that curled in towards its body.

Both Silmar and Jiutarô spun about looking for the source of the energy bolt.

The air in the centre of knoll gave a shimmer like a huge bubble and out of it stepped a figure. An aged man – no, not a man but an elf, stood before them. Although of a great many years, he stood with a regal dignity despite the grey tatters in which he was dressed. His white hair was sparse but very long. Deep lines were etched into his face but these were merely a product of age. He was not tall but his back was as straight as an arrow for one so aged. He carried a staff upon which he leaned for support. A smile gave him a kindly, perhaps a benevolent appearance.

The two warriors stood together in a defensive posture. *What is this new threat?*

Silmar waited for a feeling of pain and nausea but felt no effect from the artefact.

The aged elf smiled. "You see – I am not evil! Your, er, burden tells you this, does it not?"

"But, how –?" Silmar started to speak in his confusion but the figure seemed to become stern and perhaps a little less dignified. Silmar hesitated and then bowed to the figure. This was repeated to a lesser degree by Jiutarô. The figure gently nodded his head as if in response.

"You came in answer to my summons, Silmar Galadhal, Prince, son of Faramar, lately of Refuge. I have been waiting for you to appear for a long time. Your part in this tragedy has been foretold. You did well to come through the forest. There are many hazards here but one of the most perilous is now destroyed. It has caused some years of disquiet in the forest, believe me. It was only one of many of its kind, unfortunately."

"Lord, can I ask who it is that has brought me to this place?" Silmar asked. "Who speaks to me now?"

"You may. I am, or was in times gone by, the Lord Olorinuil, once of the Royal Court of Faerhome. The Court war-mage, Antheuseolin, was partly instrumental in its protection but he failed in the end. He lives still, older than I but grief-stricken over his failure long ago, residing deep in the great forests of Vale of Celesta where he bends his will in the defence of that troubled land. We meet, on occasions. It is he who informed me of your quest."

"Antheuseolin!" cried Silmar. "Many times have I heard that name spoken in tales by my father, and he learned of it from his father. I thought the great mage was just a character from old stories, a legend, even a myth!"

"Hah! He is more real than that and, young elf prince, he now knows of you by name as does Count Coldharth, the Lord of Celesta in his high tower that he wrested from the Darkling a great many years ago. A good man! Rejoice, for many are aware of your coming but the secret is being kept safe, for now. Keep it that way. Ah yes, I knew your father's father, an elven noble and Knight of the Court, the hero Drusilmar Galadhal. When the majority of the elven population of Faerhome fled and scattered during the Elven withdrawal, your father took his family towards the Sword Coast and I never heard of him again. Until recently that is."

Silmar was transfixed by the story. "But why am I here? Why did you call me?"

"I am old; my time draws towards its end. I have been blessed with the ability to perceive choices – in this instance your choices, Silmar Galadhal. A soothsayer, you may think of me perhaps, but no." He gave a low chuckle. "Consider me as the corner of your mind that will allow you judge your choices so that you may carefully make the right decision. You may even say I am an oracle, perhaps. No matter. Know then these things. You have but two choices. Choose one and it shall bring failure to your quest but that will be tinged with joy. However, choose the other and it will herald your quest's success but will be tinged with doom and will be signified by your wearing the trappings of disease."

Silmar bowed his head and closed his eyes. He took a deep breath and released it slowly. "Then it seems that whatever choice I take will be bittersweet!"

"Trust in yourself. Trust in your friends. Your coming shall be as the ball of ice that starts an avalanche. But who will be destroyed by the avalanche's power? You alone can influence that from the moment that you step out from this forest. I can answer no more questions now. The light has gone from my sight. Travel well master elf." He turned to face Jiutarô. "And you too, stranger from the stars. The fulfilment of your duty to your murdered master *shall* reap its rewards. You will have travelled a long road. Only he who has travelled the long road knows where the holes are deep."

Jiutarô looked to Silmar with a vague expression and then back to the enigmatic Lord Olorinuil.

"Where do we go now, Lord?" asked Silmar.

"I advise that you continue north direct to Carrick Cliffs but do not follow the road towards The Vale before turning north for it is watched by agents of your dark foe. There is a path that will take you through the Barrier Peaks. The way is firm and the trail you can follow with ease. There will be two water courses to cross but one is no great obstacle unless the rains come. The other can only be crossed with the aid of the ferryman. Now, you must be on your way. Stand together, with your little dragon." He chuckled again. "Have faith in my words. Close your eyes and open them after a dozen heartbeats. Farewell. Mention me to your father. He will remember the name of Olorinuil of the Royal Court."

The elven Lord Olorinuil faded from sight. The two warriors stood together on the knoll still panting from their exertions with the beast. Sushi landed on the ground and leapt up to settle on Jiutarô's shoulder. The carcass of the monstrous spider remained where it had fallen. Birds were wheeling in the sky. They closed their eyes and waited.

When they opened their eyes, they were at the eaves of the forest at the point at which they had entered.

"We have been just a few hours," said Silmar. "Let us hurry back."

Within two hours they strode into the campsite. Their friends were there waiting, looks of concern etched onto their faces. Caeron threw herself into Jiutarô's arms and showered his face with kisses.

"Thank the gods you've returned, what 'appened?" gasped Jasper. "Where've yer bin? Yer bin more'n three days. We was gettin' very concerned! Jiutarô's little lady 'ere was beside 'erself with worry. Made our lives a choddin' misery, she 'as!"

"But we only left here this morning," replied the elf. "Didn't we? You are serious, are you not?"

Jasper, Taura, Falcon and the others merely scowled at Silmar.

"Were we really three days?" he asked.

"What 'appened?" asked the dwarf.

He described the Lord's depiction of Silmar's forbears but intentionally omitted some of the details about the elven Lord Olorinuil's cryptic predictions. He emphasised instead the advice given to him about the perils of the normally-used road northwards to Carrick Cliffs and the recommended pathways through the Barrier Peaks. He did add that he was advised to trust in himself and his companions. The elf couldn't help but notice the fleeting look of doubt that crossed Taura's face.

A while later Taura took hold of his elbow and led him to one side. She looked directly into his eyes.

"There was more, wasn't there," she said. "What was it that you did not tell us?"

He took a deep breath and exhaled slowly. For a brief moment he considered denying her claim. "Did you use your scrying on me?" he asked.

Her face was a picture of shock, tinged with anger. "I would never do that to a friend," she growled, a little too loudly because a few heads turned towards them. "How dare you even suggest it, Silmar. The others may not have noticed it but I have sufficient knowledge of the ways of people to know when something is amiss. Well?"

He explained that Lord Olorinuil had told him that he would have to face two options the meanings of both which were unclear to him at this time. He tried to describe them to her but was unsure as to whether he accurately represented the aged elf's words.

"Perhaps they will become clearer at the right time," she concluded and walked away.

Watching Jiutarô and Caeron together gave Silmar memories of a young human girl he had left behind in the city of Westron Seaport. Sheena was very young, by now almost seventeen years, an age at which most girls would have been betrothed or even wed and with babies. Sheena had been a street urchin forced into a life of petty crime to support herself and a younger sibling. After a failed attempt to cut his purse from his belt, the elf had discovered her working as a scullery maid in the Ship's Prow Tavern in the city, the very establishment that Silmar and his new friends were staying. He and the girl had become close, very close, despite the warnings his father had given him about the consequences of an elf and a human forging a relationship.

She occupied his thoughts more and more these days.

৯ ৵

Two days later, they found the narrow, little-used track leading north through the mountains. Groves and small forests of coniferous trees dotted the lower slopes of the mountains through some of which their trail took them. From time to time they could see over to the east the great arid plains of Kamambia beyond which, far beyond their sight, the huge and densely-forested Vale of Celesta lay.

Sushi was becoming more and more excitable as they neared the forests and constantly craned her long neck to look towards the trees. Occasionally, she gave a shrill screech and chittered.

"What is it, little one?" asked Jiutarô softly.

"What's the matter with her?" asked Caeron. "Do you think she can detect danger?"

"No. No danger. I not understand what she see. But she happy to see something there. More cleret-wing dragon maybe. She say to me she fly soon."

Very shortly afterwards, however, she launched into the air and sped off towards the trees.

The Samurai became very concerned when she failed to return within an hour. There was no empathic link between him and the little dragon. Caeron, too, constantly looked about them and behind as they continued their march northwards.

"Perhaps Sushi is home now," she said.

"Hai, perhaps so," he regretfully replied after a moment.

They followed the trail as it ran parallel to a swiftly-flowing river. By late afternoon they came to a wide pool where the flow was steadier. A shack and a wooden pier marked the ferry. A wizened man, smoking a stained pipe, sat on the stoop. Taura paid him a silver coin to ferry them across the river.

"Don't get much on this road no more," grumbled the wrinkled old man. For all his advanced years, the man was lean and carried whipcord muscles on his arms and shoulders. "Why are yez using this road? It only goes to Carrick Cliffs and that's closed to visitors now. Nobody goes there and nobody leaves. So it is said, o' course. Yer me first travellers in months. Glad of the coin though but it'll cost a silver for each o' yez and one for the donkey. Where're yez going the?"

"We're travelling through," replied Silmar. "Making our way north, passing Carrick Cliffs towards Zhand's Trading Station."

"Oh yeah? Another shit pit, that is. Oh well, you know yer own business I guess."

"And our business is our own," said Taura as the group trod onto the ferry craft, a flat raft with rails down each side.

"Yez all's a heavy load," he wheezed, coughing thick smoke from his mouth and nose. "Will want some o' yez to help pull the ropes.

The ferry man said no more and, with Falcon, Varengo and Jasper adding extra muscle, just hauled on the rope, hand over hand, until the raft, with its cargo, reached the opposite side.

That evening, the companions made camp in the foothills of the mountains within a small grove. Jiutarô was now very worried for the cleret-wing dragon. It was by far the longest period of time that she had been away from him. He slept badly that night. Caeron slept well though, and shared her watch with Silmar just before dawn. She gazed to the east from time to time but there was still no sign of Sushi.

"Worry not, Caeron," said the elf. He noticed her concern and tried to offer her words of comfort. "She will

641

return, I am sure. It is quite possible that these hills and woods are her home land. Perhaps she has heard the calling of her kin."

"Yes, perhaps that is the reason," she answered shyly. "Then maybe she will stay and not come back to us. Jiutarô is very anxious." It was a rarity that she spoke to anyone other than Jiutarô.

"Once the loyalty of a cleret-wing dragon has been given, it is not usual for it to desert its human, or elven, partner except when it gets to maturity. Sushi is very young."

She nodded. "Jiutarô still feels the loss and I feel it for him," she said quietly so that Silmar had to strain his ears to listen through the morning sounds of song birds. "I know that one day I shall feel his loss too for he will return to his world and will die there. He has told me this and advised me not to love him. But I do, Silmar as I know he loves me but has not said the words."

"Ah, so he told you. We will all bear that loss with regret and sadness for he has become a good friend and a valiant warrior. If only I could wield a bow as he does."

"Practice, practice, practice, Silmar-san! Hai?" Jiutarô stood to one side with a wan smile. His eyes darted to the east but quickly returned to Caeron.

"Hai, Jiutarô-san," replied the elf, smiling broadly. "I also look forward to seeing someone that I miss."

"You have a loved one?" asked Caeron.

"Aye, Caeron. She is Sheena, and she waits for my return, at least I hope she still does, in Westron Seaport."

"How old is she?"

"She thought she was about sixteen summers when we left the city. She may be seventeen now. But I knew her for just a couple of days so perhaps she has moved on."

"Yer can get that idea out of yer daft head, elf!" called Billit. "She was crazy about yer. She'll be there when we get back, you'll see."

The group marched on soon after dawn.

At midday, Sushi swooped down with a high-pitched shriek and landed in front of Caeron and Jiutarô. There was no explanation of where she had been but she was excited to see the Samurai and the young half-elf.

They had no idea that their every move was being scrutinised from a distance by many pairs of eyes and were being reported back by arcane means.

᳢ ᳣

CHAPTER 45

THEY INFILTRATED our town in small numbers, slowly, in ones and twos at first, so we did not notice. They arrived for our salmon, cattle and sheep fayre that we have for two tenday weeks every year. Many people come for that. But they did not leave. Then they built wooden store sheds and started bringing in wagons. We thought they were bringing prosperity in to the town and work for our menfolk. Then more men came, in small groups, and they carried weapons and armour. By the time we noticed, they were everywhere in the town. They infiltrated the town's guard and night watch. They seemed so friendly and many were working around the town alongside our own menfolk. In two months, there were probably more than a hundred of them and that is when we started to be suspicious and troubled.

Then one night, many months ago now, the Temple of Tarne was ransacked and the visiting High Priest's eyes were burned out with a hot branding iron. The other young priest, an acolyte, rushed in with a sword but he was no match for them. They skinned him alive. He was but fourteen summers old! But, do you know? He did not scream or even cry out. Not even when they left him in the burning temple to die. Tarne

was with him then and now young Wenfro sits at Tarne's side.
This seemed to infuriate the gang's leader. He flew in on some
kind of wyrm. It is not a dragon really but a smaller, dark
brown thing with smooth skin, bat wings and a shrieking voice.

At first, people came out of their huts to see him fly but
then the destruction and death began. The beast spat a fiery
acid that burned the thatches and clothing. Its claws tore down
the wooden watchtowers with the watchmen inside them. Its
jaws bit men in half. And the rider laughed! Oh, he, or she
perhaps for the voice was shrill, laughed as men, women and
children died. And how we all cried! They feed the beast on
their prisoners – one every day. It is always hungry.

They started burning and looting, killing and raping.
So many perished. We think scores have died and many of
our young were taken away to keep the townsfolk subjugated.
Children, young girls and young lads, those who are too young
to work, are hostages or slaves. Or worse.

The Temple of Clamberhan suffered the worst. That same
night, they came with swords, whips and chains. They took
the priests, stripped and beat them 'til their backs were ripped
and bloody, and marched them in chains out of the town.
They burned the temple library and all the precious books and
scrolls were lost. But it is spoken that one priest escaped in the
smoke and confusion. There was such a fury and a young priest
of Clamberhan was executed in the market place. And then
another the next night. They made the High Priest, Gallen
Arran, watch it all. But they never found the one who had fled.
It is said that he took with him something of great value. The
priests have been taken away but we do not know where. We
believe it is somewhere up in the hills.

And now the men of the town are being forced to build a
tower of stone for this leader. They are beaten until they drop
and then they are left to die. Some are taken away by us women

before they are fed to the foul beast. But they recover only to end up back on the damned tower.

Travellers are turned away long before they reach the town. I believe that they are told that disease is rife and that the town can admit no visitors. Visiting traders exchange their wares by the Carrick River crossing.

We are doomed.

The Widow Helliol
Carrick Cliffs
Year of the Brown Bear

ᦆ ᦇ

Silmar, Jiutarô, Yoriando, Caeron and Jasper lay at the top of a small hill overlooking the Carrick River ferry crossing. They were midway between the town, to their left, and the crossing to their right. A large black wooden shed, obviously newly-constructed, stood on the far side of the river. The ferry raft was also on the far side and six men stood by it. They all appeared well-armed. Two horses were tied to a hitching rail. A wagon was parked to one side of the shed.

About three miles beyond the crossing stood the town of Carrick Cliffs. Unusually, there were no minarets or domes to show that there were temples in the town.

"Very strange," mumbled Varengo. "I would have expected to see a dome for the temple of Clamberhan. I know there was one there over to the right."

"Destroyed, do you think?" suggested Jasper.

"Aye, most likely."

"There is a little community by the river, way over there," said Caeron.

Not even Silmar, with his extraordinary eyesight had spotted the tiny shanties of the community in the few minutes that they had been looking out over the land. Caeron pointed to a spot on the river bank about a mile to the east of the town. Silmar could just see some little huts and wisps of smoke from cooking fires.

"You have keen eyesight, Caeron," complimented the elf. "Look, also, in the eaves of the little wood there."

A little shack stood midway between the community and the town. Neither Jiutarô nor Jasper could see anything at all at this distance.

"That's more 'n likely a community of outcasts," said Yoriando.

"Outcasts?" asked Taura. "Do you mean they're diseased or something?"

"Aye lady, I do. Lepers I would say. There are a few towns in this region that have small colonies of lepers. They roam into the towns to beg for food. It is considered that if they were to be killed or driven away then their curse would cause the leprosy to find another victim. So they are tolerated."

"Aye, an' do they wear filthy rags with hoods to cover their heads so their deformed faces don't frighten the people?" Jasper asked.

Yoriando nodded.

"Poor bastards," mumbled Silmar. In over a century, he had never encountered anything like this.

"There is stone tower in town," said Jiutarô. "Not tall. Many men build it, you look."

They waited for a few minutes more.

"Well, there is not much else to see," said Silmar. "Let's get back to the others."

It took them a half-hour to walk the distance through the hills back to the group. These hills that overlooked the river crossing were an ideal place for concealment and they could safely build a small fire for cooking during the day.

"What does anyone know about this town?" asked Taura.

From the little bits of information given by Varengo, Yoriando and, surprisingly, Caeron, they were able to put together a fairly detailed picture of the town.

The walled town was named after the high waterfalls above the ford on the Carrick River. The town, sitting a league northeast of the falls, was famed for its salmon which, on their return from the ocean, spawned in the river shallows. The town sat at the point near to where the River Carrick was crossed by the trail that the group had been following for the last few days. The buildings of the town were of stone to provide a safe and secure haven in a troubled land. Unusually, the steep slate roofs of the buildings enabled them to survive heavy winter snows.

There had a Temple to Clamberhan in the town and another, smaller temple to Tarne that from the distance from their observation point still showed signs of fire damage to one wing. Carrick Cliffs was still a frontier town where the law was almost non-existent, except on the rare occasion that a Priest of Tarne and his small retinue of priests and crusaders travelled from Norovir to enter through the town's gates.

A storage yard sat at one end of the town presumably to hold metal ore mined in the mountains.

"That shed's dwarven," Jasper grunted.

"How could you tell?" Taura asked him. She had the feeling that it would turn out to be a stupid question. She was right.

"Din't yer look at the height o' the doors, girlie?" He explained that the dwarves would generally keep themselves to themselves in any town across the lands of Baylea except on the rare occasion when the need to enter the town was called for.

"I was too far away to notice doors," she replied testily.

"So I wonders where the dwarves is now," he whispered rhetorically as he noted that the yard was deserted. Louder he said "P'raps they only comes into town now and then to trade their minerals."

"We have got two choices here," said Silmar. "Go in ourselves and find out what is going on or see if we can get help, maybe from the dwarves."

"Or both, if we can," suggested Taura.

"Aye, except we don't know where the dwarves are," replied Varengo. "They may not take kindly to visitors calling at their mines."

Jasper stood with his feet apart, his hands on his hips and puffed out his chest with annoyance. "They choddin' well *will* if they think their property in the town is being used or chopped up by the chods who 'ave moved in. Anyways, it won't be 'ard for us to find 'em. They got their mines up in the mountains. They bring the ore in by wagon, or they used to. There will be a track. See? Easy ain't it, human? Well, it is if you apply yer mind to it!"

"But we need to get into the town somehow," Varengo said. "It's a big town for a relatively small gang to keep control of. And even then they will have to divide their forces so that some sleep while others work or keep watch. We need to see if there is anyone there who can give us some information. So what do we need to know?"

Jasper replied straight away. "'Ow many of 'em are there? 'Oo leads 'em? Is there any Darkling? Where's that Priest of

Clamberhan? What's 'is name? Is there anyone in the town 'oo can 'elp us? Just what in the choddin' dark depths of the Void is goin' on? We gotta get someone in there. An' we need a base to 'ide out in."

"Gallen Arran," replied Silmar.

"What?" responded the dwarf.

"The Priest of Clamberhan. You asked what his name was."

Jasper looked confused for a brief moment. "Oh, aye. I did. Look, everyone. I'm going off to find them dwarf mines. They may treat me as one of their own, partic'ly if I yell at 'em that their property in the town is bein' used by the new peoples."

"Do you need someone to go with you?" asked Yoriando. "I'll be happy to come along with you."

"Nah. Them dwarves might not take to kindly *me* bein' there but if you turn up too they might get really pissed off!"

"When will you go then?" asked Taura.

"At sundown. Find the road during the night an' follow it up into the mountains. Should be easy to find the mine 'cos they gotta use wagons to bring down the metals an' stuff."

"Your God *Tarne* will watch over you, I'm sure," the priestess murmured.

"Aye, girlie. I'm sure 'e will, 'specially if you was to put in a good word for me with your Neilea! I'll need a bit o' food an' water, that's all. So what will all you be doin'!"

Silmar thought for a moment and rubbed his chin with his hand. "We do need to go in to the town but strangers will soon be recognised."

"Wait, Silmar," called Taura. "Maybe not. I have an idea."

Although the morning was chilly and heavily overcast, the rain held off. The woman rose early, just as she had every morning for many years. Her first task of the day would be to fetch a bucket of water from the river. This chore was repeated many times each day but it was part of her daily routine and she thought nothing of it. Many times lately she looked at her hands. The palms were hard and calloused from the lifting and carrying of full buckets, and the water-skins, bread and cloth that she took to the little community of outcasts along the river. They begged for coppers in the town but gave every coin to her for they knew that the coins would not be accepted by any trader in the town if they tried to spend it themselves. With the money, *she* would buy the flour and yeast to make the bread, and the sandals, and cloth that the lepers would need to cover their bodies and heads.

Her husband had died many years earlier soon after returning home from the fighting in the town. She had been unable to save his life despite her training as a Priestess of Tambarhal, the god of healing and nature. A powerful adventuring party had united the townsfolk and together, they had kicked out the Hoshite forces that had oppressed the population. The foul and vicious Hosh leader, a half-orc named Silas Hebbern, was then executed by the leader of the adventurers, a young Priest of Tarne named Halorun Tann.

Her failure to help her husband caused her to lose her faith but instead awoke in her a strong sense of compassion that now drove her to offer her care to the outcasts. Although their hovels were often little more than discarded pieces of wood and other materials from the town, they now had beds of straw packed in canvas covers, wool or linen clothing to replace those that wore out, regular food and, blessed be the gods, sandals! The priests of Clamberhan and Tarne had helped where they could but even their powerful prayers had little enough influence to slow the advance of the curse of leprosy, let alone to heal. Some of the townsfolk said she was foolish to give help to the outcasts but she reminded them that some of these lepers were their own kinsmen; she was not so naive to realise that in most cases the donations were given not out of charity but to buy their own protection in the eyes of the gods. Nevertheless, she was respected and had many friends in the town. Until recently at least. Now everything in the town had changed but the outcasts still managed to gather coppers, even from the insurgents. Only the priests in the town had known of her own lapsed priesthood.

She opened her door to change the night's stale air of her little shack. She was about to step out through the door when she froze in shock and fright.

Grey, dripping, wraith-like figures rose from the river waters and stepped onto the riverbank. The muddy river-water dripped from their hair, faces and clothing.

She gave a startled scream and dropped the bucket. In panic, she rushed back inside and bolted the door behind her. With her hands shaking, she tore open a leather bag and rummaged inside it.

"Damn!" Her voice trembled. "Where is it? Oh, Tambarhal. Don't fail me when I need you now!"

She gasped for air as her fingertips closed on a metal chain just as a voice called from outside.

"Dellie Helliol? Is that you? Is it really you, Dellie?"

Her fingers froze inside the bag and her eyes flashed towards the doorway. *The demons, they know my name! They are coming for me!*

"Dellie? It is I, Varengo. I was your husband's companion. Do you remember me? Yori is here too. Do not be afraid."

She rose to her feet and looked through a narrow crack in the door. In her hands was a leather medallion hanging from a chain. She saw a filthy but familiar, grinning face looking back at her from the riverbank.

"W-what is your business here?" she called back, her voice still trembling and her heart racing with uncertainty. "How c-can I trust you?"

"Dellie. We have come to help, not to harm. By the blessed memory of my friend Jannos Helliol, you have nothing to fear from us."

She opened the door a fraction and Varengo stepped forward. He let out a yell as the door slammed into him and sent him flying backwards. The others laughed as he landed with a thump on his behind.

"Ummph! Dear lady, that is no way to treat an old friend! Gods, that hurt!" A trickle of blood flowed from his nose and he prodded it with his finger. "Ouch! I think it's broken!"

From inside the house came the voice of the woman. "As far as I know, you may be in league with those that now terrorise the town. Now, be gone from here and leave an old lady in peace!"

"You are not old, my dear Dellie. You are –!"

"I am not your dear Dellie, or anyone else's."

"We wish to help," called Taura. "We have been tasked to try to sort out this problem in the town."

"Problem? Task? Who sent you on this quest?"

"It was placed upon us by one Halorun Tann of –"

"Halorun? Hal? Well now, that is a different matter. Why didn't you say earlier? He is known to me and is wedded to someone I know very well. Hah! Hal was here

653

during the last troubles some years ago when my Jannos died. Mmm! And very nice he was too! Ha ha! Varengo, you and the lady may come in. The rest of you had better hide in the trees and get dried off. *They* may see you from the town."

She opened her door wide. There before them stood a woman, tall, attractive and slender. Although clearly of middle years, her hair was long and black, although there were flecks of grey. She wore a mixture of clothing to keep out the early morning cold. A well-worn soft hide hose covered her legs beneath a linen dress that had seen better days. Her grey woollen cloak was covered with patches and a knitted woollen shawl was wrapped around her neck. On her feet were sheepskin shoes that were tied on with cord.

"You don't see me at my best, Varengo," she sighed. "I cannot afford anything nice these days."

"My dear lady, you look like a princess to me!" he mumbled. "You always did." He felt his cheeks flushing and was glad of the gloom inside the shack.

She slipped her right hand through his arm and smiled brightly at him. "You smell awful but how gallant you are. I'm so pleased you haven't lost your charm but not so happy about your odour. Tell me what brings you and your friends to my door. You did startle me. You all looked so fierce! Oh dear, would you like me to attend to your nose? Did I do that? Oh, poor you! Did you not notice that my door opens outwards? A fine adventurer you are! Now, keep still, this may hurt!"

☙ ❧

That evening, the companions crowded into Dellie's shack and listened to her tale. Many men, scores it seemed, had infiltrated the town over the period of a couple of months.

They had come in small groups dressed as travellers, tinkers, adventurers, miners and farmers. They were welcomed in at first and many had been accommodated in the inns and taverns. Some camped outside the town and entered during the day. Everything was peaceful at first but fights soon started between the new arrivals and the townsmen. Some market stalls and even a few homes were looted. And still more men came.

Then one day the newcomers showed their true colours and uncovered their uniform jerkins, armour and weapons. The principle town leaders and elders were incarcerated and the watch-houses were taken over. Weapons were confiscated and locked away. This happened so quickly that the townsfolk had no chance to retaliate although there was some resistance. A few days later, after much shouting and rioting, the soldiers waded in and a few townspeople were killed or injured.

"The leader of the gang, someone called Jarik Hebbern, had the three prominent town elders publicly executed the next day as a warning to the town," said Dellie. "I knew them all and they were good men."

"Hebbern? I know that name from somewhere," said Varengo as he scratched at his beard.

"Aye, and so you should," replied Yoriando. "His father was one Silas Hebbern, a half-orc renowned for his cruelty. It was he who stole the precious and sacred silver armour of Tarne from the Temple of the Just. Your friend, what's his name? Aye, the young priest, Halorun Tann, executed him after the battle to liberate this very town all those years ago. Tann and his friends were the heroes of the town. The son of the villain has come back to finish off what his father started, it seems."

Dellie continued with the more recent news of fall of the town. "The Temple of Clamberhan was ransacked and its holy symbols, vestments and paraphernalia desecrated. The sacred ceremonial dagger of Clamberhan was taken and a priest I think, although of what denomination I have no knowledge, wearing a black hooded cloak just like the dragon-rider, corrupted its goodness so it became a tool of a foul deity. But then suddenly, the dagger disappeared from the temple. Suspicion immediately fell on the captured priests of Clamberhan."

Almost tearfully, she described how the High Priest of Temple of Clamberhan had refused to disclose whereabouts of the dagger so in retaliation the leader of the organisation personally and viciously publicly executed two of the Temple's youngest priests. It seemed the artefact had been spirited out of the Temple and the town. Under extreme duress, the High Priest of Clamberhano, Gallen Arran, had let it be known that the dagger was on its way to Westron Seaport. Although a group of their soldiers and three mysterious riders dressed in hooded cloaks searched for many tenday-weeks, it was evident that the priest and the dagger were nowhere to be found.

Families in town each had at least one member taken away as hostages by the gang. This was to ensure that the townspeople remained subjugated and wouldn't retaliate. People leaving the town had to report out and in to the town guard posts daily to ensure nobody fled for help. Townsfolk were not allowed to carry weapons. Since then, the Town had been under the grip of an iron fist. Its folk remained under curfew during darkness and were only allowed out within the town walls during the hours of daylight. Land workers needing to go outside the town were under tight control, knowing that if they failed to return by sunset, they or their captive family member would be under a death sentence.

"The only people not subject to these tight controls are the handful of lepers," she said, "all of whom live in hovels well away from the town's walls but come with me into the town to beg for food and coppers."

"What happened to the menfolk?" asked Falcon. "Could they be armed to fight?"

"What menfolk?" she huffed. "They are all prisoners who are either taken away into the hills somewhere or made to work 'til they drop building the new tower. Everybody talks about *the Tower*, as if it's the name of the people and not the building."

"Perhaps it is," murmured Silmar. "Perhaps it is the name of this gang. Perhaps the term *building the tower* means more than the construction work in the town."

"We not know this for sure," said Jiutarô. "They just gang of killers, is all. But why they here?" He gently fondled the cleret-wing dragon beneath her jaw and she stretched her head forward, purring in ecstasy.

Caeron came in through the door having returned from sentry. She picked her way through the legs and feet of the companions and sat down next to Jiutarô. Vallio rose to his feet and stepped outside to take the half-elf's place.

"What did I miss?" asked Caeron.

"Just that the town is in deep shit!" replied Billit.

"You have such a way with words," sighed Taura, shaking her head slowly.

"Oh put a sandal in it, girlie!" retorted the gnome with a chuckle.

The others laughed, but there was little humour in it.

"How many are prisoners?" repeated Falcon.

"Hundreds, all the adult men mostly, except for the young and old ones who would offer little or no resistance. Those left in the town are not bothered by the brigands, mainly. A few women were taken captive to make sure their men work hard. Some young women have been abducted to serve as slaves for the leaders. It is suspected that these are being treated badly." She shuddered and cast her gaze downwards. "Thank the gods that no little children have been held as captives but most boys, and some girls, over the age of about 13 years have been. It is not known where any of the captives are being held but it is not in the town."

"I think we will need to find out," suggested Morendo, "but this will be just a bit difficult."

"Aye, you're right," answered Varengo. "We can give that some deep thought for a while."

"Do you think that there will be battle?" asked Dellie. "There aren't very many of you."

Yoriando stretched his back and stood up. "We have some ideas but I wish we had some of the old heroes. You know, like Kell."

"Aye, he would have been handy," said Vallio. "But what about Ghar Hrol? Remember him?"

"The dragon knight? Not heard of him for years," replied Morendo. "Rumour had it he was killed by a red dragon."

"Who is this warrior?" asked Silmar. "I seem to recognise the name from tales sung in the tavern in Refuge."

"A mighty warrior, much like Falcon here," answered Varengo. "He came to the western lands from the distant east some twenty or more years ago and became an adventurer. He took to riding the skies on a great bronze dragon called Violor. Nay, he's not dead, I'm certain of it. He and his party came up against a red dragon to destroy it. Strange, because the dragon spared Ghar at the end. It collected magical artefacts to study the art in the peace and solitude of the desert lands far to the east and south. Ghar Hrol became a sort of bodyguard for it. It is said now that Ghar works for the Count Coldharth, which means that Ghar has the favour of none other than the great War-mage of the Vale, Antheuseolin himself. Aye, he would be a handy ally, with his great battle-sword! Many songs of his heroism are sung in these parts."

"But we shall manage without the likes of him," murmured Taura. "We shall have to."

Silmar nodded in agreement. "But first it may be an idea to see what we are up against," he suggested. "What was this idea of yours, Taura? You know, just before we crossed the river?"

CHAPTER 46

JASPER HAD left his companions and embarked on his search to find the dwarven mines and his kinfolk. He knew that they were somewhere in the mountainous region to the west of Carrick Cliffs and that his search would take place mostly in the dark. He had the advantage of excellent night vision, an innate ability of dwarves. He had begun his search by walking during the dark hours at the end of the day and had now been on the road for a few hours. He noticed some wagon tracks that were very deeply cut into the road and they appeared relatively new.

Hmm! An 'eavy load they carry, he thought. *Weapons or supplies fer the gang o' cutthroats now runnin' Carrick Cliffs? Gotta be.*

He followed the tracks higher into foothills of the mountains. He was beginning to run short of water already and was getting quite concerned. During the night he was surprised to hear a wagon coming down the road towards him, leaping out of sight just in time as it trundled around a bend. It was drawn by four very heavy horses, a fact that aroused much curiosity with the dwarf. The drovers were dressed in the black garb, similar to the thugs he had spotted running Carrick Cliffs, cursing as they struggled to persuade the horses to drag the wagon over a rise. One rider on horseback tugged on the traces of one of the leading horses in an effort to keep the wagon moving. Following closely behind were two more riders armed with bows and swords.

Now, that's interestin'! Whatever the cargo was, it was quite small but hefty and covered in a tarpaulin. *Shit! I'd best take care in case of other riders and wagons.*

The wagon tracks eventually veered off to the left along another much narrower and steeper track. He decided to follow it out of curiosity. *Just for a while, won't do no 'arm!*

Dawn was beginning to cast its rosy hues on the eastern horizon and he was anxious that he might be spotted. Despite this, he was feeling quite at home in the rocks and crags that flanked the road, picking his way carefully and keeping the road constantly in sight.

Another wagon, with an escort of three riders, passed by on the road completely unaware of the dwarf that was watching them. From the groaning of the wheels and laboured breathing of the horses, it was another heavy load.

Another hour of trudging through the rocks finally brought him towards the rim of a large bowl-shaped valley in the hills. It was the din of stone being hammered and voices barking orders that caused the dwarf to be even more cautious. Keeping his profile as low as he could between boulders and scrub, he crawled his way towards the edge. He dropped to his stomach and inched his way to the lip.

"It's a choddin' quarry!" he muttered under his breath. "What are they up to? Ah, they gotta be blocks o' stone fer the tower! Aye, 'course it is."

As he looked across the quarry, his gaze centred over a group of workers who were wielding steel poles and hammers to cut block from the rock. Once cut, the blocks were dragged across the earth on heavy wooden sleds to other groups of workers engaged in chiselling blocks to specified dimensions. The finished blocks were lifted by block and tackle attached to an 'A' frame and loaded onto waiting wagons.

He spotted about two dozen workers labouring under the baking sun. *I bet they're captives from the town!*

One, an elderly man, was continually going from one worker to the next with a bucket of water. There were many men dressed in assorted black clothing driving the workers hard or just leaning against the wagons or fence posts. One in particular, a brute of a man who whipped the backs of each worker that he walked past, caught Jasper's attention. *I'll 'ave 'im, sooner or later!* Jasper vowed. The backs of some of the unfortunate captives were streaked with welts and drying cuts.

Four small wooden huts stood beneath the cliff edge of the quarry and on the other side was a small stockade in which another two dozen forms, obviously captives, appeared to be sleeping. *Hah, the night workers! I'll be back with a few of my kind soon to sort some of this out.*

He waited another few minutes before deciding to move. "By Tarne's plaited silver beard! What an operation!" he muttered again.

The sun was getting higher in the sky so he decided it was time for him to go. Inching his way backwards he moved away from the lip. As he started to rise he heard a shuffle behind him. He whipped his head around just in time to see a thug raise his sword to strike him down.

Two hours after dawn, a tall but shabbily-dressed woman approached the town gate on foot. As always, she held her head high with pride. She was accompanied, as usual, by a couple of outcasts. These two figures, completely covered in rags and leaning heavily on their customary thick wooden poles, were being brought into town to beg, as they always did, for coppers thrown at them by townsfolk and occasionally by members of the new administration. Coppers were coppers, whoever threw them. Everybody knew it was very bad luck to mistreat, or even shun, these outcasts. To do so would invite their curse onto oneself. Did not the town elder, Dallimore, become struck down by leprosy only ten years back? For all anyone knew, he could well be one of those outcasts who himself came into town to plead for alms. Now Madam Dallimore enjoyed his home, his status and his money. That is, she did so only until the new arrivals took over the town, its wealth and destroyed the temples, libraries and places of learning.

Two guards leaned against the hitching-rail placed just outside the gate. Few travellers came to the town these days. Most of them were turned away at the river ferry. Others that managed to get in were either put onto the work gangs or taken away to the new prison hidden in the hills.

"It's her again, Pall. I'm gonna get my 'ands on those ample charms under that tunic now, you'll see. Watch this."

"Har, har! Mebbe I'll get my 'ands in between –!"

"Yer can frackin' wait til I've 'ad mah go first!" yelled Grav. "Then you can 'ave what's left!"

As the woman approached, the man's look of distaste at the outcasts turned to one of lust as he gazed directly at the well-endowed chest of the woman.

"Go on then, Grav. Do it, do it!" wheezed the other guard.

"You again, witch? Why do you bring these – these – diseased people into town? What else 'ave you got, eh? I got orders to thoroughly search everyone comin' in through the gates. I'm startin' with your tunic then your hose." He reached for her tunic but she stepped back and to one side.

"I'm no witch, as well you know," she snapped back. You will not lay a hand on me!"

Suddenly, one of the outcasts stumbled as his pole slid across the ground. He staggered and collided with the woman. She recoiled with a stifled yell and the figure fell heavily to the ground.

Grav leapt back in terror. The second outcast shuffled over and, with some difficulty and bad language, managed to help the other back onto his feet.

"S-sorry m-m-my lady!" croaked the figure. "It's mm-m-my feet. I think I'm l-l-losing s-some t-toes!"

Grav leapt back again, his face a mask of revulsion. "Ugh! Foul! Keep those bastards under control, can't you, woman? Get them away from here. Go on through. Just keep them away from me! Don't think I've finished with you. I shall come calling at your hovel tonight so you 'ad better be more accom-, accommi-, er, more friendly to me!"

৬ ৶

Grabbing his great battleaxe in one hand, Jasper blocked the descending sword and swung it wildly at his attacker. The man was committed to his attack and was unable to leap over the swinging blade. Although there was little strength in the swing, the keen edge of the heavy blade cut straight through the man's ankles, severing his feet cleanly. The man's body crashed to the floor without uttering a sound, such was his shock. Blood spurted across the ground from the stumps of his lower legs.

Jasper's axe slammed into the man's head just as his mouth opened to utter a scream of shock and agony.

"Buggerit! Now I got meself a body to hide," he gasped.

Carefully looking about him, he was content that the area was clear and, using the tip of his battleaxe, scooped a shallow trench in the ground next to a boulder. He dragged the body, remembering the dismembered feet, into the dip and with great effort rolled the boulder over the top. He placed a few more stones haphazardly there too. He then scattered the bloodstained sand about him and, as the sun rose higher over the eastern horizon, he made his way back to the road. Hopefully, there would be little sign, if any, of the dead body and the disappearance of the man would be put down to desertion.

"Aye, with luck," he murmured.

୬ ୧

"Cleverly done, Varengo!" laughed Dellie. "I've had trouble with that one before. He's been trying to put his hand inside my tunic for ages but he's never been that threatening before."

"He'll have to answer to me if he tries that again. If he does call round tonight, I'll be waiting. He wants to put his hand on sacred ground!"

"Aye," she replied, blushing. "That place is reserved for someone special."

"Oh, I see," said Varengo. The disappointment was obvious from his tone. "Who is this most fortunate of men?"

"There could be someone who takes my fancy. He has been in my thoughts on and off for a few years."

665

"Oh! I am now insanely jealous and shall rush straight to an abbey and take holy vows! Does he know of this yet?"

"I expect not. But you may rest assured that I feel safe knowing you're there to protect my virtue, Varengo."

"I would die for you, my lady!" he whispered.

"Before you have walked that sacred ground? You had better not!" She gave a little chuckle.

Beneath his lepers' grey coverings, it was now Varengo's turn to blush.

"I would be grateful if you change the subject," hissed Silmar's voice from inside the other leper's wrappings. "This is going further than I feel comfortable with. Where do we need to go?"

They had entered the town of Carrick Cliffs and, surprisingly, there were few people about, despite the approach of mid-morning. To their right, just inside the city walls, was a small barrack block. A few black-clad men lounged nonchalantly in windows watching the townsfolk as they moved about the town square and market place. Beyond the barrack building were the partially-charred remains of another building. Dellie informed them that it had been the Temple of Clamberhan. The market square stood before them. There were a few stalls selling fruit and vegetables and some household goods. The single-storey guildhall and meeting-house stood beyond the town square. It looked unharmed as did most of the other houses and buildings. A round stone tower, under construction, rose behind the guildhall. A number of men were scurrying over the construction but the sounds of shouts and the crack of whips punctuated the silence of the town square.

Dellie's face gave a distressed expression. She spoke barely above a whisper. "Some of the townsmen are being forced to build the tower. Oh, Tambarhal! How can you allow this to happen? Varengo, Silmar, you will need to move from place to place. Nobody notices a leper. Sit for an hour in the town square, one of you on the guildhall steps and the other at the base of that statue. Then move to somewhere else where people gather. Approach no-one for you will frighten them. Let them approach you. Only then will they toss you a copper or two. Some of the ruffians may toss a coin in the horse troughs, or even in horse droppings. They will watch and laugh as you fish for it. You must do it without complaint. As a leper you have little dignity. Show gratitude and be polite. Do not enter any buildings or taverns either. Do you have any questions?"

"How many coppers would we usually collect?"

"On a good day? Twenty. But usually it's twelve to fifteen. Each. With that I can barely get enough to feed and clothe the thirty or so outcasts in the community.

"Aye, and yourself too," answered Silmar. "When do we leave?"

"We finish in the early to mid afternoon. Usually by that time the outcasts are getting very tired and the town square becomes almost deserted. You give the coins to me and I have to wash them in the horse trough otherwise no trader will take them. Until then, keep safe. Especially you, Varengo. I may have some holy ground that I want you to explore some time soon. Hahaha!"

"Madam, really!" Beneath his rags, Varengo grinned. And blushed again.

� ৎ৶

Although he was completely covered in the filthy, fetid fabric, Silmar could see quite well through the thin muslin that covered his face. His ears had caused a minor problem because the tips of them were obvious through the fabric. A strip of cloth was tied around his head to bind them. He had also taken the precaution of strapping a slim dagger to his left forearm so that its presence was not betrayed. Apart from the walking pole, he carried no other weapon. The pole itself would be a very effective weapon in his hands, nonetheless.

As he shuffled and lurched behind Dellie, his thoughts went back to the day in the spider-infested forest. The oracle, Lord Olorinuil of Faerhome, had foretold that he would have two options to choose from. Now he wore the trappings of disease! *The choice that would bring success but would be tinged with doom.* His doom? That haunted his thoughts although he did what he could to push it aside.

The statue in the centre of the town square was carved from stone. It showed a proud-looking warrior dressed in a formal uniform. The figure, standing at twice the size of its original subject, looked to the south with a stern face, shielding his eyes from the sun with his left hand and holding a pike against his body with his right. No plaque gave his name. Indeed, it was doubtful if many townsfolk knew these days the name of the hero or his history. The features were worn from the effects of weather and lack of care. Years of bird-droppings had left it badly stained. It stood on a plinth mounted on three steps. To its rear was a stone horse-trough that could be fed by water from a rusting hand-pump.

Silmar sat at one end of the steps thinking with sadness of the town neglecting the grand statue erected to honour a man of such bravery or importance.

The town square was a little busier now and many townsfolk strode through the market. The majority of the people were women except for a few elderly men. The silence was uncanny for there were no yells of market sellers shouting at the tops of their voices to compete with others as would normally be expected. A few dogs wandered through the market looking for scraps but there was little meat for them to have. There were no stalls selling weapons and armour.

But everywhere there were figures dressed in black uniforms of sorts. No one rogue wore the same uniform or armour, or carried the same weapon, as another. The only similarity was that the clothing was black and a red square was crudely painted on the fronts and backs of tunics, breastplates, chain-mail and shields. Many of the occupying troops appeared to be dressed in tattered and faded remnants of Hoshite army uniforms. The elf considered that there were some deserters or, because of their advancing ages, veteran Hoshite soldiers.

Neither were the rogues all of the same origin or species. Silmar was surprised to see a half-elf. The vast majority were humans but there were a few with more than a little orcish blood in their veins.

They are damned mercenaries! he thought. *Hired thugs.*

As agreed, both he and Varengo began independently estimating the number of *mercenaries* in the town.

After a while, he climbed unsteadily to his feet and, leaning heavily on his pole, he made his way out of the town square. Not far away, behind the guildhall, was the site of much building work. A large number of men, presumably townsfolk, were being driven hard at work by thugs wielding whips and clubs. Some of the workers were struggling to move large stone blocks from a wagon and manhandle them onto a platform. Other men used block and tackle to raise them into position on the wall.

At this rate, Silmar thought, it *would take months for the tower to be built.*

Then a shrill shout caught the elf's attention. Standing on another platform was a figure dressed in an ornate black helm, black cape and plate armour, black hose and high black boots. This person was not particularly tall, perhaps only five and a half feet, but the helm, with its horns and black plume, made the wearer appear significantly taller. The billowing cape made it difficult to estimate the figure's build. A long, slim sword hung at the figure's left hip but no other weapons were visible. A long black staff, ornately carved with arcane runes and glyphs, was held in the left hand.

A mage? Silmar asked himself.

Two more figures stood slightly behind the first. They were dressed similarly to the other but instead of helms, they wore hooded cloaks. Each also had a slim sword at the hip but no other weapon could be seen. Neither carried a staff.

A roar erupted from beneath the platform. Silmar's eyes focussed on a beast the like of which he had never seen before. A dragon-like creature, large but much smaller than he knew a dragon would be.

Not a dragon? Then what?

It did not appear to have a scaled hide but instead, a smooth grey-brown skin. Its head was also dragon-like but without the horny crest. Its eyes were yellow and cat-like. It was clearly becoming agitated and it issued another roar.

"My beast is hungry again" shrieked a voice. The helmed figure on the platform repeated the statement.

Gods! he thought. *It's a woman!*

"I want it fed now!" She turned her gaze about the area. Suddenly, her look stopped on Silmar. "Fetch me that! Now!"

The elf froze and blood turned to ice in his veins.

She shrieked even louder at a mercenary standing close to Silmar. The man was startled to see that he had been standing so close to an outcast and his face paled when the realisation dawned on him.

"Bu – but m-my lady!" stammered the man, his lips trembling with terror. "He - he is diseased. P-please, no! Your beast will become sick and die. I will die a slow and h-horrible death if I t-touch him."

Without warning, the woman levelled her staff and pointed its tip towards the terrified man. A lance of white-hot energy issued forth. The mercenary was hit in the centre of his chest and he was catapulted back many paces. He was dead before he hit the ground.

"It does not do to argue with me," screeched the figure. "Now my beast has food. Bring it here. Immediately!"

Meanwhile, in the shocked commotion, Silmar shuffled out of the area and back the way he had come. Within a few moments he was back in front of the guildhall and he collapsed onto the statue steps once again. His heart was beating furiously but he had seen something of immense interest – a very small detail that came as a surprise to him.

∽ ∾

Varengo sat at one end of the stone steps at the entrance to the guildhall and observed. He had watched Silmar rise unsteadily to his feet from the base of the statue, shuffle past the market and stagger by the guildhall towards the construction site beyond. He had seen how the people stepped well clear as the outcast, in his rags, lurched by. The elf's gait was very convincing. Both had spent a while early that morning watching some of the outcasts in their community. The shuffling and use of the pole had to convince the townspeople that the figures were what they appeared to be – lepers. Some folk held their noses as if to avoid breathing in the same air as the outcasts. Others touched their foreheads, and then their lips, and spat over their left shoulders in a superstitious attempt to ward off the curse.

"Alms, kind ma'am? Alms for a starving leper. I once helped defend these walls. Just a few coppers, that's all I ask!"

Using his charm and politeness, Varengo had collected eleven copper coins. *I'll add a few more to it,* he thought to himself.

To the left-hand side of the guildhall was a large stockyard and at the rear of that stood a large stone building, a storehouse by the looks of it. It was probably the largest building, measured in ground-area, in the town, measuring about forty paces long by twenty wide. It had a pair of wooden doors large enough to admit a large wagon and two other doors that Varengo could see. Strangely, these doors were quite low, no higher than four feet tall, he reckoned.

Of course! It's the dwarven store shed we saw from the hills, he thought. *Interesting, this gang is using it now.*

Even more interesting to him were the dark caped and hooded figures he saw walking past the sometimes open doors in the dim light inside the shed. They looked like priests or mages; one couldn't always be sure. Other figures also walked around the shed, both inside and outside – these seemed just to be the rank and file gang members. None of the hooded figures came outside the structure however. But it did cause Varengo to think about where he had seen similarly-dressed characters.

Surely not, he mused. *They could be though.*

Then, suddenly, a cry sounded from inside the building. Carefully, so as not to arouse suspicion, he turned his head towards the sound. The sound had been like that of a woman in despair rather than in pain. It had faded to a sob and then silence.

Slaves? Prisoners?

Nothing else happened while he watched and a couple more coppers landed at his feet. He quickly grabbed them and croaked his gratitude to the elderly woman who strode past. "Bless you ma'am. Bless you."

He was about to rise to his feet when he spotted Silmar hurriedly shuffling back from beyond the Guildhall and fall onto the statue steps but he soon rose to his feet again. As the elf took a wide path around the market place, Dellie appeared through the small crowd and made her way towards him. Varengo watched with interest as the two conversed quietly but he rose, with apparent effort, as Dellie beckoned him over to her. He leaned heavily on his pole and limped across.

"Time to go back to the commune now," she said quite loudly. "I know it is early but you both look tired. Have you had a good morning?"

Both outcasts nodded and passed her the coins. She took them and washed them in the trough by the statue.

"So many? Almost thirty coppers! No, wait! That is a silver coin. Well done, I haven't seen one of those for such a long time. People can be so kind. That is the most I have ever collected for the commune." She strode over to the market and bought bread, vegetables and meat and fruit.

"Did you put that in yourself, Varengo?" whispered Silmar.

"May have carelessly dropped it in! Can't remember!"

Fortunately, the two guards who had caused Dellie such a problem earlier that morning were not at the gate as the trio passed through. Together, they laboriously struggled back along the river towards Dellie's home.

From the scrub, a few hundred paces from the town gates, a pair of eyes watched their slow progress.

From a much greater distance, many more pairs of eyes also watched the trio.

❧ ❧

"Darkling! I'm convinced of it."

Silmar had been quiet during the taxing walk back to Dellie Helliol's shack. As he discussed the morning's revelations he grew more and more angered by them.

"I did not have the burden with me," he explained, "but I didn't need to be carrying it to feel the presence of *that* menace. It was different though. I felt something else. Another evil!"

"What is this burden you speak of?" asked Dellie.

"Ah, I carry a magical item and it alerts me to the presence of evil. But the thing itself is evil. Do not concern yourself with it. It shall be dealt with soon. But there is something else. Who is that mage in black? It is a woman, I am sure. She wields magic of awesome power. Her face was hidden but I caught a glimpse of grey-white hair beneath her helm. If she's *not* Darkling then I would be surprised."

Varengo sat opposite Silmar in the circle of companions and spoke. "I may have said that you are mistaken had I not caught sight of black-robed and hooded people in the store shed. The assassin you saw in Westron Seaport and all the way through Icedge, then to the City of Shade, the Darkling in the Shadow World and on our journey to Cascant. Now Darkling in this town. It has all been connected."

"Did this mage show any diff'rent magic?" asked Billit. "What did she use?"

"It was like a blast of lightning," replied Silmar. "It came out of her staff with a great *crack,* killed that soldier immediately and threw him back about five yards."

"Anything like the one I used on the alligator?"

Silmar thought for a moment. "Now you come to mention it, aye, it was, but a lot stronger."

"Maybe she ain't any big problem! She has prob'ly put a few of those spells in 'er staff and blasts 'em out a couple at a time. It's called *imbued* spells, it saves 'er 'aving to prepare it and all she 'as to do is speak a trigger word an' point the staff. It's a bit like a magic wand in a way. It's always good for showin' off to her adorin' public! I got an idea about dealing with the likes of 'er! I needs to spend some time studyin' 'cos I don't know what she is capable of an' I might need some ideas."

"We might be able to work together if we can come up with a plan," suggested Taura. "What's the worst thing that can happen to a mage who is in the middle of spell-casting?"

Billit looked puzzled. "His pants fallin' down? I dunno, what do you mean?"

"If you were really concentrating and firing off a spell and Falcon stuck his tongue in your ear?"

"That's not nice - ugh!" gasped the Barbarian.

"You mean – a distraction?" laughed the gnome. "Like someone throwing stones or kicking them in the arse?"

"Exactly!" replied the priestess.

"Yer not daft for a girlie, are you?"

The slap sent the little mage flying backwards across the legs of the others.

ॐ ॐ

A little before midnight, two figures strode along the road from the town gates towards the little shack by the wood. Both were obviously drunk and were weaving unsteadily.

"I'm gonna have that woman an' then have her again!" slurred one. "Remember that very young wench we took behind the inn, Pall?"

"Aye, Grav, I do. Gods, did she squeal? Shame we 'ad to kill 'er though. She was so pretty. But this time let me go first, aye? I wanna do 'er first. You hold the top end. I don't like sticky sec-!"

"You will wait for me, you slimy bastard! I told you earlier. Now, be silent."

As they silently approached the door they drew their daggers and reached for the handle. Twisting it slowly and carefully they pushed the door to open it. It didn't move.

"Pull, not push," whispered Grav.

As he began to pull, the door flew open and powerful hands dragged the two figures inside. Both men were dead before they hit the floor. Within half an hour there was no trace of the bodies or that the two men had ever been there.

❧ ☙

CHAPTER 47

JUST BEFORE dawn, Varengo woke up. It was still dark. Dellie slept peacefully next to him, her hair spread across his shoulder. He kissed her cheek and she stirred, stretching a hand for his face. He pulled the blanket closer around her, slid off the bed and pulled on his clothing. He reached for his weapons and stepped outside. A hiss from the side of the house reassured him that the watch was still alert, as he had expected it to be.

"You are fortunate indeed, friend Varengo," whispered Yoriando. "But luckily, the nights are getting a little warmer for us unfortunate mortals who have to sleep outside, eh? Hahaha!"

"Are you jealous, my old friend?" chuckled the warrior. "I have loved her for many years but have been unable to tell her. Last night I did. Aye, I am indeed fortunate for she said the same to me. Look, the dawn comes. We shall need to catch some food to eat for the dawn meal."

As if in answer, Caeron and Jiutarô stepped from the wood and waved towards the two veteran soldiers. Within a few heartbeats they had again melted into the grey gloom of dawn.

"There are two more fortunate people who are off hunting. We shall probably eat quite well for our dawn meal for the little one is a canny hunter and uncommonly good with a bow."

An hour later the group was once more sitting around a little fire deep in the wood. They used dry kindling and wood to avoid telltale smoke. They had eaten well on a deer-like animal that Dellie confirmed was an antelope, and some of the meat from the carcass had been cut into strips and was drying above the fire. The rest would be made into a broth that Dellie would take to the outcasts later in the day.

"Where d'you reckon they are getting those blocks of stone from?" asked Yoriando.

"Did ya see any sign of other buildings bein' torn down?" asked Billit. "Mebbe that's where they get them blocks from but I doubt it."

Silmar looked thoughtful for a few heartbeats and replied "No, I wouldn't think so. The stone being used for the tower is much bigger than anything used in the town for the ordinary buildings. It has to be to support the weight of the tower. I think they must be bringing in by wagon from a quarry somewhere."

There was a small crack of a twig breaking underfoot and every head whipped round. There stood Dellie with a wide grin across her face.

"Call yourselves professionals?" she laughed. "That is exactly what they do – bring in cut stone by wagon. About twenty deliveries a day, each with two or three blocks depending on their size. Most of the wagons arrive during the night but the workers are being driven hard so some wagons are now dropping off stone during the day now. Each wagon has two drovers and there are two or three horsemen as well. I think they come a long way or the road is difficult because the horses and men are very tired when they get to the town and need to rest for a few hours before leaving again."

"You see much," said Silmar. "My compliments ma'am."

"It is not just me," she replied. "There are many of us who look and take note in the hope of rescue one day."

"In which case I would ask that you tell nobody for now that we are here, or if you *have* already spoken of us, make sure the others keep their silence of it."

"Be assured that the two I have told will keep quiet. Neither of them would have any profit to make from the telling of it. One is Breagga, an elderly woman who has a knack of remembering facts and figures. The other is Lalla Dallimore, the widow of the senior town elder and she is without children. She would dearly love to see the thugs come to a very gruesome end. Her husband succumbed to the terrible leprosy a few years ago."

Taura had been listening absent mindedly this morning. She had not felt very well when she awoke beside the great Barbarian although now she was beginning to recover. "Who is carving out the stone blocks?" she asked. "And where? I can't imagine the mercenaries doing it."

"That means that there are menfolk being used to hack it out," suggested Morendo. "So there would have to be more hired thugs to guard them."

Jiutarô arrived at the camp after a check of the perimeter. "Dwarves cut it maybe, hai?" he said. "If we get in, make them free then we start army of our own!"

Dellie jumped to her feet. "I think I can help there," she said excitedly. "Lalla Dallimore and I were talking together yesterday. We do most days. It is such an old routine of ours that nobody notices two women gossiping. We do have to be very careful these days though because you never know who is listening. We even have our own code now."

"To the story, my lady," chided Varengo.

"Oh, yes my love. Well, you want to equip an army? Then you want weapons, right?"

"Aye, we do," replied Silmar. "Well?"

"I think I know where the townsmen's weapons were taken!" She stood with her arms crossed and with a triumphant smile on her face.

There was a stunned silence.

"Er, aye? Where?" chided Varengo, again. "In the town?"

"No!" she replied. "They took them away in wagons with the first batches of captives. They were the older children, clerics and town elders who were taken away somewhere as hostages."

Varengo rubbed his scalp through his long grey-brown hair. "I heard a woman, or girl, cry out from inside the great store shed yesterday. Have they got women, or anyone there as hostages or captives?" he smelled his armpits. "Ye gods, I need a hot bath!"

"Aye, you do that!" replied Dellie with a mischievous grin. She winked at Taura who laughed in return.

Dellie thought for a moment. "There have been high-sided covered wagons coming through the town late at night for many tenday-weeks. They are always surrounded by escorts and outriders. We know there are people in them but we don't see them because they are driven straight into the great store shed. Then, again in the night, another wagon will leave on the north road. We don't know who the passengers are or where they come from or where they go. We do know that on rare occasions some are dead when they get here because you can smell the burning of the bodies in the great iron ovens. Ugh!" she gave a shudder.

"Slaves!" exclaimed Silmar. "There *is* something bothering me about this. I can't put my finger on it though. But is that the fate of the captives taken from the town?"

"Mebbe the slaves ain't from the town 'ere but are just being brought through the town on their way from somewhere else," suggested Billit.

"You mean to say that we might be sitting on a slave route?" asked an incredulous Taura.

"That's sort of what I was I was wondering," admitted Silmar, "but there has been no rumour of it that I am aware of."

Taura, once again, was thoughtful for a little while but then she stood up and rubbed her aching legs. "If all those men and wagons are going west to east with slaves, then sometime they have to come back west again with empty wagons. It would take forever to go round by sea so unless they sell their wagons, which is a possibility, we would still see large groups of riders travelling back to the west coast, or wherever."

Quietly, Silmar was considering how he might send word back to Kell or even the Princess Regent.

"Aye, or more likely a few small groups so as to avoid arousing suspicion," suggested Varengo.

"But let us get back to those stone blocks," insisted Silmar. "Our conversation is wandering to across something we cannot yet prove. Dellie, have you seen these wagons delivering the stone blocks?"

"No, I haven't," she replied. As the faces around her fell in disappointment, she added "But Madam Dallimore has! So naturally we talk about it!"

"Then perhaps we need a volunteer or two to follow a wagon," murmured the elf. Louder, he asked "What say you all? Who would take this task? It will be hazardous, to be sure."

Immediately, Yoriando, Caeron and Vallio raised their hands. Seeing that the two seasoned fighters would be the obvious choice, the half-elven hunter lowered her hand in disappointment.

"Yori, Vallio, I understand your desire to be off campaigning again, but I really do think this task would be ideal for you, Caeron," suggested Varengo. "What say you on this, Silmar?"

At this, Caeron's lovely face looked up in surprise while Jiutarô's registered deep concern. She gave a gasp and then a great smile. Jiutarô placed his arm round her waist and she leaned her head on his chest.

The elf winked at Varengo. "I agree. She will be ideal. If she moves out of sight of the wagon as it travels then she won't meet anything coming the other way on the road. But I would also suggest the other two follow a mile or so behind her in case she has need of them or should she want word to be sent back. What say you, Caeron? What will you find out for us?"

For the first time since she joined the companions, she spoke confidently before the assembled group. "Thank you for your trust. I shall find where it is, how many guards, how many townsfolk there are and if they are chained, if there are huts where guards or the workers sleep, if the guards are well armed and stuff like that. We can't plan a rescue until we know what is going on. I shall do what I can. Best that we leave after dark but I shall prepare now."

A short while later, while the half-elf readied her weapons, food and water, Jiutarô walked over to Silmar and Varengo. He gave his customary short bow. "Varengo-san; Silmar-san. That a great thing you do for Caeron. I worry about her long time for she speak so little. Now she strong and proud. I proud for her too."

"We would not send her if we thought she could not do it, Jiutarô," said Silmar. "But I have an idea for you too, my friend. We now need to discuss the problem of the hostages from the town."

❧ ❧

"Your son? Since when did you 'ave a son, woman? You kept that frackin' quiet, dittn't ya?"

Jarik Hebbern sprawled across a wide, well-padded sofa in the main Assembly Chamber of Town Elders in the Guildhall and stuffed handfuls of meat into his already over-filled mouth. A large roasted ham sat on a platter on a low table in front of him and beside that was a small jug of honey and a large pitcher of ale. His features were those typical of a half-orc although a few generations of inter-breeding with human-kind had made his human characteristics a little more dominant. Although grossly fat about his stomach, his shoulders and arms showed signs of considerable strength. His face, although dark-skinned, was a mass of scars, one of which ran from the top of his nose up through his hair to the crown of his head. He looked as if a handful of his long, lank, black hair had been ripped from his head, so cruel-looking was that scar. His porcine tusks were much shorter than would be seen on an orc and they protruded less than an inch up from his lower jaw; it appeared that they had been filed short. A long, sparse black beard hung down his chest. Like all the other thugs around the town, he was dressed completely in black, the only difference being that the red square painted on the front of his tunic had been more ornately fashioned such that it clearly resembled a castle tower as viewed from above.

Beside him, propped against the end of the sofa, was a great war-hammer. On the floor next to it lay a large round shield. It too was painted black and on it, once again, was the red square.

He smelt foully.

Madam Lalla Dallimore had asked for an audience with the gang leader that morning and, unusually, her request had been granted.

When one of his mercenaries had announced that she was waiting outside to see "That Hebbern bully!" he had responded by saying "Oh gods! Not 'er again! She thinks I'm a bit of shit on the underside of her boot! Let the cow in!"

She entered and immediately informed him that her son was coming back to the town.

"Why's he comin' ere then? A bit blootty stoopid, innit? Dittn't ya tell 'im that we ain't welcoming visitors 'ere?"

"He always comes to see me at this time of year. He finishes his sea journeys and looks for work as a mercenary for anyone who would have need of his skills. Hmmph! I told him last time that he should join the Corps of Foresters! But I am getting old and he will look after me now that my husband is, um, *dead*. He would probably be interested in what is going on around here."

Hebbern was not sharp enough to recognise the barbed comment with which Madam Dallimore finished her explanation.

She thought back to the chat with Dellie earlier that morning. *Yes,* she had said. *My son, if I had one, would be very interested indeed. He who will be acting as my son will be no less interested, I think. A lovely young man, that Falcon, so you say, young Dellie?*

"Hah! Looking for a job, is 'e?" spluttered Hebbern, with bits of half-masticated meat spraying about him. "Tell me 'bout im? A fighter, is 'e? Woss 'is name?"

"Yes, a fighter indeed. His name is Falcon and he fought in the orc-wars in Triosande. He brought home the ears of many orcs. And half-orcs!"

"Watch your mouth, Lady!" spluttered Hebbern. "If you're tryin' to taunt me it won't work. There weren't no 'alf-orcs in that war, nohow. Look, there's no problem with 'im visiting you but if 'e's coming to make trouble then 'e'll answer to me. And we'll be invitin' 'im to join our organisation. You can advise 'im that it won't be a good idea to refuse. He'll end up in our gaol and eventually take 'is place on the work gangs."

"I'll speak to him. He should be here today or tomorrow."

With no further word, Madam Dallimore spun on her heel and swept out of the room, her head held high with dignity.

"Cheeky frackin' bitch!" yelled Hebbern. His hand slammed on the table so hard that the platter and its large ham clattered onto the floor. The little honey jug fell onto its side. "'Oo does she think she is?" Traditionally, Hebbern liked the power that came with him telling his visitors when they were dismissed. This woman hadn't given him the chance.

"Pass the word," he instructed a manservant, an ageing man who had once been an elder of the town. Tell 'em to watch out for this, this Falcon. Any trouble from 'im, just chuck 'is ass in the cells. An' get that mess on the floor sorted out before the dogs get on it. An' get me some more o' that ale. It ain't bad. Any word on those two missing men yet?"

"Nothing found at all, General," replied the manservant.

"The bastards 'ave deserted! Absconded! That twenty we've lost in the past month. I wanna bounty on these buggers, an' on all the others. Five gold on each of 'em! Fifteen gold if the both of the last two get brought back alive."

"It's being said that these two were going calling on some woman. No-one knows who she is but it seems she'd promised them a night of passion."

"Nah! All the young good-lookin' ones are up at the stockades. There's sod-all left in this place to give a man any pleasure. Nah! That was a ruse so they could disappear. *She* will not be a happy little squirrel. Blame it on me, no doubt."

♿ ♿

It was mid-afternoon when a runner was sent from the gate to inform Hebbern that Falcon Dallimore was entering the town. Hebbern was surprised to learn that the visitor was massive and dressed almost like a Barbarian. The half-orc stamped up the stairs so that he could have a better view across the town.

"Bugger me wiv a pike-staff! 'E's frackin' huge! Is that a war-'ammer that 'e's carryin'? It's bigger'n mine. Gods, 'e must be strong. I do 'ope 'e's on our side – 'e'll make gravy out of most o' my men! Where's 'is blootty muvver? Is that 'er?"

From his vantage point, Hebbern saw Madam Dallimore stride purposely out of her cottage to meet the young giant. He saw the mighty Falcon whisk his mother into a gentle bear-like hug.

"Put 'er down, ya monster!" the thug grunted. "You'll crush every bone in 'er body!"

The half-orc could barely hear the excited exchange of greetings as Falcon and his 'mother' walked arm-in-arm back to her house.

"Send a couple of men out to keep an eye on 'im. Don't want 'em gettin' mixed up in a fight with 'im, 'e'll just leave snot an' a grease-spot on the ground where they used to be!"

෨ ෬

Madam Dallimore had been waiting by the window of her house for Falcon to appear. She was shocked to see such a large man walking through the gates but she knew instantly that it was him. She left the house and briskly strode to meet him. She was not prepared for the way in which in which he greeted her – he swept her up in his arms and kissed her on the forehead.

"Mother!" he called. "Wonderful to see you!"

"And you my dear Falcon," she breathlessly replied.

Together they made their way back to the house.

Later, after dusk had fallen, Falcon left the cottage and made his way to a tavern by the town's market square. There were a few oil lamps around the square which gave enough light to ensure the townsfolk walked with some safety. He had one objective this evening and would enjoy doing it. He did not expect to be returning to Madam Dallimore's quaint little cottage that night.

෨ ෬

Caeron swiftly made her way at a distance around the town's walls. Although she knew that Yoriando and Vallio were behind her, she was determined to be independent and act as if they were not there. She had total confidence in her own ability to evade watchers and, if truth were to be told, she feared more for the two human warriors behind her. Her night vision was excellent as was her ability to hide in shadows. Had she not watched the Darkling in the forest, just yards from them, for two full days without being detected? Silmar, the elf warrior, had seen her only because of his own dark-vision ability. Admittedly, she herself had become distracted when the group arrived in the forest. That enigmatic human warrior, Jiutarô, had been there and she had felt an attraction almost straight away. And he had been so kind to her and had expected nothing from her in return. *Giri* was all he would say when she asked him why he would have to leave her one day. Some sort of burden or duty he had explained it as being. *Damn!* She forced the thoughts of him from her mind. She could not afford to allow them to distract her now especially as she could feel tears welling up in her eyes.

It took her an hour to skirt the town to its south and west. She was thankful that the ground for a mile or so around the town had not been cleared for a very long time. The scrub and bushes could hide an army if it decided to advance on the town during the night. But this night it hid her from any eyes that would otherwise see her from the town walls.

But not from the eyes that watched from the south side of the river. And the owners of those eyes reported back everything they saw including information about the two human warriors who followed the half-elven hunter a half-hour later.

The taproom was crowded but very few in there were townsmen. Even the barkeeper wore the gang's black uniform, filthy though it was. Falcon had left his war-hammer in Madam Dallimore's cottage but, for show, wore a very old and battered longsword in a sheath on his left hip. He felt the gaze of many eyes watching him as he made his way to the bar. He noticed how space seemed to grow around him as the crowd parted to let him through. He knew that this had nothing to do with good manners. Rather, his sheer size generally made many people feel very intimidated.

He leaned on the bar with a quart of foaming ale and wondered how to make his first move.

A tap on his shoulder solved his problem.

"Hey, ya big oaf! You bumped into my friend when you came in. He spilt his ale on my shoes. What are ya gonna do about it, eh!"

Ah, problem resolved, he pondered.

The owner of the shoes was very tall but not as broad as Falcon. As the Barbarian was leaning on the bar, he did appear somewhat shorter than he actually was. The man face was bland but the lip sneered in such a way as to show blatant aggression.

Falcon looked down at the man's boots but there was no sign of damage or wetness caused by ale.

"Did you hear what I said?" said the man, persistently. The smell of stale sweat, stale smoke-weed and stale ale from him was overpowering. "I don't like your face, boy! C'mon, what are ya gonna do about my boots, huh? Well? Don't just stand there!"

Falcon stared impassively ahead across the bar. "I will do nothing so why don't you just turn around and take your face outside for a shit?"

The taproom went deathly quiet.

The man suddenly swung his tankard but, as Falcon straightened up to his full height, the man's arm suddenly lost its power and the tankard bounced harmlessly off the Barbarian's shoulder. Falcon followed this up with a hammer-fist blow on top of the man's head. He went down in a heap, out cold.

Suddenly, the taproom seemed to explode in a flurry of noise and activity. Falcon found himself being brought down to the taproom floor by a host of black-uniformed thugs. A blow from something hard on the top of his head knocked him senseless.

୭ ଏ

CHAPTER 48

CAERON CROSSED the road that led up into the northern end of the Brash Barrier Peaks. She had seen no sign of the two warriors, Yoriando and Vallio. She hoped they were safe. No doubt they would turn up soon. She found a niche between two large boulders that would offer her a good hiding place and an ideal defensive position if she should need it and settled down to wait.

An hour passed before she heard the rumbling of a wagon. But it was coming down from the mountains and towards the town. As it passed below her hiding place, she craned her neck to get a better look. The wagon, drawn by four horses, was definitely carrying a heavy load and the drover was using the brake handle to try to stop the wagon from pushing forward on the slope. The cargo was partly covered by a tarpaulin but there was enough uncovered for her to just catch a glimpse of the edge of a stone block. Behind the wagon were three riders on horseback.

Ah, the escort! thought Caeron. *How easy it would be for me to pick them off with arrows in the darkness. But not this time, sadly.*

The escort and the two drovers were chatting and laughing with not a care in the world. They continued down the steep road towards the town and were soon out of her sight and hearing.

A while later there was the sound of another wagon but this time it came from the direction of the town and towards the foothills of the mountains.

She shifted her position slightly to allow her a better look and there, fifty paces down the track, was the wagon once again drawn by four horses. This time it was not encumbered by a heavy load and was moving at a steady pace. The two drovers and three outriders were chatting and laughing, completely oblivious to Caeron's watchful eyes.

As it passed her on the road below her hiding place, she looked back along the road. With her extraordinary night vision, she spotted, very briefly, Vallio and Yoriando as they darted across the road. *Good! They are safe.*

She rose to her feet and set off to shadow the wagon to its destination.

৯৯ ৶

Falcon raised his head carefully. He was lying on a rough wooden floor in a dark room. The blow on the back of his head had not been heavy enough to render him unconscious for more than a few moments. He had been fully aware of being carried out of the tavern by at least six toughs from the taproom. Despite their number, they struggled to carry the apparently unconscious Barbarian and twice, one of them dropped a leg or shoulder causing all of them to let go. Each time, Falcon was dumped unceremoniously on the ground. Eventually, the gang took him into a building. He heard the screeching sound of a rusty iron door being unlocked and opened. He then felt himself being roughly dragged into the cell and heard the loud clang as the door was shut and locked.

His hands were tied, so were his ankles. *I shall worry about that later,* he thought.

There was some light. A grill high up on a wall allowed some of the light of the night sky into his cell. He struggled to a sitting position. The walls appeared to be made from very thick wooden beams. As his eyes slowly adjusted to the light, he began to make out some of the features of his cell. It was about three paces by two in area and, should he have been standing upright with his hands free, the ceiling would have been beyond even his reach. He could just make out a crude wooden cot in one corner. It had a network of thick canvas webbing which criss-crossed the cot frame, lattice-style, for the incumbent to lie on. A canvas bag, stuffed with straw, served as a bolster. There was a bucket in another corner. The cell had an overpowering stench of faeces, urine and vomit.

Well, I am exactly where I intended to be, he thought to himself. *I do hope Silmar and Jiutarô are successful with their part.*

Falcon shuffled over to the cot and eased himself up onto the webbing lattice. Although the frame creaked as he carefully rolled his mighty body onto the cot, it was surprisingly comfortable after the years of discomfort he had experienced in his travels up till now. He was soon dozing lightly.

❧ ❧

"And another over here," whispered Vallio.

The pair had been following the road in the darkness using the cover of the rocks and hills high above it. They had seen a wagon coming down the road and almost immediately after, another making its way up. They had found themselves becoming breathless with the exertion of the climb until Vallio pointed out that they were probably rushing more than was necessary. Dawn was breaking and it would not be long before sunrise. It promised not be a bright day though for clouds were rushing in from the west, borne by winds that were already tugging at their clothes. They both hoped that the rain would hold off.

He pointed to the soft ground and, sure enough in the increasing light, there was the print of a small boot that he recognised as belonging to Caeron.

"Well, she's alright then, thanks be to the gods," replied Yoriando. "I can't help worrying about her being up there on her own."

"I have a sneaking suspicion that she is probably more adept than we are at this sort of thing, Yori."

"We've not seen anything of her since we left Dellie's hut but seeing the footprint gives me some comfort. That I cannot deny. What's this?"

He indicated another footprint. It was not much longer than Caeron's but was considerably broader.

"Look at the marks of the studs beneath the foot," gasped Yoriando. "That's a dwarven iron-shod boot, or I'm very much mistaken. And who do we know who wears them?"

"Jasper!" whispered Vallio. "Then he has followed this road too. And, like us, from high above it so he must have spotted the wagons going up and down it."

"Very interesting!" murmured Yoriando. "Oh well, on with it!"

ج ح

Caeron had also noticed the strange footprints. They were not of a type familiar to her, being short but broad. *What manner of man wears such a boot?* she thought. *No man. Nor an elf. Orc? Nay. Dwarf, to be sure. Jiutarô's friend Jasper perhaps?*

She had been following an animal trail when she could during the night, keeping the wagon in sight or within earshot. She decided that Vallio and Yoriando would need to know she was ahead and safe so she occasionally left a single tell-tale print.

Although they had agreed that the two men would travel at a pace that suited the terrain and the darkness, she was surprised to have spotted them earlier during the night. They had probably been no more than a half mile behind her. She increased her pace for a while, using her good night sight to guide her, but still kept quite close to the wagon.

She was determined to show her independence and to prove to them all that she could reliably bring back the information they needed. She hoped fervently, that she would not need to call on the two warriors who were shadowing her. More than anything, she wanted Jiutarô to be proud of her. Perhaps, then, he would cast aside this *giri* thing and stay with her. Perhaps.

Dawn was breaking. She bent down by a stream to splash the refreshing cold water on her face and to take a badly-needed drink and then she sat back against a rock. She did not see the three horsemen who rode over a rise not two hundred paces away. They were heading down the slope at quite a fast trot.

A snort from one of the mounts caused Caeron to whip her head round towards the sound.

Damn, how could I have been so careless? she thought. *Oh gods! They are riding towards Vallio and Yoriando.*

As the riders disappeared behind a stand of rocks and boulders, Caeron decided that the wagon was not her immediate priority and rose from her resting place. She gathered up her bow and pack of arrows and raced off in pursuit but soon the riders were a long way in front of her.

৯৯ ৶৶

It was still dark when Falcon heard the rattle of keys at his cell grate. The yellow glow of a lantern showed that there were some large figures outside. His eyes had become accustomed to the darkness and even the dim light from the lantern caused him to squint.

"Let me introduce meself," a large man said. His voice was deep but slightly husky. "I'm Gen'ral Jarik Hebbern. I command the army that now looks after this town and I like it peaceful here. And you are called Falcon Dallimore, I believe. You're a guest here in this little establishment o' mine. I must say you really don't look like you come from this town. You look kind o' eastern, like one of them shit Barbarian types. Can you count on all yer fingers? There are ten, you know, unless you got six on each hand! That would make – ooh, let me see and feel free to correct me if I'm wrong – twelve, right? Now, to make your stay in this town easier for you, and therefore easier for me, co-operate with me, young 'un. Otherwise I may make it easier for you to count yer fingers on account of there being a few less. Where's yer piggin' great big war-'ammer then?"

"I lost it!"

"Not a clever answer." Hebbern gave the Barbarian a back-handed swipe to the side of his face. Blood trickled from Falcon's lip.

"Horse-shit! Guess my men will 'ave to visit yer ma then and 'elp 'er find it!"

"Leave her alone! She is an old woman. You won't find it. One of your men has already been there and confiscated it earlier. That's the truth. It was worth a pot of money, he said."

Hebbern stood pensively for a moment. "Look, if what you say is true, then that's all to the good. Look 'ere, Falcon. I can offer you somethin' better'n what you're used to. We 'as a lucrative trade 'ere. One that can make you a rich man very quick if you decide to come in with us. I can use a man with your strength and yer ma will live in luxury, I promise you that. I need good, strong people to 'elp me run the new town militia."

Falcon shook his head. "After what you've done to this town and its people? No thanks. This was a already peaceful town but then you and your murdering scum came."

Another back-handed swipe started a swelling to the Barbarian's left eye.

"See now, Falcon. I'm standin' up with my 'ands free. You're sat sittin' there with your 'ands tied up. Surely your tiny mind should say that I can beat the pink shit out of you an' you can't fight back. So don't you think you should be a bit more polite to the Gen'ral? And, for your information, the people of this town killed my father and sent his soul to be tormented by Terene the Lunatic for all eternity."

"That was many years ago and he did the same as you'e doing – treated the town folk badly."

Once more Hebbern struck at Falcon's jaw but this time the Barbarian dipped his head so that the back of the half-orc's fist connected with the hard bone of Falcon's temple.

"Ah, shit!" grunted Hebbern as he rubbed his hand and flexed his fingers. "I can be a reasonable man and a generous boss. I'll give ya a chance to reconsider while yer sat in my gaol. If ya refuse a second time you'll eventually be placed on the work gang. Make him comfortable, boys."

As he left the cell, three burly thugs entered and went to work on re-arranging Falcon's features.

§ ↦ ↤

Vallio and Yoriando were caught in the open space midway between what would have been two ideal areas offering cover when without warning three riders, two armed with bows, the other with a heavy broadsword, came thundering towards them. Clods of damp turf were flying from the snorting warhorse's hooves and the riders yelled confidently at the tops of their voices.

Immediately, Vallio nocked an arrow onto his bowstring and fired it off. He was too hasty. The arrow missed the lead rider's chest by inches. Yoriando cast his bow to the ground and stood with his longsword in his hands. Hurriedly, Vallio readied another arrow.

The riders were now barely fifty paces away and closing fast. Instead of aiming at the rider, he fired directly at the heaving chest of the nearest horse. The arrow slammed home with such force that only the fletchings showed that it had hit. The horse screamed and pitched forward nose first to the ground. Its rider went flying over the horse's head but his stirrup had not released the foot inside it. The man was jerked backwards and was thrown headfirst to the ground.

The other two riders were on top of the fighters before Vallio had a chance to make ready another arrow. The horseman with the bow used it as a quarterstaff to smite Yoriando but the seasoned fighter was too quick for him. Swinging his longsword with all his strength, he intended to sever the rider's left leg but succeeded only in cutting deeply into the horse's flank. Once again, a horse fell to the ground, its legs thrashing in panic and agony but crashing into Yoriando. The fighter was thrown heavily to the ground. This time, however, the rider expertly leapt from the saddle, threw away his bow and advanced on the fighter who was now struggling to his feet. The black-uniformed man raised his sword above Yoriando but hesitated. His expression had turned to one of shock and he fell forward to land on top of an equally-shocked Yoriando, stone dead.

The last rider, a burly veteran with battle scars over his face and arms, had dropped from his horse and advanced on Vallio with his broadsword swinging and circling. It was clear that this man was no stranger to battle. His smile showed two rows of brown, decaying teeth as he engaged with his intended victim. Vallio parried the sword-strike, the force of which numbed his sword-arm. A flurry of swings caused Vallio to take a number of steps backwards. Suddenly, Vallio's right heel struck a protruding stone and he fell backwards onto the rocky turf. Seeing an easy victory, the thug raised his sword and then screamed in agony as an arrow struck him in the side of his chest. The third mount bolted northwards as it heard the death cries of the other horse.

Yoriando pushed the body of his dead enemy off from the top of him and only then noticed the arrow that was embedded in the man's back.

"Just as well that I am here to protect you!" laughed Caeron as she ran down the slope towards them. "It is not good that you fail to notice when danger is near! Perhaps you would prefer that I tell no-one when we get back? Hahaha!"

"You have our gratitude, mistress," replied Vallio, also with a wide grin.

"And you fully deserve to tell your story yourself when we do get back," said Yoriando.

"Which we shall, of course, deny," responded Vallio.

"Ah, men shall be as boys!" answered Caeron. "Taura tells me this. A quotation from her god, Neilea."

"Perhaps it is as well that we travel together but you shall be our tracker," suggested Yoriando. "If that is acceptable by you?"

"It is, if only that I can keep you from a certain death!" answered the half-elf. "We have lost the wagon so must wait for the next one to come. We shall not be able to hide the bodies of the dead men *and* the horses."

"That is right," agreed Yoriando. "We must trust in the Lady of Serendipity that they are not discovered soon." He was quite impressed by her logic but decided to say nothing of it.

She paused to cut the purses from the belts of the dead warriors.

"It makes no sense in leaving these to fall into the soil," she said quietly. "Dellie can use them to care for her colony."

Rain was falling now and it grew steadily harder as the little band continued across the hills. They kept a very careful watch and moved parallel to the road until they found an ideal place where they could rest, eat, doze and wait.

❧　❧

An hour after dawn, Dellie and three outcasts entered the town through the gates. Torrential rain had been falling since a little after dawn and water had turned the road by the gate into mud. The little group were let through by the soaked guards without questions. Two of the outcasts limped away and took up their customary places on the guildhall steps and by the statue.

The town streets were virtually deserted and, shuffling along behind Dellie, Taura had found it easy to slip unnoticed behind Madam Dallimore's cottage. Dellie hammered on the back door and it was promptly opened.

"My dear Dellie," cried the old woman. "Come in. Come in out of the pouring rain and warm yourself by my stove!"

The poor woman recoiled in terror as Dellie was followed in by an outcast. But Taura cast off her rags and the woman was relieved to see that her visitor was not a leper.

"Lalla! What has happened to you?" cried Dellie. "Look at your face!"

She had clearly been treated roughly and had a dark bruise on her cheek but she did not appear to be badly hurt

"Hebbern and a couple of his men came to my door and when I opened it they pushed their way in," the old lady began.

"What were they after?" asked Taura.

"I think Hebbern covets dear Falcon's war-hammer. The brute was asking me about it. I told them it was not here but he hit me. It hurt but I was determined not to show it." She explained how she had continued to retain her dignity. But her house had been almost ransacked.

"They didn't find it, you know. I hid it. It was so heavy but I lifted a floor board and pushed Falcon's hammer underneath. He is such a nice boy. Are you the young lady that he told me about? He is very keen on you, my dear."

"Oh, that is so nice," said Taura. "Yes, I am. What did you tell them about the war-hammer?"

"I told Hebbern that one of their *heroes* had already been here and confiscated it. I said that he had told me it would get him a fortune at a market. Well, Hebbern was furious and started smashing up my furniture. He said he would find that man and hang him by his testicles in the market square. Oh, excuse my language."

As she told Dellie and Taura her tale, she broke down in tears. Taura rushed over to her and placed a comforting arm round her shoulders.

"We are going to put this right," said the priestess. "It is starting to happen as we speak. "Stay in your house. Fear not. We shall leave now for we have much to do."

Dellie and Taura spent a while helping Madame Dallimore tidy her house and then Taura replaced her outcasts' rags. The two visitors left the house and made their way back to the market square. The rain was still torrential but soon reduced to a fine drizzle. A heavy mist had settled over the town and it was becoming difficult to see all the way across the square. The market was deserted, the traders having decided that it was pointless to set up their stalls in this weather. The pair was soon joined by Silmar and Varengo, both of whom were soaked through. They stood quite close together in the shelter of a market stall. Rainwater ran off the edge of it onto the muddy ground.

"The conditions are ideal," Taura muttered from beneath her rags.

The other two 'outcasts' nodded slightly.

"I am tempted to send more than just one of us," whispered Silmar.

"Probably not a good idea," replied Varengo. "If this mist clears any more may become exposed."

"Aye, you're right. We must stick to the plan. We can always follow up with a night raid if we can raise a big enough force."

"Look!" gasped Dellie. "A wagon is coming out from behind the watch house. It's the wagon they use for taking away the hostages and prisoners. It's too late to change your plan now, anyway."

Three captives were tied up in the back of the wagon, one of whom was Falcon. In addition to the wagon drover, there were two large guards in the back as well. As the wagon and its four outriders passed by the market on its way to the gate, the little group was horrified and angered to see the state of Falcon's face and neck. His cheeks were horribly cut and bruised. Taura gave a gasp of anguish. One of Falcon's eyes was completely closed by a dark swelling. His lips were bloody and swollen too and dried blood covered the left side of his face and the top of his torn goatskin tunic. His hands were bound behind him and his head hung on his chest, swaying with the movement of the wagon.

"We'll get them, Taura, don't worry," whispered Silmar. "Falcon was aware this would happen. He's tough enough to shake it off."

She said nothing but the grim expression on her face needed no explanation.

CHAPTER 49

The wagon trundled through the town gate and took the road eastwards away from the town.

One of his guards was taking pleasure in tormenting Falcon with the point of a rusty shortsword, drawing small beads of blood with each prod.

"So where's yuh fancy war-hammer then, sheep-shit?" growled the man, giving Falcon another prod with the tip of his sword.

Falcon did not respond to the guard's taunts and the thug soon lost interest.

From a vantage point on a rocky hilltop not far away, Jiutarô watched through the mist. Dressed once again in his *gi,* the tightly-fitting dark blue-grey costume, he would be difficult to spot in the shadows.

From high in the sky above the wagon, the cleret-wing dragon watched the surrounding countryside. From time to time, the samurai warrior caught sight of the view from Sushi's eyes in his own mind. This was a wondrous gift that he was still coming to terms with.

❧ ❧

The drizzle was relentless. It found its way through Jiutarô's clothing and even into the tight-fitting hood of his *gi*. He ignored the discomfort though; it was not that different to the seemingly constant rains of the early summer, and the late summer come to that, in his home land. The difference, however, was that if it was not raining in Nippon, it was about to. It was said that if you could not see across the rice paddy-fields, it was raining, but if you could see across, the rains would soon arrive.

Sushi seemed to enjoy the cooling rain. She had swooped up into the misty air some minutes after the wagon, with a sullen Falcon dozing in it, had rolled past. Jiutarô hadn't seen her for a while but her subliminal messages to him, more visual than spoken, told him that she was close and watchful.

The Samurai kept close to, but out of sight of, the wagon as it was driven eastwards. The escort riders were not particularly watchful, probably doubting the sanity of anyone who would be foolish enough to venture out this day, but every now and again two riders would double back a little way apparently checking for followers. Jiutarô smiled at the thought that the riders were blissfully unaware of his presence.

The fools speak loudly enough to let anyone know they are there, he thought.

Indeed, they almost shouted at each other to make themselves heard over the rainfall and the sloshing of their mounts' hooves on the sodden track. Their tack and weapons rattled and clanked as they rode.

Jiutarô shook his head. *Disgraceful! How did they ever stay alive?*

By mid-afternoon the wagon was led by one of the outriders up a narrow trail leading north-west off the main track. The four horses pulling the small covered wagon did not struggle overmuch at first but soon the steep, wet, chalky, track caused them to slip and slide.

Jiutarô watched with interest, and more than a little humour, from a vantage point high above the track. The lead horses were dragged by their traces by the two escort riders but it didn't stop one of them from going down onto the ground, its legs thrashing in fear and panic.

⁍ ⁌

An hour had passed. Vallio gently shook Caeron and Yoriando in turn. They were both fully awake in an instant. From their hollow between the rocks they could all hear the creaking of a wagon as it was driven along the road past them. That hollow had given them almost perfect protection from the deluge during the night but now puddles were collecting between the rocks and it was time for them to move. Another hour of trudging through the rocks behind the wagon finally brought them to a track that led off to the left. It was narrower than the one they had followed up until now but, judging by the wheel-ruts and hoof-prints, it was well used.

The wagon was gradually getting further ahead of them and, despite their haste, it increased its lead. It didn't matter though. Soon, the muffled sounds of raised voices barking orders, of hammers against rock and the cracking of whips filtered through the mists.

The trio crouched down behind scrub and watched as the wagon appeared above the tops of the low mounds that flanked the road. The two escort riders looked about them to satisfy themselves that they were not being observed but, because of the mists, they saw nothing of the three watchers. Almost immediately, the wagon and the three riders disappeared down a slope and out of sight of the trio.

"That's gotta be the quarry d'you reckon?" whispered Vallio.

"Nay, it's a bordello, you idiot! C'mon, let's have some fun!" replied Yoriando.

Making the most of every available bit of cover, the trio made their way forward towards the rim of what was a large bowl-shaped valley in the hills. The clamour of stone being hammered and voices barking orders was louder, encouraging them to exercise more caution. Keeping their profile as low as they could between boulders and scrub, they crawled their way to the edge. Dropping to their stomachs, they inched their way to the lip.

"Isn't that the dwarf's boot-print?" enquired Caeron.

"He's been here then," whispered Yoriando.

As they watched across the quarry the mist was slowly being burned off by the sun. Their gaze centred over groups of workers wielding steel poles and hammers to cut blocks from the rock. There were more than two dozen workers watched over by a dozen men dressed in black clothing. Many had whips which they used to intimidate the workers.

"Time to go," said Yoriando. "Jasper should be up here somewhere."

They eased away and began to crouch back through the patches of scrub.

Suddenly, Vallio tripped and fell to his knees. "Ahh, shit!" he exclaimed. "What in the hells of the Void is that?"

"It is a body," replied Caeron.

"Jasper's?" asked Yoriando, his face showing shock and concern.

"Nay. Look, there," gasped Caeron.

A large boulder, almost the size of a horse's body, had a mound of soil and gravel next to it. Atop this mound was balanced a smaller boulder but from beneath this a human hand protruded.

"Gods!" exclaimed Vallio. "This isn't the burial of a townsman. Look, a black sleeve!"

Caeron examined the ground. She spotted familiar footprints. "The dwarf has been here!"

"One of their sentries has been buried. Well, I'll be damned! Jasper must have been in a fight with a sentry and finished him off. Let's get back to the others. Watch carefully. They obviously patrol these hills."

❦

"You! Out of the wagon, monster!" roared the drover. He cracked his whip inches from Falcon's face. The Barbarian did not flinch. "Get that horse back up on it legs and drag it up this slope."

Slowly, almost casually, Falcon uncoiled himself from his seat and dropped to the ground. As he landed, his foot slipped on the slimy surface and he landed in a heap on his rump. He awkwardly rose to his feet but, with the heavy chains around his ankles and his wrists tied behind him, was unable to maintain his balance. His feet slid once again this time making him stagger against the back-board.

"Get on your feet! No tricks, you!" growled one of the escorts, his bow ready and the arrow aimed at Falcon's heart.

Falcon rose, still slowly, to his feet. "Untie my hands. I can do nothing like this."

"No tricks, monster." The drover produced a knife while one guard held the tip of his sword against Falcon's throat.

The other still aimed his arrow at the Barbarian's chest. The rope was cut and the chains removed.

He strode round to the panicking lead horse that struggled to regain its legs. Falcon uncoupled the traces and stood by its head. With a soft word and a gentle tug, the horse slowly stood up and Falcon was able to reattach the traces.

"Take their reins, scum!" growled the guard. "I'll see you dead if you try one false move."

Falcon did as he was bidden and gave himself a little smile as he led the horses, with the wagon, up the steep slope. He had seen, through the mist, the familiar bat-winged shape of a cleret-wing dragon. The cold rain had done much to relieve some of the pain and swelling on his face but some blood still matted his beard.

Although the road soon began to level out it continued to gradually climb higher into the hills.

୨ ୧

Keeping parallel to the road, he followed the wagon northwards for many miles as it rattled over rocky terrain. Eventually, the trail sloped gently downwards through a damp wood until it emerged onto firmer rocky ground. Falcon and the two other prisoners swayed with the movement of the wagon as it bumped and ground its way once again across the rough terrain. Gorse bushes, sedge and many boulders littered the landscape but it was increasingly difficult for Jiutarô to find cover. Sushi followed either at a safe distance or high in the sky out of sight in the thinning mist.

How easy it would be for me to take them all, one at a time, thought Jiutarô, not for the first time.

The outriders remained poorly disciplined and, time and time again, one or two of them would stray out of sight of the slow-moving wagon or the other riders. Jiutarô noticed that the trail clearly showed the passage of previous traffic and had been much used. As he climbed higher into the hills the low cloud gave him ample cover so much so that he decided to follow the track rather than the wagon. He was soon a long way ahead of the wagon and its escort.

Sushi was occasionally connecting with him through her eyes. She could not be more than a couple of hundred yards away and the scene showed the road becoming winding and narrow. As she soared above the track, she could see how the trail passed between two very tall monolithic rocks behind which squatted two rain-soaked guards dressed in the familiar black garb. These two were talking and laughing loudly enough for Jiutarô to hear them well before he got close enough to see them. *The fools, more of them!*

The Samurai dropped down onto his belly and crawled silently over the muddy ground and between the clumps of scrub and rocks. As he got nearer to the guards he could see that they were deeply engrossed in some kind of dice game and were taking no notice whatsoever of the approach to their entryway. *I could easily silence these two.*

The two dice players did not notice as the darkly-clad figure slid ghost-like past them in the mist. Neither did they notice the cleret-wing dragon watching them like a gargoyle from the top of one of the great monoliths marking the entryway.

৽ ৶

Falcon was angry. He had not felt fury like this since his days in the Barbarian Lands north of the Dragon's Teeth

Mountains when he could still raise the *Berserker* rage. The damned guard, sitting in the wagon with the three prisoners, had obviously become bored and had started tormenting him once more. Since being prodded back into the wagon, the Barbarian had had his feet shackled and now a chain linked between his hands and ankles, totally inhibiting his movement. Not only was the chain rusty and one of the links broken, the pin holding the shackle around his right wrist had shaken itself out of its barrel. Any minute, the shackle would be off his wrist and he would be able to yank the chain with his other hand to break the link. His ankles would still be chained so he would not be able to run. But he knew that he should do nothing yet. Jiutarô was close. The Barbarian had momentarily seen the cleret-wing dragon. He would soon be on his way back to his friends. Rewarding the guard could wait. Falcon pushed back the pin into the shackle but it soon slid out a little once again.

The fine drizzle had almost stopped but the mist was heavier still. It was cold here now but Falcon was no stranger to that. All through his childhood he had lived in the mountainous regions of the Barbarian Lands and nature had provided his people with the food and clothing to sustain them through the long, bleak, cold winters. Moving from place to place, following the herds of bison and elk, as they themselves moved in search of grazing grounds, had enabled him to grow accustomed to adverse winter conditions. A cold day like this was nothing.

He was very concerned for the older of the other two captives. The man was clearly ill with a wracking cough. Falcon placed a piece of canvas about the man's shoulders but the coughing didn't stop. The guard merely sneered at Falcon's gesture of compassion. The third captive was a young teenager who seemed close to tears on many occasions and made no effort to communicate. Indeed, he wouldn't even look Falcon in the eye.

Dusk was approaching as the wagon trundled round a right-hand bend and rumbled to a stop in front of a huge pair of rock monoliths. Two guards swaggered out to meet them and words, in an eastern dialect that Falcon barely recognised, were exchanged. A stale smell of urine assaulted Falcon's nose as the wagon took them in between the rocks. The track rose steeply and became slippery where chalky dust and mud had mixed together in the earlier rain. This time, however, the horses kept their footing.

꙼ ꙼

Keeping a little distance away from the track, Jiutarô continued up a steep slope. The rumble of a distant storm to the west seemed to be getting closer surprisingly quickly. A cold, blustery wind pushed the mist away from the high ground and tugged at his loose garb but he gave it little heed - the weave of the cloth was fine enough to resist all but a heavy shower. He felt he was now close to finding the gang's prison. Less than a hundred paces ahead of him, the slope appeared to flatten out although he could not see the crest despite the disappearing mist and the rapidly approaching gloom. Surprisingly, the undergrowth had not been cut away or controlled in any way and Jiutarô considered that it would be dense and high enough to conceal an attacking band of warriors.

At the top of the slope he dropped to his hands and knees and crawled forward. In front of him, dim now in the failing light of the day was an unexpected sight.

Rain began to fall again and was soon whipped by the wind.

The Samurai was on the edge of a high circular plateau, the diameter of which was hard for him to determine through the rain and the residual mist which still hid the distant boundaries. A fortress of sorts dominated the centre of the plateau. Jiutarô ran forward to get a better view. He stopped beside a large growth of gorse and sedge and crouched beside it.

From his new vantage point, he could just see that the outer wall had four small towers placed at regular intervals. The wall to the left of the gateway was badly damaged and no attempt had been made to rebuild it. An inner defensive wall had been built between the towers on the outer wall to the immediate left and right of the gateway and had itself a gateway to allow access to the tower. Similarly, this wall had also been severely damaged to the left side of the gateway.

The keep itself stood on a raised mound inside the outer defensive walls and had yet another defensive wall built around it. This wall appeared undamaged except for the gateway which looked as if it had long ago been blasted apart. The top of the keep was also badly damaged and much of it was still blackened as if it had been assailed by a great heat. The lower levels, however, looked undamaged. To the right-hand side of the keep were some structures that looked tiny from Jiutarô's vantage point but he considered that they were probably huts for the guards or some of the prisoners. He hoped to find out after darkness had fallen.

The wagon carrying the mighty Falcon creaked and groaned as it was pulled towards the keep. It was now becoming far too dark for the watching Samurai to see any more. A sudden rushing sound in the air behind him put him on full alert but he realised from a subliminal message that Sushi had landed close by.

"Good, little one!" whispered Jiutarô. "It is time for us to move closer and see what is there. Come!"

Sushi chattered and emitted a little whistle of excitement as he fed her a large chunk of the meat Caeron and he had recently hunted.

◈ ◈

Falcon was pushed unceremoniously off the back of the cart and, because of his chains, he was unable to avoid landing on a heap on the ground. The two other captives jumped down onto the ground although the older man, who was now coughing and shivering uncontrollably, was unable to stand without Falcon's assistance. The third captive, the sullen young man who had still not spoken a word throughout the journey, made no attempt to help the other. Rain was beginning to fall, driven almost horizontally by the north-westerly wind.

"On your feet, scum!" bellowed the fat guard who had been tormenting him all night. Falcon's arms and shoulders were covered in cuts and blood where the man's sword-tip had dug into his flesh with each cruel prod. "Wait here and keep still." To his men, he asked "Where's these three buggers going? Anyone know?"

When no answer was forthcoming, he bellowed "Then one of ya frackin' find out!" A rider rushed into the keep.

Using the back of the wagon for support, Falcon struggled to his feet. The escort riders had dismounted and one of them led the horses away. While he waited for whatever was to come next, Falcon looked around him. He had taken in as many details as he could while the wagon was taken through the first, and then the second, set of gates.

The outer wall of this keep would stop no enemy, he thought. Indeed the destroyed gateway had been cleared of much of its detritus and gave full access to the main tower. There were six huts to his right-hand side which were in darkness but a man, armed and dressed in the customary black garb, paced around the area struggling to light the ensconced torches around the keep's outer wall in the face of the rain and wind.

Falcon watched the man struggle to light the torches. *The extra light will be helpful!*

One hut, smaller than the rest, appeared to be too small for use as guard's quarters. A chain secured the door. Behind the huts was a large stockade. Its stout walls had been constructed using upright posts driven into the ground and cut to a point at their upper tips. A gate, strong and solid, was hung between two great posts.

Two wagons were parked between some of the huts but of horses there was no sign. Many crates and barrels were scattered about the fortress compound.

Apart from the Wagon drover, the fat guard, the escort-riders and the lamp-lighter, the only other people within the outer defensive walls were two guards by the stockade gate. They were sheltering as best they could from the rain. Falcon was also surprised at how few gang members there were. He had seen two sentries by the monoliths, two more at the front gateway and had also spotted a solitary figure in the dim light at the top of the tower. No doubt there were others though. *In the huts?* He could also hear faint shouting from inside the tower.

Suddenly, a door to one of the huts opened and from it stepped a man. He was quite plainly drunk. He scowled towards the fat guard, belched loudly and then proceeded to urinate against the side of the hut. Finishing his business, he reeled back inside.

The rider returned from the keep and whispered into the fat guard's ear.

"Oh! 'E frackin' does, does 'e? Well, we better frackin' put these frackers away an' then frackin' go. It took us all frackin' night to get 'ere an' 'e wants us to go straight frackin' back. No frackin' sleep for us then?"

A deep voice, almost unintelligible in the rain and wind, sat on the air. They could all hear it, but it was as if it were on the edge of hearing. "Do you have a problem, Emsell? Do you object to my request?"

"N-nay, Lord. I, er, just, er, I m-misunderstood your orders. Er, Lord."

"Then you shall leave without recourse to profanity."

"Aye, Lord. Immediately, sir, er, Lord." He waited lest further words came carried on the wind but there were none.

The guard turned to the prisoners, his face a mask of fear, hate and fury.

"Move!" he bellowed. The remaining escort riders withdrew their swords and prodded the three prisoners towards the stockade.

❧ ❧

Jiutarô paused. From behind the debris of the breached outer wall of the keep's courtyard he had a good view of the compound. To the left he could see a corral holding a dozen heavy horses and beyond that were three wagons. A hitching rail in front of the main keep had five horses, four of them probably belonging to the escort riders who had recently arrived with the captives. In the darkness, the Samurai could see one guard climbing a narrow stone stairway to the top of the keep's outer wall – he would have to deal with that one soon.

Two other guards were walking out to the main gate to relieve those on watch and a couple more of the gang were stepping inside one of the three huts to the right of the tower. A great cooking-pot was being carried out of a narrow gate in a dark stockade just behind the tower but Jiutarô's view of that was not good from where he now crouched.

Falcon and the two other captives were being prodded at sword-point towards that narrow gateway and then disappeared from his view. The Samurai noticed that the Barbarian was almost carrying one of the others. The cleret-wing dragon stood perfectly still beside him as he idly fondled her behind her stubby horns.

It was not until the guard at the main gate was relieved once more that Jiutarô made his move. His joints had become a little stiff in the chill darkness but a simple muscle-stretching exercise soon loosened them up. He flitted forward to a new position close to the outer wall and made ready for his next action.

The two relieved guards hastily made their way back to the huts. They didn't hear the two arrows that streaked through the darkness, hitting them with precision at the top of their vertebrae. Both were dead before their bodies slumped to the damp ground. Within a few moments both bodies were in a wagon and concealed under a filthy canvas cover.

A hiss from Sushi warned him of a three-man horse patrol coming in through the front gate, their hooves splashing in the mud. He hid behind the wagon unnoticed as the riders dismounted, tied their horses to the hitching rail and went inside one of the huts.

Except for the two guards at the main gate, the compound was quiet once more.

ೲ ಲ

Falcon was still furious. Today had been the closest he had come to feeling the power of the *Berserker* rage surging within him. He knew that it would be folly to give in to the temptation by slamming the fat bastard who had taken great delight in prodding him with the tip of his sword. What was that Samurai phrase that Jiutarô said he had used? *I shall receive his death!* Aye, that was it. *And I will,* thought the Barbarian, *soon!*

Falcon easily supported the weakening captive who had been in the wagon with him. Inside the wooden stockade were about two dozen iron cages. Horizontal and vertical flat bars had been riveted together on all six sides of the cubic cages. On one of the sides of each of them was a doorway that was secured by a simple but strong locking mechanism. A wooden roof overlapped the cages on all four sides and a large pile of straw was heaped in each as bedding. Most of the cages had four to six people, mainly adolescent men-folk as far as Falcon could see. There was no sign of the women-folk.

The captives were prodded to a cell at sword-point by the fat guard and the escort riders. The three men were thrust through and the door was slammed shut behind them. The Barbarian and the morose young man remained on their feet but the other fell down onto the iron struts on the floor. As he rolled the poor man over, Falcon could see blood seeping from a cut on the man's forehead. He lifted him over to the straw heap and laid him on top. It was surprisingly dry and very comfortable after the rough ride in the wagon all day.

After a few minutes, a one-eyed man, obviously the gaoler judging by the bunch of keys at his belt, swaggered down one side of the cage and round to the doorway. His black garments were torn and extremely filthy as were his face and hands. He pulled at the door to test the lock was secure and grinned at the captives. The man's teeth, what few there were, were blackened with decay. Falcon kept his distance. He had no doubt that the man's breath would rival that of a rabid wolf.

"I do hope this inn is to your liking, sirs," wheezed the man. "If there is anything I can get you then please ask. A hot bath perhaps? A couple of hot women to screw the night away? When I finish with 'em first, of course. Hahaha!" His laughter caused his great belly to shake as he turned walked away into the night.

As silence descended on the compound, broken occasionally by wails and cries from captives in other cells, Falcon rose to his feet and started to examine his cell thoroughly. The cage was about three or four paces wide in each direction and its bars were made of flat strips of iron on all four sides and across the top and bottom. Although the wooden boards across the tops of the cages would normally keep much of the rain from falling into the cage, it was until now driven almost horizontally by the wind. Fortunately, the straw had been heaped into the drier part of the cage.

The rain stopped sharply, the wind dropped and soon the clouds began to break allowing Falcon to make out more of the details around him. He took the opportunity to attend to the sick man. The gash was not as bad as Falcon had feared and the poor man was sleeping. His coughing had stopped too. The Barbarian moved over to a corner of the cage to study its assembly. As he did so, he worked at loosening the shackle on his right wrist. The loose pin easily slid out of the barrel and, with a tug, the shackle opened. It hung by the chain from his other wrist.

"What are you doing?" whispered a voice behind him. The morose young captive stood there scowling.

"I'm looking to see if we can escape. You want to escape, do you not?"

"You will get us killed! Stop now – *stop!*"

"Hey, keep quiet!" Falcon hissed. "Do you want to stay here or do you want to help us get out and get the town back?"

"We will all be slaughtered." Panic rose in his voice. "Guards! Gua-!"

The young man collapsed to the ground as Falcon's fist landed on top of his head. The Barbarian dragged the unconscious lad over to the straw hoping that the gaoler had not heard the shouting but a yell and the stamp of feet showed that the one-eyed man had been alerted.

"What's this noise?" a gruff voice yelled. "Keep that man quiet or I'll slit his neck!"

"It's alright," said Falcon softly. "He just wanted water and he panicked. If you can get us some water I promise that I will keep him quiet this night."

A wooden bowl, small enough to be slipped beneath the cage door, was placed just within arm's reach and the gaoler marched away muttering to himself. Falcon took the water and carried it over to the sick, elderly man who had raised himself on one elbow when the commotion had started.

"Here, water. You drink some now then sleep more."

As bidden, the man took a few sips and then sank back. After a few coughs he was soon asleep.

Falcon returned back to the corner of the cage and, using his fingers as well as his eyes, continued with his study of the assembly. His eyebrows soon raised and a smile spread across his face. In the darkness he had found a potential means of escaping from this cage but it would need all of his strength.

He took the pin that he had removed from the shackle on his right wrist and inserted it into the corresponding barrel on his left wrist. The pin there was much tighter and wouldn't move. He wedged the iron band that he had already removed on the ground and steadied it with his feet. He now had an anvil, of sorts, that he could use to push out the tightly-fitting pin on his other shackle. A little persuading with the freed pin soon moved it and, at last, the other shackle was off.

He rubbed his sore wrists. Those shackles had been tight. He could now concentrate on the bands around his ankles. These took much longer to remove and by the time he had succeeded in a similar fashion, his ankles were sore and bleeding. But he was free of the chains.

He was about to start work on the corner of the cage when a low growl and a hiss from just outside the cell froze the blood in his veins to ice.

❧ ☙

CHAPTER 50

"You crazy dragon!" gasped Falcon as he waved his arms in the air. "You made me jump! Where is your stupid Samurai friend, huh?"

"I am here, Falcon-san," whispered a voice. Falcon jumped again. "I watching you take your chains off; I know you busy, I wait for you to finish. Ah, Falcon-san, you take such long time! I hope you quicker take your clothes off for make love with your holy lady priest! Now just need to opening door."

"Not without the key you can't."

"Hai, that a problem. What you think we do 'bout that?" Jiutarô gave an almost childish smile as he watched Falcon.

The Barbarian rubbed his bearded chin as he thought about the problem. "No problem, I can lift the roof off."

"Ah! Good idea, Falcon-san. You strong enough?"

"May need help, Jiutarô."

"Good. You start then, I help if you be quick."

Falcon lifted his arms and pushed up against the roof. It lifted a little but it was heavier than he expected.

"You want me help you now?" asked the young Samurai. A mischievous grin once again spread across his face.

"Aye. Er, hai!"

The sound of a click followed by the cell door opening came to Falcon's ears and immediately Jiutarô's arms reached up beside the great Barbarian to help Falcon lift the roof.

"Where you want me holding, Falcon-san?" The samurai was not tall enough to reach anything useful but then realisation dawned on the young Barbarian's face.

"Wha-! What?" stammered Falcon as he released the corner of the roof. "You fool! You had the key all the time!"

"Hai. One-eye gave it to me." Jiutarô's head bobbed up and down as he spoke. "He not need it back for now he sits and speaks with his ancestors. I don't think they very proud of him now."

"You do good, Jiutarô. Good."

"Ah, *domo*, Falcon-san. *Domo arrrigato*! Hey! I been finding things."

Falcon looked at him suspiciously. "What did you find, Jiutarô?"

"I find hut with all weapons!" Jiutarô gave another rare, almost boyish smile.

"What? By the gods! Did the guards see you?"

"Nay. They sit now speaking with their ancestors!"

"By the gods, Jiutarô! Oh, right. What about the wagon master and the guards?"

"They, sit, speak with –"

"With their ancestors?"

"Nay." He shook his head. "With each other on road to Carrick Cliffs. Haha! They leave long time gone and make loud talking to wake the dead. Hahaha! Hey, we go in castle now. They got a man with great magic in there, I think!"

"A mage! Oh *good!*" Falcon gave an almost despairing expression – this was the last thing he needed. "We better open some cages and give the keys to somebody while we go and finish the fight. We also need to seal off the main gate in case somebody tries to escape and ride to town. We cannot allow that. Keep everyone quiet because the rest of the mob is sleeping in the huts."

In fact, keeping the hostages quiet as they were being released was not as easy as they had hoped but very soon, over a hundred captives, young and old, some ill with malnutrition and very angry, were ready to fight and deal out revenge.

Jiutarô had killed the two gate guards outside the stockade with arrows and had propped them up against the wall to give the appearance that they were still alive and in deep conversation. The mighty Barbarian wrenched the hasps from the door of the small hut and Jiutarô stepped inside. He handed a collection of bows, arrows and swords to the waiting crowd and these were eagerly taken. Many were ready to rush off and it took a lot of effort for Falcon and Jiutarô to keep them under control.

On a pre-arranged signal from Falcon, some of the men thrust lighted torches through the windows of the other huts and waited. It was not long before the doors burst open and dazed and choking men rushed out with swords drawn.

Falcon and Jiutarô rushed towards the tower as a hail of arrows were fired at the black-clad men. Although far from being expert with bows, sheer weight of numbers meant that many of the arrows found a target. The townsmen yelled at the top of their voices as they had been told to do by Falcon. A few thugs raced through the swarm of arrows to engage the townsmen in hand-to-hand combat and blades clashed and rang as battle was fought. The thugs knew they were fighting for their lives against determined and resentful townsfolk who would show no mercy or give any quarter after months of deprivation and hardship.

✑ ✐

As Jiutarô and Falcon strode to the entrance to the tower, Sushi and the Samurai exchanged a look that was full of subliminal message. She stretched her neck and launched herself almost vertically from the ground near Jiutarô's feet.

Jiutarô and Falcon quietly stepped through the partly-open entrance of the tower. The iron-studded wooden door hung precariously on its lower hinge. It looked as if the lightest touch would send the door crashing to the ground. The floor of keep, just inside entrance, was littered with debris, dead leaves, broken furniture and smashed statues. In the dimness, they could see a dented helm lying on top of a pile of rubbish in front of another closed door. A single lit torch mounted in a sconce near the foot of a wide flight of stairs was the only source of light. The three other torches, similarly in sconces, were unlit. They had either burnt out or had been deemed unnecessary. The flame of the single torch gave barely enough light for them to see. Three doors, two of which were ajar, led to other chambers or areas of the keep but no light came from the open doors.

Suddenly, there was a sharp yell and two figures rushed down the stairs. A glint of light from their weapons showed that they had not come to give Falcon and Jiutarô a pleasant welcome. An arrow from Jiutarô stopped one – the man fell down the last few stairs and lay in a crumpled heap at the bottom. The blade from his broken sword skittered across the floor. A dark pool of blood spread from beneath the man's head although the arrow had struck him in the centre of the chest.

The second man faltered in his stride, his face showing dread, but then he glanced up to the floor above and rushed in blind panic towards the pair. A single hammer-like blow from the heel of the Barbarian's hand propelled him back the way he had come towards the foot of the stairs. The crack of bone and the angle of his head showed that his beck had been broken by the blow and the jaw horribly dislocated.

"Somebody they greatly fear is up those stairs," whispered Falcon. Jiutarô nodded and nocked another arrow onto his bow.

A low, deep, mirthless, mocking laughter came to them from the darkness of the floor above. Falcon and Jiutarô glanced at each other but without hesitation they approached the bottom of the stairway. They were a few paces from the stairs when a small figure stepped into the dim light at the top landing. A very elderly man, dressed in a dark gown and carrying a battered staff, looked down at them with an almost paternal expression.

∾ ∿

In the courtyard, not everything was going favourably for the freed captives. The elderly man that Falcon had helped lay sprawled across a pile of debris, his right arm bent at a grotesque angle and his eyes staring sightlessly at the sky. The young lad who had originally objected to Falcon's plan for freedom sat weeping as he stared at the bodies lying around the courtyard.

One of the black-clad men stood close to the keep's door, a huge brute with a massive dark beard, was holding four attackers at bay with a huge, spiked, blood-spattered battle-hammer. Around them were spread the bodies of almost a dozen ex-captives. But he was tiring. A slash from a broad-sword caught him a deep cut on his arm. The battle-hammer dropped and his four protagonists rushed in raining slash after cut after thrust with their blades. They did not stop until the body was unrecognisable as being that of a human.

        ᔋ ᔐ

Within seconds of gaining flight, Sushi was circling the ruined top of the tower and, using her exceptional night-vision, she could make out the dark square opening in the roof marking a way into the inside of the keep. She had also briefly spotted the corner of a dark cloak as it disappeared down into the darkness. She gave out a high-pitched growl and dropped towards the roof.

Silently landing by the gap, she looked down into it. There was enough light for her to see the beginning of a flight of stone steps leading down into the tower but apart from that, she could see nothing.

Cautiously and silently, using her heightened senses, she crawled into the void and made her way down.

        ᔋ ᔐ

"You are either brave or foolish. Both, I would say from the look of you. You disrupt my home, free my captives and kill my men. That I shall not tolerate. Your lives are now mine for me to do with as I will. You cannot fight me for I have formidable powers at my command through which your weapons cannot pass."

"Hai, that nice for you," mocked Jiutarô.

The wizard, elderly and thin, stood at the top of the stairway. His dark cloak was stained and tattered. It had been badly patched with a random assortment of cloth pieces and its bottom hem had long been worn away. His white hair and beard were matted with grime and his fingernails were long, dirty and uncared for. Pointing his shaking finger, he fired three magical fire-darts that streaked towards Falcon, catching him high on his chest.

The mighty Barbarian gasped, took two staggering steps back and dropped to one knee.

Instantly, Jiutarô released an arrow at the man who, smiling almost benignly and displaying teeth black or lost to tooth-rot, made a large circling motion with his hand, creating a rigid, shimmering shield of power. The arrow bounced harmlessly off it, as did the next. A word and a flick of the man's wrist sent forth a burst of energy that held the Samurai rigid – he could not even release his bow to drop it to the floor.

Falcon climbed up onto his feet and rushed to the foot of the stairs towards the mage in an attempt to engage him before he could raise another spell. He was still more than ten paces from his foe when the old man raised his staff with one hand, wove a complex gesture with the other and began a high-pitched shouting arcane words of great power. "*Granna-Ammana Notrii-notrii. Bei-Dar-Ammana Notrii–*"

The air about him glowed and crackled with esoteric power but the words stopped in his mouth as a whipping sound echoed through the chamber. A dark shadow had silently descended over the mage's head. Needle-sharp claws raked the mage's face, ripping an eye out of its socket. A scream of agony emitted from the man's wide open mouth as his hands fluttered in a vain attempt to protect himself. With almost slow and deliberate precision, Sushi inserted her venomous tail-barb through the mage's clutching fingers into the empty eye-socket. Within moments, yellow saliva frothed from his open mouth as the cleret-wing dragon's venom passed through into him. Immediately Sushi backed off away from him as the mage's magical power imploded upon itself.

The very air around him seemed to glow a bright blue as sparks danced around his face, hair and beard. His staff was burnt black, as was the hand that grasped it.

"Aiiaagh!" was the only sound now to pass his lips before he slumped sideways to the stone floor but then slid slowly down the first few stairs, the head bumping on each step. He slowed to a stop and did not move although the one remaining eye looked sightlessly towards Jiutarô. Thin tendrils of smoke rose from his hair and his lips, beard and nose were burned black.

Sushi hissed at the figure and, leaping onto his chest, raked his face once again with her claws before chittering and gliding down the stairs. She landed and waddled over to Jiutarô.

The *holding* spell on Jiutarô had dispelled the moment the old mage's body had slumped to the floor. The Samurai fell to his knees, his chest heaving as he tried to fill it with air. Sushi nudged her head against his hip and purred in an attempt to encourage a response from him. Falcon hurried across to him and helped him to his feet.

"Hai, little one," the wheezing Samurai said softly. "You did well. I need learn this magic – that was clever! Hey, big man! Are you hurt?"

Shouting and the clash of steel upon steel came to their ears from outside the keep. A man dressed in filthy grey clothing suddenly crashed through the half-open door to the keep and fell to the floor. The door itself crashed to the floor close to him, narrowly missing him. Undaunted, he scrambled to his feet and rushed back out again, yelling at the top of his voice.

"Hah! The shooting fire burns in my sheep-wool tunic," murmured a triumphant Falcon. "Little burn it did on my skin. Gods! The stink! Ach! It does pain me though." He pulled away the smouldering sheepskin tunic to reveal nasty dark-red burn-marks at the top of his chest. Blisters were already forming but there was little treatment that could be given at that moment.

"Wet burn in cold water and slow count to five-hundred before you stop!" suggested Jiutarô. "But now we have battle to fight, hai?"

"Aye. Er, hai. Five hundred? That is so many."

The pair leapt onto the wooden door at the entrance and hurried out into the courtyard to find the battle in its final stages. There were five remaining gang members who were standing back to back with their weapons whirling in a desperate attempt for survival. They were completely surrounded by a mob of angry ex-captives, mostly adolescents and elderly, who were eager for revenge and reprisals. A number of dead bodies, some in black garb and others not, were scattered about the courtyard. As eager as he was to charge into the fray, Falcon was without weapons of any kind. Even if he had been armed, he would not have been able to get close to the desperate survivors. In barely a minute, the surviving gang members flung down their weapons and begged for mercy. It was not to be, however. Swords and axes rained down upon them and they died where they stood, such was the fury of their erstwhile captives.

"Stop – now!" roared Falcon. The carnage halted and the townsfolk looked at the huge Barbarian who stood before them. Slowly, they moved back from the bodies of the mercenaries.

"You are like animals," he continued. "You are not like them. Don't become like them. Clear up this mess and let us look to bury and honour your dead friends. You must find food and water, clothing and weapons ready for the march back to Carrick Cliffs."

A roar of approval burst from the townsfolk. The rain had stopped completely and stars could be seen through breaks in the clouds.

"Where are the women and girls who were brought here?"

One man stepped forward. He was elderly but with a dignified demeanour. "They are in the keep. I believe they have been put in the dungeons and are being made ready to be taken east in a few days. They are, or were, to be sold as slaves in the markets of Livuria. Wagons are to be brought here from the eastern ports to take them away then more will be taken from the town. I believe the priests of Clamberhan are in there too, bound so they cannot make holy magic."

"No longer!" gasped Jiutarô. "We come here in time. We lucky, hai?"

"Aye. Release them and care for them," ordered Falcon. "They will be greatly affected by their imprisonment in the dark. Come to the town unseen in the early morning three days from now. Be by Dellie Helliol's hut but in the wood next to the river and we shall plan how to get your town back."

Another roar of approval burst from the townsfolk. The elderly man, accompanied by a few others, hurried into the tower.

Falcon continued with his yelling of orders and instructions. Other men ran into the huts in the courtyard and came out with weapons, coins, food and clothing. "Who of you have been soldiers or adventurers?" he called.

A few of the older men stepped forward. He tasked them with planning a surprise reception for the wagon drovers and the riders who would undoubtedly be escorting them. He emphasised that none should escape to warn the town's gang-leaders but advised restraint in the treatment of the prisoners. "You have a day or two to practice with bows and weapons," he advised. "Spend it wisely."

The women began to emerge into the courtyard. They blinked at the light from the burning torches which were bright to their eyes after long tenday weeks or months confined in the keep. Behind them were led, or carried, the four surviving priests of Clamberhan. These men were in a very bad state, having endured torture, starvation and countless indignities. The young men and women crowded around and, the fury of the fighting having now dissipated at the sight of the priests, gave what care they were able.

Despite desperate objections and pleading from the freed captives, Falcon and Jiutarô insisted that they had to leave immediately and that the townsfolk should fend for themselves provided they return to the town in three days, as they had already been advised.

A few minutes later, Falcon, armed with a pair of battle-hammers, smaller than he would have preferred, and a long, heavy sword of questionable quality, all retrieved from the gang's cache, left the tower courtyard with Jiutarô on the way back to Carrick Cliffs. After a careful journey, with aerial patrolling by the little cleret-wing dragon, the pair arrived in the evening darkness at the wood behind Dellie

Helliol's hut. They slept long and deeply that night and told their tale next morning to the rest of their companions.

❧ ❧

"All of them?" gasped a stunned Silmar. "You released them all? What about the black-garbed ones? Are they in the cells now?"

Dawn had just broken as the companions gathered around a little fire in the wood. Falcon explained to the grim-faced group what had happened but there was some sympathy for the fury of the liberated townsfolk after months of harsh treatment that they had been subjected to.

"Good, so they are here in two days. That gives us just enough time to get up to the quarry and bring back the townsmen from there. Now, how do we do that?"

"I suggest we all go," said Varengo. He stood side-by-side with Dellie, his arm around her waist. Caeron had not left Jiutarô's side since he had arrived the previous evening and Taura stood arm-in-arm with Falcon.

"That sounds logical," said Silmar. "We should leave at dusk."

❧ ❧

The dark figure paced from side to side in her chamber in the guildhall. She was angry and a little concerned. She had not removed her horned helm or her black cape that shimmered and reflected the light in a myriad of colours when it caught the sun's rays just right.

Her chamber was the largest room in the building – it had once been the meeting room that had been used to discuss trade, farming, warehousing, taxation and prices, and even the defence of the town. Now, however, the great table had gone and the chairs had been taken away to be sold at the auctions, along with their main human merchandise, in the cities to the east. A large, black, heavy curtain hung across the room at the furthest end from the door. From the other side of it could be heard a deep rumbling sound akin to that of a large sleeping cat.

"What is he playing at now?"

"He appears to be sleeping, exalted one," replied the woman's companion, an elderly Darkling whose voice trembled with fear.

"Not my special pet behind the curtain, idiot! I'm talking about the doddering old fool of a Livurian Shadow Mage up in the hills with the prisoners. If you don't have anything constructive to contribute then say nothing."

"He probably sleeps also, exalted – !"

"Did I not just tell you to shut up? If I wanted you to state the obvious, I would ring a bell. I have a mind to feed your testicles to my special one!"

"No!" he whined. "No, please not, my dearest daughter! I only wish to serve you. I only meant to say that he has probably taken his dark powders again."

"I grow increasingly ashamed that people know you are my father. I shall soon find a way of ridding my life of your whining and wheedling! Be careful what you eat, father!"

You take care too, daughter! You may have cleverly disposed of your mother and sister but I am constantly aware of my surroundings and your scheming, was the thought that entered his head, not for the first time.

"If I hear nothing by sunset, I shall send my beast to present the damned Mage with a *loud* message!"

The ageing Darkling backed away a few paces and bowed. He sat on a small, hard chair near the door and waited for her next rant, which was sure to come. A *loud message* usually meant an incendiary blast delivered by arcane means. Her high-pitched, rasping voice had roused the creature that slept behind the curtain for the rumbling had stopped and the noise of movement could now be faintly heard. He pushed back the hood of his cloak to reveal a face that had turned from black to grey with advanced years. His hair had once been long and yellow-white but now thinning and lank with a need for washing. The tips of his ears were bent outwards by the years of wearing headwear or a hood. One eye was swollen and his lower lip was split and scabbed. His daughter was not a tolerant person.

The woman reached up and removed her helm. A stunningly beautiful, jet-black face, framed by long, straight silvery-yellow hair, was now uncovered. The visage was marred by a cruel mouth with down-turned corners that gave the impression of a perpetual spiteful sneer. She smoothed her hair back to reveal the characteristic long, pointed elven ears. She unclasped the front of her cape and, with a flourish, draped it across the only remaining ornate wooden high-backed chair. She wore a tight-fitting black leather costume of vest and leggings that revealed a slim but athletic physique. A slim short-sword at her left hip sat in a black scabbard that was as ornate as the belt on which it hung. Similarly, a curved matching dagger sat on her right hip.

"Time to see my darling," cooed the woman, showing a tender side to her nature for a moment. She stepped to the curtain and raised her hand to pull back one of them. The old Darkling fidgeted nervously on his chair and turned his head away.

A great spherical beast, its body a yard or more across, stood on bird-like legs in the gap between the curtains.

It had no wings to match the legs nor did it have arms. A massive single eye, the size of a dinner plate, in the centre of its forehead spread its gaze over the room, taking in the Darkling woman and her terrified father. Two stalks, each a foot long, sprouted from the top of its bulbous body, each having a single eye at its tip. The most fearsome feature on the orb, if the great eye alone was not enough, was the mouth – a gaping maw, two feet across. Long, needle-sharp teeth were bared and the dark-red tongue flickered hungrily across the thin lips.

This was a monster spawned in the Void, an *ogharii*, a mouth-monster the likes of which had long ago struck terror firstly to communities around The Boil, the Sea of Turbulence far to the south and then further afield as they spread their menace, devouring and killing as they went from one village to another. It was of a species of magic-using beasts of old that had probably emerged from the Void in the far-distant past and now usually dwelt in the deep subterranean places. It was rumoured they were the servants of Darkling or other dark or evil races and had a formidable magical power of their own. Its stalked-eyes could send forth a magical spell of *holding* that would paralyse a victim enabling it to be devoured alive; the power of the spell would be relative to the maturity of the beast.

The old Darkling cowered at the sight of the fearsome beast despite having seen it many times before. The ogharii darted towards the Darkling and uttered a rasping hiss before stopping a few paces short. A shudder took the old Darkling and he released the contents of his bladder.

"Get out!" shrieked the Darkling woman. "If you have pissed on my floor, you shall be the next meal for my beautiful friend here."

With a wail and with panic etched across his old face, the Darkling fled from the chamber.

"Hahaha!" laughed the woman. "The last time you put the fear of Terene into him, he did shit himself as well as piss his pants! The smell! The filthy old bastard! Haha!" Similarly, the ogharii gave a wheezed attempt at laughter although the emotion did not come naturally to it. "Are you hungry my sweet?" she purred.

"Ahh – yesss," was its reply. The tongue flickered once again and the ogharii glided back through the curtains into the darkness beyond.

The woman stepped over to a gong and rapped on it twice with her knuckles. There was no gong-striker – she promised to remind herself, not for the first time, to have something provided. A human collar-bone perhaps! Perhaps something would remain after…

A man, human, dressed in the predictable black livery of the gang, came into the chamber, bowed and stood stiffly at the attention.

"My friend is hungry, bring it food," she instructed. "It would like something fresh and tender this time, not the tough, gristly meat you brought a few days hence. And be quick about it."

The man bowed and stepped back out, his face an expression of disgust. She had seen it and mentally disdained the man for his weakness. *Typical human!*

He returned a few minutes later with a young girl, probably no more than thirteen summers, and then made a hasty exit. The girl was obviously terrified and shook violently from head to toe. She was unbound and her face was covered in bruises from beatings she had recently received.

"Come over here child," ordered the Darkling female softly. "You have nothing to fear from me. Have you been beaten? I shall deal with the person responsible. It is time for you to be returned to your family but, oh! Look at those dirty clothes! You cannot go home like that. I wish you to remove all of your old clothes here and then step behind the curtains. There are better clothes there for you. Then you may leave and return to where you belong. Worry not. I shall not hurt you my dear. This I swear."

CHAPTER 51

CAERON WAS given the honour of leading the group into the mountain foothills and up towards the quarry. Many of the group had seen her grow in self confidence over last few days and none more so than Jiutarô. She was speaking with much more confidence to the others now.

Visibility was very good after the recent miserable weather. Although the waning moon was low on the horizon, it was bright enough for them all to see where they were putting their feet. It would be even lower in the sky and hidden behind distant clouds soon enough though. But that would be at a time when it would be welcome.

Behind Caeron, Jiutarô and Silmar walked looking left and right. Billit and Taura followed just in front of the mighty Falcon. The four warriors, Varengo, Yoriando, Vallio and Morendo kept a careful watch to their rear. Jiutarô also had the benefit of the cleret-wing dragon's height as it flew overhead. Sushi's excellent night sight would alert them to any danger long before it became a risk for them. Only once did they take cover as a wagon, laden with stone blocks and escorted by three riders, trundled down the hill. Even without Sushi's warning, the group would have been alerted long before it got to their position – the voices of the drover and the rider, raised in laughter and joking, could be heard many for minutes before it was adjacent to their concealments and after it passed them by.

Their plan was simple but it was also hazardous because of their low numbers. When it would finally come to a pitched battle, they expected casualties from among themselves and particularly from the townsmen for whom they could offer little protection during the fight. It was a risk that made them all very anxious but they had little choice. Surprise would be their ally in the darkness but that would be short-lived.

Silmar and Varengo had discussed their options earlier that day with some of the others. They each had suggested alternatives but whichever they tried seemed to have its problems. Forty or more mercenaries were in the hills but more than half of them would probably be in their beds that time of night. That still left twice their number who would be ready to fight within a few seconds of the group beginning their attack.

"And how do we actually get into the quarry?" Yoriando had asked. "There is only one way in and the walls are sheer and high."

It had been Caeron who had provided a solution. "Wagons!" she had said, almost matter-of-factly. "Intercept some, kill the drovers and riders, tip out the stone blocks and climb in. Wear some of the black clothes and make lots of joking and small-talk. Just like *they* do."

"By the gods!" Silmar had gasped. "She's right. Two or three of us with bows up on the rim and Billit up there too hurling magic! It seems ideal. How easy is that? An excellent idea, Caeron."

They had discussed it and looked for problems but there were few. Now the group was settling down at the junction where they would need to take the track to the right. It was almost time to capture their first wagon.

"I really do wish we had a few more fighters," said Silmar to nobody in particular.

"'Ow many does yer need then, yer pointy-eared chod?" The voice was gruff – and familiar.

The elf spun round with his hands flying to his two blades. There, leaning on a huge battleaxe with a broad grin across his rugged, bearded face, was a familiar figure.

"Jasper? Is it you?"

"Aye, it's me! Well, it was last I looked. Did yer say that yer needed some fighters?"

Silmar stepped over and placed a hand on the dwarf's shoulder. "I never thought I would be so glad to see a short-shit like you but this one time I can make a huge exception! Welcome back."

The rest of the group crowded around and slapped the dwarf's back as he replied.

"Aye! Never thought I would miss takin' the piss outa a pointy-eared idiot like you but it's good to see yer again. An' all o' yous too. What 'ave yers bin up to?"

"It will take too long to tell you everything but we are all on our way to rescue the townsfolk at the quarry."

"What? Just a few o' yer? I bin up there a few days ago an' 'ad a look at it. Ain't easy. You could use some 'elp, elf!"

"Your being here will help us, dwarf. Did you not get any help from the mines then?"

"Oh, aye got a few of me kinfolk wi' me. The trouble I 'ad tryin' ter find the mines. They're not in the mountains at all. They're in hills on the edge of the desert. I 'ad ter walk fer miles ter find 'em. They was very upset when I told 'em,

I can tell yer, that some gang 'ad taken over their store 'ouse. So a few of 'em came up 'ere with me to help get it back!"

"Thank the gods! How many?"

Jasper gave a low whistle. A few bearded faces rose up from behind the rocks and bushes. Not one of the group, even Sushi, had seen them in the darkness.

"'Bout fifty."

"Wh-what?" stammered Silmar. "H-how many?"

"About a 'undred actually. I dunno, don't do numbers. An' some of 'em got bows too. An' you didn't knows we was 'ere! Hah! No wonder you didn't 'ear us, ya elf. Yer must be deaf wiv pointy ears like that! Haha! Hahaha!"

"I maybe didn't hear you but I can smell you all."

Morendo trotted over to them. "Quiet! Wagon's on the way up from the town."

"Leave this one to us," laughed Jasper. "The boys 'ave got this itch in their hose and they wants to scratch it by dealing out some payback!"

The dwarves and the companions moved swiftly into cover and waited. A few minutes later, two horsemen rounded the bend, closely followed by the wagon and the third rider.

Suddenly, a small, squat figure carrying an impossibly large battleaxe, stepped into the centre of the track.

"Gennelmen," called the figure. "Although I must apologise fer callin' you that 'cos yer obviously nothin' o' the sort!"

The riders reined in their mounts and stared open-mouthed at the lone dwarf.

"Allow me to introduce meself. I'm called Goffe the Nasty an' I'm a mean an' nasty bastard. Please don't bother to tell me yer names 'cos I'll prob'ly forget so I'll just remember you after yer dead as Piece-of-Shit-One, Piece-of-Shit-Two, an' so on."

One of the riders edged his mount forwards a pace and, leaning forward in his saddle, called to the dwarf, "Haha, you jest, short-ass. Now get out of our way else you die."

"Can't do that, you see. I require the use o' yer wagon so that I may take it to the quarry and wipe out the members of yer little gang an' free the townsfolk that you is illegally usin' as slaves. So get down please, so that I may allow all of yous ter live out this night. But knowin' yous, you'll be too bloody stupid an' will want to attack me an' you'll all be dead in less than a minute."

The rider looked with a bemused face to the left and right of the track. Satisfied that he could finish off this foolish dwarf he drew his sword. The other two riders lined up behind him, their faces amused.

"He's mine," cried the horseman as he spurred his horse forward.

As if from nowhere, a number of dwarves materialised on the track. The lead rider pulled up with a look of surprise and fear on his face. He was no longer confident as even more dwarves began to surround him. His mount stamped and snorted and was unable to gallop away, despite the frantic use of its rider's spurs, as strong hands gripped its saddle and tackle. Similarly, the other riders had nowhere to go and all three fought for their lives. One dwarf, being too close to the lead horseman, went down as a sword-blade chopped into the side of his neck. Almost immediately, all three riders were torn from their saddles by the angry dwarves and were carried off, kicking, screamimg and struggling, into the darkness.

The drover used his whip to keep the dwarves at bay but they merely laughed as two of their number climbed up the back of the wagon and drove their axes into his back. The wagon horses reared in terror and panic at the noise of the brief battle but were soon calmed as Jiutarô and Caeron appeared there to take control of them.

The dwarves wasted no time in hiding the bodies and collecting the stray mounts. Within half an hour another wagon rattled down the track from the direction of the quarry. This time however, there was no play-acting from Goffe the Nasty. Instead there was an unannounced ambush. It was yet another hour before a third wagon came up the track from the town. By then, the companions were satisfied that they had sufficient to mount their raid on the quarry.

℘ ℘

Back in the town of Carrick Cliffs, a large, sleek, dark shape slowly beat its wide bat-wings and soared somewhat awkwardly into the night sky above the half-completed tower. A terrified mercenary had affixed a leather cylinder to the unoccupied saddle. The beast knew from a subliminal message received from its owner where it was bound.
Many eyes watched from afar at the rapidly-climbing beast. One pair of eyes watched intently. The owner of those eyes instantly rose from the resting place knowing that it was time to act.

℘ ℘

"You interrupt my leisure time to tell me that a wagon is late in arriving from the quarry?" Beneath the bed sheet it was obvious that she was naked. She was sitting astride another jet-black figure that was also naked.

"Damn you, human!" She slammed her fists down on her companion's chest in fury and his face contorted in silent agony. "Well, have you lost your tongue? Speak, human, or I shall have that redundant tongue burned out of your mouth!"

"Exalted Nameless One," he began in a quavering voice. "The wagons are rarely more than a half-hour late. This one is now almost two hours behind and there is still no sign. I would send a force but I must have your personal authority before reducing the town's militia."

Now that his eyes were becoming accustomed to the gloom, the intruding guard could see the blood smeared all over the bedding but the male black-skinned elf did not seem to show any sign of pain or suffering. *Yeesh! He wouldn't dare*, thought the sickened guard.

"You have it. Send twenty fast riders immediately. I want a full report by dawn meal. When did my beast return from the tower in the hills?"

"It has yet to return, exalted one."

"What? It should have been here by now. Perhaps the old mage found my warning. If my beast is not back by dawn meal send out those same riders to the keep. Now begone! I am busy."

The guard, now feeling a wave of nausea flooding through him, hastened out of the chamber. The Darkling she-mage picked up a small blood-caked blade from the bed and placed it back on her companion's lower abdomen.

"Now where was I? Ahh yes!"

Her companion arched his back violently as the two-inch blade was pushed through the skin and fatty tissue and into his stomach muscles. His face was contorted in silent agony, his lips drawn back and every sinew in his neck straining.

Her reaction was more euphoric and she moaned with ecstasy.

ꞩ ꞩ

The great bronze dragon with the mighty weapons-master and dragon-knight, Ghar Hrol of Celesta, sitting astride the saddle on its lower neck, had sped off in pursuit of the Nameless Witch's dragonkin beast as it clumsily gained height over the town. The dragon-knight was bemused at the dark wyrm's relatively poor flying ability compared to that of his own mount, the much larger and sleeker dragon, Violor.

Ghar Hrol was not complacent however. He knew the foul beast still posed a threat with its acid-like breath weapon and there was a possibility that, like most other dragonkin, it had other breath-weapons in its arsenal too. But Ghar and Violor would be prepared nonetheless, to meet with the wyrm head-on if the necessity arose.

For more than three decades Violor and Ghar Hrol had fought foes across the length and breadth of the continent of Baylea. Once again, Ghar had responded without question to an instruction from the leader of the Society of Sentinels, the reclusive mystic Antheuseolin of the Vale of Celesta who wielded immense arcane power in the lands as the Society strove to protect the unknowing populations from tyranny and cruelty.

Following the dark beast from a distance and at a much higher altitude, they finally swooped to intercept it as it circled to attack the recently released townsfolk that filed through the tower's half-ruined bailey and out through the gateway.

Already screaming with terror or wailing and cowering from the *dragon-fear* at the sight of the dark brown wyrm, the townsfolk had no defence as it spat its first stream of acid towards them. One youth was caught in the acid and he collapsed to the ground, his flesh dissolving from his bones. His pitiful screams quickly stopped as he died. Climbing and circling to commence another attack gave moments for a few of the braver townsmen to yell "Flee! Run! Run for your lives!"

Many of the people scattered amongst the undergrowth but many more just cowered and covered their eyes in their fright as if it would be sufficient for them to escape their inevitable doom. They had seen this beast before but, strangely, this time there was no dark figure sitting in the saddle.

The coming of a second, much larger dragon only added to their terror and they wailed and screamed even louder in their utter despair. But their cries turned to shouts of joy and relief as the second dragon swooped down and poured fire into the dark wyrm. Shrill bestial screeches of pain and fury assaulted the ears of the townsfolk as they rose from their hiding places and they clapped their hands to their ears to block out the sound.

Round in circles the dragons flew, weaving and dodging as the mighty Violor, his bronze scales glistening in the early dawn light, chased the dark wyrm. The treetops waved and twigs and leaves rose up from the damp ground as the draught from beating wings disturbed the air. It was obvious that the smaller of the beasts had the advantage of manoeuvrability and, indeed, its turns were quicker and tighter as it changed direction to avoid another searing stream of flame from Violor.

But it was beginning to tire. Violor changed his attack, this time blasting a cone of ice and frost at the beast that it dodged just in time. The smell of burning flesh told of the flame-damage that had first been inflicted on the wyrm and it now seemed to be taking its toll on the beast. With a roar, that was more like a deafening, high-pitched shriek, the wyrm swooped to treetop level and sped off to the north.

Violor, with Ghar shouting words of encouragement and praise in a language that no other could understand, circled over the keep for a few minutes but the dark wyrm did not reappear. Even with his incredibly sharp eyesight, the mighty bronze dragon caught no more sight of the foul beast.

Slowly and cautiously the townsfolk gathered together. Many were sobbing uncontrollably at their narrow escape and many others were still affected by the *dragon-fear*. Little was left of the flesh that had adorned the bones of the unfortunate victim of the wyrm's first attack, such was the potency of the acid.

Many of the frightened townsfolk nervously walked over to greet their saviour as Violor landed on the sward before the tower's outer walls. The dragon-knight effortlessly slid off from his saddle and stepped down onto the ground. To the people before him, he looked every inch the warrior of myth and legend with his shining dragon-embossed breastplate, his massive two-handed great-sword and his ornately-plumed helm. His manner was haughty and grim as the first, and bravest, of the townsfolk apprehensively approached him. The towering form of the enormous bronze dragon behind him only increased his anxiety.

"Master, you have saved us!" cried the man as he fell to his knees before the warrior.

"Will the beast return?" asked another.

"Are we in danger?" questioned yet another.

"Shall you come with us to Carrick Cliffs to defend us?"

All of these questions and many more from a fear-ravaged group of young and old townsfolk, showed their dread of their journey yet to come.

Ghar Hrol spoke clearly and firmly and a hush descended on the growing crowd.

"Continue on your journey. Use the trees and bushes to give you as much cover as possible. Make no fires. Travel in small groups of no more than twenty. Keep the group in front and that behind in sight. Tarry not, nor must you move too quickly. The beast lives but it lick its wounds and will in all probability return to the town where its owner can heal it. It will not attack you in full daylight where it can be plainly seen – it has no dragon scales and can be killed by arrows if they are shot straight and true by men who remain valiant. Dawn is here and the sun is rising. At this time your greatest enemy is fear. Well, fear not. Be of brave heart. There is another battle to come. You will be needed if your town is to be free once again. You will have much aid in this battle. Others will aid you."

With a final flourish, Ghar Hrol remounted the bronze dragon and, amid pleas for him to remain with them to give them protection, he sped off into the brightening morning sky. The townsfolk stood in silence as Violor disappeared from view but very quickly natural leaders stepped to the fore and organised them all. Before long they were all moving forwards in groups on their journey just as the dragon-knight had advised.

༄ ༅

Closing the door to the chamber, he leaned back against the wall and wiped his sweating brow with the back of his sleeve. He had seen so many horrors since having signed on with this militia. This foul Darkling witch was cruel and bloodthirsty and her chamber stank like a charnel house. Aye, the rewards were good and, although he resisted the temptation, there were young girls available for his pleasure. *Too damn young! It's immoral.* It had broken his heart when he had had to take the poor young girl to the witch's mouth-monster in her chamber. He knew that beast fed every three days and another feeding was due on the morrow. But he had a plan and now had the means to carry it through – a powerful drug and a suitable candidate.

He was not the only one to lose his belief in this cause. Despite their bravado and the jokes, more and more *blackies* were carefully and quietly voicing their displeasure. Scores had deserted already but some had been brought back only to be brutally and hideously tortured and executed by Hebbern.

But they had found someone who would listen. A *townie* woman was co-ordinating something, the gods knew what, and *he*, Triffner, had been recruited along with a growing number of his highly-trusted friends. Aye – time to right a few wrongs.

ର ଜ

The plan was absurdly simple. Everyone with bows and crossbows, and Taura and Billit, would place themselves around the rim of the quarry and then the rest of the dwarves and some of the companions would charge down the track in their wagons or on foot straight into the quarry. The bowmen (*and women*, as Caeron pointed out) would protect the townsmen by picking off the black-garbed figures that came too close to them and the dwarves would finish of the remainder.

Fast and simple, as Jasper had recommended.

At about three hours after midnight the assault commenced.

It began badly.

∾ ∾

Three wagons, each loaded with as many dwarves as could be carried, clattered and swayed down the track that led through the narrow entrance into the quarry. The uneven track caused the dwarves to grasp tightly onto whatever hand-holds were available, even onto each other. Almost ninety others, with Falcon, Jasper and Vallio, followed swiftly on foot. The remaining companions and the six dwarven crossbow-bearers, had placed themselves around the edge of the quarry cliffs ready to loose off arrows and magical fury at black-clad targets when the opportunities would present themselves.

Things went awry as the wagons, hauled by cantering horses, rushed through the gateway. The guards, having issued a challenge, flung bucket-loads of caltrops in their path. The track was covered in the metal objects which, when landed, presented very sharp two-inch spikes that would incapacitate whatever stepped onto them.

One of the two horses on the leading wagon stepped onto a caltrop and reared in pain causing the other horses to panic. The wagon swung violently to the right throwing its passengers to the ground as it tipped back over onto its left side, two of its wheels splintering into matchwood. All four horses crashed to the ground, with their legs thrashing and their bodies covered in caltrops. One dwarf lay still among the caltrops and did not get up. Of the others, three lay injured and pierced by the spikes but were protected by the remaining five.

The two other wagons were pulled up just in time to avoid a similar catastrophe. These dwarves grouped with those from the first wagon and began throwing and kicking the caltrops towards the doors of the huts. The rest of the dwarves, with Falcon and Vallio in the lead, had been left some way behind by the fast-moving wagons and had yet to pour in through the gate.

Black-clad men swarmed towards the small group of dwarves by the wagons and immediately began the attack. Swords clanged and sparked against axes and shields as man clashed with dwarf. The swish of arrows and bolts was almost lost in the melee but many found their mark. Both men and dwarves occasionally stepped on caltrops that littered the ground.

Suddenly, the doors of the huts burst open simultaneously and more mercenaries swarmed out to join the fight. They were not expecting to step onto the caltrops that covered the ground outside their doors. Some of them screamed in agony as the needle-sharp spikes were pushed through their feet and as some fell to the ground the spikes found their way into their bodies too. However, the majority of the mercenaries managed to step through the writhing forms of their comrades. Arrows and magical energy found new targets and men began to fall.

Just as things were looking desperate for the little group by the wrecked wagon, the main party of dwarves, with Falcon and Vallio well in front of them, poured at last through the gates and into the quarry. His voice raised in a deep baritone battle-song, the Barbarian swept away foe after foe with his two battle-hammers.

Jasper was yelling at the top of his voice. "Protect the fallen lads! At 'em, boys!"

Falcon's voice boomed across the din. "We need some alive!"

Although arrows and spells played their part, it would be the hand-to-hand fighting that would win the battle. The mercenaries knew that they could expect little mercy from the townsfolk that they had treated with cruelty were they to just lay down their weapons and surrender. They were hopelessly outnumbered, fighting desperately for their lives and were cutting down some of the ferocious dwarves. Inevitably though, they themselves were chopped down one by one until only a couple survived. These were spared and would soon face harsh questioning.

The dwarf who had been thrown heavily when the wagon crashed was dead, his neck and back having been broken. Four others had been killed in the fighting and many others were with broken limbs, battle injuries and damage to their feet from the caltrops. They would be too badly injured to march to the town.

Initially, the townsmen had rushed to safety when the wagons arrived through the gates but as mercenaries began to fall some of them emerged from concealment, grabbed tools and discarded weapons and joined the fighting. A few were dead including one who had been strangled, later accused of complicity with the gang and having caused the recent death of three other townsmen at the quarry.

The remaining townsmen however, were released although some were in a very poor condition through overwork, oppression and malnourishment. Those who were still strong enough were tasked to scour the huts for clothing, food and water, weapons and any items that could be useful. The companions came down from the lip of the quarry to help the dwarves with organising the townsmen and caring for the wounded. The eastern sky was lightening with the onset of dawn and the carnage in the quarry became clear to see.

Taura looked at the wounded, sighed and rolled up her sleeves. She was going to be quite busy for quite a while. She looked dejected as Silmar stepped over to her.

"I'm not sure I will have enough in my healing pack for all these injuries," she mumbled. "I'll have to attend to the worst of them and patch the rest up the best I can."

"Ahh, Taura," the elf replied. "I am certain many of them will feel better just to hear you pray to Neilea over them." He strode away to see what was happening. He was troubled and decided to speak with Varengo.

"You are vexed, friend elf!" the warrior said as Silmar approached him. "Speak with me and share your worries."

"Aye. I have no doubt that the town will send up a force of riders to find out what happened to the wagons. We shall have another battle, I fear."

"Well, I am sure you are right, Silmar. But if we expect it then we can prepare. I shall order that the quarry be cleared of the dead and all signs of the battle cleaned up. Then we shall make ready. I shall send up some watchers."

The dwarves took away their own dead and placed them in graves freshly cut from the rock. In a sombre ceremony, Jasper explained that the bodies merely rest here for the time 'til the end of days when *Tarne* would return to claim them back as his own. Meanwhile, the spirits of those killed in the battle would reside in the halls of their forefathers.

Dawn had passed but the sun had yet to appear over the lip of the quarry. As the last signs of the fray were cleared and the dwarves had equipped the more capable townsmen with weapons, the cleret-wing dragon swooped down out of the sky and lightly landed on Jiutarô's shoulders. Many of the townsmen and some of the dwarves blanched at this and had to be reassured that this little dragon was not a harbinger of doom.

"Sushi tell me many riders come," cried Jiutarô. "All wear black but much time away."

It was time to put a prearranged plan into operation.

๛ ๙

Varengo and his men, and the dwarven archers, rushed out of the quarry and up towards the rim. Half of the townsmen trotted back into their stockade, but this time they had their weapons with them. The remainder returned to their original workplaces and began hammering rock but with little enthusiasm. The dwarves crowded into the huts or concealed themselves around the quarry. Once Varengo and his team reached the edge of the quarry they backed away out of sight. The only sound now was the hammering of iron on stone and a few voices shouting orders. The small army waited.

Moments later the sounds of hammering and yelling were drowned out by the echoing thunder of galloping hooves as riders descended the slope through the rock and into the quarry. Suddenly, the riders burst through the entrance and across the quarry floor. A small group of men stood before them – but no, not just men! There were indeed men amongst them but a disparate collection they were, one almost a giant and another with very strange garments and a long, slightly curved sword tucked into a wide blue sash. But there were also an elf, a gnome and half a dozen dwarves.

The riders, twenty four of them, reined in a few paces in front of the little group and fanned out to either side of their leader. Jiutarô was quite impressed by the disciplined way in which these riders performed without direction from their captain. Their uniforms were virtually identical and bore the red square of their organisation on their breasts.

Hoshite uniforms, thought Silmar. *These are Hosh deserters!*

Their captain, an arrogant young man whose confidence was bolstered by the well-trained riders to either side of him, looked around in surprise as townsmen rose to their feet with an assortment of weapons in their hands.

"What's this?" he demanded. "Where are my men? Who in the seven hells are you?"

Silmar, Jasper, Billit, Jiutarô, Falcon and the five dwarves stood there, quiet, undaunted by the array of well-armed riders but all looking the captain directly in the eye. Jasper lifted one leg and noisily broke wind. The others all laughed.

"Speak now or die," demanded the now extremely irritated young man.

It was Jasper who spoke first. "We shall not die today, you young piece of horse's dung. But I thank you for your kind offer. No, this morning you have that privilege. Goodbye!"

The man's jaw dropped in surprise. Immediately, the riders reached for their weapons. A hail of bolts and arrows fell among the riders and four of them dropped heavily to the ground. The doors to the huts flew open for the second time that morning and a mass of dwarves surged out. Many of the townsmen, still thirsting for revenge, rushed from the stockade. The riders, their faces contorted by fear, were torn from their saddles. Weapons rose and fell indiscriminately.

The companions were powerless to stop the maniacal slaughter by the townsmen and some of the dwarves.

The young captain was the only rider that was not caught up in the ferocity. His horse had bolted with him still astride the saddle but stopped suddenly as an elderly townsman, the man who had fed water to the workers, rushed from the stockade and plunged a spear into the mount's chest. The captain was thrown to the ground and immediately seized by a group of townsmen. He was brought, hands bound, before Silmar, Jasper and Varengo.

"*She* will finish you!" he panted in defiance. "Or *it* will – ugh!"

The man doubled up as Jasper drove the butt of his great axe into his stomach.

"I don't remember invitin' you to speak," said the dwarf. "Did I ask 'im to speak? Does anyone else remember?"

Heads shook in agreement as he winked at his companions.

"Oh bugger this! Let's give 'im to the townsmen. Tie 'im to the rail."

"Who is this she-woman?" Silmar asked the man.

"My name is Captain Fra- ugh!"

"Wrong answer," said Jasper as he drove the butt of his great axe into the man's stomach once again. "Don't wanna know yer name. I shall always remember you as Piece-of-Shit- er, Number Four? Nah, Five!"

"Think it's Six!" another dwarf called out.

"What? You will find out about *her* the hard way," gasped the man.

"One thing you will find out when talking to us is that a nice answer gives a nice response," growled Jasper, quietly and softly as he walked round to the man's left side. He struck the man's thigh with the butt of his axe and the man dropped in agony on one knee to the ground.

"Who is this she-woman?" asked Silmar once again but with a menacingly calm voice. "Just who is this nasty little Darkling witch?"

"Ah, so you know of her," replied the captain. "She will burn you with her awesome power."

"I have seen this power. Billit?"

The little gnome mage stepped to one side and, with a phrase and a gesture of his hands, sent forth a stream of bright-blue energy towards a barrel by the cliff wall. In less than a heartbeat there was a blast of flame and heat as the barrel exploded. Everybody in the quarry felt the blast and shielded their eyes from the intense light.

"Is that how her power works, Captain Fra-ugh?" asked the elf.

The captain's face suddenly paled. "Aye. Er, aye it does. Just like that. Aye. By the gods!"

"I 'ope she can do more'n that," moaned the gnome. "I wants some sort o' challenge. She sounds a bit feeble if that's all she can do. Hmmmph!"

"What is this *it* thing you spoke of?" asked the dwarf.

"That will be her brown dragonkin beast," said Silmar. "I saw her feeding one of her own men to it."

"Hah! You think so?" replied the captain. He was still shaken by the display of magical power shown by the little gnome. "No, there is another beast of magic. It has a huge eye and a huge mouth. It also feeds on captives and has a good appetite. It has great magic that even your mage will not counter."

"Great eye and mouth? Two little eyes? An *ogharii?*" gasped Jasper. "Is that what you mean? Aye? Oh, ye gods! One of those all but wiped out my first adventurin' party nigh on eighty years ago. Hmmph! Seems like only yesterday. Me an' Jedd were the only survivors an' poor Jedd 'ad 'is mind ruined. Aye. Terrifying it was. All the others 'ad their 'eads chewed off while we watched." The old dwarf was physically shaken and sat down on a crate.

"Aye," agreed Silmar. "I know of these. Fearsome indeed. Their eyes on stalks have the magical power to hold its victims still while it eats them alive. This is a foul beast. They are totally evil. A huge ball of ugliness that walks on legs like those of a great bird. Ugh!"

"I know all about that, elf!" yelled the dwarf. "I never thought to see one o' them again. I would rather face a black-hearted dragon alone on a hilltop than meet with one o' those mouth-monsters. We gonna need to talk about this before we meet it. I wasn't ready afore. Take that bastard renegade 'Shite away from me afore I bash 'is tiny warped brain out!" He indicated over to the Captain.

A handful of townsmen took the man away. The dwarf was shaking so badly that Taura stood behind him and, with her holy symbol of Neilea in her left hand, placed the palm of her other hand over his brow. Almost immediately, the whole group felt a warm calm descend over them. The dwarf seemed to relax and became quiet.

A townsman had found some bread and, surprisingly, full barrels of ale in one of the huts. Pitchers and mugs were filled and passed around the group along with hunks of the bread.

"What in the seven hells of the Void do we do about this mouth-monster?" asked Varengo.

"Same as you would do with any magic user," suggested Taura. "I am certain it can only do one spell at a time. It's the small eyes that will give the *holding* spell but the great eye has a devastating killing spell. If I remember rightly, it is spoken that it will only use that one last of all because it will be temporarily exhausted after all the effort."

"So does that mean we let it use up all its magic on us so we can attack it when it's tired?" asked Jasper. He was still upset with the very prospect of meeting an ogharii once again.

"No of course not," replied the priestess. She was a little annoyed with the dwarf's response but chose to ignore it. "But we can do what fighters often do to fight against a mage. Distract it, confuse it or perhaps we can blind its small eyes simultaneously."

"What?" asked Jasper.

"She means all at the same time, idiot!" explained Silmar.

"Then why didn't she say so?"

Taura continued, shooting a look of annoyance at Jasper. "Aiming arrows at its great eye and Billit or me putting a spell of darkness or light on it may work but aiming is critical especially if it is moving. It may have the means to dispel Billit's spells too. That, Jasper, means to counter the spell."

"Aye, girlie, I know what *dispel* means!"

"Remember, it can move fast on those legs," Silmar warned them. "If it can be made blind then it can be attacked and hopefully destroyed. But the great eye is lidded and will still be a danger. The mouth is dangerous too and can bite a head off as quickly as a snake. Overwhelming it is probably the best approach but it will be at great cost."

Varengo had been sitting on a small barrel but now stood up and rubbed his aching backside. The barrel tipped over as the warrior carelessly knocked against it. "We have 'til early tomorrow morning to prepare our assault on the town. The Darkling witch will be getting suspicious that her patrol and some of the wagons have gone missing and may send out another force, one even greater. That's all for the good for it will be all the less for us to fight but they may even barricade the town gates."

"Aye, you're right," replied Yoriando. He had been rubbing at a toothache all night and Taura had promised him a piece of bark which, she said, would ease the pain if he chewed it – quietly! "The folk from the prison in the hills will arrive at the river before dawn and we can't have them hanging around. We need to rest awhile, get some food and prepare for another group of riders who might come here."

A townsman was asked to bring the captain over.

"I'm sorry, good sirs," replied the man, nervously. "You see, he fell over and bashed his head against a fence post and when we tried to help him up his neck was broken."

"Look," yelled Varengo loudly enough for everyone in the quarry to hear. "Killing prisoners must stop. We are not animals. Do *not* become like them. The next time it happens, the person responsible will be dealt with by me! I hope that is damn well clear to everybody."

Townsman quailed at the sight and sound of the warrior's fury.

"Er, what's that comin' out o' there, Varengo?" asked Billit. He indicated the barrel that Varengo had knocked over when he stood up. A thick black substance was oozing out from the displaced stopper.

"Now what is in these damned barrels, townsman?" asked Varengo.

"It's a sort of thick oily substance that comes up through the ground over there in the corner. It's not much good for anything but we use it to grease the wagon wheel axles. It's difficult to light but if we pour it on a big fire, it flares up and explodes."

So that's why my spell went so well. Surprised me, that did, Billit smiled as he thought to himself. Aloud, he said "Gives me a bit of an idea though. We could do with takin' some with us."

❧ ❧

CHAPTER 52

"What happened to the squad that you sent to the hills?"

"Ex – Exalt-t-ted One!" replied Triffner. He was panic-stricken. "Th-they didn't return from the quarry. I w-would have expected them b-back at dawn. That w-was three hours ago."

"I know when dawn was, you fool. I was up when it happened. And my beast?"

"S-still n-no sign, Exalted One."

Triffner was terrified. His predecessor had disappeared – absconded, it was said – a tenday-week ago and now he had been promoted into the position of Captain of *her* personal guard. It was more likely that the man had been a meal for the disgusting mouth-monster. Triffner wasn't a guard! He wasn't even allowed to carry a weapon in the presence of the Darkling witch.

"Something is going on here!" she screamed. "Wagons and men not coming back from the quarry, my beast missing and no word from the keep. Right! I want a squad of forty, nay, fifty, riders armed to the teeth and ready for battle to be sent to the quarry. Keep a few riding some distance behind the main squad in case they are caught in an ambush. I'll want someone to bring back the information. Send Hebbern to me now. I want all of our militia to make ready. And my special companion will need feeding tonight! Begone!"

There was a low growl from behind the heavy curtain.

Triffner hurried out and breathed a sigh of relief. Something had gone seriously wrong – or right!

Aye witch, your beast will be fed tonight!

ॐ ॐ

The day was oppressively hot and humid. Almost ninety dwarves, fifty townsmen and the companions left the quarry soon after midday. Many rode on horseback although the dwarves preferred to walk. Despite their short stature, they could cover the miles at a good speed when the need arose. Jiutarô, Caeron and Silmar were some distance in front of the mass and Sushi, the little red cleret-wing dragon, took to the skies. Two wagons, driven by the dwarves, carried injured and sick townsmen. Taura had administered them as best she could for her stock of healing materials in her healing bag was exhausted. Taura's prayers to Neilea had helped those with the worst injuries.

They had just joined the main road leading to the town when Sushi swooped down and landed by Jiutarô.

"Many more horse soldiers come. More than before. Riding fast!" gasped the Samurai.

Silmar wasted no time. "Back to the others, quickly!"

The majority of the dwarves and men immediately split into two halves, each of which went up the banks on either side of the road. Laying down flat on their stomachs, it was hoped they would remain unseen as the riders sped past.

Jasper, Falcon, Varengo and Morendo, and a dozen or so dwarves stood in front of the wagons that now blocked the road. They were at the back of where the large group had been and now waited for the horsemen.

It didn't take long for them to appear.

Once again, Jasper stood in the road to greet a group of riders but this time he was not alone. Also, this time, there was no stopping to exchange niceties. The riders drew their swords and sabres and charged at those standing before them. As they entered the trap a voice, Varengo's, shouted "Arrows!" and a hail of arrows poured into them. Dwarves and men flung themselves from the tops of the banks onto the horsemen and dragged many to the ground.

Hand-to-hand fighting commenced but, amid panicking and rearing horses, the riders were quickly overwhelmed. This was the bitterest fighting so far. Neither side gave any quarter, nor did they expect it. This time though, the townsmen were fighting for their lives because they were more likely to be engaged by the riders as an easier target. But the dwarves ploughed into the fray. The militia fighters fell quickly but so did many townsmen and a few dwarves.

This was a bloody fight at the very end of which Yoriando fell with a devastating blow from a sword that severed his left arm just above the elbow as well as biting deeply into his chest. The stricken man screamed in pain and Varengo rushed to his side. Blood poured from the wound. Using a belt from a fallen mercenary, Varengo looped it around the stump and pulled it tight to staunch the flow.

There were still some sounds of fighting but it rapidly quietened. Varengo knelt down and lifted his old friend up onto his knees.

"Has... he killed... me, Varengo?" Yoriando hissed through the agony.

"You shall not dare die, old friend. I am here for you as you have been for me these years."

Tears flowed from Varengo as Yoriando slumped in his arms. Taura was there in an instant. Already tired from the earlier healing work and the fighting, she nevertheless attended to Yoriando straight away.

"Give me some space please Varengo," whispered the priestess. She took from her pack a cotton tunic, rolled it into a ball and pressed it against Yoriando's chest wound. His breathing was shallow and laboured and he was now unconscious.

She began her chanting and slowly rocked to and fro as she implored her God to grant the gift of healing. After a while, a faint blue glow appeared under her hands and spread to the injuries to the man's arm and chest. Sweat poured from her face.

To one side, Silmar and the others looked on. Of the militia riders, not one was left alive. Jiutarô had let them know that the cleret-wing dragon had seen a number of black-shirted riders turn and ride swiftly back to the town. There would now be no doubt that the Darkling witch, Hebbern and the mercenaries would know of their presence, if not their numbers, within the hour.

"The town will be closed against us," said Vallio. Deep concern was etched on his and Morendo's faces for their friend. "We may have to mount a siege although this will be difficult with just a hundred or so of us."

"I think perhaps not," said Billit. "Those barrels? The oil, right? Remember that blast when I showed my magic to that captain? I did it on the barrel. That's why it was such a big bang. Think've what a few barrels up against the town's wall or the gate will do!"

Suddenly, Taura gave a sigh and fell limply to her side. She was totally exhausted. Varengo rose to his feet and looked to his friend. Yoriando was still unconscious but his breathing was not so weak. Nor were his wounds bleeding. It was a few minutes before Taura had the energy to speak.

"He will not die now, I am certain of it, thanks to Neilea's blessings," she panted. "But I cannot do anything for that arm, even if I were fully strong I could not. But he will mourn the loss of his arm and will need understanding but not fussing over. Care but not caring for. He will adjust and will obviously still wield a sword but not a bow. Do not grieve for him or with him but encourage him in all things. With the return of my strength I shall attend to him more."

"You speak wisely, Mistress," said Varengo softly. "I shall say my thanks to the Lady of Serendipity this evening but I now offer you, and Her, my personal thanks too."

Taura was helped to the wagon and the group set off towards the town. They had lost twelve townsmen and three dwarves and their spirits were low.

∽ ∾

"Hebbern! Prepare the town militia for, oh gods, I don't know! An attack of some kind! A battle! A siege! Seal the gates and man the walls, or whatever it is you surface-dwellers do."

"Aye, right now, exalted one."

"Has the mounted company arrived back from the quarry?"

"Six riders returned, exalted one. They report the sound of a battle and fear that the rest of the company was lost."

For the first time, the witch was lost for words. There seemed to be a large force coming towards the town from the west. Surely not the captives at the quarry; they were thoroughly subjugated. Who then? And what happened at the keep? That old mage, a member of the *Shadow* sect that still cast its mischief and evil in Baylea, had not replied to her probing magic. She had trusted him with the simple task of keeping control of the prisoners there and something had gone awry. Her dragon-kin beast had been dispatched but had failed to return. There must be a strong power to have caused this much mayhem to happen. What of the captives there?

"Spread the word around the town that the peoples are to remain in their homes. Anyone out on the streets not wearing uniform is to be executed on the spot. Dismissed."

The half-orc bowed and left the chamber.

ஒ ஐ

By late evening the sun had not yet disappeared behind the mountains to the west as the force of dwarves and freed men, and the group of companions, marched past the town in full view of its occupants. There was no longer any need for secrecy. The dwarves beat their shields powerfully and rhythmically and chanted war songs at the top of their voices. They had a vast array of weapons that had been taken from the mercenaries that they had fought and beaten and they kept these clearly on display. They spread out along the road to make their numbers look greater as well as to present a more difficult target should arrows, or worse, be fired from the tops of the walls almost three hundred yards away. Nothing was. As many as were able to ride a horse did so; they had plenty of mounts after all, and this also served to make the force look greater than it was.

An hour after the small army camped by Dellie's hut and had a perimeter watch set up, the large group of freed prisoners arrived from the keep in the hills, almost doubling the size of the force now arrayed by the river. Admittedly, half of the latest arrivals would be non-combatants but they would have other uses. The four Priests of Clamberhan, including the High Priest, Gallan Arran, and the women who had been locked away in the tower dungeons, were attended to by Dellie. The skills she had learned many years before when training as a Priestess of Tambarhal, the Godess of Healing and Nature, she had long believed were lost to her. Over the last two days she had prayed and implored to her Goddess to give her the strength and return to her the healing skills she knew would be needed. She looked for a sign that these were coming back to her but there were none. That day she had been in tears and had continued to beg for the wisdom to heal the injured. Taura had not recovered well from her exertions, she knew, so it was now up to her, Dellie Helliol, to do what she could. When the sick and wounded started to appear outside her hut she almost went into a panic.

The first person she attended to was a young girl who had been unconscious since being taken out of the tower dungeon. Dellie, with her heart pounding, spread her hands over the girl's head and began to sing words that she believed were long-forgotten. Her voice quivered but she continued with the chanting. But there was no feeling of power or flow of energy.

Suddenly, the girl's eyes flickered open and the she whispered "Hello Madame Helliol!"

Dellie sat back in surprise but then dissolved into laughter and tears at the same time. The girl smiled, yawned and then sat up. Greatly encouraged, and thanking her Goddess over and over Dellie moved onto the next person. It was Gallan Arran. Although most of his old injuries from the whippings and beatings that he had received were healed, he was unable to speak and his mouth was covered in sores and scabs. His tongue was swollen. He was sitting propped up on someone's backpack, extremely weak from malnutrition.

Dellie set to work immediately and once again, with her hands placed over his face, she began her healing songs. With much more confidence, her voice now infinitely more self-assured than before, she sang clearly and beautifully. Almost immediately she felt the warmth of healing strength flow through her hands and the faint blue glow of holy power appear over Gallan Arran's face. His bloodshot eyes closed and he seemed to relax, almost sleeping.

Varengo watched her from a few paces away, his heart swelling with pride and emotion. He watched as she stopped her song and withdrew her hands. He also saw Gallan Arran's face, his mouth and tongue now appear less hurt and swollen. The old man placed his hand on the side of Dellie's face and smiled serenely at her.

She wiped her perspiring brow and took a deep breath.

The other Priests of Clamberhan were also suffering from maladies and afflictions and, moving from one to another, she gave some divine healing each in turn. Before long, however, she began to weaken but not before she was able to use the last of her strength in attending to Yoriando. He had not regained consciousness since the last battle and having been carried in the back of the wagon, he was once again breathing raggedly. By the time she had sung her long healing song and poured into him the last of the healing strength she had in her body, Yoriando had slowly awakened to an overwhelming pain.

Dellie slid to the ground but Varengo picked her up and carried her into her hut, gently placing her on the bed. When he returned outside to his old friend, he knew he would have the unenviable task of telling him what had become of his arm.

"Aye, my friend," Yori said softly. "I know this already. Gods man! I was awake when I saw the arm fly away. It's my left arm, Aye? Well then, I can still fight with the right and I can still lift a flagon of ale – but not at the same time!"

"You will find it difficult to hold an arrow with your toes and the bow with your right hand too, old comrade!"

"Dammit, dammit! I gave that no thought. I'm hungry! Oh, did you take the ring off my finger, you know, on the lost hand?"

"You already wear it on your right hand. Come, Yori. My time for eating; your time for sleeping! I shall put aside some food for you. Then I must attend to my beloved."

Before midnight, the Priests of Clamberhan, the God of Knowledge and Learning, were recovered sufficiently to attend to the majority of the remaining sick and injured but only for a while before fatigue overtook them.

As people were settling down, Dellie called to Varengo and the others of the companions.

"We have some help from within the town," she explained. "Some of the witch's militia, probably fifty or more will daub a green splash of paint upon their chests in the morning and will create havoc. Some will open the gates if they are able."

"Hmmph! Buyin' their freedom," grunted Jasper.

"No, I think not," replied Dellie. "Many of them have been carefully voicing their dismay at the treatment of the townsfolk. One of them, Triffner, has been speaking with Madame Dallimore for a couple of tenday-weeks now. I know him. He is the witch's manservant. Madame Dallimore trusts him."

"We can reserve judgement for when the fighting starts," said Varengo. "If they are there to help then all to the good."

People ate and slept during the night knowing that there would be fighting again in the morning. The second battle for Carrick Cliffs would begin.

Chapter 53

IN THE EARLY hours of the morning, Triffner received the summons he had been waiting for. His heart pounding in his chest and mouth dry, he rapped on the door to her chamber.

"In!" came the harsh response.

He opened the door and stepped inside. His legs shook and he could barely breathe. *She knows,* he thought. *Gods give me strength.*

"My dearest friend is hungry," she shrieked. "Bring food. I want something substantial so that my pet can be prepared for the great battle. A bigger meal, ready naked, drugged to bring on drowsiness, and blindfolded. Is that clear?"

Triffner bowed and left the chamber. He had not trusted himself to give a spoken reply.

He walked to the end of the corridor and made his way clumsily down the cellar steps. He called to Pradoe, a campaigner he had known and trusted for many years.

"Old friend," he said softly. "I have done many foul things for that witch and can take it no longer. I shall make amends this morning. I have one last job to do and need your help and your courage, Pradoe. Help me this one last time."

"Aye, Triff. But I won't storm her chamber with sword in hand. Neither with you nor with a company of men."

"You'll not need to, just take the beast its meal."

"Ye Gods, Triff!"

Triffner stripped off his clothing and held to his lips a bottle containing a massive concoction of the slow but deadly poison given to him by Madam Dallimore.

"No Triff!" gasped Pradoe. "I know what you intend. Don't do this. Let's leave this place now. You 'n' me. Together."

Triffner said nothing except to swallow the entire contents of the bottle, stifle the choke and direct the shocked Pradoe to bind his wrists and place a hood over his face. Two minutes later an ashen-faced Pradoe led Triffner up the stairs and along the corridor.

Gods! The pain in his gullet and his stomach was excruciating – *The poison creeps through me! Will I make it?* It was all he could do to keep from doubling up in agony as the cramp in his stomach grew with each step and each heartbeat.

Pradoe, gently holding his doomed friend by his shoulders, took the ogharii's meal in to the witch's chamber.

❧　❧

As dawn broke over the town of Carrick Cliffs, the dwarves had already assembled in groups of twenty or thirty, ranked in lines abreast, two deep, outside the closed gates. Chanting their traditional war songs and beating the butts of their spears and battleaxes on their shields, they looked fearsome but disciplined. The group in the centre was the largest and in it were the dwarven crossbow bearers, Jasper and the companions. Behind them, on horseback, were Varengo, Vallio and Morendo, wearing breastplates and helms that they had spent a few hours during the night polishing until they shone. None of them had slept. Yoriando had been mortified when forcefully told he would take no part in the battle.

Arranged on the flanks, in small groups of ten or so, were many of the townsmen, and a few women too, all armed with spears, swords and even a few bows. Every face showed a grim determination; a few also showed a measure of fear.

Varengo was given command of the attacking force and had warned every person to be ready for a siege but that they may be given the chance to make a quick entry into the town.

Leading his two men, Varengo rode to the front of the centre group and raised his sword high.

"Courage, my people," he yelled. "We shall win through."

Billit stepped forward and with his hands held high, fired an energy bolt at the gates. He gave a mild expression of dismay when the bolt appeared to be absorbed by the gates.

"Bugger!" grunted the gnome. "A protective magical shield. Next plan!"

Billit had explained his second plan to blow open the town wall using the barrels of oil and a magical energy bolt and was about to make ready when the gates were thrown open to reveal a number of militia with splashes of green on chests and shields – the friendly *Greenies*, as they were referred to.

"They've opened the choddin' gates for us!" yelled Jasper. A cheer rose up from the ranks of dwarves.

The *Greenies* were already engaged in fierce hand-to-hand fighting inside the gates and from where Varengo and his force were waiting they could see figures falling.

"Forward," yelled Varengo at the top of his voice. "Into the town! Remain in your groups!"

And forwards they all charged. First through the gates rode Varengo with Morendo and Vallio on either side of him. They immediately engaged with the militia, their swords slashing to both sides of their horses. Close behind charged the dwarves and the companions and soon the battle intensified. Some of the *Greenies* had been killed or wounded but twice as many of the militia had fallen too, having been taken by surprise at the treachery of their comrades, as they perceived it.

The companions and dwarves, supported by the *Greenies*, soon finished off the militia but as they stepped back to reform, Falcon yelled "Hebbern!"

Across in the market square strode the huge form of Hebbern, flanked by thirty or more of his militia bowmen. The bowmen spread out side by side and reached for their arrows.

Jasper yelled for everyone to mingle with the dwarves. "Shields up!" he bellowed.

With practised precision, the dwarves raised their great wooden shields and formed a protective shell around themselves and the companions. The arrows flew but not one found its mark.

Beneath the shield cover the only person in difficulty was the mighty Barbarian, Falcon. He was crouching uncomfortably but with a huge grin on his face as the arrows rattled onto the shields around him. Many of the dwarves roared with laughter.

Another call from Jasper resulted in the mass of bodies beneath the shields shuffling forwards towards Hebbern and the bowmen. More thuds on the shields indicated that there had been another arrow attack. Seconds later this was repeated but this time one of the dwarves fell with an arrow through the side of his head.

At this, the protective shield cover disintegrated and the dwarves surged forwards in fury at the bowmen. Falcon was at their head, singing a great Barbarian battle-song at the top of his voice. Arrows continued to fly and some found their target. Suddenly, the bowmen were overwhelmed. Many ran for their lives but most were chopped and hacked to death by ferocious and angry dwarves.

As the dwarves turned to face the half-orc, Falcon stepped in front growling "He's mine!"

Falcon stood facing Hebbern. The great Barbarian wished once again he had his own massive war-hammer. He missed the ornately-carved handle and the weight of the hammer-head as he swung it about his head. Instead, he had been given what he considered were a pair of lightweight weapons more useful for banging nails into wood. His own had been hidden in Madame Dallimore's house some days earlier.

Hebbern gave coarse verbal taunts and abuse at Falcon who stood there with a wry smile on his face and said nothing. This only caused Hebbern to lose his temper even more.

"I gonna kill you, bastard," grunted the half-orc, spittle spraying from his mouth with each word. "Then I gonna take your woman and split her from neck to crotch. Then your mother too!"

Again, Falcon said nothing. But the wry smile had faded. Hebbern knew he had hit a nerve.

"Which one is she? The Helliol woman? The priestess? No matter, I have 'em both naked and bound in my chamber tonight."

Having had little response from his taunts, Hebbern knew it was time for action. He swung his own war-hammer, a vicious, spiked weapon from Falcon's left to right side. Had it struck the Barbarian warrior, it would have disembowelled him and ended the fight. As it was, it knocked one of the Barbarian's hammers out of his hand. Falcon leapt back and the war-hammer swished by him. At the end of its swing, Falcon swung his remaining weapon at it and hooked it down towards the ground. The half-orc was caught off-balance and stumbled forwards.

The Barbarian hooked his left arm around Hebbern's neck and brought his hammer down onto the centre of the half-orc's back. Instead of the satisfying crack of bones, he struck the centre of Hebbern's wide, thick belt. The half-orc straightened up and this time hoisted Falcon off his feet. The great man was thrown to the ground and Hebbern launched another swing with his war-hammer.

Before he could bring the weapon down onto Falcon there was a loud clang and the half-orc stumbled to his side, dropping his weapon. Behind him stood the little, frail form of Madame Dallimore with a skillet in one hand and dragging Falcon's great war-hammer along the ground with the other.

Hebbern quickly rose to his feet but still had a vague, dazed expression on his face. Seeing that his attacker was standing close by, he lashed out with his huge hand and swiped her across the side of her head. She fell to the ground out cold dropping the great weapon.

Hebbern sprang forward reaching for Falcon's weapon. He had dropped his own and it was out of his reach. Seizing an opportunity, Falcon kicked out catching his foe high on the chest and the half-orc fell backwards. As Falcon reached down to retrieve his beloved war-hammer, Hebbern rolled to his side, sprang to his feet and, clutching at his own weapon, ran off.

After checking that Madame Dallimore was alive and breathing, Falcon very quickly sprang off in pursuit.

ॐ ॐ

"She's there, look!" gasped Billit.

There on the platform that she had once stood upon to witness the building of her precious tower, the Darkling witch now watched the progress of the battle.

"Let's get the bitch!" growled Taura.

Billit took Taura's hand and, using his newly-learned *Jump* spell, transported them both to the top of the tower.

"Wow! That was good!" gasped the priestess, her head reeling from the sudden disorientating spell.

"Not done that before," the little gnome admitted.

There before them stood the Darkling witch. Wearing her many-horned helm and her glistening cape, she looked almost invincible – a vision of beauty, of power, of terror. She held in her left hand the staff of her magic and her slim sword hung in its highly-polished black scabbard at her hip.

"Remember, missy," whispered Billit, "all that staff's got are the spells that I got except I don't need no stick to 'old mine!"

"So who do we have here?" called the witch. "Have you come to do battle with me? A Gnome who can probably do little more than parlour tricks and a – a priestess? Of what god? Some little-known godling who has given you the power to heal scratches? Oh how tiresome!"

She raised her staff and pointed the lower, iron-shod end of it towards the pair.

A blast of ice flowed across the space between the pair and the Darkling witch – but it came from Billit, not the witch.

The Darkling's expression turned from bored confidence to one of astonishment. As she became swathed in ice Billit and Taura exchanged a look of achievement but this soon evaporated as the ice disintegrated into vapour with a magical dispelling.

The witch quickly responded by sending a swarm of bees from her staff towards the pair but Billit, using a similar magical dispelling, soon disposed of that threat.

"So are we to trade tricks all day?" called out the Darkling witch. "Or shall we find out just who is the superior power here?"

With a word and a gesture, the witch disappeared from sight.

క్ర్ ఎ్

Many of the mercenaries had scattered when the dwarves had stormed into the town. The militia bowmen had also scattered when the enraged dwarves had lost one of their number beneath the protective shields. Now, the townsmen, helped by the *Greenies*, were scouring the town for their foes. They met with pockets of resistance and, if it were not for the more experienced *Greenies* stepping to the fore, many more townsmen would have fallen.

Individual mercenaries, and there were many hiding about the town, were beaten or hacked to death by groups of dwarves, *Greenies* and by the townsmen who were out for revenge. The *Greenies* implored the townsfolk for more leniency and when it was not forthcoming, they separated away to seek their own battles.

The townsmen, dripping in the blood and gore of their foes, continued their search for a while longer but started to lose some of their number as a few of them fell mortally wounded by the arrows and blades of the militia. It was only then that calm and control finally replaced their blood lust.

❧ ☙

"Where in the bloody Void 'as she buggered off to now then?"

Billit was somewhat frustrated with the latest spell cast by the witch. He knew that if she was invisible, she could cast a spell while remaining unseen but, even though as soon as it was cast, she would become visible once more, it would be too late for them to protect themselves from it or dispel it. This was often seen as a limitation in spell-casting that had been imposed by the Goddess Neilea. She had made magic available to those who developed the strength of will to control it, except for priests and others who relied on the gift of their deities, and despite the mage's good or evil purposes, could draw upon the sun for their magic. In Her wisdom, she had ensured that no mage could cast more than a single spell while invisible.

"There she is!" whispered Taura. "Up there on the top floor of her tower."

"Right then. 'Old on again, missy. We're on our way up to her one more time."

Once again, Taura felt the disorientating sensation as she and Billit were magically transported to the top of the tower by the little mage's *Jump* spell. As they suddenly appeared on the tower it took a couple of seconds for Taura to gather her wits but in that time the witch let out a shriek of laughter and blasted her off the tower with a burst of magical energy. The power took the priestess in the chest like a massive punch and she lost every bit of air from her lungs.

Billit was already preparing his own enchantment but on seeing Taura pitching over the edge of the tower instantly changed it to *Floatfall* to allow the priestess to drift to the ground. He suddenly found himself crushed to the floor under an invisible weight.

Taura lowered safely to the ground

᧡ ᧢

A sudden whoosh interrupted the various battles and skirmishes as the familiar shape of the brown wyrm soared over the tower. A terrifying, ear-splitting shriek caused every hand-to-hand battle to pause as the protagonists looked up to investigate the cause of the noise.

"It's the witch's beast!" cried one voice and the warning was taken up by many others. But *dragon-fear* affected everyone and soon the warning cries turned to wails of despair as terror took its hold on townsmen, dwarves and mercenaries alike.

All eyes turned as they followed the flight of the terrifying beast. Everybody knew that when uncontrolled, as it now appeared to be, it would be indiscriminate in who or what it attacked; especially if hungry. All fights were forgotten as every fighter, warrior and townsman held their hands to their ears to protect them against the deafening high-pitched screeches.

The beast circled once more and then swooped down to land on one of the platforms before the tower. It was from here that the witch had usually stood to watch the building of her tower.

But the wyrm did not land gracefully. It almost slid of the end of the platform as one of its hind legs buckled beneath it. Another shrill roar split the air and fighters fell to their knees in horror and terror.

Another scream sounded but it was not of the wyrm's making. The Darkling witch, standing atop the incomplete tower cried in anguish and, using her own *Jump* spell, disappeared from the tower and immediately reappeared on the platform beside the beast.

The wyrm instantly snapped its jaws at what it saw was an intruder and the witch just leapt away in time. She bent down to examine the wound on the beast.

"Oh my baby!" she crooned. "What have they done to you?"

Looking closely, she was shocked at the severity of the wound. Clearly, it was no ordinary wound but one that could only have been made by a great power – arcane being more likely than mundane.

"Who did this to you?" she yelled in a coarse, shrieking voice. "I shall kill him by inches!"

She passed her hand over the long scorch injury in an attempt to apply a healing spell but she knew that her skills in this were basic. There was little improvement. The beast merely raised its head and emitted a howl of pain.

At that moment there was a swishing sound and flurry of crossbow bolts struck the beast in its chest. The beast roared again and rose up on its back legs. Its injured leg buckled once again and the wyrm crashed back down onto the platform.

The witch spun and her gaze fell upon a small group of dwarves who were standing at the corner of the guildhall. Raising her staff, she readied her spell and released a blast of power at the dwarves. As one, they all leapt behind the building less than a heartbeat before the blast shattered the corner of the guildhall.

"Damn you!" she shrieked. "Damn you all!"

The wyrm spread its bat-like wings and launched itself from the platform. As it tried to push off with its back legs, the injured leg was unable to take the pressure and the wyrm crashed to the ground landing heavily on its rump, emitting another ear-splitting shriek.

The witch called out to the beast in an unknown language and it lumbered off through the arched entrance to the tower. The witch once more used her *Jump* spell to return to the tower just as Falcon, Jiutarô and Caeron rushed past the six shaken dwarf crossbowmen behind the guildhall.

"The bitch is over there with 'er beast," cried one of them.

"You mean the witch?" asked Caeron.

"Aye, but I think I called 'er aright, Mistress!"

One of the dwarves was peering through the devastated corner of the guildhall.

"She's gone back up to the top an' the beast 'as gone inside the tower. It's in a bad way by the looks of it."

The three companions looked at each other and, without a word being spoken but just a nod from each, they charged forward towards the tower entrance.

❧　☙

CHAPTER 54

THEY PULLED UP short as they ran into the tower through the arched entrance. A great mouth, full of fangs the length of short-swords, snapped towards them.

The dark wyrm, a creature of the Void, looked massive in the tower's dark hallway. It emitted a screeching roar and, fearing an acid attack, the three warriors turned their backs and covered their heads with their cloaks.

But the acid did not come. Instead, the wyrm flapped its wings and, despite the relatively small space, it rose a few feet above the floor. The downdraught from the beating wings disturbed dust and gravel which stung the eyes of the three fighters.

Holding his war-hammer in both hands, Falcon swung it at the chest of the beast but it had moved beyond his reach.

Before Jiutarô had a chance to stop her foolhardy action, Caeron rushed forwards and leapt up to grab at the wyrm's foreleg. The beast's skin was unexpectedly smooth and she was unable to take a grip. She slipped back down to the ground. Undaunted and knowing now what to expect, she tried once more. She made a grab for the beast's foreleg and held tightly onto the ankle. She swung her leg, hooked it over the clawed foot and started the long and unsteady climb up the leg towards the beast's chest.

"Caeron!" yelled Jiutarô in despair.

The wyrm was now aware that something had attached itself to its leg and lowered its head to investigate. Caeron's eyes opened wide in horror as the wyrm's gaping maw inched towards her. The smell of its foul breath almost made her retch and she knew that if it bit her she was as good as dead.

Falcon, on seeing the beast's head come down, was determined not to lose this opportunity and slammed his great war-hammer into the side of the beast's head, crushing the eyeball into a gory mush. The vitreous spattered across his face and arms and he leapt back once more.

There was another screeching roar and the beast whipped its head up high and away from Caeron. The wyrm frantically beat its wings and their buffeting caused both Jiutarô and Falcon to stumble to the floor. Regaining his feet, Jiutarô fired arrow after arrow into the beast's neck.

Caeron was now finding it very difficult to climb any further up the slick body of the beast. Its bucking and shaking caused her to lose one grip after another and it was only by a miracle that she didn't plummet to the ground. She had managed to plant her feet on the knee of the beast when an idea formed in her head.

She made a desperate lunge for the wing-root of the wyrm. She swung beneath the beating wing and was just able to keep her hold. Swinging up, she grappled the beating wing, gathered in and squeezed tightly as much of the flapping membrane as she could. With the flying capability of the wyrm much reduced, it crashed to the floor landing on one side.

Falcon and Jiutarô narrowly escaped being crushed beneath the wyrm. As it landed, Caeron leapt from its wing and, as it struggled to get back onto its feet, the three warriors attacked the beast's head with war-hammer, katana and short-sword.

As the wyrm howled and flailed its jaws, Jiutarô leapt beneath its long neck and plunged his katana deeply into the beast's chest in an attempt to find the heart. On his second strike, the wyrm shuddered and dropped to the floor, stone dead.

The three friends looked at each other in amazement. They had done it! But they were exhausted from their exertions. Caeron and Falcon were bleeding from many cuts. Jiutarô gently took Caeron outside of the tower and into the sunlight.

Falcon had already decided to climb the stairway. He climbed up two levels and almost ran straight into the ogharii.

❧ ❧

Silmar, aided by Varengo and his three friends, were picking of targets with their bows but with so much hand-to-hand fighting the situation was becoming difficult. There were considerably more mercenaries than they had expected and these were now furiously fighting for their lives.

Suddenly, the sky darkened as a huge flying beast circled overhead. One dragon and six smaller flying beasts almost silently flew lower and lower. Once again, the faces of friend and foe looked up in terror but a voice boomed out.

"A bronze dragon! Cleret-wing dragons! We are saved!"

The fighting continued on but with the appearance of the great dragon, the mercenaries were losing the enthusiasm for battle. One by one they dropped their weapons and begged for mercy. A few others fled.

The great dragon came in to land by the gates in the town's wall; a figure dropped down from its saddle and strode towards the group of companions.

"I am Ghar Hrol," announced the figure. "Dragon Knight, and this is my companion Violor the Magnificent."

Some townsmen, who had already met Ghar Hrol only a couple of days earlier, rushed forward and prostrated themselves at his feet. With a smile he said "Oh for the sake of the gods, get up and save your town."

At that moment, a lone horse-rider galloped through the gates just as seven hippogriffs, each with a rider, flew overhead.

"It's Kell!" exclaimed a laughing Silmar.

"Well met, comrades," boomed Kell. "I expect I've missed all the fun. I think another friend of yours has just arrived. Is there more fighting left to do?"

"I believe there is a witch still around but hopefully Billit and Taura are keeping her under control," said Varengo grimly. "I think we should try to find them though."

The group moved through the market square.

All of a sudden there was a commotion to the left side by the Mayor's house and a group of a dozen or more mercenaries charged out of the building with weapons whirling.

Ghar Hrol rushed ahead with his enormous two-handed great-sword raised and laid about him. Mercenaries fled before him as his battle-cries brought terror to them. Kell and Silmar, along with Varengo and the others, were soon in the thick of the battle, fighting face-to-face with desperate mercenaries who knew that they had nothing to lose by fighting for their lives.

Within a few minutes, most of the mercenaries had been cut down. The few that were left threw down their blades and begged on their knees for mercy.

❧ ❧

Jiutarô and Caeron joined Silmar and the others but were dismayed to see that Falcon was not with them.

"He must still be in the tower," gasped Caeron.

"Then we must make our way there for I would not be surprised if Taura and Billit are there too," urged Silmar.

As they were about to leave, seven figures dressed in silver armour and white capes strode up to them. One of them smiled broadly and held out his hand to Kell and then to Silmar.

"Greetings Silmar, Prince of Refuge," the man said. "I am Telemar Habin, Knight Commander and Paladin of Tarne the Just. I can feel that you still bear the item entrusted to you many months ago. I have followed your progress – do not ask how, suffice to say that I did so. You and your friends have been busy. These are my six warrior priests. My goodness! So what is the situation in the town now?"

As they strode to the tower, Silmar and Varengo explained what had happened and what they knew. Caeron spoke about the death of the wyrm, which raised many an eyebrow, and spoke of the Darkling witch.

"She stands atop the tower – there look," cried Morendo.

As they looked, the witch pointed her staff at the group gathered below.

"Oh no you don't," gasped Telemar and he sent a magical beam to envelop the witch and hold her immobile. But in the blink of an eye she had disappeared.

"Where is she?" growled the Knight Commander.

"There! To your right!" replied one of the six warrior priests of Tarne.

The witch now stood atop the platform. She raised her staff once more and a beam of power streaked towards Telemar. Two of the paladins simultaneously raised their holy symbols of Tarne and an invisible shield deflected the energy back to the witch. Telemar staggered backwards but stayed on his feet. The witch, however, was blasted off the platform and crashed to the ground.

ၷ ᆽ

The ogharii knew something was wrong. That damned human meal! It was diseased or it was poisoned. The ogharii had tried to bring up the contents of its stomach when it felt the sickness well up in its gut. When the sickness turned to pain, as if acid had been poured inside its gullet, it knew it was too late to do anything about it. The ogharii had drunk water by the gallon and it had felt some relief. Then the dizziness and disorientation descended upon it. It couldn't think. *Where was – where was the Darkling mistress? She would help. But she would – she would have – to be damned quick.*

The battle had started a while ago. It could hear the noise of fighting. Its magic would be needed to augment the witch's own enchantments. *Damn the pain!* It had been waiting inside the tower and the sound of fighting was getting louder and louder, closer and closer. It was time. It stumbled to the foot of the stairs and climbed on the first step. *Damn!* It collided with the walls on both sides in its agonised effort. A few more stairs. As it rose through the opening onto the top level, it almost collided with a human warrior. The warrior was very large.

A mage of some kind was at the top of the tower sending magical fire-darts, one after another, into the body of the ogharii. The beast spun around to engage what turned out to be a little gnome and then the human warrior laid into it with his great war-hammer.

The ogharii, spun about again. Using what little wits it still had, it fixed the gaze of its great eye on the Barbarian warrior who very quickly reacted to the heat caused by its spell.

Using a shard of rock, the gnome started to prise the stopper out of a small barrel. The stopper shot out and oily contents splash over his little boots. Fortunately, the ogharii had its back to the gnome who lifted the barrel and shook its contents over the beast.

The mighty Barbarian warrior fell to his knees. Unable now to lift his war-hammer because of the constricting heat of the *iron-sear* spell, he could not breathe. He tried to tear at the bindings of his breastplate but his fingertips could barely touch the scorching metal.

The ogharii spun about again. His great eye took in the little figure before him. The small gnome mage, almost insignificant to look upon normally, fired a magical fire-dart at the ogharii, immediately igniting the oil. More fire-darts struck the beast, the last of which rebounded off the great eye catching the little gnome at the top of his chest. He fell to the floor clutching at his throat.

Through the spreading flames, the ogharii sent a last magical blast which caught the mighty Barbarian and sent him toppling over the edge of the tower. A cry of distress erupted from the gnome, he knew he was too late to save Falcon from crashing to the ground.

The ogharii uttered a deafeningly loud, shrill shriek and slumped, burning and poisoned, to the upper floor of the tower.

From the base of the tower, many feet below, a wail of anguish rose, trembling at first but then ending in a scream of "NOOO!"

৯৯ ৶

The half-orc was desperate. The battle had not gone well and *she* will be looking for a scapegoat. His sword-arm was numb from the battle against that Barbarian. He just needed a few moments to recover. Six of his men remained with him but whether through fear or loyalty he could not tell.

That's better than nothing, he thought. *I can take these men out there with me and find that bastard Falcon Dallimore.*

From his place of hiding, in an alcove behind the guildhall, he had seen small pockets of his militia as they mounted sporadic resistance against the poorly-trained townsfolk. *Damn!* Some of them were being helped by those who had been his own men – gods-damned turncoat mercenaries!

A flurry of fighting broke out around the corner of the building where he and his men were hiding.

"Out and at 'em, boys!" he yelled and rushed out with his spiked war-hammer raised high. He turned his head to rally his men but they were not there. Before him, legs wide and a massive two-handed sword held resting at the ready over his left shoulder stood a warrior the like of whom Hebbern had never seen before.

"Who the frack are you?" growled the half-orc.

The warrior, wearing a gleaming chest-plate and very ornate, visored helm, smiled. "Let me introduce you to the last person you will ever see on this fair land! I am Ghar Hrol, Dragon Knight of the Vale of Celesta."

"That sword looks far too cumbersome for use in battle. Let *me* introduce you to the weapon that will crush your skull!"

The half-orc made a great swing at the top of Ghar's right shoulder but the warrior merely stepped back with his right foot and Hebbern's weapon slammed into the ground. He had left himself wide-open to a devastating swing from the gleaming sword but the warrior just placed his foot on Hebbern's hip and pushed hard. The half-orc stumbled sideways but did not fall.

"Ghar Hrol?" growled Hebbern. "I know that name. You can't be 'im, he's frackin' dead. They sing songs of his demise from Lopastor to Livuria."

"Yes I know. I helped pen them with my old friend, the Bard Crystel Brightblade from the Home Territories; a formidable fighter and the most delightful of ladies – if I may be so bold to admit. She has a charming smile and a beautiful singing voice. These tales come in handy. It gives me time to be with my family."

Hebbern swallowed hard. His mouth was suddenly dry. The songs written of this man were sung in taverns and inns across the length and breadth of Baylea. A dragon-knight! This was not going to be easy!

With a lightning-fast draw, Ghar Hrol swung the huge sword in an arc that took the tip of the weapon across the bridge of the half-orc's nose. Dark blood ran thickly down Hebbern's nose and chin. In reply he launched a figure-of-eight attack and Ghar stepped back. As the war-hammer took its second pass across the warrior's body, he blocked it with an almost effortless thrust of his sword.

Once again, the impact had a jarring effect on the half-orc's arm and he almost dropped his weapon. The two antagonists spilt out onto the market square, the clang of steel and shower of sparks was taken into the shadows of the market stalls. Blade and spiked war-hammer cut through the wooden poles and benches as Hebbern and Ghar dodged and circled each other.

Hebbern knew that Ghar Hrol would not be the certain victory he had hoped for. He leapt up onto a table but misjudged its strength – it could not, and did not, take his weight. He fell through the shattered timber planks and landed on his rump amid discarded vegetables and fruit of the previous day. Ghar planted the tip of his massive sword into the ground and roared with laughter, his hands on his hips and his long black hair waving from beneath his helm as he rocked to and fro in his mirth.

Hebbern roared with anger and humiliation and climbed to his feet. "Bastard!" he growled. "You're gonna die damned slowly and may your soul rot for eternity in the Void!"

"Not this day!" Ghar's blade whistled within inches of the half-orc's neck and continued its swing through the pole supporting the wicker stall shade. It crashed down onto Hebbern and he leapt clear just in time to avoid being covered in the debris. In doing so he tripped once again, this time backwards, falling into a horse-trough.

Ghar seized the opportunity and leapt across the remains of the low table. Dropping his great sword, he grabbed his foe's weapon-arm and forced it onto the side of the trough. But the half-orc, panicking in the water, attempted to drive his knee towards the warrior's chest. With a twist, Ghar dodged the knee and pushed his hand onto Hebbern's face, forcing it under the water. Hebbern spluttered and struggled but Ghar had the full weight of his powerful body bearing down on the half-orc.

In a desperate effort to lift himself out of the trough, Hebbern braced his elbows on the edge but he was unable to do it. Ghar's thumb made contact with the half-orc's right eye and the warrior pushed it hard. The thumb drove through the eye, mashing it to a pulp, and continued through to the thin bone at the back of the eye socket.

With the half-orc now pinned to the bottom of the trough, Ghar gave a final push of his thumb. It cracked through the bone and found the soft tissue of the brain. Water trickled in past Ghar's thumb. Jarik Hebbern gave a shudder and the struggles stopped. The water above the half-orc's head clouded red and obscured the open-mouthed face.

Ghar Hrol's face was grim as he dragged the dead body of the half-orc out of the trough and dropped it onto the ground. He picked up his great sword and turned towards the sounds of battle still being fought just as Kell came running up.

"Dead?" asked Kell.

"Very," replied the dragon-knight.

Halorun Tann, High Knight Commander, Priest of Tarne the Just God, had seen Falcon plummet to the ground seconds after the witch had fallen from the platform. With all his priestly powers, and of those of his paladins who were gathering around him, there was nothing he could do to stop or slow the mighty Barbarian's fall. It had happened so quickly.

Taura sprinted the few yards and crouched at the side of her beloved Falcon. Plainly distraught, she sang healing songs in a tremulous voice. There was no movement or sound from him; no rise and fall of his chest; no flutter of his eyelids. In her heart she knew there never would be, despite her frantic efforts to try to revive him.

Halorun and his paladins, including Telemar Habin and his warrior priests, rushed to the platform, beneath which the Darkling witch was sprawled on the ground but as they approached it the supine figure of the witch shimmered and disappeared once again. At the base of the tower, almost obscured by the platforms, they could see the little figure of Taura as she crouched over the still body of the mighty Falcon.

Jiutarô and Caeron raced across to join Taura but Halorun bade them stand clear.

"Atop the tower again, High Knight Commander," gasps Telemar. "Look how she totters!"

"Billit up there too, is he not?" called Jiutarô.

"I do not see him," replied Caeron. "Does he still live? – Oh gods! I saw Falcon fall. It was such a long way down." She buried her head into Jiutarô's shoulder.

"I regret that there was nothing we could do to arrest his fall," answered Halorun.

"Observe! The Darkling witch directs a beam of magical light into the storage sheds yonder!" growled another paladin.

As her beam stopped, she turned to the group below and, once again, raised her staff and shrieking words of arcane power.

Caeron swiftly nocked an arrow, took careful aim and fired it, the best of her life, and pinned the sorceress's left hand to the staff. With the din about them, no-one could hear the scream of both pain and fury of the witch.

"Finish her now!" cried Halorun.

As one, the six paladins raised their hands and bright white shafts of divine light lanced towards the Darkling witch. The shafts bored through her body in an instant and her chest shattered asunder under the intense power of Tarne, the Just God. She immediately fell to the floor, out of sight of those gathered below.

As Jiutarô and Caeron rushed over to join Taura, Halorun and the paladins stormed through the tower archway.

လယ

The sounds of the dying battle were no longer as loud as they had been. Smoke drifted across the market square as a couple of small buildings burned. Surviving militia, their red tower symbols still showing on their chests, were being rounded up by townsmen and dwarves. Now came the wails of those who had lost husbands, wives, mothers and fathers, and children in the fighting.

Taura was sobbing uncontrollably. "Leave me alone!" she wailed. "For a few moments, please!"

Jiutarô and Caeron stood and moved back a little as Silmar, Jasper, Varengo and his men ran up. Concern was etched over every face as they looked down at the lifeless, broken body of Falcon. Taura continued to wail as she rocked back and forth with the head of the dead Barbarian cradled in her lap.

Halorun emerged from the tower entrance bearing the limp form of the Gnome mage but, just as he was about to lay him on the ground, the gnome's head popped up and he struggled to free himself from the High Knight Commander's grip.

"Put me down, you great clod! Leggo of me!"

The gnome was struggling so hard that Halorun almost dropped him.

"Holy One," panted one of the Paladins. "We must go to see what the beam of light was that the foul witch directed into that building."

"Yea, that is so," replied the High Priest of Tarne. "But there is much healing to be done by us. Others must investigate the sheds. I dread to imagine what she has started in motion. It looked like a signal of some kind."

As one, the companions stepped forward to offer to investigate the witch's light beam while Halorun and the paladins gave healing to the wounded.

Jiutarô, Caeron, Billit and Vallio ran through the stockyard towards the low doors to the shed.

ॐ ॐ

CHAPTER 55

"We best watch our step when we go in," advised Vallio as they rushed towards the low, wide doorway.

It must have been two or three minutes since the Darkling witch had projected the beam of light through the end window of the long, low shed. They stopped outside the entrance and looked at each other grimly. With a nod from Jiutarô, Caeron and Vallio fitted arrows to their bows and the samurai drew his katana, giving it a practice swing. Together, they charged inside.

After the brightness of the day, the inside of the shed seemed almost pitch black. Clear to all of them, however, was the low-pitched chanting of clerics of a religion unknown to any of them.

Billit immediately cast a *Day-Light* spell and as it flared they were all startled to see five black-robed and hooded figures swiftly dropping down through a large open trapdoor in the centre of the hard-packed mud floor. The archers quickly loosed off their arrow and two of the dark figures fell, rather than jumped, through the trapdoor without trying to stop their fall.

A sixth dark figure remained however.

Darkling!

With a harsh laugh, he scattered widely about him what appeared to be many handfuls of white seeds or small pebbles over the shed floor. Then with a gesture of defiance he dropped through the trapdoor just as Caeron fired another arrow at him. The arrow missed and embedded itself in the trapdoor just as it crashed down. They heard the sound of two heavy bolts being shot.

"Damn!" exclaimed Vallio. "Darkling bastards got away!"

He rushed over to the trapdoor with Jiutarô and Caeron close behind. They could not budge it, even using the tip of the samurai's katana as a lever.

Meanwhile, Billit looked with a puzzled expression at the floor but shook his head.

Standing up, Caeron strode over to him.

"What do you look at, Billit?" she asked. "What do you see?"

"Dunno! Not sure. I didn't like the look on that bugger's face when 'e scattered those things about."

"I wonder what they were."

"Don't know but I got a bad feelin' 'bout this. Oh Shi-! RUN!" he screamed at the top of his voice. "OUT – GET OUT!"

In seconds Vallio, Caeron and Jiutarô were outside the door with their weapons still at the ready. They stopped dead when they realised the little mage was not with them.

"Where Billit?" Jiutarô asked.

The gnome appeared at the doorway but stopped and turned to look back in.

Jiutarô looked at Vallio. "What was-?"

"RUN!" Billit yelled again. "Keep running, fools! It's gonna be an army of skeletons! Too many fer us! 'Undreds of 'em! Warn everyone."

As they ran yelling at the tops of their voices, many heads turned and even the townsfolk guarding the captive militia stopped their goading.

"The skeletons won't stop to see who is friend or foe," shouted Billit to everyone. They'll kill everyone living by overwhelming. We're all on the same side now!"

The shouts of warning were taken up by everyone and spread around the town. "Danger! 'Ware, skeleton army comes! Everyone – to arms!"

Within a few heartbeats, the first of the skeletons came out of the buildings. In ones and twos they emerged at first, slowly and fairly cautiously, but then came more and more. Soon there was a flood of them pouring out through the low doors. They were no longer vigilant.

They were mostly armed with old, rusting swords and some also with battered and even severely battle-damaged shields. Others carried hand-axes and spears. They made no sound except for the clacking of their feet against stones on the ground or the rattle of their weapons. One small group of mercenaries emerged out of a side passage towards the skeletons believing that they now had new allies but they were instantly cut down and their bodies trampled over as the massive undead army continued its relentlessly slow march towards the large mixed group of dwarves, companions and townsfolk that awaited them. The two surviving mercenaries flung down their weapons and vowed to fight alongside the defenders and face the consequences afterwards.

Skeletons continued to emerge from the shed. Many still had remnants of decaying flesh and tatters of cloth on their bones. The smell was increasingly and overpoweringly foul.

"'Ow, er, 'ow many w-would you say," stammered Billit. He was shocked at the number of skeletons arrayed before them.

"About f-four hundred, I would say," replied a very nervous Caeron.

"Still they come from shed," added Jiutarô.

"More like six hundred," said Vallio. "And, aye, they still come!" His eyes were wide with shock at the huge undead army. Never had he seen such a frightening sight in all his years of soldiering and adventuring.

Slowly, inexorably, the mass of undead advanced towards the town's defenders. One by one, a sword clashed against sword, axe against war-hammer and sword against shield as a skeleton came up to a dwarf or a man. The defenders quickly learned that the only way to destroy a skeleton was to bludgeon it with their weapon or shield; even to chop it with their sword. But scores died before they had time to learn that lesson. But the calls went around.

Slowly the skeletons overwhelmed the defenders. The situation was hopeless. The men and dwarves were slowly being cut down and pushed back.

But then came a shriek as a great bronze dragon swooped down and poured fire over a swathe of undead. Its great clawed feet scooped up and crushed many more and its tail swept skeletons against the sides of buildings where the bones shattered. A great cheer went up from the townsfolk and the fighters. The defenders pushed the front line of the skeletons backwards a little way. A gap opened up between the skeletons and the defenders but the skeletons mindlessly started forwards once again.

Suddenly, Halorun Tann, the High Knight Commander of Tarne, and his six paladins dressed in their white armour and flowing capes, entered the gap from one end and skeletons fell away from them, shattering as bones separated and clattered to the ground. Telemar Habin, the Knight Commander, and his six warrior priests, four men and two women, entered the gap from the far end. The skeletons there also started to disintegrate.

As the paladins and warrior priests stepped forward in line, the bones of the undead skeletons disintegrated to dust. Not one skeleton could withstand the godly power of Tarne, the Just God, that emanated from their raised sacred symbols. Very slowly, the front rows of the skeletons crumbled into the ground.

But there were too few priests and paladins and too many skeletons. That is, until another great cheer went up and Gallan Arran, Loremaster High of Clamberhan, and his three priests, also joined the advancing line of Tarne's Priests and Paladins. Together, they shattered the lines of skeletons. Many of the undead skirted around the priests and attacked the flanks of the defenders but, much heartened, the dwarves and men charged forward into them. Axe, hammer and sword, and even shields wielded two-handedly, rose and fell as the town's defenders hammered the fleshless bones.

A skeleton having had its legs smashed away could still wield a sword with its arms, as some of the defenders found to their cost. They learned quickly that day the importance of the best ways to destroy a skeleton lest it destroy them first.

Once again, the great bronze dragon, Violor, with Ghar Hrol riding upon him, used his fire, his tail, his clawed feet and his great mouth and destroyed skeletons by the score with each low pass across the battle lines. The massive dragon would also carry scars of that battle throughout his remaining life but they would be small and trivial. His presence contributed to turning the tide from the threat of defeat to one of glory.

The skeletons were brainless automatons, having been raised from the ground to do one thing – kill. They continued the fight until the last was smashed to the ground by a tall woman wielding a round shield. Dellie Helliol, with her man Varengo beside her, was blood-spattered and exhausted. But she carried no injuries of her own. Varengo stumbled and she quickly supported him with her arm.

The town's defenders were quiet. Not a word was spoken anywhere in the market square. The skeletons had killed many people: townsfolk, dwarves and mercenary. Even horses, cats, dogs and chickens had been cut down by skeleton blades.

Other dogs began to bark. Children stood in doorways and cried. Women began to cry in anguish as they stumbled around the battleground searching and grieving for lost ones. Women had died too and men grieved for them also. Slowly, the many survivors began to talk. Priests and paladins began to heal where they could. The dead were taken to be buried. Heaps of bone, skulls and rusting weapons littered the market square and townsfolk began to arrange parties to move the putrid-smelling mess. But Halorun Tann bade them not to – he would request Tarne to help with this task. The market square was cleared of the dead defenders and mercenaries and of the living too.

Halorun Tann and his paladins implored Tarne for his help and, after a long while, a strong wind blew across the market square. Dust from the ground and smoke from the smouldering buildings obscured the market square for many moments but when it eventually cleared, there was no vestige of undead remains to be seen. Even their weapons had been erased from the town.

Townsfolk slowly emerged from behind buildings and other places of hiding to look at the spectacle. But it was not the absence of the remains of the undead that caught their attention. They saw a shimmer in the air by the ruined gates to the town.

Chapter 56

STANDING IN THE centre of the market square was the figure of a warrior, standing very tall and noble. He was wearing gleaming chain mail armour almost to his knees that was so bright that the onlookers could barely look upon it. His great helm was also shining. He wore an impossibly-white cloak and was bare-legged. On his feet were simple sandals but with thongs that were criss-crossed up his lower legs His face was broad and strong and his blond hair fell almost to his shoulders. His beard looked unkempt and uncared-for. A broadsword hung at his right hip and a war-hammer at his left. Both weapons were ordinary, being unadorned in any way.

Immediately, Halorun Tann, Telemar Habin, the paladins and the warrior priests dropped to one knee and bowed their heads solemnly.

A second figure emerged as if out of nothingness. A woman, tall and lithe, dressed in a long, flowing, blue and silver dress, walked up to the warrior's left side and took his arm. Her hair was long, platinum-blond and unbound. Her face, though, was regal and kindly, with a slim nose and high cheekbones. She carried no weapons.

Taura stumbled forward and fell to both knees. Her face, already streaked with dirt and dried tears as she grieved for her loss now bore fresh tears.

The figure of the warrior turned his head to the grand lady beside him and smiled. "You look lovely, my dear," he spoke in a husky but strong voice. "As always, of course! I have never seen the daughter of Amae and Oeni looking anything but her best!"

"You never cease to cast the nicest of compliments to me, kind brother. But I shall not ask you to stop for it does appeal to me so." But her eyes fell upon the figure of Taura kneeling before her.

"I suggest you keep that discussion to yourselves until such time as you both return to your own halls," spoke a voice from the air around them.

A third figure emerged into view high above them but gently lowered to the ground to stand at the right side of the warrior-figure. This man was elderly, tall and distinguished, and exquisitely dressed in a long gown with a black satin sash with a beautifully-painted medallion-type buckle. His hair was neatly cut short and a very short beard adorned his face. He carried under one arm a stringed-instrument made of white sandalwood.

"Words of wisdom, as always from the learned one," said the lady in a soft, musical voice.

Gallan Arran and his two priests knelt before this latest figure to arrive.

The Gods: Tarne the Just, Neilea the Lady of Fate and Serendipity, and Clamberhan the Lord of Learning and Knowledge, had come down.

Puzzled, the crowd murmured amongst themselves. They saw nothing except the shimmering of the air the priests and those who had come to save their town, all falling to their knees as if in worship. The townsfolk began to return to their homes in utter confusion. Silence soon descended on the market square.

෨ ෯

Tarne was the first to speak. He called Jiutarô and Caeron up to him. The Samurai had the little cleret-wing dragon on his shoulders.

"Yazama Jiutarô, A Samurai of the Ako Province, I believe. Is it right that you have another title now that your master is dead?

"Hai, Lord. I am now *Ronin* – no master now, um, I am *wave man*."

"It is time for you to go, wanderer from the afar! Kiss your lovely lady. It is time for you both to part. I would suggest that your little cleret-wing dragon is cared for by Halorun Tann." It was more an instruction that suggestion.

Jiutarô turned, embraced Caeron tightly and kissed her tenderly on the lips while placing his hand gently on her cheek. "Time is come," he said softly, kissing her tears as they ran down he cheeks.

"No, Jiutarô! Noooo!" cried the half-elven archer tearfully, but Jiutarô was already fading. In seconds he has gone and Caeron wept bitterly. Sushi screeched and then let out a baleful howl before settling down to a gentle whining.

Tarne gestured to Sushi who lifted her head. The God whispered quietly to her and turned his eyes towards her and the little beast hopped from Jiutarô to Caeron's shoulder. She affectionately nuzzled the half-elf and then glided over to the still-kneeling figure of Halorun Tann.

It was then the turn of Clamberhan to speak. He called forward Gallan Arran and Silmar.

"Bring forth your burden, Silmar Galadhal, Prince of Refuge," ordered the Lord of Knowledge. His voice was barely audible but they heard it clearly enough. The elf took off his pack and removed from it the box with its artefact inside. Already he felt the nauseating effect of the dagger.

"Be so good as to open it for me," Clamberhan instructed.

Silmar opened the wooden casket and emptied its contents onto the ground. Pain lanced through his head as the full impact of the dagger's evil influence took hold. Amongst the shards and pieces of lead lay the dagger. All three of the Gods turned their faces away with expressions of distaste.

"As we expected, this precious artefact has been corrupted by that soul-damned monk-mage of the Shadow sect." Clamberhan's voice was hard but he continued to speak with a low and gentle tone. "He is dead so will do no more harm with his madness. Now, to put it right. It will take the combined concentration of the three of us in order to restore this abomination to its original condition and beauty."

The three gods moved to the dagger and immediately, a white glow streamed from their foreheads onto it. For twenty of more heartbeats the power surged into the dagger and then, just as suddenly, the power stopped. The dagger lay on the ground. It looked no different than it had before except that the crudely scratched glyph upon it had disappeared.

"Gallan Arran," called Clamberhan. "Take up the dagger and return it in its rightful place for now until such time that a permanent resting place has been constructed. Place upon it a protective warding in my name and never again shall it be removed except by those whom I grant the right to do so. When your friends, the dwarves, tear down the tower, use its stones to rebuild the temple. I understand that the Lord Tarne also wishes for the stone to be used to rebuild *His* Temple here in Carrick Cliffs."

"That is so, Learnéd One," replied Tarne the Just with a slight bow. Halorun Tann shall soon dispatch priests to occupy the new Temple from his own great Temple in the Western Heartlands."

There was a sudden disturbance as a former mercenary stepped forward. He had a splash of green paint daubed across his chest.

Unable to see the deities arrayed before them, he spoke directly to Halorun, Telemar and Gallan Arran. "M-my L-Lords," stammered the man. He took a deep breath and continued. "My name is Pradoe. I was the manservant to that foul witch. I would just like to say, er, to let you know, er, to tell everyone, that my friend Triff, er, Triffner, gave, er, sacrificed his life to poison the mouth-monster. Madame Dallimore helped him. Well, he died when the monster ate him. That's how he poisoned the beast you see – he poisoned himself first, you see? Well, I fear that his soul shall be lost for eternity. Please be his saviour and say prayers for him. I beg of you, m'Lords."

"Dear Pradoe," rumbled Tarne.

Pradoe looked around for the speaker with the powerful voice. On seeing none, he turned towards those stood by him, his expression one of fright.

The voice continued, "Do you think I have not been watching the events unfolding? Your brave friend, Triffner, will sit in the halls of the Just God with honour, if he wishes it. And he will be made most welcome. Fear neither for him, nor for yourself when your time comes. It takes much courage to take your friend to his doom."

Pradoe fell to the ground with his mouth wide open in confusion and dread, his hands held tightly to the sides of his head as if shutting out a terrible sound. After a short while he rose back to his feet, smiled broadly and stumbed back to the town.

"I am sure he will be honoured by the town too," Tarne continued. "A new statue, perhaps? Why not replace that awful one there which honours a man who got someone else to do his heroic work for him. That is why I encouraged Lady Trangath, the *Forest Mother*, to charm her birds to crap all over it!"

"Lord Tarne!" exclaimed the Lady of Serendipity. "How could you use such words? Indeed! I have words of my own to speak now, if I may?"

Tarne, suitably chastened, smiled nevertheless and bowed his assent.

Neilea turned to her distraught priestess and took her arm gently to lead her to one side so that she was out of earshot of the others.

She said, "Taura Windwalker, you have already been selected to be my Chosen One. I understand the anguish and pain you are suffering at the loss of one dear to you. Know then, that you carry his child inside you. Falcon's legacy to you, and to your comrades, will be a child who will be favoured by me and who will be special, much loved, protected and watched over when you travel in my name. I said to you that you are my Chosen One. Beware that this may cause you to be singled out from time to time by others who would wish you harm. But you will be able to protect yourself better. My past Chosen Ones have benefitted from my favour when it comes to their need of my blessings. Use wisdom in selecting those sacred spells which I grant you. You still have much learning to accomplish but my gift to you is that the learning will always come to you with your dedication."

Leading her priestess back to the others, the Goddess proclaimed to all, "My favoured priestess carries the unborn child of Falcon of the Barbarian Tribes within her. Care for her and protect her during this time."

At this, Taura's comrades gathered around the priestess to hug her and kiss her hand.

Jasper, laughing, said, "Ye Gods, yer strumpet! I didn't even know yer had bin misbehaving!"

Taura smiled thinly.

Laughing heartily, Neilea continued. "Know you all that she has a personal task to accomplish and that for her to progress in my ministry and be of greater benefit to me and to ensure the baby is to be delivered safely, this task needs to be attended to with the greatest urgency. My priestess will need the courage and support of her friends in this challenge."

One at a time, Neilea faced Silmar, Caeron, Billit and Jasper and said "I have read the minds of you all and I am pleased that you are all resolved to help my chosen one in her test."

Finally, she turned to a still-sobbing Caeron. "My goodness, how one so young has achieved so much. You are worthy of a special gift. You have shown allegiance and loyalty to this group of adventurers. I have thought long about the gift I would choose for you. With the intervention of Tarne, The Just One, it will come to you in the fullness of time. You will know it when you see it."

It was now Tarne's turn to speak once more. His grey eyes looked across them all.

He sits at the head of the great Pantheon of Gods, thought Silmar. *Yet here He is, with two others of such greatness and among us.*

"With mine and Neilea's blessing, you have all benefited from this gathering. The artefact has been restored and will once again be guarded by the House of Clamberhan." Tarne bowed at the mention of the name of this God of Learning. "Falcon, the Barbarian now sits at the right hand of his own God and is at peace. He shall visit the hall of his forebears and will hold his head high with pride. Of your other friend from afar; grieve not for him for his destiny will be fulfilled with honour. Remember that death is part of life and together they are a circle. Go with the blessings conferred upon you by myself, The Lady Neilea, and the Lord Clamberhan."

The God of Justice joined his left hand with Neilea's right and together, they faded away. Clamberhan bowed to Gallan Arran and his priests and similarly faded away.

Silence descended on the still awestruck party.

၅ ๛

Madame Dallimore was unanimously elected as Mayor of the town of Carrick Cliffs. She had been badly injured by the blow she received from Hebbern but with healing and rest she was soon able to take on her duties. This she did with an almost ruthless efficiency. Triffner's friend, Pradoe, was given the tasks of supervising the repairs to the damaged buildings and re-establishing the trade routes with neighbouring towns while Madame Dallimore enlisted Dellie Helliol's help to recover the morale of the townsfolk.

The greatest task however was to dismantle the tower. Every sign of that accursed structure would be erased from the town. The dwarves took on this task with much gusto and enthusiasm and their songs could be heard throughout the hours of the days as they worked. They broke open the trapdoor in the floor of their store-shed and followed the tunnel that was exposed for some distance. Many of the stone blocks were used to seal up the tunnel to quite a depth underground.

The surviving *Greenies* were given the choice of whether or not to stay in the town and help form the town's official militia. They all accepted. The other mercenaries who had helped in the fight against the skeleton army were not given the same opportunity – they were banished from the town.

Varengo, Yoriando, Morendo and Vallio were asked to lead and train the Militia. They readily agreed and Dellie was greatly heartened by this. She insisted that she would still care for the outcasts.

"There are no outcasts, ma'am," came a voice. "Their camp is deserted and they stand outside the town, apparently cured of their malady." A man stood before her, still wearing some of the rags that he had once been forced to dress in.

Dellie leaned against Varengo's shoulder and laughed. She continued to laugh until tears ran down her face. Her sacred symbol, now worn openly on her chest, suddenly glowed brightly and then the glow faded once more.

"Tambarhal!" she exclaimed. "My prayers have been answered. This is far more than I ever dared hope for."

The town of Carrick Cliffs would recover in time.

❧ ☙

One evening, in the town's tavern, Silmar, Jasper, Billit, Taura and Caeron sat together with Halorun Tann, Ghar Hrol and Kell.

Ghar told of how he and Violor had watched the town from the hills and had done battle with the witch's wyrm. He had been called to action following a request from the mystic, Antheuseolin, the Archmage of the Vale of Celesta.

"Antheuseolin," said Ghar, "had in turn received a visit from a Druid who had received a call for help from an exhausted and bedraggled cleret-wing dragon who bore the outlandish name of Sushi!"

Kell took over the story by explaining how he had been secretly sent by the Count Coldharth of the Vale to report on the movement of strange and unknown travellers who journeyed through the western passes into Cascant, to try to ascertain their purposes and discern whether they were the group who were carrying a certain artefact.

"I had based myself in the little town of Hills Edge," explained Kell. "My friend, Borgan Drogarn, is the lord of the village and a friend to all who look for aid against those who use fear and cruelty as their weapons. He had spotted your little group of travellers and I followed you. I must admit that I was impressed by the way you all wiped out that gang in the swamps. They had been terrorising travellers for many years."

Halorun Tann had sat quietly but then informed the group that he and the paladins would be leaving that afternoon. They would be in Westron Seaport within a week and would call in on Half Jasper at the Ship's Prow to inform him of the events. He would also be investigating *The Tower* organisation in the city.

"That is what the slave trading and artefact thieving organisation is known as. The Tower. The fat trader whom you saw treating with the Darkling in the city, Silmar, is deeply involved in this and I must try to find out how. There may be a task for your group when you return, you never know. The Magelords of Westron Seaport will be very interested in this, not to mention the exploits in this town."

Caeron was very much fascinated by Halorun Tann's eyes. They were completely black although the pupils were only slightly visible. He looked as though he was blind, a characteristic that he had been able to use to his advantage on many an occasion.

"So, Carrick Cliffs has been saved for a second time," boomed a voice from the tavern door.

An elderly man stood there, framed in the doorway so that, with the light behind him, nobody could make out his features.

"Come in, Master, and join the throng!" called Kell. "My ladies and gentlesirs, allow me to introduce the Archmage Antheuseolin of the Vale."

As he sat on the bench at the table, he lifted one buttock and let loose a resounding fart. "Ale is all I need, not to sit here listening to the witterings of a bunch of adventurers! I shall not tarry here long. Suffice to say, friend Kell, our plans came to fruition and the peoples of the lands were able to do most of their own problem-solving. About time too. Glad you didn't need me because someone else did – The Witch Queen of Livuria. She likes a little attention from me from time to time and it helps keep her mind from conquests of a more territorial nature."

A quart tankard of ale was placed in front of the archmage and he downed it all in a single go. With a belch and a wipe of his hand across his small beard, he stood up and strode out of the tavern without so much as a 'Good-bye'. Billit, hoping to speak to him rushed out after him but the man had disappeared. The gnome went back inside shaking his head in wonderment.

Kell continued. "As I was saying, the town will be better defended and should never again be taken by surprises such as this. The tunnel beneath the dwarven store shed has been sealed and permanently warded. The townsfolk will now need to finish their grieving and recover from months of trauma. I expect you will all be returning to Westron Seaport soon?"

"Aye," replied Jasper. "We must get this pregnant lady back afore she drops the baby by the roadside!"

"Who's got a story to tell?" asked Silmar. "A tale or something? We've not told any for ages."

"Aye, here's one," replied Jasper. "If I remembers it aright. There was a pretty young blond woman in Westron Seaport, see? Lovely round, firm brea–! She was unlucky in love an' really depressed so she decided to end 'er life by throwing 'erself from the 'arbour wall. She went down to the wall an' was about to leap into the frigid water when a 'andsome young sailor saw 'er tottering on the edge of the wall, crying.

"He took pity on 'er an' said 'Look, lass, you 'ave so much to live for. I'm off away to far off lands in the morning an' if you like I can stow you away on my ship. I'll take good care o' you an' bring you food every day.' So 'e moves closer, he slips 'is arm 'round 'er shoulder an' adds, 'I'll keep you 'appy an' you keep me 'appy', right?

"So the girl nods 'Aye'. After all, what did she 'ave to lose? P'raps a fresh start in far-off lands would give 'er life new meanin'.

"That night the sailor brought 'er aboard an' 'id 'er in a cutter."

"A what?" asked Billit.

"A cutter – that's a little boat they gets in if the big one sinks. From then on, every night 'e brought 'er three chunks of bread an' some cheese an' fruit an' a bottle o' wine. Good eh? Then they makes passionate love 'til dawn.

"Three weeks later, durin' a routine inspection, she was discovered by the captain. 'What is you doin' 'ere, girlie?' asks the captain. She says 'I 'ave an arrangement with one of the sailors an' 'e stowed me away. I gets food an' a free passage to the far-off lands an' 'e's screwing me.' The captain says ''E certainly is, dear. This is the Westron Seaport harbour ferry!'"

The group around the table dissolved into laughter. Kell banged his hand on the table in his raucous laughter and Ghar Hrol rocked back in his chair so far that he almost tipped over backwards. Even Taura and Caeron managed a wan smile.

Two days later, the little group left Carrick Cliffs. The good-byes had been said and words of prayer had been said over the grave of Falcon. Kell rode with them for two tenday-weeks until they were well inside Cascant. The remainder of their return journey took them along the major routes where they hired themselves as guards for traders' wagons. They steadily earned themselves a reasonable amount of money.

Midwinter came and went and in the early days of spring, over a year after they left Westron Seaport, the travellers entered Casparsport in Lopastor. They had a new task to fulfil; one they had promised to Taura. They would find out what had become of her family she had last seen when she was a very young child.

EPILOGUE
RETURN TO KYOTO

OCTOBER 1701

I, YAZAMA JIUTARÔ, *Ronin* though it upsets me to mention it, was much disorientated. I still carried my weapons and I still had my horse. I ran my hand over the horse's flanks and, *hai!* it was the very same horse I had ridden on my long and demanding journey from Ako in the Harima province, through the mountainous regions to the Straights of Shimonoseki. But that horse had been left at a village – I could not remember its name – in the strange dream-land prior to meeting with a monstrous man, a vampire the, ah – priestess called it. Taura was her name? The dream fades in my memories.

Stone markers on the road showed the symbols or writings of Nippon, my homeland, but I did not recognise the place names. Grazing on the side of the road not fifty paces away was another horse. I approached it cautiously. Apart from raising its head to look at the approaching intruder, it did nothing else except, perhaps, to continue tearing at the tufts of coarse grass. It was my pack-horse – the one which had perished, or I thought it had, when I had regained my consciousness in the little boat. Yes! There was my precious *yoroi* armour from which I had painstakingly removed the symbol of my former master, Takumi no Kami.

None of the items I faintly remembered having when in the strange world recently, were with me here. No coins – only those of Nippon. I shook my head vigorously. Had it all been a dream? The elf, Silmar, with the long, pointed ears? The lovely Caeron with whom I had enjoyed a brief time of intimacy? I miss her greatly – or the memory of the dream of her. A tiny gnome, was it? who could hurl magic like a child throws a wooden ball? Monsters and dragons? And, hai – Sushi, a tiny dragon with which I had had a special bond? Were they just memories left over from a vivid dream?

Well, now it was time to find out where, and when, I was. I knew that I had a debt of honour to repay, with the rest of the forty-seven *Ronin*.

Taking up the rain-sodden rope dangling from the harness of the pack-horse, I led it over to where my riding-horse stood. Soon, I was riding in a northerly direction. The muddy path was narrow and badly maintained. Within an hour I arrived at the top of a path that led steeply down to a jetty. Before me, sparkling in the misty sunlight, stretched the Straits of Shimonoseki, the narrow channel of sea that separated the mainland of Honshu from the southern island of Kyushu. Beyond the channel, in the hazy distance, rose the steep dark cliffs of Honshu.

It was the same boatman that had taken me across the straits such a long time ago. As before, he had been drinking – I could smell the stale *sake* on him – but I do not think he was inebriated this time. His wife had been frightening – no wonder that the man took to strong drink.

The boat-man nodded his head slowly in recognition. "Five yen?" he asked, remembering me from before.

"What is the day today?" I asked him.

"Aha! You have been at the *sake* for too long my *Ronin* friend!" he wheezed. "Hai, I know of your provenance for you hide it poorly. Summer draws to an end and the leaves fall. That must give you an idea." He tried to laugh but finished with a fit of coughing.

"I shall remove that head of yours if you do not keep a civil tongue within it," I replied with vigour. "I asked you a question – answer it cleanly. The day and the year?"

"I meant no offence, master. It is more than a year since I saw you last. I believe it is the year seventeen hundred and one and the autumn descends upon us. As to the day of the week, the date and the month, I have little need to remember those details. I estimate mid-winter to be eight to ten weeks hence. Begging your pardon, master. The fare?"

"I shall give you one gold yen now and another on successful landing on the other side but only if you keep your tongue behind your teeth for the remainder of the day."

Three hours later, the boat bumped against the small jetty on the other side of the Straits. The crossing had been unsteady, as expected and I had to lash my horses to the sides of the boat to keep them from tumbling. The man's wife was nowhere to be seen. It would not have surprised me to learn that she had taken a long walk off the short jetty – at the point of a sword – such was her unpleasant demeanour on my last crossing. But no doubt that was wishful thinking on my part, and perhaps on the boat-man's part too.

Moving mostly at night and resting in small villages during the periods of bad weather, I rode using the long roads to the city of Kyoto. There, just three weeks before the midwinter, I met Oishi Kuranosuké, my erstwhile captain, outside a drinking house. He looked terrible. His clothing was torn and filthy and his once perfectly-groomed hair now hung long and unkempt over his shoulders.

"Oishi-san!" I gasped. "It is I, Yazama Jiutarô."

"Begone!" he slurred. He stank of stale sake. "Away with you!" He shoved a hand in the small of my back and propelled me towards a stable.

What had happened to the man I once admired. But it was strange that he should push me in that direction – it seemed intentional if not irrational. I waited in the darkness of the doorway. I heard a whisper behind me and spun around, wakisashi in my hand. I could see nothing.

Suddenly a voice murmured. "Are you going to kill me, Yazama-san? Are you going to kill us all?"

"Wha-? Toshiro-san? Toshiro Yoshisuke? Is it you?" I stammered.

A hooded lantern was uncovered and I stood there dumbfounded. Before me, hidden in the gloom of the stables, was a mass of smiling faces – my comrades. Another push from behind me and there stood Oishi Kuranosuké.

I was astonished. "Oishi-san! But-! But you are recovered!"

"Quiet, Yazama-san," he whispered. "We are the last ones here. You were the last to arrive. Every one of us is ready. For me it was an act to fool the spies of Kira Kotsuké no Suké into believing that I was no longer a threat to his safety. I must go out into the street to resume my charade. It is like acting in a *Noh* theatre drama! Speak with the others. They will tell you what has happened and what is happening."

Like a ghost, Oishi-san moved to the doorway. Then he stumbled drunkenly out of the stables, pretending to do up the front of his trousers. He threw up, gods know how, in the middle of the street and collapsed in the gutter. Two shadows moved across the road but didn't approach him.

Yoshisuke spoke first. "We shall be riding this night, Jiutarô," he began. The others, about a dozen of them, crowded around. "Most of us have already left or are in Yedo already. It is to Kotsuké no Suké's castle there that we shall travel. It is just as well you turned up early. We were getting a little concerned. We shall leave in groups of five, at three-hour intervals. You, Oishi-san and I shall be in the last group. So we shall have an opportunity to speak about what we have been doing for the last year or more."

That was a subject that I may find it difficult to impart on my friends – they would never believe me! I am not even sure I can remember much about it.

It took many days to travel the wild and treacherous roads to Yedo, or Edo as it was more commonly known nowadays. Oishi-san let it be known that he had killed the two spies who had been watching him for so long. He had cleverly hidden the bodies in the stable where, because of the rapidly approaching cold weather, they wouldn't be discovered for a long time.

We entered Yedo at different gates. An hour later, we assembled at a ruined temple. All forty-seven of us were there. Little was said on our first meeting, the grimness of the task before us filled our minds, but we then separated and found ourselves temporary lodgings around the town.

We bided our time patiently.

❧ ☙

While on the long journey to Yedo, I learned much of the sacrifice made by Oishi-san.

Oishi Kuranosuké had been absent from the castle when his master, Asano Takumi no Kami had been in the affray with Kira Kotsuké no Suké. Had he been in attendance, he may well have been able to offer council to his master or at the very least, restrain him from the disastrous act. He had already felt the guilt of not having advised Asano to take with him a present for Kira. He blamed himself for the death of his master and the ruin of his house. Not one of the other forty-six Samurais considered this of him.

The vast majority of the other forty-five, I believe I had been far away of course, had scattered and disguised themselves as merchants, carpenters and craftsmen, teachers and messengers. From time to time, some of them would surface in Kyoto and cautiously make themselves known to Oishi-san. He had returned to the city and built himself a modest house in the Yamashina quarter. When his friends saw him however, they discovered a man who had taken to frequenting houses of the very worst repute and given to drunkenness and debauchery. Had the plan of revenge been ignored or forgotten?

The treacherous Kira Kotsuké no Suké, on the other hand, suspected that Asano Takumi no Kami's former Samurai band would be scheming against him so he sent spies to Kyoto to keep a watch on Kuranosuké and to keep a thorough account of all that the man did. Kuranosuké, however, was determined to completely delude Kira's men into a false sense of security and went on leading a sordid life with harlots and drunkards. When Kotsuké no Suké's spies reported what they saw to their lord in Yedo, he was very much relieved by the news and doubtless felt very secure.

Oishi even drove away his wife of twenty years and two of his three children in his strive to prepare for the coming day. His eldest son, Oishi Chikara, remained with his father. Oishi Kuranosuké soon after, bought a concubine and continued his life of drunkenness while the spies looked on and reported it all back to Kira Kotsuké no Suké. Oishi-san's plan was working well. Too well for he had made sacrifices.

He believed Kira had begun to think that he no longer had anything to fear from the cowardly, drunk former retainer of Takumi no Kami, our lord Asano, so little by little he kept a reducing watch and sent back half the guard that had been lent to him by his father-in-law, Uyésugi Sama. He was falling into the trap laid for him by Oishi Kuranosuké.

Many of the other forty-six, using their various tradesmen's skills, had been able to gain entry into Kotsuké no Suké's house. They made themselves familiar with the arrangement of each of the rooms and made a plan of the building. They studied the inmates, who all seemed to be loyal to Kira, and sent the reports to Kuranosuké.

He was delighted when the report arrived, shortly before midwinter's day – the day appointed by them to meet and carry out their revenge – that Kotsuké no Suké's guard was thoroughly down.

EDO – MIDWINTER 1701

MID-WINTER HAD arrived and with it came the bitter, icy cold. On the night agreed by us all so long ago, there was a heavy fall of snow. The night was very dark and few were the lights that shone out onto the streets. The city was hushed and men everywhere slept deeply on their *tatamis* and *futons* unaware of the deeds that were to be committed this night.

Oishi-san announced that the night would be favourable for our impending task and the opportunity must not be squandered. Every one of us voiced his agreement. After sitting in assembly together it was agreed that our group would divide into two bands. Using the plans and drawings of the palace, each man was assigned his post. One band would be led by Oishi Kuranosuké and would attack the front gate. The other band would be led by his son, Oishi Chikara, and would attack the postern of Kotsuké no Suké's castle. As Chikara was only sixteen years of age, Oishi-san appointed Yoshida Chiuzayémon to act as the boy's custodian.

The signal for a simultaneous attack by both bands would be the beating of a drum at Oishi-san's order. If any man was to slay Kotsuké no Suké and cut off his head, he was to blow a shrill whistle to summon all of his comrades who would rush to the spot. The head would be identified and taken by us all to the temple at Sengakuji and laid as an offering before the tomb of our dead lord.

Our next act would be to report our deed to the Government and await the sentence of death that would surely be passed to us. In this, every one of us was truly pledged. The hour of the attack on the castle of Kotsuké no Suké would be midnight.

We partook of a last farewell feast together and were not sombre. I told tales of my battles against goblins and foul beasts and was congratulated for my story-telling which lifted the hearts of all of us. Little did they know that I believed that I had actually fought these battles – but perhaps these tales came only from my vivid dreams.

Oishi Kuranosuké rose from his bench to address the band.

"Tonight we shall attack our enemy in his palace," he announced proudly. "His retainers will certainly resist us and we shall be obliged to kill them. But to slay old men and women and children is a pitiful thing. Therefore, I pray each one of you to take heed not to kill a single helpless person."

We all applauded Oishi-san's speech by banging our cups repeatedly on the tables and we each prepared ourselves, in our own ways, for the coming battle.

≈ ≈

Our two bands set forth at the appointed hour. The wind howled with unexpected fury and drove the snow into our faces. But we gave scant heed to the wind and snow as we hurried along the streets, eager to get on with our retribution. I was with Oishi-san's son, Chikara. We numbered twenty-three. The postern gate loomed out of the driving snow and we waited while I and three others of our number used a rope ladder, hung onto the roof of the porch, to gain entry into the courtyard.

We saw signs that all of the occupants of the house were asleep as was also the guard in the porter's lodge. These we bound before they had a chance to wake up but when they did, they were terrified and begged us for mercy. We agreed to this provided that they gave us the keys to the gate. We were informed that these keys were kept inside the house by one of the Samurai officers and that they had no means to obtain them.

"Damn them," I growled and took up a hammer with which I strode to the postern and dashed to pieces the large wooden bolt that secured it. With a well-placed kick from outside, it flew open and Chikara and the remainder of his band rushed in through the postern gate. I was fearful that my rashness might have woken the occupants but of this there was so sign.

At this point, Oishi-san had arranged to send a messenger to the neighbouring houses to warn the occupants that we, the *Ronin* formerly in the service of Asano Takumi no Kami, were about to break into the palace of Kotsuké no Suké to avenge our lord and that we intended no harm or hurt to neighbouring houses. Kotsuké no Suké was vehemently disliked by his neighbours, so they did not feel inclined to offer him assistance. As a precaution, Oishi Kuranosuké stationed ten of his archers on the roof of the four sides of the courtyard with orders to shoot down any of the retainers who might attempt to leave the palace.

With his own hand, Oishi Kuranosuké struck the drum and gave the signal for the attack.

The beating of the drum rudely awakened ten of Kotsuké no Suké's slumbering retainers. Drawing their swords, they rushed into the front room to offer their master some protection. At the same time, Kuranosuké's *ronins* burst through the main door of the room and engaged the retainers in combat. The fighting was furious and desperate. While this melee was raging, Chikara led us through the garden and forcibly entered the rear of the house.

Fearing for his life, a terrified Kotsuké no Suké hid, along with his wife and female servants, in a closet on the terrace while the remaining retainers, who had been sleeping in the barrack outside of the house, made themselves ready to affect a rescue.

Kuranosuké's *Ronins,* who had engaged the ten retainers in the front room, had by now overpowered and slayed them all without losing a single one of their own number. Forcing their way towards the back of the house, they were joined by Chikara and his men, with me among them, and were reunited as a single band. The campaign was progressing to plan.

The fight became a single general battle as all of Kotsuké no Suké's retainers joined in. Oishi-san was sitting on a camp-stool giving out his orders and directions to us *Ronins.* I had tried to cleave the head of one retainer from his body but my sword had become wedged among his neck-bones. With a hefty kick, I managed to pull my blade free and looked for another engagement.

Very quickly the retainers realised that they were no match for us *Ronins* so they tried to send messengers out with pleas for aid to Uyésugi Sama, their lord's father-in-law. The messengers were shot down by Kuranosuké's archers. With no aid forthcoming, the retainers fought on in desperation knowing we would give them no quarter.

"Kotsuké no Suké alone is our enemy," Kuranosuké cried out aloud. "Let someone go inside and bring him forth, dead or alive!"

Standing in front of Kotsuké no Suké's private rooms stood three of his bravest retainers with their swords drawn and ready. These were the infamous Kobayashi Héhachi, Waku Handaiyu and Shimidzu Ikkaku. All were good men who were loyal to their master and known to be expert swordsmen. So well did they wield their swords that they kept all of the *ronins* at bay and for a moment even forced us back. Unfortunately, I was too far down the corridor to give any useful fight to them.

Oishi-san was so furious with the failure of his men to return the fight to these swordsmen that he yelled "What? Did not every man of you swear to lay down his life in avenging his lord? And now you are driven back by three men? Cowards! You are not fit to be spoken to! To die fighting in a master's cause should be the noblest ambition of a retainer!"

Then he turned to his son, Chikara, and said "Here, boy! Engage these men and if they are too strong for you – die!"

I was shocked by the ferocity of these words. Never had I heard such rage from his mouth as he condemned his own son to death, albeit a noble end.

Chikara however, was much encouraged by these words, took up a spear and engaged Waku Handaiyu in fierce battle. But he could not keep his ground and was driven backwards into the garden by the swordsman. Chikara slipped on the icy ground and tipped into the freezing pond. In his attempt to kill him, Waku Handaiyu, looked into the black pond. Chikara lunged with his spear and cut his foe in the leg causing him to fall. Crawling out of the water, Chikara finished off the swordsman with a great thrust.

By now, Kobayashi Héhachi and Shimidzu Ikkaku had been killed by me and three of the other *Ronin*. For the first time, I valued the fighting and swordplay that I had done during my *dream* time. Of all Kotsuké no Suké's retainers, not one survived. On seeing this, Chikara went into a back room with his bloody sword in his hand to search for Kotsuké no Suké. All he found, however, was the lord's son, Kira Sahioyé, who was wielding a halberd. Sahioyé attacked him but was quickly wounded and he fled. Although this marked the end of the fighting, there was still no sign of Kotsuké no Suké.

Kuranosuké divided his men into several parties and we searched the whole house but there was still no sign of our prey. At this, we forty-seven began to lose heart.

One said "Oishi-san. I am prepared to commit seppuku if all are agreed here and now!" Others took up the cry but I was not convinced that we had searched thoroughly enough.

"Oishi-san," I called, bowing deeply. "It is not too late to continue and widen our search. The archers would have seen if Kira had run away but they report nothing. He must still be here. One more careful search, I implore you."

He replied grimly. "Hai. We shall make a final effort. Look in, under and behind everything. Leave no door, window or hatchway unchecked. Question every woman, child and servant but harm none of them unless they harm you. Keep to your parties."

Kuranosuké went into Kotsuké no Suké's sleeping chamber and touched the bedcover with his hand and called aloud "I have just felt the bed-clothes and they are yet warm and so I say that our enemy is not far off. He must certainly be hidden somewhere in the house."

We *Ronin* were much encouraged. Chikara and I examined the sleeping chamber and, there in the raised part of the room, near the place of honour, hung a tapestry. I tore it down to reveal a large hole in the plastered wall. I took the spear offered to me by Kano Kiyomasa, one of my companions, and thrust it through the hole into the darkness but could feel nothing to impede it.

Kiyomasa took back the spear and climbed into the hole to find a little courtyard on the other side in which stood a small outhouse for storing firewood and charcoal. Looking inside he could see a white shape at the far end and he thrust his spear at it. Two armed men suddenly sprung out at him and tried to slash him down with their weapons. He kept them at bay until I came up and killed one of them with my wakisashi into his throat. How his blood spurted at me! The second one then set about me so I killed him too, without effort.

Meanwhile, Kiyomasa entered the outhouse and slashed about with the point of his spear. Seeing another flash of white, he struck at it with the spear and heard a rewarding cry of pain. He rushed forwards towards the sound of the cry but a man dressed in white robes, who had been wounded in the thigh, drew a small blade and aimed a strike at him. Kiyomasa roughly wrested the blade from the man and, grasping him by the collar, dragged him out of the outhouse. I took hold of the captive by the shoulder and thrust him hard down onto his knees.

Kuranosuké and the some of the *Ronin* arrived on the scene and together, we all examined the captive carefully. We saw at once he was noble-looking and of about sixty years of age. He was richly dressed in a white satin sleeping-robe which was now heavily blood-stained from the thigh wound inflicted by Kiyomasa. I was convinced that this was none other than Kotsuké no Suké's and Kiyomasa agreed with me. I asked him his name but he offered no reply.

Kuranosuké gave the signal whistle and soon the other *ronins* arrived. A lantern was passed to Kuranosuké and he examined the old man's face.

It was indeed Kotsuké no Suké and this was borne out by the scar he still carried across his forehead from where our master, Asano Takumi no Kami, had wounded him during the affray at the castle in Kyoto.

Oishi Kuranosuké went down onto his knees and said to the old man, respectfully, "My lord, we are the retainers of Asano Takumi no Kami. Last year your lordship and our master quarrelled in the palace and our master was sentenced to commit *hara-kiri* and his family was ruined. We have come tonight to avenge him, as is the duty of faithful and loyal men. I pray your lordship to acknowledge the justice of our purpose." Having no response, Oishi-san continued. "And now, my lord, we beseech *you* to perform *hara-kiri*. I myself shall have the honour to act as your second and when, with all humility, I shall have received your lordship's head, it is my intention to lay it as an offering upon the grave of Asano Takumi no Kami."

Taking into consideration Kotsuké no Suké's high rank, we *ronins* offered him the greatest courtesy throughout and many times did we implore him to perform *hara-kiri*. But, on his knees, he trembled and blubbered and said nothing.

Kuranosuké saw that the entreaties to persuade the nobleman to die an honourable and courageous death were in vain. He instructed "Yazama-san, take his head carefully in your hands."

And I did, knowing what was to follow.

Kuranosuké took up the blade that had been carried by Kotsuké no Suké. I forced the man's head down and Kuranosuké removed it cleanly. The blade was the same one that Asano Takumi no Kami had used to take his own life.

I was somewhat surprised at how heavy the head was, having expected it to be lighter. A bucket was brought forth and I placed the head inside it, being glad to be rid of it. We were all of us elated at having accomplished our honourable action and made ready to leave. Acting on Kuranosuké's instructions, we carefully extinguished all of the lights and fires in the place to avoid any accidental fires from breaking out and causing suffering to neighbours.

৯ ৶

Dawn broke just as we forty-seven were making our way to the suburb of Takanawa towards the temple known as Sengakuji. People flocked out to see us and, although our arms and clothes were still heavily bloodstained for we must have presented a fearsome appearance, everybody praised us and marvelled at our valour, faithfulness and honour.

We all expected that at any moment Kotsuké no Suké's father-in-law would attack us and carry off the head and we were constantly prepared to die bravely with sword in hand. But we reached Takanawa safely to hear that one of the eighteen chief *daimyos* of the land, Matsudaira Aki no Kami, of whose house Asano Takumi no Kami had been a cadet, had been extremely pleased when he heard of last night's work and he had been preparing to assist us *ronins* in case we were attacked. So now Kotsuké no Suké's father-in-law dared not pursue us.

At about the seventh hour of the morning we arrived opposite the palace of Matsudaira Aki no Kami, the Prince of Sendai, who sent for one of his councillors. We, meanwhile, sat on the cold road and waited in silence.

The Prince reputedly said to his councillor, "The retainers of Asano Takumi no Kami have slain their lord's enemy and are passing this way. I cannot sufficiently admire their devotion so, as they must be tired and hungry after their night's work, do go and invite them in here and set some hot gruel and a cup of wine before them."

The councillor bowed to the Prince and went outside to speak to Oishi Kuranosuké. He said, "Sir, I am a councillor of the Prince of Sendai and my master bids me to beg you, as you must be worn out after all you have undergone, to come in and partake of such poor refreshment as we can offer you. This is my message to you from my lord."

Kuranosuké replied, "I thank you sir. It is very good of his lordship to trouble himself to think of us. We shall accept his kindness gratefully."

So we all entered the palace and feasted well on the gruel and the wine. All of the retainers of the Prince came out to give us praise and to hear our story.

Kuranosuké then turned to the councillor and said to him, "Sir, we are truly indebted to you for this kind hospitality. But as we still have to hurry to Sengakuji, we must humbly take our leave."

After giving our gratitude and praise to our hosts, we left the palace and hastened to the temple where we were met at the gate by the abbot of the monastery. He led us to the tomb of Takumi no Kami. Kiyomasa, who had been carrying the bucket, took out the head and washed it in a well close by. He passed it to me and I, in turn, to Kuranosuké who placed it on the tomb as an offering. Kuranosuké burned incense and then so did his son, Chikara, followed by the other forty-five of us. Kuranosuké then requested the priests of the temple to come and read prayers over the tomb.

Kuranosuké then gave to the abbot all the money that he carried, saying "When we forty-seven men shall have performed *hara-kiri*, I beg you to bury us decently. I rely on your kindness. This is but a trifle that I have to offer. Such that it is, let it be spent in masses for our souls."

The abbot was astounded at the courage that we all showed; although for us we would have shown nothing less. With his eyes brimming with tears he solemnly promised to honour our wishes.

We, the forty-seven ronins, having completed our sacred task and with our minds at peace, left the temple and waited patiently to receive the orders of the government.

JUDGEMENT

WE WERE puzzled somewhat that it took some days before we received the summons to appear at the Supreme Court. However, news reached us daily that the governors of Yedo found difficulty in agreement of our fate. Some, it was said, argued that we had righted an unjustified wrong by taking direct action against a dishonourable man. The Prince of Sendai was said to have spoken vociferously in our favour. Others though, were concerned that this kind of action could set a precedent that would result in a massacre of *daimyos* across the country and could therefore, not be condoned.

We expected the worst and we were prepared.

The Governors of Yedo and the public censors had assembled and, after some debate and confirmation of the agreements reached, passed sentence upon us.

A spokesman said, "Whereas, neither respecting the dignity of the city nor fearing the Government, having leagued yourselves together to slay your enemy, you violently broke into the house of Kira Kotsuké no Suké by night and murdered him. The sentence of this court is that, for this audacious conduct, you perform *seppuku* by *hara-kiri*."

Ritual suicide by the stomach cut. There was not a sound from among us as these words were spoken.

I am pleased to announce that at that moment my heart did not sink, neither did my courage fail me. Nor did the courage of any one of my comrades' fail. My thoughts immediately went to the lovely Caeron. He face still shone clearly in my mind although the memory was surely nothing more than that of a dream.

When the sentence had been read, we forty-seven *ronins* were divided into four parties and handed over for safe-keeping to separate *daimyos*. We were treated most respectfully and were not locked in rooms or cells. We were fed very well and kept warm that night. Court officials were despatched to each of those *daimyos* – in their presence we would perform hara-kiri. In my party was Oishi Kuranosuké, but not his own son, Chikara fortunately, and my friend Toshiro Yoshisuke.

In the courtyard we were lined up. I was second in the line, with Toshiro Yoshisuke beside me on one side and Yoshida Chiuzayémon on the other, and at the end of the line was Oishi-san. He smiled and bowed to each of us in turn. I felt much encouraged.

The manner in which we would die was read out to us by a court official. We would carry out the act simultaneously. We would all meet our death nobly.

In a light-headed daze, I knelt on the ground in line with my comrades and straightened my back. On the call from the official, I began the ritual, plunging my *tanto* blade into my abdomen and drawing it from left to right. I had to bear the pain and shock long enough for me to replace the tanto into its sheath and place it down respectfully on the tatame mat in front of me.

A face seemed to swim before me – *Caeron!*

– A blinding light and a rushing sensation.

– Nothingness.

THE END

AUTHOR'S NOTE

THE ACCOUNT of the Forty-Seven Ronins is a true event in the rather exceptional history of early eighteenth century Japan. Strangely, little is known of it in Western Europe although it is recounted in the USA. I have made every effort, using various accounts primarily from the Internet, to faithfully narrate the known facts of the legend of this group of Samurai retainers, or *Ronin*, as they became after the death of their master, Asano Takumi no Kami. Obviously, I have embellished the tale to account for the actions of my heroic figure, Yazama Jiutarô, without altering the events to accommodate this. Yazama Jiutarô was actually one of the forty-seven as were the other named characters in the first and last parts of my novel.

Once Asano Takumi no Kami was ordered to commit ritual suicide, his lands and goods would have been confiscated, his family ruined and his retainers made into Ronin, or 'wave men' (being those that are tossed about uncontrollably as if on the crests of waves). As such, being masterless and without means of support, they are forced into a position that is somewhat dishonest, menial and humiliating.

Accounts vary as to the aftermath of the battle at the castle of Kira Kotsuké no Suké. It is said by some that one of Oishi's warriors was killed but other reports do not mention this. Other accounts describe one of the retainers having ridden back to Ako province to describe the events to the Asano family, whether under the direction of Oishi or as an excuse for escaping the probable consequences. Notwithstanding this, the remaining forty-six or forty-seven who survived the final battle went together to the authorities and proudly proclaimed what they had achieved. The fact that hundreds of townsfolk followed them through the streets demonstrated the high esteem to which the Ronin were suddenly elevated.

Unfortunately, the government had now been placed in a quandary. Oishi Kuranosuke Yoshio, Asano's principal counsellor and leader of the retainers, had been a pupil of one Yamaga Soko, a learnéd Japanese philosopher and strategist during the Tokugawa shogunate who, in his work, *The Way of the Samurai (Shido),* applied the Confucian idealogy of the *Superior Man* to the Samurai class. His description of *bushido* (the way of the warrior) as being "duty above all" had earned enormous respect from Samurai leaders.

The magistrates unanimously agreed the forty-seven had fulfilled their honourable duty, nevertheless, and they were undecided as to whether to punish them for murder by vengeance or to reward them for behaving more like true Samurai than any had for a long time. But the decision was eventually reached that the law must be upheld. The possible consequences of giving official approval to a vendetta were too ominous to contemplate so the Ronin were ordered to commit *seppuku* (ritual suicide) by *hara-kiri* (stomach-cut), a course of action for which they had been prepared from the outset. Therefore, having proven their valour and duty, all forty-seven Ronin were given an honourable burial at the Sengaku-ji Temple in Edo (now Tokyo). This was the last resting place of the heroes which was to become something of a shrine to the Samurai virtues and attracted numerous pilgrims, as it still does to this present day.

No other act of Samurai sense of duty was to have such a profound effect as the legend of the forty-seven Ronin. With their deaths they became martyrs to the cause of bushido and even though the years leading up to the Meiji Restoration from 1868, which led to major changes in Japan's political and social structure, were to see many such assassinations, none would produce adulation, nor generate plays, stories, wood-block prints, films and mementoes by the score.

In Japan, to this day, this legend is referred to as *Chushingura*, literally meaning the Loyal League and has been described as the country's national legend in much the same way as being equivalent to one of the great Shakespearean dramas or the Robin Hood or William Tell myths.

The 2013 film, 47 Ronin, bears almost no relationship whatsoever to the real events.

Hara-Kiri

To modern westerners the act of hara-kiri is a gruesome spectacle. The kneeling Samurai would be required to produce the notorious stomach-cut on himself using the wakizashi short-sword or tanto knife to cut a deep wound horizontally across the stomach. At its end the blade would be turned downwards cutting vertically and allowing the entrails to spill onto the ground. He would then slit his own throat, severing the carotid artery. In the moment of his death he would replace the blade in its scabbard and place it on the floor or surface in front of him. This is indeed a display of immense courage.

I sincerely hope that Yazama Jiutarô would not mind me having selected him as an adventurer in my rather frivolous tale.

About the Author

Paul Boyce began creatively writing during his time in the military and as a civil servant when producing reports for his managers and industry. He spends many hours in planning cunning ways in killing off his wife, stepson, son and daughter-in-law, and anyone else foolish enough to partake in a certain fantasy role-playing game. Unfortunately, he was recently diagnosed with MS which gives him plenty of time to tap away on the keys of his laptop. He still has a very high respect for the use of punctuation, a dying art these days, and cannot abide the puerile use of text-speak especially by the over-thirties (LOL!). He was somewhat disappointed to hear, quite recently, a man in a pub say to his wife "Don't bother using punctuation in your text, you don't need it!" What is the world coming to when the semi-colon is consigned to history?

He has already commenced the follow-on manuscripts for Black Harlequin and Far from Home.

For information about the Continent of Baylea on the World of Amaehome, please go to:
www.amaehome.esy.es
This may soon change to www.amaehome.co.uk